Jane of Annaluca

A Jane Pace Novel

E.V. Comfort

<u>Warning</u>

This title contains the following:
Graphic language, sexual content and violence.

JANE OF ANNALUCA

Front Jacket Artwork: Jon Hrubesch

JANEPACE.COM

DEDICATION

For the Jane Trio:

Kristi Cardarella Mottla

Missy Aronoff White (the real one)

and

Micah Comfort

Pure gratitude.

`

BOOK 8 PREFACE, AS WRITTEN BY THALBERG ABRAMS

Good morning.

While I am not the first non-Pacey (a Pacey being a refugee of the long-destroyed colony of Pace-Pallon) to write a preface for my friend Jane, I do have the distinction of being the first non-organic life form to do so. This makes me quite proud for I take my distinctions where I can find them. My name is Thalberg Abrams and I was created and brought into sentience by David Abrams, space ship designer, medical innovator and all around genius. Since I carry the residual memories and personality traits of his late father (downloaded into my programming) I am both father and son to my creator. An interesting position to be in to say the least.

This, however, is Jane's story of which this is the final chapter...

We will start the preface as they have all started, with an explanation of the types of people involved in these adventures. Jane's stories deal primarily with three types of Human peoples: 'supernormals' (Telepaths, Telekinetics and various forms of Empaths, etc.), 'normals' who are everybody else and 'Heelies,' who are Humans who were genetically modified to be amphibians. There are also two kinds of 'aliens' (though the term alien, I have to say, all depends on who is talking) from the Rian Nation. The space-dwelling Deneth Rian and their sister race, the gravity-tolerant Tarine Rian, who fly on gossamer wings.

Jane Pace, a powerful non-Heely Human Telekinetic, or TK, is a refugee of the above-mentioned Pace-Pallon colony. She was genetically engineered to be extraordinary and everything in her life is (unsurprisingly, at least to me) affected by this. She is known throughout the Galactic Union as the lethal Red Angel, a moniker she detests even when it proves useful.

The supernormals run as follows:

Micro-TK – Micro-Telekinetic. Move small things (and very small things) with their minds.

Macro-TK – Macro-Teleknetic. 'Lifters' that can move large things with their minds.

TP – Telepaths. Mind-readers.

Emps – Empaths. Read and project (limited) emotions.

MEmps – Manipulative Empaths. Can read and project/manipulate emotions both individually and on a group scale. Very rare and never occur naturally.

Pre-cogs – Pre-cognitives, seers of the future.

Picture-Makers – Can make a person 'see' and 'live in' anything the picture-maker has in his or her mind.

There are also the occasional hybrids such as Jane, who is a Macro-Micro and Daniel Pace, a TP-MEmp, but those are extremely rare.

Jane's most important (to her) friends and colleagues at the time of this story were: Dr. Wilby Quinn-Pace (Micro-TK), who lived on Novy with his adopted daughter, Shira, his husband, Nathan (Judean Master Assassin), and the last batch of purely Pacey babies just out of the gestational 'tubs.' Felix (Macro-TK), Atalanta (MEmp) and the afore-mentioned Daniel (TK-MEmp), were a Trio and worked for the Three Furies Mercenary Fleet. High Admiral Samuel Armstrong commanded the Union Navy and was, by then, a legend himself through "victories" at First and Second Heliot. Garrett Pace-Taylor (Macro-TK) and his lawyer husband Derek (a Terran 'normal') lived on Terra 1 while Garrett assisted the High Admiral along with Colonel Alex Couvillion, son of the Corsican Emperor. Another old friend from Pace-Pallon, Stuart (TP), lived with the mother of his child, Prince(ss) Pilar Julia-Callas of the Kingdom of Gloriana-Levvon and her husband, Prince Ronnie (long story). His Excellency, Charles Fitzroy, the Corsican Ambassador (the Ambassador with a difference, see Book 6) and ally to all freaks, continued to work towards equality within the Union. There was also my son (of sorts), the calculating and brilliant David Abrams, the richest man alive, now married and a father to four young children. He had sworn to get his ex-lover, Jane, back even though she was very much in love with someone else. He had told Jane that he had a plan and though I'd been sworn to secrecy, I knew he was telling the truth.

This was what Jane had been up to by the end of Book 7:

Book 1, Jane of Pace-Pallon: Evil crab-like creatures invaded Jane's home system of Pace-Pallon and ate it. Jane and her friends barely escaped.

Book 2, Jane of the *P.S. Scylla*: Jane fell in love with then General Armstrong, who united everyone to beat off some evil Paceys and destroy the Pace system to keep the aforementioned evil crab creatures (the *tapetia mortis*) from moving on to consume new planets. Jane and the General broke up, suffered, and everyone went to Terra.

Book 3, Jane of Terra 1: President of the Galactic Union Archer brought legislation that would catalogue supers while also secretly encouraging a war with the semi-amphibious Heliot Empire. Jane and her friends infiltrated the Union Legislature to try and protect the supers and ended up saving hundreds of lives when a Heely missile arrived at Terra to destroy the planet. Jane, in an act of supreme desperation, flew into the air and broke the missile in two (and her back at the same time), saving the lives of many including that of Ambassador Fitzroy, who became her friend. The supers then left Terra and went to work for the Pacey-run Phoenix Independent Mercenaries (the P.I.M.). Jane was paralyzed from the waist down.

Book 4, Jane of the P.I.M.: David Abrams, genius inventor of pretty much anything (including yours truly) you could name, took an interest in Jane and her spine and fixed it. President Archer launched a new vendetta against all freaks and all Paceys, even the Pacey 'normals,' including now-Admiral Armstrong. She sent his Union Fleet to Heliot just so it would be decimated (this was the "victory" of First Heliot). It was, but some survived (including the Admiral) because the P.I.M. had come to the rescue. In an effort to stop the Heely War the good guys, led by Fitz (Ambassador Fitzroy), needed to know who had been bankrolling and supplying technology to the Heelies. The P.I.M. decided to find out, going back to the Heliot Home World. They found out who it was (Vega) but, through an Archer-designed betrayal, the Heliot Home World was destroyed (the Battle of Second Heliot), allowing the War to escalate. Jane and Abrams became briefly involved romantically, but it fell apart quickly due to Abrams' underhanded agenda(s). Wilby had been the only super to stay behind on Terra (for a noble cause) but had ended up tortured by Archer's people. Jane rushed in to save him and killed Archer in deserved revenge. I'd never met her, but from what I have heard she deserved what she got and more.

Book 5, Jane of Thao: Jane and Wilby assumed new identities and settled in the Kingdom of Gloriana in the Thao Protectorate. Their boss, Prince(ss) Pilar Julia, picked Jane's ex-boyfriend Stuart as her mate and got pregnant with her long-awaited heir. Jane, Wilby, Quinn and Stuart took on the task of starting a school to train super refugees from Terra for the Glorianan military.

The Pacey supers (and friends) had been on the trail of an all-powerful and psychotic Pacey super named Tristan who murdered and raped for his own sadistic pleasure. They eventually found him and Jane took him out but not before he had done even more damage to good people. Jane survived that just in time to have her current lover, the sweet high-class rent boy Stoney, stab her in the heart with her own knife. He had, we found out soon after, been 'programmed' months before by Tristan to do it (very much against the poor boy's will) as a final act of revenge.

The constant danger that Jane faced proved too much for Fitz and he flipped out and refused to be her friend anymore. At the end of the book, preparations were underway for the politically motivated wedding of Prince(ss) Pilar of Gloriana and Prince Ronald of Levvon who seemed like a waste of space (but actually wasn't). Jane recovered slowly. Fitz sent flowers and asked for forgiveness for panicking. Jane sent the flowers back.

Book 6, Jane of Gloriana-Levvon: Jane and friends were still living under assumed names (fallout from the murder of President Archer) in the Kingdom of Gloriana. Pilar's political alliance with the Kingdom of Levvon proceeded and she (while still being in love with Stuart) married its Prince Ronnie in the royal wedding to beat all royal weddings. Jane realized that she was in love with Fitz, but said nothing since he had a mistress.

On a rescue trip to the colony of Vega, Jane and company found the Winters, a family of amoral geniuses who'd created most of the technology that had allowed the Heely War to be so devastating (including the missile that had almost destroyed Terra years before). Prince(ss) Pilar blackmailed them into creating a weapon for *our* side to use to win the War, which they did. Eventually the Winters escaped and Jane's people followed them to Torva, one of the two last great slave-creating colonies (Napia, which is dealt with in Book 7, being the other). The students on Gloriana that Jane,

Stuart, Wilby and Quinn (and others) had been training were put through a trial by fire—the Liberation of Torva. David Abrams used technology (that was needed, frankly) to influence the mission and tried to muscle Jane around. Much as I love my son I wasn't surprised when it didn't work. Bullies only make Jane mad.

The supers arrived at Torva and liberated the slaves. They also captured the Winters and handed them over to Admiral Armstrong (recently arrived with his Fleet) for trial on Terra for Crimes Against Sentients. Jane was injured during the assault, losing the use of her right arm in an LPG blast. The mission was a tremendous success with the exception of the escape of the Master, the mysterious and murderous leader who had ruled Torva with an iron fist.

Once back on Terra "Irena LeJeune" became Jane Pace again. Or, I should say, she was reborn as Jane Pace, the Red Angel, Hero of the Union, in the eyes of the universe.

Jane stayed on Terra 1 to re-start the ESTF (with her friend General Manthorpe) as a training program within the Union's Academy (the *Schola-Terra*) for top supers. Then, out of nowhere, she got the terrifying news that someone had tried to murder her Fitz. Jane immediately took off for Corsica.

Book 7, Jane of Novy: Jane arrived on Irena (the Corsican Capital) to find Fitz seriously injured but alive and figured out that a Pacey, former ruling class nexus pre-cognitive Whitman, was not only responsible for the attack but had married into the Royal Family before anyone had realized that he was the culprit. Stuart (TP), whom Jane had picked up on the way, 'reprogrammed' Whitman to use his remarkable abilities for good in the service of the Corsican Emperor.

Jane's right arm, still useless and painful from her injury on Torva, was 'fixed' by the genius of my David, but only after her friends had badgered her into letting him. Idis, Fitz's lover, kindly looked after Jane during the surgery to make sure everything was all right.

The Pelann of the Rian Nation hired the Three Furies Fleet to free five hundred creatures from the final slave-creating colony, Napia. Once rescued it was revealed that these beings were a genetically modified (and formerly extinct) gravity-dwelling sister race to the Deneth, the Tarine, brought back by the Pelann; having grav-tolerant (but still Rian) representatives would give her more power in the Union Government.

Eriss, a young and incredibly powerful Tarine TP, was their leader. In the course of the liberation Quinn was tortured in order to get revenge on Jane and, unable to stand letting her friend (and Quinn's husband) Wilby down, Jane lost touch with reality. Eriss and Ian Armstrong brought her back to sanity. Quinn realized he was jealous of Jane and Wilby's bond.

I, Thalberg, decided to leave David Abrams and come work for Jane. Because there was no precedent for non-organic citizenship, Jane was forced to take legal possession of me.

The newly (and forcedly) reformed Prince Whitman was enlisted to help Ian Armstrong's lover, Arrow Peters, who had been overwhelmed with painful and terrifying pre-cognitive visions for years. Unfortunately, however, and despite everyone's best efforts, Arrow took her own life, shattering both Ian and her father, Samuel.

Sang Heelies (anti-Terran Heely Humans) prepared to attack Novy Heliot, David Abrams' planet, home to peaceful Heelies and refugees of all types. A Union Fleet, led by newly promoted High Admiral Samuel Armstrong, arrived at Novy to defend it both from the Sangs and from the renegade Denethians working with them. Devon Pennock, a former Macro TK student of Jane's, revealed that he had orchestrated the battle to get her attention. When she rebuffed his unwelcome romantic advances (again) he vowed revenge before killing himself. In the vicious battle that followed the Union and its supers beat and destroyed the Sang Heelies and their Denethian collaborators.

Wilby broke with Jane, telling her that a jealous Quinn couldn't handle their friendship anymore. Wilby and Quinn then got married without her.

Fitz met with Jane and told her that he loved her and that his mistress, Idis, had given her blessing for them to be together when Fitz was on Terra. Jane was deliriously happy, as was Fitz.

The book "Tales of the Blackbird," written by the late Devon Pennock, appeared on the newsstand soon after, and it told of the salacious, violent private and public life of a woman identical to Jane. The fictional "Miri Pallon" was a whore, an adulterer and a pathological murderer and therein lay Mr. Pennock's revenge as it cruelly altered the reputation and legend of the living breathing Red Angel.

Now we come to the final chapter (that I'm calling Book 8: David did WHAT?) of the story Jane wished to tell. For those of you who have made it to the end, however, I should warn you to hold on to your (proverbial) hats and get ready to say goodbye to more than just Jane.

As the Paceys say…

Godspeed,

Thalberg Abrams

Abramstown
Novy Heliot
December 24th, 2899

Part 1

2873-2874

ENTRY 1-8-84

<u>11:00 – Bookseller, Terra 1 Space Station, Terra, September 15th, 2873</u>

I'd been waiting impatiently for the arrival of Charles' ship from Corsica. Waiting to be finally united with the man I loved. Killing time I'd started wandering the vendor stalls in the station, but my progress had been stopped by something.

It was a large window display, the cover of a book enlarged to Denethian height. The cover held a tall intense-looking woman with long black flowing hair, dressed in black, leaning seductively forward. Her eyes were brown and she looked familiar. She appeared to be floating in a long corridor that disappeared behind her. That corridor was filled with men and women. Naked men and women.

I looked again at the 'familiar' face of the woman on the cover and could no longer deny what I saw. That face. That face was *mine*.

Tales of the Blackbird: the Adventures of Miri Pallon, the Union's Most Dangerous Lover

A work of adult fiction by
Nora Archer and Devon Pennock.

I, hand shaking, reached out and picked up one of the actual paper books and turned to the back cover.

> *Experience the lurid exploits of a rare supernormal, a Pace-Pallon refugee whose bed has seen the most famous men and women in recent history: the Admiral, the Trillionaire, the Doctor, the E05s, the Princes, the Ambassadors, Denethians and Heelies and even the President of the Union!*
>
> *She starts wars and finishes them, saving billions of lives while breaking hundreds of hearts.*
>
> *No one, man or woman, can resist the charms of the galaxy's most infamous and lethal lover.*

Can you?

I don't really remember what I did after that, aside from puke.

14:30 – Ambassadorial Apartments, Corsican Embassy, Terra 1, Terra, September 17th, 2873

"We clearly have a case of 'actual malice,'" Tall Attorney said.

"Meaning," Charles said quietly, "That Nora and Devon knew what they said was false."

Charles looked at me, I could tell because his head turned in my direction, but I was staring off into space, only listening enough to follow along. I was still in shock, I knew, and it had been two days. Two days of reading and re-reading that horrible, nasty book. Seeing how much of the rumors had been turned into fact—and how distressingly often she'd gotten things right. I knew Charles had called in his troop of lawyers to try to help. He'd been beside himself when he'd found me huddled in my bed in the apartment, Thal standing guard. Charles wanted to stop the book, punish someone for hurting me. He was a dear, even if it was no use. I knew that Nora was many things but stupid wasn't one them and that these couldn't possibly be the first set of lawyers to look over her foul words.

"Yes, Ambassador," Tall Attorney nodded.

"This is a clear case of Defamation, Sir," Frowning Attorney said. "Since the Commodore is a public figure, she can even sue for damages."

"I am no student of the law, Mr. Mason," Charles said to Frowning Attorney, "but the Commodore cannot prove loss of income or revenue from this abomination of a book."

"She can if she gets fired because of it," Bald Attorney said.

I felt a stab of fear then, but almost immediately returned to my dazed state. Even if the ESTF fired me, Ian would take me. I'd always be able to find work and, I thought bitterly, since the "Blackbird" had racked up an even higher body count than the Red Angel, my reputation as paid psychopath was more enhanced than anything else. Blech.

"General Manthorpe would never fire her," Charles said dismissively.

"With all due respect, Ambassador, he was tainted in this, too," Tall Attorney said, "and his wife." Yes, apparently I'd fucked Thelonious Thorpe and his Heely wife. Among thousands of others.

"Something must be done, however," Charles said, his voice low and angry.

"I hate to say this, Sir," a new voice said, a deep, kind and reasonable voice, "but there isn't anything to be done." We all, myself included, looked to the man I had insisted be present, my personal attorney, Derek Pace-Taylor. "Nothing at all."

Charles looked from Derek to me as I forced myself to meet his almost golden eyes for the first time in ages. He regarded us, then looked at the other legal minds and said, "You may go." They immediately left. His presence, his command, made sure that they moved their asses. It would have been funny, if anything had been right at that moment, but nothing was.

I was distraught and defeated at the same time. Furious at the betrayal and heavily depressed. What I really was, however, was deeply embarrassed. Yes, the book was full of sex and violence. I wasn't ashamed of my sexual history (with a couple of exceptions), so it wasn't that. The thing was that this story, the bastardized version of my story, wasn't only mine. It was Wilby's and Samuel's and Criss' and Stoney's and Stuart's and Fey's and so many others. Their lives were violated, too, because of their time with me and some of that time had been intimate and personal and wonderful and now anyone could read it. Surprisingly Charles had been left out entirely, either as Ambassador or Emperor. My guess was that even Nora's lawyers hadn't had the balls to go there. Or maybe her husband, Albert Nylander, had put his foot down then. We hadn't heard from Albert, though he'd been the first person Charles had tried to reach. That was going to be an interesting conversation, assuming Albert didn't just run for his life.

"We're going to do nothing?" Charles prompted.

Derek hesitated and looked at me. I knew he needed my permission to break attorney client privilege. I nodded. "If Jane starts denying things, the press will start looking item by item." He let out a breath. "The underaged and adulterous affair with the High Admiral," he said with an apologetic shrug to me, "the condoning of incest with his son and daughter," god, would Ian never be free of that? and, "the murder of President Archer." Oh, yes, and that had been in there, too. Nora hadn't been a witness, but I'd told her what I was going to do and then had done it.

"Not to mention the ménage a trois with the Pacey doctor and the highly respected attorney," I said quietly. There was no surprise in Charles, not in his expression or his body. Odd that. Right that minute, though, my concern was Derek. "I am so sorry, Derek. For you and Garrett…"

Derek put a hand on my shoulder, now *that* made Charles tense, though only a Micro could have read it, "Now stop right there, Jane. We three chose to play that night. I am not ashamed of my choice and my reputation will be just fine." He gave a squeeze and let go. "Don't worry about us."

I shook my head. "But *I* am ashamed. Not of what I did, but that everyone I have ever known—and some people I've never even met—is going to be looked at now. Stared at for bedding the freak." I caught Derek's deep brown eyes and uttered the deepest of my fears. "What about Samuel?" Would all our sacrifices be for nothing? Would this scandal rob him of his job when he'd finally reached the top of his profession? I couldn't bear to contemplate it.

"With your permission, I will visit him and tell him the same thing I'm going to tell you."

"Which is?"

"Laugh it off."

Charles said nothing but shook his head.

"Laugh it off?" I repeated dumbly.

Derek nodded. "Make a joke of it. Pretend it doesn't bother you and mock it when you can."

"I don't know if I'm up to that right now, Derek."

"I don't blame you, Jane, but you can't fight this and, since the stupid thing is racing up the best seller charts, it isn't going to go away."

I laughed humorlessly to myself. "He said he would be the second line in my obituary." Devon, Devon had said it.

"He said that?" Charles asked.

"Right before he killed himself."

"Father in Heaven," he murmured.

"He was right, wasn't he, Derek?" I asked.

Derek sighed unhappily, "He may very well be, Jane, and for that I am truly sorry."

"Thank you, Derek."

"Any time, Jane."

Charles rose and Derek seemed to sense that the interview was over. I stayed put in my chair, too off to move. I knew Derek was right…about everything, though I didn't think I'd be up to joking or mocking anytime soon. Jane Pace was horrified at the invasion of her privacy, but the Red Angel was a bad ass and the Red Angel would find all of this ridiculous. The Red Angel might have been a little bit nuts.

Charles took a step towards me, but his comm beeped and he turned his head to answer it. "Fitzroy, here." He listened. "Play the Countess' message now."

Idis.

Shame.

The shame I had been keeping at bay overwhelmed me and I stood up. Charles, probably misinterpreting my action shook his head at me, "You don't need to leave, my dear." I sat back down, but my brain reeled with misery. Charles was a public figure, more public than most people knew. It was one thing if he and I knew my past (as well as the people with whom I'd actually lived it) but it was another for the entire Union population to know, or think they did once they found out that we were together. He would be a joke. A joke. Not Charles, not my Charles. Fuck, and here I was again. Making the man I loved *less*. I just couldn't win. Should I just leave? Take my fucked-up-ed-ness and run?

I was, to my own surprise, not being visited by dead Soames, not throwing up, not anything. I was calm and my determination to do the right thing, again, was growing.

I just needed some clothes, Thal, and my <u>Jane Eyre</u> that I'd brought from the *Liberty*. Within ten minutes I could be gone. I stood up again.

I hadn't realized that Charles was watching me intently as he listened to Idis's message. He turned his head to click the comm off and said only one word, "No." To me. I looked up at him in surprise and he held up a finger, silently telling me to wait as he walked quickly into the other room.

I stayed where I was. Charles walked slowly into back into the room. His heart rate was elevated and adrenaline was singing through his body. He was carrying something. A file.

"Idis said you would run. In her message."

I looked at him in surprise. "She did?"

He nodded, moving closer. So handsome. I took a step back, but he took three steps forward. "She agrees there is nothing we can do without making everything worse, but she was worried about you. You can't go."

Didn't I have to, though? To do the honorable thing and protect him? "Charles, I…"

"I know you can read me, Jane."

"Of course."

"Do you know why I wasn't surprised when you mentioned being with Wilby and Derek years ago?"

That *had* been odd. "Why?"

"This."

He held the file out and I took it, sitting on a nearby couch to read it. He sat next to me. My eyes went wide as I thumbed through it. It was all about me. It was lovers and after-action reports and Tristan and Devon, the sex dungeons on Gloriana, Criss Utat, even the one night with Synon. A few things (that I thought of later, I was too inundated with the volume of information to think of much else right then) were missing and a few things weren't quite accurate, but most of it was right and there was a *lot*.

"Why would you have something like this, Charles?"

His cheeks reddened slightly, "Idis had you investigated after meeting you on Corsica."

"*Idis* did?"

He shrugged. "Corsicans don't like being blind-sided. She suspected we cared for each other and she was looking out for me. She liked you, despite her worries, and was curious."

"You've read this?" I said, handing it back to him with a hint of disgust.

"Yes. After you left, after Louis' funeral."

"And none of it bothered you?" I asked skeptically. It was a very thick file.

"Some of it did." He looked down and away, uncomfortable. "The parts where you almost died."

"What about the other things?"

"No." The way he said it, though, made me catch his eye and hold it. He broke away first. "I wondered if..."

"Charles?"

"...if our version of monogamy would be...boring for you, that's all."

I shook my head. "It wouldn't have been," I said as I rose. To my complete surprise he stepped in front of me, suddenly angry.

"You aren't going anywhere, Jane."

"The hell I'm not."

"You aren't."

I put my hands on my hips, almost amused. He and I both knew he couldn't actually stop me. And I really wanted to stay, of course, I just didn't see how I could. "It can't work, Charles. You are an Emperor, for god's sake, and I am damaged goods at best." I took another step towards the door.

"Damn it, Jane, I'm not Sam!" he almost yelled.

I just stopped.

"What did you say?"

"I'm not Sam," he said with deliberate emphasis.

"What the fuck does that mean, *Charles*?" Seriously.

He walked in front of me and grabbed my wrists hard, his golden eyes going black. "You've told me the story of how you and Sam fell in love and then you let him go for his own good."

"For his career," I said, still not sure where the hell he was going with this, "so he wouldn't be the joke with the child bride."

"Yes, yes," he said dismissively. "It was all very noble and painful, but the part you leave out of the story is his part."

My gut clenched. "His part?"

He paused as if making sure I was really listening. "The part where he lets you."

I felt like I couldn't breathe. I had tried my best never to think of it that way; too painful. "But, Charles, he had to, he would have lost everything."

"He would have had you…and he let you go." Charles wasn't done, however. He shook me, still gripping my wrists. "I'm. Not. Sam. I am never letting you go. Not for my own good or yours. Never."

"But Charles…"

"NEVER."

He kissed me, pulling me to him so tightly I couldn't draw breath. I didn't want to. I pulled back for a second.

"Wait, you knew all that shit about me and still came for me?"

"Of course I did."

"So Idis's plan failed."

He frowned at that. "She may have started out with that in mind, but I think she became intrigued." I thought about her asking about my romantic life when I was about to go into surgery on my arm. Yes, she had been intrigued. "I think she found some of it pretty sexy." He pulled me close again and put his lips on my neck. I shuddered at his touch. He felt so good. "She wasn't the only one." Oh my.

He kissed me again and I surrendered. Fuck noble gestures, Grand or otherwise. He wasn't going to let me go and I never wanted him to and I was tired of worrying, tired of suffering. I wanted to be happy and I needed Charles. I attacked his mouth, pressing myself to him. He groaned and I swear it was the best, sexiest sound I'd ever heard. I pulled away to push off his suit coat, then his waistcoat, then started on his tie, but couldn't get it off. I looked up and he chuckled and slipped it off his neck in a practiced motion. I was pretty much naked by now, but I really didn't know when the clothes had come off, not that I cared. I unbuttoned his shirt, momentarily stymied by the cuffs. This was ridiculous.

"Geez, Charles, no one wears this many layers," I laughed, "who are you protecting yourself…" and his shirt was off, "…from." My voice trailed off. I'd been joking, of course, but under his shirt was another vest, thin and light and impenetrable. Personal armor. I looked up at him, my vision blurring as my eyes filled. He kissed my forehead.

"It was the only way Idis would let me off the planet."

"Thank god for Idis," I breathed and I meant it. Our relationship, hers and mine, might be tricky in future, but we were united in loving this man. It would have to be enough to make it work. "I'm glad you have it, love, but now you need to take it off."

He did, while I unbuckled his belt and dropped his pants and underwear to the floor. There was another undershirt beneath the armored vest, but finally, finally, we were actually undressed.

He took me in his arms, now skin to skin. "Promise me that we are together now. We're finished with all the rest of it. No more running away, no more Grand Gestures. We're done, Jane. This is it, forever." He held my face in his elegant, long fingered hands. "Promise."

Whther we were in a bubble or not, whether I was being selfish or not, I no longer cared. He was Charles and I loved him and that was all. I smiled. "I promise. Forever."

He kissed me and picked me up, contact with his body making me dizzy. He lay me down on the couch and it almost was a battle, both of us so desperate to touch every part of the other, but eventually I had to surrender again, this time to his mouth as he moved lower and lower down my body.

"*God*, Charles, Six, I'm…" but before I could come he was over me again and then, slowly, inside me. And we were together, and we came then, together. And for the next six hours we made love again and again. It was so much more than even I'd hoped. More than sex, more than touch, more than love even. Just more.

And while I sure as shit didn't think of Idis while I was in the midst, so to speak, with Charles, I did think of her afterwards and I was grateful. More than a little guilty, but very, very grateful.

Personal Letter from Ian Armstrong, Dep Qua, Trithicate, Rian Nation, to Commodore Jane Pace, Terra 1, Terra, September 17ᵗʰ, 2873

Dear Jane,

I've been at Dep Qua for about a month now and I swear something is wrong. I thought it even before the events of today, which I will get to in a minute. I hardly ever see Eriss. She is surrounded by people, Telepaths mostly, and is never alone, even when she sleeps. She is afraid, Jane. I can see it all over her the rare times I get to be in the same room with her. I've asked her if she wants me to leave and she says no. Emphatically. Her 'advisors' sure as hell want me gone. I haven't seen the Pelann or Lita, but Eriss has gone up to the station a dozen times since I've been here. If I had to guess, and it is clear that I do since I have no fucking information, I'd say the Pelann was leaning on her. Eriss is strong, but everyone has their weak point and the Pelann has no doubt located Eriss' and exploited it.

[It was the next morning and I was sitting at the computer in Charles' study reading my mail from the day before. Ian was worried, which was not good. He was using his real name for the first time in forever, but I couldn't tell if that was a good or bad thing. I could also tell that he and Eriss were friends but not yet lovers. That last did not surprise me. The ghost of Arrow was still too near. I desperately wanted Ian to be happy and have a future with someone terrific. Not now. Someday, though. I knew, as did Ian, that Arrow had wanted that for him, too. Maybe that thought would help him accept a new lover—once he was ready to consider it.

Just then Charles passed by the monitor. He was dressing; a process that seemed to take forever and required professional assistance from Mr. Beddoes. I, of course, had showered and dressed inside of 20 minutes. Charles was going on 45 and seemed to be only mid-way through. He averted his eyes as he leaned down to kiss the top of my head.

I smiled at this and nodded in the direction of the screen. "What do you think of this, Six?" He blinked for a second, surprised I was sharing but pleased, and quickly got down to scanning part of the letter I had up on the screen.

He frowned. "Jack is no fool, Jane. If he thinks something is seriously wrong, then it is."

I sighed. "Yeah."

I scrolled to the next part. It was not an improvement upon the first.]

You may be thinking that this is all conjecture on my part, but there is something else. Father had asked me to look at the design of the Carcara fighters when I had the chance. He was thinking that part of the new Corsican designs could include carrier ships...

[Ooh, I thought. God, I hadn't been in a fighter in ages. Fun.]

...and knew the Carcaras needed updating. So I had taken one of them out to play with around the station and I was pushing the acceleration. A bit too far, turns out, for the tolerance of the ship's skin.

["Mother of god," I muttered.]

I'm fine, obviously, and got some ideas about a Tenorium alloy that might fix the problem. Imagine a semi-transparent ship—harder to see and impenetrable! Anyway, I had to eject (don't worry, I was wearing my DSS) and made my way to the station for rescue. I was passing by the main windows of the entry hall (where you had your 'fight' with Lita) and saw something I hadn't expected.

Jane, I saw Thal.

["Holy shit," I whispered looking up at Charles whose eyes had gone wide. "What the hell is a Thal doing on Trithicate?"

"I though Thal was..." Charles started.

I shook my head. "My Thal is safely on the station. This is David's Thal."]

Now I don't know what he is doing there, but I'm asking you to please contact Quinn on Novy and try to find out what is going on. I know things aren't right between you two, but this is important and the man I know

Quinn to be won't turn you down. I will be coming back to Terra 1 in a little over two weeks for Eriss' formal introduction to the Legislature. Let's hope you can have something for us so we're not as blindsided as I feel right now.

[He wasn't the only one. What the fuck was David up to now? I wondered. Contacting Quinn? Ugh. I had no doubt that he would help, especially since the Rian were his obsession, but…ugh.

"It seems we are never free of Mr. Abrams," Charles growled in my ear. I knew I should be agreeing with him, but what I was thinking was, do that again, please, as my body shuddered. "Something bothering you, love?" Charles said, dropping his voice even lower even as he smiled. Bastard. "Anything I can help you with?"

"If you don't knock that off, you'll have to start all over again," I warned as I looked back up at him.

He grimaced at that, but his eyes were black gold. "Finish the goddamned letter, Red. And hurry."]

I'll look for your letter. I've already sent something off to Tania (and to Marston), but she may know less that we'd hope. Abrams loves his secrets.

[Charles was doing something wonderful to my neck and it was hard to catch my breath—in the best possible way.]

Give my best to Fitz.

Your friend,
Ian

The letter now read I did everything in my power to give *my* best to Fitz and he did have to start the whole getting dressed process all over again. Strangely enough, he didn't seem to mind at all.

I sent the following to Quinn while he and Beddoes (who had discretely disappeared when it was clear Charles and I were getting amorous) put the Ambassador back together.

*URGENT Personal Letter from Commodore Jane Pace, Terra 1, Terra, to
General Nathan Quinn-Pace, Novy Heliot, September 18th, 2873*

> *Quinn,*
>
> *Ian saw one of David's Thals on Trithicate. David is up to something
> (not to mention whatever the Pelann is planning) and it may fuck the lot of
> us. Work your spook magic and find out what it is, if you will.*
> *We need to know what is going on before Eriss gets to Terra. Ian has
> already contacted Tania and Marston.*
>
> *Jane*

Not the warmest letter I'd ever sent, but, hey, there wasn't a fuck you or a
'thanks for breaking Wilby's (and my) heart by separating him from his
closest friend' in there, so I was reasonably proud of my restraint.

I checked my watch. Time to get to class.

10:00 – Classroom 2 (Mine), ESTF, *Schola-Terra* Academy, Terra 1, Terra, September 18th, 2873

I stood in front of twelve cadets, the twelve cadets of my first class of the
day. They were freshmen, babies, all 18 or 19 standard years old. You may
think it strange that I had given myself this class, that my experience and
talents would be better used serving the seniors or the graduates who'd
come back for extra training. This had certainly been what Marston had
thought and we'd argued about it quite a bit, but I'd held firm. I'd spent
years 'lifting' wrong and being unaware of all I could do and the
responsibilities of the gifts I had entailed. The babies needed guidance
immediately and I needed (for my own sake as well as theirs) to be the one
to guide them. So, as a compromise of sorts, I was teaching an assload of
classes, but I got the freshmen. We were only a couple of weeks into the
semester, but I'd seen time and time again that I'd fought for the right
thing. They were out of control without a strong hand. With a strong hand
they were able to move mountains. Literally.

Today was different, though. The kids were clearly uncomfortable and
I was puzzled as to why. They'd been terrified of me at first, of course.
Having the Red Angel as your Intro to Macro Instructor was an

intimidating prospect, apparently, but they'd relaxed a bit and we had settled into a respectful rapport. Today, however, they were just staring at me.

Oh, right. The fucking Blackbird. I should still have been upset. I should have been embarrassed, but I was so damned happy right then. I just had to think Charles' name and I couldn't contain my grin. So I found, to my surprise, that Derek's advice was easy to take. Or at least eas*ier*.

"So I suppose most of you have either read or heard of that Blackbird book."

No one said anything, but most of the kids looked guiltily away.

I smiled. "Don't worry kids, it's not me."

I felt some of them exhale in relief. Some didn't, however, and I really needed to put this to bed, er, rest. Fine. "Questions?" I asked.

"But," a young woman, Caroline Tellesco, "you have done some of the things the Blackbird lady did." She looked around defensively when several people frowned at her. "Don't look at me like that, it was in the news."

I felt a lump in my throat at the students' protective reaction. I hadn't expected it at all. (An interesting side note on the last name thing. Caroline had been Caroline Ohanesian before she'd enrolled at the *Schola-Terra*, but had changed her last name almost immediately. She'd told me that she was a Tellescan, but she was also a freak and she wanted everyone to know it up front. Sure the last name Tellesco didn't have the caché (shudder) that Pace did, but it still made a statement. Who could have expected that my choice years ago to go by Jane Pace could have ended up affecting the newly renamed Caroline Tellesco? I'd thought it was pretty fucking cool and I'd told her so.) I respected her (not just because of the name thing) and owed her an answer—even if my answer wasn't the whole truth.

"I'll be honest with you all," I said thoughtfully, "and I'd appreciate it if what I am about to tell you stays in this room." They all nodded, transfixed. It was adorable. "Caroline is right. Some of the Blackbird's adventures and mine overlap. This was done deliberately." I sighed. "I've lived a very full life to this point," I had to grin, "though I think I would have to be three times the age I am now to have done all the things, not to mention beings, the Blackbird has done." The students chuckled, obviously relieved that I was making light of it. "My real life has made me some enemies, though, and two of them wrote this book."

I saw understanding dawning in their faces.

"So when I say the Blackbird isn't me, I mean it."

Caroline smiled shakily. "I'm glad, ma'am," she said. "I didn't want to think you'd actually killed President Archer."

Breathe. Breathe, Jane. "No, of course you wouldn't, and I didn't, for the record."

"What about sleeping with the Denethian Ambassador?" someone murmured. I knew who it was (Blake from Cyrillic) but I pretended I didn't.

I couldn't help grinning at that one. "No comment."

Some laughed. Some looked horrified. Some just stood there, trying to work out the mechanics.

I purposely switched back to Teacher Voice. "All right, kids, pair up. One of you will spot, the other will be lifting…" I 'lifted' out six sets of weights ranging from 6 ounces to 1000 pounds, "these."

Dutifully they paired up and we got to work.

12:10 – Aronoff's Bar & Grill, Terra 1

The repercussions of the Blackbird were felt throughout the rest of the day. Not all of them, surprisingly, were bad.

"Jane?" a light soprano voice said quietly as I took a bite of my lunch. I swallowed hurriedly and looked up to see the pretty face, spectacular cleavage and smile of Missy Aronoff, the owner of this, my favorite restaurant in the universe.

"Missy, hi," I said a little warily.

"May I ask you a personal question?"

I looked over at her and she was just waiting, not nervous, just friendly as she'd always been. "Sure thing."

"Look, sweetie," she said as she took a seat next to me at the bar, "I know that book was sensationalist garbage and that you weren't actually in it no matter how hard the whores that wrote it tried to put you in there." She laughed. I did, too, though my laugh was a tad more forced. "I did want to ask your advice on something, though. A side issue, really."

"Go ahead."

"General Synon has been stationed here off and on for the past couple of months," she said.

I nodded.

"And today they're going to announce that he will be the Novy Heliot Ambassador to the Union."

I sat back in my chair. Holy shit. "He'll do a great job." Then I realized what she'd said. Or why she could have said it. "Wait, how did you know that if it hasn't been announced?"

"Hello, little lady," a deep reedy voice said behind me.

Suddenly there he was, all seven feet of Heely bad-asshood. Yes, I know that isn't really a word, but it still fit him perfectly in my mind. "Hey, Big Heely."

Synon grinned at me and kissed Missy on the cheek. Well, then. Synon, you dog.

"I'll join you in a minute, Sy," Missy said. That was all she said, but she practically glowed when she said it.

"Good," was his response, but I was pretty sure he was doing the Heely version of glowing, too. "I'll be seeing you, Jane."

"Uh huh," I said, amused, as he took his leave. I turned back to Missy, eyebrows raised. "He certainly seems smitten."

Missy looked after him fondly. "It's mutual, yet..."

Her hesitation was so unlike her that I had to prompt, "Yet..."

"It's a bit confusing."

"How so?"

She bit her lip. "He sought me out. He...told me that we were bonded."

I just blinked at her for a second, astonished. "He said *what?*"

"Bonded," she repeated. "That it had happened the second he met me." She laughed a little. "Happy Hour the Friday before last."

"That..." and I thought of Marston and Tania. Heelies usually didn't, even couldn't, bond except with other Heelies, but it had happened for them. "That is incredibly rare."

"That's what he said," she looked away from me, bemused. "He said he loves me."

Well, that is what the bond is all about, is what I thought, but what I said was, "And how do you feel?"

"Like I've been put into an arranged marriage," but she turned her eyes back to him, "with someone wonderful."

"Do you feel the bond, too?"

"Yes," and this came out very low. "It just wasn't what I'd ever expected."

No shit. "We go where the universe takes us, Missy." It felt nice to quote Idis just then, but to business. "So what was your question for me?"

"Two, really. If the book is to be believed, you've been with him."

"Don't go by the book, but yes, I have." I'd also almost killed him, but she wasn't a super so I didn't feel I needed to bring that up. Didn't seem helpful.

"Is he a good being?"

I could tell she was holding her breath, waiting for my honest response. Thankfully, the one I could give was a good one. "He is."

She exhaled. "Good."

"And your second question?"

She smiled. "What do I need to know to fuck his brains out?"

My grin almost split my face. "Get me some paper and a pen and I'll draw you a picture." She ran away and was back with them really, really fast.

So I gave a little lecture to Missy.

I got flowers the next day from Synon with a card that read:

> *Thank you, little lady.*
> *Your friend,*
> *Sy*

12:57 – Classroom 2 (Mine), ESTF, *Schola-Terra* Academy

I rocked back and forth on my toes, a move (Marston's standard) that was being witnessed by Marston himself on my right. He chuckled, though I could sense his tension, too. There was a large almost coffin-shaped box behind us on the table. I kept eyeing it as the two of us waited for our single student to arrive.

"I know you and Tania," Marston said, "agree on this and, for the record, so do I, but it is a lot of pressure to put on him."

"It is," I agreed, "but someone has to be first."

That someone was a person that had been in Terra 1's Infirmary, healed from moderate injury, but still in the Infirmary, I was sure, because no one had known where he'd belonged. It had been about a month ago that Marston had gotten the call. Dr. Kirsten Bruce, a tall, pale woman with a shaved head and boundless energy had asked him, asked both of us, to meet a patient of hers. This was, in and of itself, unusual, even unprecedented, since we kept tabs on all our people.

She'd met us at the Infirmary's entrance and took us via lift down, down, down into the bowels of the station. Far enough that I was pretty sure we weren't even in the official Infirmary anymore.

"It isn't anything I'd run across before, Marston," she said quietly, her voice musical and calming. Nice for a doctor, I thought distractedly.

"Where are we going, Doc?" I asked. Crap. My voice sounded so…flat by comparison. Blech.

"Well, Commodore," she said, hesitating, "You know we get all the refugees here." Marston and I nodded. "We check them for everything, treat them if they need it and then move them on to be registered and catalogued and Lord knows what else."

"Sure," I said encouragingly.

"Part of what we do is a kind of preliminary sorting. Planet of origin, date of birth, family history. It all goes into the file. We also," and she gave me sort of a sidelong look, "look for any *extra* abilities."

"You have a super down here?" Marston said as the lift finally stopped.

Dr. Bruce grimaced. "Yes and no. He's one, I'm sure of it, but he won't even discuss it and," she shrugged, "one doesn't push a nearly seven foot potential Macro-Telekinetic."

"Wise choice," Marston said dryly as the lift continued to descend.

"We're so far into the station I'm surprised we're not back on the planet, Doc. What's going on?" I asked, a bit impatiently.

"I know where we are," Marston said suddenly, looking sharply at Dr. Bruce. "We're in Max."

Max was short of maximum security holding. Impossible (to date) to escape from prison cells where we kept the worst of the worst. Who the fuck were we going to see?

Marston was thinking, however, his avuncular face creased with concentration. Then his expression cleared. "Oh my God." He shook his head. "These aren't refugees, Dr. Bruce. These are P.O.W.s."

My mind was racing. The only people we'd fought that we would have gotten Prisoners of War from were… "You are taking us to see a *Sang Heely super*?" I almost screeched. At least I hoped I almost screeched. I was so shocked I didn't even know how to respond. This was both a fascinating opportunity and a chance to get seriously killed by a violent racist.

Dr. Bruce exited the lift and we followed her down the hall and turned right. She stopped in front of a clear Tenorium Door. A young Heely sat inside on his bunk, eyes closed. The room was starkly bare, even for a prison cell. Odd, I thought.

"I think you should both meet him first before you judge," she chastised gently, "and," she deliberately caught my eye, "it is only something I strongly suspect, Commodore."

"What have you seen?"

She nodded. "He has nightmares. He nearly killed one of our nurses when she tried to help him. He never touched her, but everything in his room seemed to 'attack' her."

"Is that why his room is empty?"

"He insisted." Dr. Bruce stepped closer, all seriousness. "He won't talk about it. He just apologized and shut down."

Ah, OK. Shame. "So, he's not so much super, right now, as freak."

"That's exactly it, Ma'am."

"What do you want us to do?" Marston said, his eyes on the still form of the young Heely.

"Help," Dr. Bruce said simply.

"All right," I said. "Let us in."

Dr. Bruce paused a second as if she wasn't sure this was as good an idea as she'd originally thought, but I formed my shield around Marston and myself and nodded. She keyed open the door.

"Wylan, I have some people I would like you to meet," she said as the door slid back. "Commodore Jane Pace and General Marston Manthorpe."

Wylan, apparently, this was the young being's name, opened his eyes warily. He said nothing, did nothing, just watched us as we stepped into the room.

"Good afternoon," I said in Heely. I felt his body tense in surprise, but still he remained quiet.

"We wanted to talk to you, Wylan," Marston said kindly, also in Heely.

Wylan glared at us and spoke in heavily accented Standard. "The Terran Doctor told you what I did? What she thinks I am?" There was so much anger, so much self-loathing in those words it hurt to hear them.

"She told us what she suspected," I responded in Heely.

"You can drop your shield, Commodore Jane," he closed his eyes. "I am awake. I am in control."

"I don't think so, Wylan," I said. His eyes snapped back open and he frowned. "You can earn my trust, but you must actually earn it." His angry expression faded just a bit. I had passed some test, I guessed. "And you are *not* in control."

"You and your friend, the husband of the *teputa* Queen, are trying to convert me?" he said angrily.

I had never admired Marston's control more than at that moment. The 'whore Queen' was Tania, you know, his beloved wife, but Marston did nothing. Actually he smiled. "You fight your battles with name calling, do you, son?"

Suddenly Wylan was on his feet. Dear god, he was almost as tall as Synon and clearly still had growing too do. I wasn't afraid, but it did take me aback a bit. Trust me, you would have been taken aback, too. Apparently Standard was too difficult because he launched into a steam of furious Heely. "It's bad enough I'm a [no translation] freak! They'll put me to death for my crimes and I will go back to the Mother knowing I did my job. That I fought on the side of right!"

But…but there was something wrong with that. He was lying or guilty or something. His body had read with suppressed violence right up until the end. That last sentence had made his stomach clench. It had clenched, I thought, when he'd spoken what he hadn't believed. Aha. I felt Marston's tension relax, too, and wondered if he'd come to a similar conclusion through 'normal' observation. All very interesting.

"Sit," I commanded and I stared at him until, eventually, he did. "Thank you."

I modified my shield and moved it to cover Marston only as I knelt down in front of the young Heely. Wylan tensed but stayed put. "I know you think I want to control you. I don't. I want to guide you until you can control yourself." He huffed and stared straight ahead. "I can't make you un-super." No, I couldn't do that, but perhaps I could offer him something. Something I'd needed as much, perhaps, as this boy did. A place in the universe that was *his*. Well, it was worth a shot. "I can give you a place to learn," I heard Marston's quick intake of breath—yeah, we were going to discuss *that* once we'd left this cell, "what you can do and what you can't. I can give you choices." I blinked quickly to hide my emotion from this damaged boy. "I can give you chances to be proud of your work and what you can do."

He turned his green head to me, his fin tight against his scalp. "Add 'for the purity of our nation' and that is almost word for word what they said to me before they took me away from my *Demna*."

Now my heart ached. Poor, poor kid.

I nodded approvingly. "I am glad you are smart enough not to take me at my word. I am a stranger to you no matter what you've been told about me."

"Do you know how many of my people you killed, Red Angel?" he said venomously.

"Do you know how many of *your* people the Sang Heelies killed, Wylan?" I responded firmly.

He quailed at that, though he tried to hide it.

I rose and headed for the door. "I'll be back tomorrow."

"Of course, you will, Red Angel. Brainwashing can't be done in one day, can it?" he sneered.

Oh, I liked this feisty boy. "Un-brainwashing can't either, young one. See you then."

Marston and I made it out the door and it was only when it had shut behind us that Marston rounded on me. "Have you lost your mind, Jane? You're going to put that kid in our program?"

"Maybe. It's up to him, though he'd never believe that now." Then a thought occurred to me. "That isn't the whole picture, of course." I turned to Dr. Rogers. "Has he been formally charged?"

"No," she said, looking at Wylan though the Tenorium. He was sitting, mimicking his pose of earlier, but his massive hands were in fists now. "As far as I can tell, he didn't actually *do* anything in the Battle of Novy. He was there, yes, but someone shoved him in an escape pod when ships started exploding. Even the JAG," Judge Advocate General, "couldn't find a single witness that saw him kill anyone. He was still a trainee, apparently." She shrugged. "The other Heelies sang (ha!) like Terran birds about each other, but barely seemed to remember he was there. I think the ones that 'got away' were the ones who hadn't really wanted to be there in the first place, honestly."

"The True Believers all died for the cause," Marston murmured.

"Well, that is one way to cull the herd," I said.

"They…they *spit* when I mentioned Wylan's name," she confided in a whisper, horrified. "They said he was unclean, defective." I didn't know the specific significance of a water-based people wasting body water like that, but the act clearly wasn't a nice one. They hated him because he was different—easier than being jealous of the incredible things he could do, I supposed with an internal sigh. Racists begetting racists. Yikes.

"I am pretty sure," Dr. Bruce said, recovering herself, "that enrollment in the *Schola-Terra* would show that he wanted to be a part of society and even the 'in the wrong place at the wrong time' charges would go away."

I looked at her in wonder. "You're trying to save him."

Dr. Bruce shrugged. "I have a teenaged son myself. They are all attitude and hormones and sure no one understands them—mostly because they don't understand themselves. That boy in there reminds me a lot of my Kevin." She grinned. "Fins notwithstanding."

"Ok, then." I cocked my head at Marston. "So, I'm coming back tomorrow?"

Marston narrowed his eyes, but then sighed. "You're coming back tomorrow." He put his fingers on the bridge of his nose. He turned away and started down the corridor, but then stopped and said, over his shoulder, "Welcome to motherhood."

I stopped walking at that word and stood there long enough that Marston had to call to me to catch up. He was chuckling as he did it. Asshole.

So the next day, before my first class, I had shown up at Wylan's cell with weights. My usual 6 ounce to 1000 pound weights. I had demonstrated moving them and juggling them. I'd encouraged questions, but didn't ask him to try anything. I'd stayed about an hour and left the weights (my spare set) with him.

When I'd come back the next day they'd been moved, but I'd said nothing about it. I'd brought feathers this time and explained how I would use the same amount of effort to move feathers as to move the thousand pound weight. I amused him (though he tried to hide it) by 'moving' them into patterns of animals of all kinds. I left the feathers behind.

The next morning I'd come back to find a rebellious Wylan and shredded feathers. Since I'd detected traces of feathers under his nails/claws, I knew he was probably not a Micro. Or not *also* a Micro. That day I'd taken him to the Heely pool within Terra 1. It was a new addition, a concession to Queen Tania's new influence (not to mention David's) within the Union and I'd gotten to see genuine joy on Wylan's face as he swam circles around me in my protective suit. At one point I'd noticed he was staring hard at me. Holding quite still I just watched him, but after a moment he seemed to change his mind and swam on. I made a note to come back to the pool as often as possible.

The next day I'd taken him to the main shuttle bay, where I'd hastily moved my *Liberty*. I'd had him put his massive webbed hands on my shoulders as I'd lifted the shuttle up over our heads. The most important thing I would ever teach my kids, aside from basic control, was that the physical body had nothing to do with 'lifting' with the mind. It was, I'd known, a daring move on my part. Not because of any possible sexual tension (I got a strange vibe from him on that) but because he was at my back. Aside from his hands trembling a bit, however, his touch was respectful and I think he got the point. Then I let him ride back with me on my *Liberty* as I put my baby back at its docking slip. It was the right call—he'd loved my little ship.

"Do you teach your cadets to fly ships in your program?" he'd asked as if he couldn't help himself.

I'd smiled. "We teach all kind of flying, Wylan."

His pale green eyes went wide at this. "You can really fly, Ma'am? I thought that was just a myth." Or he'd been told it was a myth. By the same people that had treated him like a pariah.

"Any properly trained Macro-Telekinetic can fly. It is one of the most liberating things we do and," I grinned, "it's a hell of a lot of fun." I let him absorb this only for a second. "Could you request clearance to dock, please?"

He tried, bless him, to play it cool, but it came out, "Dockingcontrolthisis122402requestingclearancetodock."

I'd said nothing as an understandably confused Docking Control had him repeat the request.

The day after that we'd gone back to the pool and that time, instead of taking off into the deep blue, he'd stopped and stared at the air above the water. I felt it; he was making a shield. For what purpose, I wondered? The shield wasn't what I would have expected either; whereas my shields were usually a wall this was a…ball. Holy shit. Then he 'pulled' the ball (and that took a bit of strength since it wanted to be buoyant) down into the water and around me. If it looks like a Macro, I thought, and acts like a Macro, and 'builds' kick-ass shields like a Macro…

"You can take off your mask, ma'am, if you want to," he said shyly through the water in lower Heely. "It's OK if you don't."

Christ on a bicycle. I felt a second of panic. This was fucking dangerous, Jane, and everyone you know would kill you for even considering it, I thought, but, another voice in my head said, you wanted the kid to trust you. I closed my eyes and took a deep breath…and pulled my helmet back.

Oh wow. I could breathe and I could see everything. "This is amazing, Wylan," I said in lower Heely, "I've never even heard of anyone doing this before."

"Thank you, ma'am," he said with quiet pride, but I could feel the strain in his body.

"We can train for this, if you'd like." An interesting application of 'mass means nothing' that was for sure.

He could only nod then as he started to shake.

"I'm going to put my helmet back on," I said gently, and I did, trying not to look like I was rushing. I checked the seals. "You may release now."

He did.

You know how heavy water is, especially Heely water? Really fucking heavy.

I woke up on the ground next to the pool, a very panicked Wylan standing over me. I'd felt, not coincidentally, like I'd been hit by several tons of Heely water. My head hurt, but I was basically unharmed. That suit was damned incredible.

"Great Mother, ma'am!" he gibbered. "Are you alright?"

I sat up. "I'm fine, Wylan. Don't worry." His eyes kept darting to the nearest door. Fuck me running. "Who'd you call?"

"You were unconscious, ma'am."

A feeling of dread infused me. "Who did you call, Wylan?"

"Well," he gulped. "Everyone."

Then, as if his words had summoned them, Dr. Bruce, Marston and a whole Med Tech crew appeared with a stretcher. Everyone was glaring at Wylan and he backed up in the face of their fury. I had to nip this in the bud.

"Hold on, everyone!" I said loudly as Marston opened his mouth to speak. "Wylan and I were experimenting with shielding within Heely water and I let go at the wrong time and got smacked with tons of it. It knocked me out. I'm fine."

"Thank goodness," Dr. Bruce said, looking at Wylan, then guiltily at me. "I mean, I'm glad you're not hurt, Commodore."

I suppressed a giggle. Thanks, Doc. Marston, however, clearly didn't buy my little story one bit, and gave me a significant look which I returned with equal significance. I really hoped we were being significant about the same thing. He then looked from Wylan to me and back again.

"You should be more careful in future, Jane." Thank goodness.

"I will be, Marston, I promise."

"You, son, will you take the Commodore's mistake to heart?" Oh, yeah, Marston knew the score.

Wylan nodded spastically. "Yes, Sir. I will."

Such a good kid, I thought.

"It's a great responsibility, being a Macro, isn't it, Wylan?" I said with a smile. What I was thinking, however, was admit it, admit who you are.

He let out a great breath and finally said, "Yes, Ma'am, it is."

I exhaled, too. Finally.

After that, Wylan had no longer pretended to be uninterested in Macro training. I'd also made a note to do more research on underwater 'ball' shielding and how to turn it off without knocking out or killing the person/people inside it. Probably should have thought about that before I'd gone into one of the things, but we all know that thinking ahead isn't necessarily how I learn. Ah, if only.

So, back in the present, Marston and I waited for Wylan to show up to the first ever Heely Macro Class; currently a class with only one student. He had been 'paroled' to the *Schola-Terra* ESTF and would be a free being if he graduated at the end of four years. Dr. Bruce and I had vouched for him. Queen Tania had even sent him an encouraging message, though that hadn't gone over as well as it could have. Wylan no longer insulted her, at least out loud, but he'd looked distinctly uncomfortable. One step at a time.

Wylan entered the room nervously (his hands were trembling), but tried to hide it (by clenching his fists). "Ma'am. Sir."

Marston and I both grinned. "Welcome to the Class of 2877, Wylan."

His smile just glowed. He was so happy he'd forgotten to pretend he was too worldly to care. "So, I'm a Cadet?"

"You are," I affirmed, "and as such, you need a uniform."

"Thank goodness," he said slyly, "now I'll blend in with everyone else."

Was that an attempt at humor? Who knew he was even capable? He had a point, however, as I looked over his almost seven foot frame. Blending in? Nope. "You are the first Heely super in the *Schola-Terra*, Wylan, but we hope you won't be the last."

"Hear hear," Marston agreed.

I 'lifted' the large box from the back table and 'maneuvered' it until it was on the ground in front of him. He looked from the box to me, silently asking permission to proceed. I nodded and he pulled open the lid.

It was a uniform, yes, but one with difference.

He picked it up reverently, but frowned when it didn't fold. Or bend. Or lose its shape in any way.

"Ma'am?"

"Marston, would you explain?"

Marston stepped forward and pointed to the uniform, or should I say, suit. "The Commodore and I were thinking about the problem of a Heely living in a 'dry' environment." He shrugged. "Training can be tiring, time can be short. Sometimes you won't be able to get to the pool. So we brought," he tapped the suit, "a bit of the pool to you."

"I don't understand."

I stepped forward. "Most suits, like the DSS and the DPSS are made to keep things *out*. This DSS, the first of its kind, far as I know, has been made to keep Heely water *in*."

"You mean you can fill this…" he trailed off astonished, unable to take his eyes off our creation.

"With a small amount of Heely water. Enough for almost a week, if it comes to it," Marston said with more than a hint of pride in his voice.

"A week?"

"We checked it with the Doc and she suggested a filtration system which my friend Thal was able to implement and add to the small pack at the back of the neck." It had been surprisingly easy to do, actually, once we'd come up with the initial idea. Thal was a god-send. He just *saw* what needed to be done and did it. Well, he'd been created from the personality of David's father (though this Thal rarely alluded to it) and David's inventing abilities had come from somewhere. As for the suit, Wylan would be our tester and, if things went well, we'd pass on the idea to Synon, Tania and their people. Thal would hold the patent.

"It still looks like a uniform," he said in awe.

"A cadet needs to follow dress code, Wylan."

"Yes, Sir."

He stared at it a while and felt the material. Stiff but not uncomfortably so. The wrists and ankles had a seal so he could use his hands and wear regulation boots. *Pretty damned cool, if I did say so myself.*

"May I go try it on?"

"Of course," I said, but then I realized we had one more bit of information we needed. Something I'd asked him to think about. "I need to know; have you decided on a surname?"

His body language instantly changed to rigidity. "Smith."

What? "Smith?"

"Yes," he said defiantly. "I read a book once that said that Terran humans emigrating often lost their real last names when they came through immigration. Unusual to impossible to spell ones became things like 'Smith' and 'Jones.' If I'm really no different than any other émigré," his chin lifted at this, "I can be a Smith, too."

"Of course you can," I said faintly.

Marston looked as perplexed as I felt. "Most supers take either the name they were born with, or that of the planet they're from, like Commodore Pace did, and I know Heelies don't usually have last names, but I assumed you would take the name of your clan. Your *Demna*."

"I don't have a *Demna*, Sir."

"You must have had at one point."

"Yes, Sir." Wylan, however, remained silent.

I couldn't let it go, though. I had to know. "What was the name of your *Demna*, Wylan?"

"I was taken from my parents when I was young. I never really knew anyone there. My parents had escaped..."

Now Wylan looked really uncomfortable.

"Escaped from where?"

"The Homeworld."

I felt the room spin a bit. *The Heliot Homeworld that I had seen destroyed by Samuel's Fleet, though it hadn't been his fault.*

"The Sangs wanted the blood-line," he said. "Until they realized that I was...wrong."

That he was a super. Heelies weren't supposed to be supers. Why would I think...? Then I thought I knew. *Oh, crap.* Marston's face was all surprise, shock even. He was looking at the kid with new eyes, as if trying to make pieces fit.

"You'll think it means something it doesn't," Wylan said, the old defensive kid I'd met a month before.

"Wylan," I said, a hint of steel in my voice.

"My *Demna* was called *Indus Felae.*"

Like Tania's. So this boy was *family.* Well, well…hell.

I took a breath then said, "Go put on your uniform, Cadet Smith."

He nodded, the tension draining out of his body. "Yes, Ma'am."

18:00 – Classroom 2 (Mine), ESTF, *Schola-Terra* Academy

Wylan had done well learning one on one. He'd been quick to learn and was very intelligent—when one could fight through the occasional attitude flare-ups to get to it. He was worried about mixing with the general cadet population, especially since the Heely War had ended so very recently, but I could only reassure him a little. Truth was, I didn't know how it would go. There would be problems, of course. We had a whole batch of Tellescans whose entire planet had been consumed because of the Sang Heelies. I could enforce our Rules of Conduct, but I wouldn't be there to nanny him through every moment. I'd start, however, by making announcements in every class about fairness, etc. I just had to hope that they were all still intimidated enough by me that they would leave the kid alone. I shook my head mentally as I dismissed my Terran human students for the day. At least the motherfucking Blackbird had made me to be even more of a son of a bitch than I actually was. Let's hope this would be helpful (at least to Wylan) instead of the constant clusterfuck it seemed to be.

Soon I was alone in the classroom. The class I'd just finished was in hand to hand—no abilities. I was sore and bruised. My bad shoulder ached. It was kind of a frustrating class, but a core requirement in the curriculum. Most of the kids hated it and since it was an advanced class and since some of the kids were getting to be better fighters than I was, it was a bit of a drag for me, too. There was always someone with attitude when the semester started ("I can crush a shuttle *with my mind,* ma'am, why am I doing this exactly?") that had to be lectured ("a super who knows how to fight *without* abilities will be an infinitely better fighter *with* them," you little punk). I pictured myself having to do this semester after semester and the thought was depressing. I needed a teacher. A teacher who was strong, disciplined, tough, fair and, most importantly, not me. I'd been thinking this since the previous semester and, for once, the universe dropped someone right in my lap.

"You're still protecting your back," a dry female voice said from the back of the room as I was wiping the sweat off my brow. Well, that was a bio-signature from the past.

"I didn't know you were on station, Mallory," I said by way of a greeting. She walked over to me, all whipcord muscle and control. She was in her fifties now and age had softened her face (she didn't look as leathery as she had when she'd been our fighting instructor on Pace-Pallon) if not her body. I extended my hand and she shook it once she reached me. She smiled.

"I got back yesterday."

"It's good to see you," I said, though I didn't really know *why* I was seeing her. The last time I'd been in the same room with her had been Arrow's funeral. I pushed the inevitable sadness that came with that thought away and focused on my former instructor.

"And you."

While definitely a Pacey, Mallory was not a super, technically, but she was far from ordinary. Her parents had, Samuel had told me ages ago, used all five of her legally allowed modifications on strength and improved reflexes. She had mentored both Felix and Arrow and she was incredibly strong and lethally fast. An impressive fighter—because she'd been designed to be so and because she'd worked her ass off to be one.

"Are you looking for a job?" I asked, speaking before I really thought.

She laughed. "I am, as it turns out. Why? Do you need someone?" She looked at me, drenched with sweat and sore. "Yes, I can see you do."

"It's that obvious?" I asked, chagrined.

"To me, yes." Mallory nodded and her tone changed to the one of strength and kindness that had made her such a good teacher at the School. "You've done really well, Jane. You've come a long way."

"Thanks," I said softly, embarrassed. It was nice to hear, though. Really nice. "I'm getting in over my head, as you can see, and I'm overbooked as it is, so it would be great to have you here."

"I would love to work here."

I expected her to say more, but she fell silent. "But…"

A regular, normal (ha!) woman would have hemmed and hawed, but this was Mallory, who was fearless. "That ridiculous book put the Blackbird as the love of Admiral 'Lindbergh's,'" she shook her head in silent condemnation of the book, "life." She cocked her head to the side. "I know you were with Sam and that he loved you."

"Yes."

"Does he still?"

"No." It didn't hurt to say that anymore. The fact that it didn't almost took my breath away. Wow. I'd never thought I'd actually get there, but it was such a relief. I was pretty sure that was Charles' doing, though the amount of time that had passed had probably helped, too.

"Do you still love him?" Mallory asked.

"In the romantic sense, no."

She nodded briskly at that. "I'm glad you still care for him. We all need good friends we can depend on."

"True." Where was she going with this? Oh. "You love him." Geez, Jane. Subtle.

Mallory nodded again, unperturbed. "I have for a long time. Longer than you've been alive." They'd been lovers years ago, right after his first divorce, but it had been merely an item in Samuel's sexual history when he and I'd discussed it. For him at least, it hadn't been a great love or even love at all, which sucked for Mallory for whom it, apparently, had been.

"I don't think he knows that," I said truthfully.

"He doesn't."

"Why not?"

"I knew I wasn't what he needed. Not then and maybe not now, either," she rubbed her forehead.

"But you want to try now and you need to know I won't be in the way."

"Yes."

"I won't be."

"The physical you won't be. The memory of you may be a problem." Blunt but true, but there was nothing either of us could do to help that.

"All I want is for Samuel to be happy."

"I believe you." She looked at me. She was my height, something I'd never noticed before. She'd always seemed taller than me, larger than life. "Are you happy now? Separately from Sam, I mean?"

Charles, I thought, and the smile I didn't want to fight took over my face.

She grinned back, probably unconsciously. "I'm glad."

"Thanks." I still wanted her to teach, however. I still wanted to unload this fucking class and all like it. "So will you take the job?"

"I will."

"Thank you." I wanted to cheer, but didn't of course. Not cool. Inside my head, though, I was cheering my head off. Mallory smiled and turned to leave, our interview apparently over.

"Mallory?" I called after her.

"Yes?"

"Be good to him."

She paused. "I will, Jane. If he'll let me."

19:00 – My Apartment, Terra 1

"So, Captain Jack saw Novy-Thal on Trithicate Station," Thal (my Thal) repeated gravely.

We, and by we I mean I, had sat down to dinner at the small table in my equally small apartment. Charles had some Ambassadorial function to attend that I was thrilled I didn't have to go to so I was on my own for dinner. Thal, wonderful Thal, had cooked. I wasn't much into food (food = fuel) but what he'd made (something delectable called Beef Corsica that was, according to Thal, a delicacy on Berria. Beef wrapped in something tasty and that wrapped in something else tasty wrapped in a pastry. Heaven.) was delicious. How Thal knew what he was cooking was even edible was beyond me, since he didn't eat, but he was a terrific chef.

"Yep." I took a bite. Yum. "I know you've been prohibited from talking about David's work, but I wanted you to be up-to-date."

"Thank you." Thal pursed his lips. "This is beyond my personal experience with Mr. Abrams," he blinked thoughtfully, "so I think I am safe to theorize."

I put down my fork in surprise. "Really?" Thal nodded. Nice loophole, Thal, I thought, amused. "So what do you think David is trying to do with the Rian?"

"I don't know, though I have to assume that it is all tied to the introduction of the Lady Eriss to the Union."

"I agree."

"I may, possibly, be able to get some information on that."

"How?"

"In a roundabout way." He folded two of his hands in front of him. "Mr. Abrams considers his experiment in self-directed sentience to be a failure." I shrugged sympathetically since the translation of that was that David considered *Thal* to be a failure. That bothered me a lot, for Thal's sake, but there wasn't much I could do about what David thought. Not that I hadn't tried. "Which means, very likely," he continued, "that Novy-Thal's free will has been compromised."

"That sounds about right."

"It is also likely," he sighed, "that any attempt to 'turn' him would be a waste of time."

"Yeah," I said glumly.

"However…" and here Thal gave a wicked grin that I'd never seen on his mobile plastic face before. It was startling and wonderful, "…he may have outsmarted himself."

"That would be a first," I muttered.

"You mean aside from giving me the ability to say 'no' and leave him?" he asked, smirking.

"Point taken."

"The thing is that he is very ambitious, as you know," he said. I nodded. "He needs to be several places at once." I nodded again. "So, if I were Mr. Abrams…" he trailed off. "Miss Jane, do you know for sure that that was Novy-Thal?"

I stared at him for a second and had to admit, "I just assumed… Oh my."

"Mr. Abrams is paranoid in the extreme. He cannot trust beings he cannot control." Well wasn't that the goddamned truth, I thought. "As I've said, however," Thal continued, "he needs to be in several places at once— what with ramping up the Novy shipyards to compete with UNav and Corsica, the medical business, actually running Novy (there is only so much he will let Queen Tania do), whatever he has going on with the Pelann and his home life. He doesn't just need a right hand, he needs…"

"…an army." My eyes actually hurt, they went so wide. "Holy shit, Thal."

"My thoughts exactly, Miss Jane."

I pushed my plate away from me, no longer hungry, which was a shame. "You said you think he's outsmarted himself?"

The wicked grin returned. "There is a protocol in my system that does something quite interesting. Mr. Abrams always thinks ahead and he inputted a program into me, and all Thals I have to assume, that allows us to communicate with and monitor each other."

"All of you?"

"It seems so. He based it on the ability of Denethian families to, under certain circumstances, act as one."

"But, Thal," I cried, dismayed, "I thought he couldn't control you. He swore and so did Affy…"

He put his two right hands up in a calming motion. "That has not changed. If I access the program, which until now I hadn't thought was relevant to anything, I will be able to 'hear' what is going on and 'hear' the orders from Mr. Abrams, but my ability to choose for myself will remain intact and I should," he grimaced, "be able to get an idea of how many of my brethren we are dealing with."

"Will you do that?"

He looked surprised by the question. "Of course."

"Thank you." Then I had another thought. "How will you do it? You can't let David know you are 'listening in.'"

"I believe I can get in passively, but even if I can't I'm not really all that worried about it."

"Why not?"

Thal shrugged. "Mr. Abrams wants obedience and thought within very strict parameters. I would be very much surprised if he found out." I looked askance at him. "If he doesn't directly *ask* the Thals about someone monitoring their network (or get the idea to look on his own) they will have no reason to tell him." He looked angry then, his lips becoming a thin line. "They have been programmed, neutered. Their opportunity to be loyal, to be devoted, was taken away before they even had a chance to know what it was."

"It's not right, losing your liberty, Thal. Even if they don't know they could have had it."

"It is what it is, Miss Jane." Thal rose from the table, taking all the dishes (four arms really came in handy for that sort of thing) and headed for my miniscule kitchen. "I choose to focus on our freedom," he said seriously. "The future may be uncertain, but at least it is ours."

I watched him quickly and efficiently clean up dinner. "There is that," I murmured to myself.

23:45 – Ambassadorial Apartments, Corsican Embassy,

Breathing hard, I collapsed on Charles' broad chest and tried to recover from some serious love-making (what my friend Felaysa, the E05, called 'hot monkey sex'). Wonderful wonderful wonderful. Charles sighed contentedly and tucked me to his side as he stroked my back.

"Well, my darling, that was worth sitting through that dreadful dinner."

"I aim to please, love," I said with a chuckle. "Was it really that bad?"

"No, not really. I think my tolerance for the posturing and intrigue is just getting less and less with age."

"Age, huh?" I teased.

He sighed with amused tolerance. "I saw Alex today."

"How was he?"

"He says he's fine."

Something about the way Charles had said that made me think Alex wasn't fine at all. "The report from Novy," the only time I'd heard from Wilby even if it had been in the most impersonal way possible, "said the treatment for his skin was a success." Or, as successful as it could have been considering the damage involved. I'd been fascinated by the whorls and swirls left on Charles' son's skin after he'd been dipped in the poisonous Heely water, but I was a weirdo. I couldn't hope that everyone else would find them as interesting.

"Idis says…" and then he stopped.

I sat up, resting his arm on my lap. I brushed his red hair from his forehead. "Idis says…"

He laughed awkwardly. "Forgive me, Jane. I don't know what I'm allowed to say and what I'm not."

I thought about it for a second. "How you talk about me, if you do at all, when you are with Idis is something you'll have to negotiate with her. However," I grinned, "as long as you don't spend all your time saying, 'well Idis does it this way or Idis is so much better at this or…" I felt myself get quieter, "'Idis is a grownup, why can't you be one, too?'" I'd started off joking, but had unintentionally landed myself in a pit of insecurity. Charming, Jane. Bet Idis wouldn't have done *that*.

Charles, alarmed, sat up, too, and took my hands. "I won't do that, Jane. We have to figure this out and since we all want it to work, I think we will."

I nodded, believing him because I loved him more than anything and because I really didn't have much choice.

"I don't want you to pretend she doesn't exist…"

"You just don't need her in our bed."

"Yeah." I smiled at him, feeling better. "So, what does Idis say?"

He pushed back so that he was leaning against headboard and he brought me with him, tucking me back where I'd been before. Perfect.

"She says that I focus on little things and let them drive me crazy." He grimaced. "I know I do that, but still…"

"You saw something about Alex."

"He was wearing gloves," Charles said.

I sat with that for a minute. I might have noticed that myself or I might not have, but I did think it was significant, now that it had been pointed out. "So he's hiding the only part of him that was marked that anyone, outside of a doctor or a lover," Alex would probably have said disfigured, not marked, "could see?"

"Yes."

"I'll talk to him this week and see what his thinking is. What he probably needs, Six, is time. It's a big change for him."

"I know, I just can't stomach my son thinking he's wrong somehow."

I moved up so I could kiss his cheek. "I'll do my best. I promise."

"Thank you, Jane." He looked sad and vulnerable and while I felt privileged that he was showing this to me, what I wanted right then was for him to be happy. "So, tell me about your day, love," he said.

I ran my hands over his chest, delighting in his shudder of arousal. "Later." I kissed him and I'm pretty sure he forgot all about either of our days, if only for a while.

Sometime later I again rested on his chest, after a much needed (not to mention exciting) shower, and traced the faint bullet hole scars with my fingers. Charles lay there contentedly, eyes closed but very much awake, stroking my back.

"So young Wylan Smith is a full cadet now?"

"Yes."

"Good. The Union could do with a reminder that Heely humans are still humans." He sighed. "Not that that should matter."

"It shouldn't." All sentients deserved respect.

"I wonder how closely related he actually is to Tania."

I hadn't thought about it. "Why?"

"If he's biologically related he could be an heir," he explained. Well, that whole heir/dynasty thing was in his wheelhouse so I was hardly one to argue. "After her children."

Was this an issue of actual bloodline? "Her kids are all adopted."

He thought for a second then nodded. "No cross-breeding with a Terran human husband."

"No."

"Interesting wrinkle. I wonder what General Manthorpe is discussing with his wife this evening?"

"I wonder, too."

He sighed and moved on. "The blasted Blackbird is here to stay."

"Apparently."

He snuggled me closer. "Will you talk to Sam about it?"

I sighed. "I've made an appointment to see him tomorrow."

"Will you be all right?"

"Me, sure. I can always find work somewhere." That, I was pretty sure, hadn't been what Charles had meant, but I was worried for my ex-lover. How many Admiral jobs were there in the universe?

"He's tough, Jane. He'll weather this just fine."

"Yeah, but what about Albert?" Albert Nylander, Nora's spouse. Still MIA.

"I issued an Imperial Order today recalling him," Charles said grimly. "He'll show."

"Good."

Charles was tense now and angry at the mention of his possibly traitorous (or at best disloyal) old friend. I needed a change of subject. I then realized I had something, something I'd been curious about and regarding my favorite topic, no less. "Question?"

"Hmm," was his only response.

I bit my lip, trying to figure out how to phrase it, "In terms of physiology, most men, you know, wear out at a certain point…in bed…" He didn't. Like, not at all.

I felt the muscles in his freckled face pull into a huge grin. "Ah, that."

"I'm not complaining, mind you," I clarified, "I'm just surprised."

He chuckled and said, "Well, my darling, it all goes back to my 48 times grandfather, also a Charles."

"Of course he was."

"It goes without saying." He took my hand, the scarred one, and threaded his fingers through mine. "*That* Charles didn't really like women."

"So he married a man..?"

"Oh, no, he didn't like men much either, but he did his duty by his wife and Kingdom and fathered ten sons and eight daughters."

This was centuries before 'tubbing' had even been invented. I shuddered. "Poor girl."

"Indeed, but he'd married an experienced woman of twenty-five. A widow with, according to legend, an exceptional appetite for sex."

"Right..?"

"He'd emerged from their wedding night furious that he couldn't have as many orgasms as she."

"He hated women because he was jealous of *that*?" I giggled.

"You'd be jealous, too, I think, if you came twice to my forty times."

Now I sat up, staring at him. "Forty? Really?"

He nodded. "The Palace staff used to listen outside her bedroom door and place bets."

Now I liked a good orgasm (who didn't?) but that seemed excessive even to me. "So what did he do?"

"He had his male children...modified."

"Genetically engineered modified, you mean? Really?"

Charles nodded. "He tweaked it more with the grandsons and the great-grandsons and so on." He pulled me closer. "It is the only real reason I can think of to keep the Couvillion-Bourbonais line as pure as possible."

"So all the men in your line can do this?" I asked, dumbfounded.

"Uh huh." He started kissing my neck.

I laughed, even as I enjoyed what he was doing. "So we're both freaks, then, aren't we?" He started to answer, but then I reached down and touched him and he only moaned. "I'm afraid you'll have to continue to prove this to me, love. It's a lot of take on faith."

His eyes had been closed as I touched him but they snapped open now, black gold, twinkling with merriment. "I bet you cry 'uncle' before I do."

I quickly straddled him. "Not a chance, Six." He growled at me and I laughed.

"You'll regret those words, Commodore."

Sure I would. "Make me, Your Highness."

He rolled us over and soon we were both lost to sensation. We both did our best and, as we eventually, hours later fell asleep in the midst, shall we say, it wasn't clear who'd won and I had to smile as I drifted off. I'd accidently fallen in love with a man as insatiable as I was. He'd thought I might be bored. I snuggled closer and slept.

ENTRY 2-8-85

08:00 – Ambassadorial Apartments, Corsican Embassy, Terra 1, Terra, September 25th, 2873

My alarm buzzed and I flung out my hand to turn it off. Nope. The buzzing got louder. My hand searched but only succeeded in knocking my watch off the nightstand. It was blissfully dark in Charles' room and the warm man wrapped around me was every temptation to stay in bed forever. Unfortunately the stupid alarm was almost deafeningly loud now. Where the fuck was it?

"Jane, love. Have pity," Charles mumbled into my shoulder sending shivers all over me. "Dresser."

Oh, right. I sighed and kissed the top of his head as I rose and stumbled over to the dresser and switched off the bastard alarm. I shook my head to clear the cobwebs and had to smile. Yes, bed had become such a wonderful place that I'd been nearly late to work every morning in the last week. Much as I loathed having to get up, however, the facts were that I needed to do it. Grownups with responsibilities did that sort of thing, hence the alarm set across the room to make absolutely sure I got my ass out of bed.

He rolled onto his back and stretched. Damn. He opened his eyes and smirked at me. "What do you have this morning?"

"Class at 10:00," I said, as I grabbed a clean uniform and underwear and efficiently stripped off my sleep shirt and panties all within about thirty seconds. "Why?"

His eyes had gone black gold as he'd watched me. "Come here."

This was why I'd learned to set that alarm earlier than I'd actually needed to get up.

Things were just about to get really interesting when my comm beeped in my ear. "Damn it," I muttered as I froze. Charles immediately stopped the delicious things he was doing.

"What's happened?" he said quietly, knowing I had an 'emergency's only' edit on the comm at this hour.

I shrugged and turned my head to click the comm on.

"Pace here," I said and then listened. "Right. I'll be there in 20." I listened to Marston again and finished with. "Fuck off, Marston. See you in a bit."

Charles looked at me with raised eyebrows.

I rolled my eyes. "Trouble with Cadet Smith."

"What, again?"

"Yes, love, and I have to get ready," I said regretfully. I kissed him quickly and rose, quickly re-grabbing my uniform and underwear from the floor. "Rain check?"

"With interest," he growled.

"Stop that," I laughed. "Do you think I won't make it up to you?"

"Oh, I know you will," he said, dropping his voice further because he knew it turned me on. Evil he was. God, I loved him.

"Back in a second," I said as I practically ran for the shower.

"Jane?"

"Yes, Six?" I said.

"Why did you tell Marston to fuck off just now?"

"He said Wylan needed his mummy," I grimaced.

Charles looked thoughtful, but was silent long enough that I took the opportunity to get going.

8:30 – My Office, ESTF *Schola-Terra*, Terra 1

Yes, I have an office. I rarely used it, but Marston had said that a person in my 'position' should have one, so I did. When I arrived Marston was already there, as was Wylan, stoned-faced, and Cadet Petros Nitsa, 23 and handsome in his olive skin and curly hair. Nitsa wearing his standard expression of smugness. This was our third little dispute with Mr. Nitsa and I wanted to smash that smugness right off his face. I felt proud of myself for not actually doing so.

Mr. Nitsa was from Prado, a small, unremarkable world that had become an unwilling Heely colony just before First Heliot. His family had been one of a few hundred survivors and those survivors had only made it because they had been off planet on their private yacht at the time of the attack.

"Good morning," I said testily. "What is it now?"

"Good morning, Commodore," Marston said grimly. "Cadet Smith has requested a repair on his uniform."

I rubbed my forehead. "What kind of repair?"

"A puncture. One that renders his suit useless."

I looked at the Heely and noticed that he was wearing an ill-fitting cloth uniform, not the super special one we'd made for him that was essentially projectile-proof. A puncture in his real one would keep the thin coating of Heely water from circulating within the suit. Only a real dick-bag would put a hole in it. Meet Mr. Nitsa.

"You think that Cadet Nitsa is responsible."

"I do." Marston glared at the Mr. Nitsa who smugged back at him. I was pretty sure I wasn't the only one who wanted to deck the guy.

"Mr. Smith, do you make this accusation?"

"No, ma'am."

This did not surprise me. Wylan never said anything, never reported anything.

"What do you say to this accusation, Mr. Nitsa, being well aware that this is grounds for dismissal from the Academy."

"I deny it. If there was tampering, ma'am, I had nothing to do with it." He seemed vaguely amused by the whole affair. Standard for Nitsa. He never admitted anything. Well, I'd had enough. My door chimed. Excellent.

"Enter."

The door slid open and Brady Carmichael stepped in. Mr. Nitsa's eyes went wide, fearful for the first time I'd seen. It was a good look on him. Brady Carmichael was an instructor at the Academy. He was slight and unassuming; someone you'd never notice, a fact he used to his advantage. His prey never knew who'd scanned their innermost thoughts until it was far too late. I tried to hide my smile. Yes, Mr. Carmichael was the second most powerful (human) TP I'd ever known, after Stuart. (Daniel was probably third.)

Such a shame Mr. Nitsa hadn't learned to fully close his mental 'door' yet.

"You can't scan me," Nitsa said, trying to recover his superior tone, "I have rights."

"No, Cadet, you don't," Marston said, all traces of his usual jovial manner absent, "you signed several documents when you entered the Academy giving us the right to scan you if we can show cause. Which we can."

"But he hasn't said anything," Nitsa said, still a bit panicked.

This seemed to rouse Wylan from his impression of statue. "Where I come from, we don't tell on bullies."

Nitsa flushed. "No, you just let bullies kill billions of people." His patrician face changed into a sneer, "Billions of *Terran* humans, I should say. Worthless lives to you, but not to me and not to a lot of others here."

"I had nothing to do with that," Wylan said defensively and, I thought, a bit guiltily.

"Says you," Nitsa said.

"Says me," Brady said quietly. He had one of those voices that people heard though he spoke barely above a whisper.

Nitsa swallowed, clearly loathe to argue with a man that scared him, but unwilling to give up his point.

"You remember me, Cadet?" Brady asked.

"Yes, Sir."

"You remember the scans we did before your admission?"

"Yes, Sir." Nitsa went pale. Yes, that had to have been unpleasant. He'd never met a TP before (his family seemed to breed Macros and nothing else) and Brady was a tough one to meet as your first. I hadn't envied Nitsa or any of the hundred other potential Cadets Brady had scanned. I'd pitied them then, but found I didn't much care now.

"You were, by virtue of your prejudice..." Brady started, but he saw Nitsa blanch and smiled, "You didn't think we knew? I saw a lot in your head, young man. Your younger brothers were more open to the idea of working with Heelies as equals," yes, that question had been added to the list of standard ones this year and thank goodness it had been, "but you were always...borderline."

Nitsa said nothing now.

"All I have to do is scan you and you will be free and clear," Brady said.

"But...but I didn't *do it*." Nitsa looked at me pleadingly. "I swear I didn't."

"Not this time," I said.

"No, ma'am," and then he surprised me and straightened, "I admit I did the other things I was accused of." (Tampering with Wylan's jet pack and adding something to his food to make him sick, just enough to skew an exam, in case anyone was wondering). "I shouldn't have lied about it, but I didn't do this."

This was not news to me, of course. Nitsa was smart but not clever when it came to dirty deeds. We'd have to work on that as his future profession demanded it. Here, of course, it worked to our advantage.

"Both those offenses are grounds for dismissal, Mr. Nitsa." It was hazing and I hated it.

"I know," the Cadet said, now sounding a bit defeated. "I can do better. I can."

I regarded the little weasel thoughtfully. He did have some brains and a great deal of talent, however, as did his brothers and he really wanted to stay in the program.

"Two conditions, Mr. Nitsa."

"Yes, ma'am," he said with a small exhale of relief.

"One, you go on probation for the next two semesters."

The boy nodded foolishly. Yes, I know he was only a year younger than I, but a boy he very much was.

"And two, anything, and I mean *anything*, that happens to Mr. Smith from this moment on will result in your immediate dismissal."

"Anything?" His eyes moved back and forth as if picturing all the things that could go wrong for which he would be held responsible. He wasn't the only person who wanted the 'Heely Abomination' gone; he was just the most noticeable.

I waited for him to get it.

"For how long, ma'am?"

"For as long as you both are here."

He digested this for a minute. He would be Wylan's shadow, which, from Wylan's body language pleased Wylan just as much as it was pleasing Nitsa.

Nitsa was silent a long time.

I regarded the boy thoughtfully. "May I have a word with Cadet Nitsa alone, please?"

Marston nodded and herded Brady and Wylan out.

"Petros?" I said, the steel gone from my tone for the first time since I'd entered the room.

"Yes, ma'am?"

"You must get over this."

"Yes, ma'am," he said because he had to.

I stepped closer. "Your pain and your loss are very real, but the Heelies are being reintegrated and they are strong. Mr. Smith is our first Heely super, but I can promise he won't be our last. You must find a way to see him as a Heely *human*. As a being like yourself."

He exhaled hard and I finally saw his defensiveness and his privilege drop away for the first time. "I don't know how to do that, ma'am."

"I will tell you how," I said as I smiled kindly at him. "First, you will fake it."

"Fake it?"

"Exactly. Then, over time, you may find you aren't faking it completely."

"All right." He looked up at me. "I don't want to be forced to be his friend, ma'am."

"I am not asking that."

"You're not?"

"No, Petros." I sat on the edge of the desk I never used. "Think of it as a lesson, one of many that you won't exactly get in the classroom. He is a member of your team, as all the other Cadets are. You don't have to like your team to back it up and they don't have to like you to save your ass." Then I had an unbidden thought that made me laugh a little. "Actually, I have found that working with people you really care about personally can throw your game a bit."

He looked askance at me.

"Going into a mission can be easier if you are all professionals instead of friends or lovers or this person's father, etc."

He frowned as he tried to picture it, but he had never been tested that way. It would come, I thought, unfortunately. It was the only thing I really hated about teaching; knowing that the innocence and the petty worries that so preoccupied students would soon be lost to gruesome experience.

"If you say so, ma'am."

"I do say so, Petros. Now," I rose, "do we have a bargain?"

"Yes, ma'am, we do." He said softly, "thank you."

I nodded. "We are counting on you. We count on each other." I patted him on his shoulder. "Dismissed."

He saluted and left.

I waited and Brady, Marston and Wylan trooped back in.

Marston was the first to speak. "So?"

I sighed. "I think he'll be fine. Eventually." I turned to Brady. "What did you get?"

"He's…cogitating," was all Brady would volunteer.

Well, it would have to be enough.

Brady, though, then cocked his head to the side and regarded all of us. "So, who punctured the suit?"

I blinked at him innocently. "What?"

"It wasn't Mr. Nitsa, which Marston knew, as did Cadet Smith here," Brady said. My 'door' was a vault it was shut so tightly. "So, I should keep looking for the culprit?"

"I don't think that will be necessary, Brady."

Brady rolled his eyes at me, but smiled slightly. I'd never seen him smile before. "Was there even a hole in the first place?"

"Funny thing about that," I said, as I headed for the door. "Turns out that nothing readily available in the ESTF can puncture that suit." I winked at the three men I was leaving behind. "Who would have thought it?"

"Good God," Brady swore under his breath. "I hope this works."

"Especially since I am now saddled with this asshat for the rest of my life," Wylan said under his breath.

"What was that?" I asked a little sharply.

"Nothing, ma'am," Wylan said, cowed.

You called me half an hour early, Marston, was what I thought, but I had class so I left.

12:34 – My Classroom, ESTF *Schola-Terra*

A couple of hours later I was cleaning up after my baby Macro Class and silently cursing the day wax bullets had ever been invented. Seriously, they splattered everywhere. It wasn't as bad with my Tuesday Micro Class; they could manipulate them one at a time, but the Macros could only grab them as a large mass. I frowned at the large human-sized metal cut out we'd been using for target practice. There was more wax on the wall behind it than on the target. Bet they'd hit more if I'd told them to miss the target, I grumbled in my head as I used my 'fingers' to scrape the wax off the walls. It was early days, I reminded myself, and they could clean the shit up themselves next time. I felt better immediately and did my best to work faster. I was looking forward to lunch at Aronoff's. More accurately, I was looking forward to gossip at Aronoff's. Missy had been either off or swamped with work over the last week, but I had hopes for a good dish session today.

Naturally my comm bepped.

"Pace here." I listened and immediately 'dropped' the bits of wax I'd been 'holding.' "I'll be right there, Charles."

Albert Nylander had returned to the nest.

Oh, and in case anyone was curious about my meeting with Samuel of a week ago, well, it was (at best) anticlimactic.

I'd arrived at Samuel's Office to be greeted by a harried-looking Alex (wearing gloves as he had for his father) and had been quickly ushered in. Garrett hadn't even been there. Off on assignment with the X-ships apparently.

"Jane," Samuel had said from his desk. I heard his voice, rather, but could barely see him, there was so much stuff in the way. Manuals and reports and two flexi-monitors as well as his actual computer, books and assorted other things including, I was pretty sure, a half-eaten sandwich.

"Samuel?" I said tentatively. Charles may have had an eye for little details, but any moron could see that Samuel was overwhelmed with work.

"One minute, please."

"Of course."

I waited for about ten minutes, feeling foolish for bothering him when he was clearly dealing with actual Big Picture issues and I opened my mouth to apologize and leave when he looked up at me and smiled. It was a tense smile, but I didn't get the feeling that the tension had anything to do with me.

"I'm sorry to be so busy and I really don't have much time, so may I have this conversation for the both of us?"

I took half a second to catch up, but I had to smile. "Go ahead."

"Your ex-student and ex-room-mate screwed you over and exposed a good deal of your private life in that motherfucking book and you are pissed but helpless to fix it."

"Correct."

He stood and started walking over to me. "You are deeply embarrassed by it all, as anyone would be, and you want to apologize to me for possibly ruining my career when we did everything we could to save it."

Unbidden came thoughts, unleashed by Charles, of how Samuel had let me go, and that didn't feel any better than this unwitting betrayal of our personal lives had. He must have seen my face fall. "The reason I wanted to see you was to tell you that I am not angry with you, that it wasn't your fault, that you couldn't have known what would happen and that I will be all right."

I stared at him a second, trying to take all that in. He'd just condensed the long, painful and (probably) tearful conversation I'd expected into about thirty seconds.

"Ok." I gulped. "Thank you?"

He chuckled. "You're welcome. Hugh isn't going to investigate an allegation from years ago when I wasn't High Admiral—aside the fact that, even by Terran standards, you were only underage by something like a week when we…"

…started fucking, fell in love, did it in a chair… I finished for him in my head, and only in my head.

"Derek told me to laugh it off and I am." He was in front of me now. His (to me) beautiful brown eyes were kind and his handsome (to me) face was gentle, but there was no pull towards him anymore. Not even a little bit, though he was still very dear to me. Ah, Charles.

"So, don't worry. Besides with all the changes happening around here, the last thing Hugh wants is his High Admiral replaced."

"Right."

He smiled and clapped his hand on my shoulder affectionately. "I really have to get back to work." He started back towards his desk. "I could use your help in the near future, if you have the time."

Well, dear, compared to you I appear to have all the time in the world. "What can I do?"

"Meet someone with me. A new," he grimaced, "ally. Who will arrive next week."

I didn't think a new Heely ally would have elicited that response so it had to be… oh. "The Denethian Commander?" I'd expected him before this, but apparently all of Samuel's stalling tactics had worked well. Until they hadn't.

"Yeah."

"That ought to be interesting."

"Yeah," he said again, but this time with a large helping of chagrin.

"Let me know where and when and I will be there."

"Thanks." He sat down behind his desk and picked up one of the fleximonitors. I headed for the door.

"Jane?"

"Yes?"

"I ran into Mallory yesterday and she said you'd given her the job at the ESTF." He seemed pleased. And Mallory 'ran into' him, my ass.

"I'm happy she accepted it. We need her."

"She is the best," he said, a bit distractedly, as his work was pulling him back into its thrall. "We're having dinner tomorrow night. Care to join us?"

Man, it was hard not to snicker. I was just imagining Mallory's face when she saw me arrive to third wheel her alone time with Samuel. I could tell the Infirmary when to expect me. "Thanks, but I have plans."

"Oh, well. Another time." Now oblivious to anything but work he frowned at the screen in front of him.

"You bet."

I left quickly and waited until the door shut behind me to roll my eyes and cackle quietly to myself.

"The High Admiral said something amusing, Commodore?" Alex said, his golden eyes twinkling.

"He did, Colonel, though he didn't know it," I responded but I was now focused on those damned gloves. Alex hadn't noticed and I almost started laughing again. Poor boy didn't know me well enough to know that he should be running for the hills right now. "Do you have time for lunch, Alex?"

Alex looked at his watch and his eyes lost focus as he ran through his responsibilities. I waited. "A quick one, Jane. That would be nice."

Poor, poor boy.

Missy was there and Synon was not (just the opportunity I'd been hoping for, damnation!), but my nosy curiosity about the newest Heely human/Terran human coupling would have to wait. My nosy curiosity about Alex, well…that would be up to Alex.

We made small talk; he was doing well at work and so was I, blah blah blah. He didn't ask about his father and I was relieved, though I wouldn't have minded certain questions. I think he thought that his reticence would cause me to be reticent, too. Like I'd said before, he didn't know me that well.

The food arrived and the gloves stayed on, even while he was eating.

"So, Alex. The gloves."

He swallowed and speared another bite of salad with his fork. "They save awkward conversations."

"I see." He ate the bite and stayed silent. "Are they temporary?"

He shrugged. "An awkward conversation today will be just as awkward in a year or ten, so I don't think so."

I paused, mostly so that he would be prepared for a more invasive question. "Are you seeing anyone?"

He snorted, so inelegant (yet human) of a Prince. "You must be joking."

"Why would I be?" I goaded.

He put his fork down and looked directly at me. "You are the only person, woman," he corrected, "I know who wouldn't be horrified by how I look and you are currently sleeping with my father."

Currently. "*Permanently* sleeping with him, yes, but I'm not so unusual."

His eyebrows had raised at my wording, but he shook his head. "Don't kid yourself, Jane, you are *very* unusual."

Somehow I didn't think that was a compliment. I wasn't hurt by what he'd said, though. I was a freak. I wasn't ashamed of it. Or I wasn't ashamed anymore. The door, however, had been opened on discussing my relationship with Charles, for better or worse.

"Are you going to marry him?" he asked unexpectedly.

What? I realized I wasn't breathing and that was probably a bad thing. Things were starting to gray out and I couldn't let that happen. In. Out. In. Out. "No. Why?"

"Oh." Alex actually looked forlorn. "Why not?" A touch of anger crept into his voice. "Or does 'permanently' mean something different where you come from?"

"It doesn't, asshole." Alex's eyes went so wide I thought they would fall out of his head. "Forever doesn't always have to mean marriage, you know."

Alex sighed, his snark dissipating. "It figures that father would fall in love with two women who didn't want to marry him."

"It's not that," I said, stumbling for words, "it's that I don't want to be..." Empress or Princess or whatever. I couldn't say it, not there, but he knew what I meant.

He nodded. "That's what Idis said, too." He speared another bite. "Ironic that a million less worthy women would commit murder to be in your shoes, and Idis', and yet..."

"...and yet." I watched him eat. He seemed down, more down than when we had started lunch. "Why do you care, Alex, whether or not he marries?"

His face reddened slightly and his ears turned pink with obvious embarrassment. "It's part selfish, part not." He straightened. "I want father to have a *good* marriage." He stared at me defensively. "He's never had one, you know."

I did know. I'd heard about it in broad strokes, from Idis, though Charles himself had barely discussed the late unlamented Empress Marianna. "The selfish part?"

"If he marries and has another child, then I don't have to be…" Emperor, "…to take over the family business."

"Oh." I felt that old familiar feeling of guilt, of letting Charles down by being with him, but I pushed it aside. Charles knew me, knew that I didn't want the risk of having a child out there in the universe for anyone to hurt that hated me, and he wanted me anyway. We'd promised each other we were together no matter what. I had to trust that, but I did feel badly for Alex, all the same. "I'm sorry, Alex."

"It was just a thought," he said, his mouth full of food.

We'd eaten in near silence before we'd returned to our respective jobs. I'd, as I'd prepared for my next class, wondered how much of that conversation I'd be mentioning to Charles.

Back in the present I headed quickly back 'home' to the Ambassadorial apartments on the station.

Mr. Beddoes met me at the door and silently ushered me towards the Audience Room, the most formal of the Ambassadorial Rooms within the suite. It was, I thought as I entered it, a room that was very reminiscent of a throne room. I'd passed through it once or twice on my way to the private apartments, but had never spent any time here. My 'business' with Charles was always personal. I knew this long-awaited meeting with Albert was, too, but it was also real business.

Albert Nylander stood off to the side. He was tall and, shall we say, comfortably built. He'd previously given the impression of robust health (when I'd seen him within the Legislature years ago), but now I could see bags under his eyes, pallor to his skin and feel the vague shakiness that comes with adrenaline burnout. All was not well with Albert.

"Commodore," Albert said quietly with a deep bow of his head.

"Mr. Nylander," I responded. He turned away from me and faced the double doors in front of us expectantly. It was obvious to me that nothing was going to be said until Charles arrived and that was fine with me. I wondered what this man near me was thinking.

The doors opened, by Mr. Beddoes, I noticed, and Charles entered. I tried not to stare at how resplendent he looked in a very formal suit, superb vest, glossy tie and, my heart stuttered a bit, his gold and red ring of office. His body was singing with tension and he had that oh-so-determined look he got right before he let someone have it. Albert's respiration quickened and he started to sweat. If he hadn't known he was in deep shit before, he certainly knew it now.

Charles looked at Albert and held out his left hand (the hand with the imperial ring) palm down. "Albert."

At this command Albert stepped forward and knelt, kissing his monarch's hand, though I felt his stomach clench when he did it. I wondered if Albert had ever had to do that outside of an official occasion. These two had been friends their whole lives.

Albert stayed down, waiting.

"Rise."

Albert rose. Charles then walked over to me and gently put his arm around my waist. His stern face softened when his eyes met mine. "Thank you for coming, Jane," he said as he kissed me gently on the lips. I knew he was marking me as his in front of Albert, making certain he knew the current lay of the land.

"Father in Heaven," I heard Albert gasp under his breath. I thought he might throw up. He hadn't known. Nora had screwed her own husband over, too. What a bitch.

"Of course," I said.

Charles let me go with a squeeze and moved back to his place in the center of the room.

"Well, Albert?"

Surprisingly, Albert seemed to decide bravado and feigned annoyance would save him and he sighed. "Are we done with the display, now, Toff? Couldn't I just have admitted your dick is bigger than mine?"

Charles let out a huff of air. "Shut up, you idiot." I felt the corners of his mouth turn up just a tic probably in spite of himself.

"It isn't, for the record," Albert said, though he studiously didn't look at me when he said it. That was, apparently, too far even for him.

Charles rolled his eyes. "I need you to be serious, Albert."

"Yes," Albert said, tension returning as his bravado faded. "I know. I'm sorry. Sorry for everything."

Some of the anger left Charles, I could see it go. Just a bit, but not nearly all.

"That's it?" Charles said, the warning very clear in his voice.

"No," Albert said sadly. "I...fell in love with the wrong woman, Toff." He looked at me guiltily, "She lied to me about you." He turned back to Charles. "Nora said that the Commodore was out to expose your secret and ruin you and that discrediting her *now* would help discredit her *then*..." His expression became pleading. "You have done everything to stay Ambassador and have held on longer than I'd ever thought you could or would."

Or would? I thought. What did that mean?

Albert shrugged with affected casualness. "I didn't see the harm."

Now Charles was furious again, his face flushed and his heart racing. "You are telling me that a *Corsican* thought there was no harm in exposing the secrets and private life of anyone, let alone the woman who saved my life?"

Albert looked completely ashamed of himself now. "She said it was a necessary evil," he said in a low voice.

Charles nodded. "Evil. Yes, that is a word for it."

Well this wasn't getting us anywhere.

"Do you know why she hates me, Mr. Nylander?" I said suddenly.

Both men looked at me.

"I told you why," Albert said.

I shook my head. "Nora doesn't give a shit about Charles or about anything other than Nora."

Silence from Albert.

"She does, however, have a talent, apparently, for revenge." I looked at Charles. "You know she was my roommate on Gloriana."

"Yes."

"Well, she was in love with our other roommate and he wasn't interested." I clenched my fists. "I noticed how *that* little tidbit was left out of that fucking book."

"That other roommate was," Charles' golden eyes went wide, "Wilby. Now that is someone to be obsessed with," he said thoughtfully.

"What is so amazing about Wilby?" Albert asked, dismissively.

Charles laughed. "If you saw him, you'd know."

I smiled at my lover, amused.

Charles shrugged, "Even I can appreciate that sort of beauty." Now I grinned as a little color painted his cheeks. He was so cute. His expression clouded then, "You *were* with him, so…"

I shook my head. "He was my friend, but we were never in love, as you know."

"She thought you 'stole' him."

"She did."

"So, that's all?" Albert asked, dumbfounded.

"No, because she located someone just as interested in getting back at me as she was."

"Devon Pennock?" Albert asked.

"Yes," I sighed. "He'd been my student, my best student, and had made a pass at me, but I was already deeply in love," I smiled at Charles, who smiled back, "and was not available. He took it about as badly as anyone could." I rolled my shoulders, trying to loosen them. "At least no one has died from that damned book."

Charles glared at Albert, but there wasn't very much anger in his look anymore, "Not yet."

Albert made an exasperated noise. "Look, Toff, I said I was sorry and I meant it. I'm divorcing her and I'm willing to, what is the phrase, throw myself on your Imperial mercy. What more do you want?"

This was the wrong time for him to be flippant because all of Charles' anger came flooding back. "What do I want? I want to break that bitch's neck and yours with it for hurting and embarrassing Jane. I want both of you to suffer for making a woman I love upset and for opening her private life to ridicule. She has broken bones, risked her life again and again for the greater good and loved who she wanted to love and she gets punished for it by this shitty exposé. What do I want?" he was yelling now, "I want to rip Nora's fucking head off, that's what I want!"

Albert's face was ashen and he stood there a second with his mouth hanging open in complete shock. He looked around him, at a loss for what to do. He came up with nothing so dropped back down to his knees, head bowed. His breathing was labored and I started to be afraid he would pass out.

As for me, my eyes were full. Charles was protecting me. God, he wanted to fix it and couldn't and it was killing him. He was wonderful and I loved him so much. I needed him to let it go now, now that he'd finally found someone to rail at…and had had his railing, so to speak.

I walked over to him and put my hand on his shoulder firmly. "Charles?"

He might have been made of stone he was so full of rage and suppressed violence. I reached over and gently but firmly grabbed his chin, making him look at me. "Charles?"

He said nothing, but I felt some of the tension go.

"Thank you."

He took a big breath, trying to calm down. It worked a little.

I stepped up to him and put my arms around him. Albert wisely stayed where he was, eyes still fixed on the carpet. Charles did not move. I pressed myself to him and buried my face in his neck. I tried to stifle a sob, but he felt it anyway and his arms closed around me almost instinctively.

I wanted him to know how moved I was. That I was always the protector, a role I loved, but that this was monumentally important to me. Overwhelming emotion prevented it, though, and I just clung to him.

"Darling," he whispered. "Don't cry."

I nodded into his now very wet neck. I pulled away just a bit to look him in the eye. "Just…thank you."

"I haven't done anything, Jane." He shook his head. "I can't *do* anything."

I wiped my face with the back of my hand. "Sorry to sound cliché, love, but you have and it means everything to me." He pulled a handkerchief out of his breast pocket (he always had one) and pressed it into my hand, then kissed me gently. He took another deep breath. I could see it, then. He was himself again. Thank goodness.

I inclined my head in the direct of Albert and Charles rolled his eyes.

"Get up, Bertie. I promise I won't do anything awful to you today."

Albert got up shakily. "Wasn't so sure there, for a minute."

"I wasn't either."

Charles kept a good hold of me and I was happy right where I was.

"So you can't you do anything to them?" Albert asked carefully, meaning Nora and Devon.

"Devon killed himself on Novy," I said dryly as Albert blanched. "Though he deserved worse."

"I didn't…and Nora?"

"I'll revoke her Corsican citizenship and expel her from the Empire," Charles said, and then added with a grumble, "which is, apparently, all a 'civilized' Emperor can do in this day and age."

I kissed my lover on the cheek and broke away from him, holding out my hand to his oldest friend. "I think that's enough for today."

I looked over my shoulder at Charles, silently asking his approval since this really was his party and not mine. He nodded.

"Yes, thank you, Commodore," Albert shook my hand, looking wrung out. I think we all were. "I am truly sorry for everything."

Well, that would have to do for me, too, wouldn't it? "I know." I smiled tiredly. "Call me Jane."

"Albert."

I nodded. Albert bowed to his Emperor. "Charles."

Charles waved a dismissal, but his gesture was tired and no longer angry. Albert left and I went back into my man's arms. He held me close and said, "It may take me a while to forgive him."

"How long have you been friends?"

"About forty years, give or take."

"Then you have time, love."

I kissed him, touched him and, eventually, took him to our bed and made love to him to make sure he knew just exactly how much he meant to me.

14:00 – Large Gun Lab, ESTF *Schola-Terra*

My Friday afternoon Micro Class meeting, for the first time, in the biggest of our stationside Gun/Weapons Labs. We actually shared time on it with UNav since we didn't work with projectile weapons every day. Today, of course, that was all we were doing and this was the safest place onstation to do unsafe things. It was a cold, echoing, indestructible room deep within the station.

The Micros were Seniors, mostly, with one or two Juniors who'd shown exceptional control. These kids had promise and had demonstrated that they wanted to do well, plus they'd had to 'audition' to get in. I'd kept the class number small (just six), partially because I really wanted to be able to give everyone as much attention as possible and partially because these were the elite of the fourth year Micros and they would be active as soldiers/spies, etc., after next year. Kids now, colleagues soon enough.

I was assisted by Captain Dalia Kovshevnikov (not, as you might have expected, Dalia Cyrillic, since the Cyrillites had no problem with anyone, human or not, super or not, as long as no one was a slaver) who was one of our instructors. Not a lot of power to her talent, but she utilized it with tremendous delicacy; the Micro's equivalent of having a surgeon's steady hands. She could remove, as she put it, your knickers without you knowing 'till you had to take a piss. (She also had helped the actual surgeons on a couple of occasions at the main Infirmary when they'd asked. I'd thought for a minute that I might lose her to medicine, the way (well, one of the ways) I'd lost Wilby, but she told me she found medicine necessary but boring. It had been a relief.)

Today's lesson was a new one, both for them and for me. I honestly wasn't sure that it would have any actual application in battle, but the idea had come to me and I was curious to see how the kids handled it. Dalia had immediately been onboard, curious herself.

The bell sounded and the Cadets, who had been talking quietly immediately, turned to me and became expectantly silent.

"Good afternoon, class."

"Good afternoon, Ma'am."

I opened my hand and in it sat a metal bullet. I 'lifted' it into the air in front of me. They knew what the projectile was, of course. Micros were the best at controlling bullets fired from a standard projectile weapon and we had worked endlessly with them to make sure their control was automatic and their aim impeccable, but that wasn't exactly what we were going to work on today.

"As you remember," I said, "a typical bullet has five parts." They nodded. "The bullet itself, or the part that actually shoots out of the barrel of the gun, the case, the propellant, usually gunpowder, the rim and the primer."

I 'turned' the bullet around in the air, the metal gleaming as I did so. "You pull the trigger on a handgun and the hammer snaps forward causing the pin to strike the primer. This creates a spark that ignites the gunpowder, and the explosion propels the bullet out of the gun."

They nodded again.

"What I want to do today is figure out how to 'shoot' this bullet without the gun."

Cadet Wilson Jackson said, "You mean, Ma'am, that you don't know how to do it?"

I smiled. "I think I do, but I want to see if you can figure out how and, I hope, how to do it better than I would do it."

They stared at me. Some looked excited. Some looked nervous. All were surprised. I 'brought' the bullet back to my hand, which brought their attention fully back to me.

"I will tell you something that we don't tell our younger students. Your instructors, myself included, don't know everything." I smiled and I flicked my eyes to Dalia who was smiling, too. "Most of the things we have taught you here were 'discovered' by people just like you trying things. As far as I know, no Macro had ever 'flown' before I did it on Novy and that happened only because someone, a non-super, for the record," David, for the record, "suggested it. A Micro friend of mine saved High Admiral Armstrong's life by breaking up a blood clot, not because he had been trained to do it, but because he didn't want his boss to die. All of your instructors have taken chances and learned much, some of which we will teach you here. Very often things didn't work out but some of the time we ended up with the ability to do things we would never have dreamed of before they happened. We," and I indicated Dalia again, "still know a great deal more than you right now, but I hope you will surpass us eventually. Push your limits. Try the impossible—safely, please, but you may find that the impossible can be done."

I gave them a second to digest this. "Now, ideas?"

First, however, everyone had to get into protective gear including helmets with face shields made of micro-thin Tenorium. Someone getting mildly hurt didn't really bother me (I didn't want it, of course, but things happened and it reminded everyone of the stakes) but seriously hurt, or seriously dead, would be, you know, bad.

Thal, actually, had come up, after commandeering the ESTF's lab, with the Tenorium formula that had allowed the creation of the face shields. Apparently Tenorium was trickier than it looked, especially considering how common a substance it was. It needed a certain thickness to maintain stability and if you went a micrometer over/under its limits when you were manipulating it it would shatter. No exceptions. Plus it distorted what you saw. Something about light refraction that I didn't really follow. It didn't matter for space ships and stations. The distances and sizes involved usually made the distortion negligible, but up close was like looking in a fun-house mirror. Not the best thing for a face shield, especially with Micros whose bread and butter was precision. So, making the face shields was not the easy thing it would be appear to be. While I was daunted (and strapped for time, not to mention lacking in chemical knowledge), Thal had been intrigued and then obsessed. Ian's letter about the possibility of semi-transparent ships made with Tenorium alloy had been his inspiration. It had been an idea written in passing, but Thal had run with it.

It had taken him a little over two days. Not the 'two days' someone who had to sleep and eat would have taken, though, but fifty-three hours of constant effort and failure after failure. I could understand persistence if someone's life was in danger—as in, if you didn't figure it out immediately the one you loved was going to have their head blown off—but we had other helmets we could have used. They were more cumbersome and not nearly as cool, but we had them. No, this was Thal tinkering because he wanted to do it. Because he needed/wanted to solve a problem. Like David and, I assumed, like David's father.

I'd asked Thal about it early in the second day after admitting that I would have given up about six hours in (if that).

He'd replied, "I know I can solve this, Jane. It's almost in my grasp."

I'd been so astonished he'd forgotten to call me 'Miss' I'd found it difficult to form words, but, it was me, so I'd gotten my voice back quickly enough.

"Don't you get discouraged?"

He folded two of his arms across his chest. "Of course, but you cannot, *cannot*, learn without failure. Sometimes failure is even the point, for it may send you in a completely different direction." He reached down (with a hand that was free) and typed on a flexi-monitor. "It's most instructive. Both Mr. Abramses knew that."

That made no sense to me at all. Well, intellectually it was nice, I guessed, but failure was just that to me...failure, but I was no scientist. For me failure meant people died.

"May I ask you a personal question, Thal?"

"Of course," he said as his mobile synthetic face frowned at the beaker of hot goo in front of him.

"Is this you doing this, or is this...you." Meaning, of course, was this Thal, the construct of David, acting or Thalberg, the memories and thoughts of David's father.

Thal hadn't even paused in his contemplation of the goo. "Both, I think."

"I haven't seen much of Thalberg since you came to live here," I prodded gently. He looked over at me, but I smiled. "I like you however you are, Thal, I was just curious."

He sighed and I'd felt I could see the transformation into Thalberg happen. His body language became looser, more organic and his expression rueful. "My son told me, before I left, that the Thalberg part of me would cloud things, bring emotion into issues that didn't need it."

That sounded like something David would say. "So you've tucked Thalberg away, for the most part."

"Until I get my bearings." He stuck his finger into the boiling substance and I jumped instinctively, almost feeling the burn myself. His eyes twinkled when he saw my reaction. "It is a strange thing to be me, Miss Jane." Damn it, the Miss was back. Oh well. "I am not human, but I am. I have feelings, but they are almost borrowed. I don't really know what my place is. Not yet."

I understood that right down to the ground, so to speak. "I want you to be the being you need to be."

He smiled, "I know that, Miss Jane. It's one of the reasons I'm here."

"I'd understand if you wanted to move on," I said kindly. He looked stricken and I hurriedly added, "I don't want you to go, Thal, you've made yourself indispensable, but..." He looked a bit nonplussed, as though leaving hadn't even occurred to him, but then guilty because part of him had apparently thought about it a lot.

"Thank you," he said uncomfortably, "but what I need to be right now is the being that figures out this fucking formula."

I grinned, letting him off the hook (at least for a while) for the conversation that he didn't seem ready to have. "Then I will leave you to it."

So I had.

Eighteen hours later, Thal had scared the crap out of me by waking me up in the middle of the night, burned, scarred and triumphant, holding a small piece of what looked like glass but was (he'd informed me) the thinnest piece of Tenorium alloy ever created.

The joy and pride I'd seen on his face had been all Thalberg and beautiful to see.

My mind back in the classroom now, I watched my kids as they tried all sorts of things and asked all sorts of questions.

"We're not altering the bullet, Ma'am?" Cadet Tolliver asked as he stared at the object.

"No. Standard bullets only."

"You want to be able to mimic the gun so that we can replicate its effects?" said Cadet Sugawara.

"I want to be able to use the bullet," I said thoughtfully as I turned it over in my mind, "as a weapon." I smiled. "Creating a 'gun' to do it seemed logical."

Hisa Sugawara grinned. "It's a good place to start at least."

I nodded at the girl. "It is."

We started simply. Cadet Pittle 'held' the bullet in the air and Cadet Hjort created a tiny vortex that he used as a 'pin.' The bullet 'fired' when the 'pin' hit but the bullet went only a couple of inches after a loud bang and then dropped to the floor unimpressively, which I'd known it would (the barrel of a gun wasn't just there for decoration after all) and now they knew it, too.

The next step had Miss Pittle creating, after many attempts, a 'barrel' and Mr. Hjort 'firing' the bullet yet again. This was better, but still much less effective than the real thing because, we'd (or they'd) figured out, there were no grooves in our invisible 'barrel.' The lack of grooves played havoc with trajectory. We could control the bullet, of course, once it was out there, but it would be nice not to have to do every damned thing to get this to work. We got a bang and a crack this time, however, like you would when firing with a real gun. (The bang is the muzzle blast and the crack is the sonic boom made when the bullet breaks the sound barrier. Bet *that* little tidbit won't be on my UEL 2 exam.)

There were three groups of two working with Dalia and I circulated among them, offering suggestions but mostly just observing the ideas as they flowed.

Miss Sugawara asked, "What if we twist the 'tube' as the bullet fires?"

Mr. Hjort frowned condescendingly. "And you can do that?"

Well, after about ten tries, yes, yes she could. The 'gun' fired and the bullet went reasonably straight, but it took two Micros and a lot of concentration to pull it off.

It was Mr. Tolliver, however, the youngest of them, if only by a few months, and the smallest and shyest, that gave us something new to think about. "Ma'am?"

"Yes, Mr. Tolliver?"

"Do you have a bandolier?"

"I do," I said, wondering why he wanted one. I quickly 'opened' the far cabinet door and 'lifted' a pocketed leather belt full of ammunition out and 'brought' it over to us. I'd previously shown them a bandolier as an example of what the more heavily armed bad guys carried their ammunition in. I'd never found any real use for it, though, beyond the example. Toddy (his name was Todd, but no one ever called him that) Tolliver looked at me for permission, which I gave, and took the bandolier from me and put it over his gear.

"Ooh," Dalia purred, "I love a man in a bandolier."

I was pretty sure little Toddy's head was going to burst into flame, his face was so red, but he persevered despite his mortification. He took a breath and his color got a bit better. "What if you fire the bullet, right where it is, but stop it from propelling?" he asked as he looked down at his chest.

"You'd have…" Miss Sugawasa said slowly, "fifty tiny bombs on someone's chest."

"Or in someone's clip," Sherry Pittle said. "It might not injure anyone…"

"…but it might be a good distraction, not to mention making the ammunition itself useless," Mr. Hjort finished approvingly.

Oh, this was good. I stepped forward and gently 'turned' the bandolier so that all the bullets were pointed directly into Toddy's chest.

Dalia laughed, "Or fifty guns at point blank range."

"That is so cool," Cadets Pittle and Hjort said at the same time.

Toddy looked a little green at the sudden arsenal now pointed at his vital areas. Smiling, I made the bullets lie flat again.

"Well done, kids," I said happily. I glanced at the clock on the wall. Close enough to the end of the lesson. "Dalia, do you have the..?"

Dalia 'lifted' out a large box and 'opened' it while it floated in front of the Cadets. "These are practice bullets. Same weight but no gunpowder or other propellant."

"We want you to take these and practice your control," I said seriously. "I have set a schedule for this room and I want you all to use it at least once before we meet again Monday. Ideally, I want each of you to be able to 'fire' the 'gun' on your own with some semblance of control."

They looked daunted. I didn't blame them. "Stick to the same pairs you used today and make sure you wear your protective gear even if you are sure you don't need it." I gave them all a stern look. "You do."

"Yes, Ma'am," they said.

"Very well. Dismissed."

They quickly got out of their gear and put it away, then filed out. I smiled at the shyest of them as he passed me. "Good job, Toddy. Keep it up."

The boy blushed bright red again, but this time I could see it was pride that did it. "Thank you, Ma'am."

They left.

"Want to bet which of us just went into that boy's spank bank?" Dalia said, amused.

I sighed, playing it off, ignoring the sudden feeling of dread in my stomach. The thought of another student crush was unnerving at best. "His bank is not my problem."

Apparently I wasn't as good at hiding my unease as I'd thought because her amusement faded. "Jesus, Jane. I'm just teasing you. You're always so serious."

I was abruptly angry. Angry at her off-hand attitude, angry that an innocent potential crush could flip me out and just…angry. Thal's words about failure echoed in my head, not easing my anger.

"If you'd failed as many times as I have, Dalia, you'd be serious, too."

Stricken, she started to say something but I held up my hand for silence and got the hell out of there.

Getting back to my apartment helped nothing since a letter from Quinn awaited me.

URGENT Personal Letter from General Nathan Quinn-Pace, Novy Heliot to Commodore Jane Pace, Terra 1, Terra, and Ian Armstrong, Trithicate Station, Rian Nation, September 24th, 2873

Ian and Jane,

I don't have much to give you, Huong did her best but she and her G-L contacts have come up with almost nothing. I know, Jack, that if you think something is wrong it is. The only thing I was able to get from anyone was worrisome but not helpful. All access has been denied to Dep Qua during *this "time of transition" (as they put it) and the Ambassadors that live there have been encouraged to return home for the welcoming ceremony. The few Ambassadors on Dep Qua would have been going anyway, but the fact that they were, once again, encouraged to take their entire staffs with them is odd.*

That wasn't the truly strange thing, though. It was something I read in a confidential report by Cyrillic Ambassador Gureyev to her High Command. All very standard stuff except for one comment at the end. She'd said she missed seeing the Tarine flying around. She hadn't seen them in a week before she left.

Lady Eriss has been sighted often publicly on Trithicate station, sometimes with you, Jack, but never without a dozen Terran humans and Deneth, too.

Where are the other Tarine?

Let me know if you know anything. I'll keep looking into this.

Quinn

Now my stomach hurt in earnest. I called Thal over and had him read the letter, which he did almost instantaneously. He frowned.

"Any luck in your passive snooping, Thal?"

Thal shrugged, his movements more tight and polished than they were when he was Thalberg. "I have a theory, an unsatisfactory one, I'm afraid." He glanced back at the letter. "Especially in light of…"

My eyebrows rose. "You do have one, don't you? You've figured out what they're doing?"

He sighed. "I have a guess. The thing is that they aren't going to say, 'By the way, what is our plan in case anyone has forgotten, and what is the one thing our enemies could do that would stop us?'"

I giggled. "Beings can be so unhelpful."

He rolled his eyes at me, with tolerant affection. "Indeed. So," he became serious again, "I traced the movements of the Thals over the last week."

"What have they been doing?"

"This," he pressed a button on the table next to my desk, "30.5 hours per day in the week I've been paying attention." An unusual system, I thought, with that many hours in it's day. It wasn't Terra, obviously.

At first all I could see were little red lines, twenty or so of them, that moved fairly quickly over what appeared to be nothing, but as the lines continued to move a shape began to emerge. The negative space inside was a large ball. No, I corrected myself, it was a dodecahedron.

"That's Trithicate station," I said, surprised.

"It is." Thal pressed another button and the red lines sped up.

I frowned at the image, trying to make it look like more than just a bunch of artificial life forms crawling like ants all over the outside of the station. "What the fuck are they doing to it?"

"As I said, this information is, unfortunately, not as helpful as I'd like," he said, chagrined.

I looked at Thal. "And your theory is..?"

"I'd hazard a guess that they are doing a structural check," Thal said thoughtfully. He pointed at the places where the red lines were darker, more intense. "They're making repairs, it seems, in these places."

"So, this appears to be a large scale station overhaul?" I said, confused. "That's so...boring."

"Agreed." Thal folded his arms (both sets) across his chest. "I suppose we should be happy that the most obvious explanation is so benign."

"Yeah," I said, still unsatisfied. I leaned against the kitchen counter. "It's not as if they haven't had to maintain the station all this time, though. It's over a thousand years old. Nothing survives that long in space without anyone paying attention to it. Why ask David to help, though?"

"I couldn't say, Miss Jane."

I sighed. "Thank you, Thal. Please keep an eye one this in case more information makes this clearer."

"Of course."

I smiled weakly. "Maybe it really is exactly what it looks like."

"It is possible," Thal said while managing to convey that it really wasn't all that possible.

"I'll let Ian and Quinn know what you've found."

"Very good, Miss Jane."

So I immediately set out to do just that.

URGENT Personal Letter from Commodore Jane Pace, Terra 1, Terra to General Nathan Quinn-Pace, Abramstown, Novy Heliot and Ian Armstrong, Trithicate Station, Rian Nation, September 25th, 2873

Dear Ian and Quinn,

Thal has done some digging and it appears that David Abrams has assigned his Thals to check and repair the exterior of Trithicate Station. We do not know why this needed to involve David, nor why any of this needs to be done right now.
I will let you know if Thal finds out anything else.

Jane

I did some work in the apartment, lesson planning, etc., and Thal cooked dinner. I tried to be optimistic about what we'd found. That optimism lasted about an hour.

MESSAGE RETURNED
URGENT Personal Letter from Commodore Jane Pace, Terra 1, Terra to Ian Armstrong, Trithicate Station, Rian Nation, September 25th, 2873
MESSAGE RETURNED

Holy crap. Where was Ian? What the hell was happening to him?

That feeling of dread I'd been trying to forget about was apparently here to stay. I dashed off another letter to Quinn, letting him know that Ian was unreachable (in case he didn't already know) and checked my mail for the hundredth time in the last three weeks. Nothing from Atalanta, Felix or Daniel. Very odd. I realized, though, I didn't have time to deal with that now. A check of my watch confirmed this. It was time to meet Samuel and the new Denethian Commander.

18:00 – Cargo Bay 7-11, Terra 1 Station

Samuel awaited me at the airlock, looking sharp in his dress uniform, jet pack securely on his back. I felt…strangled in *my* uniform, though I'm sure I appeared respectable enough. God, these stupid collars. Why did uniform fashion have to choke the life out of those who serve?

Out of nowhere, though, I remembered that I was standing next a person who would be even more interested in the well-being of Ian than I was.

"Samuel, we can't reach Ian, I'm worried he is…"

Samuel looked concerned, but I was interrupted by the opening of the airlock door.

"When we're done here," he said quietly. I nodded.

I felt seven Denethian beings inside the Cargo bay. One of them would be the person we were there to meet.

The beautiful masculine/feminine face of a Denethian warrior appeared in the doorway. "High Admiral, Commodore, pleasse enter." The sibilant 'esses' reminded me of Criss, but I saw no warmth in the person before me. I suppressed a shiver.

We nodded and entered, quickly adjusting to Zero-G.

There, floating in the center of the large metal space, was a being who could only have been the new Denethian Commander for UNav. I could tell this from the way the other six warriors were stationed around him in a half-circle and from the confidence he emanated. He was smaller than most Deneth, smaller than I was, even, at a little over five feet in length. His black hair was short (!) and slicked back to his head and he wore a UNav Uniform (with a special hole for his tail.) He looked as assimilated into Terran culture as an alien could look. I didn't like it at all. I didn't like it because I had a philosophical objection to people pretending to be other than they were, but also because I knew the Pelann was constantly moving towards…something. It worried me a great deal that I didn't yet know what it was.

"High Admiral," the Denethian smiled coldly, "and," his dark eyes crinkled in surprise, "Commodore. An honor. I am General Rnn," he said in unaccented Standard.

"Delighted to make your acquaintance, General Rnn," Samuel said in pretty damned good Denethian.

"Sir," was all I contributed, also in Denethian since mine was much more limited speaking-wise, despite the traditional Pacey flare for languages. I had, also, guessed that the General was a he. Seemed I was right since no one had corrected me.

The Denethian looked pleased and I had a fleeting thought that he might actually *be* pleased. Interesting. "I'm planning to go by General

Ravven, here on my new home." He leaned in a little bit, confidentially, "Humans do love their vowels, don't they?"

I smiled. "I suppose so, General Ravven," I said in Standard.

The General's tail swished as he moved forward, extending his long-fingered hand with the extra joint for Samuel to take. "Your excellent reputation precedes you, High Admiral." Samuel shook the offered hand without hesitation though it wrapped entirely around his. "I'm looking forward to working with you during this transition."

Transition from what to what, I wondered. He could merely have meant from no Denethian involvement to some in the UNav, but this thing with the Pelann had me spooked and I was reading much more into it. I couldn't, however, dismiss my feelings as mere paranoia—even the paranoid were right sometimes.

"I wish I could say the same, General, but" Samuel chuckled, "the Pelann didn't let anything get through to our intelligence network."

The General smiled, "Her Holiness sees all, High Admiral."

"Indeed."

Now it was my turn. Hand extended, I shook it. "Commodore," he said, "I wanted to talk to you about future plans, for your school."

"My school, Sir?"

He nodded, released my hand. "I know the Union allows training on home planets if the members so desire," which was true. Most of our UNav soldiers were trained that way. Only the best of the best came to the *Schola-Terra*. Now I could guess where this was going.

"You want Deneth and Tarine," I'd added the Tarine part just to make a point, "to be graduates of the *Schola-Terra*?"

I sensed Samuel's stomach clench but he said and did nothing.

Ravven inclined his head in my direction, a token of respect, I thought. "Her Holiness wants as much parity as possible in all parts of Union life."

My mind was reeling with the implications, not to mention complications of such an audacious concept. "I can't say as I blame her, Sir, but we are still new and just starting to introduce Heely Humans to the program, though," a thought occurred to me, "you mean the regular Cadet Training, don't you, Sir? Not the ESTF?"

"There are Heely Humans in the ESTF?" Ravven asked in shock. "After all that happened?"

I didn't want to let him goad me, but I bristled anyway, "We are starting small, but I know you have Denethian Telepaths," and Tarine TPs, but I didn't know if I was supposed to know that so I didn't mention it. "Do you have other types of supers as well?"

"Her Holiness is looking into it."

Thank you for that non-answer. "Any Heely Humans that qualify for the *Schola-Terra*, as well as the regular UNav, are those who have been cleared of any charges of treason and are subjected to rigorous Telepathic scans to make sure nothing squirrelly is going on in their heads."

Nothing on the outside of the General changed, but inside I felt tension, tension, tension. Ooh, he was not happy.

"They dig into the minds of all recruits? From all worlds?"

"Of course," Samuel chimed in. They did no such thing, of course, but I, now that it had been brought up, really thought they should. "You don't want someone at your back that you don't trust." He smiled. "It is mandatory, but no one forces anyone to apply." His message was clear: our way or the highway.

"I wasn't aware of this procedure. I will have to let my people know. We're not used to dealing with this sort of thing." He pasted on a totally unbelievable smile. "We will adapt, of course."

"That is good to hear," Samuel said implacably.

I was watching the six goons who were floating almost motionless around the General when I was struck with a thought.

"You know what would be fun, General Ravven?" I asked.

"No, Commodore?" he responded, amused.

"We Macros have a Griit Ball league, well, an adaptation of Griit Ball we call Macro Ball that we play in a grav environment, since those are much easier to come by for us."

"Are you suggesting a match, Commodore Pace?"

I shrugged. "Training, then, yes, a match. I think it would be quite eye-opening to compete with and against beings who've played the game their entire lives."

Ravven chuckled, this time thoroughly amused. "You may get more than you bargained for."

"I'm sure we will. One of the High Admiral's assistants, Captain Pace-Taylor, runs our league and I'm sure he'll be up to the challenge." Garrett was going to shit himself. Plus it was a terrific way for my baby Macros to see what exactly they would be up against if it came to it. The Deneth were brilliant in Zero-G. Brilliant and fucking scary if provoked.

"I will run the idea through channels and let you know," Ravven said.

Now we knew that Ravven wasn't going to wipe his ass without permission. Great.

"Wonderful, Sir." Then, because I couldn't help myself, I added, "Sport is a great way to make friends."

The tension in Ravven's body increased. Oh brother. "I am sure Tfr has a Griit Ball tucked away somewhere. I see no problem with having a, what's it called, a game of catch?"

So he wanted the conversation with me to end and was giving me this to make that happen. This was fine with me since I didn't have anything more to say.

"Thank you, General Ravven."

Immediately Tofor produced a ball and we started tossing it around. Not a real game, but still fun. Man, those articulated fingers gave them a grip of iron. I gave half my attention to the little game we were playing while the other half was on the conversation the General was having with Samuel.

"So this is the hold designated for the Denethian garrison, High Admiral?" Ravven said quietly.

"It is, General," Samuel said, "We have received your requirements and will begin work tomorrow. I would hope that you will have some time to supervise construction, just to make sure everything is as you would like."

Ravven nodded and he looked around the metal box his people were to live in. "No windows."

Samuel grimaced. "We will install a small Tenorium section, but I'm afraid there were too many concerns from the structural engineers to allow a full wall."

Ravven sighed. "Her Holiness understands. We're just used to being in the vastness of space—even when we're technically indoors."

"I hope it won't be difficult for your people."

Ravven waved a hand to drive the concern away, "Warriors adapt."

I felt Samuel look in my direction as I tossed the ball to a higher Deneth. "That they do."

"If I may make a rather bold observation, Samuel," Ravven said quietly.

The ball came back to me and I 'caught' it reflexively. The Deneth I was playing with were suddenly much more attentive. One of them, whom

I was pretty sure had no Standard, gestured to me to 'throw' it back, which I did.

"Sam, please," Samuel said a little tightly. "Go ahead, Ravven."

"Sam, then. Now that I've met her, the Commodore doesn't seem to me like either an Angel or a Blackbird."

I 'caught' the ball again, but my mind was on my ex-lover. I could feel Samuel blinking rapidly at the jump in subject while his chest got tight the way it did when he was angry. "How do you mean?" he asked without inflection.

I 'tossed' the ball over to the Denethian on the far right.

Ravven shook his head, "Do you know *Ml Ebat*?"

The returning ball almost hit me in the face, I was so surprised to hear that name. Ml Ebat, more commonly known by humans as Mila Ebata, was the hero of one of the greatest series of adventure stories ever written. She was a Denethian ship captain in the middle of nowhere who always seemed to find herself in the worst situations and come out of them in ingenious ways.

"One of my favorites," Samuel said, his voice flat, clearly not liking where this conversation was going.

"One of her Holiness,' too."

"The Pelann thinks the Commodore is Mila Ebata?"

"She does," the General's expression turned cold. Like cold as space cold. "Do you remember how the series ends?"

Samuel nodded, still staring at me. "Mila sacrificed herself saving an entire planet from destruction." Yeah, it was brave and awful. When I re-read the series I always stopped reading before the last book. Brave and awful, yes, but depressing as hell, too.

The General patted Samuel on the shoulder. "Thus cementing a legend." He smiled joylessly as he stared at me. "Her Holiness, the Pelann, will mourn her when she goes. There will never be another Red Angel."

The space of the cargo hold was heated, but it felt cold as hell to me right then.

I don't know how Samuel kept up the conversation about deployments, etc., for another twenty minutes after that, but he did. I was glad when we were done, however, and soon we retreated to the safety of the grav corridors within the station.

"So her Holiness hasn't forgiven you," Samuel said dryly.

"Apparently not."

"What's this about Ian?"

"My letter to him today was returned," I said, rubbing my forehead, trying to get rid of an incipient headache. I quickly brought him up to date on what little we knew about Trithicate and Dep Qua.

"Odd, but not conclusive," Samuel said as he leaned against the wall.

"I just wish we knew what the cunt was up to."

Samuel laughed quietly. "You sound like Mallory."

I did? "How is she?"

"Good," and I felt his cheeks heat. "We're having dinner again tomorrow." I noticed that he didn't ask me to join them this time. I did not grin, but it was difficult not to.

"That's good. You must need the break with all this going on."

"Yes," he said, but he seemed lost in thought, in a memory perhaps. The corners of his lips were slightly turned up.

"I have to get going," I said. "I'll let you know if I hear anything about Ian."

"Thanks, Jane." He turned to go, but then looked back at me. "I've hired the Furies to help keep an eye on things during Lady Eriss' introduction. To see things us regular folks will miss."

I couldn't help but grin. It would be so great to see everyone after so long, but my initial reaction quickly faded by the seriousness of his expression. "You *must* be worried."

He shrugged. "It's just a feeling. Perhaps it's nothing."

"We're all on edge. I don't think that's nothing."

"Who knows, Jane?" He smiled. "Maybe this time we're wrong."

"That would be a nice change, Samuel."

He nodded. "Good night, Jane."

"Good night, Samuel."

22:03 – Corsican Embassy, Terra 1

I found that despite having had a long conversation with Felaysa at the ESTF (on a very non-ESTF topic, more on that later) I had still managed to beat Charles back to the Embassy's private apartments. His working dinner had run long, according to Mr. Beddoes, and I took the opportunity to send the following off to my friends in the Furies who were currently stationed on a 'keep the peace' contract out in the boondocks:

Dear Atalanta, Felix and Daniel,

Samuel just told me that we would be seeing the Furies during Eriss'
introduction to the Legislature. I'm so happy I'll be seeing you all. Feels
like it's been forever. Much is going on here and I'll tell you all about it in
detail when I see you next week, but here is a brief summary: we've lost
touch with Ian on Trithicate. Trithicate Station is being overhauled by
David's people and we don't know why. Dep Qua is closed to everyone
and the Ambassadors and staffs have all been politely expelled. Here on
Terra 1 the new Denethian Commander, General Ravven, is a piece of
work and freaked out at the idea of TP scans of all his people before they
could actively serve UNav. I'm sure Samuel is making that official policy
even as I write this. Something is up, though none of us seem to have a clue
what that 'something' is.
The ESTF keeps going and, for the most part, classes are going well.
The absorption of the Heely boy, Wylan, has been tricky, but I think we
might have it in hand. I wouldn't mind the three of you taking a look at him
while you're here, if you wouldn't mind. While I do my best I'm the wrong
kind of super to try to see what he's thinking and feeling. Marston calls me
"Mama Heely" and thinks he is funny as shit. So if he is slightly damaged
when you see him, you'll know why.
It's been a long time since I've heard from any of you. Is everything
alright?
I can't wait to see you three.

Love,

Jane.

That accomplished and with still no sign of Charles I went off again in
search of a drink. There were several bars and restaurants on the
Diplomatic level of the station and I headed into the first one I found.

I was surprised to find Albert Nylander there, seated on one of the
stools and several drinks ahead of me. I plopped down next to him, but it

took him a minute or two to notice I was there. Spirits were good for that for that sort of thing.

"Hey, Commodore, I mean Jane," Albert said, only slurring slightly.

"Hey, Albert," I said, signaling the bartender for a drink. "How are you?"

"Peachy," he said, taking a gulp of whatever his drink was. He then stared at the glass for a while, as if trying to make his brain form words. "I really didn't know, you know. About you and Toff."

"I know," I said as I received my own drink. "Why do you call him 'Toff'?"

Albert snickered. "He really wanted to be 'normal' when he and I started school." He swept his arm front of him, knocking over an empty glass. "No private tutors for the Prince. He wanted to be just like everyone else at school." He snorted. "He was very attached to the idea."

"I take it that didn't happen?"

"Of course not. It's not as if everyone wasn't aware of who he was. Every time he tried to act like a regular boy he just…did it wrong."

Poor Charles. "What is a toff, exactly?"

"A dandy. A swell. Someone more, I dunno, self-consciously grand than the rest of us." He laughed into his glass, the contents bubbling up as he did so. "You can't take the Prince out of the boy."

"So no friends?"

Albert shrugged. "Aside from me, no. Social climbers, trying to get into his 'set,' but that didn't last. He didn't like any of that shit. Reminded him too much of dear old mum." He leaned back to stretch. "They called him Toff because he wouldn't play the game."

"Why do *you* call him that?"

"I never called him that in school. Now I call him Toff to remind him of who he is." He drained the glass. "Went to all that trouble to escape his mother and then went and married that bitch who was even worse than she was."

"You didn't like Marianna?"

He shook his head. "No one did, once they got over her manners and beauty. The woman underneath was a cold, cold person. Not the right woman for Charles." He sighed. "We were all dazzled by her at first, though, even me. Until she tried to seduce me a week into the marriage."

I cringed. "Yuck."

"Yes. Yuck indeed." He looked up at the bartender. "Another, please." He waited for the drink then continued. "I was so glad when he met the Countess."

"You like her?"

"I admire her as a person," he said cagily as he took a sip. "She's fiercely loyal to Toff and that's all I can ask." He looked at me out of the corner of his eye. "You must have been a surprise."

"To all three of us," I said almost to myself. "Will I be a problem for you? Honestly?"

"If Idis has passed you," he said as I looked at him in surprise, "then it isn't my business."

"How did you..?"

"I know Toff," Albert said as his mood darkened. "He hates lying and keeps his promises." He stared at the half empty glass in front of him. "Even if you have to wait forever and a day for him to follow through."

I was sure he wasn't talking about Idis, Charles and I anymore and I started to wonder about it but my eye fell on my watch. Time to go. "I'll see you around, Albert."

"You sure will, Jane." He downed the rest of the glass. "I've got nowhere else to go."

I nodded, unsettled, and headed back to the Embassy.

23:17 – Private Apartments of the Corsican Embassy, Terra 1

It was an hour or two later and I lay comfortably next to Charles, tucked under his arm.

"I'm happy for Sam," Charles said quietly as he stroked my naked back.

"Me, too. Mallory is a good woman. I hope it works out." I ran my fingers over his chest eliciting a shiver. "I spoke to Alex today."

"What did he say?"

"The gloves are here to stay."

"Damn," he said quietly, but then he turned his head to look at me. "So, what's your plan?"

I grinned. Now *this* man knew me pretty damned well. "Working on it."

"Good," Charles laughed and I felt the vibrations through his chest. Lovely.

I hesitated now, but pushed through. "Alex wants us to marry and have a baby so that he's off the hook." Wow. Subtle, Jane, as always.

Charles sighed. "I wondered when he would bring that up."

"You did?"

"He had the same conversation with Idis ten years ago." He closed his eyes. "I assume you set him straight."

"I did," I said softly as a wave of guilt washed over me. "Charles, you know that if I were to marry or reproduce with anyone it would be with you…"

"I know that, love." He turned his whole body towards mine now. I tried not to see the sadness he was trying so hard to hide and focused on the love that was there instead. What else could I do? I couldn't go the traditional route and he knew that. "We are perfect, just as we are."

"You really think so?" I asked a little shakily.

"I promise."

He kissed me.

It was the middle of the night when I was lying in my lover's arms when I remembered something Albert had said that had stuck with me. I could sense that Charles was awake, though his eyes were closed.

"Six?"

"Hmm?"

"I know you had planned to give up being Ambassador when you became Emperor."

Suddenly Charles's previously relaxed body was tense. I wanted to drop it right then because his reaction had already given me the answer to my next question, but in for a penny…

"I changed my mind," he said lightly, though I knew the casualness of the answer was a put on.

"Who would have been Ambassador if you had stepped down?"

A long pause as he stared at the ceiling.

"I promised it to Albert." Twenty years ago? Holy Mother, that was a long time to wait for a gig.

"Oh." I thought a bit more. "He still allowed that book to come out to protect you, so you could keep being both Fitz and Emperor."

"Albert's cockeyed loyalty," was his only response.

I had to ask, "What will you do?" for Albert. Because it seemed to me, in my own cockeyed version of justice, that Charles owed him. Despite everything. Albert had resigned from the Legislature when he'd married, probably at Nora's insistence. More control over what he heard and saw, I guessed. Horrible woman.

"I don't know. Something."

I fell silent. Charles tossed and turned for a few minutes then apparently gave up and rose, kissing me on the forehead as he did so.

"I have work, Red. Go back to sleep."

"All right, love."

I closed my eyes and feigned sleep as he headed for his dressing room.

I lay awake after he left, however, until it was time get up.

ENTRY 3-8-86

<u>13:45 – My Apartment, Terra 1, Terra, October 2nd, 2873</u>

I waited a little nervously in my tiny living room. Thal had discretely left on ESTF business so I was alone. I checked my watch. Time. The entry chime rang.

"Come in," I said.

"You wanted to see me, Jane?" Alex said as he entered looking both curious and confused, as well he might. He really was very handsome, I thought. A younger, prettier version of his father if, and only if, he was covered up from the neck down (this was his opinion and not mine, of course). I tried not to look too obviously at his gloves, those gloves that had so worried his father.

"I did," I said as I gestured for him to sit. "Thank you for coming."

Alex nodded and sat, I joined him. Now he waited.

I cleared my throat. "We are connected, but we don't actually know each other that well."

He smiled. "I suppose not."

"I consider you a friend, Alex. I would have even if I weren't involved with your father."

"I appreciate that, Jane," he said, clearly trying to get his bearings in the conversation.

"The problem, though, with being my friend is that I am," I searched for a word that painted what I was about to do without a too negative connotation, "a meddler."

"Oh."

"I want the people I care about to be happy. So, I interfere."

His posture straightened and the tension in his body became a palpable thing. "I'm fine." He started unconsciously pulling at the fingers on his gloves, but then realized what he was doing and stopped.

"You are functional," I said, "but you aren't fine." He wasn't. I'd asked around. He was eating in his room. He never socialized, didn't date, and barely spoke outside of work unless he was forced to. He was faking normalcy and, in my opinion, doing it really badly.

He stood up. "I have to get back."

"Please, Alex," I said gently. "I have a friend coming who would like to have a conversation with you."

He shook his head agitatedly. "A psychiatrist. I'm not crazy, Jane. I'm…" he threw his hands up, "ruined."

"Not a psychiatrist, love." I rose, too. "My friend, Felaysa, the E05."

His eyebrows almost hit his hairline in his astonishment. "You got me a *hooker*?"

"Lord, no!" I said, almost wanting to laugh. "Please never, ever use that word around an E05."

"Sorry," he said reflexively. "So you're not telling me that you want me to have sex with Fey?"

"No," I said soothingly. "I want you to *see* Fey." The door chimed again. "She had her memory of Corsica wiped," well, 'safed,' "so she doesn't remember you or know who you really are, Ok?"

"Jane…"

"Come in."

Felaysa entered, wearing something white, sleeveless and soft. She was her usual almost black with short cropped white hair and bright blue eyes. She could assume any persona, depending on what was required, but today she walked regally, like a queen. "Colonel Couvillion," she extended her lovely hand, "I am Captain Fey Torva. It is a pleasure to meet you."

"And you, Captain," Alex said, once again reflexively. I wondered how much of his courtly training carried him through odd situations without his ever realizing it.

Fey and Alex took the sofa and I went to a nearby chair.

"Are you familiar with E05's, Alex?" Fey asked. Alex immediately turned bright red. She laughed, "I can see you are. Don't worry; this isn't going to be about sex."

"It isn't?"

I couldn't tell if he was relieved or disappointed.

"Not today."

"What does that..?"

"There is more to being an E05 than just sex."

"I didn't know that."

"Jane didn't either. Most people don't. Sex is the…flashiest of the things we do." She settled back, completely comfortable unlike the rest of us. "When people hire us they don't always want sex, or if they do it is as part of something else."

"Part of what?"

She paused, as if thinking of the right way to say something, though I was pretty sure this was a pose and that she had said this little speech many times before. "Touch."

The tension was abruptly back in Alex's body. "No."

She nodded. "I understand." She leaned forward just a bit. "I have, however, seen people with injuries, dysfunction, fears and loneliness. A lot of it can be accepted."

"Accepted?" Alex said scornfully.

"Do you like how I look?"

He regarded her as though it were a trick question. "Why wouldn't I?"

"What is your type, exactly?"

"You'll do," he said.

She smiled. "Thank you. This," she indicated herself, "is a very popular incarnation, but it isn't me."

"It isn't."

"No." She closed her eyes for about fifteen seconds and when she opened them all pigment had disappeared from her body (except in her hair, of course). I'd seen Stoney do this once on Gloriana (a memory I treasured) and it was no less impressive here.

Alex gasped and drew back.

Her skin was fine and so translucent you could see veins and muscles and even the bones of her hands. "This is my true self. I can be anything anyone wants and I would be, but this is really me." She extended her arm towards him. He stared at it, fascinated. "What do you think?"

"I…I don't know," he said honestly.

"Touch," she ordered gently.

He reached forward but she turned her eyes towards his gloved hand and shook her head. He hesitated, clearly debating whether it was worth taking the glove off. He sighed and, with a quick glare in my direction, pulled off the glove on his right hand. The skin was still marked on the top with the ridges and whorls of his torture. His hand shook a bit, but he was determined and he carefully touched her forearm. "It feels the same," he said with an unconscious smile.

She reached out her other hand to cover his. He jumped, but didn't pull away, though I could tell it was an effort for him not to do so. He held his breath as she ran her fingers lightly over his skin.

Then she blinked rapidly, as I'd known she would, and the skin on her arm, and only her arm, started to change again. First it became a kind of pinkish white (the kind redheads like Alex usually had) and then, slowly, patterns emerged. They were Alex's patterns, texture and all, on Fey's forearm.

Alex snatched his hand away. "What are you doing?" He stood, backing as far away from Fey has he could in the small room.

"Touch," was all Fey said.

He folded his arms over his chest, almost hugging himself. "No fucking way. That's disgusting. Why would you make yourself disgusting like that?" Like him.

She looked at him thoughtfully. "I am not disgusting, Alex."

"You are," he said, face red, breathing hard. "You are gross and maimed and abhorrent." I could feel the tears building in his eyes. They were building in mine as well. Fey, however, remained calm. "You need to stop this, change back. No one will want you. You'll," he wiped his face and laughed bitterly, "you'll lose your job."

She shook her head. "Wanna bet?" She patted the sofa. "Please sit."

He did reluctantly as far from her as he could on the couch. Small couch, though, as I've mentioned before.

"Jane?"

She startled me, but I did my best to respond. "Yes, Fey?"

"If you were single and I propositioned you, would you say no to me if I looked like this?"

"Are you crazy?" I asked with a laugh, "I'm just sorry you didn't think of this when we were playing around."

"You? And...?" Alex stuttered.

I snorted inelegantly, "You don't turn down a lady like Fey, Alex." I rolled my eyes, "She's..." and my mind flashed through all kinds of inventive erotic memories, some of which Fey herself wouldn't remember, "...the best."

"I am. I know better than anyone else how much appearance matters when it comes to sex," she shrugged, "and who we are in general." She smiled. "It matters less than you'd think but, that being said, you can't just assume what people want to see."

Alex, however, wasn't hearing it. "Change back, Fey. I mean it."
Panic, sheer panic.

She shook her head.

"*Change it back!*" he roared.

She closed her eyes and became translucent again.

Alex was taking big ugly gulps of air as he looked at her through wet lashes. "No, back to how you were before."

Fey smiled at him sadly. "This *is* me, Alex. This is who I am," she whispered.

"Stop it. It isn't the same."

"It's the same enough," she said.

She moved forward and gently put her hand to his wet face. He flinched but she kept her hand there and he let it stay.

"I can't even look at myself anymore," he mumbled.

"*I* can see you, Alex." She stroked his cheek. "You are beautiful."

He shook his head wildly. "I make myself sick."

"You. Are. Beautiful."

"Saying it," he whispered, "doesn't make it true."

She took his scarred hand and held the back of it to her lips. "'There are more things in heaven and earth, Horatio, than are dreamt of in your philosophy.'"

She rose and stood before us.

"For my very first client." She blinked and her skin faded to an eerie pale lavender, her eyes went white and her posture changed to slumped over. Her breasts and hips seemed to enlarge, though that was more illusion, not enough time for a real transformation.

"Oh my," was all Alex said.

"A VIP last year." She blinked again, this time more rapidly, and she appeared to get taller, leaner, more graceful. Her hips narrowed, her breasts seemed to disappear and her shoulders got broader. Her skin turned pale blue that darkened to black at her extremities and her eyes became dark as space itself. Lack of tail and long hair notwithstanding, she was a Denethian.

"Whoa," Alex said almost to himself.

Belatedly I realized I could be scanning him for a physical response. Fey sure was, in her own way. Alex…liked it. A bit. It was a start.

Then she used the 'real' magic of her gift. She started small adjustments, taller here, no, then smaller. She was reading Alex. Slimmer, yes he liked slimmer, then muscles, no, no bulk. She read him over and over, hundreds of adjustments and changes. Eye color, posture/carriage, voluptuous versus slender, but I noticed something as the changes happened quickly in front of us. Fey was growing uneasy and I couldn't figure out why.

Alex was looking at her steadily now, his fear subverted to determination.

She paused again, almost staring him down. He stared back. After a second she dropped her head in acquiescence.

Then she became translucent Felaysa again. Alex's body became, not aroused, but relaxed, which was, for the purposes of this exercise, much better. He'd realized what she was doing and skewed the reading. I bet that had never happened to her before in her life. I was impressed in spite of myself.

"Fair's fair," Alex said quietly.

"Yes, I suppose it is," she responded, clearly unsettled.

She sat down on the couch, momentarily lost in thought. He reached out and took her almost clear hand in his gloved one. Then he pulled the glove off, deliberately not looking at the red texture and patterns on his skin.

Fey blinked again and her whole body became the pattern, even her lovely face. She was both, I thought, stunning and fascinatingly grotesque.

He dropped her hand as if stung.

"Will you say I'm ugly?" she asked.

His golden eyes were huge as he looked at her in horror. "Yes."

She blinked again and was her original self. "I'm not, love."

"But I am. I wish," he said painfully, "I wish you could take it away like that."

"I would, love, if ever I could, but this is you now."

He let out a sound that was half groan, half sob and surrendered. Surrendered to grief and surrendered to Fey. She quickly moved closer and held him to her. He shuddered in her arms, stiff at first, but then he clung to her and cried, really letting go, probably for the first time since it had happened.

This was part of being an E05 that no one talked about. It was too perfect, too generous, too private to brag about. She'd told me about it when we'd spoken the previous week, but witnessing it was something else. I kept blinking, trying to see, but it was difficult. I hated seeing men cry, but, man, if ever anyone needed to, it was Alex.

Fey gave me a significant look over Alex's shoulder and I rose.

"I have class, love," I said softly. "I'll see you later."

I don't know if he heard me, but it didn't really matter. He was in good hands, so I quickly pressed my hand to the top of Fey's head, a tiny gesture of thanks for this gift and left.

12:03 – Hallway Outside Cargo Bay 7-11, Terra 1 Station

I was on my way to lunch, but had taken the long way (very long, actually, since Aronoff's was on the other side of the station) to assuage my curiosity about the Denethian contingent of UNav. Yes, I was spying on them and yes, I didn't care that I was. Something was up and I couldn't let it go, but when I arrived at the airlock to the Cargo Bay that had been assigned to them I was surprised to see Synon coming in the opposite direction.

I looked at the tiny Tenorium window in the airlock. Something was in front of it blocking the view. Of course it was. Synon stopped in front of it and grimaced.

"I see I'm not the only one curious," I said by way of a greeting.

"If by curious you mean worried, then you are correct," Synon said.

"Something's off, Sy."

"Tell me something I don't know, Jane." He looked in the direction of the airlock. "What are they doing?"

I concentrated, feeling for movement inside the Cargo Hold. What I did feel shocked me.

Sleek Denethian bodies streaking through the (comparatively) small space, so quickly they were like slivers of light.

I looked at my friend, eyes wide. "Speed drills."

He nodded. "When I passed by here this morning I heard the distinct sound of metal hitting metal."

Weapons drills. Great.

"Everyone arrives tomorrow," I said. Dignitaries, diplomats, legislators, even T.I. stars and the ultra-rich. All wanting to be part of the spectacle and meet Eriss.

"The ceremony is the day after," Synon nodded.

"They are training awfully hard for something."

Synon rubbed his jaw. On a Terran Human he might be scratching his beard, but Heelies had no hair. "How are your Cadets at attack formations?"

I frowned. "I haven't covered it."

"Perhaps," he said, putting my arm in his as he started us walking, "My people and I can help with that, Commodore."

"With jet packs?" I asked.

He chuckled. A deep sound that seemed to come from his toes. "Eventually."

I felt a little better about our impending doom as he laughed. "What did you have in mind?"

19:00 – My Apartment, Terra 1

"What are we having tonight, Thal?" I asked as I entered the apartment. Class was over for the day and I was in a good mood, despite the impending doom. Fey had given me no report on how things were going with Alex, but she'd told me beforehand that his privacy was the most important thing. I'd agreed (who wouldn't have?) but that didn't make me any less curious. This was me, after all. The one thing she had told me was that she was going to meet with him again, several more times if he was willing. I'd thanked her repeatedly for taking an interest in my friend. She'd said it wasn't necessary to thank me. She liked him and wanted to help. She also thought it had been terribly clever of me to pick the one person who was so right for helping him. The amount of smugness on her lovely face was impressive to say the least and it reminded me of another friend. A friend I hadn't heard from for over a month now. What the hell was going on with the Trio?

"Cyrilliac Festrel with anise," Thal replied cheerfully.

"What in the world is a Festrel, Thal?" What the hell was anise, anyway?

"Something they had at the market, Miss Jane."

I smiled at him, bemused, "Are you being deliberately vague, Mr. Thal?"

Thal smiled back. "I am."

Since Thal was an excellent cook and I had loved everything he'd made thus far, I let it go…at least until I realized that he had set out two places. That was something I had to ask about. "I didn't think you

condescended to eat, my friend. Or have you been keeping this ability from me all this time?" I teased.

"No, secrets, Miss Jane," Thal said confidently. "I thought, however, you might want me to feed…" the door chimed, "your date. Come."

The door opened revealing Charles.

I'm sure my face was full of delight as my man came through the door, but if there had been any doubt as to how glad I was to see him, however unexpectedly, I'm sure it was dispelled when I threw myself into his arms. Charles laughed as he held me a second, then kissed me before letting me go.

"I thought you had a dinner," I said, taking his hand as I led him to the little kitchenette.

"I did, but one of the perks of being…whatever I am," he said with a grin, "is that I can cancel the unimportant stuff if I want to." He leaned over and kissed me again. "I guess I never had a good reason to before."

"And your reason would be?" I asked, giggling.

"You've been raving about Thal's cooking and I wanted to see for myself."

"Of course." I led him over to Thal who came around the little island. "Ambassador Fitzroy, I would like you to meet my assistant and friend, Thal."

"A pleasure, Mr. Thal," Charles said.

"Good to meet you, Sir."

No one shook hands. One didn't with servants, I supposed. Corsicans were really strange. Or maybe it was an Emperor thing.

"Mr. Beddoes said that you were most helpful in setting up dinner."

"Seemed the least I could do, Sir," Thal said modestly.

"Thank you."

"Of course, Sir."

I seated Charles at the one other chair at the island and sat in mine. Thal plated and set out the food, which looked delicious.

Charles grinned. "Festrel. My favorite."

I looked at Thal who winked at me and had to laugh. Between Thal and Mr. Beddoes we were apparently quite taken care of.

Thal headed for the second bedroom which was his work room (since he did not sleep), but Charles stopped him.

"Excuse me, Mr. Thal, but may I ask you a question?"

Thal turned back around, his mobile face expressing surprise that quickly faded into professionalism. "Of course, Sir."

Charles looked a bit uncomfortable. "I do not mean to pry into your personal affairs," I could feel the posture of my friend shift from Thal to Thalberg since this was going to be a private issue, "but the Lady Idis is a lawyer of some repute on Corsica and she had a question for you."

She did?

"The Countess of Boulton had a question for me?" Thalberg asked, just as surprised as I was.

"Yes. Do you wish to be free?"

I just stared at him. So did Thal. Charles hastened to continue, "I don't mean quit your job, I mean 'own' yourself. Legally."

Now I could really see Thalberg coming through as he leaned forward with both elbows on the counter, something I could never have pictured Thal doing in a million years. Charles' eyebrows rose as he saw this, but he didn't remark on it.

"Eventually, yes, Sir, but…" he trailed off. "I think that's what Miss Jane wants."

"It is," I said, "from the beginning." I shrugged. "I only took 'possession' of him to get him out of that damned cargo delivery area." I looked quickly at Charles, now scared. "Did I fuck everything up by doing that? Does Idis think I screwed Thal's future by doing that?"

"No, love, she agrees it was the only thing to do at the time, but," he sighed, "under Union law it made this being, Thal, a 'thing' rather than a 'person.'"

"Oh god," I said guiltily.

"Miss Jane, please," Thalberg said, his expression soft, fatherly, "I am happy where I am and you yourself said that if I wanted to go, I would be able to." He smiled kindly, "I trust you not to do the wrong thing."

"Thank you, Thal, but being told you're the nicest slave owner around isn't a compliment I'm comfortable with," I said as I patted his arm to soften the sting of my sarcasm.

"Miss Jane, I…"

"The Countess had an idea," Charles said, effortlessly diverting the coming circle of apologies. "A test case." He sighed ruefully, "She does love her test cases."

"What is it, Charles?"

"A woman on Adgar created a test. A test of sentience." I looked at Charles in surprise. "She is an explorer, a prospector, really."

"Like David's..." and then I realized to whom I was speaking and finished weakly, "parents."

Thalberg's expression clarified. "Dr. Buerki. She needed to be able to classify any alien species she ran across. For threats to humans, diseases, planetary resources and...sentience."

Charles nodded.

I had to ask. "She can determine sentience in a *questionnaire?*"

"A questionnaire of sorts," Thal answered. "The test has been approved by the Wild Catter's Association this year, though it hasn't actually been used but once."

"The Olla," Charles said. I looked at him for an explanation. "Sludge-like species. Non-threatening, but definitely alive. Just not sentient."

"You both knew about this how?"

"I keep up with the journals," Thal answered promptly. "There was no mention of a test."

Charles shrugged his answer, "Idis."

"It isn't common knowledge," Thal said.

Charles nodded. "I think they wanted it to find something before they made it public. Unfortunately, or fortunately, alien species are incredibly rare."

They were. The last encountered alien species had given the Union the Black Blood disease that had killed everyone (non-alien) that it had come in contact with the exception of Thalberg and Annabelle Abrams (who were carriers) and David. Poor David, who would suffer from the effects of the disease for the rest of his life.

"So you think we can use this test to prove I am sentient, Sir, thus giving me my freedom?"

"Yes, I think and, more importantly, the Countess thinks it might." There was something, however, about it that was making Charles hesitate.

"And the catch?" I asked.

"Adgar is a Corsican Colony."

"Sure," I said.

"Idis can only work within the Empire."

"Right."

"So you, Jane, would need to become a Corsican citizen in order for Idis to sue on your behalf."

I was puzzled. "Why do you look like that? Is the test hard?"

Charles grinned. "No test." He turned to Thal. "Is this something you would like us all to pursue, Mr. Thal?"

"I don't want anyone to go to any trouble on my behalf…"

"The Countess likes this kind of trouble," Charles said, positively.

I patted Thal's arm again. "I think this is right. I hate the idea that I own a person." I shuddered. "It's wrong."

"Then, yes, please."

"Thank you, Mr. Thal," Charles said in kind dismissal.

Thal looked at us both thoughtfully, but retired to his room.

I looked at Charles curiously. "Why are you acting as though becoming a Corsican Citizen is scary, Six?"

He leaned back in his chair. "Because Corsicans, even naturalized ones, must be 'approved' by the Emperor himself."

"You have to approve every Corsican that has been born on any of your worlds *yourself*?" I asked, aghast. "How would you have time to do anything else?"

He smiled, "It's an ancient custom and rite of passage for our culture. Almost all of it goes through an office that handles everything and I sign something twice a year, but," he clarified, "the high profile cases, like Nora Archer-Nylander," he said with distaste, "are personally approved by the Emperor."

I laughed. "You mean Idis?"

"When I'm away, yes." He leaned forward and took my hand. "All the lists, whoever approves them, are public Union-wide. It's the law."

"Except when you are sneaking slave refugees in," I chided gently.

"Except then, but were you to become a citizen, it would have to be known outside Corsica for two reasons. One, you are a public figure yourself and two, it gives you grounds for the legal case for Thal."

"I see," I frowned. "Still not seeing the problem."

"The journos will link us. We won't be secret for long."

"Oh." I thought for a second or two, absently turning his hand over and tracing the lines on his palm. "No more bubble." I mean, we hadn't really been hiding anything so it wouldn't have been hard for anyone who was really determined to figure out that we were together, but we weren't 'out' as a couple either.

"Is that something you are worried about, love?" Charles asked. "There really isn't any hurry, you know." I looked into his golden eyes and saw nothing but patience and affection. The last time a relationship of mine (not counting Devon) became public was with David and that had been without my consent. What a difference trust made.

"How long could we keep the journos away from this if we held on as is and did nothing?"

"Not too long," he grimaced. "I've changed my schedule, something I've never done in all my years here and, as Bertie told me earlier today, I 'look like I'm getting some.'" I had to laugh at that. Charles joined me in laughter. "My monk-like solitude has been a source of curiosity for two decades. It will come out, Jane. I'm sorry."

"I'm sorrier for you, Charles," I said sincerely. "Your privacy…"

"My privacy has caused you and me a great deal of grief," he said a little angrily. "I am tired of keeping the women I…" and he stopped, cut off by that still-new confusion about when to put Idis's name with mine.

"You want to stand with the women you love." My heart was full. I got up and climbed onto his lap. "You should, Six, both here and there. So let's do it."

He wrapped his arms around me, partially to be close and partially to keep me from falling. I was pretty sure the chairs at the kitchen island weren't made to hold two people. "Are you sure?"

"As sure as I can be without knowing what will happen."

"I guess that is the best we can do." He kissed me gently. I kissed him back much less than gently. "None of that, now, love." I pouted for a second, but he chucked me under the chin teasingly. "You have visitors coming."

I grinned, my pout gone.

"When do they get in?"

I checked my watch. "In about an hour."

He lifted me easily off his lap and deposited me back on my chair. "So, let's eat."

We ate for a bit, chatting about small things. I can't tell you how much I loved that sort of thing, the little mundane stuff you could talk about when you shared your life with someone wonderful.

Before I knew it, it was time to go; Charles back to work and me to the shuttle bay. Thal reappeared as if magically sensing when we'd finished eating and started cleaning up. Charles thanked him for a wonderful meal and we both headed for the door.

He leaned down to kiss me goodbye and said, "There will be a ball."

"A ball?"

He nodded against my hair. "To celebrate the introduction of the Pelann's Heir-Designate to the Legislature."

Oh, right. A ball for Eriss. I'd read something about it in the dispatches, but I'd had too many other things on my mind to really care.

"Want to be my date?"

I looked up at him, his freckled face flushed, his eyes black gold. I really wished we didn't have to be other places right then. "I've never been anyone's date," I said without thinking and then realized it was true. Huh.

"Is that a yes?"

"Yes."

"Good." He kissed me again, his kiss promising much more and we left, going the opposite directions down the same hallway. He to the Embassy. Me, well…

The Furies were back!

21:23 – Shuttle Bay Alpha 7, Terra 1

I waited impatiently for the Bay to repressurize, staring at the red light until it turned green, then burst through the airlock to see my fellow Furies.

The first people I saw were two Captains, Freya, the Heely Captain of the *Indus Felae* and the Boss, Captain Paul Friedman, who was temporarily running the Furies while Ian was at Dep Qua—or wherever he actually was. I hugged them both and guiltily tried not to look as though I was scanning the small crowd for other people I wanted to see more.

"How was New Jakarta?" I asked.

"Interesting," Paul said dryly. He looked mostly the same, still tall with red hair that stood up like straw, but he seemed thinner and there were bits of gray in his hair that hadn't been there before. Responsibility had put them there, I wagered.

"How so?"

The Heely looked at Paul for permission and getting his nod said, "There was a new colony on the outskirts of the system."

"On one of the moons?" I didn't know if the system had any moons, I'd never been to the Indonesian Republic.

"In a way," Freya started.

"Orbiting," Paul said, dropping his voice lower. "It was a Denethian refugee colony. A new one."

Freya nodded. "About a month old. They were adapting an old ship as a station."

"Why didn't they just go to Novy?" I asked, perplexed. The Denethian presence around Novy was small, but well established.

"I think," Paul said, "they don't want to attract the attention of the Pelann."

"That's why you were hired? To protect the Deneth?"

"No," Freya said with a bit of venom, "we were hired to clean them out, though that was never put in writing."

"That isn't what you did, of course," I said, hoping that came out as a statement and not a question.

"No," Freya said, "after we established that there was no territorial issue…"

"Your friend Derek advised us," Paul interjected.

"Derek knew about a Denethian colony and didn't tell anyone?" I said, appalled.

"No, Jane," Paul said, "it was a blind question about jurisdiction." He rolled his eyes, "Their *Demna Trenni* Larna, or Lrn, as she prefers, made us swear to give nothing away to him."

"How did the good people of New Jakarta feel about this?"

"They were not pleased."

"So you didn't get paid?" I asked.

"Oh," Paul grinned toothily, "we got paid, just not by them." He folded his thin arms over his chest. "We handed them off to another mercenary group when the time for this contract drew near." He leaned in, "Jack told me that requests from either his father or you took precedence."

I smiled. "That was nice of him."

Paul's expression grew serious. "Have you heard anything from him, from Jack?"

"We haven't heard a peep in over a week. You?"

"No, nothing."

I saw two familiar figures walk out of the shuttle and managed to say, "We have to be here until after Lady Eriss is introduced. We're all worried that something is going to happen."

"So I gather," Paul said. He saw me looking at my approaching friends and grinned. "We'll catch up with you later, Jane."

"Good to see you both," I said, almost over my shoulder as I moved quickly into the embrace of two people very dear to me. Only two, though, not three.

I pulled them close and they held on tight. My own personal Pacey sandwich, I thought, as I kissed the top of Felix's head then Daniel's dark cheek.

"How are you? I've missed you so much," I gushed. They stepped back, but neither would look me in the eye. Fear knotted my gut. "Where is 'Lanta?" Now I thought I was going to throw up. "She's not..."

"No, Jane," Daniel said in his deep calm voice. "She's fine. At least, I assume she is."

Felix stared at the shuttle bay floor.

"What do you mean you assume she is?" I said, afraid for a different reason now. "Where is she?"

"On the *Ouranos*."

"Why? Why isn't she with you? You...had a fight?"

"Not exactly..." Daniel started, but stopped, clearly at a loss.

"It's over, Jane," Felix said, his voice strangled.

"She dumped us," Daniel said in a low voice.

Time seemed to stop, just for a second.

"But...but..." and I was at a loss, too. "When?" Like it mattered, but it was the only question I could think of to ask.

"Right before we went to the last job. We were on that new station outside of Esperanza and..." Daniel said.

"She didn't break up with us. *We* broke up with *her*," Felix growled.

"Because that's what she wanted, Fee!" Daniel whispered angrily, obviously rehashing an old argument.

"We gave her no choice," Felix hissed back.

"*She had a choice!*" Daniel said loudly, as people turned to stare. He then stopped talking and took a big, deep breath, trying to calm himself down. He turned to me and smiled a smile I didn't believe even for a second. "I cannot tell you how much I do *not* want to talk about this again."

I really, really wanted to know what the hell was going on, how the seemingly perfect Trio had fallen apart so quickly, but I could also see that Daniel and Felix were dying to take a break from it, even if only for a little while. I would hunt Atalanta down (oh, and I would) once I'd paid some attention to the two of her Trio who were left floundering.

"Are you staying on the *Indus* while you're here?"

"No," Daniel said, relieved that I wasn't going to push, "we got a room on the station."

"Good, then let me buy you a drink."

"That would be great, Jane," Daniel said.

Felix, however, said nothing as he took my hand. My heart broke for him, broke for both of them. What the hell had happened?

I got nowhere that evening, however, in my quest for information. I'd tried to see Atalanta, but had been informed, to my surprise, that she'd been in the middle of a sublight engine refit, so I'd gone home to my man (after getting the boys seriously drunk and seeing them safely to their room) to wait and try again in the morning.

I didn't, it turned out, have to try all that hard.

09:00 – Ambassadorial Apartments, Corsican Embassy, Terra 1, October 3rd, 2873

Charles and I had just finished breakfast in the sitting room of his apartment.

He had risen from the little table Mr. Beddoes fed us at and was saying, "I have to get a letter off to Idis before my day starts. She'll be thrilled Mr. Thal is on board with the test case…"

A throat cleared at the door and we both looked up.

"Captain Atalanta Pace is here for Miss Jane, Sir," Mr. Beddoes said. He looked both surprised and curious.

"Well that's a time saver," I murmured. "Would you please show her in, Mr. Beddoes?"

Mr. Beddoes' eyebrows had raised at this…impropriety, but Charles had nodded with a smirk. "It's all right, Beddoes."

Mr. Beddoes retreated, radiating both disapproval and amusement. Neat trick.

I looked up at Charles, who had already checked that his robe and pajamas were in good order. A reflex with years of practice behind it. He put them on when we got out of bed. More propriety, since he never wore anything when we were in bed together.

"Sir, Miss Jane." Mr. Beddoes bowed and ushered in, "Captain Pace."

I wouldn't have known her if I hadn't had her bio-signature down cold. The woman before us was small, slight and almost frail. Her usually lustrous dark hair, of which she had been so vain, was cut short around her face. No cosmetics. Her uniform was standard issue and free of the usual tweaks and tucks she would normally have used to accentuate her fantastic figure. It was only those big brown I eyes that I really recognized. They were still beautiful, despite Atalanta's best efforts, but they were the worst of all to see for they were full of despair.

"Miss Atalanta," Charles said graciously. "It is a pleasure to see you." He walked around the table and kissed her hand gallantly.

Atalanta smiled tiredly, "I doubt it, Fitz, but I appreciate the thought."

"Hey, 'Lanta," I said quietly.

"Hey, Jane."

"If you ladies will excuse me, I'm afraid I have to get about my day," Charles said.

Atalanta said nothing, but I said, "Of course, love."

Charles inclined his head in farewell and disappeared into his dressing room, Mr. Beddoes following to assist the never ending process of dressing a head of state.

Atalanta sat down heavily on Charles' abandoned chair and closed her eyes. It was nice that she didn't even wait for me to ask. "It all started with this job offer."

"Yeah, what's that about? They told me you were refitting a sublight engine," I said, mystified. "I know you're crazy smart, 'Lanta," no preening from my friend, no response at all, not good, "but I didn't know you knew how to do that sort of thing."

"One learns," she said with a wave of her hand. "So, it turns out that there really isn't much use for a MEmp in a mercenary fleet."

"I'm sorry to say I've never thought about it."

"Why should you? You're not a MEmp." She shifted in her seat. "A Macro or a Micro or a TP, now those are people with a valuable skill set. I used my 'talents' to get the Denethians at New Jakarta to listen to us instead of fight and be destroyed out of their own fears of the non-Rian." She sighed. "It was the first time I'd used that aspect of my abilities in I don't know how long." She snorted. "Ironic that that would happen *after* I'd taken the new job."

"What new job?"

"I'd been under-utilized, as I've said, and bored, but I have experience and brains and had worked either for or with some of the best tacticians around, so I talked to Paulie about it."

"'Paulie' Friedman?" I bet only Atalanta called him that.

"That's the one," she said colorlessly. "He said he had a problem, too. Anyone he would have wanted for his second-in-command was either unavailable or already Captain, since Freya was promoted and Captain White has taken a commission at UNav under Admiral Tree. So, Paulie offered me a chance to train and, after a six month period if all went well, the job as his second-in-command."

"Wow," I said, flummoxed. "That's quite an honor, 'Lanta, but I would have thought that he would have asked Felix before anyone else, no offense."

She shrugged. "He had asked, apparently, and this was news to me," she grimaced, "but Felix had turned the opportunity down for, he'd said, personal reasons."

I frowned. "Personal reasons that you didn't know about, I'm guessing."

"Yeah," she said bitterly. "So I said that I would love to accept, but that I had to run it by the boys first. Paulie understood and I went to talk to them." She paused a long time now.

The suspense/dread was killing me. "'Lanta…"

"They want to have a baby, Jane." She took a shaky breath. "I don't want to."

Holy mother. *This* was the problem? Holy mother again. "And they talked this over amongst themselves and decided to do this, Felix even turning down an amazing job because of it, and never bothered to discuss this with you??"

Her brown eyes looked dead and flat. "Yep."

I was angry so quickly I felt momentarily faint. "Those…fuckheads!"

"Yep."

"So how did they explain themselves, exactly?" I said, fists clenched in fury.

"They said, well, Daniel said, Felix just looked guilty as sin, that they knew I wasn't 'keen' on the idea of motherhood but that they wanted to find the best way to broach the idea with me. They were afraid," and here she laughed mirthlessly, "I wouldn't take well to the concept."

"At least they got one thing correct," I said, but I was thinking hard. I looked over at my oldest friend. "And you're sure you don't want children? Completely sure?"

She exhaled hard. "Aren't you?"

"Yes."

She looked around her as if she was going to rise and possibly pace, but relaxed again as if realizing it was too much trouble. She tapped her foot agitatedly against the chair leg instead. "I don't know why they had to even go bring this up. Our life was so good, perfect even. We'd worked so hard to get there and now they want to bring a baby into it. And our lives will be about the baby, which is how it should be if you have one."

"If," I said.

She leaned forward and took my hand, clutching it convulsively. "I know my reasons for not wanting kids aren't the same as yours, we don't have the same pressures you do, but you do understand, don't you? A little?" She was pleading. I hated that Atalanta was pleading for my approval.

"I do understand, love." I put my other hand on top of hers. "Because I know that when you love you love with your whole heart and you would adore that baby and everything around you would change, because that's what happens when you love that much."

"I'm glad you don't think I would just walk away."

"Only someone who doesn't know you would think that. Someone who doesn't know like I do," and her men also had to know, "that inside that beautiful bitch exterior is a heart of pure mushy gold."

"Not so beautiful now," she said tiredly. "I guess they banked on my pure mushy heart falling for the idea of a child and that that would make the choice for me."

"And when you said no..."

"I didn't say no, Jane," she said.

"You didn't?" I asked, dumbfounded.

"Of course not. I said I wasn't sure. That I'd never thought about being a mother. And they dribbled on about how easy they would make it for me. That they would do all the work, blah blah blah." Tap tap tap went her foot against the chair.

"That's when you started plotting your escape because you didn't want to shit on their dream." Oh yeah, I got that.

"Exactly."

"So, how?"

"First I accepted the job with Paulie and requested to be berthed immediately on the *Ouranos*." She seemed to realize the foot tapping was getting out of control so she stopped it. "He granted my request and didn't ask any questions, which was nice, and I moved my things out while the boys were at work."

"And then..?" because none of that would have been enough. She'd needed a clean break. Something decisive.

"That night I went to Esperanza Station, consumed a lot of alcohol as well as an aphrodisiac the HM's call the 'horny' pill and fucked the brains out of the first hot man I saw at the bar." She reached for my tea and took a swallow. "I was *very* thorough."

"Then you went home and told them about it? Or let them," shudder, "find some evidence?"

"My dear, Daniel is a Telepath, or have you forgotten?"

Oh god. "You *showed* them?" I gulped. "Everything?"

Atalanta's jaw was clenched. "Not the spirits or the pill, but yes, everything else." She fixed me with a determined look. "They had to know I wanted it."

Decisive. Yes, that would have been just that. I sat there in shock that she would do something so brutal, though part of me was impressed. She hadn't half-assed it. She hadn't left a trail of breadcrumbs or the door open even a little bit. It was done. I looked over at the wreck my friend had become. What a cost.

"I'm so sorry, 'Lanta."

"Don't, Jane-love," she said, her voice wavering a little. "I can't stand pity or blame right now."

"All right," I said, understanding that, too. "Are you on leave until Eriss and party arrive day after tomorrow?"

"Yes," she laughed miserably, "worst time to have nothing to do."

I rose. "Let me get dressed and I'll ask Thal if he'll look after you today. Maybe you can help him get some more information on Ian."

"I want to say I don't need a minder, but that sounds good, Jane, thanks."

"No problem." I headed for the massive closet, but Atalanta called me back. "Yes?"

"You're worried about Ian, aren't you?" she said.

I smiled ruefully. "I'm worried about a lot of people, love. Be right back."

I left her there to her cold tea and walked into the closet to find a half-dressed Ambassador/Emperor holding several ties in his hand.

"I sent Beddoes to bring Miss Atalanta a good breakfast," he said quietly, "I have a feeling she hasn't eaten in a while."

"That's nice, my love. You heard all, I take it?"

He looked abashed, "I'm sorry for eavesdropping. I was worried for her. She's been your friend for so long and…"

"It's all right, Charles." I tapped his nose playfully. "Saved the recap later."

"What will you do?" he asked as I picked one of his ties for him to wear. He shook his head and selected a different one. I rolled my eyes.

"I don't know, yet. Maybe nothing can be done."

"That doesn't sound like my Jane at all."

"Your Jane has to think and," I checked my watch, "get moving. I have class in half an hour." I kissed him quickly as I headed to my tiny part of the closet. "I'll see you tonight."

"That you will, love," he said thoughtfully.

11:00 – Heely Water Tube, *T.F.S. Indus Felae*, Three Furies Fleet

I stood in front of my Senior Macro Class clad in my anti-Heely water suit, helmet off. Six students waited for me to speak, but I was waiting for two helpers. One a kid. One a pro. They weren't there yet, so I got started.

"Welcome to the *T.F.S. Indus Felae*, a mercenary ship that is part of the Three Furies Fleet. This ship was the first of its kind to be designed with both Heely and Terran Humans in mind," I raised my arm, indicated the tube of beautiful dark blue water behind me. The kids looked at it in awe as it seemed to glow behind them. The tube had been designed to be a jewel in the middle of the large room. This was so because the designer was David Abrams and he believed in beauty and function. The pool on Terra 1 had an observation window, but wasn't, aside from that, much more than a metal box with lights and water in it. It was a good useful pool but nothing more, but *not* designed by David, so even if the kids had seen the other pool, they'd never seen one like this.

"Today we will be adjusting to Heely water, hence the suits, and learning control within it."

"Do you anticipate our fighting in Heely water, Ma'am?" Caroline Tellesco asked.

"Not specifically, no, Cadet," I answered, "There are almost two dozen worlds with Heely oceans now, however, and it never hurts to be prepared."

"But," Cadet Blake Sheffield almost whined, "We won. Why would we have to fight the Heelies again?"

"Learning to adapt to any situation is never wasted effort, Mr. Sheffield, and who said anything about fighting Heelies?" I regarded him with my best stern teacher face and he quailed a bit. "Many of those worlds are abandoned now. Abandoned by *Heelies*, at least, and nature abhors a vacuum."

"Yes, Ma'am," he said, chastened.

"At least we taught those Eels a lesson," Sinata Dawes said under her breath.

Ah, yes, the fun new nickname that had popped up over the last months since the Heely War had ended. You know, Heely = Eely = Eels. Because Heelies are amphibious, get it? Yep, super clever. (Good to know my sarcasm gene was still functioning properly.)

Upon hearing that nasty word, well, if I had been a Denethian my claws would have come out, I would have bared my teeth and seemed to double in menacing size. As it was I am proud to say my fury at this racist and unfair term did not go unnoticed.

Everyone backed up.

"This is not a perfect Union," I said in a low and deliberately scary voice. "Reintegration will be a pain in the ass, but that is not a word that should ever be used or even *thought* within the confines of this school. All of you have been treated as less than equal because of who you are and should know better than to single out beings because they were born different." So much for not making windows into men's souls, Jane, I thought dryly. That word had to go away, though, at least while they were on my watch.

"Hear hear," a deep voice said behind me.

I took a breath, giving calming down my best shot, and looked over my shoulder to see the two, make that three, people I'd been waiting for. The first was…

"Kids, this is General Synon, Novy Heliot Ambassador to the Union," I said, smiling at my friend who smiled back. "He's agreed to help us today in the pool."

The over seven-foot Heely walked forward all muscle and subtle menace. Call him an 'Eel,' I thought, I dare you.

"Sir," they all said in response, some as if barely breathing. Good.

"Some of you may know Cadets Smith and Nitsa who will also be joining us."

Of course everyone knew these two. My Macro class tried to look friendly, or at least not antagonisticly towards Wylan. If any of them entertained the idea, however, the fierce look from Petros (who wasn't a small guy for a Terran Human) killed it. Excellent.

Then, to my class' continued surprise, eight Heely soldiers (2 Teams) appeared. No, I corrected myself. Seven more Heely soldiers, four females, three males. They stood in a double line behind their General and said not a damned thing. I noted that, unlike Synon, they were all, to a Heely, on the small side, each about six feet tall. I caught Synon's green eyes when I made this mental observation and he twinkled at me. All by design, that twinkle said. Actually it said more than that. It said that he was happy. Wonderful.

I also noticed that the Heelies wore light combat gear; a very tough wet suit equivalent with bandoliers for knives and projectile weapons. All looked well-used.

"General," I prompted.

"My friend, Commodore Pace, and I wanted to show you some of what Heely Humans bring to the table," Synon said, with an incline of the head to me. "While Heelies have great physical strength at any time, Terran humans have, out of the water at least, speed and agility on their side. In Heely water, however, we have the edge, not surprisingly."

Cadet Dawes raised her hand.

"Yes, Cadet…" Synon said.

"Cadet Dawes, Sir," she said carefully, "does Heely Human speed and agility apply to fresh and salt water as well?"

Synon smiled, showing a lot of teeth. The kids looked a bit unnerved at this, though I was sure that was not the intended effect. "It does, though, as you'll see, Heely water is much more viscous," he saw someone frown, "or thicker," he clarified, "than either fresh or Terran ocean water." He looked at me. "We've been experimenting on the planet."

"Where?" I asked, now sorry I'd missed it.

"A fresh water lake in North America, the Indian Ocean, the Mediterranean Sea and the Dead Sea." He scratched his arm in memory. "The Dead Sea made us itch for the rest of the day. All that salt."

Cadet Holter grinned, nodding.

Synon laughed. "You know the Dead Sea, Cadet?"

"Yes, Sir. My neck of the woods, so to speak."

"Beautiful country. Nothing like back home. Though," he said, looking around, "neither is this."

"No, Sir," the Cadet said and I felt him relax a bit. They all did, a bit, even Petros who, poor fellow, must have been constantly on his guard.

"To answer Cadet Dawes' question: the fresh water seemed like mist and the salt water seemed like air. It was as if we'd moved to a planet with half the gravity. It was an experience, but I admit I prefer working in the dark blue." He looked over his shoulder at the beings standing still and silently behind him. "So today we will, with the aid of Teams Wanhatta," loose translation 'Big Tough/Hard Head,' really, "and Lau-Tresca."

I was so surprised I started to cough to cover my laugh. I caught the eye of one of the female soldiers and she gave me the slightest of eye rolls. Lau-Tresca meant 'Four Cocks.' "Sorry, General."

I noticed that several of my students were trying to catch each others' eyes, trying to confirm what they suspected about the name. Language training was an essential part of the education here at the ESTF. Heely, upper and lower, as well as Denethian were drilled into their heads from the moment they walked in the school. We did not, however, spend any class time on the swear words. Marston liked to dole those out on a reward basis. Apparently he hadn't gotten to everyone in the Macro class yet. Pity.

"Cadet Smith?"

"Sir?" Wylan answered startled, as if he'd been caught napping. He hadn't been, of course.

"I assume you remember your basic drills and formations?"

"Yes, Sir."

Synon nodded his approval. "Join Team Wanhatta for this exercise."

"Of course, Sir." Wylan scrambled to get into position.

Synon turned back to my Cadets. "We will demonstrate six formations twice. Then you Cadets will join us in the water and learn them. This will be only a taste of what we can do, however," he looked over at the giant tube of deep blue water, "since a lot of our abilities require the space and speed you can only get in an open ocean, but you'll get the general idea."

Synon turned to his men. "Wanhatta, Lau-Tresca, *andomene.*" Rough literal translation: Dive in. Rough more poetic translation: return to the Mother.

With telling fluidity, all nine Heelies walked quickly to the stairs that curved around the tank and up to the platform at the very top. Synon immediately dove up in the air, twisted five times as he flew and entered the water, barely even breaking its surface. The other eight, including Wylan, followed, diving with equal precision if much less flash. I didn't blame Synon for showing off a bit. Heelies did this shit all the time, how many times would you have a chance to impress anyone who couldn't already do what you were doing?

I looked at Synon floating motionless in the center of the pool, his natural swim bladder keeping him at whatever depth he chose and he tapped his temple.

"Helmets on and comms," I ordered and we all put on and sealed ours. 'We will use the comms only for this part, the observational part, of the demonstration so you can hear the commands. Once you are in the water yourself they will be switched off.'

'Yes, Ma'am,' the Cadets answered in unison.

'*Prestatu,*' Synon ordered his teams in lower Heely. Prepare.

Synon faced us and the Heelies formed two lines behind him.

'*Bat.*' One.

They fanned out behind and out from him in a "V" pattern.

'*Bi.*' Two.

The "V" split and they spread out further and in four spikes from the center.

'*Hiru.*' Three.

The four spikes moved forward, stretching over Synon and widening out. Cadet Tellesco took an involuntary step back.

'*Lau.*' Four.

The two Teams continued advancing as they drew their knives in both hands. All except Wylan who had none. It was hard to notice, though. The Heely knives were bloody huge.

'*Bost.*' Five.

The soldiers started spinning, knives flashing in the lights of the ship and pool. Corkscrews of death coming at us.

'*Sei.*' Six.

They darted at each other, crossing each other's paths, narrowly missing, but never touching. They spun around perfectly, moving around Synon, creating a perfect bubble of bodies and steel around him. Their green skin glowed in the blue water, their eyes were clear and sharp. Wylan moved with them flawlessly. Aside from the lack of weapon and difference in uniform, you would never have known he wasn't part of the team.

'*Hasita.*' Beginning.

They instantly moved to their original position in two lines, resheathing their weapons as they did so, behind Synon. Synon himself had never moved. He'd never needed to.

'As I mentioned to Cadet Smith, this was a very basic form, used from childhood. You have seen it now at one eighth speed.'

'Jesus,' Cadet Bridges muttered. Get ready, kid, I thought with an evil internal chuckle.

'*Prestatu,*' Synon said, his voice strong and commanding. '*Abiatura.*' At speed.

A pause. I could feel strong muscles gathering. My own heart raced. Blow me away, friends. Knock my socks off.

That's just what they did.

'*Bat.*'

At seemingly blinding speed they fanned out behind and out from Synon in a "V" pattern. Everyone gasped, even me. He barked the next command almost before they were in position.

'*Bi.*'

The "V" split and they spread out further and in four spikes from the center, but this time the outer ring of four circled clock-wise while the inner one circled in the opposite direction. The disturbance in the water made what we saw distort alarmingly.

'*Hiru.*'

The four spikes moved forward, stretching over Synon and widening out, the circling grew stronger, but not faster. Tons of water was being moved now.

'*Lau.*'

The two Teams continued advancing as all but Wylan drew their knives in both hands.

'*Bost.*'

The still turning soldiers started spinning individually, knives flashing.

'Looks like they're going to core us,' Cadet Dawes whispered.

'Yeah,' Cadet Holter said with a shiver.

It was Cadet Petros Nitsa, however, who was the most awestruck. 'I've never seen anything like it.'

I leaned closer. 'This is only the beginning, Petros."

I saw he was watching his charge move with his Heely brethren, Wylan holding out his hands as though he, too, held invisible blades.

We weren't done yet.

'*Sei.*'

Knives very much in hand the Heelies abruptly stopped circling and darted at each and over each other, crossing each other's paths, narrowly missing, but never touching in a perfectly choreographed and deadly dance. They moved around Synon, created a sphere of steel around him at dizzying speed.

Impenetrable. Lethal. Beautiful.

We would never have beat them on their home turf, I knew. In space, however, all Humans were equal and, I grimaced, the Deneth Rian waited to wipe the floor with us there if they so chose.

'*Gelditu.*' Synon nodded at his people. They stopped in position and waited. '*Urratzen.*' The soldiers put their weapons away and headed for the surface and some much deserved air. They were breathing hard, I noted with relief. It would have seemed unnatural had they not been.

Synon gestured to us to come in and swam up to the top for his own dose of air.

'You're joking, Ma'am,' Cadet Blake said, dismayed. 'We can't come close to doing that.'

'You know this how, Mr. Sheffield?'

Blake stuck his chin out. 'Because we are finless wonders, Ma'am."

Well, that was a different spin on our genetic differences. I cleared my throat instead of snorting. 'That may be, but we are *Macro* finless wonders.' I raised my voice for the others. 'So let's be grateful they are our allies, find our balls and get in the water. *Berehala!*' Immediately. So they immediately did just that.

13:17 – Heely Water Tube, *T.F.S. Indus Felae,* Three Furies Fleet

I sat hard on the bench in the viewing area next to the Heely water tube and closed my eyes. My kids had done well, actually, for their first time. The

Heely soldiers had been patient and helpful and if they'd thought the Terrans were clumsy idiots, they'd kept that to themselves. It had been work for everyone, but these were my best student Macros and they weren't just the best because of their abilities; they were extremely tenacious as well. That was a trait the best *Schola-Terra* Cadets, whether super or normal, had to have in common. Those that didn't were sent home.

The kids and soldiers had just left. I was freshly showered and in a clean spare uniform. There was something wrong about getting out of the water soaked with sweat, but working hard in your adapted DSS suit and never actually *touching* the water would do that for you. I needed to head back to the station, but didn't feel like standing up. Not yet. Swimming, even our Macro version of it, for an hour and half was work. Actually, what I really wanted to do was find one of the regular water pools on the station and swim the old fashioned way. You know, and actually get wet.

A large form settled on the bench beside me. The same bench, ironically, he'd picked me up at (literally and figuratively) many months ago.

"Hey, Big Heely," I said as I opened my eyes.

"Hey, little lady."

"You were amazing today, thanks."

"I was that," he said with a smile. "And you're welcome." He leaned back comfortably. "Her Majesty is very worried about the reintegration so I thought this would be a good opportunity to show what we can do."

I ran my fingers through my still wet hair. "I remember having similar discussions with Samuel, that's the High Admiral to you," I said teasingly, "on our way to Terra after Pace was destroyed." I leaned my head back against the back of the bench. "Offer them something they need that no one else can do and they'll be forced to want you."

"It's a start at least." He inspected the webbing between the fingers on his right hand for a minute. "Wylan Smith wishes he was Terran. To fit in."

I shrugged. "It's a natural feeling when he's so outnumbered and so young."

"I wonder what my sons and daughters will think when they start growing up."

I looked at him in surprise. "Is that something you need to worry about this soon?"

Synon snorted, "No. Not just yet, but I can't help thinking about it."
He sighed. "The future is a funny thing, Jane. I'll have a Terran wife and
we'll have Terran babies and Heely babies and they will grow up together.
And they will fight like siblings do and love each other like siblings do
and, if Missy and I have done our jobs properly, will wonder what the fuss
is about."

"We can hope, Sy." I put my hand on his for a second. "I'm very
happy for you, you know. For you both."

"Thank you, Jane. I'm very lucky."

I stood and stretched. "I have to get back. Micro class in less than an
hour."

"You know, your friend Marston said something to me yesterday," he
continued as if I hadn't spoken. I paused indulgently.

"Yes?"

"Not all Heelies bond. Did you know that?"

I sat back down. "No," I said, surprised.

"It isn't something we talk about outside out own *Demnas*. People who
don't or can't bond are looked on as defective."

"That's horrible, Sy."

"It is."

"You were one of those people?"

"Until I met Missy."

What a gift, I thought, but what I said was, "So Marston?"

"When I told him that I had found my mate, he'd congratulated me and
said that that was the fourth Heely/Terran bonding he'd heard about in the
last month. He said he'd always thought that his meeting Tania was a
miracle—and it was, but..."

Four Heely/Terran couples? In a fucking month? My mind was in
shock. "Why now?"

"His theory was that the Terrans had split themselves by making the
Heelies and the reason we seem to bond when we come together is because
we aren't artificially separated anymore."

Made sense. Once the Heliot had been created the two peoples had
rarely, if ever mixed without either prejudice or bloodshed. "So all those
un-bonded Heelies..."

"Were probably missing their equally un-bonded Terran partners."

"Wow."

"It gives me hope, Jane. Maybe in a hundred years we won't be able to fight each other. Perhaps our two peoples will be so intertwined that it would be impossible."

To me this scenario sounded like a good set up for a very bloody civil war, but no way was I going to rain on his parade of rainbows and kittens.

"We can only hope, Sy."

I rose and kissed him on the head fin, then headed for my ship and the station.

18:56 – Aronoff's Bar and Grill, Terra 1 Station

Felix, Daniel and I in a booth with a view of the stars and delicious (I assumed) food in front of us. We pretended to eat, but didn't even bother to pretend to talk. All I felt was depressed in their presence and for the first time in forever I didn't feel like butting in. It was all too sad. I took a bite. I couldn't even tell you what I was eating. I just thought of Atalanta, heartsore and alone when two months ago she'd had everything she'd ever wanted. This all just sucked.

"Jane," Felix said. Or I thought he'd said it. I wasn't sure. I watched a ship pass by the Tenorium window.

"*Jane*," Felix said again, an edge to his voice.

I looked over. "What, Felix?"

He exhaled hard. "I thought you were meeting us to read us the riot act."

I shrugged.

"You're saying we don't deserve it or that you don't care?" he said bitterly.

"I care."

Daniel continued to eat as though we were at another table.

"You think I don't know how fucked up this is?" Felix asked, pushing his uneaten plate away.

"I have no idea what either of you are thinking," I said honestly.

I could read the tension building, the knots in his stomach as Felix's impotent anger built. "So you, who always has something to say, stay quiet."

"I'm...dismayed."

"Dismayed," Felix repeated, getting more and more pissed. "That's it?"

"I guess."

"Daniel and I, the two of us, lost the best thing that has ever happened to us and you are 'dismayed?'" he asked incredulously.

I felt a stab of anger burst through my depression, which I was sure had been the point of his question. "Yeah," I said through clenched teeth.

"I *knew* she didn't want children," he said, glaring at Daniel, who still looked only at his plate, "I *knew* it."

"*Then why the fuck did you do this?*" I asked, now furious.

Now Felix was silent. He looked at me, but not at Daniel.

"Because of me. All this was because of me," Daniel said quietly.

"I know," I said, because I did somehow. This wasn't Felix. Felix knew better.

Daniel sighed and I could see how tired he was, how beaten down. "This was what I wanted. It was selfish of me. I am a selfish bastard," he said, rubbing his forehead with his palm.

"If you want children, though…" I started.

"Not more than I want her, or want us," he growled, finally showing signs of a pulse.

"Then why, Daniel?"

He sighed again. "I saw what I wanted to see. I would ask her questions about kids, you know, in passing and she would never actually *say* she didn't want them. They were deflections, always, but I didn't get it. Had she definitively said…"

"You *do* want children." He said nothing then. So I turned to Felix. "What was your excuse?"

"A dream."

"A dream?" I asked, nonplussed.

Felix nodded. "Daniel broadcasts our thoughts to each other, usually only when we are being intimate, but sometimes he forgets to shut it down when he falls asleep." He stared at the stars. "I saw her dreaming of a baby. A beautiful son. He had her eyes and he was dark like Daniel and his little hand was around her finger and I thought maybe…maybe…"

"I didn't know you wanted kids, Felix."

"I don't know, but that baby was perfect and I knew Daniel wanted children so when he brought it up I went along with it."

"But it was just a dream." God, if I got all the things I dreamed about…I shuddered to think. "So you were trying to please Daniel? Or yourself?"

Felix said absolutely nothing to that. It was for Daniel, then.

I turned to Daniel. "So, go apologize and fix it. You say you are willing to live without children to have Atalanta so prove it."

"Because you think she'll be willing to take me back thinking that I will give this up for her?" Daniel scoffed.

No, I didn't think that, but something had to be tried. "Then convince her."

"I can't, Jane. I…" Daniel put his hands over his face covering suddenly wet eyes.

"Why? Because you don't believe it?"

"Because I see her with that man over and over in my head." He dropped his hands. Tears were leaking down his handsome face. "You want to talk about dreams? That is all I see when I close my eyes."

"She did that for you. You know that, don't you?"

"I know!" Daniel almost shouted, but then his voice dropped to almost nothing. "Only someone who loved that much could be that cruel." He picked up his fork then threw it down, it bounced noisily off his plate to land on the table. He rose then abruptly. "Now I get to keep the knowledge that she was thinking more about me, about us," he said, indicating Felix, "than I thought about her." His guilt was a palpable thing as he threw his napkin down and stalked away.

"Danny…" Felix gasped as he, too, rose.

"You have to do something, Felix."

He looked back at me blankly as if he'd forgotten I was there, too wrapped up in the despair of the lover he still had.

"Felix."

"I don't know how to fix this, Jane."

I stood next to him and grabbed his arm in a firm grip. "You are the best tactician I know, aside from the General. You are still better at this than 'Lanta. Outflank her or something. Figure it out."

I squeezed his arm hard, silently telling him I had faith in him and I headed out. I wanted Charles. He would be home, now.

I made it to the door, but then looked back at my friend. I could see his small form in shadow against the starry night. He was still standing there as I left.

120

20:06 – Ambassadorial Apartments, Corsican Embassy, Terra 1

I poured Charles and myself spirits. He leaned back against the breakfast table and watched me. I handed him his drink. He silently toasted me and took a sip.

"People will start arriving tomorrow."

I nodded.

"One in particular should interest you," he said. "Sam let my people know about it just before I left the office."

"Who is coming?"

"The Station Master got a request for a high security mooring for the *N.H.S. Foudroyant*."

"You're kidding."

"If only."

David. David was coming to Eriss' coming out party. "Why on Earth?"

"From what we've seen there will be more than one reason, but only Abrams will know what they all are."

"True. Well, he always makes things more interesting."

He barked out a little laugh, but I didn't think he really cared about the usual havoc David brought, not really. Charles stared at his drink, then downed it all at once. He read tense and tired. I put my glass down, walked close and wrapped myself around him. It only took a second but I felt him relax. I snuggled closer and he relaxed even more.

"So work was tough?" I asked. He'd spent most of the day on-planet in the Legislature. Talking, lobbying, keeping an eye on things. He liked this part of the job. He liked telling me about the personalities involved and what they were trying to do, whether altruistic or nefarious. Nothing was perfect, of course, but days on-planet were usually calls to action. Today, however, he seemed a bit shaken.

He sighed into my hair. "Katja Gureyev resigned today."

"Why?" I would have thought she'd only have resigned her Cyrillic ambassadorship for the Presidency itself.

"The Senior Senator, Tikonov, from Cyrillic was lobbying all the Legislative Members to push through *Hominum* Bill 61874," he grimaced, "*before* the representatives from the Rian could be seated."

I leaned back a bit though I stayed in his embrace. "What kind of fast one were these worthies trying to pull exactly?"

"A Union-wide Law that allowed each *Hominum* District to decide whether Heely/Terran segregation was in their best interests. The majority would rule."

I buried my face in his neck. So much for the civil rights of Union Citizens. "I'm shocked but not surprised." I raised my head, "Katja actually resigned over that? Really?"

"I'm as astonished as you are, Jane, but I really think that, for the first time in her opportunistic power grab of a career, she finally found something she just couldn't do."

"Was the bill defeated?" I had to guess that it was since he seemed more disappointed and tired, rather than afraid (for the Heelies) and furious.

"It was, by an overwhelming majority." The 'this time' was implied.

"Thank god." I reached up and massaged his scalp gently. "This is how reintegration should go, isn't it? Small battles, big ones, victories and losses."

Charles nodded. "Yes, but, love, I have to take issue with that word."

"What word? Reintegration?"

"Yes. Everyone uses it, I've used it myself, but it isn't the best description. Heelies and Terrans have *never* been integrated. They've never been assimilated. Their culture was created out of whole cloth by humans with a great deal of imagination and not a lot of sense."

"Sounds like they were created by Paceys."

"It does," he smiled down at me. "So this isn't a case of going back to something we had before. This, shared genetic heritage aside, is entirely new."

"I agree to a point, love, but let me tell you what Marston said about…"

I froze. A commotion outside the Embassy. Weapons pointed. Soldiers on alert.

"Jane?" Charles asked sharply, all his relaxation gone.

I kept scanning but soon looked up at my Six puzzled all to hell. "The guards were surrounding someone, or a couple of people and…now they're at ease again." I frowned. "Three are coming. Mr. Beddoes," my eyebrows rose, "Thal and Atalanta." The fuck?

Charles and I let each other go but stood side by side. He automatically checked his tie, coat and cuffs. He probably didn't even realize he was doing it, it was so ingrained.

There was a quiet knock on the door completely at odds with the excitement of the people on the other side of it.

"Come." Charles was instantly the Ambassador. I couldn't really tell you what had changed about him, but it was definitely there.

"Miss Atalanta and Mr. Thal, Sir, Miss Jane." Mr. Beddoes looked quite put out. "They insisted that it was extremely important."

"Then I am sure it is," Charles said with a hint of dryness, implying that it had better be. Charles dismissed Mr. Beddoes and both of us turned to 'Lanta and Thal for an explanation.

Atalanta waited, apparently, for Thal to say something, but Thal just bit his lip. She put her hands on her hips, irritated.

"Thal, you tell them."

"You noticed it first." Thal looked ashamed of himself. Like he'd missed something or failed, but I couldn't imagine what.

"*Thalberg*," she ordered.

"Sir, Miss Jane..."

"Yes, Thal?" I prompted gently.

"Trithicate Station," Thal said, his four hands clenching over and over.

"Yes, Mr. Thal?" Charles said.

"It's gone, Sir."

ENTRY 4-8-87

<u>20:15 – Ambassadorial Apartments, Corsican Embassy, Terra 1, October 3rd, 2873</u>

"It's gone, Sir."

Thal's words sort of echoed in the room. Or maybe that was in my head, but Charles and I just stared at Thal and then at Atalanta, too, in shock. How could an entire fucking Denethian space station be…gone?

"Was there a debris field?" I asked, because wouldn't that be the nicest easiest solution to the mystery of the missing Trithicate Station. Well, not the nicest. Actually that would be very bad for the Deneth but *so* much simpler for the rest of us.

Atalanta shook her head, "No, Jane it's not destroyed, it's…" She looked unhappily at Thal, but it was Charles who either got there first or just admitted a truth.

Charles rubbed his smooth chin. "Well, I guess we know why Abrams' people were shoring up the structural integrity of the station."

Thal nodded. "It's moving." He grimaced. "It has moved."

He opened his chest cavity and drew out a holo projector disk which he placed on the breakfast table and pressed a button on it. The room filled with dots of light of various sizes. Planets and suns.

"The station was, for over a thousand years, here," Thal pointed and one of the balls of light turned red. "The Trithicate system," he explained or reminded, depending. "When I checked in this morning it was here." He moved his finger many, many light years away to a position near the Devrah System, his finger making a red line as he did this.

"What did you get yesterday?" I asked.

Now Thal's cheeks turned bright red with obvious embarrassment. "Nothing, Miss Jane. No reading. Nothing."

I really didn't want to be angry at my friend. I really didn't, but this was a fuckup. How could he not have said anything? So *I* said nothing, not trusting myself not to reveal my disappointment. He was clearly beating himself up enough for both of us.

"I thought it was an error with the Thal communication grid." His mobile plastic face fell. "I am so sorry, Miss Jane."

"Miss Atalanta," Charles said, very professionally, "noticed the position change today?"

"Yes, Sir."

"Only because Thal was going over equipment reports at the time, Fitz," Atalanta said calmly.

"What is their course?" I asked quietly. "And why did they stop near Devrah? Because they are no longer in Devrah, correct?"

"They were at Devrah for about an hour then returned to hyper," Atalanta said. "I think they were testing their hyper engines so made a relatively short jump."

I wished Felix was with us. In fact, I wished a lot of people were with us. Yes, that was a good idea. "Excuse me," I said as I turned away to switch on my comm.

"Commodore Pace for High Admiral Armstrong."

Behind me I heard Charles say, "That was an extremely gutsy move on the part of the Pelann. I doubt those engines had been used since the station was put into place millennia ago."

"I agree," Atalanta murmured as Thal stayed quiet.

They continued talking as I spoke into my comm. David was coming to Terra, I thought, as I went through layers of gatekeepers to get to the people I was trying to reach. Is this what David had wanted? Had he just been hired for a job and nothing more? I shook my head at my own naiveté but then stopped the movement because I was in danger of switching off my comm. Within a short time my calls were all placed and I looked up.

"They'll be here in ten minutes."

Mr. Beddoes opened the doors, apparently summoned by Charles.

"Tea, Beddoes."

"Very good, Sir."

I looked at Charles in wonder. Bad shit was going down and we were going to drink tea while we waited for it. I sighed. Well, why the fuck not?

Ten minutes later the room was much more populated. Samuel (representing both UNav and President Leder) stood next to Mallory (!!), and Synon towered over everybody as he spoke to the Terran Ambassador to the Union, the Honorable Ut Phan. Slender and barely five feet tall she made quite the contrast to the Big Heely. Atalanta stayed off to the side, near a corner of the room. Hiding. We waited for two more.

Thal was in another corner unmoving, almost as if he'd shut down. I was glad I had said nothing before if just my silence had knocked him down this hard. I felt bad, but he *had* screwed up.

"Thal?"

He looked up.

"Beings make mistakes."

"I don't."

I had to smile. "Sentient beings *do*." I leaned against the wall next to him. "I've messed up in so many ways, my friend, over the years."

"What do you do about it?"

"Fix it if I can and if not, feel bad for a while and try to do better." I shrugged. "What else can you do?"

"The last time I made a mistake…" he stopped. He was referring to the time a previous Thal had attempted to assassinate David and myself, and a soldier had died because of it.

"It wasn't you," I said automatically, but then I stared at him. "Someone told you about that?" Why would anyone do that? Just to be cruel?

"I have access to things you wouldn't believe, Jane," Thalberg, and right then it was Thalberg, slumped against the wall.

"Screwups are part of existence. A lot of mine have been more embarrassing than anything else. Some," I took a breath, "not."

"I don't want to let you down."

I took his lower left hand in mine. "I know that, love. Nor I you. How could we trust each other without that?"

Thalberg's face turned to mine, his expression so sad I wanted to look away, but I didn't.

Just then Paul(ie) Friedman and Felix arrived. Atalanta didn't outwardly respond, but I felt her body tense and her stomach knot. I patted Thalberg's hand and let it go. "Showtime, Thal," I said. Thalberg straightened and it was Thal who headed to the center of the room where the holo projector still showed all the planets. The red line was temporarily gone.

"High Admiral, Captain Faro," that was Mallory, "Captain Friedman, Captains Pace and Ambassadors," Fitzroy, Phan and Synon (the place was lousy with them). "I am Thal, an independent sentient construct created by David Abrams, and I currently assist Commodore Pace."

The Honorable Ut Phan nodded. Either she'd heard of him or she was so *sang froid* that nothing phased her.

"It appears Trithicate Station is on the move."

"Trithicate *Station* is on the move?" Felix asked, incredulous.

"Yes, Captain," Thal said seriously. "As some of you know, David Abrams has had a small army of constructs similar to myself working on the station for over a week. We have been monitoring the activity of these 'Thals' covertly. Our theory had been that the station was being checked and repaired structurally."

"How did you do this?" Ambassador Phan asked.

"There is a passive communication system, a network of sorts, between Thals. I was able to access this and see their activity."

"The activity, however, though apparently unusual, was no cause for alarm until today," she said.

"Yes, Ma'am," Thal said. "We could get no reading yesterday, but I assumed, mistakenly, that it was a communication error."

"Because," Samuel said in his rich voice, "the Station was in hyper, I assume."

"Yes, High Admiral."

"Where is it now? Or do we know?" Samuel asked emotionlessly. His body, as were most in the room, was singing with tension. Outwardly everyone (except Felix who looked really agitated) could have been discussing lunch plans. Humans were so weird.

Thal did the same trick he had done for us earlier with the holo projector with the red line showing the trip to from Trithicate to Devrah. "As of this morning."

"I assume, Mr. Thal, that the station is no longer at Devrah," Paul said.

"That is correct, Captain."

"So where is it going?"

"You mean aside from 'anywhere in the goddamned universe'?" I asked dryly. Half the people (well, actually almost all) rolled their eyes at me.

"The Pelann is not going to do something this big without a plan, obviously," Samuel said thoughtfully. "So it all depends on her goal."

"Which is?" Ut Phan asked.

"If I may, Sir?" Felix stepped forward. Samuel nodded and Felix said, "The Pelann's ultimate goal is power, of course."

We all nodded. What else could it be?

"Captain Friedman and I think that her first effort will be peaceful. Or peaceful enough." He looked unhappy, though. "It's when it doesn't work that we're really in trouble." He walked up to the holo model of the near universe and pointed at Devrah. "The Pelann has a list of, shall we say, unfriendlies." He pointed from Devrah to, "Novy Heliot," where a red line appeared, to, "the Thao Protectorate," a different red line to "Corsica, to…" another line and the final one, "Terra."

"How the hell do we know all this?" I had to ask.

"Quinn sent the General, you and I an urgent message fifteen minutes ago," Felix said. "I got it right as we were heading over. It's why we were late."

"What did it say?" Samuel asked for all of us.

"That the Pelann was on her way and that she would be there to make sure the power was equally shared."

I saw Charles flick Samuel a knowing look. Neither of them looked surprised.

"What?"

Charles shook his head. "Two thoughts. One, no one who wants power wants to *share* it." All the professional diplomats (and Samuel) nodded over that one. "Two, we know where she is going."

"Yeah," I said eloquently. Terra. Not home, but home.

Felix wasn't done, however. "The source also said that she'd emptied out the reserves of Deneth warriors." Oh, so not good. "Apparently there are Denethian ships all over the quadrant that look manned but that are almost empty."

"Mother of god," I said quietly to myself. "Who was the source? Did Quinn say?"

Felix shook his head.

"So," Ut said, "The Pelann's only pretending to want to do this the 'right' way."

"I don't think, though, that this was how she'd planned it all to go," Atalanta said suddenly. Samuel and Mallory, getting their first good look at her, hid their signs of surprise at their very altered former student. Felix swayed slightly in shock. He'd been avoiding looking at her, but now he'd been forced to see the devastation their breakup had caused. I wanted to go to him, but he was all the way across the room and it would have brought attention to his plight so I stayed where I was.

"How so, Atalanta?" Samuel asked.

128

"I was there when Jane and company played and won that little game on Trithicate Station." With the race and the unexpected (to the Pelann) introduction to the Union of Eriss. "The Pelann was very, very angry to have Eriss seen by the T.I. public before she was ready." Atalanta's lovely, if wan, face was deadly serious. "Murderously so. She will never forgive Jane for that, for stealing that moment she'd worked twenty years to achieve."

I shrugged. People wanted to kill me all the time. Charles frowned, not as blasé about death threats as I was. That would come with time, I supposed.

"The reason I bring this up now is due to something I discovered during a 'tap' I had performed yesterday."

"You had a 'tap' performed?" Felix said, horrified. "By a *stranger?*"

Ut Phan and Synon looked around, wondering how they seemed to suddenly be in a family drama. Everyone seemed to be uncomfortable enough that no one (who didn't know) even asked what a 'tap' was and they really should have.

Atalanta realizing this, ignored Felix. "A 'tap' allows a Manipulative Empath, such as myself, to purge memories and, if desired, pick through them for more detail, as if they were put in slow motion." Ut Phan nodded her understanding. "Something about the Pelann's anger felt…off and when I went over it I felt something I hadn't expected: Jealousy."

"Jealousy?" I said, "Of Eriss?"

"Yes," Atalanta said firmly.

I looked at my Six, "You know her a little, Fitz." Ut's eyebrows went very high on her forehead. Such familiarity! She had no idea. "Does that sound plausible?"

Charles nodded thoughtfully. "She has been the Pelann for twenty years. She is worshipped and absolutely obeyed, but," he looked around him without seeing any of us, "because of tradition she cannot be photographed and cannot speak in her own voice. She is famous but not known at all." Yes, Charles knew all about that, that was for sure, I thought. "She, as has happened to every Pelann and most hereditary heads of state, can only be the job. Plus she is head of the church, infallible. She is a symbol. My guess is that these truths, combined with the fact that she can never set foot in the Legislature because of the gravity issue, have given this very powerful and ambitious being a feeling of impotence. An intolerable feeling for someone with theoretical absolute power."

"I thought," Ut said, "she'd solved it by creating the Tarine, by creating and training Miss Eriss."

Here Atalanta nodded. "It is a good plan, but, when it came down to it, it wasn't enough. Eriss has turned out to be strong-willed, difficult to control, but even if Eriss were completely under the Pelann's thumb, she would still be just a surrogate. The Pelann would stay on the sidelines, a place she is very tired of being. Aside from the fact that," Atalanta grimaced, "the Pelann made a tactical error in designing Eriss."

A *huge* error. "She made her a Telepath. An extremely powerful Telepath," I said. The most powerful I'd ever seen, bar none.

"Exactly," Atalanta said, "and by trying to give herself too much of an advantage she ended up giving that advantage…"

"To Eriss." I looked at my friend in horror. "The Pelann can't kill her. Can she?"

"Welcome to the one good thing that came out of that early introduction of yours, Jane. My guess is it is the only thing keeping Eriss alive."

"What about Jack? I mean Ian?" Paul asked, looking in the direction of Ian's father. Ian, yes, Ian. With all the rest of the mess that was going to come with Trithicate Station, was the overwhelming need to get Ian, and Eriss if she would come, back. I only hoped that was still a possibility. I started going over the plans for the station, what I remembered of them from our last visit, in my mind, trying to figure out where he would be held. A daunting task since the station was fucking huge, but it could be done because it *had* to be done, and the Furies and I were the ones to do it.

"If I know my son," Samuel said, and I stifled a gasp; that was the first time he'd publicly acknowledged the parentage. Of course he would only do so now because Arrow (poor Arrow) was gone. "He's doing everything to protect Eriss." He opened his mouth to say more, but then shut it and fell silent.

"Who is Jack/Ian?" Ut Phan asked.

"My boss, Captain Jack Fisher, who commands the Three Furies Mercenary Fleet," Paul said obliquely, "is the High Admiral's son, Ian Armstrong."

"Oh," was all she said as if that were a reasonable statement.

I covered a giggle with a cough. Smooth.

"Sam?" Charles said calmly, "when is the Pelannate-Heir-Designate expected to arrive the day after tomorrow?"

"12:00," Samuel replied. "We can bet she'll be on time since the Pelann will want all the journo coverage she can get for the big entrance." He exhaled. "I will brief the President." He looked at all the rest of us. "I will be coordinating with the Furies for any UNav response," he caught the eyes of Synon, and I was so glad there were finally Heelies to be included in UNav, "but I need everyone to keep what we've discussed here in the room, at least until all this becomes common knowledge."

We all nodded our agreement, including the very bemused Ut.

Samuel nodded and we started to disburse. Atalanta darted out of the room first, escaping any possible conversation with Felix. Synon clasped my shoulder briefly in farewell after nodding to Charles, Ut Phan leaving with him. Felix, seemingly lost in his own mind, left slowly. Paul followed him concerned.

Thal paused in front of me as I stood by Charles. "Miss Jane?"

"Atalanta?"

"Of course," he said and he left, too, to find 'Lanta and make sure she got back to the Furies all right. She had work to do now.

I'd turned to Charles to say something when I noticed that Samuel was hanging back, though he should have been the first one to leave. He whispered something to Mallory who frowned but went out the door anyway.

"Samuel?"

He hesitated, looking rather guiltily at Charles. "I need to say something, but I don't want to put ideas in your head."

I felt Charles tense behind me.

"I can't wait to hear what comes next," I said very, very dryly.

He narrowed his brown eyes at me, "Let my people rescue Ian and Eriss."

"Oh, you wish," was out of my mouth before I realized it.

"Jane…" Samuel said, but I talked right over him.

"Am I not a member of both the Furies and UNav?"

Suddenly I saw the light of triumph in his eyes. "I *order* you to stay out of it."

I put my hands on my hips and cocked my head to the side.

Charles just stood there watching our interaction with a kind of fascination.

Samuel stared at me. I stared at him.

Eventually he sighed in defeat. "I just don't want you to get hurt because of…" He looked a bit guilty when he flicked his eyes to Charles'. Charles did not respond, his diplomatic poker face in place.

"Because of you, or Ian or even Eriss," I finished for him. "I'd be concerned if you did." I smiled at him. "But this is what I do. It's what I'm good at." He had to know that while we were pretty sure Eriss had to be alive, there was, unfortunately, no guarantee *Ian* was. I knew the universe didn't owe us shit, but that was too much. Suddenly emotional, I channeled my fears into fierce determination. Ian had to be alive. He had to because Samuel would be destroyed if he wasn't.

I knew my eyes were too bright, but I ignored that when I said, "It will be all right, Samuel. If there is any way for me to make it all right, I will do it. I promise you that."

I felt Charles exhale hard just as Samuel looked away.

"Thank you," was all Samuel said because there was nothing else he could say. He looked at me one last time, then at Charles and left quickly.

I turned to my Six and gasped in surprise. His eyes were black gold, so much that the gold was almost gone. I opened my mouth to speak but he crushed me to him before I could, kissing me with a desperate passion he hadn't shown before, even when we'd first come together. He took my breath away, both literally and figuratively, his hands shaking as he cradled my face. He was worried, which I hated, but that wouldn't change anything.

"Jane," he whispered hoarsely.

"My Charles," was all I could say before he picked me up and carried me away.

We made love, of course, or rather, he made love to me. It was beautiful and sweet and sad somehow. I clung to him afterwards as I lay across his chest.

He *was* afraid, but he never told me not to go or even asked me if it was a good idea. He never said anything about it at all. This was who I was and we'd been through far too much for him not to know it. So he kept quiet and there were no words to tell him how much I loved him for it.

So we said nothing at all and pretended to sleep (though I knew neither of us did) until Mr. Beddoes knocked at the door the next morning and it was time to get up and get on with what had to be done.

And since I had a small amount of time to prepare for all hell (possibly) breaking loose, the first thing I had to do was talk to my kids.

11:00 – Large Assembly Hall, ESTF *Schola-Terra*, Terra 1,
October 4th, 2873

I stood in front of all of the ESTF students. My fellow instructors—Brady,
Fey, Dalia, Mallory and the rest—stood behind me. Marston stood at my
side. Synon, there as a favor to me, stood on my other side.

"Tomorrow is a big day for the Union, as you all know," I said. "For
the first time in history the Rian will have representation in the Legislature
in person and in the Diplomatic ranks." The one thing that had barely been
mentioned in the journo feeds was that it wasn't just Eriss who was coming
(as Pelannate-Heir-Designate and newest Ambassador to the Union for the
Rian), but two Tarine Senators and six *Hominum* Members ("elected" by
station population instead of by any district associated with land, the way it
was done everywhere else—no one had supervised the Rian elections, of
course, we'd just been told who would be coming and from where) were
also on their way to Terra to be true constituents at the Union table. The
Pelann had gone to a lot of trouble to play this game if that indeed was all
she was doing. "Many of you have seen the report from Trithicate that was
on many months ago," who was I kidding, everyone had seen it, "and I
know the Lady Eriss personally so I can say that we need to give the
Tarine the benefit of the doubt the way we would want them to give us the
same."

"They really fly?" Cadet Blake said quietly, with awe in his voice.

I smiled. "They really do. It is quite something to see." I became
serious again. "I have known several Deneth Rian who are good, generous
people. The first one I met was Ambassador Criss Utat."

There were several looks from person to person. Yes, that rumor that
either the Blackbird or the Red Angel had slept with him (and survived!)
were never going to really die. Why would it? It was too good.

"The day the Sang Heelies sent that missile, the Aquaformer, to
destroy Terra he piloted the ship into Earth's gravity, knowing full well
what would happen to him if he did, to make sure that supers, myself
included, made it to the planet alive so that we could stop it."

"He did that?" someone gasped.

"He did," I said sadly. "He was one of the bravest beings I've ever
known, and I've been lucky to know a lot of brave people." I shook off the
sadness that always came with talking about Criss. "You simply can't

assume that either the Deneth or the Tarine are either all good or all bad, any more than you can do that with all supers, Terrans, Heely Humans, Tellescans, etc., and if something happens, you follow orders and fight, but it isn't always as easy as 'they look like this or they can do this, therefore they must die.'"

The dismay on the faces of the Cadets was to be expected.

"We have only to look at the aftermath of the most recent war to be reminded of this." I looked at my friend Sy and he nodded.

"Something to think about," I added, "but what I called you here to say, aside from the fact that classes are cancelled starting today and for the rest of the week," the students were too flummoxed to cheer, "is that if something happens tomorrow, you must not get involved unless directly threatened." Oh Mother Irony that I would be saying this after my conversation with Samuel.

Some of the kids looked relieved, some looked mutinous.

"As long as you are Cadets, General Manthorpe is your CO and you must obey him and your teachers."

"But Ma'am…" Caroline Tellesco protested.

"You are all very talented, but still green, and, while your hearts may be in the right place, your more seasoned supernormal brethren will have to spend more time protecting you than doing their jobs and if that happens people could die."

I stared everyone down at that. I could not have been more serious and I knew it showed.

"Now, if General Manthrope tells you to have at it, then you do so," I said, nodding at Marston, "but other than that you will stay in the ESTF on lock down until he tells you to leave."

"This is an order, Cadets," Marston said, equally seriously, "and disobeying will get you brought up on charges and expelled."

"Does everyone understand?" I asked.

They nodded.

I softened my tone when I said, "Your time will come. Unfortunately, there will always be more battles to fight."

I turned to leave when Cadet Toddy Tolliver spoke up, "We're going to war, Ma'am?"

I looked him in the eye. "I certainly hope not, Toddy." I raised my voice. "You are all dismissed to the confines of the ESTF until further notice."

I headed for the door and saw Wylan, Petros in tow, heading for Synon. They spoke briefly, but Synon shook his head. Wylan left, head down. I knew he wanted to go with Synon and the other Heelies, but I couldn't allow that. He was a Heely, yes, but he was a Cadet first and Cadets had to stay put for their own safety.

Marston caught up with me with Mallory right behind him so I paused.

Mallory, never one to beat around the bush, said, "Twenty-four hour schedule for the Cadets: 8 hours guarding perimeters, 8 training and 8 rack time. They need to stay busy."

Marston nodded, "Coordinate with me and the other instructors."

"Of course," she said. Then to me, "You are off to the Furies?"

"Yes." For a moment I thought of sending Thal to the relative safety of the ESTF, but realized I was marginalizing him again. We needed him with the Furies and not just because of the information he might be able to glean from the Thal communications. He was a hell of a fighter without being affected by the vacuum of space or its chill or lack of air. "When does Tania come?" I asked Marston.

"Tonight," he said, and even the stress of the unknown couldn't completely dampen his happiness at getting to see his wife.

I gave him a smile and got out of there.

13:12 – Main Briefing Room, *T.F.S. Ouranos*, Three Furies Mercenaries Fleet, Terran System

It had taken me longer than I would have thought to get things in order to go to the Furies, but I was in the Briefing Room at last. Thal was with me, loaded for bear. He had accepted my order to accompany him without question or complaint and I think was even a bit flattered that I had finally decided to let him into my full professional life. We'd been delayed while he had loaded his inner cavity with weapons, grappling hooks and all sorts of other potentially useful items, but it had seemed necessary to be as prepared as possible. As for me, I had a bag with my DSS Suit, projectile guns and my three knives (the Agni Katar and two butterfly knives). I refused to carry an LPG out of principle. I wished I could convince everyone else to do the same.

At the head of the table stood Paul Friedman and to his right was Felix who was frowning intensely at the holo of Trithicate Station floating in front of him. Atalanta, as Paul(ie)'s acting second-in-command was there, as were Daniel, Captain Freya (*Indus Felae*), and the four other Captains.

Oh, and one other person that I'd met, very unexpectedly, on the way into the room.

Quinn.

His adrenaline had been up, his nerves as close to frayed as I'd seen them. Apparently he'd left Novy at the same time as his last letter. He'd stood in the hallway outside the Briefing Room door, clearly waiting for me.

I'd stopped short in surprise, almost causing Thal to bump into me.

"Jane, I wanted to say…" Quinn began.

"Fuck off, Quinn," I'd muttered and I'd walked right past him and into the room. I'd picked the closest empty chair and flung myself into it. I didn't need this shit now, but, I had to admit, we needed Quinn. He'd been right to come even if he was one of the last people I wanted to see right now. The other one, David, was coming later today. Quinn slunk in a few seconds later and took the seat opposite me. I studiously ignored him.

Everyone, the disbanded Trio especially, watched the two of us with interest, but when we'd done nothing long enough, they gave up.

So the briefing began.

Paul paced in front of all of us. "We are, from a previous mission, familiar with the basics of Trithicate Station. From the intel we have we can assume that the Captain is being held, if he is alive, somewhere on station in order to keep the Lady Eriss in line throughout her introduction to the Legislature. As to where he would be held…" he inclined his head in Quinn's direction.

"I would have bet money that the Pelann would be holding Jack in the center of her private domain, the most heavily fortified part of the station," Quinn said, pointing at a ball shape in the middle of the dodecahedron that was Trithicate Station. "Unfortunately, due to a side mission that had taken place at the end of our last visit," where he and Felix had broken into said private domain and stolen the records of the Tarine language to give to Eriss, "I cannot imagine she will still have confidence that it's secure. This," he sighed, "makes our job much more difficult."

I looked at the holo of the huge station, built for tens of thousands of Deneth Rian. "Or impossible."

"It is worse than just that," Quinn said gravely.

"Worse how?" Paul asked.

"I got one last message from my source as I was leaving to come here. I was glad I'd happened to catch it, since it changes the game yet again." He took a breath. "It said, 'she'll never leave without her sisters. Tell *Shann* I'll do everything I...' and then nothing. I assume she was found out and had just managed to send that."

I had sat up ramrod straight, as if I'd been shocked, which I had at that word. *Shann*. It meant something to... My eyes went wide. Oh no.

"Who was your source, Quinn?" Even though I knew.

"Lita Utat," he said quietly and with sympathy.

"*Shann* means lover or beloved, correct?" Freya said, trying to work it out. "Whom did she mean?"

I raised my hand, "She was my friend, it...it was complicated." It *was* complicated because I was pretty fucking sure that Lita was dead. She had risked everything and gone against her spiritual and temporal leader (which considering the cultural conditioning must have been unspeakably hard for her) and had paid the price. I wondered if there were any of the Telepathic Utat family left, generation after generation of stewards to the various Pelann. My guess was that they were all gone by now. God, it was heartbreaking, but there was no time for grief now. Later, I thought. Later.

"What Lita did was incredibly brave," Paul said, "but it gives us more to do."

"Indeed," Quinn said firmly.

"So the 'sisters' she was referring to..." Atalanta said.

"Are the Tarine the Pelann is no doubt holding hostage somewhere," I said flatly. "It's a quirk of the language. 'Brothers' are the Deneth and 'sisters' are the Tarine, regardless of the actual sexes involved." I sighed. "At least we know where the Tarine went." I looked at Quinn, forgetting for a moment how angry I was at him. "They're still alive, you think?"

Quinn nodded. "I do. Another benefit of that broadcast. At least *some* have to be in existence or the journos would be all over it."

"How many Tarine are there?" Freya asked, staring at the hologram.

"We picked up five hundred from Napia," Paul said.

"That will make them easier to find, if they're being held together," Daniel said.

Quinn snorted, "Which means they won't be. Were I the Pelann," he said, "I would have them in small groups, twos and threes, spread out all over the station, very effectively slowing us down so that even if we freed some, we'd be caught before we'd freed all."

"Assuming they *want* to be freed," Freya said unexpectedly.

I had to nod at that reminder that not all slaves wished to be free. I didn't get it, but I didn't have to. People needed to choose for themselves even if their choices were really stupid.

"We have to give them the option," Atalanta said. "Besides, you can bet Eriss won't leave without them."

"I think you are kidding yourself that Eriss will leave at all," Freya said.

"She's a prisoner to an evil homicidal bitch," I sputtered along with many others, "you can't even suggest that she'd stay."

"I don't have to, Jane," Freya said very seriously. "The Rian and the Heliot Nation have very little in common, despite what some bigots may say, but the one thing we do have is a very strong set of clan bonds. Heelies have our bonding to our mates and our *Demnas*, and the Rian to their bloodlines and Pelann. The normal sense of duty that any ordinary Deneth/Tarine/Heely would feel to their people would be infinitely greater in a being who'd been raised specifically to rule. You may all think she can walk away, *but you will be wrong.*"

I sat back hard in my chair. An exchange I'd overheard between Ian and Eriss before he'd initially left her on Trithicate came back to me. He'd tried to convince her to leave with him, once they realized how dangerous staying would be for her, but she'd told him that that was precisely why she had to stay. I realized that even though I didn't want to hear it, Freya was correct. Fuck.

"Ok, then," I said, walking over to the holo. "Then we have to make sure she *can* stay."

Then the real planning got under way.

A Note on Trithicate Station

Trithicate Station itself was a wonder of engineering. Its twelve-sided shape (a dodecahedron) was huge, five miles in diameter at any given point. Each face, of the twelve, was thick Tenorium, giving both a window out and a rather fascinating window in. Inside was indeed a rabbit warren of tall tunnels, each room seemingly on a different axis, giving those of us used to 'up' and 'down' as being concrete concepts, a real headache. Offices, work areas, troop garrisons were all just inside the Tenorium (or in the next circle in). The next layers were businesses (shopping, restaurants, etc.). Then came living quarters for both the civilian population and the military one. Then came the prison complex, a thin impenetrable band of highly fortified cells for the beings the Deneth really didn't want to get out. The innermost circle held the important stuff—the Temple of the Righteous and the official quarters of the Pelann herself once unofficially visited (and robbed) by Felix and Quinn.

Trithicate Station was a fortress but also a true city with everything that came with it including a population of tens of thousands of Denethians. It wasn't the most modern or the biggest of the Rian stations (that honor went to the station orbiting Paragon several light years away) but it was the first, the oldest and the most sacred and it had been Criss and Lita Utat's home for their entire lives.

What mischief was the Pelann planning for it to bring it away from its home for the first time since its creation?

We spent the next six or seven hours planning the assault. The real problem with the station like Trithicate was that it was so old and had been altered by every subsequent administration in so many ways that it was no longer the regular installation that it had started as. The only good news we seemed to find was that the military sections which comprised the second ring of the station were, of all of them, the most regular. Unfortunately, they were, aside from the Pelann's sacred space, the most protected. The station was so big that it would be impossible to memorize the schematics completely. We had all of them loaded on our DSS suits of course, but the station really was enormous, easily five times the size of Terra 1, and Terra 1 was known as the biggest station within human space.

It was going to be a massive mission. Every single member of the three Furies would be used, one way or another. There were actually four objectives, five if you counted my personal objectives of rescuing both Ian and the Lady Eriss. Seven assault teams would be used to breach. Six teams from the Furies, each led by a Macro with a Micro, a TP, and six Marines. The Marines were responsible for podding and removing any Denethian soldiers or civilians we ran across. Unfortunately, we couldn't count on the Pelann to have evacuated the station of nonessential personnel and that made our job infinitely more difficult. The six Furies teams were to get into the station and go room by room, ridding the station of all the Denethian warriors. Macros were to do the heavy lifting, as usual, and the Micros' job was to incapacitate hostiles.

The team leaders, in order, were myself (with the Micro Dalia), Felix (with a newly recovered Akiko), Hannibal (the recent heavily tattooed 50-year-old ESTF graduate), Alicia Knight, Trent Torva, Dennis Napia and Anupam Khan. All were Macros and seasoned veterans, whether of the Furies or of other military or mercenary work. The Marines had been hand-picked by Col. Rodriguez, including the two teams of Heely Marines working with Team Delta and Team Echo. It was their first major mission as Marines, but the Col. was confident in their abilities and training.

Looking over the list of our best people, I was once again very relieved that more and more supers were being trained and, hopefully, trained well. It was depressing that our numbers never seem to grow all that much, despite the occasional influx of new blood.

The seventh team, the only one from UNav, was led by Capt. Garrett Pace-Taylor and its sole purpose was to arrest and detain her Holiness, the Pelann of the Rian Nation. Now, you may think that was premature. It was. Aside from being exceptionally manipulative, the Pelann had not actually done anything wrong as yet. Union President Hugo Leder and Samuel, however, had no illusions about the Pelann's surprise visit to Terra being anything other than the opening move in a violent confrontation. Perhaps not violent initially, but they had too much experience with the greed for power to feel that it would go any other way.

Every other Furies member who was not required to actually run any of our ships would be out in space waiting. They would be waiting with their weapons and their jet packs to catch or stop any being attempting to leave the station and attack either Earth or Terra 1. In case you were concerned that the Furies were vastly outnumbered by the possible 10,000 Denethians (or more) on Trithicate, you weren't the only one. We needed help. The good news was that Paul, Felix, Quinn and I (after a very quick dinner) were going to a meeting where help was at hand.

We were going to UNav headquarters.

20:00 – Large Briefing Room, Union Navy (UNav) Headquarters, Terra 1

High Admiral Samuel Armstrong and Union President Hugh Leder sat at the head of one of the largest tables I'd ever seen. Garrett was next to them, as was Alex (without gloves!), completely absorbed in their conversation. The rest of the room was full of men and women in uniform, but that wasn't what struck me when I entered the room with my friends and Quinn. What struck me first was the level of noise.

Some people were murmuring at each other. Some were yelling. A couple were getting in each other's faces. One woman pushed a man hard in the chest and glared at him.

Surprised, I looked all the way over at Samuel. His expression was blank, but I could read his body as he spoke to his companions. I felt stress and the certain tightening in his chest that he had when he was annoyed, but since I also felt a bubble of laughter there, too, so I knew he was at least somewhat amused by what was going on. President Leder was leaning back in his chair idly drumming his fingers on the tabletop.

The four of us leaned against the wall and waited for some sort of signal that we were to come fully into the room. Samuel had silently acknowledged us when we'd arrived, but had given us no indication as to what we were to do. So we waited.

I felt the door behind us open and a small familiar form slip in. I looked at Samuel in surprise, but then realized what he was doing and had to smile. He gave me the smallest of winks and darted his eyes behind me to nod at, of all people, Atalanta.

I felt her nod back as Samuel rose.

The conversations and arguments continued unabated.

Samuel looked over his shoulder at the Sargent-At-Arms and raised his hand for a minute, indicating the Sgt. should do what he did best.

"*Attention!*" The Sargent-At-Arms barked in a voice designed to carry across space itself.

Even with their years and years of training it took the dozens of officers in the room a second to snap to attention.

It was really, really hard not to laugh.

"As you were," their High Admiral said.

Everyone returned to their seats, but their attention had been commanded, literally, and they were focusing where they should have been.

"The time for discussion is over," Samuel said, his rich voice impossible to ignore, "we have identified a very dangerous potential threat to the safety of the Union. I know that no one likes the fact that we aren't completely sure what, if anything, will happen. This is hardly a simple assault, or simple search and rescue."

I saw the defensive expressions of the officers start to fade and calm a bit, full of renewed confidence in their esteemed commander. Interesting. And artificially created, I thought. I looked over my shoulder at Atalanta, whom I knew was the author of the feelings of everyone in the room, and gave her a proud smile. She tapped on her temple once, indicating that I should open my mental 'door,' which I dutifully did, and went back to concentrating. Sweat was beading on her brow, but her focus remained perfect.

Samuel continued, "Some of you object to working with a mercenary group such as the Furies."

I sighed internally. The UNav officers considered themselves serious professionals and us a typical band of misfits and weirdos—not that we weren't, but it was a clichéd judgment. My guess was that they figured that if any of us had been any good, we'd be in UNav, not running around lawlessly on our own. The difference between being good and being able to work within the military machine was, apparently, something most of these people could not comprehend.

"You do not trust mercenaries very much in general and trust mercenary supers not at all, but I can tell you that these particular mercenaries have done more to protect the freedoms and lives within the Union then anyone outside of the Union Navy has ever done."

Nice point, Samuel, I thought. Talk us up without slamming the Navy.

"They have proven their loyalty to the principles of freedom and of law…"

I tried not to snicker at that one, I mean, how many hundreds of laws had we broken over the years?

Samuel continued, "…time and time again. This is a prejudice that those of you who hold it must put aside."

I felt Samuel's anger and disdain, some of it projected by Samuel himself, wash over the room. I wondered how many of them were remembering, right then, that Samuel, while not an official super, was very much a Pacey. The broadcast emotions then slid into resolve and pride.

"I do not want us to have to fight tomorrow. The idea of many Union members fighting one Union member seems to me obscene." The emotional tide grew. "The real problem here is that we are not completely sure who our enemy is. The President and I are at least holding out the hope that it is *not* the Rian Nation." He paused. "Each of you knows that there is a point in every military endeavor where one has to ask the question, am I only as good as my commander?"

"With all due respect, Sir, you want to lay all of this at the Pelann's doorstep?" a heavily decorated General asked, his voice deliberately calm.

"I would rather, General Craig, lay this madness on her doorstep, even if only temporarily," President Leder responded laconically, "than sanction genocide."

I felt Atalanta broadcast relief and even some affection in relation to the President's good sense.

"I am not unaware," Samuel said, "the irony of giving you orders that you may not agree with while giving the benefit of the doubt to Denethians who may be following orders *they* possibly do not believe in." He nodded. "Today's plan, however, has the chance to let more people live who perhaps should not die," and he smiled, though the smile was not a friendly one, "and while we may be defending a democracy, *this* isn't one."

No one laughed, no one cracked a smile. Samuel was done with fucking around.

Resolve from my friend the MEmp. I watched her, knowing she was 'listening' to what they were all feeling as well as projecting. I felt Samuel watching her. She nodded. They were ready, or as ready as she and Samuel could make them.

"You are dismissed to your own departments until 08:00 tomorrow morning when we will reconvene here," then Samuel turned to President Hugh to say something, giving his people no more of his attention.

With that almost all the couple dozen military personnel quietly filed out. The second they were all gone Samuel looked up. "Thank you, Atalanta," he said with a smile, an affectionate one this time.

"Anytime, Sir," she said. She bowed her head quickly in farewell and left without once looking at her former mate. I felt Felix close his eyes for a minute in pain.

Samuel gestured us over to the front of the room. Two Generals and five Admirals remained, along with the President.

They sat. We sat.

"I've been looking over the plans you sent me," Samuel said, "and they are, I think, the best that can be done with the information we have." He grinned at Felix. "Your fingerprints were all over them, son. Well done."

"Thank you, General," Felix mumbled, his cheeks pinking with happiness.

The President was watching them thoughtfully. "Seems a waste to promote you, Sam," he said. "To your Paceys you will always be the General."

Samuel cleared his throat and said, "I did have one suggestion, for Quinn."

Quinn looked up, surprised.

"From the information I have, you are the person who, aside from Jane, knows the Deneth, and specifically the Pelann better than anyone. You need to lead Team Hotel with Garrett. We need the Pelann to come quietly."

"She hates Quinn, Samuel," I protested.

"Jane," Quinn said.

I gave him a 'fuck you' look and kept on. "She'll try to kill him as soon as she sees him." Just because I was pissed didn't mean I wanted anything to happen to him. Wilby would never forgive me if I did. Yes, I know that sort of feeling got me into a mess before but it was still there. Sorry not sorry.

"I can take care of myself," Quinn said angrily.

"Obviously," I said, my sarcasm like a knife.

Garrett spoke up, breaking our little battle of wills. "If she does then that's what I'm there for, among other things."

I had to stand down at that statement. I found myself staring at Quinn's ruined nose, so had to look away.

"What do you think her opening move will be, Sirs?" Felix asked, bringing us back to the matter at hand.

"Our first thought," Samuel said, "was that she would invite all the powers that be to a reception on Trithicate, and she may still do that. She knows everyone is dying to see the station and that doing so could be a once in a lifetime opportunity."

"Once in a millennium," the President said. "Even *I* have never been there." He straightened the pens in front of him on the table. "It would be a strong temptation."

"She has to know that we would never allow that," Quinn said.

"And hand her the best package of hostages ever? Not bloody likely," I muttered under my breath.

"She could be counting on the leaders all going their own way and coming anyway, but..." Samuel started.

"...they wouldn't have survived a day in their jobs by being that stupid," I finished.

Samuel sighed with fond exasperation. Funny how often I got that response from the people I loved. "Yes."

"So," Hugh said, "we figure she will try to lobby each individually. It will seem safer to them."

"Lobby?" I asked.

Samuel and Hugh nodded. "Manipulate, try to form alliances, that sort of thing."

"How does David Abrams fit into this?" Felix asked.

As one all of them turned to look at me. Yep, meet Jane Pace, David Abrams expert and prognosticator. I'm so lucky.

"Well," I said, "David never does anything without an agenda, an agenda that is usually at least three-fold deep. We know he is worried about building his business in relation to the Union Shipyards and the new ones at Corsica, so my guess is that his primary motive will be to either protect or increase his ship-building profile. We also know he has a deal with the Pelann for Denethian ships now that that market has opened up. He provided Thals to her as well so she may be expecting his support, whether or not he has overtly given it to her."

"His support being a not inconsiderable thing," Samuel said.

I inclined my head in his direction, acknowledging his point. "Personally, I think he's here to see which way the wind is blowing and make sure his interests are covered no matter how this shakes out."

"The second objective?" Samuel asked, his face carefully blank. I found myself wondering what he was thinking about this dissection of the motives of my biggest romantic error.

I had to think a second. "He'll probably be testing technology, something unusual."

"Something he's probably given to the Pelann," Samuel said thoughtfully. "A weapon perhaps?"

"Unfortunately, that is very likely."

"Great," Felix said.

"You think, Commodore," President Hugh said with deliberation, "that David Abrams would side against the Union?"

"No, Sir." Of that I was sure.

"Out of loyalty," Hugh said as he started rearranging his pens as though the answer didn't matter to him.

I quickly decided that snorting in front of the President was bad form so I refrained. "I wouldn't put it like that, Sir." I leaned forward and rested my elbows on the table. "David is first and foremost a pragmatist. He will back whoever seems to fit most closely with his interests and his interests are his businesses and his ships. A take-over or coup by the Pelann would disrupt trade, cause a war and wreak havoc with his production schedule and sales. He will not back the Pelann when it comes down to it, though he will play with both sides until the very last second."

"Can we count on him as an ally or not?" one of the Generals I'd forgotten was there asked impatiently.

"*I* wouldn't."

"So, Abrams thinks of the Union as a means to an end," the President confirmed.

"For David Abrams, Sir, I believe everything is a means to an end," I said honestly.

"Have you figured out the third of his three-fold objective?" Alex asked, clearly fascinated by this shadowy figure of David Abrams.

"Only David knows that," I said, feeling cowardly for hoping to dodge what I knew was David's third objective.

"Jane," Quinn said, irritated that I was being coy. "Jane is always the third objective."

"Quinn," I said through clenched teeth.

"Be embarrassed on your own time, Jane," Quinn said. I glared at him. What an asshole. Even if he was right. "He almost lost the Heliot War for us because he was trying to keep you safe."

Well, that was too much. "That's not true."

"It isn't entirely *un*true either," Felix said slowly, fearing my wrath, as he should. I shook my head in denial. The President paused in his pen rearranging, then went back to work.

"Will you, Commodore Pace, be able to use your relationship with Mr. Abrams, should the need arise, to help us?" President Hugh said, turning his dark, penetrating eyes on me for the first time.

I had to think. Getting in bed (even metaphorically) with David was… I shuddered at the thought, but he was waiting for an answer. "I will do whatever it takes to protect our people, Sir, but whatever these men," and I indicated Quinn and Felix, the rat, "think, any time I have attempted to change David's mind on *anything* I have failed."

The President made no response.

"What will we tell the Ambassadors, Mr. President," Garrett asked, "if and when they are asked to the station for tea?"

The President looked at Samuel who answered, "Obviously we can't condone their going to that station."

I felt a coldness in my belly. Wait, the *Ambassadors*? No, not... "General?"

Samuel looked surprised. I don't think I'd called him that in years. A sign of my panic if ever there was one. "However," Samuel concluded heavily, "we can't legally stop them. Not without causing an intra-Union incident."

"Who will the Pelann ask?" Felix said, with dread in his voice. I was starting to feel sick.

"If I were she," Samuel said slowly, "I would start at the top, since if any of those people fall under her sway it would influence others." He took a breath. "President Leder, Queen Tania, Prince Pilar and Ambassador Fitzroy."

Just as I'd feared. No. No. Not Charles. I looked at his son pleadingly, but Alex, while he looked a bit green at the prospect, shook his head. No help there.

We all looked at the President who was still calmly playing with his pens. He looked up as if surprised we were staring at him. "Don't worry about me. I'm staying right where I belong." I think we all heaved a sigh of relief, though I hadn't really thought he would go.

"As for the others, however, I need to meet with all three and two of them have yet to arrive," Samuel said, his rich voice professional, but also calming.

"Of course," I think I said, but I wasn't completely sure, so wrapped up was I in fear, "you will encourage them not to go." A question disguised as a statement.

"As hard as I can, Jane," Samuel said, voice deliberately cool. I tried to breathe, but it was difficult. *Charles.*

"One thing is clear, however," Hugh said, watching me closely, "if any of them is stupid enough to accept her invitation you, Commodore, must lead the team that accompanies whoever goes."

Now there was a flurry of protests from Felix, from Garrett, Paul and even Quinn, but a stern look from the President brought them all to silence.

"Thank you, Sir," was all I could muster. Even if Charles wasn't the one going, these were my friends. I would rather be there than off on the sidelines if they were going to be in danger.

"With respect, Mr. President," Felix said carefully, "the Pelann hates Jane as much as she hates Quinn, if not more."

"Yes, but who would be better than she to protect Ambassador Fitzroy, Captain Pace?" Hugh said lightly. He knew. I looked at Samuel who now looked uncomfortable. He'd told him, told his boss about Charles and me.

"Yes, it isn't just about using her attachment to the *Ambassador*, is it, Sir?" Quinn said, keeping his anger simmering just below the surface.

Hugh cocked his head to the side, appraising Quinn. He nodded, pleased. "No, it isn't."

Then I got it. It was about that, yes, but it was also about David. David would never knowingly allow anything to happen that would hurt or kill me. Putting me on that station was its insurance policy.

I inclined my head in respect towards the President and he gave me the ghost of a smile in return. It was a smart move, putting me there, worthy of David himself. That comparison didn't make me happy, but it was what it was.

"So," Samuel said, not meeting my eyes anymore, "UNav deployments…"

Two hours later we were done having tirelessly gone over ships and men in great detail. I had calmed down a little bit, or enough, to seek out Alex as we were all leaving. I didn't have much time before Samuel, Quinn, Alex himself and I were going to meet with the Dignitaries Most Likely to Be Accosted By The Pelann, but I wanted just a second with Alex and his scarred hands.

I walked up to Alex, who was waiting for me by the door, and hugged him hard. He laughed as he hugged me back and didn't even flinch as I took one of his marked hands and playfully squeezed it.

"How do you feel, Alex?" I asked in a low voice for privacy.

"Better, Jane, not," Alex exhaled, "completely myself, but better now that I'm not hiding."

"Do you get asked about this," I asked, squeezing the hand I held, "a lot?"

"Directly asked, no," he said ruefully, "but I get 'looked' the question all the time."

I could believe it. It *was* hard to miss. "Do you say anything?"

"The first dozen times I got 'the look' I launched into my story." He shook his head. "The first time, oh, that poor woman. I think I had her there for ten minutes, explaining and apologizing for being this way."

"God, Alex."

"I know. The next time the story was shorter, then the time after that, shorter still." He smiled. "Finally I had it down to 'tortured by Sang Heelies during the War.'"

I nodded as I traced the whorls on his skin, still fascinated.

"That got me sympathy and few free drinks. Then yesterday morning someone gave me the look and I'd had enough of explaining myself, bleeding so that the other person could feel comfortable."

My eyes went wide. "You didn't hit anyone, did you?"

Alex's gold eyes twinkled with amusement and his Corsican accent became much more clipped and grand. "My dear woman, how could dare suggest such a thing!" he said. I laughed. His speech returned to normal (for Alex), "Not that it didn't occur to me, but no. They looked the question and I said, 'Cyrillic Grass Shark Attack. Barely made it out with my life.'"

I giggled in spite of myself. "Cyrillic Grass Shark? Is there such a thing?"

"I have no idea," he said with a huge smile. "The next one was 'Satanic Moon Orgy, but I didn't know I was allergic to melon.'"

I sighed wistfully. "I never get invited to the good parties anymore."

"A tragedy. The last one was just before the meeting. 'My girlfriend's learning to be a tattoo artist. What do you think?'" He was laughing now and I had to join him.

"I'm really glad, Alex. Your father will be, too."

He shrugged. "It still bothers me, when I forget, but I *am* doing much better." He looked in my eyes. "Thanks for asking Fey to help. It's made all the difference."

"I'm glad it did help, love," I said as he blinked at the endearment. "Meddling doesn't always pay off, but I'm glad it did this time. So you'll continue to see Fey?"

"Yes, despite…"

Oh, lord, what now? "Despite?"

"I asked her to marry me."

"You did what now?" I said and realized my voice was a little louder than it should have been. Samuel and Garrett looked in my direction, rolled their eyes, then turned back to their own conversation. "What did she say?" Well, that would be an interesting pairing.

"She just laughed," he said with chagrin.

Poor lamb. "Are you in love with her?"

"I thought so," he said quietly, "but I think she was right to laugh. Well, not to *laugh*," he said through slightly gritted teeth, "but she knew what she'd given me had made me have delusions of grandeur, I guess."

"She made you feel normal."

"Yes."

"Cheer up, Alex," I said. "The universe is full of oddities. You are a good person. You'll find someone."

"You're so sure," he said, but his expression was shyly hopeful.

"Hey, I am the biggest oddity you will *ever* meet and it happened to me." Charles, my Charles.

His expression softened. "That it did."

23:49 – Formal Reception Room, Corsican Embassy, Terra 1

Samuel, Felix, Quinn, Alex and I entered the room quickly. Thal had already arrived. Samuel had felt that my assistant should be included in as much as possible since, aside from myself, he was our best hope in understanding David's part in all this, though, currently David wasn't foremost in my thoughts. Not with Trithicate Station mere hours away from breaching the Terran home system. Samuel, as it turned out, was prescient in including Thal. Or he got really damned lucky. Either way it was a good call.

Standing in the center of the room was Charles, my Charles, formally dressed and looking quite dashing in my less than unbiased estimation. There was a small crease on his brow from worry, but the beautiful smile and the black gold eyes of the man I loved made me smile back reflexively. Alex, right behind me, bowed to the man few of us knew as his father.

"It's good to see you again, Ambassador," Alex said with a twinkle in his eye.

Charles looked at Alex's bare hands and I felt some tension leak out of him. "You, young man," he said, twinkling back, "are looking well."

"Thank you, Sir," Alex said. I suppressed a smile and continued into the room.

The second person I saw was the lovely and exotic Queen Tania of Novy Heliot, Marston by her side. She was wearing something comfortable and white (apparently her favorite color) and looked tired from her trip, though still stunning.

"Ma'am," I said as I rushed over, "it is good to see you." I didn't move to hug her as I usually would have, letting her decide how informal we were going to be, in a rare (or even unheard of for me) example of consciousness of protocol.

She seemed to sense my hesitation and embraced me with a tight squeeze. "Jane!" She let me go only partially, her hand in mine. "And Captain Felix, Mr. Thal, Colonel Couvillion, General Quinn and the High Admiral. Marvelous." Then she searched the worried faces of the people she'd just greeted. "Or is it?"

"Welcome back to Terra 1, Your Majesty," Samuel said a bit stiffly.

"Ma'am," Felix, Alex and Quinn said at the same time.

Tania frowned, too. "What's happened?" She looked at her husband who shrugged his ignorance. She gave me another squeeze and let me go. "What was so urgent? We just arrived not twenty minutes ago."

"We're just waiting for one more pers…"

Just then Lord Miller, Stuart Pace to us, walked in the door, glowing with health and happiness.

So, not Prince Pilar after all. I had to grin. The G-L contingent was safe from Shirin's machinations at least; no way was the Pelann asking a brilliant Telepath into her secret space lair.

Any thoughts of protocol flew from my head, though, as I launched myself into Stuart's arms. He laughed and hugged me back. I could sense the tension that had started when I'd hugged Tania grow in Charles' body.

"How's baby Hector?" I asked.

"Hector and Persephone Jane are fine, my friend," Stuart said, his brown eyes dancing.

That stopped me short. "Persephone *Jane*?"

I thought his grin would split his handsome face. "Yep. Born a bit on the early side *very* early the day before yesterday, but healthy and safely transferred to a tub to finish gestating."

"Pilar is..?" I asked, apprehensively.

"Pilar is fine and resting. Ronnie is looking after her," Stuart said. So this all explained why Stuart was here and not Pilar, but…that Persephone Jane? Really?

"You really named…" I was immensely flattered. What a crazy honor. I was speechless and stood there dumbly while everyone crowded around Stuart congratulating him.

Stuart caught my eye and laughed at me. "You have a Princess named after you and that is all you have to say?" he teased.

Pretty much. My mouth continued to flap uselessly, but Charles rescued my by saying, "What she means is thank you from the bottom of her heart and she will thank the Princes," yes, Ronnie would have had to approve the name, too, god, "as soon as all this is resolved."

Stuart's relaxed expression became very focused and he was suddenly the man I had known back in the day. Clever, kind but fierce. "All *what* is resolved?"

Charles turned to Samuel and all of us turned with him.

On the spot Samuel switched on that presence he had, the presence that commanded with fathomless respect. He never asked for it; it was just given. It was interesting to see him project like this in the room with two other people (Charles and Tania) who had that ineffable presence, too. He didn't, in this moment, cancel them out, he was just…more.

"We have reason to believe that the Pelann is bringing Trithicate Station to Terra."

Everyone seemed to react at once.

"How is that even possible?"

"Here? Are you sure?"

"She's going to start a war on our turf?"

"Has she lost her mind?"

"What about the Tarine?"

Samuel, Quinn and Felix fielded all questions, but I was watching Charles who'd remained silent (since this wasn't news to him) as he stole quietly over to me. I didn't see fear in his gold eyes, but I know he saw fear in mine. He moved closer and gently rested his large elegantly fingered hand on the small of my back. It was a small amount of contact but it was all I needed to mentally ground myself. I exhaled and leaned back a little into his hand.

Finally the initial flurry of questions slowed and Tania asked, "What will she do?"

"We think," Samuel said carefully, "that she will try to recruit one or all of you."

"Against the Union," Marston said as if the words made no sense to him.

"Against the Union," Samuel confirmed.

"David Abrams' ship is moored on the leeward side of Terra 1," Marston said darkly as Tania tensed. "No good can come of that either." So Tania had not yet forgiven David, her old friend, for gambling with the lives and future of Novy Heliot during the end of the War. I couldn't blame her even if it had all turned out well. It might not have. Tania's pale green eyes flicked to Thal who looked on with deliberate blandness.

"True," Samuel said.

"How will she do it?" Tania asked. "Blackmail?" and she looked at Charles. Now *I* was tense, irrationally angry that Tania would bring up Charles' great secret. Charles' hand rubbed gently at my back.

"Blackmail?" Quinn asked as his eyes darted towards Charles, but then bit his lip as if he could take it back. He looked at the floor. No one loved intrigue more than an historian and a spy and Quinn was both. It was then I realized that he was the only one in the room that *didn't* know Charles' secret. I am ashamed to say that made me feel a fucklot better. "My apologies, Sir."

"Don't let it trouble you, General," Charles said mildly.

Charles pulled me to him, putting his arms around my waist. I looked up at him adoringly. Let Quinn think that was the secret. Well it was a secret, at least until the 'welcome to Terra' ball for Eriss that I wasn't quite sure would actually happen now, but it sure as shit wasn't *the* secret.

"We don't quite know. Unfortunately, all of this is speculation at this point."

Tania shook her reedy head, "If she thinks I am going to put myself under her power then…"

Just then we were all startled by Stuart's cry of either pain or surprise. The attention of the room whipped to him in time to see his eyes go wide with terror as he swayed on his feet. He dropped to his knees. Hard.

"Stuart!" I cried as I raced to kneel next to him, taking his hands. He stared into space unseeing. "What's wrong?" I frantically started scanning him but was finding nothing other than huge surges of adrenaline.

Then he spoke, but the words he said as his lips moved were in my head. In all our heads.

"Le haxhaith, réuch, an bent wicket an boxha, téanann siat réith a arrow ar an teaxhrán a shoot sa torchatas ax an uprixht i xcroílár."

Tania had put her hands over her ear holes, but immediately took them down when the words continued unaffected. "What was that *noise*?" Her hands shook. That noise that sounded like bats dying. That noise I hadn't heard in so very long. My hands shook, too, but for a different reason than Tania's. I looked at Samuel, Felix and Quinn. They looked as sick as I felt though Samuel looked worst of all.

"That was Pacey," Felix said as he sought a chair to collapse into.

"What did he say?" Charles said sharply.

No one who understood Pacey wanted to translate, but someone had to. I didn't look at Charles when I answered the question.

"He said, 'For, behold, the wicked bend the bow, they make ready their arrow upon the string to shoot in darkness at the upright in heart.'" I gulped and I was surprised as a shadow of a childhood memory put it in context for me. "It's from the Ju-Christ Bible, I think."

"Psalm 11:2," Charles said quietly as he went white as a sheet along with Tania, Marston and Alex. The rest of us, of course, were already there.

"Why would you say that, Bobby?" Tania asked Stuart using his official name. Stuart, however, was too wrung out to form an answer.

"*He* didn't say it, Ma'am," Felix answered from his chair, his head resting on his hands. "He just transmitted it. Through the most powerful Telepath I've ever seen."

A movement out of the corner of my eye caught my attention. I looked over in surprise to see Thal, no Thalberg, leaning hard against a chair. He appeared...sick. What the hell?

"Thal?" I asked quietly.

He shook his head violently.

No one else noticed this and it was Charles who looked at the silent Samuel who of all of us looked the most shaken. "Then who is warning us, Sam?" Charles asked lowly.

Samuel was so non-plussed he hadn't bothered to project that he wasn't. I'd recognized the mental voice immediately, as all the Paceys in the room had, even channeled as it was through Eriss.

"My son," Samuel said so quietly we had to strain to hear it. "Ian warned us that the end is coming. *She* is coming."

Something, though, was really wrong with Thal. He knew something, of that I was sure.

"Thal," I said, an edge on my voice, "what does that message mean?"

All eyes turned to my assistant, who put his hands over his face. "You can't ask me that, Miss Jane."

Then I understood. This fell under the proscribed list of things he couldn't discuss. Well, fuck that shit.

"*Thalberg*," I said through gritted teeth.

"What is going on?" Samuel asked.

"A condition of employment, Samuel," I answered, never taking my eyes off Thalberg. "In order for David to release him, there were two things he had to promise not to discuss with me: Family and technologies."

Samuel moved closer to Thalberg. "So this has to do with Abrams."

Thal just stared at him, eyes full of fear. Fear and guilt.

"Was there a message or deeper meaning within the verse my son transmitted to us?"

Still nothing from Thal. Samuel took that, as I did, as confirmation he was on the right track.

Samuel said the words his son had given us again slowly, watching Thal for any sign, any clue that would give things away. "For, behold, the wicked bend the bow, they make ready their arrow upon the string to shoot in darkness at the upright in heart."

Thal's face remained unchanged, though tears had started to fall. Poor, poor Thal, but what could we do? If there was a weapon, we needed to know.

It was when Samuel said the word 'arrow,' however, that Quinn stood up straight as if he'd been shocked.

"Quinn?" Samuel asked.

"Arrow," Quinn said excitedly, but then looked abashed at the small frown on Samuel's face at the mention of his daughter's name. "Sorry, Sir, but I don't think that your son using that word is a coincidence." Quinn walked over to Thal and said right to his face, "Is it, Thal?"

Thal stared at the massive Quinn for a second, then dropped his eyes in surrender.

"Explain, General," Samuel said a bit impatiently.

"We, the spooks network, including Huong on Gloriana-Levvon, have been hearing about designs for a weapon, a simple, brilliant weapon," he said excitedly, as if forgetting in his love of technology that often the best weapons had a side effect of creating a fucklot of death. "Jet-controlled twenty-foot long tubes of solid tungsten, coated in Tenorium that, if properly guided to hit the surface of a planet or moon, will obliterate it." He nodded to himself excitedly, clearly sure he was on the right track. "Abrams Arrows." He looked around at all of us, remembering himself. "That's what we've been calling them," he said, sounding less pleased with himself. "The P.A.U. records have them just as a project number."

A moment of digestive silence, then people were talking again, over and around each other. It made sense to me that weapons like that would have only a number and I was sure David would never name them after himself. Even *his* massive ego went only so far. I remained lost in my own thoughts along this line, but most everyone else continued talking, processing what they'd just learned.

Samuel stayed out of the fray, brow now furrowed in deep thought, but only for about a minute, then he took a breath and said, "Put the Fleet and the Station on Full Alert." His rich voice was firm and unwavering and I felt relief and, honestly, gratitude. This was the man who lived to command and to lead his people to victory through the most dangerous times. "Everyone return to your ships." Samuel headed for the door, Alex hard on his heels. "We have Armageddon to prepare for."

"Thank you, High Admiral," Charles said.

Samuel nodded and he and Alex left. Tania and Marston followed almost immediately. Felix and Quinn moved towards the door, Stuart right behind them. He looked back grimly at me. "Just like old times, Jane."

"Unfortunately, Stu," I replied but I had turned to Charles. I kissed him and he held me to him for just a second. "I love you," I whispered.

"And I, you," he whispered back.

I pulled away and held out my hand to a clearly shattered Thal. "Come, my friend," I said gently. Thal moved quickly towards me, putting one of his hands in mine as if grabbing a life line. I squeezed the hand, cast one last look at Charles and we went to work.

Excerpt from an interview of Ian Armstrong conducted by Jane Pace on July 11th, 2898.

I sat down opposite my longtime friend and turned on a recorder.

"Are you comfortable?" I asked.

"Tremendously," Ian said with amused sarcasm. I flipped him off and he laughed. "Happy 50th by the way."

"Thanks, Ian," I said. Usually I forgot my birthdays, but this one I had remembered, mostly because both Idis and Charles had reminded me of it countless times. They seemed to think it was important. I only thought it had significance because I was still around to have it. "Enough stalling," I teased.

He nodded. "You want to know, for the record, what was going on in those missing two weeks before Trithicate Station arrived at Terra."

"I do." Since history was written by the winners (or in this case, survivors) I wanted his first-hand version.

He sighed. "Only for you, Jane." He made himself more comfortable in his chair. "Let's get started."

I'd gone to Dep Qua mid-August of 2873 (about six weeks before Trithicate Station came to Terra) to check up on Eriss. I couldn't fight the feeling that she was in over her head so I'd gone.

To say they were not glad to see me was an understatement.

Oh, they made sure I had an audience with Eriss that first day. I assume they only did that so that I wouldn't go poking into things I shouldn't looking for her. It was strange, though. The city, while still beautiful, seemed colder somehow. It was two weeks before I heard from Eriss again. I had nothing to do, but remained unwilling to leave when something was clearly wrong. I'd gotten to the Trithicate system via the *T.F.S. Rauschenbach*, our newest and largest assault shuttle, and we'd temporarily refit it to hold two *Carcara* fighters so I could play with them since dad had asked me to. I was worried and bored so I started doing *Carcara* drills towards that end around the non-station side of the planet. No one stopped me.

I saw Eriss a couple of times but always, as I'd mentioned to you in my letter of September 17th, with an army of human and Denethian TPs. I had my 'door' shut when I was around them, of course, and I wondered what, if anything, she was allowed to hide from her minders. She started going to and from the station a great deal, but I never saw her alone.

I wanted to see if I could get anything from flying abound the station so changed my flight plan and, if you remember, blew apart my *Carcara* doing so. Then I saw Thal and all I could think was that I had to let you people know. The Denethians rescued me and firmly returned me to Dep Qua. I sent the letter.

The next day I went out in the other fighter, trying to figure out a way to get closer to the station when I saw something coming at me, a small figure in a DSS Suit sort of floating in my direction. One of its jets was on, pushing it, but the figure itself wasn't moving. I used the (crappy) grappling arms of the fighter to pull the person to the ship and headed back to the planet's surface. The grappling arms had broken the arm of the small Tarine man, but I soon realized that it hadn't mattered.

The poor thing was both violently decompressed and frozen solid by space itself. One of his wings had been torn off, a hole left in the back of the suit. It wasn't until I was back in Dep Qua that I found, pressed against his back, beneath the layers of DSS and an undersuit, a small thin package with Eriss's seal on it.

It was a Denethian-Tarine dictionary and pronunciation guide. I know this because the friendly Tarine inhabitants of Dep Qua helping me burst into a stream of what had to be Tarine when they saw it. It appeared that Eriss had been busy. I had to assume, then, that it was for me to learn so I did. The Tarine helped. It actually is a beautiful language, a softer cousin of Denethian (a language I already spoke), related similarly to it the way Terran Spanish is to Terran French or Italian. I didn't know why she wanted me to learn it, but I studied it anyway. At least it was a bit of a distraction from the endless waiting.

Over the next few days I noticed some of my Tarine friends weren't around anymore.

When I asked where they had gone the only response I got was a fearful look and the one word, 'Tris,' which was the Tarine form of the Denethian word 'Trith,' which meant 'Home.' 'Trithicate,' when very literally translated from Denethian meant 'Home Safe.' I was pretty much convinced that this was some kind of code for heaven or the afterlife, but couldn't get a straight answer out of anyone. It was either the language barrier or their fear that kept me from the truth.

Soon after I was 'relocated' to Trithicate Station and the Tarine were left behind. I saw Eriss more, but only in passing and never alone. I was cut off from the planet now and had no idea what was going on, if anything.

September 24th I received that very worrying letter from Quinn, the last letter I received from anyone while I was in Rian Space. I was surprised, actually, that they'd let it through (I was sure there was no privacy of any kind on the station) but I could see why they would. The Tarine were gone, now, and the Ambassadors and their staffs expelled from Rian Space. They, led I was sure by the Pelann herself, were using Quinn's words to scare the crap out of me and it was working.

The letter you, Jane, sent me the following day was one I never received. I didn't know that the Thals were preparing the station for hyper. Such an idea would never have occurred to me.

It *didn't* occur to me…until I woke up one day and we were in hyper.

I was against a wall in a strange room, my arms bound behind me and my feet tied together. I was still in Zero-G, so still on the station, and didn't feel impaired in any way, just restrained. The now worn off drug they had given me, piped into my room no doubt, had apparently only been used to make moving me easier. It's so nice, I thought bitterly, that they didn't consider me enough of a threat to keep me drugged. For the millionth time I mentally cursed my beloved parents for not making me any kind of freak. Of course, I had to admit, I'd probably have been dead by then if I had been.

A figure floated above me, tail swishing agitatedly. I looked up, hoping to see Lita Utat, but it was a stranger. I hadn't seen Lita for a while and I had to assume that she was dead, caught, as so many of us were, between her ideals and the shitty time she was living in. Just out of curiosity I opened my mental 'door' and filled my mind with horrible images of carnage and destruction, our standard TP flushing out trick. The figure above me was unaffected. Damn. I felt a stab of pity for Telepaths (an unusual feeling for me). How many Deneth and Tarine ones were even still alive?

That thought brought me back to Eriss. God, Eriss.

A chime. The Denethian guard moved gracefully aside as a door in the ceiling opened. Five more guards (all huge fuckers) flowed in, followed by the Pelann herself. I watched her move into the center of the room. She looked ancient and, I thought, a bit strung out. Worn thin. Yes, taking over the universe is stressful, isn't it, you grasping bitch.

She hovered in front of me, her black eyes staring as if trying to bore into my soul.

I had a thought, then. Even Jane had been momentarily intimidated by the Pelann (though she'd recovered), but when it came down to it, this was just a being. She could torture me or Eriss or the Tarine or the remaining TP Deneth or anyone, but her actions weren't mine. She could only kill me once. I didn't want her to (and I didn't have any romantic notions of being united with Arrow in death), but if it was going to be then so be it. She had no power over me. I had to admit, however, that that was because I had no power of my own. Not here. Maybe not anywhere. Was I scared of pain? Not really. Don't think that's some stoic nobility talking. Pain was the body telling you to stop doing whatever was being done to it NOW. I would scream and curse and tell people to stop hurting me, but was I afraid? No. I was a soldier. Physical pain could be dealt with if not actually enjoyed.

"I assume, Ian," the Pelann said suddenly in crisp Denethian, "that you know why you are here?"

So it was Ian and not Jack, which meant she knew who I was. I sighed. Of course she did.

"Bait," I said. Because of course I was.

"Your last letter was received," she said, pleased. "and now they are dithering about whether or not I mean to cause trouble or will I be reasonable and do things legally." She shook her head at the inherent stupidity of all non-Rian. Well, she had a point, I had to admit, since I was on a giant metal Ball of Doom hurtling through space to start (and end) a war. "Everyone knows of your attempt to save the poor little Princess for love." She laughed. I wanted to punch her in the face. "I, however, needed to issue someone a specific invitation." I had no doubt Jane (and Felix and everyone) were already planning the assault to free me. They were beautifully predictable that way. "Siobahn Archer brought your Commodore from across the galaxy by torturing another of her friends. Why mess with success?"

Yeah. Because for all my brilliant epiphanies about the Pelann being the only one responsible for her own actions and no one forcing anyone to do anything blah blah blah, there was one person in particular who would never believe that and who thought that everything was her responsibility no matter whose it actually was. I had to ask, though, "Do you *want* Jane to kill you?"

The Pelann smiled. It was not pretty.

She made a clicking sound as she quickly backed up and out of the way.

Immediately six very large Denethian warriors swarmed towards me. Dear god, anyone would have wanted to back the fuck up at that one and all I had behind me was a wall. Well, I may have been philosophical about death and torture, but I really didn't *want* any of that. So I punted using cultural conditioning as my ball.

"She will know if I'm dead, Your Holiness," I said as I stared down what seemed like endless claws and teeth. "We are *Shann*."

I saw, just for a fleeting second, a hesitation, perhaps even a look of guilt on the Pelann's face. Jane wouldn't have any idea if I died, of course, but the Pelann didn't know that and even if she did, her guards didn't.

Her eyes narrowed, but I was watching her men (some of whom were probably female, but what the heck). They had stopped moving when I'd used that word, the word for a lover's bond, but now that the Pelann was challenging it, they looked confused. "Terran humans will have sex with anything or anyone. Using that word is an abomination."

The warriors turned towards me, anger on their faces, but I stood my ground, as much as I could bound to the wall. "No. I love Jane. We are bonded even if we are not together. We are *Shann*. If you kill me she will know."

"You are the son of her first love," she scoffed.

"Which is why it isn't common knowledge," I raised my head challengingly. "Ask her when she comes for me." I hadn't lied even if it had been an embarrassing episode in our lives that we'd both rather forget. I stared the Pelann down, but I was speaking to her men. "*Shann*, Your Holiness." Then I dug the knife. "A bond not to be interfered with."

Her eyes widened and I knew I had her. Her claws retracted. "I will ask her, Ian Armstrong, and know that such a connection is never to be lied about." She looked at her men for the first time. "The penalty for such a lie is severe." One of the warriors nodded. By his/her standards this was right. Interesting.

"I understand, Your Holiness." Bitch cunt whore. This I added only in my head, pretty sure that there were no TPs alive, except for Eriss, anywhere anymore. Poor Lita.

<u>A Note on the Denethian Cultural Concept of Shann by General Nathan Quinn-Pace</u>
Published March 8th 2871 (two years before Trithicate Station arrived at Terra)

The one instance of sexual intercourse between a Terran human and Denethian has been documented for posterity (and for the sake of titillation). Sexual contact between Denethians themselves is much less fraught with physical danger but has peculiar issues of its own. There is no casual sex with the Deneth. There may be sexual relationships that do not work out (incompatibility, separations because of distance or work, etc.) but a bond is created by sexual congress that remains important throughout the lives of both (or all) partners.

This is doubly complicated by the fact that Denethian families share intense feelings and relationships as though they were their own. Jane had sex with Criss Utat so, by extension, she'd had sex with all the Utat (in their minds at least) and thus the bond proliferated. Therefore a conscientious Deneth will choose very carefully whom to take as a lover (there is a lot of incentive to be smart about your choice since you'll have your whole family furious with you if you saddle them with some asshole for eternity) which makes Criss Utat's choice of Jane all the more extraordinary. By making her his Shann *he bound her to his family, giving her a small level of protection. He also sacrificed himself for his* Shann, *binding her further. It could be argued that it was his way of standing up to a Pelann he knew was evil long before anyone outside of the Rian Nation had any idea.*

Shann *are bound but unmated (by which I mean they have not created young through their bond.)* Shann Da *are those that have mated and produced offspring. A* Shann Da *can only be killed by their mate, according to custom. It was thought that only one's mate should have the power to decide their partner's life or death; only he or she could know them well enough to be able to make such a call. That sort of thing made Denethian capital crimes very interesting, to say the least.*

Shillin, the Pelann who preceded Shirin (her father) had theorized that the Shann *bonds served a twofold purpose: to encourage the young to take mating and sex (and the creation of children) seriously and to ensure a tie between all Deneth so strong that civil war would be too complicated to wage. It seems that, for good or ill, he has been correct thus far.*

I stayed against the wall for a long time. About a day, according to my internal clock. You know the one thing that never gets mentioned when someone is confined for a long period of time? What to do with bodily functions. Well, since you asked, all I'll say is it ain't pretty. I was starving (though food became less appealing from a, uh, sanitary stand point as time went on, if you get my meaning). So I was relieved, literally, when the door to my little prison opened and some (I assume) cleaning staff came in to make me presentable and give me some food. I wondered who was coming. They left and the door opened again after a small respite.

Eriss floated in.

She looked like utter shit.

Yes, her clothes were perfect and her hair impeccable, but she had become a wraith with her suffering and worry. Her lovely face was lined and her lips drawn and thin. It was hard to see. Impossible to see.

"Are you all right?" I said, my voice rusty from lack of use.

"Are you?" she responded quietly.

"Yes."

She floated closer to me, her delicate wings moving her seemingly without effort. "That was quite a bluff with the Pelann."

Jane being my *Shann*. Right. I opened my mouth to answer and she looked around the room pointedly, only her large eyes moving. People were listening. I should have expected it. I didn't know specifically why she was here, but I was sure she was on a mission of some kind, whether her mission or the Pelann's remained to be seen.

"It wasn't a lie, Eriss," I said, wincing internally, not knowing if this admission would hurt her. "We were lovers and I do love her."

She said nothing for a minute, but she appeared to me even more beat down than before. Crap.

"Jane and I aren't together, my dear, and we won't be," I said. Damn that Pelann anyway.

"So you didn't come here to be with me?" She looked forlorn and my heart went out to her, but I couldn't forget we were playing to an invisible audience. I had no idea what she actually felt, if anything. I still hadn't liked telling her about Jane. I refused to examine why.

"I…" I had to stop. Why had I come? I shook off the thought. If people were listening the truth, even if I figured out what the fuck it was, was the last thing I needed to be sharing right now. "I was worried about you."

"I have my brothers and sisters to take care of me, Ian."

"I know, but you are my friend. Friends worry."

She looked over her slight shoulder at the door. "I should go." She made no move to actually leave, however.

"Eriss," I said and she turned back. "Why are we in hyper? We can't be going to Terra. That's suicide." I struggled with my bonds, but gave up almost immediately. "Is that where we are going?"

"The Pelann has not shared her vision with me." She looked me in the eye, though, and blinked slowly.

Mother of god. We (those of us on the station) were going to be slaughtered, but what could we do?

"Why would she want war? Hundreds of thousands, if not millions of beings could die."

She frowned. "You forget yourself, Captain. Her Holiness is governed by the Holy Mother. If She has told her what to do, then we must allow her to guide us to Her purpose."

What did the Pelann have on Eriss that would make her spout this horseshit? Almost as soon as I'd had that thought, however, the answer came to me. It was so obvious I would have smacked myself in the head had I had use of my arms. The Tarine. She was buying time for her sisters.

I nodded. "I understand the importance of sisters, Eriss." I did my best to avoid that pit of sadness in my chest whenever I thought of my Arrow.

"Do not forget your brothers, Ian," Eriss said with infinite sadness. "Your family is unusual, but it is still family."

"I would die to protect them."

"That is what family does."

So Eriss was well and truly fucked. She needed to leave, she needed to fight, but right now fighting would get the Tarine wiped out for the second time and help no one. Was she waiting for an opportunity to resist? Did she have a plan of some kind? Or was she just…waiting. As in waiting to die like everyone else was going to when the station entered Sol's orbit?

She reached out and scratched an itch on her forehead. No, I corrected myself, she'd tapped her temple and had made it look like a casual movement.

I opened my mental 'door.'

She spoke aloud, however, not in my mind, as her expression became seductive. "You can't tell me you came all the way across the galaxy to talk to me about family, Ian."

So, she was giving me a cue and, hoping information would soon follow, I tried to take it.

"Yes, I've come a long way," I said, only some of my irritation feigned, "but now I wonder why. You teased me on Terra 1. I've been here for weeks and this is the first time we've been alone." Then I glared at her. "Tying me to a fucking wall for days on end doesn't help either."

I saw relief on her features. I was apparently playing this correctly.

"You have to understand...

"I have to understand," I repeated, my tone mocking.

"I'm sorry," she said, sounding anxious, as if worried I wouldn't want her anymore. "I've been so busy, Ian

"Now I can't even touch you." I looked away, playing up a lover's frustration.

"I can touch *you*," she said, giving a full dose of maidenly hesitation.

"Come here," I ordered, thinking that we were both lucky I was so damaged because being aroused right now would have been way too distracting.

She moved closer to me, much closer. Soon her delicate but strong body was against mine, her face so close. This time, though, the physical response I'd had (and had felt guilty about) months ago was nowhere to be found. She was still beautiful and I still liked her, but my heart had been thoroughly broken and getting turned on was still the last thing that was going to happen.

Then there was a whisper in my mind, so soft I could barely hear it. The whisper was, I was sure, a targeted Telepathic contact from the being pressing against me, in Tarine, just to make sure that it wouldn't be overheard or, at the very least, understood.

'Abrams gave Shirin guided weapons, something called the spooks have nicknamed 'Abrams Arrows.' Apparently they're planet-killers if enough are used together. Or so his Thals promised the Pelann.'

'Abrams deactivated the guidance systems, I assume?' I thought back. He liked to give weapons that looked functional that weren't. It was a specialty of his.

'They were able to reactivate them three days ago.'

An Abrams specialty no more, apparently. Fucking fantastic.

"Ian." She kissed me, a full on gorgeous kiss that unbroken Ian would have thoroughly enjoyed. Broken Ian gave a master class in acting.

'She's keeping me alive to distract the Union while she launches her attack.' She paused in her kiss. 'Say something out loud, Ian.'

"Get me free, Eriss," I groaned and I kissed her back. Not original, but I was trying to keep up and faking several things at once.

"You know I can't do that, lover," she said with a small nod. I guessed I was doing well with the charade, but I still needed information.

'But why now?' I thought back. 'I know this wasn't her plan. Why bother to create the Tarine at all if she was just going to start a fight?'

Eriss bit my lip, teasing it with her teeth. "I knew you wanted me, Ian." She smiled at me (a smile I didn't believe for a second) and kissed me again.

"Of course I did," I gasped, but thought, 'tell me.'

'She has 20,000 Denethian warriors hidden within the station.' I stiffened (and not in the good way) in shock. Eriss moved against me, covering my reaction. She continued, 'Shirin is dying. She only has a year or more to live. No one knows this except Shirin, myself and now you.'

So the Pelann had nothing to lose and all of us to lose it with. 'Fuck me running.'

Now Eriss actually laughed. If her laughter was slightly hysterical, then I couldn't really blame her.

There was a knock on the door and Eriss jumped a bit against me.

"I have to go, lover," she said aloud in Denethian.

'You have to let me warn them,' I thought frantically, but said aloud, "Eriss, take me with you."

"I will wait for you," was what she said, but she thought, 'When we are close enough,' she promised. 'Keep your mind open.'

'I will.'

She kissed me quickly and flew away towards the door.

I was left alone.

Another day passed with me attached to a wall. I tried to sleep, knowing I would need my wits about me when shit came down, but it wasn't easy. Wall-sleeping was yet another talent I seemed to lack. Eventually, however, even the uncomfortableness of my position wasn't enough to keep me from dropping off and I had the strangest dream.

I was floating, no, flying, my wings beating slowly as I moved down one of those topsy-turvy corridors in the station. I was tired, so tired and on the verge of emotional collapse. I looked down at my hands as they straightened my blue flowing dress and noticed the extra knuckle and pale blue skin. I floated past mirrored Tenorium and saw myself. Ah, I was Eriss. Around me I/Eriss felt the body heat of six huge Denethian guards and two Terran humans. They were too close, but every time I/Eriss moved they moved with me, their distance remaining constant as if it were a dance and not a mobile prison.

A thought, in Terran accented Denethian, came into my head. 'Fifteen minutes, Your Highness. Not a second more.' One of her Terran TP minders. 'We will be moving them tomorrow.'

I/Eriss didn't respond. I/Eriss knew there was no need. This was clearly a regular thing.

We approached an airlock in the wall, up to the right and we all moved towards it. I/Eriss could hear the hiss of the jet packs of the humans. I felt a wave of Eriss' hatred towards them. As Ian I thought I understood the reason for the hatred. As Ian I was wrong.

Several codes were punched into the door and it soon opened.

As Eriss I went in alone.

It was a large hall, one that was probably used for performances or theater. The first thing I saw were bed pods. Hundreds of bed pods attached to the walls, most occupied.

Here were the Tarine. Hundreds of Tarine, probably, I thought later, all of them.

Most of them didn't even acknowledge me/Eriss when I came in. I saw movement out of the corner of my eye and followed it to the ceiling. A couple dozen Tarine were floating there aimlessly. The way they floated was wrong, though (I thought this as Ian, Eriss was used to what I was seeing). The Tarine were always so graceful, but this… The way they were moving reminded me of that poor Tarine man I had tried to save in space.

That poor Tarine man that had been missing… Oh god.

I/Ian was abruptly awake, back in my cell.

All of them, every Tarine I'd seen, had had only one wing, the other having been cut off their bodies.

One wing missing.

They couldn't fly.

They were maimed and Eriss was brought to see them, probably every day in case Eriss ever forgot her duty. In case Eriss ever forgot her*self*.

I wanted to scream. To throw up. To kill someone.

I didn't, though. I just waited.

Six and a half hours later I felt her, Eriss, in my mind once more, speaking gentle Tarine.

'Tell them, Ian.'

I had wracked my brain, trying to think of a way to let my people know what was going on, but without giving everything away if the message was intercepted and understood by unfriendlies. The irony of an anti-religious Pacey using a bible passage was not lost on me, but I was sure it would do the trick *if* the right people heard it. Saying, "Hey, the Pelann has planet-busting weapons and an assload of Denethian warriors and we're all gonna die," didn't leave a lot for interpretation. The only real chance we had was to prepare while the Pelann didn't know we were preparing, hence the verse from the Ju-Christ bible.

'Tell them *now*,' Eriss ordered.

I nodded though she was on the other side of the station and thought in Pacey words I trusted her to broadcast over an incredible distance, *"Le haxhaith, réuch, an bent wicket an boxha, téanann siat réith a arrow ar an teaxhrán a shoot sa torchatas ax an uprixht i xcroílár."*

Because, though I hadn't known it at the time, father was correct.

Armageddon was coming.

Entry 5-8-88

<u>11:48 – Space Outside Terra 1 Space Station, Terra, October 5th, 2873</u>

It's Jane again and I was in the middle of getting us prepared for the shitstorm.

The first thing we had done was disarm and confine the Denethian contingent of the UNav. It had been a clearly illegal action and entirely my idea. They had gone, surprisingly, without violence. Samuel and I had handled it and the procedure had been almost depressingly civilized. No one within UNav command or the President's office had raised any kind of objection and, while I wasn't looking for conflict, I had to admit it had kind of bothered me. It was racist, or alia-xeno-phobic, or whatever, but on the other hand, we just couldn't have anyone attacking us from within while we were being attacked from without. Especially since I couldn't be sure we were going to win Big Picture-wise.

So now we waited. The shit was going to hit the fan at noon and we were almost there. I had my Team Alpha with my Micro, my TP, and my cadre of Marines and we floated in the cold beauty of space where Terra 1 usually stayed. Yes, we'd moved the station. Seemed like an ironic parity that in the incipient arrival of Trithicate, the station that had never been relocated in a thousand years, would cause the removal of Terra 1, a station that hadn't been moved in over a hundred. The trouble was that Terra 1 hadn't been designed to do much more than correct its orbit as needed. It didn't have hyper capability and would have fallen apart had we even been foolish enough to attempt it. It was hiding in the shadow of the moon now, staffed with Tellescan soldiers and my ESTF students. All non-essential personnel, including Derek Pace-Taylor, had been evacuated to Luna itself. Anyone who could have left Earth behind had gone as well. That had been tricky to arrange, though, since we were supposed to be preparing for a celebration, not a war, and keeping the journos silent had required an Executive Order from Terra's President Mahajan. Union President Leder had handled all of that. David and the *Foudroyant* had retreated to Luna's shadow as well, though not without a fight. I think he'd just resisted being told what to do even if he'd known it was the smart thing, but David was a stubborn dick just because he could be so often, so what could you do?

I looked around me as I loitered in space with my Team. Sixty-five Union ships were ringing Terra, gleaming in the light of Sol, though most concentrated in the area where I was, where we expected Trithicate to go. Terra 2, the smaller of the two stations orbiting Earth, had also been moved and was slowly, too slowly, heading out of the system. Only fifty years old it was faster (something I had never thought about in relation to a space station until recently) but also not hyper-capable. I had a feeling that would soon change, assuming any of us survived the next few hours. I sighed in frustration into my helmet. Every new conflict always showed us new ways we were vulnerable. We should just encase the whole damned system in a Tenorium box and be done with it.

The Union ships directly led by High Admiral Samuel Armstrong (who was on his new flagship, the *T.S.S. Scheherazade*) formed what the journos were told to call the Union Alpha Welcome Fleet. We called it Fleet Terra-Omega.

Those sixty-five ships were a supposed honor guard and were loaded with two types of projectiles—one set that would explode with pretty colors (fireworks, essentially) and one set that would explode with, well, death.

11:58.

Admiral Jennifer Tree, who was Samuel's second-in-command for Terra-Omega had just finished receiving status green from each ship in her Fleet. Now it was our turn. I felt my hands shake a little, my body's not so subtle way of letting me know the adrenaline was really flowing.

'Furies Teams report status,' Paul Friedman's voice said calmly over our comms.

I quickly checked my display. All good.

'Team Alpha ready,' I said.

'Beta ready,' I heard Felix say.

'Charlie ready.'

'Delta good to go.'

'Echo is green to proceed.'

'Foxtrot ready.'

'Team Hotel is ready,' Quinn's voice responded.

A short pause, then Atalanta said, '*Ouranos* shows green across the board.'

'*Tisiphone* ready.'

'*Megaera* shows green.'

'*Alecto* also shows green.'

'*Gaea* optimal.'

'*Indus Felae* ready,' Captain Freya said.

'High Admiral Armstrong,' Jennifer Tree said solemnly, "Terra-Omega is ready."

'Acknowledged, Admiral Tree, Captian Friedman, stand by,' Samuel's rich voice said in all our ears.

12:00.

I was pretty sure I wasn't the only one holding my breath as the seconds ticked by.

'Contact! We have contact, Sir!' someone's tactical officer (Samuel's, I had to assume) called out. He gave the coordinates. Right outside the Terran system. 'It's confirmed, Trithicate Station, Sir, heading on a direct course for Terra at maximum sublight.'

'Here we go,' Felix said softly into his mic.

Then a different, soft feminine voice came over our comms and, I assumed, all the journo feeds within the Sol system, 'This is Trithicate Station requesting permission to enter Terran orbit, pleasse resspond, Terra 1 Control.' It wasn't Eriss, it was someone else, but hearing a Denethian voice, finally, notched my adrenaline up to sky high levels. It kinda made me nauseous.

'This is High Admiral Samuel Armstrong, Trithicate Station,' Samuel's voice said rather unexpectedly. A warning. 'We welcome you in peace to Terra.'

'Thank you, High Admiral,' the Denethian voice said.

'Please proceed to the following coordinates,' the Docking Master said over the comm. Usually he handled larger docking/orbital issues for Earth from his post on Terra 1. Today, I knew, he was on the *Scheherazade* with Samuel.

'Acknowledged, Docking Control,' the Denethian voice said. 'Incoming message from the Pelann-Heir-Designate.'

Here we go.

I had no visual monitor feed on my helmet, nor did anyone else who was already in space in DSS Suits, but (I was told later) people onboard ship saw Eriss, dressed in white trying not to look tired, her hair tied back, unexpectedly, in the style of a Denethian warrior.

'Stay on your toes, kids,' Samuel said quietly even as Eriss began to speak in flawless Standard.

'*Good afternoon, fellow members of the Union. As you may know from our previous introduction,*' her voice changed a bit as though she were smiling, "*I am Eriss Fenton of the Rian Nation, the Pelann's Heir Designate, and the newest Ambassador to the Galactic Union.*'

I 'pushed' my senses out to their limit, trying to 'feel' movement in the space around me. Problem was the distances, even just around Terra were pretty damned big. I focused on Terra 2, a station I'd never even set foot on but had no intention of our losing, still making its plodding way out of the system. Happily it wasn't alone. Ten, very large, very new Terran built battle cruisers flanked it. Sure, it was their virgin cruise and they weren't fully staffed and all sorts of other things, but they were there, populated mostly by Novy Heelies and led by a person who had no love for the Pelann, General Synon. I could make out the distortion (no other way to put it) around Terra 2 that was these ships, but I wasn't looking for that. I was looking for something, or somethings, else.

There.

'*As many of you may know, the Tarine Rian, of whom I am one, are a sister race to the Deneth Rian. We are a gravity-friendly people, ready to take our places within the Legislature and the Diplomatic Corps to try to build consensus and assist Terran and Heely Humans in the growth and prosperity of this our Union.*'

Felix said it first. 'There's a cluster of ships coming at Terra 2, Sir,' Felix said over his comm. The expected Denethian fleet, or at least part of it.

'How many?' Samuel asked.

'Too far away to tell,' he said. 'Fewer than twenty? Jane?'

'That's all I have, too,' I said, frustrated.

'Seventeen,' Garrett said.

'Scanning confirmed seventeen hostiles,' a crewman said.

'Nice, Garrett,' I said.

'*Some of you have been to my home on the planet Trithicate, Dep Qua, and the rest of you have no doubt seen it on the journo feeds. It is a beautiful place. My Tarine brethren and I are so happy that we will be able to see, finally, the birthplace of Humans, Earth, in person for the first time.*'

'Can you identify the model of the ships?' Quinn asked suddenly.

A slight pause. 'Crea Warbirds,' the tactical officer said.

'Well, that is unexpected,' Quinn said.

'What is it, Quinn?' I had to ask.

'Those are older ships, Sir,' he said, answering as though Samuel had asked the question, 'of Deneth manufacture, not the newer P.A.U. designs, and very labor intensive to run.'

'How labor intensive?'

'Even a skeleton crew would have to be five times one on a similarly sized P.A.U. design that the Union uses. Actually a skeleton crew and a fully-staffed crew wouldn't be different enough to bother with.'

'So Lita was wrong?' I asked, astonished. 'The ships aren't emptied and the crews stuffed aboard Trithicate?' My stomach dropped sickly, 'Or did she lie?'

'*Friendship between the Humans of the Union and the Rian has already begun,*" Eriss continued, "*from the many Ambassadors we've hosted on Dep Qua to the close relationship that has developed on a personal level between many Humans and our people.*'

Where was she going with this?

'Sir! Terra 2 is under attack!' Samuel's tactical officer said tensely.

'Monitor the situation, but General Synon has it well in hand.' I didn't even need to be there to know he was projecting confidence.

'I don't think she lied, Jane,' Quinn said, 'but I think the Pelann is too smart and determined not to use a TP's gifts against her at least once.'

Misinformation. Fucking great.

Eriss was still speaking, '*For it is to those old friends and the newer ones I hope to make now that we are here that I wish to send a special message.*'

All chatter on the comms went deadly silent. What the fuck was she doing?

'*We are more alike than we appear.*' There was a noise in the background of the transmission. Someone told me later that large figures then appeared in the background behind Eriss. The figures surged closer.

'*Sáxháil an Rian, tá an Pelann ixithe xheabhaix!*'

'*Save the Rian, the Pelann has gone mad!*' but it was in our heads. In Pacey.

God, she was begging for help.

The last thing we heard just as the feed was cut were two more words from her, this time in Standard. She said 'Godspeed,' and the screen went black.

'Multiple object launch!' the tactical officer said excitedly.

'How many, Williams?' Samuel asked, but I could already feel them, a couple hundred or so of them fanning out silently from Trithicate Station. Simple weapons of incredible destructive power. I shivered, despite my heated suit.

'Scanning reports…two hundred-fifty…'

'…Abrams Arrows,' Samuel completed with obvious distaste.

'Yes, Sir.'

'Course,' Samuel demanded, though their destination wasn't much of a mystery.

'Terra, Sir,' he responded. 'Fanning out around the planet.' David, I thought, I swear someone is going to put a bullet in you and, at this rate, it probably won't even be me.

Then another voice chimed in, 'General Synon's group has been fired upon, High Admiral.' A pause. 'They have engaged.' Yes, I felt the distant burn of SLPG fire around the still escaping Terra 2.

'Furies Teams stop the projectiles…' Samuel started but then I felt something that really scared me.

'Fuck me running.' My eyes went so wide they hurt.

'Jane?' Samuel asked warily.

'Mother of God,' Felix breathed as he felt it, too.

'Hundreds of Deneth warriors have launched themselves from the Station,' I gasped. The Station seemed to almost *leak* warriors as they streaked, almost invisible in their black uniforms and unsurpassed speed, towards…towards, not the Abrams Arrows as a protective measure, but towards the Union ships. 'Sir, they're coming for the ships.'

Samuel said. 'Jane, get to Trithicate. Leave the rest to us.'

'Yes, Sir,' I said, but my mind was racing. 'Furies Teams, disable anything hostile you run across, but our goal is the Station. Let's go.'

'Yes, Ma'am,' I heard a bunch of people respond.

We 'flew.'

We were so very fast and so very murderous. The Marines, Micros, and TPs used LPGs to kill anything that got in our way. The Macros broke necks. The Station loomed closer. How to play this, though? How to exploit every advantage? I didn't know if Eriss was alive or dead. I also didn't know if she'd even had a plan once she'd called for help. I knew jack shit, apparently, but something was niggling at my brain.

Thal. Yes, Thal.

A giant SLPG beam sliced through the starry darkness. I looked up at the rapidly approaching Station that had produced it. Well, it couldn't have been unprotected, now could it? I wondered if David had 'improved' that, too. That son of a bitch had a lot to answer for.

'Connect me with Thal on the *Ouranos*,' I said into my comm. Another new beam sliced through. I knew the burns it cast. God, I hated those things.

'Yes, Miss Jane?' Thal responded almost immediately.

'Are the other Thals still on Trithicate?'

'Yes, Miss Jane.'

'I need you to go see David and override their programs. We need their help.'

'He won't want to do that.'

'You need to *make* him, Thal. So get your ass over there. Understood?'

'Yes, Ma'am.' He disconnected. I didn't really know if it would help, but I didn't think we could do any worse.

Twenty Denethian warriors converged on us as we finally reached the Station.

Just as a second wave of 'Abrams Arrows' left it for Earth. We let them go past unimpeded. We had to. We had to trust that Samuel's people would take care of them. Damn it.

The warriors were getting too close. I had to pay attention or a no-contest mini-battle was going to go very badly very quickly.

'Hold the LPG fire,' I said. We were in close and I really didn't want to get hit by another blast. 'Macros.'

Eight warriors were dead within fifteen seconds, the rest knocked out and podded, and we were untouched. (I'm sorry to say that killing is faster but we did the best we could—we really didn't want this to turn into a self-genocide for the Deneth, though it was going to be touch and go no matter how careful we were.) We left the bodies of the dead floating in space.

Okay. We'd made the Station. 'Pull up your Station schematics and head for your assigned airlocks. Signal when you've reached yours. Go.'

I felt the other five Teams scatter like ants across the skin of the station. Why airlocks, you ask? Why not just blow holes in the Station? Because depressurization was a weapon of last resort, especially when we were going in as blind as we were. Actually, it wasn't the weapon of *last* resort, but it was pretty damned close.

My team and I moved quickly across the Station, skimming it like birds crossing the surface of a lake. God, it was fucking huge.

'Team Beta has reached airlock 12,' Felix said.

We continued to move very quickly. I felt the dimple in the Station's skin that belonged to our airlock. We stopped as I rested my gloved hand on it.

'Team Alpha has reached Airlock 7,' I reported.

I waited as the other four Teams reached their destinations. I felt the battles going on around us, over the glorious vista that was Terra spread out below us all blues, greens and silver cities sparkling here and there along the landscape. Such a lovely planet, I thought. I wanted to be out there. I wanted to be in the fight with the ships and my people, but this was (with Felix's help) Samuel's plan. If there were two people in the universe I could trust to put personnel where they needed to be and when they needed to be there, it was those two. So, stay put, Jane, I ordered myself. Stay put and do your fucking job.

'Team Charlie in place at Airlock 3.'

'Team Foxtrot at Airlock 17.'

'Team Delta has Airlock 12.'

Then lastly, because the Station was huge and they'd had the furthest to go, I heard Garrett say, 'Team Hotel has reached Airlock 9.'

Ok, then. 'Go to work, friends. Godspeed.'

Putting my rarely used lock picking skills to use (it was a physical lock, easy-peasy) it was barely seconds before I had the outer airlock door open. The eighteen of us crowded into the surprisingly large space. When I say it was surprisingly large, I mean we weren't quite as crushed as I had anticipated. Our Marines were very large/strong men and women and their equipment made them positively enormous. Dalia, Aki and I looked like children next to them.

'We have a green seal on the outer lock,' Marine Captain Parnell reported over the comm.

I felt the pressure start to equalize within the room and started to work on the inner door's lock. The indicator on the door glowed blood red. The gears were a bit sticky and I had to guess that this one wasn't used all that much. No matter. Click. Click. Click. Click. Click. Big Click.

'Geez, you're fast, Jane,' Dalia murmured.

The door's readout turned green and unlocked.

Without another word we moved silently into the Station, the Marines, Aki and Dalia utilizing their jets with enough skill to rival my own ease of movement.

We made it halfway down the hallway before we encountered our first hostile.

I never stopped my forward velocity. I put up a shield and 'flew' right by as fast as I could. Even the burn of LPG fire on my shield was a fleeting thing as Dalia 'pressed' the proper artery in the warrior's neck (she really was good at that) and knocked him out. Like lightning one of the Marines pushed forward, punctured an obviously large hole in the skin of the being's arm, curled him into a ball and podded him. (The puncture served two purposes: 1. it delivered a powerful sedative that would, depending on body weight, etc., render the being unconscious for up to twelve hours and 2. keep him out of open space until it healed since a break in the skin rendered him vulnerable to all the nasty things the rest of us were vulnerable to.) The Marine did this with such perfectly controlled effort, that I was sure they'd practiced. He then passed the pod containing the unconscious Denethian down the line of Marines to the end. The last Marine would put the pod on a tether on the outside of the ship until we were ready to leave. Two Marines would stay behind and guard whatever we put there. I didn't have time to 'feel' it but I knew the other Teams were doing the same thing. We would save as many as we could, but at some point I knew we would run out of time (not to mention access to the airlock) and the chips would have to fall where they would. I just hoped the only chips falling would be Denethian.

I kept us moving, following the schematic in my helmet. We had thirty or so Denethians podded within about ten minutes. Two of the Marines had been hit by LPG ricochets, but the injuries weren't serious enough to send them back (not possible in any case) and their DSS Suits had supplied anesthetic and healed over the wounds almost instantly.

We went right, then left, then up and over (and god, these hallways and tunnels were enough to drive you mad they were so all over the place) and we entered the main exhibition hall/banquet area (where the infamous race had taken place months ago) and we stopped.

About a hundred armed and angry Denethians waited for us. I quickly threw up a shield to cover all of us.

I screamed as a wave of LPG fire blasted it. My people did not move, did not flinch. We couldn't fire back either, with the shield up. The Denethians weren't stupid, however. They kept the burning fire going, alternating firing groups to save the batteries in their guns. They knew I would break eventually. They were very nearly right.

'Aki!' I screamed into my comm.

The Deneth weren't Telepaths and we didn't want the wrong people knowing we were there if they already didn't. We didn't have the comm frequency for the Deneth either. So how to communicate?

Aki pulled back his helmet and yelled in perfect Denethian, "Where is the Princess Eriss?!?"

Some of the Denethians stopped firing. Some.

Aki 'listened.' He looked at me and nodded as he pulled on his helmet back on.

'I know where to go, Commodore,' he said.

'Good,' I responded, 'give it to them.'

The constant LPG fire hitting my shield just *burned*. I felt tears running down my cheeks, which was both annoying and ticklish because, of course, I couldn't do anything about them.

Aki projected through our minds and through the minds of the Denethians in front of us, 'This is the Three Furies Mercenary Fleet. We have boarded your Station and will kill anyone who does not immediately surrender to us. That is all.'

Aki looked at me now expectantly and I could feel Dalia and all the Marines turning towards me, but also focusing on our enemies.

The Denethians continued to fire. They started advancing towards us.

I dropped the shield and my people, Aki and Dalia included, put up a blistering field of projectile weapons fire. Not LPG.

I then formed another shield, a long one, as Dalia and the crew moved closer to the Deneth. Dalia quickly crumpled the noses of the Denethian LPGs. She moved lightning fast and the fire we were drawing was lessening mercifully. The excellent design of the DSS suits was protecting my people well. Every few seconds someone cried out in pain, but the suits sealed up again and we moved on.

The Denethians could not see or, at this point, feel the shield. They were getting closer, tossing their weapons now as Dalia wrecked them. My people kept firing. The leader of the Deneth got closer and I could hear his tail swishing in the Zero-G. His black eyes turned blue with blood lust, his body seeming to enlarge and his lethal extra claws came out.

My people may have been thinking, 'fuck me, that's fucking scary,' but they said nothing.

The hundred or so Deneth warriors bared their claws, moving closer like a cloud of ravenous predators.

I waited until I felt they were close enough.

I took my long, flat shield and smashed all of them, all hundred or so Denethian warriors against the clear Tenorium of the outer wall. Then I pushed. And pushed.

Some died with the force of the initial impact. More died as they were crushed with their brethren and the rest died within the six inches I left between the shield and the unforgiving Tenorium. And why, you ask, didn't we try to pod these folks? Because we didn't want to die. Stupid question.

I dropped the shield and looked at Aki. 'Where?'

Aki looked a bit pale, but was all business, 'Sector 21, Pelannate Apartments.'

It appeared on my helmet readout as he said it.

I 'pushed' myself towards the proper exit, feeling worn out. More than I would have expected, which surprised and worried me since this was just the beginning. Perhaps, I reasoned sarcastically, murdering scores of beings at once is more tiring than you'd remembered, Jane. In the end it didn't matter. I just needed us to hurry hurry hurry. I had to get back into space and help.

We flew through the fun house corridors of the Station immobilizing as we could, killing when we had no choice.

'Status on the projectiles,' Samuel said over the comm, cutting through the chatter.

'The second group is still moving into position,' Atalanta's voice replied.

'Why aren't they all heading for the surface?' I asked. 'Why are they waiting?'

'We'll be able to pick off a couple here and there while they're lining up,' Felix replied, 'but once they all launch at the planet we won't be able to be everywhere at once.'

'Final number on the projectiles?' That was Samuel.

'Four hundred ninety-eight.'

Almost five hundred. Something about that number bothered me. What it was, though, was beyond me.

'This is the *St. James*,' an unfamiliar voice said. 'Four projectiles were destroyed by our Marines.'

Four hundred ninety-four, then.

There were still so many of them, I thought as we 'flew' nearer the Pelannate apartments.

Then, out of nowhere, over my comm a completely unexpected voice said, 'I'm not taking sides, Thal. Though apparently you have.'

My god, it was David's voice, his tone bitter, but how the hell..?

'I need you to override the constructs, Sir,' Thal's voice said sternly.

I could easily picture David, his metaphorical back against the wall, shaking his head. 'No.'

'You can't play both sides against the middle anymore,' Thal said impatiently.

'The Denethian contracts...' David protested, sounding a little less sure.

'Damn it, David!' Thal almost yelled, his voice now full of emotion. That was Thalberg, no longer 'son' but angry 'father.' 'You fix this mess you helped create or I will never, ever forgive you.' Then Thalberg's voice dropped. 'Think of the others in your life who will hate you if you let Jane and her people die today.'

'They won't die,' David whispered.

'Can you guarantee that, son?'

Dead silence from David. In the background I could dimly hear the ship-to-ship babble of battle. I was pretty sure this transmission had been meant for me only. I really hoped I wasn't missing anything crucial in the larger scheme of things.

Wait a minute, what the hell did 'the others in [his] life' mean?

'Davy,' Thalberg said gently.

David took in a big breath and let it out slowly.

'I'll think about it,' he said quietly just as the comm feed was overridden with dozens of voices shouting.

'They've hit Terra 2!'

'The station's sublight is disabled!'

'She's starting to drift—pulling back into...'

'What are they *doing*?'

I felt something…break. Like someone had snapped the station clean in half.

'Synon,' Samuel said in his commanding voice, 'report!'

I felt a burst of heat. It was tiny at this distance. Too tiny for me to localize. God, no. Please not Sy's ship.

'The *Penelope* is gone, Admiral,' Synon's voice said quietly.

Three more bursts of heat. It felt like my heart stopped. Oh god.

'She'll have company,' he growled.

'Three hostiles destroyed,' someone reported.

I let out a breath I hadn't realized I'd been holding.

Synon continued, professionally unfazed, 'Our engines have been disabled, Sir, and the station has been decimated.'

'How many of your ships have mobility?'

'Only two, Sir, and…'

Small blips that felt like SLPG fire, then two more bursts of heat.

'I've given the evacuation order, Admiral,' Sy said.

'Status on station trajectory.'

'The station halves are headed out of the system.'

I exhaled hard with relief. Despite the heavy losses he'd accomplished his objective of keeping Terra 2 from smashing into Terra itself, but what a cost.

'Collect your people and get out of the way, General. Captain Friedman,' Samuel said calmly, though there was no way he was actually calm, 'send a ship for any stragglers.'

'Yes, Sir,' Paul answered. 'The *Megaera* is on its way.'

'Terra-Omega,' Samuel then said, his steely voice sending shivers down my spine, 'target Trithicate Station.'

Within that same Station we were finally where we needed to be; the door to the Holy of Holies, the black inner ball-shaped room that was the Pelann's private apartment. Twelve very large Deneth guards flanked it, floating in a rather threatening formation.

"Her Holiness is waiting for you, Commodore," the tallest one said in Denethian.

"Thank you," I responded in the same language as I nodded to Dalia. Ten seconds later the guards were all unconscious and punctured. 'Quinn? Where are you?' I asked into my comm just as I felt his Team Hotel approach. Quinn said nothing, just moved to my side.

I scanned inside the apartment. The Pelann's bio-signature. Ian's. Not Eriss'. I frowned. Just the two of them? Where was Eriss?

'Just the Pelann and Ian,' I said.

'We've reached the security level, Jane,' Felix said over my comm. 'But…'

The Pelann's door opened. I could see her, the Pelann, floating. Watching.

'…the Tarine are gone,' Felix said, his voice full of dread.

I felt sick. Were they already dead? Murdered by their re-creator? Was everything Eriss had sacrificed for already gone? Shirin, what have you done?

'Felix,' I said, 'neutralize as many of the warriors as you can and shut down those SLPGs.'

'We can't *find* any warriors to neutralize, Jane,' Felix said.

The Station rocked with a Union SLPG blast. The Station rocked but we, not standing on it or touching it, stayed still, completely unaffected. Surreal.

'We have to get off the Station,' Felix said.

It was Garrett who added, 'Before the Admiral destroys it.'

'You have your orders,' I said sternly. 'We're going to save the Station if we can.'

'*Save* it?' someone cried in disbelief.

'The Deneth will need to have somewhere to live when they lose. Pace out.'

The Station rocked again, this time harder. Alarms started screaming, but silenced after fifteen seconds. Someone was working, repairing as the damage to the Station grew. Technicians, engineers, support staff. Where, though, had the rest of the warriors gone?

The open door seemed to call me. It was time to see what the bitch's play was.

'Aki,' I said softly into my comm. He did not respond verbally, but I felt him nod as he turned on his exterior mic, both recording and broadcasting (to Samuel) what would come next, however it turned out.

"Come in, Commodore," the Pelann said in Standard. "You may bring your people, but helmets off. It's so impersonal speaking with someone through a mask, don't you think?"

I sighed as I pushed my helmet off the back of my head. Comm chatter continued uninterrupted through my earpiece. The sooner we heard her speech maybe the sooner we could arrest her and move on to bigger problems.

I moved into the apartment quickly, Dalia and Aki at my side. Some of my Marines came with me and the rest stayed outside, weapons ready.

My eyes immediately went to the wall where Ian was tied in a seemingly ceremonial fashion to a set of fixed silver handholds. The set-up looked very well-used. He was unconscious, but alive. Blood dripped from cuts on his face, his left eye was missing, but it felt as though the rest of him was in pretty good shape, considering the situation. I guessed that the visible injuries were there to provoke a reaction—and if I hadn't been able to scan and gauge the whole story that might have worked, the eye being a nice touch. On the 17 year old Jane it would have succeeded either way. Though I hurt for Ian I was, however, no longer green and seventeen.

"Release my friend," I said quietly.

"Of course," she said with a scary smile. Well, that was…easy. Seeing the not very well hidden look of surprise on my face, she explained, "He has served his purpose."

"Getting me here."

"Of course," she said again.

She pressed a button on her wrist cuff and the restraints on Ian disappeared into the wall and he floated, still unconscious, into the room. I looked at Captain Harley, my closest Marine, and he grabbed him. Ian was in uniform, but had no DSS. Captain Harley appeared to check over Ian for responsiveness, lingering on his face for a second. Ian twitched but then lapsed back into slackness.

All this I noticed, but what I was really doing was waiting for the other shoe to drop.

"Where is Eriss?"

Her smile grew wider. Fine, then.

Now Quinn took a breath and said, "Ma'am, I am arresting you on behalf of the Union for the crime of attempting to incite war."

Her good humor, if you could call it that, faltered. "*You.*" She turned to me. "You brought a thief to arrest me?"

"No, President Leder *sent* a thief to arrest you," I said.

I felt something, Denethian fury/adrenaline/something start flowing through her body. Her eyes turned from black to blue. Oh shit.

"Engage engines," she said to, apparently, no one.

At once I felt the hum, the vibration of the sublight engines for the Station come on. Full sublight.

Full sublight but only on one side of the Station.

The side away from Terra.

"Commodore," Dalia said, her voice shaking, "she's pushing the Station towards the planet."

I just stared at the Pelann. She watched me, fairly vibrating with contained violence. "Felix, belay the previous order. Disable all Station sublight engines immediately."

The Station shook again and once more with the SPLG fire from Samuel's Fleet, but I could also feel the blistering response from the Deneth.

I could also feel the Station moving. It would have been barely detectable to the naked eye, but I knew that the supers could feel it, not to mention the sensitive instruments on the Union ships.

"I was wrong, you know, Jane," the Pelann said, her voice almost calm.

"About so many things, Shirin, but what in particular were you wrong about today?"

"That a seat at the table would make the Deneth equal players."

I cocked my head to the side, regarding her. "You should have trusted the plan you made. It was inspired."

"Your approbation means so much to me, Jane, really," she said scathingly.

"I knew it would," I returned with saccharine sweetness. "Where are the Tarine?"

"The Tarine are on their way to Earth," she said with a tiny hint of triumph. "They should be there any minute now."

"On their way…" but how? The only things that were 'on their way' anywhere were… My eyes went wide. Five hundred Tarine had been 'made' by the slavers to the Pelann's order. There were almost exactly five hundred… "They are in the Arrows. You put them in the Arrows." Mother of god. The impact would kill them. Destroying the tubes they rode in would kill them. We'd already, unwittingly, killed at least four of them. "You really are a monster, aren't you?"

"If you like." She raised her head proudly. "My error was that I thought we could compete with gravity dwellers, but we can't, not if the only playing field is a planet."

'Reaching engineering now,' Felix reported in my ear, breathing hard. He'd obviously been 'flying' as quickly as he could to get there in time to… 'Fuck me running…' he gasped. I heard a battle scream that could only have come from the Deneth.

God, Felix. I needed to stop fucking around with Shirin and help my friend. More bad shit stopped me, however, before I could.

The Station went into hyper.

For two seconds.

Just enough to put it within Earth's gravity well.

I wanted to weep at the overwhelming odds against…anything. I just shook my head at her, ashamed of her, really. Humans and Rian were dead and dying, and there wasn't anything to say.

"The Deneth need to play a game they can win."

"Only a coward would start a war she can't possibly live to see finished," Quinn said contemptuously.

The Pelann's composure flickered for a second. "Ah, yes. Another error on my part, giving the apostate Tarine Telepathy." I really hoped Eriss was still alive. "I am no coward, General Quinn. Tell me," she leaned closer to him, "if you had a year or even a day to live, would you give any of it up before you had to?" Quinn swallowed, flicked his eyes to me then looked away. "Give up a second of the time you could be spending with your husband and your children?"

Quinn said nothing, but his answer was clear. Of course he wouldn't.

"I have a billion children," she said. "I won't see the end of the first battle."

I felt Earth's gravity lock greedily onto the massive object that was Trithicate Station and start its inexorable pull. We were very high over the Legislature, over D.C. All timed perfectly. I was impressed, or I would have been had I not had work to do.

"Gravity is impossible to overcome once it has you, Jane. The rest of the Deneth will fight to avenge me and the Tarine you Humans killed today. We will destroy your ships. We will vaporize your shipyards. Keep you trapped, isolated on your planets."

I nodded. "We'll be back in the pre-space age."

"You'll be more than that, Jane."

"We'll be slaves."

"Yes."

"I thought you had no love for slavers," Quinn said.

"Times change," she said quietly as she pressed another button on her wrist cuff.

I felt a jet of air disturb the space around us. No, not air.

"Pod Ian," I said as I watched Shirin, the last Pelann of the Rian convulse and seize before floating bonelessly in front of us. Captain Harley snapped Ian efficiently into a pod.

Shirin was dead, however. Her warriors no doubt were dead as well.

I inhaled just because I still could. Everyone had balked at the uncomfortableness of the nasal implant, but Quinn and I had guessed correctly that we'd need it. A tactical choice since an airborne poison was one of the easiest ways to disable a super. Ian, should he survive this, would probably be pissed that Harley had forced one up his nose when we'd arrived, but he'd have to be alive to be angry, so I wasn't worried.

'Felix!' I called.

'Here, Jane,' Felix said, sounding off, injured. 'The Denethians are all dead.'

'Status on our people.'

'We've lost some, but we can still cause damage before this thing hits the planet.'

'Get all the Macros outside the Station and rip out the sublight engines. I'll get between us and the planet. Everyone else needs to go capture all the Abrams Arrows.'

'Capture?'

'The Tarine are inside them. Godspeed.' Please let Eriss be in one of the ones that wasn't already destroyed. There was something else. Right.

'Admiral? Ian is alive. I'm sending him to you, but we don't have enough people to save all the projectiles.'

I imagined Samuel thinking, but apparently he'd already thought. 'Union Marines are being dispatched to assist in retrieving them. We'll save as many as we can.'

'Captain Harley, take Captain Fisher to the *Sheherazade*,' I said. The Captain immediately headed for the door, a floating Ian in tow. I looked at the rest of my people. 'We need to get out there.' I gritted my teeth, 'Follow me.'

I knew where the planet was. I pictured a corkscrew in my mind, turned it into a vortex in the direction I needed to go and 'pushed.'

The tough skin of the Station gave way like butter touched by a hot knife. Six minutes later we were out in space. There were no SLPGs now. There was no *one* to fight.

There was only a Station five miles across heading to destroy Terra.

I sent everyone away except Quinn who wouldn't leave and I didn't have the time or strength to argue with him. I put myself between Earth and the Station and I hovered there in the dark, the ship blocking the sun completely. I was glad Charles was safely far away. I was glad the people on the ships would at least survive. I was glad Wilby was safe on Novy. I was tired. I felt ill, weak, but there was no time for weakness.

Father in Heaven that Station was huge.

Then I heard a voice over my comm. 'Jane,' David said.

'It's too big, David,' I whispered.

'I know, love,' he responded calmly. Why was he calm? 'Divide the work.'

What the fuck was he talking about? The Station was still getting closer to the planet, almost in the atmosphere.

'Tell Sam to carve it up.'

Yes. *Yes.* 'Samuel, use the SLPGs!'

'Roger that,' was all he said in response, but within second the darkness was lit up with the holy horror of the beams of death slicing, dicing that Station into pieces.

I felt twenty humanoid shapes coming at us but took no action, too distracted to do anything more than create a shield bubble to protect Quinn and myself.

'Master Abrams sent us, Miss Jane,' a not-my-Thal voice said in my comm. 'The Denethians died too quickly for us to assist before, but we will act now. We are,' he laughed, 'Construction Constructs. We can move almost anything.'

Thank you, David, but I didn't have a chance to give voice to my gratitude. A large chunk of Station, about the size of a small ship, flew off to the left of us. 'Can you take that?' I asked the closest Thal to me. 'Protect the ships and the planet.'

Without a word he jetted through space, so quickly, even faster than I could move when I put my mind to it. He grabbed the chunk of Station and the back of his torso seemed to light up when he ignited an auxiliary engine. He pushed the hunk of debris. He pushed and pushed and slowly the metal stopped moving forward. Then it stopped moving at all. Holy crap.

Now my attention was focused on another section. I could feel Union ships moving closer, trying to get close enough to pull the bits of Station into their tractor beams.

I kept my eyes on the Station, barely hearing the constant stream of reports Samuel was hearing. One Arrow hit in the desert in Africa, wiping out a village. Another in the Indian Ocean, setting off a tidal wave. Ten were rescued by Marines. One more was stopped feet from the ground in Shanghai. One made it through to strike Vladivostok taking the city off the map. More were saved.

I watched the Station as it was shaved off bit by bit. The largest piece was coming at me. The piece I knew held the Pelann's body. All the Thals were engaged. The Pelann's Piece (as it would later come to be known) was coming at me like a slow meteor.

I put Quinn behind me and 'pushed.'

It was so big. Bigger than the *Scylla*, larger than the Octos of Napia.

Garrett, Felix and the other Macros had their hands full with the other bits, keeping them from hitting the ships, from hitting Luna, from making their way to Terra 1.

I remembered that mass meant nothing. I really did. I didn't tense up. My spine wasn't in danger, but all I could do was slow it and I could barely do that.

I could feel the buildings far below me. I could almost feel the burn of reentry through my DSS as we passed into the atmosphere.

'Felix!' I screamed.

'All Macros to Jane,' Samuel ordered.

I felt them coming, tiny supers moving from space into the thin air above the planet.

Too fast. It was still falling too fast.

The Legislature is empty, I kept telling myself. The Legislature has been evacuated, but an object this size would destroy the planet when it hit. The damage as bad as it had been when we'd fractured Pace 3.

I 'pushed' harder. It slowed just a bit more.

'We're coming, Jane,' Garrett said.

Tell Charles I'm sorry, I thought, not daring to be clichéd enough to voice the words aloud.

Clouds passed me by, getting my DSS wet.

Still I 'pushed.'

God, it wasn't going to work.

'I can't get in front of it in time!' Felix said.

'Pull, then!' Quinn growled. He grabbed me around the waist.

'Let me go, you idiot!' I said through clenched teeth. 'Get out of here!'

'Fuck you, Jane,' was his tense reply. Fair enough. I had no more energy to devote to his stupidity. I only had enough to spend on mine.

But I felt the 'pull' on the Pelann's Piece. My friends, I couldn't even figure out how many now I was so tired, were slowing it.

I summoned all the strength I thought I had (and a bit more) and 'pushed,' using the might and solidity of Terra itself to brace me.

We were slowing. Slowing.

It slowed more.

I heard one of the Macros scream. I could hear Garrett breathing into his mic like he was running.

The buildings were visible now, though they were far enough away to still look like toys. It was raining beneath the cloud cover.

I put my hands out now as the giant wall of metal came closer to me. I'd run out of room to retreat. I'd run out of room entirely.

'Jane,' Quinn pleaded.

The ground.

I found my back was on the grass, Quinn beside me. The same grass we'd run over to get into the *Hominum* years ago. Off in the distance was the clearing where Criss had died. Fitting, I thought distractedly.

I looked up at the mass of metal and Tenorium, at the Pelann's tomb, the rain falling on it now instead of on Quinn and me.

I 'pushed' and 'pushed.'

The Pelann's Piece still slowed, then slowed some more, then swallowed me up, just as I felt the large body of Quinn cover me.

Quinn grunted and I felt a sharp pain in my shoulder. The pain was impossible and I passed out.

Journo Conference: High Admiral Samuel Armstrong speaks to the Union, October 8th, 2873

"This is Tabitha Carson, Union One Galactic Journo Coverage, with an exclusive report on the violent and unprovoked attack by the Deneth Rian on the gravity-dwelling members of our Union." An exquisitely dressed

woman with shiny black hair, luminous brown eyes and a small 'serious face' frown stared at the camera. "We are expecting word from the Admiralty and the Union President's office momentarily, but before we hear the official version," her sneer made it clear that anything official would be a lie, "of these distressing and deadly events, this reporter has received information that the attack, which the President's Office has called 'rogue,' is actually the start of a larger war."

Images filled the screen, amateur photographs of a ball of fire in the sky. Another of it closer and larger.

"The Residents of the District of Columbia that defied the evacuation order saw something yesterday that none of them had ever expected to see again. Death raining down on the Union Government. The following still images were taken from amateur video recordings made at the scene. The man in the pictures has been identified as Genral Quinn- Pace and the woman is, of course, the Red Angel herself."

An older male voice spoke over the images, "That thing was [beep]ing huge. I almost [beep] myself when I saw it comin' down on us."

The next picture showed two tiny figures between the giant torn block of metal and the ground. Then another was a similar picture in profile. Earth, two small dots and the Pelann's Piece.

The man continued, "That's twice in less 'n ten years we almost got [beep]ing squashed."

Now two pictures: the space-suited Jane Pace had her back to the planet, her arms outstretched, pushing at the air. The much larger (also suited) man held her around the waist and the metal hovered over them both. Their suits were wet with rain. The second picture was almost the same, except the two humans were now in the shadow of the object.

"And how do you feel about this, Mr. Parker?" the voice of the on-scene reporter asked. The T.I. cut to an older man, bald with a large bulbous nose and beady black eyes.

"If that Red Angel girl hadn't stopped this [beep] we'd all be dead, but who knows if she'll be here next time somethin' happens?" He scratched his head loudly. "Women. You can't depend on those [beep]s for nothing." The reporter coughed loudly. The old man looked at the camera. "The [beep]ing taxes are killing me, too." He glared at the reporter. "I'm [beep]ing leaving."

Miss Carson back in the studio smothered her amusement. 'Serious news' face firmly back on she said, "Civilian casualties have been at a *minimum, but many military lives were lost, though we will get more details of these losses at the journo conference that is about to start. A source within the President's Office is sure, however, that President Leder will be doing everything in his power to downplay this attack in an effort to stop a war." She paused for effect. "A war that may already have started."*

Her expression softened slightly as she paused. "There are two questions, however, I would like to put to President Leder and High Admiral Armstrong: one, even if we can buy the idea that the Pelann was off her rocker and acted unilaterally, how can we just forget images like these?"

The picture showed the barest second before the Pelann's Piece touched the soft grass of the field in front of the Legislature. "Mr. Parker spoke of the Red Angel, Commodore Jane Pace. Here she is moments before being crushed by the Pelann's plans." Jane stared at the mass above her, the enormous man with her was just a blur of motion, already in the process of throwing himself protectively over her.

Then the second image, a beautiful one in its starkness, was of the large piece of the thousand year old Trithicate Station imbedded in the ground. The still pristine Homimum stood in the background. The detail on the Pelann's Piece in the picture was incredible; visible were corridors, wiring, broken windows, doors askew. The two humans were gone from sight, but there were three bodies, all Denethian, lying dead on the grass. One with long, white, ornately-braided hair.

Miss Carson continued, "And two: where is the Red Angel?" She paused as if listening to something and then nodded. "We're going live to the journo conference as Union President Leder prepares to take the stage on the lawn in front of the Senatus building."

The image then shifted to an outdoor stage set up. President Leder moved behind a podium at the stage's center. High Admiral Samuel Armstrong stood next to him as did the President of the Senatus, Terran President Mahajan, the Speaker of the Hominum, assorted Senators and other worthies as well as Captain Friedman and Marston Manthorpe. The white bulk of the Senatus took up the rest of the frame. President Leder looked directly into the bank of journo cameras and mics.

"Good evening to all members of our Galactic Union." He took a breath and looked around him at what was probably a large crowd of supporters, reporters and the generally curious. "Yesterday was a difficult day in our history, but we have prevailed thanks to the dedication, bravery

and sacrifice of our Union military personnel. High Admiral Armstrong will give you a more detailed account of what happened and why, but first I would like to say how proud I am of our team. As bad as this was, it could have been catastrophically worse. Admiral Armstrong led a team of our best people, of Terran Humans, Heely Humans, and supernormals and they fought cleverly and fiercely to protect what is ours.

"Of our defenders, it was the Heely Humans and the supernormals who suffered the greatest losses in this battle. General Synon of Novy Heliot," Leder gestured over his shoulder and the big Heely (who had not been visible before) stiffly rose from a chair to his feet towering over everyone, "lost half his force while keeping the debris from Terra 2 Station from damaging both Terra and Luna. Thank you, General, for your efforts." Leder bowed and Synon bowed his head, closing his eyes as he did so. The camera moved closer, bringing the new deep scars over every visible inch of his green skin. Leder gestured for Synon to sit back down and the Heely did so.

"There are those who command our Union supernormals, General Manthorpe of the ESTF and Captain Friedman of the Three Furies Mercenaries Fleet." Leder gestured to Marston and Paul who also bowed their heads. "They entrusted their people, the Marines, the Telepaths, Telekinetics, and staff with the future and safety of all our peoples. They did not let us down, though they paid dearly."

"They are not the only ones that paid, though, for it wasn't just Humans that suffered. Our newest Ambassador, Eriss Fenton of the Rian, and her fellow Tarine Rian were also victims of the Pelann's scheme." His expression turned grim. "Over two hundred of the previously almost five hundred Tarine died yesterday. There will be a memorial for them in two days' time, but," he looked up, "the Pelann's genocidal plan, like all her others, failed."

There was a collective gasp as a slight feminine figure dressed in black hovered, delicate wings glistening in the light, then landed next to the President. He smiled at her as he took her hand then kissed her cheek. "Ambassador Fenton has pledged to get justice for all our people, punish those who have wronged the Union and help put right what could have gone so terribly wrong."

There were many murmurs in the audience at that, but he ignored them. "The Deneth Rian are, as yet, not our enemy. The Pelann was dead by her own hand as Trithicate Station met its end. Ambassador Fenton and *her people, supported by the Union, will be traveling to the other Denethian Stations to find answers."*

Now the murmurs became a roar. He held up his hand for silence and got it, but just barely.

"Then lastly, before I finally let the High Admiral speak, many of you want to know how and where Commodore Pace is." His eyes flicked to the Admiral for a second, but the Admiral had no reaction. "She is alive and recovering in a private location."

"So, she's all right?" someone shouted out. "She'll be back?"

Leder's expression remained unchanged, "She is alive and recovering." He turned to Admiral Armstrong. "High Admiral, if you would..?"

Admiral Armstrong stepped forward after shaking Leder's hand. "Thank you, Mr. President." He took his place behind the podium. "The first thing I have to say is that, while we were good, we were also lucky. The Tungsten 'Abrams Arrows' that the Pelann sent to destroy our capital planet would have succeeded in doing so had they not been hollowed out in order to hold the Tarine Rian. The damage from the projectiles that got past us was terrible but not catastrophic because of this. It does not change the losses incurred, but it could have been so much worse."

He took a breath, having gotten that out of the way, and said, "The on-planet death tolls are, as of this hour, as follows..."

From evening of the day of the battle, the day before the journo conference...

11:49 – Jane's Infirmary Room, Washington General Hospital, Washington, D.C., Terra, October 7th, 2873

I opened my eyes and stared at the pale beige walls of what had to be an Infirmary ceiling. Well fuck me running, I was alive, and, apparently, so was everyone else since I could feel the slow steady turn of Earth below me. Excellent. I heard voices speaking softly outside my partially open door. Samuel, Ian (something was over his left eye socket, a patch I guessed), Atalanta and someone I didn't recognize who I assumed was a doctor-type. It was then I realized I was not alone in my room; Quinn was slumbering on the other side of the curtain. That was a relief.

I scanned him. He was heavily bandaged on his left side and hooked up to all kinds of monitors. I felt a stab of guilt. I hadn't wanted him to get hurt protecting me, of course, even if I couldn't forgive him for separating me from Wilby. I 'looked' inside him to see what was under the bandage and felt, instead of the familiar slightly rough texture of bones, smoothness. I had a flash of him over me and his grunt of pain as part of the metal of the Pelann's Piece went through his flesh and into…mine. I involuntarily felt my (already) bad shoulder. Bandages. Lots and lots of stitches, but the same old crappy bones underneath. So no surgery for me, but plenty for him. Not what I'd wanted, but I'd told him to leave me, damn it. Yeah, that sounded defensive and guilty even to me.

The voices outside the room raised a bit, someone getting quite agitated. Ian. Everyone was speaking except, I frowned, except Atalanta. Odd. I crept out of bed silently and made my way to the door to eavesdrop.

"We need to figure out how to tell her now before she wakes up," Ian said angrily. "She needs to know."

The strange voice, the doctor's, I had to assume, said, "I, for one, am just relieved that we didn't have to operate on her. Too dangerous in her condition. General Quinn saved more than just her life today."

That didn't make any sense to me, but I didn't pay too much attention to it.

"Is his husband on the way?" the doctor asked.

"Yes," Samuel answered, "I got a message from Dr. Quinn-Pace late last night. He should be here tomorrow."

"Jane will have to be out of here by then," Atalanta said, her voice tired and flat. Yes, yes I would have to be. Fucking Quinn.

"Why would she have to leave..?" Samuel started.

I felt Atalanta shake her head. "A reason too idiotic to go into, Sir."

"We should be able to release her later today," the doc cut in smoothly, "and she'll just have to check in every couple of days so that we can keep an eye on her wound."

"What about the baby?" Samuel asked.

There were a few seconds there where I swear the word 'baby' had no meaning for me. It was total gibberish.

Then my brain caught up, at least part way.

There's a *baby*?

"She'll have to be told," Atalanta said, her voice sounding even more dead.

What baby?

"You're sure she has no idea?" the doctor said, then she seemed to correct herself, "She would never have risked herself if she'd known." She said with confidence.

Samuel barked out a laugh and Ian said, "I don't think we can definitively say that," I felt him scratch his chin, "though we've never seen her in this situation before."

What fucking baby?

I felt a wave of panic coming. I stomped the crap out of it.

"I'll tell her when she wakes up," Atalanta said quietly.

"Thank you, Atalanta," Samuel said kindly.

"I just don't understand how this could happen," she said, then she paused to allow the men their snickers. "She's on the ten year shot, we all are. We got them when we came back to Terra. I *know* she got it and I *know* she doesn't want children."

I was having real trouble convincing myself that she was talking about someone else. It seemed impossible (not to mention really stupid) that I was even trying, but my brain just couldn't compute the obvious. It was, however, getting harder to hold back the panic.

"According to her Union Med records," the doc said as she, I guessed, checked my file, "the injected prophylactic was still in her system in late 2870 when she was discharged from this facility after her...accident."

"After she broke her back stopping the Aquaformer from killing everyone," Ian almost snarled. "That the accident you mean?"

"I'm sorry, Captain," she said, embarrassed.

"Forget about it."

"But there is no trace of it in her system according to the Phoenix Independent Mercenary exam records from February of 2871." After my back had been repaired and I could walk again. "It had to have been counter-acted somewhere in that period of time."

I heard Atalanta's sharp intake of breath. I felt a bit dizzy myself.

There was only one motherfucker who could have nullified my birth control.

"What happened in the time in between these two exams?" the doc asked.

I hardly heard her now being kind of overcome with chills and nausea. Don't forget the panic which was getting harder and harder to deny, either. Moth-er-fuck-er.

"Abrams," Atalanta said quietly.

"Mother of god," Ian murmured. Samuel said nothing, but I felt him tense up, stomach roiling with anger.

Still safely on the other side of the door, I knelt to put my head in my hands over my knees.

This can't be happening.

It can't be.

I can't be a…

"You think David Abrams deliberately counteracted her medication?" the doc was horrified. She had never met David. Obviously. "Without her consent?"

I felt my friend shrug.

"I think," Ian said carefully, "Abrams should get the hell out of the system. Once you tell Jane, she'll…"

Atalanta nodded. "You're right. I'll take care of it and look after her when she wakes."

"She's still asleep?" the doc asked, dubiously.

I felt the muscles on Atalanta's lovely face pull into what had to be one of the most genuine fake smiles of all time. "Poor girl is exhausted. I'll go in now and wait." I moved quickly back into bed, wincing a bit as I pulled my stitches. I closed my eyes in a poor semblance of feigned sleep.

Then, unexpectedly, I heard Atalanta say, "Ian, what's wrong? Why are you so guilty?"

Ian leaned hard against the wall. "I know the name of her daughter."

What the ever living hell?

"What do you mean?" Samuel asked sharply.

"Arrow," he said, swallowing as though his mouth was dry, "she saw it. She said that the little girl would be unusual, like her mother, and I asked who her mother was and she said…"

"Jane," Samuel breathed.

"Why didn't you say anything, you asshole?" Atalanta said tearfully.

"I…I forgot," he said guiltily. "I'm so sorry."

"You've known how long?" Samuel let some of his anger show through.

"Since last year," Ian said listlessly, "I should have told her, but things were so awful with Arrow and it was the only vision she'd had in months that had made her happy. It got lost in everything else." He hung his head. "I'm not sure I really believed it."

However, Arrow was never wrong, I thought. He'd known that and he'd said nothing. I was angry, true, but being angry at Ian was different than being angry at David. Ian'd suffered so much and though he could have prevented it had he said something, this wasn't his fault. I knew I wouldn't have been so forgiving if Arrow were alive and happy, but she wasn't. Atalanta seemed to have reached the same conclusion because, for all her spike of fury, she just said, "Oh, Ian."

"What is the child's name?" Samuel asked.

"Lucy."

"It's a nice name," Samuel said thoughtfully.

"Arrow thought so, too," Ian said sadly. "I...I...Eriss is expecting me."

"We need to look at that eye, Captain Armstrong," the doctor said.

Right, Ian's missing eye. His eyes were always so beautiful.

"Fuck my eye," he said angrily. "I'm going now."

Samuel nodded. "I'm due at the Admiralty."

"I'll let you know if there is any change." Atalanta's voice was confident. Everyone, even Atalanta, which was odd, walked off.

I waited. Five minutes. Ten. Fifteen. What the heck?

I tried to push away everything, but every minute I was alone made that more and more difficult.

Ian had *known* and, apparently, knew I was going to keep and raise the baby. My daughter.

But...

What if she gets hurt?

What if she gets sick?

What if she hates me because I'm a killer?

What if she just hates me in general?

What if the child hates freaks?

What if the child *is* a freak?

What if someone hurts my baby because they want to punish me?

What about Idis? How could she see this baby as anything other than a betrayal of the spirit of our too-new arrangement? Would she forgive me? Should she?

Will Charles hate me?

Will Charles hate me as much as I hate myself for not wanting this child?

My wheels were spinning out of control. I stood up. Sat down. Lay down. Stood up again. There was no physical relief and no mental relief either. I wanted to throw up, but that wasn't happening, for once. I was having trouble breathing.

The most important recurring thought I had, however, was something Atalanta had said when *her* life had fallen apart. She'd said there was a difference between not wanting a theoretical baby and saying no to a real one.

I *could* abort; I was a Micro, for god's sake. I could say it was a miscarriage, go back on the shot (or just have myself sterilized permanently) and everything would be back to normal. When it came down to it, though, I couldn't do that to Charles. I just couldn't. It wasn't in me. I had lost. Arrow had been right again. She was right and I was trapped. Trapped forever.

My vision was starting to blacken scarily. I lay down on the bed before I fell down.

Finally, Atalanta strode in and quietly closed the door behind her. She was carrying a medium-sized black bag that looked familiar. Once she was inside, however, she hissed, "Jane!"

I opened my eyes but couldn't see her. I was falling down a well of fear.

"Oh, Jane," she said sympathetically and she moved over to me quickly and put her soft small hands on either side of my face, pumping a huge drugging dose of calm and affection into me. After a minute I could breathe. She helped me sit up.

"I'm so sorry, love," she said.

"Not sorrier than I am, 'Lanta," I said. I felt a tear fall. I wondered what had taken it so long. "Thanks for letting me listen in. It was easier that way." I snorted, "Well, not easier exactly."

"No, but no one needs an audience for that sort of revelation."

Those big brown eyes were so sad. "I'm sorry, too, 'Lanta."

She shook her head, "You can't apologize for getting accidently knocked up by your son of a bitch sociopath ex-boyfriend."

"Not for that."

Her expression softened. "Not for keeping the baby, either." She leaned forward and kissed me on the cheek. "Ok?"

Not even close. "Ok."

She looked at her watch and immediately stood up, her comforting body language gone in a flash. Now she was all adrenaline and excitement.

"We have only a couple of minutes before someone realizes that I didn't warn Abrams that you were coming for him."

"What?"

"Focus, Jane. The *Foudroyant* is still moored by the station. Take this." She handed me the bag. I held it numbly, my mind stuck on what she'd said.

The *Foudroyant*. Where my treacherous ex-lover had taken away my protection and then, if memory served, had tried to fuck me into oblivion in the days before I'd finally left him. God, if he'd managed to get me pregnant I would never have been free of the bastard. Not, I thought bitterly, that I was all that free of him now, but I *could* be. I could be permanently free of him. I started stripping and putting on the DSS. Oh yeah, I was going to see that motherfucker.

"You can't kill him," she said sternly.

"There is no one I can't kill if I really want to," I said angrily, "you know that."

"No shit," she said, miffed, "but you can't allow yourself to do it. *You* know that."

"I want him to pay and I want him out of my life, 'Lanta."

She nodded. "So punch him in the nose, yell at him, but," she bit her luscious lip, "he's a father of four and you are going to be a mother. Not a mother on the run or in prison." Her eyes twinkled. "Just a regular run-of-the-mill supernormal teacher who can lift buildings with her mind and take out any enemy with a thought in love with the baby's father who happens to be an Emperor." She smiled, her cheek dimpling.

"Oh, one of *those* people," I scoffed, amused in spite of myself.

"So punch him in the nose, or in the balls if that will make you feel better, and move on."

Unfortunately, I would have to face all of it then. Once I'd moved on. I felt the panic start to return, sweat beaded my brow. Atalanta's eyes went wide with alarm and she took my hands, but this time instead of pumping calm, she pumped fury. I exhaled hard. Yes, anger now, despair later. Or something more. I felt, for the first time in a while, that pull to crazy that took it all away. Yes, I thought. I could go back to the farm. Until my child is eighteen. A funny thought, though I was pretty sure part of my brain wasn't laughing.

"So, to recap: punch him for Jane and *don't kill him* for…"

"Lucy," I said. Wow. I'd said my daughter's name for the first time. So strange.

"For Lucy. Now get your ass out of here before they try to stop you and you have to make a mess." She went to the window and opened it wide.

"You're too good to me, 'Lanta," I said as I 'pushed' myself off the ground.

"You don't have to tell me," she preened, sounding much more like her old self.

I sealed my helmet and 'flew.'

The relatively short journey to the *Foudroyant*, unfortunately, gave me more time to think. Mostly what I thought was thank god for those stupid annoying sex socks (condoms) that they'd required on Gloriana-Levvon since I had had a *lot* of (apparently) fertile sex in the last couple of years. Obviously I knew that this was Charles' baby, but I couldn't help wondering what would have happened had it been...Wilby's, Stoney's (though I was pretty sure HMs were produced sterile), Synon's (nope, not genetically compatible) or, god, Samuel's. He would have had a new baby when he'd lost Arrow. Would that have helped his grief at the loss or... No, it was best not to dwell on that, though I wondered if the thought had crossed Samuel's mind. No, if this had to happen, Charles would be the best man to be Lucy's father. Hell, he already was an excellent father. He could make this child a good one even if her mother was a complete waste of time. It was a comforting thought. Mostly.

The elegant bulk of the *Foudroyant* finally loomed in front of me. I turned my head to switch on my comm. "Commodore Pace hailing the *Foudroyant*."

"*Foudroyant* here, Commodore. What may we do for you?" a sterile male voice answered. A not-Thal. I wondered if he had any humans working for him at all anymore. It made sense; humans had never meshed well with his need to control everything in the universe. What an asshole.

"I need to see Mr. Abrams privately. I'm outside Airlock A."

"One moment, Ma'am."

A pause. An interesting one, for me anyway, because I felt a humanoid-ish presence come up behind me. My Thal, if I could call him that. How did I know it was my Thal? Because I'd asked him to modify one of his servos (in his neck) so that it was just slightly off, just miscalibrated enough to make a vibration I could 'feel.' He pulled up next to me, floating in space with the help of his built-in jets.

"Miss Jane."

"Atalanta asked you to come?"

"Yes and no," Thal equivocated over my comm. "I knew I needed to be here in any case."

"Why?" I laughed bitterly.

"Insurance."

For whom, I wondered. I looked at my friend and was surprised by his expression. He wasn't suited, of course, which made him much easier to read. His posture told me he was Thalberg, but also told me something else. That he felt guilty. Horribly so.

Then I knew why.

Because he'd known. *This* was the thing he'd been prohibited from telling me. (It only occurred to me much later that it had been naïve of me to assume that only *one* thing had been kept from me in reference to David, but it was what I'd thought at the time.)

"Are you going back to him, Thal?"

"No. Not even if you send me back," he sounded tired but resolved. His voice dropped. "Or away."

I thought about it, but that was a purely academic exercise. Thal was my friend and he was a victim of programming as much as…well, as much as David was. Thal would stay, had to stay because I had offered him my friendship. I was trapped there, too. The calm of the crazy called me harder than it had last time. No, I told it, not yet. David first. "If you have to choose between him and me, whom will you choose? I need to know."

He straightened, somehow managing it even in zero-g. "He is my son and I will never give up on him, but you are my first friend. I chose you and I still choose you."

I felt a traitorous lump in my throat. "Ok."

The voice from the ship returned in my helmet, "Commodore, you and your Thal have been cleared to enter through Airlock A. The Master will meet you there."

So they'd scanned and found Thal. Or just looked out the Tenorium window. I didn't care. One more question. "Are Mr. Abrams' children onboard, Thal?"

"No, Ma'am," the Thal responded sounding slightly surprised. I was relieved. His kids didn't need to see what their son-of-a-bitch father looked like after he'd gotten what was coming to him.

"Opening outer Airlock door now," I said as I pressed the green button and pulled the door open.

"Acknowledged, Commodore."

Thal and I went in and the outer door shut behind us. We waited in silence as the small room repressurized and we were able to stand in the artificial gravity. The inner door went green and I pulled off my helmet leaving it hanging off the back of my DSS. I scanned on the other side of the inner door. "David and two Thals."

"Not unexpected."

"Yeah."

The door opened away from us (into the body of the ship) and there David was. He looked fine. For about ten seconds.

"Jane, I…" was all he was able to say before I stepped into the corridor and punched him square in the nose breaking it soundly. Best crunch I'd ever heard. He dropped like a stone.

He screamed, mostly in fury that I'd gotten the drop on him, and yelled, "Thals!"

I looked expectantly at his mechanized henchmen, ready to take them out, but they stayed where they were. David screamed at them again through the veil of blood covering half his face, but still nothing.

Then he turned his furious glare to my Thal. "What the fuck are you doing?"

"Making sure you get your comeuppance, son, and," he looked pointedly at me, "nothing more." I shrugged. I was still furious, but I'd gotten a lot more enjoyment out of the nose thing than I'd thought I would. I was good. Or good enough.

David rose painfully, attempting to blot his nose on his grey jacket. The Thals stepped forward to assist him, but they were shaken off.

"What did I do now?"

I folded my arms over my chest. "You switched off my birth control, motherfucker. Want to know how I know that?"

David paled, or I think he did, the blood made it harder to tell.

"So you're pregnant?" He leaned against the wall. "With Fitz's child?"

"Yep," I said with as much venom as I could muster—and that was a fuckton of venom.

He took his sleeve from his face. The blood was seeping now instead of running, but he sounded congested. It made me happy. "You're not going to *keep* it?"

"You think I would do that to Charles?"

"If he doesn't know yet," he searched my face, "and I think he doesn't, you can end it before it gets too far."

"I know that, but that isn't how it's going to go."

"Jane," he hesitated, "you can't be mother to a helpless baby. You know that. You told me that."

It was harder to get air into my lungs. Just moving my rib cage up and down felt like too much work. "I'll figure it out, David."

"What about the danger to the baby?"

Breathe, Jane, breathe.

"You don't know what it's like to have children to protect, Angel." He shook his head, but had to stop to blot his nose again. "You were more right than even you knew. That child will *never* be safe. How can you or your precious Fitz," the name in his mouth was an insult, "be selfish enough to risk that?

My vision was going gray around the edges. I was being called back to the crazy farm.

"David, stop it!" Thalberg ordered, but David could not be stopped.

"You never even *had* parents, how can you even consider trying to be one?"

Spots. I was seeing spots while he was ripping out all my fears and throwing them at me. A Telepath couldn't have done a better job.

"Parenting is an impossible job under normal circumstances. You can never even come close to normal. You aren't up to this and you know it."

I wished he wasn't right. I *wasn't* up to this. Someone was screaming. It might have been me. It was too much. It was overwhelming, the fear, it reached up and...

...suddenly I could breathe.

I was standing on what felt like a space ship. Three robots stood around me, one of them looking with fear into my face. The lone other (Terran) human was a handsome man with a broken nose. Recently broken if all the blood was any indication. Hmm. Interesting. Had to be a story there. My hand felt sore. I looked down at the blood on it. Not mine, I guessed. Huh.

I smiled at them. For some reason this seemed to really freak the human and the concerned robot out.

"Miss Jane?" the robot asked delicately. "Are you alright?"

I nodded cheerfully. I felt pretty good, actually. Happy. "Why wouldn't I be?" I asked, amused. My name was Jane, apparently.

"What the hell is going on?" the human whispered, sweat adding to his blood. Yuck.

The robot shook his head, apparently to shut the human up. "This has happened before. Dr. Wilby told me before he left."

"What are we talking about?" I asked pleasantly. God, everyone was so serious.

"Nothing, my dear," the robot said, smiling. "My name is Thalberg and I work for you, look after you, really. Your name is Jane Pace and you are a Commodore in the Union Navy."

"Oh," I said. I pointed at the bloody human. "Who is he?"

"No one, Miss Jane," Thalberg said coldly. "Someone's disappointing son."

The human winced.

"We need to go, Miss Jane," Thalberg offered me his arm and I took it. We went into an airlock saying not another word to the dejected looking human. The inner door sealed. "Let's put on your helmet," he said gently, but he had to help me do it. The pressure left the little room and we started to float. Wonderful feeling.

"Where are we going, Thalberg?"

"On a trip, Miss, in your space ship." Thalberg bit his lip as if thinking. "After I make a few calls."

"Sounds like fun," I said, because it did. "Are we going far?"

"A couple of days' journey with one stop on the way."

The outer door opened and we went into space. I kept a good hold of Thalberg since my suit didn't seem to have jets on it. Odd, that.

"I have my own ship?" I said, enjoying the sensual pleasure that seemed to come from Zero-G.

"You sure do, Miss Jane. The *Liberty*."

"That's a nice name."

"It is," sadness flickered across his mobile plastic face but it disappeared as soon as he started speaking in a very different tone into his helmet. "This is Commodore Pace's Thalberg, I need to speak to Lord Miller on Gloriana-Levvon immediately. Yes, I'll wait."

Into the constant night we flew.

A Note from the Jane Pace of the year 2890 regarding the Jane Pace of 2873

My friend and defacto editor, Atalanta Pace, thought I should clarify something about this particular trip of mine to the 'crazy farm.' While I am, at present, as sane as I can be, I have written the following as I remembered it, as though the 2890 me was years off from existing. The experience of losing my mind (for the second time) was an unusual one and I put it in this book as I lived it. I did it this way deliberately in order to explain the toll fear of impending motherhood was taking on me to you, the Reader, but also to remind myself of the strength of feeling that comes with being young and the will needed to persevere.

10:02 – A Beautiful Room, Somewhere, October 10th, 2873

I awoke on our first morning on the planet. I was alone, something I hadn't been since I had found myself on that ship three days ago. Or was it four? Sunlight flowed in through wide open old-fashioned glass windows illuminating a wood floor covered with richly patterned carpet. My bed had partially opened deep red curtains around it and there was more of that color in the fabric on the walls. I could see a heavily carved and ornate ceiling just beyond my curtains and a stone sort of half-table thing over a bricked kind of exhaust tube on the wall. Somewhere in my head the word 'fireplace' and 'chimney' popped up, though I had the feeling I'd never actually seen such things in real life.

The breeze from outside was sweet and slightly cool. All in all it seemed a perfect place. I stretched my arms over my head luxuriously and went over once again what I had been told.

I was a Commodore, though no one would tell me what I was Commodore of exactly.

My memory was temporarily gone due to some kind of psychological trauma.

I was among friends who would try to help me get my memory back.

I was unexpectedly pregnant by the man I loved, Emperor Charles Six of Corsica. (That last had been quite the surprise, I can tell you.)

I 'felt' gently inside my body for the tiny, oh-so-tiny, heartbeat of my daughter. I hadn't told anyone that I could do this—but then I didn't know that everyone else couldn't do it either. I didn't think so, though, somehow, but I didn't want to stop being able to do it, so I kept it to myself.

Someone, Thalberg I immediately realized, knocked on the door and I stopped 'feeling' her heartbeat guiltily.

"Yes, Thalberg?"

"Someone to see you, Miss Jane."

"One second, please."

I rose quickly and threw on the robe they'd given me. It was too fancy and way too heavy, but it was pretty. Didn't seem like me (though how I'd come to that conclusion was beyond me) but I didn't want to meet some stranger half-naked. Everyone was a stranger these days.

I stood next to the bed as presentable as I was going to get and said, "Come in."

The door opened and Thalberg stepped aside to admit a tall, spare-looking red-haired man with golden eyes that turned black when they saw me. Wow. Pretty.

I smiled. The man paled beneath his freckles. I had to stop smiling at people, I thought, it only freaks them out. I dropped the smile. I saw his black-gold eyes go to my stomach. Oh.

"You must be the Emperor." And my baby's father. You know, in case you were confusing him with some other Emperor I'd slept with. Then again, who knew? Sleeping with Emperors could be my thing.

His expression turned tragic as he bowed his head. I felt tears in his eyes. "I just wanted you to know, Commodore, that you don't have to worry about anything. I will make sure you are taken care of and taken care of well. This is my home and it is open to you for as long as you need it."

"That is very kind of you, Sir."

"It's nothing I assure you." His chest was clogged. I immediately felt terrible and frustrated because my loss of memory was causing him pain. He was probably a wonderful man. Why would anyone want to forget him?

"Thank you, Sir."

He nodded.

"I am so sorry about all this…"

He waved his hand, dismissing my apology. Not as if it didn't matter, but as if it hurt too much to hear. Damn it. "I have a meeting so I have to go, but I will be back tomorrow if you don't mind."

"Of course, Sir." He turned to go, but I had been taken again by the beauties of the room and the large house it was part of. "You said this is your home?"

He turned back. "I was born here."

"It is the most beautiful place I have ever seen," I said before I realized what a stupid thing that was to say, considering. "What is it called?"

"Robin Hill." He took a breath. "Until tomorrow, then."

With that he left, I thought, before tears could fall.

I sat down hard on the bed. Here I was in the loveliest place I could imagine, apparently ruining everything for an Emperor and everyone around him.

Fuck.

ENTRY 6-8-89

11:30 – Library, Robin Hill, Irena, Corsican Empire, October 14th, 2873

Three more days had passed. I saw the Emperor every day at 10am. We didn't talk much. Mostly we just walked the grounds on the castle/house/mansion/palace. There were gardens, both the flower and kitchen kind, cozy tunnels carved out of hedges leading to nooks with benches and sun shades, and ornamental pools at interesting places. All planned to look whimsical and, well, *un*planned. There was a lake, I knew (the estate was in the middle of it), but the Emperor's face had fallen at its mention, so I'd never asked about it again.

Once the Emperor returned to work I had the run of the house. No one pushed me to remember anything. They watched me, though. It turned my visit to Robin Hill into a sort of 'waiting for the bomb go off while on a nice vacation' affair. It was odd, but not unpleasant.

I did have a constant companion, however, aside from the discretely ever-present Thalberg. It was a middle-aged man, a little heavy, dark hair, dark eyes with a sallow, fattish face and a look of general bitterness about him. He'd told me his name was Soames Cherwell that first afternoon in Corsica when he'd appeared in front of me. He was a friend of mine from way back and he said no one else would be able to see or hear him since he'd been dead for some years.

"So, you are a ghost?" I asked, surprised at how comfortable I was with him. Perhaps because I'd already accepted my crazy as normal, a new twist on the old insanity. Or perhaps because somewhere in my confused head I knew and trusted him. Either way he didn't bother me.

"I am a projection of your mind, Jane. I show up when things get too hard for you to handle," he'd said with a touch of annoyance. This didn't bother me either as if I'd already known that this was just his way.

"So we are friends?"

"You were one of my only friends."

"Oh," I said, "welcome, then."

He snorted. "Thanks."

"Are you here to help me get un-crazy?"

He shrugged. "Possibly. It would be nice to think so."

"It would," I agreed. "I must be pretty upset about something to have gone off the rails like this."

"You were."

"Do you know what it is?"

"I do," he said seriously.

I felt my gut clench. "Will…will you tell me what went wrong?"

He shook his head. "I don't have a solution for you, Jane, so I think not. Just know that you will be yourself again when you don't see me anymore."

I thought for a minute.

"How did you die, Soames?"

His head rose, his sharp chin sticking out as he puffed out his chest in pride. "I sacrificed myself so that you could kill the man who murdered my twin sister."

I exhaled hard. "Did I?"

"You did."

I thought some more. "Why are you the one that's here, Soames? You can't be the only person I've lost."

"There is another person that wants to come here," he said, "but she's afraid to do so."

"Why?"

"Let her come and you'll see."

How on Corsica was I supposed to do that? I was just thinking this when I saw a small, athletic person materialize next to Soames. She moved like a dancer, like a fighter, her copper skin and high cheekbones accented by short dark hair.

"Jane?" she asked quietly.

Suddenly I was overwhelmed with grief, sadness, guilt.

I woke up on the floor, Thalberg shaking me. Soames crouched next to him looking concerned, but Thalberg didn't acknowledge him.

"Miss Jane! Miss Jane!"

I sat up too quickly, feeling the room spin for a second. "I'm all right, Thalberg. I just remembered something that upset me, I guess."

Thalberg's mobile features brightened. "You remembered something?"

"Someone," I clarified. I looked at Soames.

"Arrow Peters," he explained.

"Thalberg, who was Arrow Peters? What happened to her?"

Thalberg frowned as if parsing his words. "She was the daughter of your first love, High Admiral Armstrong. She killed herself a few months ago."

I was having trouble breathing. "Was she my daughter, too?"

"No, Miss Jane."

I 'felt' for the tiny heartbeat within me. Still strong. Still there. I found I could breathe again. I struggled to stand. "Sorry to have worried you, my friend. I'm all right, now."

"I should call a doctor…"

I shook my head. "No, I'm fine, really and I have visitors on the way," I said with a smile. My visits with the Emperor were formal and nice, but never relaxed. There seemed to be too much emotion, too much that needed to be said but couldn't be. That wasn't a problem with the next people I was expecting to see.

Plus I had a question for them since I was pretty sure we (as in the whole 'Jane's lost her mind what the hell do we do about it' crew) were waiting for someone. I devised a very clever plan to figure out who and why: I asked.

Which brings me to the two men I *was* expecting. Two men and a baby, actually. Or two men, a baby, assorted support staff including a nanny, and twenty-four guards. We'd stopped and picked the lot of them up on our way to Corsica. Their guards were only different from the Corsican Guards that littered the estate in that their uniforms had a brighter color scheme, but the same air of professional menace emanated from both sets. Neither the two men nor the baby paid them any attention at all. No one (but I) could see Soames making himself comfortable in a chair in the corner so he was ignored, too.

The first of the men, the one who seemed to be in charge somehow, though technically the other man outranked him, was long-haired, medium in height with a few more pounds than necessary, but a clever humorous face. His name was Lord Bobby Miller and he was (apparently) a friend of mine from way back.

The other man was an odd combination of gentle and…louche. He drawled, he rolled his eyes, he affected boredom. He stank of privilege. His uniform, unlike his companion's dark unassuming one, was distractingly opulent. Gaudy almost. I figured out almost immediately, however, that it was either a pose or just habit and not his true nature. Not just because his friend seemed to find him either exasperating or highly entertaining, but because of the two month old baby that Prince Ronald Julia-Callas cradled gently in his arms. The look of indulgent affection on the man's face gave the lie to his pose of indifference.

"So, who are we waiting for, exactly?" I asked Lord Bobby.

Lord Bobby grimaced and darted his eyes to his friend, for that is clearly what they were, he and the Prince. "We're waiting for reinforcements."

"For what exactly?"

Bobby sighed. "You have been told that I am a Telepath; I can read thoughts."

I nodded. "You want to root around in my head and shake all this loose so we can all go back to real life. Right?" Because that was the only thing that made sense.

Lord Bobby looked uncomfortable. Prince Ronald looked up from testing the baby's grip on his pointer finger. "That is essentially true, Miss Jane, but we, and your Thal, thought that any powerful Telepath could do what needed to be done."

"Because it has been done before. To me, I mean."

"Indeed," the Prince said.

"So you've tried and it didn't work?"

Lord Bobby looked embarrassed. "Unfortunately. So we are waiting for the lady who was able to do it before, but she is a very important person with a lot of claims on her time."

"Oh. Has she said she will come?"

"She has."

Prince Ronald settled the baby more comfortably in his arms. "I, for one, am looking forward to meeting her." He grinned mischievously at Lord Bobby. "Even Pilar has never met an alien of this particular variety."

"She's an alien?" I said, suddenly excited. "What's she look like?"

"Blue skin, scales, wings," Lord Bobby answered, amused.

"Oh, wow," I breathed.

Lord Bobby looked over at his friend. "Some things never change." The Prince snorted his agreement.

Soames chuckled. It was hard to fight glaring at him, but I didn't feel like giving his presence (or lack thereof) away. At least there was *some* crazy I could keep to myself.

"So who's this Pilar?" I had to ask.

Lord Bobby's eyes took on a wicked gleam that seemed to cause the Prince's eyes to roll. "The Prince Pilar of Gloriana-Levvon is Prince Ronnie's wife, my lover, and the mother of this, the second of all of our children." He bowed his head at the Prince who bowed his head back. Apparently this was a well-rehearsed routine. "She is, at present, home with the Prince's boyfriend, Chester."

The Prince rolled his eyes, "You get far too much enjoyment out of that explanation, Stuart."

I blinked for a second as I worked it out. "Do you keep all that on a chart or something?"

Prince Ronald shook his head. "It is actually far less complicated than it seems." He studied me for a second, his brown eyes piercing. There was clearly a perceptive man beneath the pose, I thought, but what could he perceive from the woman who wasn't all there? Something, apparently, because he turned the baby and then grasped her under the arms, pushing her in my direction. "So I give you, at least until she cries, Princess Persephone Jane Julia-Callas of Glorian-Levvon, third in line to the throne of Kings."

My eyes went wide and I shook my head, but the Prince would not be deterred and I ended up holding the squishy-soft little person with trembling hands. "Sit, my dear," he said gently, "it's easier sitting until you get used to it."

"Thank you, Sir," I whispered. I held the baby on my lap, her feet and legs on my stomach. It *was* easier now that she wasn't in my hands.

"Ronnie," Lord Bobby said with an edge on his voice.

"Stuart," Ronnie mocked back.

I'd been about to ask whether Stuart was the Lord's middle name when the baby smiled a toothless smile at me. It was ridiculously adorable. I smiled back reflexively and looked up to find that calculating expression on the Prince's face again.

"Am I doing it wrong, Sir?" I asked, worried.

"Not at all, Miss Jane," he said quietly. "Actually, I'd say you were a natural."

Lord Bobby growled his exasperation which made the Prince chuckle.

Right then I felt something outside the door. Something besides Thalberg, who stayed within hearing distance though rarely made his presence known. I'd been surprised that I could tell who was in my vicinity even without looking but I'd been told it had to do with special abilities I'd been born with. I guessed that also explained how I was able to 'feel' my daughter's tiny heartbeat.

It felt like a woman outside our door but it wasn't any of the house staff. She stood near Thalberg, but no alarm had been raised. Perhaps it was another friend I didn't know.

"There is a woman outside the door," I said quietly. "Someone I don't recognize."

Lord Bobby nodded and thought for a second. "Well, that is very interesting." He stared at the Prince for a second. The Prince's eyes went wide.

"She's come every day, Jane," Soames offered, "but never actually comes in to see you." Why, I wondered.

"Interesting, indeed," the Prince said as he rose quickly and went to the door. He opened it quickly, giving a brilliant smile, "Good morning, Ma'am. I am Ronald Julia-Callas. You must be the Countess of Boulton. Won't you join us?"

A few minutes later we were seated around a small table that had been brought into the Library and covered with an ornate tea service complete with cakes, cookies and other assorted delectables. The baby was back with Ronnie, cooing in his arms. The Countess of Boulton, the Lady Idis, was a rather exotic-looking beauty. Tall, slim with a warm cocoa complexion, bright blue eyes and in what seemed like the most elegant and complicated dress ever worn. It covered whatever empty space there was between the men that sat on either side of her. Her dark hair was up in an ornate style and sprinkled with jewels. She was by far the most impressive creature in the room and the most uncomfortable, though I couldn't have told you how I knew that since she appeared to be all composure.

As for conversation Lord Bobby seemed content to eat and observe while Prince Ronald kept the ball rolling. The Countess looked everywhere but at me, which made me nervous, though she clearly wasn't dangerous. I wondered what our relationship was, if anything. I had to assume that we weren't close. It wasn't long before I thought I knew why.

"This is such a beautiful estate, Lady Idis," the Prince said as he reached for a slice of cake. "It was very generous of you and the Emperor to allow us to stay here." He put the cake on a plate and deposited it in front of Lord Bobby who just shook his head in amusement. He offered her some but she declined with a smile and brief shake of the head. The Prince then took a piece for himself.

"We are honored to have you, Your Highness."

"Ronnie, please," the Prince said with his mouth half full of cake.

"As you wish," she said.

Wait, we were guests of the Emperor *and* the Countess? Was he married and no one had told me? I put my tea cup down, feeling stricken.

'It's all right, Jane,' a voice said in my head. Lord Bobby's voice. 'The Emperor hides nothing from Lady Idis. You aren't some guilty secret.'

"He's right," Soames confirmed.

That was a relief to know even if hearing someone else's voice in my head had been really weird. I still wasn't comfortable, though. This visitor brought emotional landmines with her, it seemed.

"We have nothing like this on Levvon, of course," Prince Ronnie rattled on companionably. "Living in orbit isn't conducive to lovely gardens."

"My late husband visited one of your modular cargo ships once many years ago," the Countess said with a pasted on smile, "he said they were the most efficient vessels he had ever seen."

"Efficient, yes," the Prince said with a grimace, "but not much more."

"Surely efficiency is a virtue, Ronnie," Lady Idis chided pleasantly.

"I'm afraid efficiency meant nothing to the wastrel I was back then, Lady Idis. As I recall your husband threatened to box my ears," he leaned in confidentially, "a term I'd never heard before and had to have someone explain to me, when I showed up to an official event, er, shall we say compromised." Lady Idis' expression became fixed. Why was this getting so uncomfortable? "I remember him saying, 'no son of mine would behave with such a lack of propriety!'" He chuckled. He was the only one.

I felt Lady Idis hold her breath, just for a second. It was a small thing, but I knew she was in distress. Lord Bobby knew it, too, and shot the Prince a look that clearly told him to shut up. The Prince, however, looked unrepentant.

Lord Bobby quickly said, "I have been told, Countess, that you are rebuilding the Way Point."

I must have looked as clueless as I felt because Lady Idis explained, "The Way Point was a transfer station for the Empire. It was primarily used to process rescued and escaped slaves seeking asylum."

"What happened to it, Ma'am?"

She shrugged elegantly. "One of the slavers destroyed it as well as the slaves that had been liberated."

"Mother of god," I whispered.

"Yes, one would think that making slaves to order would be too barbaric a practice to continue in today's age, but genetic 'improvements' have brought as much heartache as good, I think." Then, for the first time, she turned to me. "It was something you were quite passionate about, Jane, stamping out the slave trade. Understandable since you were one, too." She looked over at Lord Bobby, "You both were."

"We were *slaves*?" I asked, incredulous.

Lord Bobby looked uncomfortable. "We didn't call it that, but yes, we were."

I stared at Ronnie who was making absurd faces at his daughter. She gurgled in delight. I saw Lady Idis watching them longingly. I think Lord Bobby and the Prince noticed this, too.

"So were our parents slaves, too?" I asked Lord Bobby.

"We didn't have parents, Jane."

I felt the stirring of panic in my soul. Why was I panicking? It was as if the emotion belonged to someone else. Lord Bobby's eyes went wide.

"*I* wasn't a slave," Soames said smugly. "I was a *natural* Telepath and a bio-birth. Not genetically engineered like you and Stuart."

It was really hard not to throw a muffin at him.

"Goodness," Prince Ronnie teased baby Persephone Jane, "you've spit up. You are such a messy love." He turned to the Countess. "Would you mind, Lady Idis? I can't reach my handkerchief."

"Ronnie," Lord Bobby said warningly.

"No, it's all right," Lady Idis said a little nervously. I felt her hands shake slightly as she reached for the little person. The Prince handed her over as if everyone had thought it was a good idea, sparing a dirty look for his friend that the Countess wouldn't have been able to see. The Countess held the baby against her chest, Princess Persephone's little face resting on the Countess' neck. The baby immediately reached for dangling (and probably priceless) earring in front of her and the Countess laughed as she removed it and put it into the baby's chubby fist. And laughed again when that same fist shoved part of the trinket into the child's mouth. "Well aren't you precious, little one? Is it delicious? You have very good taste, sweetheart. That one has been in my family for five hundred Standard years."

"Lady Idis, I…" Lord Bobby started.

"Don't worry about it, Lord Miller," she said, amused, "Everyone knows a Princess must have jewels." She gently 'booped' the baby's nose causing Persephone Jane to giggle adorably. "It suits her even if it is being used non-traditionally."

Prince Ronnie gave a pointed look to Lord Bobby. Lord Bobby watched Lady Idis and his daughter very thoughtfully for a minute, then, catching the Prince's eye, nodded slowly.

I watched Lady Idis, too, and wondered if she had any children of her own. She looked genuinely happy with the little baby.

"Not anymore," Soames said quietly.

Panic. Again with the panic. Why was the subject of babies worrying me so much? This child inside of me was such an interesting thing, such a good thing, but the panic was there anyway. Soames leaned back in his chair, apparently done talking.

"Lord Miller tells me you are an attorney, Lady Idis," the Prince said as he reached for a second piece of cake. "That must be fascinating work." He made no move to take back his daughter, I noticed, or look for the promised handkerchief. He'd clearly manipulated the situation, but I had no idea why.

"It can be frustrating work," she said, still keeping her attention on the little Princess, "but it is worth it when any kind of reform gets through the system."

"What sort of reforms have you been working on?" Lord Bobby asked, "If you don't mind talking about them."

She laughed and fully relaxed for the first time since she'd entered the room. "You may be sorry you asked, Lord Miller. It's a subject I like talking about a bit too much."

Lord Bobby's smile lit up his face. "Not at all. Please."

We weren't bored. She ended up speaking quite passionately about the law and the antiquated system of jurisprudence within the Corsican Empire. Some of the rules on the books were hundreds of years old and beyond comprehension. She'd reformed the divorce laws, property laws (biological and otherwise) and had helped the Emperor rework the succession itself. The Prince and Lord Miller had been particularly interested in that bit of information, though I wasn't sure why. Or rather, I didn't want to think about why.

The initially uncomfortable impromptu tea turned into a fun and educational lunch. Lady Idis never relinquished the baby even though holding her forced her to eat with one hand. It was only when it was clearly time to go that she'd returned the child (soggy earring reclaimed) to Prince Ronnie with thanks.

Then it was the three (+ baby + Soames) of us again.

The Prince turned to me, his expression suddenly quite urgent.

"Miss Jane, I wonder if you would give me permission to question your Mr. Thalberg about the events leading up to your memory loss."

I blinked at him a second and shot a questioning look to Soames who nodded his approval. "Of course, if you want to."

"I do." The Prince nodded to himself as if confirming something.

"Yes," Lord Bobby said slowly, "I think that is a good idea."

"Whatever you need."

"Then we will say goodbye for now, but we'll see you tomorrow," the Prince said, surprising me with a gallant kiss on the cheek that made me smile.

Lord Bobby shook his head affectionately at his friend and kissed my other cheek. "We'll see you then."

Then they left. I had to wonder what friendly (hopefully) mischief they were up to. Soames, if he suspected, told me nothing.

The next morning I found out.

11:01 – Informal Dining Room, Robin Hill, Irena, Corsican Empire, October 15th, 2873

My day had started with two notes: the first (elegantly handwritten as if from a calligrapher) from the Emperor saying that he was sorry but that he would not be able to visit me that morning as he usually did and the second (scrawled haphazardly) for me to meet Prince Ronald and Lord Miller in the Informal Dining room at 11:00. Both unusual but not terrifying.

I walked (Soames at my heels) quickly up to the large gilt entrance doors to the dining room to find an enormous Guard Captain in front of it and voices (some loud, some not) within. Had whatever was going to happen started already, I wondered. I was only one minute late.

I looked askance at the Guard Captain. He shrugged and said, "You're not really late, Miss Jane. They've been at it for over two hours now."

The voices inside abruptly quieted as soon as he spoke.

I frowned at him, my guard now up. "At what exactly, Captain?"

The large yet friendly man just opened the door and gestured me in.

There was nothing of the relaxed atmosphere that usually accompanied my visits with Lord Bobby and the Prince. Part of that had to be because the baby was absent, but the Emperor and Countess were there instead. The other part was the extremely elegant, gold-leafed (not to mention spacious) room with the floor to ceiling windows overlooking the garden. 'Informal' my ass.

The four of them were assembled around the table which was bare of anything except cut glass candelabras with real wax candles in them. The candelabras, I thought wryly, were each half the size of the mess table in the *Liberty*. Thalberg stood just inside the mirrored doors of the room, Soames taking a seat in the corner, and dozens of Corsican and Gloriana-Levvonese guards patrolled at intervals outside on the grass. Once again, super informal.

"Please sit, Miss Jane," Prince Ronald said, clearly establishing this as his party. I sat. "I wanted to talk to you about what I am sure is the root of the problem that sent you here."

My heart raced but I nodded.

"I know that what I am about to say is a gamble, but please know that I do not take any of this lightly. We are, as you know, waiting for a Telepath who has agreed to help you come out of your fugue."

I nodded again nervously.

"I feel, however, that you need more assistance than that." His expression softened. "Part of my motivation is selfish. You helped me once when I was in trouble and I wish to repay the debt."

"Ok," I said so quietly I wasn't sure anyone could have heard me. It didn't seem to matter, though, the Prince understood.

He leaned back in his chair and steepled his hands in front of his face thoughtfully. "You heard me mention yesterday that I was a wastrel. I was being kind to myself." He smiled ruefully. "Born a Prince of a wealthy nation I had been given everything and had turned it into crap. Then my father, the late unlamented King of Levvon, tried to kill the woman that later became my wife and, though he didn't know it, her baby, our son, Prince Hector."

Lord Bobby nodded, but his expression was sad. I wondered why.

"He died during the attempt and my arranged marriage to Pilar combined the Kingdoms and I, not giving a ripe shit, continued on my merry wastrel way. Something happened, however, that I could never have expected: I was given a chance to contribute." He dropped his hands and stared at me. "I was trusted. I was forced to *earn* my rank. I could have failed and I almost did," he smiled at Lord Bobby who smiled back, "but I became someone close to worthy of what I had been given."

"You are worthy, Ronnie," Lord Bobby murmured.

Ronnie inclined his head in thanks but continued, "That was all fine until it looked like the baby was finally going to be born and what did I do?"

Lord Bobby said nothing.

"I panicked. I fell off the wagon. I did everything I could to prove to myself and everyone else that the responsibility of being a co-father was beyond me." He leaned forward. "I was an inebriated, drug-addicted whoring waste of space." Pretty much everyone in the room, including myself, winced at that harsh description. "I'd had terrible parenting and had been told (mostly by the attempted murderer that was my father) I was worthless my entire life and I believe I was—up until I married Pilar. I was convinced I was in no shape to be anywhere near a child, let alone corrupt one with my awfulness."

Lord Bobby really wanted to say something, I could tell, but he kept his mouth shut.

"I was terrified that I would make a mistake and harm or kill the baby. What if some of the people I had treated like garbage made our child feel ashamed of their father by speaking the truth about him? What if he hated me anyway? What if someone wanted revenge, either on me or on Pilar or Stuart? We have enemies, the slavers we drove out of Thao in particular, some of whom hate us just because we exist."

He exhaled as if getting all that out had been hard on him, which it probably had been.

"My friends, however, for that is who my wife, her lover and my boyfriend are, told me what I am going to tell you: you will always worry, as any parent whether ordinary or grand will, and that will never, *ever* go away. That, despite that fear, you wake up every morning and do your goddamned best to be the finest version of yourself you can manage. You have a good heart and an ability to give and to love and those are the most important things."

I closed my eyes and felt a tear fall down my cheek.

"Most importantly, you are *not doing this alone.*"

My eyes snapped open.

He took out a large flexi-monitor and unrolled it on the table. "I know this won't make much sense to your conscious mind, but please look this over anyway, Miss Jane, and think about what it says."

I could feel the Emperor and Countess staring at me, boring holes in me with their eyes, really.

It was a schedule. It had the Emperor and me (teaching at a place called the ESTF) on Terra for the Fall, I would stay on Terra to teach for the Frost (Winter), coming back to Corsica briefly for the Frost Festival, the Emperor on Corsica for the whole season, then he would be back to Terra for the Bloom. I would be on Corsica for the bulk of the rest of the year, travelling back to Terra for final exams and graduation as well for planning sessions and new cadet-screening before the following Fall. The Countess and the baby would stay exclusively on Corsica where the child would be safe, or as safe as anyone could ask for.

I felt something loosening in my chest, a tension I hadn't realized I had. They all must think teaching is very important to me, I thought, to go this far to allow me to still be able to do it.

A sob was building. I saw Soames stand up, worried.

"I wish I could say that there were guarantees, Miss Jane," Prince Ronald said soothingly, "but there aren't. You *will* make mistakes." He grimaced. "All parents do."

"It's true," Lord Bobby said.

"It is," the Emperor echoed. I remembered that someone had told me he had two grown sons. He would know, I guessed. They all would.

The sob climbed higher in my body, making its steady way to my throat. Soames was by my side, his pale hand on my arm. "Let it go, Jane. Let it go."

I was still scared, however. I still fought it.

"These are good people, Jane," Soames said. "They wouldn't be trying to help you if they didn't think you were good, too."

My eyes were full and my breathing labored. The Emperor rose in his seat but it was the Countess who spoke. "Jane, love," she smiled, her eyes full, too, "let's be mommies together."

I looked over at her though I had to blink to see her. "For Lucy?"

Stuart looked up startled. "I never told her…"

"Hush, Stu," Prince Ronnie whispered.

Idis nodded. "For our Lucy."

I let the sob go and cried with big ugly gasps of air. Suddenly Charles was on my right side and Idis on the other. I held on to them like the drowning woman I was.

When I finally opened my eyes again Soames was gone and I was back.

More importantly, I was home.

I would like to say that everything was simple and easy from then on, but that isn't how life goes, especially if you were unusual (now *I* was being kind) like me. I will say that I have never, in the many years since, been 'to the farm' again. I've felt the call a few times, but I've been able to fight it. Having Lucy, my beloved Lucy, would be the largest incentive to stay sane, but it wasn't the only one. Ronnie had been right; I wasn't doing this alone. Idis, Charles and I gave Lucy a family and a home and, along the way, I got one, too, my first real home since Pace had been destroyed. That home, Pace, had been an accident of birth, this one I *chose* and that made it all the sweeter to claim. Eventually. Once I got my head out of my ass.

First there were some issues to try to take care of, however, issues I could have handled better.

Back to the Informal Dining Room, post Jane meltdown.

I wiped my face and rose as Stuart and the Prince were discretely heading for the door.

"Sir?" I asked and the Prince stopped. "May I hug you?" He gave a watery laugh and opened his arms. I hugged him hard. "Thank you, Sir. You've saved me."

"My dear girl," he said with put-on smugness, "it's what Princes are for." The Prince rolled his still damp eyes, "What *are* they teaching children today, Stuart?"

I stepped back and laughed as I wiped my eyes and moved on to my old friend. Stuart smiled as he tried to breathe while I hugged the crap out of him. "We'll soon find out, Ronnie."

I 'opened' my mind and let Stuart feast on my gratitude and affection.

'This is what family does, Jane,' he said modestly in my head, then he kissed me on the forehead and I let him go. Both men bowed to the Emperor and his women and left.

Of course now it was super awkward. Ordinarily (were Charles and I alone) I would have tried to touch him, get some kind of physical reassurance, but I was all too aware that this was the first time the three of us had been in the same room since our initial 'arrangement' had been brokered. I was also painfully conscious that we weren't ever supposed to be the on the same *planet* at the same time, let alone in the same room. I had, unwittingly, fucked our safe 'arrangement' all to hell by getting knocked up. Charles and Idis watched me expectantly, clearly no more comfortable in this situation than I was.

"I punched David in the nose," was out of my mouth before I knew it.

"You *what*?" Idis asked and Charles started to laugh. And laugh.

I nodded. "You should have heard the crunch. I shattered that sucker." Charles laughed harder. "Blood everywhere."

Idis shook her head, but there was a smile in there. "Sounds satisfying."

"It was, actually."

Charles' laughter faded. "I'm surprised that was all you did, Jane, after such a betrayal."

"It wasn't my first thought, no," I admitted, "but Atalanta and Thal were the cooler heads that prevailed." I sighed. "They were right, of course."

Idis frowned. "You think you really would have killed him, left to your own devices?"

I thought about it. "No. I might have broken his legs or something, but I wouldn't have taken his life even though I was angry enough to." Problem was that now we were on the subject of retribution I had to address the transgression. "I'm sorry, Idis." Her expression didn't change, but her heart rate sped back up. "This must have been even harder on you than on me and…and…I'm just sorry."

It was interesting to watch her expression shift subtly from open and human to perfect and diplomatic. I saw Charles' golden eyes narrow slightly. Yes, he'd seen it, too. "Life is full of change, Jane. We adapt."

"Of course," I said, not really sure how to proceed or that I even *could* with her. She'd put up a pretty serious wall.

"You two must have a great deal to talk about and I am due back at the Palace." Idis smiled a gracious smile, inclined her head and left with a grand swishing of skirts.

I turned to Charles with my eyes wide. "What was that?"

He sighed, exasperated. "May I offer you some advice, my love?"

I was momentarily distracted by how good that was to hear and I found myself snuggled in the safety of his chest before I'd even realized we'd moved together. "Hmm?"

"She does this when she's upset," He said, his body relaxing against mine. Heaven. "Don't let her get away with it."

"So I should go after her?" I said reluctantly. I was so happy right where I was. "Now?"

"You should," he said, sounding equally reluctant. "As much as we are three, you two have to find a way to communicate as two."

"But you and I..."

"Yes, we have a lot to say to each other, but it can wait a bit," he said kissing me lightly on the lips. "I'll be in your room." His golden eyes turned golden black. "Waiting." His voice was full of heat. Oh my.

I let him go so that I could get back to him faster, "I'll be right back."

"Take your time with her, love," he said gently. "It's important."

"Ok," I said and I left.

I found her (not that she was hard to spot in her huge dress and glittering jewels) as she was about to exit the house.

"Idis?"

She stopped but did not turn around immediately. Her shoulders were rock hard from tension.

"A word, please?"

She dropped her head in defeat, her good breeding forcing her to accede to my request. What a ridiculous weapon good manners were, I thought.

"Shall we find a room?" she asked a bit cooly.

"Lead the way," I said.

We walked down this corridor and that one until we ended up in what had to be a small breakfast nook (small in this house having a different meaning than in other more normal places). She closed the door and stood with her back against it.

She clearly wasn't going to start so I jumped in. "You have every right to be angry with me."

"I told you that I am not."

I just stared at her until she came close to squirming.

"You are calling me a liar?" she said, her voice even colder.

"I am saying that you aren't allowing yourself to feel it," this was a guess, but I was pretty sure I was correct, "because you think your anger will be pointless."

"Isn't it?"

"Not to me," I said a little annoyed myself, but then I put that aside. "Perhaps you and I can only be co-parents; perhaps we can never be friends. That isn't what I want, but I have been nothing but trouble to you and I'd understand if that was what you wanted."

"What I wanted," she repeated and I was suddenly reminded of a Denethian warrior as its eyes went blue with blood lust and claws came out. "*What I wanted*?"

I wanted to get the fuck out of there, but I stood my ground so she could let me have it. Lord knows I deserved it.

"None of this has had anything to do with what I wanted, Jane." Idis' hands went on her hips her blue eyes sparking with fury. "The man I have given my heart and my life to falls in love with someone else after over ten years together and I accept that I will have to *share* him to keep him—do you think that was anything close to what I wanted?"

I waited as she built up steam.

"To know that what I gave him wasn't enough? That someone younger and sexier and more famous and interesting was going to be in his bed but that he was willing to keep me around because he had made me a promise and didn't want to look like a heel for breaking it?"

"You think he kept you solely out of obligation?" I asked, incredulous.

"What am I supposed to think? I can't compete with you on any level."

Boy was I tired of hearing that shit.

"As if I can compete on any of *your* levels? I can't be the woman who helps him run the Empire—when you aren't actually just running it outright. I'm not the one to say and do the proper thing. I don't have a yen for diplomacy or the law or the pomp and circumstance of this life. You do. You are amazing at it."

"Fine to compliment me on things you don't care about."

"Just because they aren't things I can do doesn't mean they aren't important."

"How gracious of you," she sneered.

"Then why didn't you just leave?" I asked. "Just because Charles and I wanted this didn't mean you had to allow it."

"Because this is my fucking *life*, Jane!"

"You think Charles would just kick you out if you didn't want to sleep with him anymore?"

"No," she said, "but I wanted what we had. Being on the same team, working together for the greater good, the intimacy of a shared history, of being lovers who had known each other forever. I'm not worried about job security for fuck's sake."

"Then why 'for fuck's sake' did you say yes?"

"Because at least I got to keep some of it. It was still supposed to look and feel just like it did before, even if it wasn't."

"Then I blew it all up by getting pregnant."

"Yes, you did and now everything has to be different." She pushed her palm against her forehead as if trying to force a headache away. "Damn you, anyway, Jane." She was crying. I hated it. Hated that I'd been responsible for her hurt.

"I'd offer to just disappear, but the baby prevents that," I said softly.

"Seems you are getting a good deal here," Idis said.

"I am and I know I am."

"What will you do if in ten years he meets some new woman who is fresher and hotter than either of us? You can't tell me definitively that won't happen."

It made me sick to think of it, but she was right. "Then I will adapt, but I don't know what I would do."

"You won't just make room for the new..."

"Shiny vagina in his life?" I asked. "I really couldn't say."

The words 'shiny vagina' seemed to pull her up short. Almost in spite of herself she snorted a very unladylike snort. "My mother called it a hoohoo."

"You're serious?"

She laughed. "Wish I weren't." She walked over and sank into a chair at the small table. I sat opposite her. "Charles told you to corner me."

"He did."

She sighed. "I don't want to be cruel to you, Jane, despite all the nasty things I just said."

"I believe you."

"It's stupid of me to fuss," she said, laying her hands flat on the ornate table. "Plenty of triads exist and some quite happily. It's just..."

"Not what you and Charles had planned."

"No." She looked up, her rather exotic face intense, "You see, Jane, one of the things that makes me good at my job is that I am a planner. I know the variables, I know what has to happen and how to achieve it—the way you have to know similar things to make a battle plan."

I remembered our discussion earlier in the year comparing a state dinner to a tactical assault. The tools had been vastly different, but the concept wasn't dissimilar. "Right."

"With time and experience you weed out the options that make no sense or that are too expensive or time consuming and you can be confident in your work. You can even adapt to all kinds of situations with ease, or," she grimaced, "make it *look* easy, which is more often the case. So once you've been doing this a while you start to think you've got it all nailed down as long as your obstacles fall, and this is important, within certain parameters." She leaned back in the chair, dragging her fingers over the wood of the table. "The combination of you and the baby, though, hasn't fit anything I've had to deal with before. Not on a personal level anyway." She smoothed her already perfect hair. "For the first time in a very, very long time I'm at a complete loss."

She seemed lost in her own thoughts for a minute, but my curiosity wasn't yet exhausted.

"Idis?"

"Yes?"

"When did you find out I was pregnant?"

"When you arrived. Lord Miller told Charles and Charles told me in private."

"How did you get, in four days, from the betrayal you must have felt to wanting to co-mommy with the Shiny Vagina?" I said this with a smile to let her know I was teasing. Still better than 'Golden Cunt.'

"Well, the fact that you clearly hadn't done it on purpose to trap Charles and you had been so terrified by the idea that you'd gone out of your head helped, as terrible as it sounds."

I shrugged, embarrassed, "Unfortunately, that sort of thing seems to be much harder on the people around me than on me."

"Either way it showed that you were taking all of this very seriously."

"Yeah." Massive understatement.

"I kept thinking how dare she have a baby when my Jamie was dead in the ground." Oh, that hurt. She saw it in my eyes and said, "You asked what I thought, Jane."

"I know. Sorry."

"I'm sorry, too. One thing actually had nothing to do with the other, of course. I re-realized that after a night of stewing. Then I started thinking about that baby. Not only would she be safer here, but she would need to have time to be comfortable in this world before she had to assume her place in it. That was something that, of the three of us, I would be in the best position to offer her."

Assume her *what* in it? I thought, but Idis was still going.

"What if she ends up a supernormal of some kind? How will that fit into her duties here?"

Her *what*?

"So when the Prince and Lord Bobby came to negotiate the schedule I realized that it would only, could only work if I was a mommy, too. I found that I really wanted that." Idis smiled shyly. It was a lovely smile, but I was still stuck on the words 'duty' and 'place.'

"You agreed to be a co-parent and what did Charles say?"

She blushed and looked away. "He won't tell me directly, but I think he'd always wanted us to have children, but knew I couldn't, or wouldn't," she corrected, "and had stopped thinking about it."

"He's happy about the baby, then?" I asked, trying not to betray my nervousness.

She laughed. "Of all of us he's the happiest."

I exhaled the breath I hadn't realized I was holding. "You know, this is surreal for me, too. On Pace the Government had complete reproductive control. This could never have happened there."

"No bio-births?" Idis asked, surprised. "Not at all?"

"A few illegal ones, but I'd had no idea about them until the last week we were there."

"In a month or so you can 'tub' the fetus," she said, "will you?"

I instinctively 'felt' for the little heartbeat. "No. She's with me until it's time." Funny how I hadn't had to think about *that* for even a second. "Wait. Why in a month? You can 'tub' divided cells."

Idis looked uncomfortable. "You can get into that with Charles."

Now *I* was uncomfortable. "Get into *what* with Charles?"

She rose, her skirts rustling expensively around her. "I really do have to get back, but I'm glad we spoke."

I rose, too. "Not so fast, Countess. What will Charles be 'getting into' with me?"

She sighed impatiently as if I were being dense which, in retrospect, was what I'd been. "My dear, you are carrying a child of the Emperor of Corsica. An Emperor who has two heirs who don't want the job."

I sat back down hard. "So you're saying that Lucy is…"

Mother of god.

Idis nodded. "Princess Lucy and if Charles chooses her to be…"

"…the future Empress of the Corsican Empire and its Environs," I finished for her.

Fuck me running.

14:21 – My Room, Robin Hill

I'd walked around the gardens for quite a while with Thal and a dozen guards as my really obvious shadows. I was a bit numb. How had I not thought about this before? My brain could hardly even comprehend what Idis had made me see. It was just so much pressure to put on a child. What if something happened to Charles before Lucy was ready? What if Charles pinned his hopes on her and she didn't want the job either—not that I would blame her. There was the small chance, however, I told myself, that she may *want* to be Empress. It could happen, I told myself, all the while not understanding why anyone would want to take on the responsibility of billions of lives.

But to be born into a job just seemed so unfair.

I'd been born into a job, I reminded myself, but I'd gotten out. It had taken the deaths of millions and the destruction of all life on four planets, but I'd gotten out. Had I, though? I'd been trained to be a fighter and an assassin. Aside from being a teacher wasn't that pretty much what I still was? If Lucy was a super, which was very likely, she'd have Charles' brains (at least I hoped she would) and perhaps become a force to be reckoned with. Without training and the need to do good things, however, she could become a monster. We all had the possibility within us, she would just have more power, money and resources with which to be one.

My mind was still a-whirl when I opened the door to my room. I was instantly grabbed, kissed and ravaged in the best possible way by the man I loved. It was wonderful, dirty and loving and damn, I'd needed it, needed him. It was clear he felt the same way as he held me prisoner and showed me how much he'd missed me until dawn. Mr. Beddoes discretely brought us food from time to time but we rarely left the bed. We didn't say much, but ah, it was perfect.

It wasn't until first light when Charles, holding me tightly to his bare chest, brought us back to reality. I should say *his* reality since the topic he brought up was the furthest I could think of from *mine*.

"Idis is all right?" he asked carefully.

"Getting there, I think," I said, sighing comfortably. "She really told me off and I think it helped."

"Good," he said, but then added quickly, "you know what I mean. We have to look out for each other and she wouldn't talk to me."

"I deserved it."

"No, love, but what she's been feeling was perfectly normal."

"I agree." I propped myself up to look in his beautiful eyes. "She knows you set her up."

He laughed and I could feel it resonate in his chest. Wonderful. "Of course she did."

"Will she be Ok, Charles?" Will we? Was my unspoken follow-up question.

"It will take time, but I think so. You are both remarkable women and you will, in a few months, have a common cause."

"Lucy."

"Lucy."

That made it impossible not to bring up... "She'll be a Princess and one of your heirs."

His body tensed. Just like that.

I sat up, alarmed, "Charles?"

He sat up, too, against the headboard, but didn't, for once, pull me over to him. This wasn't going to be pleasant I could tell. I was right once again.

"There is..." he stopped. He tried again. "There is a point of Corsican Law that can't be gotten round, Jane."

"Which is?" My stomach hurt.

"She doesn't have to be Empress."

"All right..."

"She *can't*, however, be Empress if her parents aren't..." big hesitation, "married."

I didn't faint or go crazy or anything, but my heart raced, I started to sweat and I felt really… I leapt out of bed and made it to the toilet just in time to throw up every delicious morsel Mr. Beddoes had provided us.

Mrs. Charles-Victor Arthur Bennett Fitzroy Couvillion-Bourbonnais. Not me. Princess Jane? Really not me. Corseted and bejeweled and smiling and diplomatic. Not me. Seating charts and court politics. Nope. People bowing. Not to me. A throne. Not for me. Why bother leading me to believe I'd get to go back and teach? My life wouldn't be mine in any way ever again.

Trapped, trapped and more trapped.

And just for a minute (a minute I am deeply ashamed of) I hated Lucy for doing this to me, for taking away my Liberty just by existing. What could I do, though? Screw her future because I needed to 'be me' more than I needed *her* to have choices? No, no I couldn't do that to her.

Everything had been so good before I'd known I was pregnant, damn it.

Fuck fuck and fuck again.

So I did what any good future mother would do under the same circumstances.

I destroyed that bathroom. Shredded it.

Through it all Charles sat forlornly outside the door, waiting for my anger to dissipate. It didn't, however. I just ran out of things to wreck.

"Charles," I said finally through the door.

"Yes?"

"I need to fly. Would you please tell your people not to shoot me?"

"Sure."

"Thanks."

I opened the window (thankfully there had been some clothes of mine on the floor that I was able to throw on (a naked pregnant woman would have been a sight for the nearby villagers)) and 'pushed' myself up into the sky.

I 'flew' and 'flew' and 'flew' until I was too high and damp and cold. Not to mention lost.

It had been a couple of hours and I was tired, but I kept going. I was being an ass and I knew it, but being in the air felt better than being on the ground with everyone's expectations so I kept going.

Suddenly my comm beeped. I answered it out of sheer instinct, mentally kicking myself as soon as I heard the voice on the other end of the call.

'Jane!' It was Idis, damn it. 'What the hell are you doing?'

'Getting my last moments of freedom in before I'm sent to prison,' I said through the wind. Like I said, I was being an ass.

'Father above, you are acting like a child!'

'At least it's still me,' was all I said.

'For the love of God, Jane, it isn't a cult.'

'Isn't it?' I flew a bit lower where it was a lot warmer. 'Didn't we already establish that I can't be you?' Then I had an idea. 'Can't you just say the baby is yours and you marry him? I can stay the dirty little secret?'

'Yes, because we have no *science* on Corsica to prove paternity and the hundreds of guards and staff, not to mention all of your friends that know, who will all willingly say they remembered the wrong woman was pregnant.' She made a very exasperated sound, 'Aside from the fact the universe would have to be blind, too, when the baby comes out looking like unbaked bread with freckles and not like warm chocolate.' Oh, right. Then, almost as an aside I heard, 'I don't know how either of you can stand to be so pale.' It was impressive how much sarcasm that woman had at her disposal.

'I didn't say it was a good plan,' I mumbled.

'Are you upset because you think you can't sleep with others if you're married? It's not as if a piece of paper could stop you if you wished to.'

'No!' I said. 'I wouldn't.'

'Are you planning on staying with Charles for the rest of your life?'

'Of course.' Because I was.

'Because Charles just offered you, in what I am sure was the wrong way, though I'm not sure there was a right one, everything in his world to you on a silver platter and you just vomited all over it. Literally.'

I just stopped, hovering over some farm. 'Oh,' I whispered as tears rolled down my cheeks.

'I've got your attention now, have I?' she said, sounding much less angry.

'Yes,' I said, chastened.

'You have experience in life but you don't have experience with this. I. Do,' she said confidently.

'How will that help me?' My voice was small.

She sighed. 'You are going to marry the love of your life, right?'

'Yeah.'

'Then I will help you negotiate how that comes about.'

She correctly interpreted my dumb silence as a request for an explanation. 'I am a veteran of both the Court and the court. The Palace will give on some things, like title and other things and you will give on others. It won't be perfect, but it will be a hell of a lot better than whatever horrors you are imagining.'

'Really, Idis?'

'I promise, Jane,' she said so firmly that I really believed her.

'Thank you,' I said breathlessly.

'Thank me by coming home and apologizing to your apoplectic lover and make it good.'

'I will.'

So I did.

I said I was sorry first with tearful confessions and apologies and second other much more fun ways. I did my best and, not to brag, my best was pretty damned good.

Once we'd caught our breath and I was securely snuggled up against him at the headboard I traced my fingers up and down his chest as he stroked my arm.

"I know too much to take it personally," he said with a small smile, "but it is funny that the two women I love more than anything in the world would rather chew their arms off than be married to me."

"Ask again as Charles Fitzroy and not Supremely Magnificent King Extraordinaire and Idis and I will be lining up."

He chuckled, "I like the sound of Supreme Magnificent King Extraordinaire. It's no less cumbersome than some of my actual titles." He leaned his head back on the headboard. "Do you still regret getting pregnant?"

I thought for a second, 'reaching' to feel the heartbeat I'd come to depend upon feeling. "No, but I'm ashamed of myself for…"

"Wishing it away. I know." He kissed the top of my head. "Want to hear my theory about pregnancy?"

I giggled. "Sure. What's it like?"

He stuck his tongue out at me, a very *not* Imperial action that was completely adorable. "That it's as complicated as anything we do. Everyone is supposed to be happy and nervous, but only in a good way, and it's all pink and blue and tiny clothes and itty bitty baby toys." He pulled me closer. "I have not been pregnant, nor am I likely to be…"

"I'm pretty sure I wouldn't be the only one freaking out if you were, Charles," I muttered against his chest.

"Can you imagine?" he said with a laugh, "but I have been a parent and, I can say from experience, that parenting is harder, more complicated, more exhausting and far more wonderful than what I'd been led to expect. So…"

"Finding yourself unexpectedly pregnant by a hidden Emperor to the great surprise of his mistress might be complicated, too?"

"It *is* possible," he teased. "So what will you and Idis be up to now?"

"I hardly know," I said, "but I feel better knowing she's on my side." We'd made plans the whole of my flight home. Or rather she'd already *made* plans and I'd agreed to them. It was a relief to be in her hands and on her turf. I was, once I'd stopped being an emotional twat, very grateful.

"She is quite formidable when she wishes to be. You two have that in common," he said affectionately. "When are you seeing Mr. Harris?" Charles smiled, "That's the Lord Chamberlain to you."

"Tomorrow afternoon. Idis and I are meeting first in the morning." I frowned. "She said something about getting me ready that didn't really sound like we were rehearsing arguments." Then I remembered something. "She told me to do some fight training with Thal tonight." I shrugged. "I'm pretty sure it was an order."

He laughed harder this time. He laughed long enough that I pouted, though I was secretly thrilled he was so happy.

"Care to explain the joke, Six?"

"I will, Red," he said with mock seriousness. "She is reminding you of who you are."

"And who am I, Sir?" I said arms folded over my chest.

"Mine," he said, kissing me possessively. "Also a teacher, a soldier, a leader, a powerful super, a friend, a protector and, though I know you don't want to hear it, the Red Angel."

"Yuck."

"I can't agree with you there, Jane, but I think borrowing the Red Angel's fearlessness is called for right now, at least until you find your own again."

I studied his handsome, pale and freckled face as I thought about it. "You're right."

"It goes without saying," he said with a grin and I swatted him playfully on the shoulder. "Now go and fight and I will see you tomorrow afterwards."

"Tomorrow?" Then I got it. Idis. "Sure." While none of the three of us had ever thought about sharing within the same house, we had to adapt. At least this was a change I could understand. I kissed him and got out of bed, his golden eyes turned black again as he watched my naked self head for the closet. "Just so you know, she thinks we look like uncooked bread. With freckles."

He was still chuckling when I was dressed and on my way.

19:00 – Gymnasium, Robin Hill

I was stretching as Thal stood unobtrusively in the corner. Much as my brain hated exercising, my body was really happy to be moving again. Yes, it had betrayed me by enjoying exercise much more than I did. I'd been a good girl, though, and had checked with a doctor to see what I was allowed to do pregnant and what I wasn't and, aside from not getting hit square in the stomach, I was allowed to do pretty much anything I wanted especially since I wasn't even showing. She'd warned me that this would change as I…expanded, but for now I was good to go.

I'd actually been sparring for about thirty minutes with a patient Thal when my guest arrived with a guest of his own.

"Stuart!" I said with a grin as I walked over to embrace him. "And Sir," I said extending my hand for a shake with Prince Ronnie.

"Ronnie was bored," Stuart explained.

"You're going to fight, Your Highness?" I asked, surprised. The concept just didn't fit him. At all.

"Lord, no, Miss Jane," Prince Ronnie scoffed, "but I thought it would be fun to watch Stu get his ass handed to him."

"Only fun for you, Ronnie," Stuart grumbled.

"Don't count out Lord Miller," I said loyally, "he was quite something back in the day."

Stuart laughed, "That was many years…"

"…and many pounds…" the Prince muttered.

"Ago," Stuart finished with a glare at his friend. He looked from his, shall we say, comfortable girth to my stomach. "Let's keep an eye on both our bellies tonight, shall we?"

"Agreed." I walked over to a near table and grabbed some water. "Do you want to warm up?"

The Prince snorted. "He's been doing all sorts of strange contortions ever since you called. He's ready."

Stuart's cheeks pinked. "Well, it has been a while."

"I have orders for you, Miss Jane," the Prince said unexpectedly.

"Your Highness?"

"From the Countess," Prince Ronnie said smugly. "You are to start small but you are *required*," he said with emphasis, "to show off as much as you can."

"Oh really, Sir?" I said with a grin that could only be described as evil.

"Am I going to die today?" Stuart asked plaintively.

"Oh, and you can't kill him," the Prince said almost as an afterthought. "He has seven or eight more children to father before we're through with him."

"Nice to know I have my uses," Stuart grumbled. Then he turned to the Prince, "Isn't it about time you let Jane call you Ronnie? She'll outrank you within the next couple of weeks anyway."

"I don't give up my privilege until the second I have to, Stuart," he sniffed, but then he grinned at me, "Will you make me call you High Exalted Jane whatever, Miss Jane?"

I snorted like the future…whatever I was going to be. "Not likely, Sir."

"Then once the ring is on your finger you may call me anything you like."

"Anything?" The mind reeled with possibilities and I started to chuckle.

The Prince started to look alarmed and conceded, "Ronnie is fine, Jane."

"Thanks," I said with a laugh. "Shall we begin, Stu?"

"Yeah."

A reluctant Stuart and I moved to the center of the mat and squared off. I held up my hand and we both stopped. "Three rounds straight fighting."

"Goodie," Stuart mumbled.

I went into my horse stance and Stuart did the same.

"Ready," Thal said, "and FIGHT!"

I punched (from the shoulder) and my fist came within inches of Stuart's chest as he danced out of the way. I followed with a sweeping kick from my left leg, aiming to catch his feet, but he grabbed my leg with surprising ease and pushed it back, throwing off my balance just for a second. He then landed a punch in my ribs that, well, didn't feel good at all.

I didn't let myself feel the pain (no time) as I moved my right arm back to wrap it backwards around his neck. I pushed myself back with all my weight and we landed on our backs with myself on top of him, my back to his stomach. I'd hit him just hard enough to wind him.

"Round 1 to Miss Jane," Thal called out. I'd forgotten he was there.

I got up and turned to offer my hand to a red-faced Stuart, who took it.

"I thought you promised not to kill me?" he whined.

"That was hot," Ronnie said. Stuart gave him a withering look. "Well, it was."

I stifled a giggle and said, "Again?"

"Why the fuck not," Stuart said.

We went into our stances for the second time.

"FIGHT!"

This time he punched one-two my hip (with his left) and my knee (with his right). He'd gotten the angle just right and I wobbled, just for a second, as I kicked him square in the chest with my right foot. He stepped back, absorbing the blow and whipped around catching me square in my bad shoulder. Ow. I went down, but used the momentum he'd forced on me to roll away from him, putting me out of the reach of his next kick. I got back up and punched like a mad woman, Stuart blocking me with his sheer determination not to go down as easily this time. I grabbed his fist and turned him around, landing several good punches to the kidneys. I moved closer to grab him around the throat when he spun around and landed a perfect kick right in the center of my chest.

I toppled 'catching' myself before I hit the ground.

"Round Two to Lord Miller," Thal said.

Stuart helped me up looking extremely pleased with himself.

"And what was *that*, My Lord?" I asked, pleased, too, though a bit worse for wear.

"Did we not mention that Bobby has been training the last month with a master in Gloriana-Levvon?" Ronnie said smugly.

I grinned, delighted. "You both set me up, you bastards."

"Never assume, Jane," Stuart said allowing himself some smugness, "You know better than that."

"Uh huh," I said. I was going to kick my old friend's ass now. Stuart paled. "Last time without abilities, ok?"

Stuart nodded and we prepared.

"FIGHT!"

This time we both moved so quickly it would have been hard for an observer to follow what was going on. Stuart seemed on fire as he whirled around, kicking like a man possessed. I kept up with him just barely, analyzing his moves, his strengths. Kick kick kick all in circular motions. He'd been training for a month. I, however, had been training for much longer. I landed a punch, but my goal wasn't to win, not yet. I was fighting a war of attrition. Sweat dripped off of us and his muscles were screaming for relief. Yes, I know, no powers, but I couldn't help this passive information from coming through. He was tired. And frustrated. And angry as he realized what I was doing.

"Damn it, Jane!" he said through gritted teeth.

All right, then.

He whirled around with an excellent kick, I grabbed his foot with both hands (a risky move) and instead of stopping his momentum, I pushed so that he continued to turn and lost his balance. I then threw myself on his back as I kicked his remaining foot off the ground and we landed in a heap on the mat with a groan (from both of us).

"Round 3 to Miss Jane," Thal said.

I got up, a little more slowly than last time. I may have been in better shape that Stuart, but that didn't mean this was a walk in the park for me. I offered him a hand, but he waved me off with a smile and caught his breath for a second.

"Nice one, Jane."

"The footwork is new."

"Work is right," he laughed tiredly. "Now one with abilities?"

"Sure." He let me help him up now and we squared off again.

"Open up, Miss," Stuart smiled, "but only passive Micro, please. Or this will all be over in two seconds." He rubbed his jaw wryly, "Not that that doesn't have its appeal right now."

"Lightweight," I teased.

"Lifter," he teased back.

I 'opened' my mind and grounded at the same time.

"Ready," Thal said as he stepped forward, "and FIGHT!"

Stuart, clearly summoning the last of his energy went for the kill with a series of kicks that were so fast they appeared to blur. I knew he'd 'read' me so I needed this to go quickly enough that his information would be useless to him. So... I 'pushed' myself up into the air, spun around like a top with one foot raised to the level of my chin and came down behind him, sending him flying to the ground. Just like that.

Stuart, now in a heap on the floor, held up his hand in surrender.

"Final round to Miss Jane," Thal said as tossed me a small towel (god, I was sweaty) and then he quickly moved over to help Stuart up.

"I want to play a game I can win," Stuart whined, but, despite a split lip, he grinned tiredly.

I, on the other hand, felt *terrific*. Like I'd stretched muscles that had desperately needed stretching. I felt like a bad-ass for the first time in a long time. It was amazing.

Well played, Idis. Well played.

Stuart leaned on Prince Ronnie who seemed to be staring at me with new eyes.

"Ronnie?" I asked.

Ronnie shook his head, his affectations gone for the moment. "That was..." He smiled. "No one is going to want to fuck with Corsica now. You know that, don't you, Jane?"

His words stopped me cold, but in a good way. It was like some piece of a puzzle had fallen into place. When I married Charles I would be (by extension) responsible for an Empire—not directly, but they would still be *my people*. I suppose it should have scared the crap out of me (being responsible for one tiny child had made me lose my mind, so why not this?) but it didn't. I could have a place here, one I understood. Ronnie's words had somehow made it Ok.

I looked at him and Ronnie apparently saw something in my eyes that made him take a step back.

"Anyone who fucks with Corsica fucks with me," I stood straighter, even though it hurt to do so, "and that would be a serious mistake."

"That was scary, Jane," Ronnie said as Stuart nodded. "Still hot, though."

I laughed and threw my sweaty towel at him.

They left soon after and Thal and I sparred until I was too tired and sore to continue.

16:00 – Lord Chamberlain's Office, Imperial Palace, Irena, Corsican Empire, October 16th, 2873

The next day Idis and I stood outside the ornate office of the Lord Chamberlin, awaiting our audience. The shuttle in from Robin Hill had brought us in a bit early. I hadn't been back to the Palace since Charles' attempted assassination and it was hard not to think about how close we'd come to losing him. That was making me scared and sad, emotions which would not be helpful today, so I distracted myself with what was to hand, namely clothes.

You may think that I, Jane Pace, don't care about clothes and you would usually be right, but this was an unusual circumstance. Idis' version of getting me ready for this meeting had been to put me into full Red Angel gear (though she'd toned the big hair down so that I could still see and hear). So I had the red corset top, the black pants and jacket and the bad-ass boots. I was a giantess. It was Idis, however, who had my full attention clothing-wise.

She wore black and red, like me, but that didn't even begin to cover it. Her dress was so large, so bejeweled, so gorgeously ornate that she positively glittered from the top of her ruby-encrusted hair to the tips of her red velvet shoes. (You, of course, couldn't see the shoes without asking, but I'd asked.) She'd had to turn sideways to walk through doors. She'd taken up four seats in the shuttle. She was a work of art. It was full court dress, she'd said. The kind one wore to coronations and weddings—the kind only someone of her rank could wear.

"What? No crown?" I'd teased.

"It's a tiara and I'm saving it for the actual wedding," she'd said, the humor leaving her blue eyes. I'd wanted to say something to make it better, but couldn't think of a damn thing that wouldn't make it worse so I'd kept silent. I thought she'd appreciated my silence. I certainly hoped so.

"So this is your 'don't screw with me, Lord Chamberlain' dress," I'd asked attempting to lighten the mood.

She'd smiled, "That is exactly what it is, Jane."

We'd gone over a couple of points, but she didn't try to manage me too much, which was nice. The Lord Chamberlain was a true snob and an appointee of the late Empress Marianna. They had been cut from the same cloth, apparently, and he lived his Court life by her grasping standard. Idis hadn't divulged too much more, but I had to think that being the unmarried

Mistress of the Palace under this man hadn't been a picnic. After the interview I was to wonder how she'd survived.

"Countess, Commodore Pace, the Lord Chamberlain will see you now," a functionary said portentously. The Countess, Idis to you, gave me a quick look, checking for nerves, I supposed, but I wasn't nervous. Not anymore. This was a man with power, but he was just a person. Just like everyone else. I could eat him for breakfast. Not literally. Too kinky even for me.

We were shown into a, once again, very fancy office. There were chairs of gold, desk of gold, really dim looking paintings and the clutter of knickknacks everywhere. I think there was at least one sword in a case. Everything said old and tradition. I couldn't have given a ripe shit.

An averaged-sized very old man with dark skin and rheumy eyes, wearing an expensive black suit and a large gold ceremonial chain around his neck that seemed to reach his navel walked from behind his desk over to us. Physically he was unprepossessing, but his manner was very, very formal and grand, not to mention off-putting. A taller blonder, much younger man stayed to the side of the desk.

Idis extended her hand for the Lord Chamberlain to kiss, which he did with a curt bow over said hand. Her expression was cool. He turned to me and I offered my hand to shake. He hesitated with a slight grimace and shook it touching the least amount of skin he could. He gave me a professionally disapproving look. Apparently I had erred against protocol. I smiled showing how *terribly* upset I was to have gotten something wrong. He frowned, my sarcasm not lost on him.

"It is a pleasure to see you, Countess, and to meet you, Commodore Pace," he said insincerely.

"And you," we said with equal insincerity.

"This is the lawyer for the Crown," he said, "Mr. MacTavish, esquire."

Now Idis actually smiled. "So they've roped you into this, Angus."

"Yes, My Lady," Angus said with a quirk of the lips. "I've been called in from the bench in your absence."

"It's good to see you." She liked him. Good to know.

"Thank you, Ma'am."

"Shall we get started?" the Lord Chamberlain said with thinly disguised annoyance.

"Of course, My Lord," Idis said.

240

We all sat around a low table, Idis and I on one side (there was a stool made, I had to assume, especially for ladies with large dresses for Idis and a regular chair with a back for me) and the Lord Chamberlain and Angus on the other side.

The Lord pulled a stack of legal documents from off his desk and put them gently on his lap. "It appears that his Imperial Highness desires to marry you, Commodore Jane Pace of Pace-Pallon and Terra 1."

What an odd, and not particularly nice, way to put it. "Yes."

He pursed his lips. "Has a date been set for the wedding?"

"Yes," Idis answered. "November 4th."

Mr. Harris pretended he hadn't heard her and looked at me.

"The Lady said November 4th," I said. What the heck?

He sniffed and made a note. "November 4th, 2874."

"No, My Lord," I corrected, "November 4th, *2873*."

His face became even more disapproving. "Plan an Imperial Wedding in two and a half weeks?" He shook his hoary head. "Not possible."

Idis was cool as always. "The Commodore has a semester to teach and she's already missed many classes. Even at two and a half weeks, she'll have been gone half the Fall Semester."

"You're putting that as a priority over the Emperor's *Wedding*?"

Our combined silence seemed to confirm this, apparently, insane thought.

"I will have to speak to his Imperial Highness about it," he said.

"If you like," Idis responded confidently.

This confidence irritated the man further. "Even *if* the Emperor approved the plan," he made this sound highly unlikely, "there isn't time to plan a wedding of this magnitude."

"Nonsense," Idis scoffed. "I have the plan together already and am meeting with my people first thing tomorrow."

The Lord Chamberlin turned to her, looking at her for the first time. "I'm sorry, Countess, but I am not sure why you are here."

Idis bristled. "I live here."

"Currently, yes," he said, "but I do not understand why you are in this room. This is Crown business." He raised an eyebrow. "We already have an attorney."

What an asshole. "The Countess is here because I have asked her to be," I said, not really sure of the play.

"How charming," he sneered, "the old guard training the successor."

I started to retort hotly, but Idis rode right over me. "Since the date is non-negotiable," Idis said with firmness, "shall we move on? Title?"

Mr. Harris clearly felt this wasn't worth his time so gestured to his colleague to continue which Angus did.

"As My Lady well knows, the consort of the Emperor will be Her Imperial Highness, Princess of Lyonesse, Royal Consort, etc. etc.. With her titles come lands and royal income on Trea, our oldest Imperial Acquisition, as well as a household and estate."

Ugh. I didn't want to be Princess of anything, but some things couldn't be avoided, so Idis and I had worked on a compromise. A compromise the Lord Chamberlain was going to hate.

"That is acceptable," Idis said and Mr. Harris roused himself to make a note on his papers when she said, "with some modifications." He stopped writing and scowled.

"Modifications," he repeated.

"Two points," I said, "I will live at Robin Hill and the Palace while I am on-planet and have no need for either a household or an estate. The Trea property can be held for next Imperial Spouse."

"How will you draw your income without an estate?" the Lord Chamberlain said, aghast.

"I have all I need." Before he could object again I continued, "My official title will be 'Commodore Pace-Couvillion-Bourbonnais of the Union ESTF, Her Imperial Highness the Princess of Lyonesse at any state functions and Commodore Pace on ordinary days."

"That is not how it is done on Corisca, Commodore," he said.

"Yet it is how we *will do it*," I said, putting a touch of menace in my voice.

"Excuse me," Angus said, clearly not wanting to jump into the fray but feeling compelled to anyway.

"Yes?" Mr. Harris said, irritated.

"I don't understand how the Commodore can be, according to the schedule you sent us yesterday, off-planet half the year and expect to take over all of the Countess' duties for the Imperium." Angus looked at all of us. "She does quite a lot, you know." His voice got smaller as we made no response. "More than most people realize…" If there had been a hole for the poor man to crawl into, he would have disappeared inside it he was so embarrassed.

I looked at Idis, but she said nothing and wouldn't look at me. We'd never discussed this, mostly because it had never crossed my mind to bring up. Apparently just as the idea of Idis having to make way for me seemed crazy to me, but that I wasn't going to oust her was crazy to everyone else including, to some extent, Idis herself.

Now, for the first time, the Lord Chamberlain looked pleased. "There will be plenty for the Countess to do on her estate on Berria," he said condescendingly. "There is no shortage of small endeavors there, one is sure, that will fill the Countess' time."

"She could go to the law full time…" Angus started, then blushed and stopped.

"The quiet of country life would be a welcome change after all the years here," the Lord Chamberlain said. "I can train you, Commodore, in the finer points of being the Imperial Hostess, etc."

I really hated that pompous son of a bitch.

It was then, however, that I realized why Idis herself had never brought this up. Pride. I technically had the power, not to boot her, only Charles could do that, but to diminish her. It would probably have been all too easy were I the sort of person who cared about status or power and currying favor at Court. Or if I were a complete bitch. I don't give myself too much credit character-wise, but a *complete* bitch I am not.

"I'm sorry the information we sent you was not clear," I said in a low voice. "The Countess' duties will remain the same in every respect unless she wishes them to change."

"Really?" Angus said, pleased, as the Lord Chamberlain gave him a murderous look.

"The Emperor will be *married*," Mr. Harris said, "You can't expect the Empire to continue to honor a…"

"…displaced mistress?" Idis finished for him icily.

"But she is not displaced," I said, taking Idis's cold and reluctant hand firmly in my own. "Before we were mistress and girlfriend to the Emperor, now we will be mistress and wife to the Emperor. The three of us will be raising the new Princess together, as a family, but aside from that things will go on as they have before." Massive oversimplification and not entirely true, but true enough for this dickhead.

"I see," the Lord Chamberlain said with quiet fury.

Well, I'd had enough. "What exactly do you see, My Lord?" I said.

"Jane…" Idis tried but I shook my head.

"I'm curious as to why he is so upset and I figure that he won't feel free to speak his mind once I have married his Emperor, so, Sir, what exactly has crawled up your ass?"

The Lord Chamberlain became silent as the grave. Oh, he wanted to tell me where to stick it, but my putting him on the spot meant anything he said would have to be outright rude. I'd taken the right of snide insinuation away from him and he was silently livid about it.

"Let me help you, My Lord, since we will be good friends for many years to come," I said with a smile. "You are sitting with the Emperor's Whores. You'd thought you'd gotten rid of the pedigreed one and you haven't, which must be disappointing, and now you have to deal with a second one. Whore #2, that would be me, is not only an interloper of uncertain lineage and no breeding but a supernormal freak possessing a functional, not to mention occupied, uterus. Your newest Princess will be half-freak and may end up being a half-freak Empress in the bargain."

The Lord Chamberlain was alternating red and white in the face, but he held his peace.

"You are also very angry that the not-displaced Whore #1 will be planning the wedding to end all weddings—an event you had expected to control." I paused for a fraction of a second. When I'd said the word 'wedding' his gut had clenched. Right then I knew I had the old fossil by the balls. Excellent. "Now you'll have to bow and scrape for both Whores forever."

"I have never said any of that, Commodore," Mr. Harris said with a kind of grand bravado (covered in a heavy sprinkling of fear). "Telling anyone I did would be an outright lie."

"True, it would," I agreed, "and I have no intention of lying to anyone, even you." I leaned forward and stared the Lord Chamberlain in the eye. "So let me be quite clear. The Countess is my friend and my partner, along with the Emperor. This disrespect, whether subtle or overt, must stop *right now*. Anyone who disrespects her will have me to answer to." My voice was quiet and gentle, which I hoped made what I was saying even scarier.

"Threatening me will not help you at Court, Commodore," he said.

"Like I care, little man," I said, preparing to strike. "If this is all too much for you I will marry the Emperor in a cabin on my ship with Idis by my side and be done with it. The journos will fall all over themselves to cover it."

"You wouldn't do that," he said openly horrified, his heart really racing now.

"Try me," I said through gritted teeth.

"She can't..." Mr. Harris looked beseechingly at Idis. Oh, so now he wanted her help?

"She can, My Lord, and she will," Idis said calmly following my lead, though her heart was racing, too. It was a bluff, well, not for me since I didn't care one way or the other, but a bluff for her. "It would certainly save us all the bother of having to pull off a 'not possible' Imperial wedding in so little time."

"We haven't had a true Imperial wedding in a hundred years." The Lord Chamberlain was quietly panicking.

I looked askance at Idis.

"The Emperor was a mere Prince and heir when he married the future Empress," she explained. "A ruling Emperor marrying would be the high point in a Lord Chamberlain's career."

The old man looked a bit lost and I would have pitied him except for the fact that I could remember quite clearly what an asshole he'd been up to that point.

"So," Idis said, "we will do this our way and you will get your crowning," pun intended, I was sure, "achievement. Correct?"

"As you and the Commodore wish, My Lady," he said faintly.

"Good."

He swallowed hard and collected himself. "When, if I may ask, is the baby due to be born?"

Idis and I both smiled as she answered, "June 11th."

The Lord Chamberlain, "Congratulations," and stared into space, defeated, at least temporarily.

It was Angus who said, quite warmly, "May I add my congratulations, My Lady, Ma'am?"

"Thank you Angus," Idis said.

The rest of the interview was much more respectful on everyone's part and we'd gotten a lot accomplished. Apparently the estate on Trea had already been established earlier in the year so it couldn't simply be disposed of, but Idis would manage it when I was gone and the income would go to fund programs to assist freed slaves. Idis and Atalanta would stand up with me at the wedding and the Princes Alex and Hal would stand up with him. The wedding itself would, because of time constraints, have to be a simpler affair (only by Imperial standards) anyway, which suited me just fine. The Lord Chamberlain had been horrified on several occasions during the discussion, but was smart enough to keep his feelings and subtle digs (for now) to himself.

I was pretty sure Angus had a crush on Idis, but Idis was merely kind and friendly to him. All of us knew where her heart was, of course, but it was really cute watching Angus adore her from afar.

<u>02:01 – Informal Dining Room, Robin Hill, October 17th, 2873</u>

Back in the Informal Dining Room Charles lay sweaty and quite pleased with himself over my partially clad body on top of the dining table. Apparently it was quite capable of holding two people. Charles hadn't been sure, but I'd dared him and it had been quite the adventure. I smiled and stroked his hair.

"I think I may have found an exhibitionist streak in you, my love."

"I closed the curtains," he protested with a laugh.

I kissed the top of his head, "But unless you gave the guards earplugs…"

He shrugged. "You'll be making an honest man of me soon enough, no one would begrudge us some illicit fun now."

"Least of all me."

He moved up the table a bit and took me in his arms. Perfect. The stubble of the beard he was growing tickled. I loved it.

"The invitations have gone out?' he asked.

"Tomorrow," I said comfortably as I snuggled closer.

"I'm sorry they had to be so limited."

"The people that need to be there will be," I said. This was true, for the most part.

"Except Wilby. Except Quinn." He felt me tense. "I'm sure they would make an exception for a wedding."

"They didn't make an exception for *theirs*," I said bitterly.

"No, they didn't." He ran his hand down my spine making me shiver. "Am I a fool for trying to hold on to Fitzroy a bit longer?"

Because I wasn't marrying Charles Fitzroy, I was marrying the Emperor Charles 6, which meant more secrecy on Terra 1, unfortunately, since a 'Princess' (ugh) couldn't be seen keeping company with the Emperor's trusted Ambassador. It also explained the beard Charles was

246

growing. The Emperor wore one, the Ambassador didn't. I was Ok with saving Fitz, in fact, I'd suggested it. The clock was ticking on Charles Fitzroy, we both knew, but I didn't like the idea of my Six giving him up a second before he had to. The look of relief and gratitude on my lover's face when I'd suggested it had made the future annoyances worth it.

"Perhaps," I said with a smile, "but Fitz does a lot of good. Keeping him alive can't be a bad thing."

"I hope it isn't, in the end." He kissed me, "Thank you."

"Anytime."

He chuckled. "Have you decided who is giving you away?"

I sat up next to him. "You know how barbaric that custom is, don't you?"

He sat up, too, his eyes twinkling, "As if you've been sold and are being handed over to your buyer, I know. Just be happy I talked Mr. Harris out of insisting on a dowry."

"You're joking?"

"Yes, indeed. You've met the Lord Chamberlain so you know what a madcap fellow he is."

Yeah yeah yeah. I flapped my hands in surrender. "According to tradition, it is supposed to be either one or both of my parents," I shrugged acknowledgement of my lack of them, "or some sort of male authority figure that has played an important part in my life. Problem is the person who fits the bill best is..."

"...Sam." Charles moved behind me, long legs surrounding mine as he wrapped me in his arms. "I wouldn't mind, you know, if it would make you happy."

"I'm just not sure it would make *him* happy."

"Probably not. Then who?"

A plain, almost ugly but truly loveable face popped into my head. "Felix."

"Felix?"

"And Daniel."

I felt his grin on the back of my neck. "I sense someone is interfering again."

"Always," I said with a laugh.

"While I applaud your efforts to reunite the Trio, you may be dealing with feelings you can't just 'fix' the way you usually do."

"I know but I can't help feeling guilty."

"For being happy?" He swallowed and his voice lowered. "You are happy, Jane, even with all this?"

I angled back to kiss him. "Too happy, Charles."

He kissed me again, this time with a bit more intent and it was seriously hot, but his words had made me think about the wedding in more emotional terms. Not *my* emotions, though. I pulled back.

"Six?"

"Hmm?"

"What would you say to spending the wedding night with Idis?" He looked at me, surprised, but considered it while I continued. "We'll have the trip back to Terra 1 on the *Lumina*, but she won't have that. I know she is strong…"

"…but this is still an uncertain time for her." He kissed my shoulder. "That is generous, Jane."

"She is one of us, love. I'm afraid she'll get scared and forget."

He smiled, his eyes bright. "I love you."

"Charles," I said, my throat tight with excess feeling.

He kissed me and we entertained the guards a bit more.

ENTRY 7-8-90

13:03 – Shuttle Landing Ground, Imperial Palace, Irena, Corsican Empire, November 3rd, 2873

Stuart and Persephone Jane had returned to Gloriana-Levvon the week before so that Pilar and Ronnie could attend the wedding. Pilar's security, including my old friend Huong, were very humorless about the safety of their rulers, and since Stuart and Pilar were *never* allowed to be off planet at the same time, my friend had dutifully gone home. I'd rather tearfully thanked him for everything and he'd (almost) tearfully said it was nothing. What were friends for? (Who would have thought that the ex-lover whose dick I'd almost pinched off would have, along with his lover's husband, saved me from my own mind years later. Fate is a brilliant bitch, isn't she?)

Pilar had arrived a couple of days ago and was luxuriously ensconced in a suite with room for Ronnie and Chester, who'd accompanied her. The reunion of Ronnie and Chester had been sweet and their kiss of greeting a bit dirty. Wonderful.

Back to the present, though.

People were starting to arrive. Lots and lots of people. Not Samuel, who had been invited but had been swamped with Union business. Not Wilby or Quinn. Plenty of other people, though. Most were coming for the pageantry, some to meet the new Imperial Consort and honor their Emperor and some because they were my friends. My percentages were low, as compared to those on the groom's side of the aisle, but they were very, very important to me, these people.

The transport from the Furies had just landed outside the Palace. I stood with Bertie Nylander. The freshly divorced Albert looked ten years younger since the decree had been speedily granted and Nora forcedly ejected from Corsica. I was very happy for him and happy for the Empire. Nora was a complication it didn't need. Charles, who was protecting Fitz's identity, had wanted to join me at the landing field, but couldn't (obviously) and Idis was elsewhere. I could only hope that she wasn't avoiding my people, who knew a great deal of the story of Jane/Charles/Idis, to save herself from understanding and pitying stares. She needn't have worried, if she was indeed concerned. We were a pretty damned accepting group.

A tall, almost delicate man with thinning red hair exited the shuttle. Paulie Friedman. Freya, the Heely Captain of the *Indus Felae* followed, an unusual sight on Irena, not just because she was easily the tallest being in the area, but because she was first Heely human to ever set foot on Corsican soil. Her pale green eyes sparkled as she scanned the small crowd gathering for the other shuttles. I could see her nod to herself as she took in the heavy security. She held the hand of another Heely, not so tall, not so imposing and with a devilish twinkle in her eye.

Bertie checked his list. "Who is *that*?"

The second Heely winked at me and I started to laugh. "Lieutenant Felaysa Torva, Albert."

Bertie smiled. "Striking a blow against anti-Heely sentiment?"

Then I had a thought and groaned. "She's going to give Captain Stanley fits," I snickered. "Five credits says she gets arrested every time she changes her appearance."

He snickered, too. "No bet." Then he stared hard at my former bed mate. "Wait, you mean she's one of *those*?"

"Careful," I said.

Bertie shook his head. "I mean an HM. I've never actually met one before."

"Far as you know," I said under my breath, but then I turned to him. "Be respectful, Albert. She's off the clock."

"Oh," he said, chastened, "of course."

The three Furies personnel we could see paused, apparently waiting for the rest of their party. Daniel and Felix emerged almost immediately and then Atalanta, still shorn and worn. The group moved towards us at last and I raced forward. Daniel and Felix quickly moved to the front of the pack with Atalanta falling far behind. I wrapped the boys up in a big embrace.

"It's great to see you. Thank you for coming. Are you all right?" I blurted. They felt thin. Their bodies read tired. Damn it. No change then, but 'Lanta would have written if there had been, I supposed.

"We're surviving," Felix said into my collar bone, gripping me tightly around the waist. Daniel said nothing at all, just hugged. "We're so happy for you, Jane." Daniel nodded.

"Thanks," I said with a grin as I let them go. I extended my hand to Paul. "Captain, thank you for coming."

He smiled. "An honor, Jane."

I shook hands with Freya and hugged Fey, then turned to my companion. "This is Albert Nylander. The Emperor's best friend and best man."

Bertie rolled his eyes. "Really, Jane, you make this sound like boarding school."

"Doesn't make it any less true, Bertie."

Bertie started meeting everyone and I stole over to the lovely form of my Atalanta. She looked like real shit. For Atalanta. Even so she was still stunning. I hugged her. She let me.

"You're evil, you know," she whispered.

"You're just realizing this now, love?" I said.

"It won't work. Just because we're in the wedding party together doesn't mean everything will be fixed."

I sighed. "Always my little ray of sunshine."

"Fuck off, Jane," she said with affection.

"I'll join you at the welcome reception in a bit."

"More arrivals?"

"Like you wouldn't believe."

She nodded then, to my surprise, kissed me on the cheek and sauntered off to join Fey and Freya. Daniel and Felix watched her go forlornly then followed respectfully behind.

"I thought they were a Trio," Albert said as he reappeared next to me.

"It's complicated."

"Isn't everything?" he said and I shrugged my agreement. Another shuttle landed. "Ah, next."

They just kept coming. Many of the new arrivals were strangers to me. People I needed to meet as part of my new 'position.' Most appeared pleasant but it was a dreadful bore.

The arrival of Garrett and Derek Pace-Taylor was a bright spot in the whole thing and their enthusiasm and happiness for Charles and me had lightened the doldrums for a good while, but it was back to the grind soon enough.

It wasn't until about an hour after they'd been taken to their rooms in one of the out buildings (only the royals and the Trio, at my request, were in the Palace itself) that another shuttle I recognized landed. Landed and almost gave me a heart attack. Mr. Beddoes had joined us by then, ready to take personal care of our next visitors. The shuttle was the *Annabelle*. David's ship. Named after his late mother. Fuck me running. Of course he hadn't been invited, but… He wouldn't, would he? He would. Wouldn't he?

"What's wrong?" Albert said. "You look pale, Jane." He frowned worriedly. "God, is it the baby?"

It wasn't, but I checked in anyway. Nope. Fine. "He can't be here," I said, almost hyperventilating.

"You invited General Manthorpe personally," Albert said, confused. "I thought he was your friend."

Marston, right. Coming from Novy with his wife. I scanned the shuttle as Marston and his Queen and…Wylan? debarked. No David. I was able to breathe again.

They came in a tight group, Marston holding Tania's hand and Tania holding the hand of a very surly looking Wylan. Coming here was clearly not his idea. Or, for that matter, mine, not that I objected to Wylan's presence. As they approached I noticed how determined Tania was and how strong her grip.

I walked forward and quickly hugged Marston and Tania. Marston looked amused. Wylan, less amused, only dropped his attitude when he recognized his superior officer. He attempted to salute, but couldn't break out of Tania's death grip.

Once again introductions. "Marston, Tania, Cadet Wylan, this is Albert Nylander. Bertie, this is General Manthorpe of the ESTF, Her Majesty, Queen Tania of Novy Heliot, and…" I raised my eyebrows at Tania.

"Wylan of the *Demna Indus Felae*, my cousin and heir."

"Holy…" I started, but caught look from Marston, "poop," I finished weakly.

Marston covered a laugh with a cough. Badly.

Tania held out her non-Wylan hand and Bertie bowed over it. "A pleasure to meet all of you," he said respectfully.

"My cousin and I thought this wonderful event would be a good time to get to know each other, didn't we, Wylan?" Tania said with a smile that was all teeth. Like hell he did.

"Yes, Ma'am," Wylan said. *His* teeth were clenched.

"We hope this addition to our party won't be too much of an inconvenience, Mr. Nylander?" Tania asked knowing full well what a breach of protocol this was. Bad form, Tania, I thought. Idis will not be pleased.

"The Countess will be happy to oblige," Bertie said with a smile no one believed. "So it is three, Your Majesty?"

"Where is Petros, Cadet?" I asked because where the fuck was Wylan's shadow?

"On the ship, Commodore," Wylan said, his eyes pleading.

I nodded. It was tough enough being a teenager in his position as resident freak at school, but being a royal hostage on top of it? Wylan needed a friend. Or close enough. "Four, Bertie." I gave Tania and Marston a brilliant smile. "Petros will get a kick out of the Big Show, won't he?"

Tania looked displeased, but inclined her head in acquiescence.

Mr. Beddoes then stepped forward, all professionalism. "Your Highness, General, Cadet, I am Beddoes, the Emperor's Valet. I will show you to your apartments, if you will allow me to escort you."

"Thank you, Mr. Beddoes," Marston said. The group started to move and I ran up to buttonhole Marston.

"What the hell is she doing kidnapping one of our Cadets, Marston?" I hissed.

He shook his head. "She's been like this since the genetic tests came back."

"He's a teenager who's been bullied his entire life for who he is and *this* is how she treats him?"

"I'm trying, Jane, but she's desperate to keep the succession going. It wasn't a possibility before." Yes, the Manthorpes had no genetic children. Six kids, but none of Tania's blood.

"She's got teenaged sons, how could she be so…" I couldn't call her stupid, not to her adoring husband, but he flushed when he got my implication.

"They're not speaking to her either."

Oh crap. Marston, Wylan and Tania had already moved on, however. Damn it.

We took a break for the welcome reception that consisted of a lot of food and drink and plentiful awkwardness. The Trio barely spoke a word to anyone, let alone each other (even when they were in the same part of the room, which was rare) and I avoided the Manthorpe party because I didn't think I could be civil to Tania. Fun. I got out of there as soon as I could and probably sooner than I should have and returned to the landing area for more arrivals. Bertie joined me a few minutes later.

Some more shuttles landed, one of them bearing (in style) a couple I hadn't seen in a long time who were specifically my guests. You'll see them much later.

The sun had started to set when the final shuttle I'd been waiting for landed. This one was a special case, for a number of reasons.

I felt Charles approaching from the Palace, a coterie of guards with him. The shuttle waited as Captain Stanley and his people cleared the landing ground. My fiancé made his way to me, pulling me close with his arm around my waist. I sighed contentedly.

"Bertie," Charles said by way of greeting to his friend.

"Toff," Bertie replied.

Captain Stanley appeared and bowed in front of his Emperor. "The field is clear, Sire."

"Very good, Captain. Please give them the all-clear."

"Your Imperial Majesty." Stanley bowed again and started murmuring into his comm.

"Bertie?" Charles said.

"Yes?" Albert said as he checked his list again.

"Would you consider going back to work on Terra?" I could feel my lover's heart rate go up. He was a little nervous.

"If you like," Albert said, mind still on his list.

"As a Senator."

Albert looked up, surprised. "Really?"

Charles swallowed. "It will be a while before you get what I promised, Bertie, but you could do a lot of good in the *Senatus* until then." He paused. "If you want to." I could feel Charles' body tense as if steeling for a blow. Not a physical blow, of course, but an emotional one. Albert had been promised the job of Ambassador to the Union more than a decade before, but he couldn't have the job if Fitz still occupied it. Albert could read Charles the riot act right now and Charles was clearly prepared to take it.

Just then two forms exited their shuttle and started to make their way over to us. One was my dear friend Ian, wearing a patch over his missing left eye, and the other was the beautiful, elegant, ethereal Eriss Fenton of the Rian Nation. I wondered why she didn't fly, but she was clearly happy to be walking by Ian's side. Interesting.

Albert exhaled hard as he took her in. She really was something. "Are there more like *her* somewhere?" Albert asked me quietly.

"There are a few hundred Tarine Rian, though," I frowned, "she's the only one that can still fly." Ah, such a tragedy. I was so glad the bitch Pelann was still dead.

Ian and Eriss got closer and Eriss was not getting any less beautiful the closer she got.

"How about Corsican Ambassador to the Tarine Rian, Toff?" He grinned at his oldest friend. "That ought to buy you a decade or so with all the shit going on right now."

"What about the Deneth Rian?" I asked.

"Zero-G makes me puke." Bertie's eyes never left Eriss. "What do you say, Boss?"

"I wish I'd thought of it myself," Charles grimaced. "Yes, of course."

I leaned closer to Albert, "I'd stop looking at her like that, Bertie. Fucking with Ian would be a huge mistake."

"Noted," Albert replied softly because they'd finally reached us.

The first thing I noticed was Eriss's smile when she saw me happily next to my fiancé, but she schooled her expression immediately. Protocol. Since I was the only one of the group that knew all five of us, I stepped forward. I knew I was supposed to give the ultra-formal introductions, with titles, etc. It's what Idis would have done automatically. It's what a Corsican Princess would do, too. Well, I wasn't one yet, goddamn it.

"Charles, this is Eriss and you remember Ian, Samuel's son." I grinned. "And this is Albert Nylander, Charles' best man. Glad you could make it."

Charles laughed. "Blessed informality."

Bertie chuckled, too, "I really wish you had done that in front of the Lord Chamberlain. Would have finished the crusty old bastard off for good."

Eriss rolled her eyes at me but stepped forward confidently. "Your Highness, it is a privilege to meet you at long last." *This* Princess, at least, knew what to say.

Charles did not bow, outranking her, but he did kiss her hand. "A pleasure..." and he waited for her to complete the sentence. Yes, what the heck title did she use anyway?

"Miss Fenton will do, Sir, though my friends call me Eriss," she said with a smile.

"Eriss, then." Charles extended his hand to Ian. "Captain, it is good to see you again."

"Congratulations, Sir," Ian said as he looked at me with his one beautiful eye. "It is good to see you both." Better than 'welcome back from the nut house, Jane.' "I'm so sorry we couldn't get to Corsica sooner." He glanced at Eriss. "Events overtook us yet again, but it seems things have worked out quite well without us." He sighed. "There are times I wish more things did."

Boy, did I understand that.

"We were hoping, Sir," Eriss said, her voice low, "to ask your advice about it all, perhaps once you have arrived back on Terra?" She glanced meaningfully at me.

"I would be glad to offer my opinion," Charles said mildly, though I knew he was dying to pick Eriss' brain on the subject. I kept my amusement at his playing it cool to myself.

I saw Mr. Beddoes moving across the lawn once again, coming to fetch the visitors to the Palace. Charles gave me a wink and offered Eriss his arm, which she took.

"Don't get any ideas, Eriss" I said, teasingly. "That one's taken." I grinned. "Twice." I saw Eriss sneak a look at Ian who looked guilty and sad. The brief glance he gave her when she'd turned back to Charles, however, was one of longing. So no progress there.

Charles snorted a very un-Emperor-like snort as he checked his watch. "Rehearsal and then that blasted dinner in half an hour."

"Ugh," I said eloquently, but much as I didn't want to go to the rehearsal for the ceremony, there was no doubt we really needed one. Way too complicated to wing it. "I'll see you then, love."

Charles' gold eyes twinkled. "Bet your ass you will, Jane."

Yes, I know I'm besotted, but that was adorable. They started towards the Palace leaving Albert, Ian and myself behind.

"I'll need to be at that meeting, about the Tarine," Albert said. Ian looked confused but I nodded.

"Don't worry, Bertie," I reassured. "You'll be there." Albert nodded curtly. "Thank you," I said, putting my hand lightly on his arm, "for letting him off the hook for a while."

Albert shrugged. "I'm learning that friends do that. Right Jane?"

I nodded. "They do." We watched him go.

"What was that about?" Ian asked as I tucked my hand into the crook of his arm.

"He's the new Ambassador to the Tarine."

"Since when?"

"Since about," I checked my watch, "six minutes ago."

"He's up for it?"

"As much as anyone, I think," I said thoughtfully. "He's a good man, Ian."

"We're going to need all the good people we can get over the next few years." His tone was bleak.

"Looks like," I said. "How are things with Eriss?"

"Please don't meddle, Jane," Ian said quietly. "With her, with...." With us, I finished in my head for him.

"I'm already meddling enough for one wedding," I said as we started to walk.

He chuckled; relieved I was moving on to a different topic and I was, for the moment. "Who is bearing the brunt of your interference this time?"

"The Trio."

He sighed. "Yes, I'm sorry about that. I liked them together and it was such a good thing for Felix."

Felix, the perpetually broken. It was unfortunate that the people who knew his secret often focused on that and not on the amazing man he was aside from his design flaw. I'd done it myself in the past, I was ashamed to say, but it was interesting that Ian had focused on *him* and not the other two. "He's stronger than he looks." Which was ridiculous. He looked plenty strong. "On the inside, I mean," I corrected myself.

"I know," Ian said quietly.

"You're saying that you're not?"

"Please don't push."

"Ok."

Then I went in a different direction. "So, what's going on with your eye?"

"Not much," was all he said, shutting me down quite effectively. Well, it was his right.

We neared the Palace.

"She's lucky to have you, you know."

Ian stopped walking and, for a second, I thought he would cry. It was a near thing, but he didn't. "No, she isn't. She won't look anywhere else while I'm with her, but," his voice dropped to a whisper, "I can't leave." Without meeting my eyes again he squeezed my hand and walked away.

I stood there awhile, sadly, then took a breath and headed for the rehearsal. Oh, Ian.

04:03 – My Room, Robin Hill, Irena, Corsican Empire, November 4th, 2873

It was the morning of the wedding, really fucking early in the morning since it was still dark, when I woke up alone. Well, almost alone.

Over in the corner my wedding dress stood on the mannequin, glittering in the moonlight like the ghost of weddings future. I shouldn't complain, though. It was by far the simplest Imperial wedding dress that had ever been worn in the Corsican Empire. The Lord Chamberlain had, when he'd seen the dress yesterday, implied that it was the simplest wedding dress that had been worn by *any* woman of *any* kind in Corsica. I'd shrugged it off. It was a simple frock, but it was also lovely. The whole affair was pale gold (not white like in some cultures) with a simple bolero over a corset-waisted Berria-silk dress with a full skirt to the floor. Petticoats galore. No train. The lack of train had been the worst offense in Mr. Harris' eyes. (I was *terribly* upset about that as you can imagine.) My long red/black hair would be intricately braided and the veil wrapped around it as it went down my back. The little yellow flowers I loved would be in my hair and in my hand. I'd refused any jewelry and I'd prevailed— with the exception of a…crown. Ugh. We'd chosen the smallest one. A child's tiara, really, just fancier. Of all the things that had come up with this fucking wedding, it was only the crown that made me feel like a fraud.

I felt the tiny, tiny person inside me shift and smiled. She seemed to do that when I got too angry or distressed. It was worth it for Lucy. And there were much worse things than having to wear a small sparkling birdcage on my head for a few hours.

I felt Charles pacing in the other room. Our night together had been good and the passion perfect, but he hadn't been able to settle into sleep. I'd been too worn out myself from the excitement of the day to stay awake, but something was troubling my boyfriend. I slipped on his robe and went to him.

He stood at the closed window (it was November and chilly) clad only in his pajama bottoms. The night sky was clear and beautiful overhead, the moon glinting merrily off the LPGs of the guards that patrolled back and forth in front of us. I went up to him and wrapped my arms around his bare torso from behind.

"You're restless, love," I said gently.

He put his hands over mine. "Have I bothered you?"

"No, but you're supposed to," I chided as I moved in front of him so that I could see his face. "Wife or no, I'm still your girlfriend and girlfriends want their man to be happy, share his burdens, that sort of thing." He kissed me on the forehead and pulled me to him. I sighed contentedly against his body. "Should I pry, Six? Or I could beat it out of you."

He chuckled. "No bruises before the wedding."

Well, that got my attention. Not *before?* "And after?"

He laughed, "We'll talk." He snuggled closer and sighed. "Stupid to worry about this now. Rationally, I know that, but the reality of actually getting married again just hit me today."

"What did it for you?"

"The sight of the shuttles arriving, bringing all the people in. People in their best clothes all excited for the special occasion."

"Even my people?"

"Your people especially, Jane." He stroked my hair. "Everyone has this extra excitement in their eyes. They are happy for us, I know, but it is more than that. They want the spectacle of a real, honest-to-god Imperial Wedding."

"You sound bitter, love," I said gently.

"I'm not, Jane. It's just that I've had all this before. The Big Show—you should have seen Marianna's dress and its thirty-five foot train covered in diamonds," I shuddered in his arms, "the flowers, the ten thousand guests, the expense, the music…" He exhaled hard and shook his head. "I remember being so happy that day, giddy. Marianna was lovely and so charming. She was perfect. We were going to be so damned happy. Much happier than my parents had been. We would be good for the Empire and good for each other…"

"When did you realize who she really was?"

Charles sat down on the bench seat and folded me onto his lap. "After Alex was born. I'd had hints of her real self before that, but I hadn't wanted to believe the worst so I didn't."

"What did she do?"

"She knew I needed an 'heir and a spare' and refused to get pregnant the second time unless I got her things, jewels, trips, clothes, more titles for her friends, etc."

"And she couldn't have gotten all of those things herself?"

"That wasn't the point. Power was the point." He looked away, embarrassed. "I needed a second child. I needed more choices for a successor. Being brother to Louis had taught all of us that the hard way."

"So you gave in and got Henry."

"I can't be sorry about that."

"Of course not."

"Part of the deal was I had to sign the papers to allow her to get sterilized once Hal was born," he looked disgusted, "and once she'd recovered she plowed through the Court like a field."

"Wait, she blackballed Idis for getting sterilized to protect herself from her rapist husband and condoned putting her in jail when…"

"She'd already gotten her freedom from fertility. She just had permission to do it, according to then-current law."

I sat there a minute running over the list of appropriate names to call that horrible woman, but swearing (for once) didn't seem appropriate. "There are no words, Charles, for how sorry I am about Marianna. She was a fool not to appreciate how amazing you are."

"You are biased."

"The point is that *she* should have been biased."

"That was the bargain, or so I'd expected when I married her."

"Did you love her, Charles?"

"I thought I did." He smiled sadly. "I just didn't know how powerful it could be until I met Idis." He pulled my chest tightly to his, "Or how passionate it could be until I met you."

We stayed close for a while and I rubbed his back comfortingly. "So you are worried that I'll turn into someone you don't know once we've made it legal?"

"No," he laughed. "I was an ignorant kid when I was introduced to Marianna. We barely knew each other when we were married. That clearly isn't the case here."

I grimaced, "You've seen me at my worst way too many times. You know all the bad. The good news is that I've stopped questioning why you still like me."

"I love you and stop fishing for compliments," he said, kissing me. "You are amazing, but that's all you get tonight."

"I'll bet," I said, waggling my eyebrows suggestively.

He laughed and I tweaked his nose to make him laugh some more. I put my arms around his neck, but slowly enough that he could guess my intent and put a stop to it if he wished. He didn't wish. I moved to straddle him and put my face close for a kiss, but stopped just shy of his lips. "We know each other. We chose each other. Shit is going to go wrong, guaranteed, but we've already made the promises that matter. Just enjoy the circus and life will go on. A good life. *Our* life. We are together, love, body and soul as long as we live."

"All right," he said and I felt him relax...in some ways and not in others. Without another word he simply picked me up and carried me back to bed.

11:56 – Imperial Cathedral, Lyonesse, Irena, Corsican Empire

The days leading up to the wedding to end all weddings had been busy, as was, I supposed, typical before anyone's wedding when they made as big a fuss as we were making. Thankfully Idis had taken care of most of it. The parts we hadn't been able to duck (fittings, etc.) we'd tried to get through with humor and patience. Naturally Charles had handled it all better than I. This should shock no one.

Pretty much every invitation that had been sent out had been accepted and when the journos had speculated about a 'shotgun' wedding Albert had simply announced that Commodore Pace was indeed expecting an Imperial Heir. We'd thought about delaying telling everyone, we certainly could have since I wasn't that far along and could have passed for un-pregnant, but our tolerance for secret-keeping wasn't what it used to be. We were keeping Fitzroy alive and that was enough for the moment. Charles's beard was in and so was an unbearded double (as Fitz) who would be amongst the guests.

The story of the Knocked-Up Bride was everywhere. The nice thing was that I was on Corsica where the media was securely leashed. Once I was back on Terra, it would be a different story, but for now I was left alone.

I waited now, very dressed up in my wedding garb, bouquet of yellow flowers in my hand, standing just off to the side of the huge double doors leading into the sanctuary. I waited for two things, well, one thing and two people. I looked behind me and smiled. Idis, dressed in satiny red with white flowers in her hair smiled nervously at me. I nodded back, not nervous at all. I supposed I should have been trembling with the thought of all those people staring at me (I had heard of many people having stage fright) but my standards for fear were different. Was anyone going to try to kill either me or anyone I loved? No? Then I was fine. It's all in the perspective. Atalanta, on the other side of Idis, stepped forward slightly as she shifted the lovely dark brown wig she wore. The contrast between the slim, tall, elegant Idis and the short, stacked and stunning Atalanta was comical (to me anyway) but I kept my amusement to myself. Just past her stood the Obligatory Bridesmaid Duchess (whose name I'd not bothered to retain) looking both respectable and, by contrast, completely boring.

Bertie (Best Man), Prince Alex and Prince Hal (groomsmen) were already at the altar waiting for the show to start. Prince Hal's no-nonsense wife, Sophia, had declined the 'honor' of being a bridesmaid with a 'you've got to be kidding' and was sitting happily in the audience. A woman who did not suffer fools and I liked her even more for that. All the men looked terribly handsome in their matching suits with long (and inexplicable) tails at the back and *de rigueur* white gloves, which had been a relief to Alex. Speaking of men who looked good, I felt the approach of the two I was waiting for: Daniel and Felix. They were also dressed in tail coats and were dapper in their starched cuffs, high collars and gloves. They both stared at the vision who was Atalanta, stunning in red, and said vision resolutely looked at anything but them. Daniel was handsome as always as he tugged at his stiff collar. He grimaced at me but I had no sympathy for him in my dress that must have weighed forty pounds and denied me the ability to take a proper breath.

"Is it time?" Felix asked quietly as he tore his eyes from his former mate.

"In a minute," I responded.

"Nervous?"

"Why would I be?" I asked, close to perplexed.

He smiled his amusement and I was struck by my friend's beautiful deep blue eyes with their flecks of black. They surprised me every time, which was ridiculous since he'd had them for years now, but my image of him in my mind was of a Felix with the non-descript brown orbs I'd first known him with. I wondered if that mental image would ever change.

"She won't look at us," Daniel said under his breath.

"Focus, Danny," Felix hissed. "This isn't about us. Not today."

Daniel turned to me, embarrassed. "I'm sorry, Jane."

"Forget about it," I said, but what I was thinking was that it isn't about you right this minute, kid, but it would be later if I had anything to say about it.

"Commodore," the Lord Chamberlain said sonorously, "it is time."

I sighed. Finally. "Thank you."

"Places, please," Mr. Harris said. I noted, as we moved into our preassigned positions, that he was dressed so formally and with so much ceremonial jewelry (in addition to the huge chain of office) that I was surprised he could move. He may have been encumbered but he was also in his element, his heart almost beating out of his chest. Well, good for him. At least someone was getting a kick out of the circus.

"Please ask the Emperor to take his place," he said into his comm. He waited. "Good. Cue the organ." We jumped as the organ (apparently the biggest one on the fucking planet) burst into musical life and started playing something…impressive. He turned to Obligatory Bridesmaid Duchess. "Go."

The Duchess smiled shakily and left the vestibule, turning the corner as the great doors opened. She walked steadily into the sanctuary, the eyes of the Union on her. T.I. cameras were everywhere and I was sure someone outside the cathedral was making the usual play-by-play that came with these events. It reminded me of Pilar and Ronnie's wedding and *that* reminded me of the first time Charles had kissed me. Who would have thought that that seemingly doomed kiss would have led us here? Not me, certainly.

Now Atalanta was walking into the fray, dazzling all lucky enough to see her.

Now Idis, whose body betrayed her as the most nervous of all. She couldn't have foreseen this either, I thought. I hoped this wasn't the worst day of her life. I really hoped it wasn't.

"Commodore and Captains Pace?"

All thoughts of Atalanta temporarily put aside, Felix offered me his arm on one side and Daniel on the other. Their grins were blinding and brought a lump to my throat.

"Ready?" Mr. Harris asked.

"Yes, M'Lord," I said, my voice strong despite my emotion.

We walked, the three of us, out of the vestibule and turned to make the straight shot into the sanctuary as the rest of the party had. I'm sure the music was deafening, regal and all that, but I tuned it out. I felt everyone rise. The cameras moved closer but it was all noise to me.

I saw *him*.

He was too far away, waiting patiently by the altar, but that would be fixed soon enough.

We started the long walk up the nave of the cathedral, the eyes of all upon us. I really couldn't have cared less, though my escorts were really damned tense.

The cathedral was both more elegant and less pretty than the other one I had been to; the one on Gloriana where Pilar and Ronnie had gotten married. I'd only been here one other time and that had been for Prince Louis-the-Unlamented's funeral. The Charles of that day had been grand and somber, dressed handsomely in unforgiving black. The cathedral itself had been covered in black crepe but today everything was cream and red with flowers on every conceivable surface. The people outside had all been carrying or wearing the little gold flowers, enchanted, apparently, that the woman who would be their new Princess had fallen in love with a bloom that came from what really was a weed (I hadn't known this, of course, I'd just liked the flower). The stained glass in the nave had been polished and bright sunlight streamed through it. So many people were smiling, I registered absently, and that was nice.

All I saw, however, was *him*.

As we made our ponderous way up the aisle he smiled. This smile was just for me and it was beautiful.

"Oh my," I whispered.

Felix squeezed my hand.

Finally, finally we made it to the goal, er, altar and got to stop processing.

The Head Officiant moved to the center of the altar space, which was our signal that the Big Show was really going to start.

The boys performed the handoff and Charles took his place beside me.

Here we go.

The Head Officiant steepled his hands in front of him and addressed us all. "The grace of our Lord God, the Universal Father and the fellowship of the Galactic Mother be with you."

Everyone responded, "And also with you."

The Officiant continued, "God is love and those who live in love live in God and God lives in them."

He paused in his slow ritualistic delivery for a few seconds, then moved on.

On a completely irrelevant side note I will tell you one thing I'd learned in the rehearsal the previous day; I needed a middle name or even two. Charles had something like forty of them (an exaggeration) and I had exactly none. It had been too late to make one up when I'd realized the problem, but it bugged me. All the vows sounded really fucking uneven as they were. You'll see. Anyway, the Officiant had gotten the ball rolling;

"In the presence of God, the Universal Father,
we have come together
to witness the marriage of Charles-Victor Arthur Bennett and Jane,
    to pray for God's blessing on them,
to share their joy
and to celebrate their love.

Marriage is a gift of God in Creation
through which husband and wife may know the grace of God.
It is given that as people grow together in love and trust,
they shall be united with one another in heart, body and mind,
as God is united with his bride, the Church.

The gift of marriage brings husband and wife together
in the delight and tenderness of sexual union
and joyful commitment to the end of their lives.
It is given as the foundation of family life
in which children are born and nurtured
and in which each member of the family, in good times and in bad,
may find strength, companionship and comfort,
and grow to maturity in love.

Marriage is a sign of unity and loyalty
which all should uphold and honor.
It enriches society and strengthens community.
No one should enter into it lightly or selfishly
but reverently and responsibly in the sight of almighty God.

Charles-Victor Arthur Bennett and Jane are now to enter this way of life.
They will each give their consent to the other
and make solemn vows
and in token of this a ring will be given and received.
We pray with them that the Galactic Mother will guide
    and strengthen them,
that they may fulfil God's purposes
for the whole of their earthly life together."

He looked us all over to make sure we'd fully digested his point. It seemed we were all taking this seriously enough so he went on. Speaking of God, god, this dress was heavy. I 'lifted' it a little and felt better. But on with the wedding of Charles-the-super-magnificent and One Name Jane.

"First, I am required to ask anyone present who knows a reason why these persons may not lawfully marry, to declare it now."

No one said anything, which was nice; since I assumed anyone who'd be stupid enough to speak would have been immediately hauled off to a Corsican prison.

"The vows you are about to take are to be made in the presence of God, who is judge of all and knows all the secrets of our hearts; therefore if either of you knows a reason why you may not lawfully marry, you must declare it now."

Nope. We were good.

"Charles-Victor Arthur Bennett, will you take Jane to be your wife? Will you love her, comfort her, honor and protect her, and be faithful to her as long as you both shall live?"

All my plans to mentally snicker about the phrase 'forsaking all others' having been seamlessly removed from the service went up in smoke when I saw the black gold in my lover's eyes.

"I will," Charles said firmly.

I had to blink away tears. Damn it. It had gotten to me.

"Jane, will you take Charles-Victor Arthur Bennett to be your husband? Will you love him, comfort him, honor and protect him, and be faithful to him as long as you both shall live?"

Charles' eyes were bright, too. I was overcome with love for the man.

"He knows I will," I said.

There was a small gasp from the members of the audience, congregation, whatever, who had sticks up their asses. My promise was made, however, and that was that.

I saw a twinkle in the eyes of the Officiant, but he continued as if I hadn't gone off script. "Will you, the families and friends of Charles-Victor Arthur Bennett and Jane, support and uphold them in their marriage now and in the years to come?"

Everyone responded, whether sincerely or not, "We will."

"Let us pray."

We all bowed our heads and I tried to get my emotions under control. It had to be pregnancy hormones, right? No, Jane, I scolded myself a second later. You are marrying the man you love. Emotion is called for, Ok?

"God our Father," the Officiant intoned, "from the beginning you have blessed creation with abundant life. Pour out your blessings upon Charles-Victor Arthur Bennett and Jane, that they may be joined in mutual love and companionship, in holiness and commitment to each other. We ask this through our Lord God, the Universal Father, who reigns eternally, in the unity of All Souls with our Galactic Mother, now and forever."

The congregation said, "Amen."

We raised our heads and hymnals were handed to us. The huge choir began to sing.

I felt a TP's knock knock. 'The Countess is crying,' Stuart's voice said in my mind, once I'd opened my 'door.' No, not that. Idis was never, ever emotional in public. Corsicans didn't... Just as I was about to turn and try to comfort my soon-to-be husband's mistress, though, Stuart spoke again, 'Atalanta will help.'

I felt Atalanta's small hand grab onto one of Idis's tightly and then Idis take a long calming breath. I was relieved and also hoped 'Lanta didn't drug the woman so much she toppled over.

'Atalanta told me to tell you to go to hell.'

I had to smile at that.

Oops, the song was over and we were back to the main event.

"Charles-Victor Arthur Bennett and Jane, I now invite you to join hands and make your vows, in the presence of our Lord God and his people."

We faced each other. Charles was directed to take my right hand in his, which he did. He repeated the following after the Officiant said it.

"I, Charles-Victor Arthur Bennett , take you, Jane,
to be my wife,
to have and to hold
from this day forward;
for better, for worse,
for richer, for poorer,
in sickness and in health,
to love and to cherish,
till death us do part;
according to God's holy law.
In the presence of God I make this vow."

Then it was my turn. I was really tempted to say, "Back at you, Six," but I didn't and repeated the same vows back to him.

The next part of the ceremony was the ring part. This had been the only real bone of contention (with my intended, anyway) in the negotiations about the actual service. I'd refused to wear one. It was that simple, especially since the man I'd be sleeping with on Terra 1 wasn't (technically) the man that would have been giving me the ring today. I didn't wear jewelry and didn't particularly feel like being publicly marked (my tattoos were private, thank you very much, most people who knew me didn't even know I had them.) The rings didn't make me married, didn't make Charles married and left out Idis entirely. It was a non-starter, for me, at any rate. Charles had been irritated at first, but had given in when I'd dug in my heels. So we'd compromised. Kind of.

I put the ring Idis handed me on the fourth finger of his hand. The ring was bejeweled with three colors of expensive stones and quite beautiful.

Charles said, when prompted, "Jane, I receive this ring as a sign of our marriage. With my body I honor you, all that I am I give to you, and all that I have I share with you, within the love of God the Father, the Galactic Mother and of All Souls."

The look in his eyes was so lovely it was too much. Damn it, get it together, Jane.

The Officiant turned to address everyone.

"In the presence of God, and before this congregation, Charles-Victor Arthur Bennett and Jane have given their consent and made their marriage vows to each other. They have declared their marriage by the joining of hands and by the giving and receiving of a ring. I therefore proclaim that they are husband and wife."

I could hear the cheers of the people outside washing over the cathedral in a wave but still all I could see was him.

Charles, eyes black gold, leaned in and kissed me gently on the lips. Then he said so quietly I could barely hear it myself, "Ours. Body and soul."

There was nothing to say because he had said everything. All I could manage was a smile of sheer adoration.

The Officiant joined our right hands together and said, "Those whom God has joined together let no one put asunder."

That was it. We were married. Holy crap on a cracker.

14:48 – Staging Room Outside Great Hall, Imperial Palace, Irena

Most of the wedding party waited for the next event in a holding/staging room just off the Great Hall. Atalanta, fixing her wig, walked into the room after everyone else, saw her two former lovers standing there with me and turned quickly around to run away. Suddenly I wasn't the concerned friend anymore, I was the pissed off friend and I was sick of these idiots dodging each other. Something had to be done.

Through the door, standing in a small ante room sipping tea before the next part of the Show, I could see Idis standing next to Charles. She was where she belonged. Soon I would be with them where *I* belonged. Hmm. Idis. Unlike the situation with the Trio she wasn't my lover and wasn't going to be, but some things were eerily similar. She kept things inside, too. Part of that was cultural, part was just who she was and the rest was probably just stubbornness. I remembered how angry she'd been at me when I'd confronted her, but I was pretty sure there was no way she would be where *she* was right now at this moment if Charles hadn't insisted on (my) getting her anger out.

Yes, I thought. Anger. Because it wasn't just Daniel who had fucked up, was it? It was a group relationship and it had taken all three of them to ruin it.

"'Lanta, stop," I ordered. I 'blocked' the door leading to the Great Hall.

"Really, Jane?" Atalanta said, her deep brown eyes shooting sparks. "You are really going to trap me in here so I'll talk to them?"

"I am," I said. "I'm sorry it has come to this, but there are some things that need to be said, especially since the three of you seem incapable of saying them without a push."

The three of them, especially Atalanta, stood there mulishly and I realized that we were attracting attention. I caught the eye of the ever-present Captain Maass (my personal Head of Security) and said to her and everyone else, "May we have the room?"

It was something I'd seen both Charles and Idis do but I'd never actually done it myself. Captain Maass simply looked at everyone and then all of them seemed to melt away. That was pretty cool, I had to admit.

Back, however, to the problem(s) at hand, starting with Miss Atalanta who was staring at me defensively.

"I don't see why *I* need to say anything," she spat at me.

Daniel mumbled something.

"What was that, Daniel?" I asked sharply. He fell silent. I could have decked him. Or asked where his balls were. Or decked his balls. "Here's the thing. You three love each other and were happy together. I don't know if you can work things out no matter how much I wish you would, but it seems monumentally stupid to just let this go without at least one honest conversation."

"Hear hear," Felix said softly, apparently channeling Charles.

"So you will indulge me since it is my wedding day and speak the fucking truth."

"You're seriously playing the wedding card?" Atalanta scoffed.

"Did you get me anything?" I'd told her it wasn't necessary. Look, folks! Jane set a trap.

"No."

"Then yes, I am." I put my hands on my hips as my dress swirled around me. It *was* pretty. "You all seem to dance around each other. Daniel wants this, Felix wants this and Atalanta wants something else."

"You don't hurt the ones you love," Felix protested.

"Because the three of you are so un-hurt right now?"

Felix became absorbed in contemplating his shoes.

I sighed. "Charles and I hurt Idis a lot by making the two of them the three of us."

Felix nodded. Daniel stared at the carpet. Atalanta studied the ancient painting on the wall.

"So I forced her to call me on the bad shit I'd done." I shrugged. "Which she did."

"That fixed everything?" Felix asked.

"No, but it was a good start," I said. "I had wronged her, even though I hadn't done it maliciously and you have all wronged each other."

"I haven't done anything," Atalanta protested.

"You sure about that?" I challenged.

She raised her chin defiantly. "I just reacted the best way I could. They needed to be free and I made that possible." She certainly had, with ruthless efficiency.

Daniel let out an angry huff of air.

Atalanta crossed her arms on her chest. "This isn't my fault, Jane."

I looked piercingly at Daniel and Felix.

"That true, boys?"

I let the question hang in the air.

"Jane," Felix pleaded softly.

"What?" Atalanta said sharply.

"Do you want to tell me why you are afraid of the truth, Felix?"

"For a lot of reasons, but I guess we have nothing to lose now." Felix looked at Daniel and took a deep breath. "We went into this with defined roles, didn't we?"

"I don't know what you mean," Atalanta said a little nervously. "I need to go."

I glared at her. She was going exactly nowhere.

"I am the damaged warrior," Felix continued, "Daniel is the emotional one and Atalanta," he looked at me, "is the perfect one."

I nodded. "Daniel is, forgive me, the one who causes the trouble, so he always gets the blame. Felix is powerless because of his genetic quirks," I gave him an apologetic look which he shrugged off, "and Atalanta is the bitchy but loyal queen of all."

"That seems really unfair," Daniel said.

"Unfairly true," Felix corrected, "but we are more than that. There is more to us than those roles."

"There isn't if you don't let there be."

Atalanta, for the first time in I don't know how long, looked really embarrassed. "I never actually *said* I was perfect."

I snorted. "You're joking."

"I *was* joking," she said defensively. "It was just, I don't know, a pose."

I shook my head. "You are the most beautiful woman I have ever seen. You are brilliant, kind, talented and truly special. Perfect, however, you are not."

She turned to Felix and Daniel, perplexed, "You both think I'm perfect?" She frowned. "Or you think that I need you to think I'm perfect for this to work?"

Both men were silent.

"Oh, for the love of Christ," I said, exasperated, "yes, that is what they think. Mother of god, you people are frustrating."

Felix snorted, the other two remained silent.

"There is a grain of truth to all this, of course. All three of you generally do live up to the roles you've assigned yourselves, but Daniel needed to be able to say what the hell he wanted, 'Lanta." Then I stared her down, "And you…"

"Should have said from the beginning that you didn't want children," Daniel said.

Finally.

I could see that Atalanta wanted to argue, that she was puffing herself up to defend herself again this charge, but she gave up almost immediately, her posture slumping. "I know I should have. I didn't want you to go and I thought you would if I gave you a definite no. I'm sorry." Big fat tears rolled down her face. She carefully pulled off her gorgeous wig, revealing her decimated hair. "Fuck, that thing is hot."

"I have loved Atalanta what seems like my entire life," Felix said softly. "I was so lucky to find you and, later, Danny." He straightened. "I can't, however, stay with either of you if it's going to be like this."

Both Atalanta and Daniel hung their heads.

"There are other TP/Emps out there. They are rare, but not unheard of. Even Heelies are popping up with abilities." Felix's voice was firm. "I am not the charity case that everyone seems to think I am. I can move on, to nothing if it comes to that. I wanted to be with you both because I got to feel, I got the connection I'd been wanting my whole life. For a while I had it all. I'm not broken. I'm just different and I'm tired of being dragged around like luggage."

"You're not luggage," Atalanta said.

"You aren't a charity case, Fee," Daniel whispered, horrified. "Don't say such a thing."

"I can say what I like, Danny, Atalanta," Felix growled. "And I'm sick of being the last consideration." He looked at Daniel, "I went along with you because it would make you happy. I would have gone along with Atalanta to make her happy. Because that's what the broken and desperate do to keep from being alone."

Daniel and Atalanta protested his words and I was starting to think that instead of making all this better that I was instead giving them a different reason to break up. Well done, Jane.

So, I tried to get them back to the initial problem. "So, I assume, Daniel, that you've been looking into adopting or fathering a child?"

Daniel's head turned so fast I thought he might injure himself. "What?"

"You were willing to destroy your relationship for a baby, so you must be in the process of getting one and you can't have mine."

"No, I..." Daniel just stopped talking, clearly flummoxed.

"He hasn't looked," Felix said.

"Not at all?"

"Not at all," Felix said, his face slightly flushed.

"Why?" I said to Daniel.

"Because I want us back. I wanted more, yes, it's true, but not more than I want us. I told you that, Jane."

"You told *me*, not *her*," I accused. Moron.

Daniel closed his eyes, as if summoning all his energy. "I want us more than I want a child, Atalanta. I want you and Felix, just like we were. I am a fuckup, I know it, but this has been killing me. Killing us."

"I can't take you back knowing that you're giving something that big up for me," Atalanta said. "That's why I never tried to fix this. That's why I ended it the way I did. So it would be done and you could move on."

"I'm not going to move on."

"You can't give this up for me," she said, weeping again.

"That isn't your choice to make, love," Daniel said. "That, at least, is only mine."

"What do I do with the guilt?" she asked.

That seemed to stymie everyone.

I was still thinking of Idis and Charles when I said, "I think we all have to admit that this relationship, that *any* adult relationship, is probably always going to be more complicated than we think it should be. We aren't nineteen, shiny and malleable. We are grownups with our own problems and worries. We are complicated people. Complicated people don't have simple relationships. Not the ones that matter, anyway."

"Jane's right. It won't be perfect," Felix said slowly, "and I think we need to let go of the idea that it could be and however halcyon our memories are it was wonderful, but it wasn't perfect then, either." He looked at me, "Another role we assumed; that of the perfect Trio."

"I suppose you're right," I said. Of course he was. It was Felix.

"I need to think about all this," Felix said.

I nodded my agreement even though I was still surprised that he had become the largest obstacle in Mission Trio: Recovery, but he was right that more than just their relationship with Atalanta needed to change. No one wanted to feel like a charity case. He looked at Daniel and Atalanta, the two people he clearly loved the most in the world.

"Will you both think, too? I mean really look at the three of you?" Sadly I added, "Or do you even want to?"

"I do," Daniel said quickly.

Atalanta's response took a bit longer, but she said, "I will think about it. I *am* sorry, Felix, Daniel. More than you can ever know."

"Me, too," Daniel said contritely.

"So am I," Felix said, his voice a little hard.

"Your Highness," the rather unwelcome voice of the Lord Chamberlain intruded. "It is time."

I sighed. "Fine." Such a gracious Princess. The wedding party started to drift back in.

It was time for the next part of the Big Show.

It was the second, or third (I wasn't sure) biggest moment of the wedding extravaganza: the official introduction of the Imperial Couple as they entered the reception hall. What-the-fuck-ever. While it wasn't a big deal for me (I met us all the time) it was, actually, a huge event for the Corsicans present. The ceremony and attendant hoopla had been broadcast on Union-wide T.I., but the parties afterwards were private, including this introduction. *This* wasn't for the masses. This was for the rich and powerful who'd actually attended the wedding. Charles and Idis walked into the holding room, right on cue, almost before Mr. Harris had finished speaking. All right, then.

After a slight pause while the makeup and hair people touched up both Charles and myself (what a nuisance) we stood in front of the gold-painted doors that led to the Grand Ballroom. I saw my reflection in an old mirror on a nearby wall. I glittered. I don't think I could ever have said that about myself before that moment. I regarded my appearance critically. Not too bad, I thought, but it's pretty obvious he married me for love, not my looks. The thought briefly cheered me up but only until I noticed Idis, Atalanta (wig back in place) and the Obligatory Duchess Bridesmaid standing off to the side with Bertie, Daniel, Felix, Alex and Hal. They all had the bored looks of supporting players waiting to support further. It was the supporting part of that, with regards to Idis at least, that really bothered me.

The Lord Chamberlain leaned in to Charles and me and said quietly, "The door will open and there will be a pause to the count of ten, then I will step forward and make the formal introduction. After an additional count of three the Emperor and the new Princess will be introduced and greeted as Imperial Majesty and Consort for the first time. Then I will precede you both to the receiving line." He looked me in the eye, backwards child that I was. "Any questions?"

"What about the Countess?" I asked. I felt Charles tense, though he betrayed nothing outwardly.

"The Countess will be following with the rest of the wedding party."

Another subtle demotion, I thought angrily. Not today, asshole. I looked pointedly at Charles who merely raised his eyebrows and waited to see what stunt I would pull.

"Countess?" I asked.

Idis looked up, her excellent control almost masking her surprise. Almost. "Your Highness?"

Ugh. "Would you please join us?"

Everyone froze in shock/horror.

"Excuse me, Ma'am?" Idis said in a small voice and I had a fleeting moment of doubt that my gesture would make her more miserable then she'd already been, but I wasn't backing down now. All the same, I hoped I was doing the right thing. It *felt* right, if only to me.

"Please," was all I said and Idis warily (but still gracefully) walked over to us. I took Charles' left hand firmly in my own. "Charles." I looked pointedly at his right hand.

A small, but beautiful smile broke out on my lover's face as he extended his hand to Idis who stared at it as if it might bite her. She seemed incapable of movement so I reached over and put her hand in his.

I then turned back to the astonished Lord Chamberlain and said, "We are ready."

Mr. Harris looked pleadingly at Charles.

"Proceed, Mr. Harris," Charles said pleasantly, but with an edge to his voice. My Six was so getting rewarded the next time we were alone. Oh yeah.

The Lord Chamberlain recovered himself and said, "It is my honor, Sire," and he bowed deeply. He then rose, took a deep breath and signaled the footmen to open the double doors. He waited ten counts, then stepped into the main room, full of nobles, commoners, an alien, a Queen or two, assorted supers, three (and a half) Heelies and many others.

"My Lords and Ladies and gentlefolk of all nations of this our Union, it is my very great honor to introduce to for the first time as Imperial Highness and Consort, His Imperial Highness Charles-Victor Arthur Bennett Fitzroy Couvillion-Bourbonnais, Emperor of Corsica and Its Environs, and Her Imperial Highness, Princess Jane of Lyonesse, Commodore of the Union Navy and Imperial Consort and," no pause, "Her Royal Highness, the Lady Idis, Countess of Boulton."

There were many gasps and a few smiles. Someone, had to be an off-worlder, actually clapped, but gave up when no one else joined in. The three count was up and the three of us stepped forward into the room. The Corsicans bowed and curtseyed in an almost choreographed movement. The non-Corsican subjects either bowed their heads or, if she was a Head of State (like Tania, Pilar and Eriss) she nodded and smiled. Some of the Corsicans, my new people, seemed actually happy (but with Corsicans, famous for playing close to the vest, who knew?) and some were wary. Some were openly hostile to the freak. Openly hostile for a Corsican, I mean. No smile. Three hundred years ago that lack of smile would have called for a duel. However they actually felt they all bowed anyway.

I found my throat tight with emotion, despite this knowledge, and my first instinct was, stupidly, to bow back, but Charles' tightened his grip on my hand and I stayed standing tall. Damn it, another moment that had gotten to me.

Charles inclined his head graciously acknowledging their acknowledgement. "This has been a great day both for the Empire and for

Ourselves personally. Within the last few weeks We have realized more dreams than We'd admitted We'd even had." He raised his clasped hands slightly. "With these women and Our daughter on the way," he smiled, "combined with the friendship and assistance of Our beloved sons, We usher in a new, happier, more prosperous age in Our history. Sharing this day with all of you has made this beginning all the sweeter." He caught my eye, then turned to smile at Idis. "Thank you." Was he thanking his guests or his lovers? He'd left it deliberately ambiguous, of course, but I saw knowing smiles amongst the crowd. Those that could be bothered to smile.

Just then Idis leaned in slightly and said to Charles and myself, "You're sure about this?" No, she wasn't asking about our three-way partnership, she was asking about the next item on the agenda. It was one we'd notified Stanley about (you'll see why in a minute) and had been my idea.

"It could go either way," Charles responded. I subtly kicked him in the shin. He sighed. I felt the bubble of laughter in Idis' chest and felt much better. People were starting to murmur, not sure what was to happen next. The Lord Chamberlain stepped forward, but a hand movement from Charles held him back. Charles inclined his head in my direction and I stepped forward, still holding his hand. Everyone quieted.

"Thank you for celebrating this day with us," I said. "I know that, in general, Corsicans distrust outsiders and I am as much an outsider as one can get." No one said anything. "I was born a Pacey, as everyone knows, but I am a Corsican now and whether any of you accept me as such *I* accept myself as a protector and defender of both my husband, his partner, and this magnificent Empire." I smiled at the assembled. Some actually smiled back. Or maybe it was only Daniel, Felix and Atalanta. It was nice anyway. "His Imperial Majesty," Charles, to you, "doesn't like it when I call myself a freak," Charles shrugged, "but I am what I am. I am no more ashamed of being unusual than you are ashamed of being Corsican," I lowered my voice, "but my skills are now at the disposal of this great Empire. I don't mean to be immodest," like hell, "but that is no small thing." Now more people, even ones I didn't know were smiling. "As I said once in a speech to the Legislature, supers are just people. Some good, some bad. Some can read thoughts, sense emotions, change their form, fly. I," I grimaced, "prefer to crush things and blow stuff up." Some chuckles. "And some can take you to the most beautiful place I've ever been." I smiled and reached out with my free hand. "May I introduce the acclaimed artist, Alma Gonzales."

There were gasps in the audience as well there should have been. The former Pasa Winter's time in exile from Gloriann-Levvon (and with Srihas) had been extremely successful. The pair of them traveled the Union in style, performing Alma/Pasa's 'stories' to small groups for tremendous fees. I looked at her assessingly. She'd been a small thing with unruly wavy hair, olive skin and striking grey eyes when I'd known her, but now she was sleek, coiffed and elegant. Next to her was her husband, my old friend Srihas, a slightly overweight man, tall, distinguished and charming. He looked the same as I'd remembered except much happier. He'd finally found his *alma,* literally, as I had found mine. I smiled at them, but only Srihas smiled back. Pasa was here to work. She nodded at me.

As Eriss herself had said to us a while ago, I said to the assembled, "Here, my friends, is Dep Qua."

I opened my mental 'door' and let Alma and Srihas in.

One second we were in the luxurious Great Hall and the next (to the gasps of the audience) we were standing (or it looked like it) on a very basic landing field with a paved area and a large low building for shuttle storage. It was terribly ordinary and would have seemed completely unremarkable had it not been for the 'trees.' The 'trees' were actually crystalline formations, living ones, coming up out of the ground. About six stories tall (average), two dozen of them lined the rectangular field dully gleaming in pale translucent blue, relatively unaffected by the small breeze. They stood quietly, overlapping in places shielding eyes from the city of Dep Qua beyond. One side of the field was open (the side farthest from the city) and the rest was closed off except for a small tree-arched walk that led to the city proper. The ground was covered (on the non-paved area) with a pale sort of fuzzy moss.

"Father in Heaven," someone murmured. I wanted to snicker, but didn't, not wanting to mess with the transmission of my strategically chosen images. They hadn't seen anything yet.

'We' started to walk down the path towards the city. The crystalline 'trees' tinkled slightly overhead while making the light on the pathway a pale blue. Soon, though, 'we' reached the end of the pathway.

"Is that…real?" I heard someone whisper. Yes, I thought, very much so.

'Shhh, *querida,*' Srihas said in my head.

'Sorry,' I thought back.

In front of 'us' the paved road sloped gently down on the left side while the regular 'ground' sloped just as gently upward. It was as if half of two opposing hills had come together in one spot. The ground on the left fell gradually away, going lower and lower as the 'up' part of the other hill climbed. What remained was a sharply defined and stark white cliff face.

With a city in it.

Not a series of rough caves, either, but a delicately carved edifice with sculptures and balconies, doors and patios. A grand three story hallway pierced the far side of the cliff-face that lead into a large internal chamber with carved columns.

It wasn't just the breathtaking architecture (which was dignified and graceful); and it wasn't that the city was so pretty, though it was very beautiful. It was also the Tarine walking on the carved stone paths both on the front of the cliff face and the road in front of it. Other Tarine were playing in the ornamental park across that same road.

There was a group of Tarine picnicking on the (clearly imported) grass that caught our attention. I remembered this moment well, but now it made me ache for the Tarine we still had left. One of the picnicking Tarine laughed, gave a little wave then rose quickly, extending his/her wings as he/she rose…and flew gracefully into air, over the road darting quickly into one of the upper level dwellings.

I could hear the people in the Great Hall murmuring things like 'beautiful' and 'amazing.' I could hear them, and they could hear each other, because Alma had willed it so. If she hadn't wanted them to, they wouldn't have. She really had a quite a talent.

We 'walked' through the main gate/entrance, and before us was a grand staircase, wide and magnificent, carved as everything else was out of native white stone. There was no painting, no other adornment such as metal grillwork or even railings, yet it was impressive and beautiful. We 'walked' down four stories and eventually reached the main courtyard. The floor was intricately laid out with white and black stones in a swirled design that had once reminded me of bird's wings. Now I knew they were Tarine wings.

We 'looked up' to the almost blinding light of the reflected suns of the planet Trithicate to see the walls of the courtyard that I knew was actually a quarter mile under solid stone. The eight levels inside the city were ringed with balconies, some grand (royal and Ambassadorial apartments) and some more ordinary. Tarine bustled about on most of the levels, all doing seemingly unremarkable things, except that when they wanted to go from one level to another they skipped the stone staircases and flew, often carrying their burdens as they did so. The wings made little shadows in the light.

Then large shadows diffused the light and we 'looked' back up at the ceiling. A single form's wings beat slowly as it descended, black at first against the harshness of the natural light. The lone Tarine descended slowly, the light filtering through the gossamer that made her wings both delicate and so strong. The other Tarine in the vision faded away and only she remained. She got closer and closer to the ground and the images of Dep Qua retreated, too, so that by the time Eriss (the real Eriss) landed she was touching the rich parquet floor of the Great Hall.

"Ladies and Gentlemen, Miss Fenton, Representative of the Tarine Rian," the Lord Chamberlain announced as he'd been instructed. Ordered.

Eriss smiled brilliantly and flew over to Charles, Idis and myself.

"That was quite an entrance, Miss Fenton."

"Thank you, Your Highness, and we Tarine congratulate you, Sir, the Princess and the Countess," nice, Eriss, "on this tremendous day."

"Thank you," he said with a smile. Charles kissed her gallantly on the cheek and, apparently dismissed, Eriss moved among the now very excitedly talking guests. I could see Ian shadowing her from a discrete distance, not wanting to seem too intimidating. I watched as people held themselves back from her at first, but then those same people soon fell to the charm of her beauty, novelty and, most important of all, approachability. She may not have been a human, but she didn't seem *too* alien. She knew, of course, when we'd discussed all this beforehand, that any friends she made here (or even non-enemies) would help her cause in the long run.

Back to us.

"That was incredible," Idis said under her breath.

"Even more so than I'd imagined," Charles agreed.

"Let's hope that was pretty enough that no one realizes how potentially dangerous a talent like that is in the wrong hands," I muttered.

Idis put a hand on her hip. "You're no fun at all, Jane." Her expression went from what appeared to be fond exasperation to resignation. "Speaking of no fun."

The Lord Chamberlain bowed in front of us and we followed him to the receiving line.

17:02 – Great Hall, Imperial Palace

What felt like ages later, and after profusely thanking Alma and a very proud Srihas, I stood just inside the entrance to the Grand Ballroom with Charles and Idis, a long, long, long, line of well-wishers needed their hands and asses kissed. It was a drag, but what could you do?

"I'd take off my shoes, but I did that once and my dress hit the floor and puffed out like a balloon," Idis said to me behind Charles' back. She did this without moving her mouth. I was impressed.

I giggled and turned to the next person. The next person was, to my surprise, Prince Whitman with his wife Princess Joyanna. They looked...determined.

Whitman bowed deeply and kissed the Imperial ring on Charles' hand. Charles' wedding ring glimmered on his other hand. It was pretty, I had to concede. "Congratulations, Sire," Whit said with sincerity.

I saw Charles search Whit's face and he must have seen something he approved of because he opened his arms and embraced him. It was brief, it was professional, but he hadn't done that to anyone else in all the guests. Even the untutored rube I was knew that people would notice. "It is good to see you, nephew," Charles said. He turned to the extremely pregnant Joyanna and kissed her gallantly on the cheek, "And my very favorite niece."

"Congratulations, Uncle Charles," Joyanna said softly, blushing. Pregnancy had softened her rather horsey face and she seemed happy. It was good to see. "It was a lovely ceremony."

"I'm glad you approve," he said watching them.

Whit cast his eyes over the three of us, resplendent in our wedding garb and his smile was thoughtful but believable, "We do, Sire. This is a good day. Finding what makes you happy and gives you purpose is the best thing, don't you think?"

"Whit, darling," Joyanna said gently.

"It's all right, my dear," Charles said, frowning slightly. "Your husband is right."

"I know, Uncle," Joyanna said unexpectedly, "and we were hoping you might see us tomorrow before you leave for…" she stopped flustered. The

Emperor Charles was going nowhere. Jane and Fitzroy were the ones returning to Terra 1. "Before the Commodore leaves tomorrow. We would be grateful if you, the Countess and the Commodore would meet with us for a few minutes at a time of your convenience."

The long long line had come to a complete stop and, noticing this, Idis stepped closer. I followed. "Is something the matter, Your Highness?" she asked Whit, with the implication that there better not be. She cast her eyes to the line, indicating that things were getting screwed up.

"My apologies, Countess," Whit said, nervously determined, "but we have a proposal."

Idis looked at Charles who gave the briefest of nods and said, "We will fit you into the schedule at 11:00 in the Emperor's private office at the Palace."

Whitman bowed again, "Thank you." Joyanna kissed Charles' cheek with a smile, took her husband's arm and they moved on.

Idis resumed her place on one side of Charles and I had to ask, "What was that about?"

Idis shook her bejeweled head, "Couldn't say. Sir?" It creeped me out when she called him that in public. Just seemed wrong.

"No idea. We'll find out tomorrow."

"We need to move this along or you'll be late," Idis cautioned.

Charles' eyes went wide then he nodded.

"Late for what?" I asked. Both Charles and Idis shrugged identically and smirked. I growled and we worked our way through the line.

19:00 –Imperial Shuttle

It had taken several hours of solid effort to free ourselves (temporarily) of the social obligations of the wedding and I was now sitting on a comfortable bench of the luxurious personal shuttle of the Emperor, snuggled up against that same Emperor. It was, miraculously, just the two of us...and twenty-four Judean-trained Corsican soldiers in the next compartment.

"Where are we going, Six?" I asked.

"You'll see," he said softly as he kissed the top of my head. "We shouldn't be stealing away like this, but I needed to give you your wedding present."

I sat up suddenly. "Shit, Charles, I had to get you a *present*, too?"

The look of horror on my face was, he told me later, priceless and he dissolved into laughter. "No, Jane, you didn't," he said, still laughing, "but I wanted to give you something anyway."

"Better not be any more fucking jewelry," I grumbled.

He pulled me back to him and sighed contentedly. "I promise you will love it."

"Okay," I said.

Five minutes later we were landing at Robin Hill. Charles just smiled at my confused look. Mr. Beddoes and Thal waited for us there, but other than a nod from both, no words were said and they made no attempt to follow us. No, I'm wrong, one word was said, but Charles to Captain Stanley, "Perimeter." Captain Stanley nodded and he and his people disappeared into the darkness.

Charles took my hand and we started walking through the beautifully lit paths around the old house. Charles offered no explanation as to where we were going and I asked for none. I was quite content to be alone with him walking, listening to the wild creatures settling down for the night, smelling late fall flowers, seeing the shadows of trees stirring in the slight wind. It was quiet and perfect and I was lost in my own pleasant thoughts so that our destination took me by surprise, though it really shouldn't have.

It was the lake.

Ah, the lake. I leaned over the edge to peer into the water and thought I caught a bit of the glow of the Lumina beneath, but I wasn't sure.

"Will you dance, Jane?" Charles asked softly, reverently.

"I would love to, Charles," I replied just as softly.

There was no music, but, as it had been the one other time we'd danced together, it was unnecessary. I 'formed' a thick, flat shield beneath our feet and carefully 'lifted' it off the ground. Charles took my hand and put his other one at my waist and we started to move. We turned and danced one-two-three one-two-three out into the center of the lake. He was smiling at me, I could tell from the muscles in his face, though it was too dark to actually see his expression. One-two-three one-two-three.

Now I could see his golden eyes as they turned black gold. And it was just as I realized that I shouldn't have been able to see them that my lover whispered, "Jane, look."

I turned my head and almost lost track of the shield, dropping us into the depths (wouldn't that have been something?).

Lumina floated all around us, glowing, lighting up the night like strangely-shaped angels.

"Oh, my."

There were hundreds of them shining their light on both us and the lake. I could see the Guards now, no shadows to hide them, and some of them stepped to the edge of the water, eyes wide with awe.

A Lumina floated slowly towards us and I admit I stared. Up close it was beautiful and not plain white at all, but full of many subtle colors. It blinked at me and I unconsciously blinked back. It kept approaching and I, without thinking, held out my hand.

I felt Charles tense behind me, but he said nothing so I didn't withdraw.

The creature slowed his approach, but still moved closer and closer until I could touch it, which I did. Its skin was rougher than I'd thought it would be and cool.

"Father in Heaven," Charles whispered.

I'd barely touched it when the creature retreated. Overwhelmed by the honor, I bowed my head and said, "Thank you."

The creature lowered itself slightly, as if it were bowing, too, and then all the light started to fade. Quickly, too quickly, the Lumina lowered back into the water and were gone.

"Charles?" I said softly.

It took him a second to answer and I could feel that his throat was clogged with emotion. "A sign, my love."

I nodded and I stepped into his arms. He took a shuddering breath.

"That will be added to your legend, wife," he said.

He kissed me as we floated over the now dark lake.

ENTRY 8-8-91

<u>23:14 – Imperial Suite, Imperial Palace, Irena, November 4th, 2973</u>

Many hours later, after talking to every wedding guest and dancing with every wedding guest (though nothing could beat dancing with Charles and the Lumina) it was, at last, my wedding night. If this were the novels I loved reading (the classics, not the dirty ones), I would be in a glorious negligee, nervously applying perfume to secret places in hopes that it would entice my husband and soothe my virgin nerves. I snickered at the thought as I pulled on my t-shirt and headed for the bedroom.

A form waited for me on one side of the bed.

"Charles," I said with a giggle. "You've changed."

"Just a bit," Atalanta said with a smile as she stretched out luxuriously. Charles was, of course, with Idis, so I'd called in the second team. Well, not the whole team, just Atalanta. The bed was big, but it wasn't that big. "You're sure Fitz is all right with this?"

"He was relieved," I admitted as I joined her in bed. "He felt guilty leaving me tonight even though his doing so was my idea."

She nodded. "Guilt is the word of the day, isn't it?"

"Yeah."

She paused, hesitating a bit before saying, "We got the invitations to the wedding while Wilby was on Terra, preparing to transport Quinn back to Novy."

I had a bunch of questions about that, but didn't want to get upset so I said nothing. Atalanta, being Atalanta, took that as license to continue talking. Of course.

"That was partly my fault," she said, guiltily, "I was so excited and kind of astonished that it was all happening so quickly that I wasn't paying attention to who was hearing me." She sat up in bed, her short hair sticking up adorably all over her head. "You know each invitation was delivered by a Corsican Guard, right? Full livery and everything."

"Oh god, really?" I asked, horrified. Had the Corsicans never heard of subtlety? Hey, just because I can't do it doesn't mean I didn't think anyone else should try.

"At first I thought I was going to be arrested or served a subpoena, it was so serious, but his emotions were proud and happy, so…" She pulled her knees up to her chest and wrapped her arms around them. "He bowed and everything." She grinned. "I had a drink with Garrett and Derek before the Furies pulled up stakes and they were like little kids they were so excited."

I had to smile at that. "I hope everyone had a good time."

She laughed, "Are you kidding? Your Countess had activities, games, spirits and enough food to feed all Tellesco at all times. The Corsicans themselves are about to piss themselves they're so thrilled to have a new 'heir-option' that nothing bothers them…it's been surreal." She patted my hand. "Wonderfully surreal."

"How do the Corsicans feel about Charles marrying a freak/commoner and keeping on his 'whore' at the same time?"

She shrugged. "I heard some unkind things, but mostly support for the Countess. The general consensus is that she's 'put in the years' and done a 'deuced fine job.' The women especially seemed happy she hadn't been tossed out with the garbage. No one seems to believe, though, that Fitz would still be sleeping with her while he has the 'Red Whore' on her knees." Atalanta made a face.

I sighed. "It's nice that Idis and I have whoredom in common."

"Don't we all?" She'd meant it as a joke, but her face fell anyway.

"Have you been thinking about the boys?"

"Yes."

I waited and she volunteered nothing. I sighed again. "And what have you been thinking?"

"That I miss them," she said quietly. "I haven't felt like myself since I left them."

"Can you let them…" but I was interrupted by a chime on my comm. I turned my head to click on. "Yes, Thal." I listened as Atalanta watched me with great interest. "This is the perfect time for a visit. Please clear them with Captain Maass, Thal, and show them in. Thank you."

Atalanta's heart-shaped face went pale. My 'door' was closed, but I knew she'd guessed correctly who was outside the door. I rose and she grabbed my hand convulsively. "Don't go, Jane. Not yet, okay?"

I nodded. "Let me get dressed, love, and then we'll play it by ear."

"Thank you."

I hugged her and she hugged back too hard, her nerves taking over her muscles. Thankfully she was a tiny person and it didn't hurt even my stupid bad shoulder. I got up and headed over to the suitcase on the floor, pulling out training clothes. I stripped and dressed efficiently, chuckling to myself that this was something, for all his brains and power, that my lover couldn't manage to pull off. Well, not without an hour to spare. And assistance.

"Your tattoo is into its second column?" she asked.

Oh, that.

"Unfortunately, yes," I answered as I pulled on my shirt. In fact, I thought, it's out of date. That was something that should be rectified.

"You carry your guilt on your skin."

"We're adults now." I shrugged. "Guilt is inescapable."

"Yeah, yeah," she laughed humorlessly, "I hear you." Her whole body stiffened. "They're right outside the door, Jane."

"Good," I said, striding for the door, "let's get started, shall we?"

"Sure," Atalanta said, looking even paler.

The door was opened by Captain Maass, one of my new life partners. Because I was such a delicate fucking flower that I needed protecting. Ah, mother irony. Anyway, I digress.

In walked a very nervous looking Daniel.

"Where's Felix?" Atalanta asked.

"I assumed he'd be here," Daniel said.

Then just like that, there he was. Felix walked in dressed in a beautifully pressed Furies Uniform, his boots striking the wood floor authoritatively. I had to smile. Whatever crisis of confidence my friend had had was behind him. He was the true motherfucking badass that had started scaring students back at the School years ago. It was good to see him.

Atalanta and Daniel stared at him. She opened her mouth to speak, but he raised a hand for silence.

"Here's where I talk and you listen," he said very firmly.

Atalanta's mouth snapped closed in shock. Well, Ok then. So we listened.

"I passed up the chance to be second-in-command to the Fleet for the three of us."

Atalanta's cheeks turned red and she stared at the floor. "I...can't give it up now, Felix."

"Nor should you," he said, his voice a little hard. Still angry, I thought. "It occurred to me, though, that I had to stop putting the needs of the three of us before my own." He clenched his fist. "That only works if your partners are doing the same." Ouch.

"Fee, I..." Daniel started.

"From now on we discuss things as real committed partners, but this was my decision."

"What was?" I asked.

"I've taken command of the *Megaera* as of this morning."

Holy crap. I stared at Daniel and Atalanta who looked just as shocked as I felt.

"Captain Duncan will stay on," Felix continued, "for a month to make sure I know everything I need to know, but he's been looking to retire, so once Paul knew I was interested, he arranged it."

"Just like that?" Daniel asked softly.

"No, not just like that," Felix said, testily, "but I pulled the trigger today."

"Oh," said Atalanta.

"Now Atalanta will have her Fleet, Daniel will still have his recruits on the *Indus* to train and I'll have *Meg*."

"You'll have *Meg*," Atalanta repeated.

"In twenty years or so when Paul wants to move on you, Atalanta, can choose Freya as your second." Felix looked at me. "People should be closer to accepting a Heely in that position by then."

"So you have Freya's support?" Atalanta asked.

"I do. She was an integral part of the discussion."

"We may even have recruited Heely supers by then," Daniel said thoughtfully.

"Recruited by you and Felaysa, trained by you," Felix confirmed. "My guess is that the next evolution of the Furies will have very few 'normals,'" Felix said seriously. "With the influx of more 'natural' supers, Terran and Heely human alike, there won't be much room for them."

I didn't like the sound of that at all. You didn't have to have abilities beyond the norm to be a freak, but that could be dealt with later. "You think the future is in Heely supers, Felix?" I asked.

He folded his arms on his chest. "I think we should be turning serious attention to the problem of Heely integration into the larger Union society, though," he grimaced, "that may have to take a back seat to the fallout from the dissolution of the Rian Nation."

My gut clenched. "*Dissolution*?" Millions of Deneth Rian with no government? No religious leader? No identity? Mother of god.

"I hope not, but there will be splintering no matter what Eriss does."

Wait a minute. Eriss. He's concerned about the Rian and Eriss which means... "Ian had a hand in this, didn't he?" I asked. Felix smiled and suddenly I felt like I was back on Pace 4 getting something right in class. "He wants to make sure there is a place for the Deneth and Tarine to go if they need it."

"An Empire like the Rian Nation will take decades to fall apart, if it actually does," Daniel said. Felix nodded. Full marks to Daniel.

"When it does the Furies will be ready to take in the qualified," Atalanta said, "having hand-selected and trained all of its people with that possibility in mind..."

"...for more than a decade," Daniel finished, staring at Felix with wonder. "Have you already placed the order for the X-ships?"

"It's being discussed," Felix answered. Yes, I thought. The dissident Deneth needed to be able to travel with the Furies without the damage their artificial gravity would do to them. Even with the ships dealing with a race so very alien would be tricky. Tricky, I thought with a touch of jealousy, but fascinating.

"So the Furies will, eventually, be mine and..." Atalanta said.

"...ours," Felix finished. "The best home we can give the freaks of the universe, whatever their origin."

"Wow," she breathed. It was then I noticed that her eyes were dilated. "I forgot how hot it is when you take charge, Felix."

His dark eyes narrowed, but the corners on his mouth turned up. "Is it?"

Daniel's breathing was shallow as well. Oh my. "Fuck yeah, Fee."

Felix cocked his head to the side, regarding them. "Jane, would you excuse us, please?"

"Of course," I said as I sprinted for the door, but Felix had seemingly already forgotten I was there. Excellent.

The last thing I heard before the door shut behind me was the order, "Daniel, take off Atalanta's clothes. Slowly."

I had to grin as I made my way to Captain Maass. "Please see they're not disturbed until morning, Captain." I made a face, "And ask someone to change the sheets." I had to giggle.

"Commodore," the Captain protested, "it's the *Emperor's bedroom.*"

I grinned. "It's my wedding night. I'm just happy someone's getting laid."

The Captain's face relaxed and she nodded. "Yes, Ma'am."

"Good," I said. "I was hoping you could help me with something."

"Anything, Ma'am."

She was well trained, I gave her that, in Corsican unflappability and didn't even bat an eye (externally) at my unusual request. Ordinary Jane wouldn't have been able to pull off what I did in the middle of the night, but Don't-Call-Me-A-Fucking-Princess Jane apparently had resources ordinary Jane did not. More on that later.

11:00 – The Emperor's Private Office, The Imperial Palace, November 5th, 2873

I'd slept on the couch on the *Liberty*, my Security Detail fanned out around the ship like lethal barnacles. It was the best place, somehow, and seemed less lonely even though I was very much alone. The nice thing was that this 'alone' was just a temporary thing. I would be with him tonight and for the next month. I had no complaints at all.

The Emperor, Charles to me, entered his private office at precisely 11:00 with Idis who looked both regal and, if I was reading her body correctly, satisfied. I kept my smile to myself, but I was really pleased. So much of *our* happiness depended on *their* happiness. This was a good start. Plus you couldn't deny that the Emperor Charles 6 was a real stud. Not too many heads of state could spend their wedding night with their mistress and make his wife happy about it.

Charles paused in front of me, just long enough to lean in and kiss me on the cheek. "How are you?" he asked softly.

"Well, Six," I said with a smile. "How are you?"

He looked over at Idis who was speaking to Captain Stanley, "I'm the luckiest son of a bitch on the planet." He grinned at me. "Aren't I?"

I laughed. "Damned straight you are."

He winked at me and gestured Idis over to us. Then we stood in the formation that would become ingrained into habit over the next few decades: Charles in the center, Idis on his right and me on his left. As such we were an unstoppable three.

"Their Royal Highnesses Prince Whitman and Princess Joyanna, Sire," someone announced.

Charles nodded and the door opened admitting the two dressed very formally, out of respect for the Emperor, followed by Captain Drea Pace, their TP on duty, who immediately found a wall and did her best to blend into it. They must want something fairly serious, I thought, to be so...glittery this early in the day. I was not wrong.

Whit and Joyanna did their usual bowing/kissing routine and then waited for their Emperor to start the conversation. Protocol, I guessed.

"What may I do for you both?" Charles said graciously.

Whit glanced a little nervously at Joyanna who nodded her encouragement. "We wanted to ask you, Sir, for a colonization charter."

What the fuck? My brain had to chew on that one, I was so surprised. I turned to Charles. "I didn't think Corsica did that sort of thing, do they? Uh," I was a citizen now, right. "Do we?"

Charles frowned thoughtfully. "We've always expanded via peaceful absorption of existing systems. We've never actually had a colony that we started from scratch. Well," he qualified, "not for a very long time."

"Aside from Corsica itself," Idis said. "Why do you want to start a colony, Your Highness?"

Charles let out a huff of annoyance. "Whit this is Idis, Idis this is Whit. Everyone clear?" I noticed he didn't let Whit call him Charles, which I thought was pretty funny, but the title thing with Idis was annoying.

"Yes, Sire," Whit said, his cheeks red. "I...I've been having difficulty reconciling life at court with my...nature or, I should say, my natures."

Charles' eyebrows raised at that. So Whit was still fighting the Telepathic modifications Stuart had made to his mind to suppress his natural ambition. His occasionally murderous ambition.

"Joyanna has been helping me, guiding me, but it is still hard. Here."

We all looked at Joyanna now.

She nodded. "I know Whit has had his nature tampered with." Well, that was news to all of us. "Some things, however, one cannot change about a person. He wants more than he can safely have here, Uncle Charles. I thought that putting his considerable energies into building a colony could allow him better choices." She looked fondly at her spouse.

"He is brilliant and driven and, with all due respect, Sire, completely wasted here."

"You think that his talents would be better used creating than marking time," Charles said a little warily.

"Allocation of resources," I said to myself. There was a logic to it. There had to be more to this than just starting a colony, however.

"There is a system that is strategically significant," Whit said as he produced a flexi-monitor. "May I?" Charles nodded permission and Whit rolled it out onto Charles' desk. "Three planets. The largest of which we could terraform to make arable."

He pressed a button on the flexi and planets appeared on the black screen. Three in green, one in gold and an area of space in red.

"You said there was a strategic advantage?" Idis asked as she leaned closer.

"This system is almost exactly between Irena and Paragon," he said looking at me as if willing me to understand something. Fucked if I knew what it was. Though that system he wanted. Something about it bothered me.

"You want to use it as a base, a fueling station for a Union Fleet," I said.

"Paragon, the Denethian Station?" Idis asked.

I nodded. "It's the largest space station they ever built," I said. "Not as old or revered as Trithicate, but easily twice as big."

Idis looked at Charles and me, horrified, "Is war so foregone a conclusion?"

"It isn't," Charles said, "but so much depends on Eriss. Perhaps too much." He cast his eyes on Whit. "So you want to build a station as well as terraform?"

"Yes, Sire."

Now Idis was frowning, her hands on her hips the way she put them when she was really thinking or upset. "There is a serious vetting process with the Union for charters, Whit. It could take months, if not years, especially if there is a prior claim. Have you researched it at all?"

Now Joyanna looked really uncomfortable, green with nerves, actually. "We have and we know that there is only one claimant, the only person who *could* inherit it, so to speak." She paused and I felt an epiphany coming. "Whit himself."

I felt the room go gray around the edges. It was hard to breathe.

"Pace-Pallon," I gasped. "You want to go back to Pace. I need to sit down," I said as a chair seemed to magically appear behind me. I felt Charles' hand on my shoulder. It weighed me down, tethered me to the ground in the best way. "You have clearly lost your mind."

Whit looked as though I had struck him. "You can't object to this, Jane, this is our home."

I massaged my forehead, trying to stop the monster headache that had suddenly formed behind my eyes. "No, Whit. This," and I gestured to Charles and Idis, "is my home."

"Of course," he kept on doggedly, though I was sure he didn't care or even understand, "but Pace made you. Gave you everything you have. All the good you have done you would never have been able to do without it."

"That is true." I stood a little shakily, but I stood. "Without illegal genetic tampering I wouldn't have been a freak," I felt Charles wince, "and perhaps I would have had parents or siblings. Maybe even a whole family." Unconsciously I found my hand on my belly. "Like Lucy will have. Maybe I could have had a home. Maybe I could have had an ordinary life that I would have wished myself out of, desperate for adventure." I took a wobbly step towards him. "Maybe I would have had choices of my own making. After all, who chooses to be a slave?"

"We weren't slaves!" Whit said, horrified.

"You tell yourself that, Whit," I sat back down heavily. "If it will make you feel better."

"None of those people, the Scientists, still exist, do they?" Idis asked, still staring at the red blob that marked the Denethian territory. Aside from Whit, I said only in my head.

"No," Whit said sadly.

"I'm correct in assuming that everything, even topographical features were wiped out when Pace 3 was broken?" she asked. I looked at her in surprise. She shrugged elegantly, "I like to read."

"That is true," Whit said.

"You would not object, Jane, if this were a system unknown to you?" Charles asked.

"No," I said, now feeling a little foolish, but still upset.

"So the question has to be, does a place have a memory?" he said. I looked at him quickly, but there was no mocking in his tone. Sympathy, yes, but no mocking. He stepped away from his desk and extended a hand to Whit. "We," the Imperial 'we' or the three of us 'we'? I didn't know which, "will give this a great deal of study and thought. Thank you for the proposal."

Whit started to object but Joyanna rested her hand on her husband's arm as she curtseyed. "Thank you, Uncle. You have been most kind hearing us out."

"Not at all," Charles said kindly. He shook a nettled Whit's hand. "You will do nothing, of course, until We have made Our decision."

"Of course, Sire," Whit said, remembering himself. "Thank you."

"We will see you both at the Frost Celebrations." Charles smiled, but it didn't reach his eyes this time. "All four of you."

Joyanna twinkled at him. "It's past time for that, Uncle Charles. Safe journey."

They bowed and left. Captain Drea started to follow, but stopped at a look from Charles. "Report, Captain," he said.

She stood at attention and said, "They are sincere, Sire. Princess Joyanna loves her husband and is very worried about him. Court life puts stresses on him that can incapacitate his mind."

"When the 'real' Whit conflicts with the 'created' one," I said.

"Yes, Commodore," she said. "Princess Joyanna feels that the reclamation work of the first 5-7 years, not the mention the construction of the space station, will be so absorbing and so, in her words, 'lacking in nuance' that he should get a respite from this constant internal struggle."

"I've spoken to terraformers before," Charles said thoughtfully. "It is painstaking work at a slow pace."

"She feels that he has the requisite determination to pull this off. That it will be the making of him."

"How does he feel about it, Captain?" I asked.

Her expression clouded. "He wants to go home. He wants all the rest of it, too. Glory for Corsica, pride in achievement, strategic advantage."

"While the rest of us are relieved his 'home' no longer exists," I said bleakly.

"Thank you, Captain," Charles said briskly, "you may return to your charges."

"Very good, Your Imperial Majesty." She left.

Charles gestured Idis and me over to a small seating area. We sat.

"This was a surprise," Charles said.

"Indeed, my dear," Idis said dryly.

I kept quiet, ashamed that this bothered me as much as it did. Charles had been right, I was afraid of a place. A place that had no resemblance to the former home I knew. There were no buildings, no fields, no School, no Government, and there hadn't been any corpses even at the time. All our history, both good and bad, had been wiped clean. Except it hadn't. Not as long as any of the original Pacey refugees were alive.

"We need much more information," Idis said firmly. She stared off into space as if an invisible checklist hovered in the air in front of her. "Terraforming experts, colonization specialists." she huffed out air. "We'd need specs on the system—new specs to determine if the planet he wants to terraform…" she looked at the flexi-monitor.

"Pace 1," I said glumly. Where Samuel had met his first wife. The most beautiful of our worlds, the breadbasket of the system. I'd never seen it bountiful. I'd only seen it from space, confirming the *tapetia mortis* had been wiped out. It had been a husk of a planet then. Who knew if it still was? It had only been a few years, but a lot could happen in a few years, the voice of the former slave-turned-Princess-of-Corsica said in my head. I told that voice to shut the fuck up.

"We don't even know if any of the original atmosphere still exists." Idis bit her lip. "No atmosphere means domes, usually, and that can get very expensive." She rubbed her forehead with the heel of her hand. My headache was catching, just for very different reasons. "We'll need to send a survey ship to get an idea what we're dealing with."

Charles leaned back in his chair. "The problem is that this isn't just an issue of money and resources, but of feeling." He looked at me, his golden eyes soft. "Whit seems to think this is a simple reclamation, but of all the Pacey refugees that are still alive, he may be the only one." He slumped against the couch now. "The political ramifications aren't going to be any fun, either."

Mother of god, I hadn't even thought about that. "They'll say you married a freak and you now want to go back where it all started and make more?"

"Jane, please," Charles said, annoyed, "that word."

"Fine, they're going to think you're going to create a supernormal printing press."

"They will probably think that," Charles nodded.

"You still want to do it, however," Idis said, shaking her head.

"You do?" I asked, surprised. Charles said nothing and I turned to Idis, "He does?" How could she tell?

"It's the way he brings up what concerns him, Jane," Idis was amused and Charles's expression was a bit sour. "He's turned on by the whole thing."

"I thought we had rules about who turned you on, Charles," I said, finally seeing humor in the situation.

Charles mock glared at both of us before shrugging, "We have rules about *whom*, my darling, not *what*. I was just taken by the idea of starting from scratch. We haven't done that as a nation since we first colonized the system a millennia ago. It would be quite the challenge."

I laughed. "You sound like Samuel," I teased. Then I had a thought. "Samuel is just the person to talk to about this, Charles. Samuel and all the surviving Paceys."

"I agree," he said, "and Whit needs to be there for it, to know what he's getting into."

"What happens if Whit turns out to be the problem?" I asked. Idis frowned. "The reason Corsica even has a claim is because Whit was part of the old system. Most of us won't want that system brought back."

"Or will they want it brought back their way," Idis said slowly.

"What do you mean, Idis?"

"What is the first thing a slave dreams of?"

"Being the Master," I whispered. Fuck fuck fuck.

"The problem is, ladies," Charles said as he rose from his chair, "that the strategic value for the system looks to be sound. Too sound to ignore."

Idis rose, too, but I stayed put, depressed by the whole topic. "You are saying that if we pass, someone else will take it."

"The Paceys will really have a fit then," I grumbled.

"One may assume that, yes," Charles said as he walked over to Idis, embracing her. "We have to depart, dear one." She melted against him and I was at a loss. Was I supposed to pretend I wasn't there? No, I thought. If they'd needed to be alone, no one was stopping them. Still damned uncomfortable for me. "You will write?"

She smiled sadly. "Reams." She kissed him, squeezed him hard and strode purposefully out of the room. He stared after her a minute, then walked over and knelt in front of me.

"She'll send a survey ship and then we shall see what we shall see."

I pulled him closer with my legs and kissed him. "We've got some ships of our own to catch, Six."

"Roger that," he said with a smile as he pulled me to my feet and led me out of the room.

01:48 – Captain's Quarters, *W.S. Liberty*, Cargo Hold B, *H.M.S. Lumina*, En route to Terra 1, November 6th, 2873

It was a little strange to be relaxing sprawled over my lover in my old cabin on my beloved ship...that was nestled inside Charles' much larger ship. I loved it, for as much as I could have a home that wasn't a person, my *Liberty* was it. It also had the added benefit of being all ours, once the Guards had checked it over thoroughly. I could passively sense the two dozen of them patrolling the cargo hold around the ship. We were safe, but we also had the run of my small ship. Mr. Beddoes had promised to appear with food periodically, but other than that we were to look after each other.

It was pretty damned perfect, in my opinion. Three days in hyper with the man I loved. Who could ask for more?

"I was doing some research in the family history," Charles began as he pulled me up the headboard with him. I snuggled close happily.

"Ok?"

"I was looking for a formal version of Lucy," he said. I looked askance. "For her official name, etc."

"What's wrong with Lucy, Six?"

"Nothing is wrong with it, Jane, and I am sure she will rarely be called anything else, but having a formal name serves two distinct purposes."

"Which are?"

"It endears her to the public," he said as he nuzzled my ear. I shivered happily. "It will be their Princess Lucy. Princess Formal Name will be for the outsiders."

I had to smile. "Makes sense and the other reason?"

"She'll know she's in real trouble when her parents call her by her full name."

I ran my hand gently over his now smooth cheek. The beard had lasted all of ten minutes once we were underway. I hadn't minded the facial hair, but I liked his face better without it. "Is that really a thing?"

He laughed. "You'd better believe it, Red. Charles-Victor was in a great deal of trouble. Charles-Victor Arthur Bennett was probably about to be executed."

I giggled and stretched luxuriously. "No wonder you dislike the wedding ceremony. Too many memories of childhood punishments."

He grimaced, "All kinds of punishments." He ran his hand down my back causing another shiver. "You've added to your list." He traced the tattooed names delicately with his long fingers. "Lita Utat and Arrow this time." How Captain Maass had been able to find a discrete tattoo artist in the middle of the night had been some kind of magic, but she'd done it.

I shrugged. "At least I'm not adding to it as often, though the losses get more painful."

"Most of these names are Paceys."

"Most but not all." I turned so that I could face him. "Some of those names are there solely because of Whit's people."

"To play devil's advocate, however, one could argue that all Paceys only exist in the first place because of Whit's people."

"That's not an argument, it's just truth." I chewed my lip. "We could hit him with a powerful partner. Tellesco, perhaps. Most of them are still unsettled."

Charles shook his head. "That puts Whit in a position of powerplays and intrigue, which is exactly what we're trying to avoid for him."

"Right." We needed someone incorruptible, loyal and tireless. I knew just the being. "We could ask Thal."

Charles' golden eyes went wide as he considered. "You really trust him that much?"

"I've had to learn to, Charles," I said with more of a touch of self-loathing, "and it took longer than it should have. But I do trust him."

"Idis' Sentient Property Case won't be on until at least next year, but…" he paused and I waited as he processed. "That could work in our favor. Whit'd be much less likely to try anything if he thinks that he'd be messing with you."

"I suppose so." Gross logic, but valid.

"Will he do it?"

I just loved that he never questioned Thal's right to say no. Well, I just loved Charles period. Have I been too subtle about my feelings for Charles? Didn't think so. "We can only ask, but I think he'd enjoy the challenge. If he isn't interested, we'll figure something else out."

"Very good," he said as he extricated himself out of bed.

"Tired of me already?" I asked.

"Even the Super Grand Magnificent whatever has to deal with certain issues, Commodore."

"You have to pee," I accused him teasingly. "Charles, I know you pee."

"Emperors do not pee," he said with mock hauteur. "We urinate."

"Please spare me whatever you call taking a shit. There are some things I don't need to know."

"Understood."

"You know," I said once his Imperial task had been completed, "You're giving up something when you let Whit go."

He sighed as he washed his hands. "Yes. His talent only works with proximity, at least in reference to me, but there are other considerations. There won't be a lot of people around the former Pace-Pallon," Charles said. He paused.

"Right…"

"We will encourage traders with the Rian to use the system as a way point as well." He looked at me. "It *is* on the way."

I sat up. "It might be a good base of operations for Eriss since, now that Trithicate is gone, Paragon is the closest Rian Colony." My mind was ablaze with possibilities.

"So we put a colony, so to speak, of UNav Intelligence on the new civilian station, let everyone know about it while at the same time sprinkling the population with our TPs…" he smiled, waiting for me to finish the thought.

Oh wow. "And feed all of that information to Whit."

"Who will send his nexus predictions to me, which I will then send on to Sam and Hugh."

"That is brilliant, Charles," I said so enthusiastically, his cheeks turned pink. Didn't anyone ever praise an Emperor? Or did they do it so much it meant nothing? I kissed him proudly. "You're pretty smart for a Head of State."

"I have my moments," he mumbled against my lips. I kissed him again but then stopped abruptly when I had a thought. "What? Tired of me already?"

"Don't be ridiculous," I said, but I sat back a bit. "You *are* giving up your advantage, Charles. If you send Whit away you won't have his insight into your life anymore. Proximity will be lost."

His golden eyes were soft as he tucked some of my long hair behind my ear. "My boys are healthy and happy and right now I have everything I have ever wanted in them, you, Idis and Lucy. If something is going to go wrong with that, I don't want to know."

I stroked his chest the way he liked just so I could watch his eyes turn to black gold and his breath catch. "Me either." I backed up so I could move down his body and he arched into my touch. I used all my Micro tricks, everything I'd picked up over the years of playing around to make him lose control, which he did. A few minutes later I wiped the sweat off his brow and he looked at me with a kind of wonder. (I can't tell you how gratifying that feeling is, to know you've blown the mind of your lover. Fucking amazing.)

"The present is more than enough for me, Jane."

"For me, too, love."

Later Mr. Beddoes brought us food, even though it was the dead of morning, and eventually, finally, sated in every way we could think of, we settled into sleep. I was almost out when I heard Charles say sleepily. "You never asked what the name was, for Lucy."

"Sorry, Six," I said trying to wake myself back into coherence. "What is it?"

"The name of a great Queen, one who ruled Corsica long before we were an Empire. It was her idea to expand through mutual interest. She set the stage for many things we've been able to accomplish since."

"What was this Queen's name?"

"Annaluca."

I wrapped myself tighter around him and he sighed happily, relaxing further. "Annaluca. What does Idis say?"

"She approves."

All right, then. "That's a good name for our girl."

He kissed my forehead and we dropped into sleep, his large hand splayed across the tattoo on my back that now read:

Lita Utat

Arrow

Adele

Stoney

Soames

Peter

Winifred

Duncan

Thal

Gladys

Criss Utat

Ian

Samuel

Wilby

Andrew

Anan

Julianne

Sig

Paulette

Arthur

Irrfan

10:00 – Conference Room, ESTF, UNav, Terra 1, March 15th, 2874

I sat with the others in the conference room at the ESTF on Terra 1 seeing what I'd expected to see: Miles and miles of dark brown earth passed in front of us as our select group sat in front of the monitors. A dead land that appeared flat at first, but soon we'd see great valleys, riverbeds and even what looked like caves in places.

That, however, wasn't at all what we were looking at as we viewed the Survey Ship data from its trip to the former Pace 1.

My hands rested protectively on my now six-month pregnant belly. Lucy was spinning around merrily, which was a strange yet very cool thing to feel.

What I was looking at, what we all were looking at, however, (we being Charles, Samuel, Whit, Joyanna, Princess Sophia, the Trio, Hannah Three and Thal) was distressing, even though I hadn't been completely on board with the reclamation project in the first place.

I was staring at a giant crater, a crater the size of a continent. Had I been there I could have felt it, but as it was we could see the shadows of its imprint on the planet through the storm of dirt, dust and debris what swirled violently across our view. That wasn't, however, all the mayhem that had been visited on Pace 1.

The view cut to rivers of black rock, cooling lava still steaming slightly. Deep fissures, new valleys and an enormous mountain range of truly stupendous proportions. All this through the constant winds and flying dirt.

Pace 1 was decimated. A complete loss for millennia to come.

"It's like Pace 3 cooled," a woman said. We all looked at her and she nodded. Hannah Three, one of the handful of non-Furies Pace 3 survivors (and the only female one I had ever met), was easily the largest person in the room, as Pacey 3s tended to be. She was scarred and fairly intimidating but whip smart. We gave her our attention easily. She would have made a good successor to Andrew, had he lived to succeed Sig, I thought. A Senior Engineer needed to be that sort of strong.

"It didn't look like that after we split 3," I protested. "I was there, I checked on it to make sure the *tapetia mortis* were wiped out." I turned to the small group assembled. "Which they were."

Hannah looked at Princess Sophia. "A piece of debris struck the planet after that, then?"

Sophia, a too-lean, too-pale, plain woman, was all focus, and you could see it in her black almond shaped eyes. They were, I thought, her best feature and also her scariest. Even if she didn't see everything you felt like she could. You always knew how you stood with her, though, even if you weren't thrilled about where you were standing. She sighed. "Yes. There is no other explanation for the destruction and that crater. We did some calculations and it looks like the planet face that was hit was turned away from the refugee fleet when it occurred."

"How did we not notice?" I asked Samuel, High Admiral Armstrong to you.

He shrugged, "We were trying not to be murdered by our countrymen at the time, Jane." Now all eyes turned to Whit, who blushed scarlet and stared at the floor. "It is true, however," Samuel continued, "that even had we known, we were in no position to stop anything."

"So there is no coming back from this, Sophia?" Whit asked in a small voice.

Sophia, who saved the world(s) with her husband Prince Hal on a regular basis, shook her head sadly. "I'm sorry, Whit, but even I can't work a miracle here." If that sounded a bit arrogant, she'd earned it. Her work on Tellesco (where Hal currently was) was yielding results at last and the level of Heely water was dropping fast. Another year or two and the Tellescans might be able to reestablish a settlement. It wouldn't be the same, but it wouldn't have been *anything* without Sophia and Hal.

"Damn," Whit said sadly.

Sophia lifted her hand to press the button on the flexi-monitor to stop the projection, when, surprisingly, Charles (playing Fitzroy today) said, "Hold a minute, Sophia."

Wait, what?

"Switch it to the third recording, please."

"Yes, Sir," she corrected herself, "Fitz, I mean."

I could tell my lover was having trouble not rolling his eyes at this near mistake. Here she outranked him, but in private and at home…not so much.

She selected the third file and we saw something completely different.

"You've been holding out on us, Fitz," Sophia said quietly, her dark eyes wide.

The world we were looking at was flat, as if the topography had been wiped clean away. There were the valleys and canyons I'd been expecting, too. There was also one giant hole, big enough to put a city in. The drone's camera stopped there for quite a while, then lowered in, showing remnants of metal, wires and tracks for what had to have been a transportation system. That couldn't be, I thought wildly. No, that can't be.

"Samuel," I asked, willing my voice not to shake. "What is that?"

Sophia answered first. "A best spot for a settlement," she said thoughtfully. "It's by far the biggest structure on the planet—which we'd need to be able to house all the workers necessary for a quick—and by quick I mean five years—turn around on the station. Having the bulk of the city underground is ideal in this environment and building a domed settlement without using this would be prohibitively expensive…" She thought aloud then, "We'd need to treat the air and terraform so that we could do massive plantings to supplement the oxygen lost in the orbital disruption, but with a temporary dome or two we could…" and then she stopped as if suddenly aware of the deadly silence that had consumed the room.

"No fucking way," Hannah breathed.

"What is it?" Sophia asked, slightly annoyed.

Samuel stood and walked over to the monitor. "It's where I was born and where the Prince was born, too."

"Me, too," Daniel said bitterly. Oh, right. Created to be an Empath cannon fodder, controlled by Tristan.

Any negative subtext was completely lost on Whit as his face lit with a smile that said 'home.' "Bane?"

"Yes, Your Highness," Samuel said slowly. "Bane."

The room erupted in outrage.

"I'm not living where those butchers held court!" Hannah growled.

"It won't work, General," Felix offered. "Too much bad blood."

"You're bringing a Scientist back to his throne," Daniel protested.

"That is both unfair, Captain Pace, and untrue," Sophia protested unwisely, "We must be practical. It's just a city. A space we can use. Almost ideal for our purposes."

"Do you know what they did to fetuses they didn't like or have any use for?" Atalanta said fiercely.

I felt Lucy kick reassuringly, but 'Lanta had a point. Arrow had also been created there, made of Samuel's DNA and the DNA of the brutal psychopath Indira Pallon. As understandable as everyone's emotions were, however, it wasn't just that simple.

"Things that went on in that place were illegal *even on Pace*," Daniel said. A terrifying statement.

On and on it went, but I was thinking hard and I could tell that both Samuel and Charles were subtly watching me, which was uncomfortable and a little weird.

Whit's face had gone white with anger and I could feel his tension and panic shoot through the roof. His fists were clenched and I knew that he was going to say something. Perhaps tell the plebes that they needed to shut their mouths and keep their place. Perhaps just scream his frustration. He stood up abruptly and opened his mouth to speak and...

"Whit, love," was all Joyanna, previously silent as the grave, said.

Whit froze and thought for a second. Then he deliberately unclenched his hands and sat back down.

Joyanna looked us all over levelly. Then she turned to me. "Commodore?"

I took a moment to be impressed. She, apparently, knew about my connection to Samuel and, obviously, to the man pretending not to be my husband. She knew they would weigh what I had to say carefully. That meant I had to weigh my own words even more carefully.

The room became silent again. Waiting. No pressure. I knew what this meant to Charles and to the Union in general. Hugh Leder wanted this to work, too, for strategic reasons, but the idea of people of living in Bane (not to mention anyone reclaiming Pace-Pallon in the first place) was frightening to me and that fear irritated the fuck out of me.

Thal looked me right in the eye and said only three words. "There is Nuta."

Then, it came to me. Whether or not anyone else would agree with what I was about to say (aside from, I guessed, Thal) was beyond me.

"Yes, Nuta," I said quietly. Nuta had been required reading on the UEL Exam Two I was currently doing a bad job studying for.

Both Charles and Samuel sat back in their chairs at the same time.

"Yes," Charles said, with a nod to Thal. "An interesting parallel."

Samuel bit his lip but said nothing and Sophia looked thoughtful.

It was left to Joyanna to ask the obvious question, "Nuta?"

I rested my elbows on the table. "Nuta was the capital city of the Pharo about six hundred standard years ago. The Pharese had previously tried to invade a neighboring system, though they didn't really have the resources to win their war, and they lost."

Felix nodded.

I continued. "The Bitta, the victorious system, had lost much and they took it out on the Pharese in thorough and cruel ways. Even after the surrender there were bombings, mass murder, conscriptions, etc. I think anyone, even the Bitta, would have agreed that life on Nuta was hell." I looked at my fellow Paceys. "Much worse than what we had to live through."

"That would be safe to say," Samuel said dryly.

"The Bitta saw the error of their mishandling of the subjugated people too late. Far too late."

"The Pharese fought back, as I recall," Felix said with narrowed eyes.

"A leader crawled out of that hell and invigorated the populace. He picked a minority, the Bitta-Pharese, refugees from Bitta proper two hundred years before, and started systematically poisoning their water and setting fire to their communities. He called it 'culling.' Millions died on the planet they considered their home."

"I don't understand how this relates…" Whit said.

"The Bitta of their home planet, under new management, recruited allies and wiped out the bulk of the Pharese, saving only the people of the resistance (Pharese or not) and all the Bitta-Pharese who were still alive. They were all given an option: come home to Bitta or stay and start again."

"Oh," was all Whit said then.

"I've been to Nuta," Hannah said slowly. "They have turned it into a beautiful world. All that's left of the regime of centuries ago is a desecrated monument to that leader and a museum of the atrocities so that no one could forget."

I nodded. "They cleaned that world of the stain of genocide and re-made it in their own image." I exhaled. "I think that if we work hard enough we can do the same with *this* world. Starting with Bane."

"Jane!" Atalanta said, clearly shocked.

"It's only my opinion." I could feel the tension in the room building, but I had a question to ask the being whose opinion would be crucial to the success or failure of the venture. "What do you think, Thal?"

He bit his lip as he sat slumped in his chair the way he did when he was Thalberg, not Thal. "I think even a world can use a second chance, Jane." I smiled at him and he nodded back. "I think we can do it." Ok, then.

The arguments and outrage started again, but Joyanna kept glancing from me to Thal to Samuel to Charles. Slowly, the more she stared at us, the more relaxed she looked.

On June 10th a massive Corsican colony ship, one third of its population Paceys, and flanked by four construction ships, one of which was captained by Hannah Three and full of Pacey 3s, left for the Pace-Pallon System.

On June 11th Princess Annaluca Victoria Idis Atalanta Rochester Pace Couvillion-Bourbonais was born after twelve hours (ugh!) of labor. Crowds cheered the name "Princess Lucy" in their delirium outside the Palace walls.

The first Corsican Colony System since the Kingdom's founding was named Annaluca in her honor.

END OF PART ONE, BOOK EIGHT

June 11th, 2874

Entry 9-8-92
Or
The Ballad of Eriss and Ian
An Unplanned Novella

[This Entry was contributed by Ian Armstrong, former Commander of the Three Furies Mercenary Fleet in place of Jane's usual ramblings. Don't worry, if you're missing her, Jane will be by in a bit.]

<u>12:50 – Shopping Concourse, Terra 1 Space Station, Terra, September 15th, 2874</u>

I, Ian Armstrong, sat at a table at a random café on Terra 1, stared at my Denethian coffee (still popular despite the events of last year) and thought about loss. Doesn't that just sound like it sucks balls? Yeah, does to me, too. I sat and waited for a friend who was waiting for another friend, but I was, as I often was, thinking of Arrow. It had been a year and two months since Jane had found my lover's space-frozen body and brought it back to Dad and me. I'd been angry and sad and numb and hopeless and then sad again over that time, of course, and I was pretty sure I was never going to lose any of those feelings completely. In fact, letting go of all my sadness seemed wrong to me. Disrespectful, even.

I saw Dad whenever I was on Terra 1 and at first we'd tried talking about her, and when that had made us both uncomfortable, then we'd tried pretending that nothing had happened, which was a different kind of worse. Now we danced around her death as if addressing it directly would unleash something highly toxic. So we flailed around stupidly, each trying our best to keep the familial bond going even though I hardly recognized it anymore. Don't get me wrong, I loved my father, I just wasn't myself and had no idea who I was supposed to be without her. I know that my favorite meddler, that would be Jane, would have pushed and pulled until we actually communicated and probably had to hide manly tears, but she had the new husband (and sort of wife) and baby. This was aside from the fact that she'd only arrived back on Terra 1 last night and was starting the Fall Semester at the ESTF tomorrow. The woman was rather busy.

The funny thing was, I thought as I took a sip of the most potent coffee ever, it appeared, to those who didn't really know us, that Dad and I were coping just fine. He had Mallory, the epitome of patience, and I had Eriss (if my 'having' Eriss meant following her around like a sad puppy dog). I worked hard for her, was devoted to her and her interests, though it was obvious to both Eriss and myself that part of my excessive dedication was making up for my failures in other areas. If I couldn't stand myself most of the time, it was no one's business but my own. I guess my super ability was denial.

I still missed Arrow, however, and it hurt so much to miss her. It was something I wouldn't readily admit to anyone, but her touch, her smell, her laugh and her fierce strong mind were never far from me. I was haunted and sad. I snorted over my cup. How could Eriss resist me? This thought brought a new wave of self-loathing and shame. I shouldn't be considering what Eriss thought, at least in that specific way. I didn't deserve anyone as wonderful as she. I knew this. Unfortunately, she didn't.

Just then a stir in the people doing their shopping caught my attention, saving me from this afternoon's pit of misery. I looked up and smiled as I saw people step aside (some bowing, which brought an involuntary chuckle) as Princess Jane of Lyonesse, Commodore Jane Pace-Couvillion-Bourbonais made her way towards me. Her expression was one of resigned annoyance but other than that I had to say that she looked good. Post-baby Jane was dressed in a simple black suit with her *de rigueur* badass boots and was, perhaps, just a bit rounder than she had been (which looked good on her, by the way), but still fit and strong, her red/black hair caught back in its usual ponytail.

Her rather stern expression melted, though, when she saw me. I found myself smiling and stood as she grabbed me into a serious hug.

"Ian, love," she said happily into my ear, "it's so fucking good to see you. Thanks for coming."

"Anything you want, Jane," I said quietly back, "you know that." We let go and she sat next to me at the table. "Though I'm not sure why I'm here."

She frowned. "I'm not completely sure either," she said a little nervously.

"You've been waiting for this for a long time," I said.

Her frown deepened. "I know I have, but now it's going to happen I'm..." she looked around her as if the concourse would give her an answer, "...confused."

"You can forgive him, you know," I said gently.

Her eyes looked bright, too bright, "Can I?" For a brief second I wondered whom she meant. Odd thought. She clenched her fists, then forced her hands flat on the table. "I've been up all night, thinking." She sighed. "And thinking and getting more and more upset."

"What have you been thinking?"

She shook her head.

I leaned forward. "Why are we meeting him in public, Jane?"

She sighed. "Because I don't know what to say."

Oh boy. She was regarding me then, and I could see a growing sense of purpose in her brown eyes, not to mention her meddler hat going on.

"Jane, you need to leave this alone..."

She cut me off as I'd known she would. "The eye patch looks good on you." It didn't, of course.

Sigh. "Eriss says it makes me look rakish." I winced because I'd mentioned her name in presence of She Who Always Knew Best.

My friend rolled her eyes but went a different way than I had expected, though I knew the overall end point would be the same. "You've been busy, I hear."

I exhaled hard because I knew what she was getting at. Still not hitting on the Eriss problem directly. I almost wished she would now that she'd brought this up. "From whom have you been hearing?"

"Fey," she said, cocking her head to the side as she looked at me. "I know she came back early from Elysium to prep for the new semester."

Yeah, I knew that, too. "I didn't think she gossiped about her clients," I said through clenched teeth. I felt my face heat, much as I willed it not to.

Jane's eyebrows shot up. "You weren't a client and you didn't tell her to keep quiet."

"Right."

"And I wasn't talking about your night with her; I was talking about everyone else."

I tipped my head back wishing I was anywhere but where I was. But, really, this was my friend Jane. What had I expected? "Criticism, Jane?"

She snorted. "Depends." She reached out and put her hand over mine. "I'm all for promiscuity, love." Now she gripped my hand. "Providing it's the right kind."

"Meaning?" I knew what she meant, but I liked the idea of delaying my confession as long as possible. Not sure why I bothered since it didn't delay it by all that much.

"The kind where no one gets hurt."

Felaysa, the beautiful, experienced and unexpectedly kind HM, had been my first sexual partner since Arrow. I'd been right to pick her (if I'd needed to pick anybody). She'd been very generous and understanding when I'd been a disaster in bed. It had been awful, but she'd made it almost ok. That took talent considering what a wreck I'd been.

"Why, then, Ian?" Jane asked gently. "You know I'll love you no matter what, right?"

I did know that and it meant a lot to me, but that didn't change…anything.

"Tell me," she commanded but with a smile.

So I did.

It had been about four months ago. I'd been training Eriss to fight. Not the looks pretty kind of fighting, either, but down and dirty lethal stuff. We'd trained mercilessly against Terran humans, Heelies and (via the Denethian ATR I'd ordered from Affie's people) Denethians. No matter how violent the attack or defense, though, Eriss moved with such grace it blew me away. I did my best to incorporate her Telepathic abilities into her advantages, but there was, as Jane had said many, many times, no substitute for knowing how to fight straight. Eriss's world was a very unsafe one right now. Terrans had died when the Pelann had attacked, as had Heelies (though they weren't a threat anymore, focused as they were on reintegration problems) and the Denethians she was theoretically supposed to rule didn't know what to do with her. As a whole they didn't, but individually some of them just wanted her dead.

So we fought and fought hard. Jane, Felix and I had worked out a training plan that would have daunted anyone except Quinn, but the results were paying off. Eriss had been forced to shed a lot of her young person innocence and protect herself physically in ways she'd never even thought of before.

When you're a fighter you have ample opportunities to know whether or not you're good. There was no hiding, either in actual battle or on the training floor, so I know I am very, very good. So the day she finally knocked me down was a wonderful shock.

I'd landed hard on my back, wind almost knocked out of me, when she glided over me, her teeth bared, fists cocked.

Of course it was at that moment that my previously dormant dick chose to wake up.

She was so very beautiful and had that dangerous edge that really did it for me. It was as if the last piece of the puzzle had been laid in place and god, I wanted her. My mental 'door' had been open (so she could read and anticipate my moves) and she'd felt everything.

She floated down and kissed me. My body couldn't have been happier about it. My brain and heart, however, rebelled. Arrow, my brain screamed. Arrow.

Eriss read that, too.

I didn't have to push her away; she did it herself.

She sat on the floor next to me, wings folded behind her, looking like a fallen spirit. I hadn't thought my heart could break again, but I'd been wrong.

"Eriss, I…"

"Do you always feel this way around me?" Too complicated a question to answer. She took my silence as confirmation, even though it wasn't the whole story. "I've waited."

"I haven't wanted you to," I lied. I lied because it wasn't fair to make her wait for me when I couldn't promise that things would ever change.

She hung her head. In that moment she looked very young and I felt like even more of a shit, if that was possible.

"Will you send me away?" I asked, trying to hide my terror at the concept. She paused and I felt like I couldn't breathe.

"No," she said finally as she rose. "I know you want to stay, though I can't think why."

I 'closed' my door fast, afraid my feelings for her would make things worse, give encouragement where it would only do harm.

"I believe in you," I said softly.

She smiled the saddest smile I'd ever seen. "I know you do, Ian." She straightened her tunic. "I will stop asking for more from you."

Dread. All I felt now was dread.

Her pale, lovely eyes were cool now. Not cold, exactly, but cool. "I'm done with waiting."

With that she flew out of the training room. I felt physically sick.

That night I saw a Terran man exit her rooms looking hastily put together. I was in the common space between the two bedrooms of the Terra 1 suite we shared. He gave me a bright 'can you believe it?' grin before he walked out the door.

The sleeve of my jacket was wet. I looked down and the drink I'd been holding was shaking so much it had spilled. I managed to put the glass of spirits down on the table without breaking it, but I couldn't stop shaking.

It sounds so sentimental, so juvenile to say that somewhere in my head I'd hoped to be her first, like I'd been Arrow's. I'd never given a rat's ass if my other lovers had been virgins, in fact, experience had been a plus. This, however, was Eriss, my Eriss. I wouldn't be her first. The thought just killed me.

I found the bottle of spirits and drank half of it as fast as I could. Eventually I stopped shaking, but found I couldn't leave my bed.

The next night she brought home someone else. Then the next and the next. Half were men, the other half, I noticed, were women as the week progressed. Jane would have been proud of her willingness to try everything. The following week it was Heelies (apparently now everyone was doing it, er, them) and they all looked satisfied by the experience, though I never saw Eriss until the next morning. I wondered why.

I found a spot in my room where I could hear into hers (to make the torture complete) and drank and listened until I had no choice but to take myself in hand, hating myself as I did so.

After two weeks of this (and a great deal of alcohol) I'd showed up at Fey's door with a broken heart and raging hard on. I don't know what had made her let me in. Pity, I supposed.

Over the last four months I'd gotten proficient at what I called self-loathing sex and bedded anyone who'd have me (which, thanks to what Jane called my 'startling blue eyes'—even though I was still an eye down—was a lot of people). Eriss could fuck Heelies? Well, so the fuck could I. Terran women? Sure. A man or two for variety? Eh, ok. (As Jane would say, not really my thing, but why not?) Then more women. It was a virtual parade through our rooms. Sometimes Eriss' one night stand and mine would go out for breakfast together afterwards.

I wasn't surprised Fey had heard about it all. I would have been shocked if anyone in the small community of the station *hadn't*. It was all quite disgusting, really. There was something so sad about even an orgasm being just another thing you got through.

Back in the shopping concourse in present day Jane looked at me and said, "Well, I think that's the most we've ever talked about your penis." Her look implied that that was the most she'd spoken to *anyone* about their penis.

"You asked," I said, a bit embarrassed.

She smiled. "I did."

"So now what?" I said, angry as if my confession alone should have fixed my problems.

She pursed her lips, thinking, then said, "Well, first I think you should stop fucking everyone, especially since you clearly aren't enjoying it."

I shrugged.

"Try a course of 'if sex doesn't mean anything let's not have it' for a while."

"Can you get her to stop doing that, too?"

"You really want me to have that conversation with her?" Jane asked, her eyes sparkling wickedly.

Did I? The idea of having Jane solve everything without me having to do much did sound great right then, still a cheat, but great. "No."

She took my hand again. "One of the things I admire about you is how devoted you are to the people you love."

"Uh huh," I said articulately, not sure I would be happy with where this was going.

"And I know that you are, for all intents and purposes, a monogamist, as am I."

"Yeah?"

"Do you know who the first person was to see Lucy smile?" Jane said, smiling herself, as she abruptly changed the subject. I was struck by how really happy she looked, how not like the vengeful Red Angel she was at that moment. Wow.

"Who?"

"Idis," she said with satisfaction. "She called Charles and me in immediately and we saw it, too," she explained with a happy sigh, "but Idis was the first one." She leaned forward. "You know my version of a Trio. You know Stuart's. You know the Atalanta/Daniel/Felix extravaganza that's the only traditional, if that's the right word, one we know of."

"What are you…" I just stared at her like she'd gone crazy, "you're suggesting what exactly?"

"That your heart and your devotion need to expand their scope, love. Widen your gaze, Ian. Keep your love for Arrow and let Eriss in."

"At the same time?"

"Yes." She sat back, pleased with herself, I could tell.

I, however, had to think about that and once I had it seemed supremely stupid. "You want me to be in a Trio with a live Tarine and…" she nodded, "…dead Arrow." The idea was horrifying at best. Every instinct rebelled. "I couldn't."

She shrugged. "It may be that you *won't*, but that isn't the same thing, is it?"

"Eriss would never understand that, Jane." My mind was spinning and all I could do was protest in hopes that it would slow down.

"Eriss is young and green, true, but that could be an advantage," she said "The young are more flexible than we are."

"You're all of twenty-five, Jane. Don't make yourself out to be an old lady." I was heading fast towards forty myself. I'd lost everything or given it away. I'd accomplished nothing. This conversation was supposed to help? A failure so far.

"Quit trying to deflect, Ian," she said, now annoyed. "You love her and she loves you. Get your head out of your ass before she really gives up on you." I opened my mouth to say that she clearly already had when she shook her head. "She's trying to get to you. Fucking everyone essentially in front of you is an immature response I would expect from *her*. From you it's just…"

"…pathetic." Another dish on the Ian is a worthless asshole smorgasbord. I needed a drink. A big one.

"I was going to say desperate. You can do better. Be happy."

"I don't *love* her."

"Please try to sound less like the oblivious hero in a romance novel," she said, exasperated.

"But…but…"

"Listen, you're not going anywhere and we both know it. She's your mate, hopefully for decades to come. Talk to her. Ask for time but tell her how *much* time. She's waited this long. My guess is that she'll wait longer if she can see that the waiting will actually pay off."

That made sense to me, but I couldn't shake the feeling that I would be betraying Arrow by touching another female I…cared for. Liked. Was attracted to. Something. Hell.

"Think about it, Ian. Think hard," she rose. "You've already chosen someone extraordinary, even if you won't follow through. Give her the chance to surprise you." She put her hand on my shoulder. "Promise me you'll really think about it, even if it hurts to do so?"

I said nothing but nodded eventually. She leaned down and kissed the top of my head. It felt almost like a benediction, that kiss, and I did feel a tiny bit better.

We stood there a second or two in companionable silence but then her whole body stiffened.

"He's here?" I asked even though it was obvious that she'd sensed him.

Jane nodded and moved closer to me, though I wasn't sure she was aware she'd done so. Her face was very pale. I really hoped she wasn't going to vomit. For all our sakes. We were in public and nothing would get more press than "Princess Red Angel Pukes on Food Court." Yes, the journos had already given her a new moniker. They were so helpful like that. Sons of bitches.

I stood up, too, and there he was. He was still breathtaking in his beauty. My small bit of dabbling in my own sex had been at best passable but no one compared to this man. I admit I stared, as did everyone else who could see him. Then the most beautiful man in the Union spoke.

"Jane," he said with evident relief.

"Wilby," she responded as if there were no air in her lungs.

Yes, the year of separation was up, I thought as Wilby and Jane suffered through what had to have been one of the stiffest (not to mention most obligatory) hugs of their entire lives. I watched their body language more closely and realized I'd been wrong in my assessment. Wilby had been fine, but Jane had been a block of wood. She'd missed him so much. Why wasn't this the joyous reunion we'd all, including Wilby, apparently, had thought it would be?

Wilby, no fool, felt it, too, pulled away and swallowed hard. "Congratulations on …everything."

"Thanks," she said. "You, too." I knew what she was thinking, that they'd missed each other's weddings, that she'd missed a whole year of his family growing up and he'd missed the birth of the child she'd never thought she'd have. Her eyes were full and I realized that she was about to lose it on the concourse. I had to get them out of here.

"Jane, Wilby, with me," I ordered and they followed, keeping their distance from each other, but not too much. Magnets repelling and attracting each other.

I took them back to my home, leading my friends quickly past the stable of guards always present at our door. Once inside we saw Eriss was sitting on the couch, studying intelligence reports (something she did a great deal of). She stood as we entered, surprised, I supposed that I would bring people I actually knew and cared for into our place instead the usual casual fucks.

I opened my 'door' for a second and thought, 'They needed a safe place to talk, my dear.'

'I'll be in my room,' she thought back, as surprised by my endearment as I was, but pleased.

'Thanks,' I said with a grateful smile, 'I'll fill you in later.'

She disappeared into her room without a word spoken aloud and I followed her slim androgynous form with my eyes the way I always did. Her door closed and I turned back to my friends who were watching me with astonishment (Wilby) and amused chagrin (Jane.)

"She's…" Wilby started, awe in his tone.

"Yes," I sighed, "she is."

Wilby shook himself out of his appreciation for my…for Eriss and offered his hand to me. "Hey, Ian. Good to see you. You look well."

Bullshit. I was half-blind and looked and felt like crap, but whatever. "Thanks. You, too, Wilby."

Jane said nothing, still on the verge of tears.

"Sit, please," I said. We sat. In silence. Now I knew how Jane felt when people were being idiots. I also knew, then, why she'd asked me to be there, to kick both their asses. That I could do, if I had to, but I was hoping they'd do most of the heavy lifting (ha!) themselves. The least I could do, though, was get the ball rolling.

"How is Quinn?" Yeah, that ought to start things going.

"Fine," Wilby said and then nothing more. Or maybe my pushing would have no effect at all. I sighed.

"He's been back with the Furies this year?" I persisted.

"He has been," Wilby responded, though his expression clouded. I didn't know what that meant.

Silence again. Jane wrapped her arms around herself, but she watched Wilby longingly, as if he were still across the galaxy and not next to her on the couch.

I opened my mouth to yell at them when Wilby spoke.

"I left him for a while. A couple of months." He looked at Jane and me defensively. "We're back together now."

"Why?" Jane asked. "I thought…"

"You thought my breaking with you would fix everything," Wilby said. "He thought so, too." He shifted in his seat. "I went along with it because I hoped he was right. We got married because I hoped he was right about that, too."

"But it didn't fix everything," she said.

"It seemed to for a while, but then he thought I liked one of the nurses. Then one of the doctors. He demanded I get them both jobs elsewhere. I refused," he said to both of us, "and he hit the ceiling." He cracked his knuckles angrily. "Then Affie and Gabriel came to check in, just to visit, and he was convinced I was going to sleep with both of them." He ran his fingers through his perfect dark hair. "It would have been fun," he said. We just stared at him, Jane looking dubious. "I didn't do it," he said, annoyed, "but the fact that I was even considering it, that cheating would have been a relief after all the shit Quinn was pulling, finally made me realize that we were in real trouble."

I nodded. I wasn't the only monogamist around (the mistake with Adele notwithstanding); there were exceptions within relationships, of course. Derek and Garrett played around but loved each other, but I couldn't share and couldn't fuck around on a committed partner (that wasn't losing her mind, anyway) and neither could Jane or, more importantly in this case, Wilby.

"So I finally found my balls and gave him an ultimatum. He told me I just wanted an excuse to stray and I threw him out."

He looked down at his lap. "We were still apart when he was hurt."

"Oh," Jane said. "When he was hurt saving my life."

Wilby nodded.

"He tried to talk to me and I basically told him to go screw himself."

Wilby took a breath. "He told me later that he had wanted to apologize and ask for your help. With me."

"Oh, Mother Irony," she muttered.

"Yes," Wilby said dryly. "I know." He folded his arms on his chest. "So I sent Quinn and Shira to Judea to visit the old homestead." He smiled then, a mostly nice smile. "He ran into some of his old Masters, ones who had trained him, and they kicked his ass. Literally and figuratively. He came back a new man." His expression finally relaxed. "A penitent man and I think he finally trusts me. It hasn't been easy but," he shrugged, "we're Ok now." The way he said it, however, gave me the impression that he was expressing more wish than fact. That sucked, but I made no comment.

"I'm sorry, Wilby," Jane said quietly.

Wilby let out a huff of air. "Me, too, Jane. I've learned there's a fine line between being understanding and being a doormat for crazy."

"I suppose so."

We lapsed into silence again, but this time it was different. It was expectant.

"I bet," Wilby said slowly, "Lucy is as beautiful as her mother. I'd love to meet her one day."

Jane nodded, as if trying to keep herself together, but let out a sob and launched herself into Wilby's lap, her arms going around his neck. They both cried and clung to each other. I was feeling a bit emotional myself at their reunion.

"Are we too broken to be friends again, Wilby?" she whispered into his neck.

"No, love," he whispered back, his voice choked, "never that."

The door chimed. I got up and opened it and there was Fitz. For a moment I was petrified. This was his wife, after all, crying all over the prettiest man ever.

"Hello, Ian," he said, "Jane's people tracked her here..." he stopped, his eyes lighting on his woman in Wilby's arms.

Crap. I scrambled to explain. "Fitz, it's..."

Then he just smiled with genuine relief. "Thank God."

Thank god, indeed.

We ended up at dinner (in the suite so Fitz and Jane could be themselves) with Eriss and the addition of the Trio, since the Furies were in town (so to speak) for repairs. Jane sat between Wilby, holding his hand when he didn't need it to eat, and Fitz, his arm around her shoulders. She positively glowed, she was so happy.

Felix was telling a story about Garrett and Derek's most recent pleasure trip. "So, Derek got a bonus for defeating some evil corporate wizard or something," Daniel rolled his eyes and Felix mock-glared at him, "well that's how Garrett put it, and they got the Platinum Package to Elysium."

Well, that got all our attention. Firstly, that was some bonus and secondly, the amount of perfect debauchery they would get with that package was overwhelming. I noticed Atalanta looking at Fitz through narrowed eyes. It wasn't an angry look, but she was focusing on him, that was for sure. I wondered why.

"I thought only heads of state or," Jane shrugged, "drug lords got the Platinum. Holy crap!"

"Well," Felix said slyly, "Derek's husband has a friend on Gloriana-Levvon." So Stuart had pulled strings for them. Well done, Stuart.

"Speaking of Heads of State, Jane, do you know any that would like the Platinum Package?" Atalanta said innocently.

Fitz coughed and turned slightly red.

"It would be quite the adventure, I hear," she said devilishly. "They really give you the works." Fitz turned redder.

Jane laughed, but tried to cover it. "Leave him alone, 'Lanta."

Atalanta smirked. "Corsicans are so easy."

Then Fitz surprised the crap out of everyone by saying quietly, "It wouldn't be prudent right now." *Right now?*

We all stared at him and the biggest grin spread over Jane's face. We all pretended not to notice and started talking animatedly about nothing in particular, but I was sure I heard Jane say, softly into his ear, "It's a wonderful idea, but I won't hold you to it, love."

He turned to her and whispered, "Do."

"Oh my," she breathed and then she kissed him a bit more passionately than she probably should have with all of us there. I looked away to see Atalanta preening and her men stifling their amusement. I leaned closer to her. "I saw what you did there."

She sniffed. "He's a very good man who has chosen well. He just needs encouragement to spread his wings a little."

I gave her a bemused look. "By having a lot of wild sex with professional strangers?"

She shrugged. "By letting Jane be a Pacey he will be more himself."

"So that was for her?"

"For them both." She looked back at Fitz and Jane, who were, thankfully, no longer making out, and her expression was soft and loving. She reached for Felix's hand as Daniel put his arm around her waist.

Daniel whispered something in her ear that caused her to shudder as Felix brought their combined hands to his lips and kissed hers.

"Where is Quinn, Wilby?" I asked, trying to pretend that most of the people in this room weren't going to be having a whole lot of sex once dinner was over. *I* wasn't, not any more, but almost everyone else. I wanted to look in Eriss' direction, she sat silently next to me, but I forced myself not to. The sex she had was her business. Damn it.

"Quinn is too fucking far away," Wilby said with a laugh. "He'll be here tomorrow to join the gang here," the Trio, "for their latest mission."

Both lust and love were in the air at this little dinner party and while I was happy for all the lovers, it was uncomfortable. I noticed Wilby frowning slightly as Atalanta said something to him I couldn't hear. Eriss, to my right, had been remarkably, almost implacably, silent throughout dinner. All of us, myself included, had tried to engage her in conversation, but we'd all failed. The Eriss they all knew, if they knew her at all, was confident, funny and charming. This silent and grave being next to me was the Eriss only I knew. I didn't know what to do for her. While I was pretty sure that all the Paceys here had their 'doors' tightly shut in the presence of the most powerful TP any of us had ever seen, she was probably drowning in the very obvious love Fitz had for Jane. If I was jealous of what they had from only the evidence of my eyes, she had to be really unhappy—unless Jane was wrong and Eriss didn't care for me as much as she'd thought. I was pretty sure, however, that Jane was very much correct about a lot of things, that being one of them.

I thought I should take Eriss' hand to comfort her, but then I thought doing so would say more than I wanted it to at present. Eriss was picking at her desert dejectedly. She had never looked so lost. My hand twitched. Yes, I would do it.

"Eriss?" Wilby's voice said out of the blue, a smile in his tone. Eriss and I looked up to see him wearing his most engaging smile.

"Yes, Doc?" She said, smiling back because she really had no choice; it was Wilby.

"I'm dying to show someone what my little Sebastian did the other day and these jokers," he said with a look of affectionate contempt at the lovers, "are too wrapped up to pay attention. Would you indulge me?"

Now her smile was one of relief. "Sebastian is your son?"

Wilby rose and walked over to her side, offering her his hand. "One of twelve."

Her look was frankly disbelieving. "You have twelve children."

"Twenty-six, actually, but only twelve are boys."

Eriss looked appropriately astonished and led Wilby over to the nearest monitor on the wall.

Atalanta disengaged from her men long enough to whisper, "You didn't tell her about Wilby's flock of kids?"

"Of course I did," I said softly back, "but she knows he gets a thrill out of shocking people with the number so she let him do it."

"Has Jane already kicked your ass about you not being with her?" The her in question being Eriss, of course.

I sighed. "Yeah."

"She always gets there first," Atalanta grumbled.

"Holy Mother!" Eriss exclaimed as she stared at the monitor. She whipped around to stare at Wilby. "But he's only three years old."

Within about ten seconds all of us had crowded around the monitor to see something I thought was truly amazing. Since we were the only non-supernormals present Fitz, Eriss and I had never witnessed a child do anything like what we were seeing.

A chubby, rather adorable boy with dark skin and black tightly curled hair stared at a wooden block in front of him. He stared hard and the block 'lifted' unshakingly into the air.

"Fuck me running," Jane said to herself, but then gasped when the camera pulled back to reveal a tower of small single blocks standing at what looked like ten feet high. She looked at Wilby. "He can manipulate the blocks *and* keep them standing at the same time?" She shook her head, clearly shocked at the toddler's abilities.

"He can," Wilby said, his voice full of pride.

"Which way is he leaning?" Felix asked.

"What does that mean?" Eriss asked. "Leaning?"

"There are generally two types of Telekinetics, Eriss," Felix said, easily slipping into teacher-mode. "The Micro-TKs, like Wilby, who can move the smallest of things, from tiny objects to immobilizing nerves, etc., and Macro-TK's who can move the biggest." Felix smiled. "I'm a 'lifter' as the Macros are called."

"So Wilby is what, a 'pincher'?" she asked.

A *pincher?* The look of unbridled glee on Felix's face was beautiful.

"No," Wilby protested weakly, though it was probably already too late to save Micros from the nickname. "We're not called that."

Felix chuckled out a laugh that seemed to come up from the floor it was so wicked. "Oh yes they are."

Eriss blushed (or its equivalent in a Tarine which was, I'd figured out, her wings twitching), "I'm so sorry." This was to Wilby.

"Forget about it. I'm actually surprised something like this hasn't happened before," he said ruefully, placing his rather large hand on her shoulder. Suddenly and violently drowning in jealousy I wanted to rip that hand right off his body and beat him with it. The feeling came on so quickly it shocked me. He must have seen my look of (impotent) jealousy and removed his hand. "To answer your question, Felix," he said smoothly as though he hadn't been silently threatened with maiming by a friend, "I think he'll be a Macro when all is said and done. Just a hunch."

Eriss frowned as she looked at Jane. "You can do both, correct?" Jane nodded. "That must be pretty uncommon."

Fitz put his arm around his wife's waist, "That she is," he said, kissing her temple.

"Yes," Wilby said with mock annoyance, "only a truly uncommon woman could pick me up and spin me around in the air until I vomited."

"Actually," Atalanta said, her smugness of old returning full force, "that little act of retribution was what made me really like her for the first time." She winked at Eriss who was trying to look blasé. "Wilby had tried to cheat on me with her, among other things." Eriss gave up the fight for detachment and just stared. "It turned out all right, though," Atalanta sighed happily. "Jane made Daniel appear out of nowhere, so she can do no wrong with me."

"I can, unfortunately, do plenty of wrong," Jane protested.

"It was literally *years* between those two events," Felix said at the same time, laughing.

"I didn't 'appear out of nowhere,'" Daniel said, rolling his eyes.

"Yes you did, love," Atalanta said with a soft smile, "Felix and I dreamed you into existence." Daniel blushed. Eriss looked uncomfortable. Too many happy couples, er, groupings.

Yuck, I thought with no jealousy at all. None. This was all going downhill very fast and I'd had enough. I was just about to tell them all to go home before the love fest got too out of control when I was saved by the door chime.

"Come," Eriss said with obvious relief.

The door opened to reveal the muscle (literally and figuratively) in the protection detail of Eriss Fenton. We had guards (the *Indarrean* Guard, if you wanted their official name), it seemed everyone did nowadays, but this other person and myself were (when Eriss wasn't at home) the ones who were with her all the time. It had galled me at first to have to bring in help, but the plain fact was that if you needed punch in this day and age, you needed a super, a real one, not one whose supernormalness was assumed because of his planet of origin like me. That assumption (and then failure to live up to it) galled me, but that feeling was pointless. The good news was that, when I'd written to Jane for advice, she'd had the perfect person for the job.

Hannibal Horowitz (Macro-TK) entered the room and we all took a step back (except Fitz because an Emperor would never take a step back), even though we all knew better. Fifty years old, he was big as a Pacey 3 and almost completely tattooed from head to toe. He looked menacing as fuck. His face wore a permanent scowl so serious you could hardly see the dark green eyes that marked him as a Judean-bred fighter. The unusual thing was that while, like Quinn, he'd been created (as in genetically tampered with though in a less drastic way than the Paceys had been) as a fighter, he hadn't been engineered to be a supernormal. *His* supernormalness had just…happened.

Unfortunately for Hannibal, supers had been new to Judea a half century ago and no one had known what to do with him. Frustrated by their confusion and occasional outright mistrust he'd run away as a boy to join a Merc fleet (not the Furies, since the Furies hadn't existed back then) and had become proficient with his abilities. He was a double rarity; a Judean who'd trained himself and an experienced super to boot. After a year of teaching at the ESTF, however, he'd wanted a different challenge. Jane had recommended Hannibal to me because he was good, unprejudiced, and he had a thing for the Tarine Rian. In specific he had a thing for Marca, an *Indarrean* Tarine that registered more on the masculine side of the scale. Since Marca couldn't fly with only one wing (of all the Tarine, you may remember, only Eriss still had both wings) Hannibal was point person on the flying problem. I'll elaborate on how we were attempting to fix that issue later.

After greetings all around our dinner guests started filing out, but not before Felix pulled me aside to ask quietly, "Any problems lately with the Deneth?"

"No," I said semi-truthfully. Aside from a small bomb scare two months before (caught in time, diffused and hushed up) the Deneth Rian weren't much of an issue when we were in a grav environment. By that I mean that the Deneth *themselves* weren't an issue in a grav environment.

Felix nodded. "You seem to have everything in hand," he said, "but call us if you need anything, ok?"

"I will," I said, trying not to sound resentful. It was an indicator of how irritated I was by my life that the word 'seem' bugged me so much, but I had to let it go.

"New threats?" Hannibal asked tersely to Eriss once my friends had finally gone.

"Some potential candidates in the security feeds," Eriss replied, unconsciously mimicking his serious mood. Hannibal was a good man, but a lighthearted man? Not that I had seen. "We have some time."

Hannibal nodded and sat down beside her, ready to go over the work. I immediately headed for the door since I had been over everything but the most recent stuff already. Besides, they didn't need me for this; Hannibal was making sure Eriss saw everything that could be dangerous. I'd get the summary when I returned.

"Stretching my legs," I said. Eriss frowned slightly. "Back in fifteen." Her frown erased itself. Yes, Eriss, I grumbled in my head, even I need more time than that to get laid. Maybe Jane was right and I did need to have a talk with my charge. Maybe if I did she wouldn't get so irritated every time I was out of her sight and maybe she would stop fucking around, too. Or, I sighed, maybe she wouldn't. Fifteen minutes, however, I thought, was enough time to get to a bar and back. The thought cheered me up slightly and I headed out.

I was on my way to Aronoff's, taking a shortcut I'd recently discovered along the outer "skin" of the station when I was grabbed, shoved into an airlock, the inner door slammed shut behind me and then ejected into space.

Just like that.

My first thought was, fuck this is cold and that I couldn't breathe. All this was expected. What I had not planned on was the wave of emotion that hit me and the thought that filled my brain as I should have known it would…

this is how she died

Thankfully, the part of my brain responsible for my survival said something else, it said…

helmet
gloves
seals
activate
distress call
tether

My fingers were nearly useless as I pulled the collapsible helmet out of the back of my uniform and over my head. The helmet (thank god) was "smart" enough to automatically attach to the neck of my skin suit if the proximity was good enough (which it was) and it did so. I then pulled the gloves out of my sleeves and got them over most of my fingers, the suit doing the rest of the job for me. The display in my helmet monitor came up and five musical tones sounded in my comm as the five major seals were confirmed. The helmet light turned green.

"Activate," I croaked. The suit would activate automatically if I was no longer conscious, but it was better to speak the word aloud. Made me feel better anyway.

"Confirmed," the suit responded.

The suit immediately stiffened and forced out the deadly vacuum while at the same time pumping in oxygen and, heavenly father, heat.

I took a ragged breath.

"Sending automated distress call to Fenton, Eriss, Horowitz, Hannibal, Armstrong, Samuel…"

Oh shit.

"Belay call to Armstrong, Samuel!" I practically shouted. "Cancel the others on the list!"

"Call to Armstrong Samuel sent, others terminated."

Well, crap, but it couldn't be helped.

I watched the station start to move away from me and remembered my final step.

tether

I pulled the synthetic rope from the zippered pocket on my pants leg awkwardly. The skin suit wasn't designed to do much more than keep you alive, which it could for hours if you were really stuck, so doing anything technically demanding was out. We had, however, practiced all of this endlessly and while it was a pain in the ass, I could do it. Also, I had to be careful not to drift since the suit was, aside from the life support functions, unpowered. They could still find me since the suit had a built-in locator but getting run over by a passing ship who had no idea you were there wasn't really an appealing thought. I used the magnetic end of the rope to attach it to the station and wrapped the other end around me.

Then I waited.

I didn't have to wait long.

The outer door of the airlock that had been used to toss me to what should have been my death opened and a head was explosively sucked out into space, quickly followed by another, then the bodies (I had to assume) that they had belonged to followed.

I had to smile.

I'd started to pull on the rope to get myself back to the airlock when I realized I wasn't moving in under my own power. I landed clumsily in the airlock and felt the slam of the outer airlock door behind me. I looked up and through the viewing glass to see the impassive face of Hannibal next to the faintly pink one of Eriss. (Faintly pink was a bad sign on a Tarine, the Terran human equivalent of bloodless.)

"Recompression sequence started," the station's computer said through my comm.

I exhaled.

A few endless minutes later the inner door opened and I told my suit to stand down as I removed the helmet. I straightened, happy that I could now move normally, and walked out into the corridor.

Dad, Eriss and Hannibal stood there along with twenty-five of our private security force (half of them one-winged Tarine). As I've mentioned before, they called themselves the *Indarrean* and they were as devoted and scary as we had made them. So goddamned terrifying. Hannibal had wanted to call them the Fedaykin but not enough of us had understood (or appreciated) the reference from some old Terran book so *Indarrean* had stood. The Tarine members especially had probably had enough of all things Terran and I could hardly blame them. On the station people were either too fascinated or outright freaked out by the Tarine. It was racist and unfair, but, for now, it was how it was.

I looked from Hannibal, who was bloody, to Eriss, who also, surprisingly, was bloody to the immaculately clean High Admiral Armstrong who was...disapproving. Or something. He looked off. What I needed, however, was the information Eriss must have acquired before she and our Macro had dealt with the assassins.

Because while the Deneth couldn't work in a gravity environment, they sure as hell could hire people who could.

"Did you get a name?" I asked. The adrenaline was starting to ebb and I wasn't feeling so great. Actually I could feel exhaustion barreling down at me, but this was key. This attack was what we'd been waiting for, though we hadn't known exactly where, when or who would be doing it— or even which of us would be the target. We hadn't known, for sure, but I had assumed it would be me. I was viewed as our weakest link, annoying as that was, and everyone knew or guessed Eriss' attachment to me. I had prepared for any eventuality but I'd known it would be me.

Eriss nodded.

"You know who ordered the hit?" Dad asked. You know, he still didn't look right.

She hesitated, as if she was holding something back, but then she said, "Tirith Ebata."

There we had it, the name of the Denethian leader who'd bucked the traditional role of following the Pelann, which Eriss technically was. There had never been a Tarine Pelann, of course. The Tarine Rian and the Deneth Rian had never really mixed though they had shared the same system, and Shirin's plan to leave Eriss as the spiritual leader of their combined peoples would only have worked if Shirin herself had lived to force it through. I wondered, in the cold light of day, if she'd ever really planned on making that happen. It had been the topic of much conversation between Eriss, Hannibal and myself. Eriss's theory was that it had merely been a stalling/positioning tactic from the beginning. I wasn't completely sure about that, but had agreed that plans had changed once Shirin had found out she was dying. Hannibal had thought that Shirin (a healthy Shirin) could have strung Eriss, and the Union, along for decades had Eriss been the drone Shirin had expected. The power play would have been subtle and elegant, a twenty-year plan at least, not the crazy gamble that bringing Trithicate Station to Terra had been. The problem was that whatever Shirin's original goals for the Rian had started out as, in the end she'd really only been out for herself or she would never have left her people in the mess they were in now.

"There are actual Ebatas?" Hannibal asked, perplexed. "I thought the last name was made up for the books."

Yes, I thought, the *Adventures of Mila Ebata*, the greatest Denethian Captain of the famous stories—and, for most Human people, the only source they'd had for information on Denethians until recently. The stories were terrific but hardly comprehensive, especially since they'd been written a couple of millennia ago.

Dad looked aggrieved. "I've run across Tirith Ebata before, unfortunately. His great-grandmother changed their family name to Ebata two centuries ago as part of an anti-religious movement against the then-Pelann, Guerin, Shirin's grandmother."

Eriss looked surprised. "Anti-religious?"

Dad equivocated with a shrug, "More like Reformists. The Ebatas were, and are, very well connected within the Rian Military establishment. They, and their followers, felt that the Pelannate had gotten too powerful, their iron-fisted rule had become absolute and, by definition, unfair since only one being's opinion mattered.

"So they aren't heretics exactly," Eriss both stated and asked.

"They would say they weren't," Dad said dryly.

"You are thinking that Tirith wanted to take us," Hannibal indicated our little band of three, "out to consolidate power and end religious confusion?" His usual frown deepened to something even more intimidating.

"Perhaps he wants to place his own Pelann, a Denethian one, in my place," Eriss said thoughtfully. "Why didn't he just send someone to kill me?" She looked right at me.

"Who says he didn't?" I said. "First they pick off me, then Hannibal," Hannibal snorted, "then you."

Eriss shook her beautiful head. "I'm never out on my own. Anyone who is paying attention knows I have at least ten *Indarrean* with me, plus you or Hannibal or both of you."

"You think it was a test?" I asked. I thought for a second. "Wait, what did you get from the attacker's head, Eriss?"

"Just a name." Tirith Ebata. There was that slight hesitation again, however. Ok, that wasn't my imagination, but she would have shared her thoughts if she'd felt she could. I'd ask her later. Eriss turned to my father. "Tirith is in the military, you said?"

"Actually, he's the Admiral-Zuerst, or First Admiral, for the Rian, since the death of most of the high ranking Denethian Admirals on Terra."

Shit. "He's your opposite number?" I asked. We were up against someone with Dad's reach, but (most likely) without his moral compass. Shit again.

"He is."

"Where is he stationed?" Eriss asked, suddenly looking determined. I did not like that look at all.

Dad didn't seem to like it any more than I did because he looked pained when he answered, "Paragon."

Eriss paused and I could almost see her mental wheels turning. "All right, then." She looked up and right into my eyes, "Then that is where we need to be."

For a second, I thought that Dad would argue, but only for a second. I realized he'd seen the look in Eriss' eyes, too. He'd seen it before (I was positive Jane had had it more than a few times before doing something insane) and wasn't going to waste the energy arguing. It was then I noticed he was leaning a little against the wall. What the hell was wrong with my father?

I looked at Eriss and noticed her glaring at me. Hannibal was asking Dad about getting blueprints of Paragon Station. I glared back. She tapped her temple and I reluctantly opened my 'door.'

'Go hug your father, Ian.'

'What?' I always have the wittiest comeback.

'You almost died and he's freaking out. Give him a goddamned hug.'

Well, I thought, that would explain why he looks ill. He wasn't even projecting that he wasn't and I was a moron not getting it. Thank goodness for Eriss.

I nodded and 'shut' my door.

Hannibal and he had finished their discussion (definitive plans of Paragon didn't exist, apparently, not even for the Deneth—too many changes over too many years) and I walked over to my father.

"We'll keep you in the loop," I said with a smile.

"You do that," he said quietly.

Then I opened my arms and grabbed him into a hug, as if we'd always said goodbye that way. He tensed at first, out of sheer surprise, but then hugged back hard.

"Love you, Dad," I said very low.

"Ok," was all he said which made me smile.

It was more than good enough.

"See you at the auditorium," Hannibal said as he walked off.

"We need to get you cleaned up," I said to my favorite Tarine, though the blood looked good on her. Perhaps I was kinkier than I'd thought.

Eriss nodded and squeezed my arm happily as we started down the hallway with the flock of *Indarrean* surrounding us. I should have been wondering what the hell Dad was going to say to the station police about the now-frozen body parts floating around in space, but what I was really thinking was what a kind heart the being walking next to me had. Ah, yes, and then the wave of guilt. Fucking great.

Plus, it was time to get some answers from my winged friend.

Eriss started walking faster, but there was no way she was outrunning my questions. I touched her arm and she stopped, staring, not at me, but at the wall. Yep, she was definitely keeping something from me.

"Eriss?"

Nothing. Her lovely eyes flicked to the *Indarrean* around us and tapped her temple yet again. I sighed and 'opened up.'

'What else did you see in their minds?'

She laughed without humor as she thought. 'Well, at least if I was going to let something slip I was glad you were the one to notice.'

I waited, desperately suppressing the thought that I was always watching her, so who but I would see all the little things. Obsession was kind of reliable like that. Unhealthy obsession certainly was. I'd read about exorcisms once. Maybe I could get one of those. Of course I'd be exorcising myself from myself in that situation, but still…

'We need to get to Paragon and talk to Tirith, Ian.'

'I agree, but that doesn't answer my question.'

Now she looked at me. 'The message I got from the men who tried to kill you wasn't something I had to search for. It was implanted specifically for me, in Tarine.'

My eyebrows raised. 'In *Tarine*?'

She nodded.

'I thought you found a name, but you said message?' She was maddening sometimes. Couldn't she just tell me?

She shook her head, having, of course, 'heard' my frustration and thought, 'I'm not trying to be difficult, Ian.' She frowned. 'I need to think.'

'The. Message.'

She smiled a little. 'His name and then three words: Look to Myrrim.'

'What the fuck is a Myrrim?'

'Not what, love, but whom,' she corrected, but I could tell she was thinking hard again. She put her hand lightly on my shoulder. My skin tingled with the contact. I wanted more, god did I, but no. Didn't matter, of course, because fresh guilt came anyway. She felt all that, of course. Ugh.

'Listen to the story at the broadcast,' she thought, 'and then you'll know all I do.'

I doubted that, I thought as I closed my 'door,' but I also knew that I'd gotten all I was going to get for now. She apparently needed to process and my bugging her was only going to piss her off.

She checked her watch and said aloud. "We're going to be late."

She was right. So we moved faster.

23:00 – Tio Auditorium, Terra 1

It was mostly dark on the large stage. Eriss stood in the middle of rings of chairs. I sat in one of these, as I always did, as did the hundred or so Tarine Rian who resided on Terra 1. Of the approximately three hundred Tarine still alive only a third were on Terra 1 at a time. The rest were divided into half a dozen groups and placed strategically within the Union. Eriss' overriding fear was of another genocide so we were attempting to spread the risk.

Two T.I. cameras floated around her, controlled by one of our Tarine acolytes. We broadcasted to the Union and beyond every week. If Eriss couldn't do it (which was almost unheard of) one of her fellow Tarine did it for her. Previous Pelann (Pelannese?) had never shown their faces on camera, but Eriss was different.

Eriss looked up at the 'heavens' and we looked up with her. Up, just below all the rigging and lights that were part of the stage, was the sky. A holo projection gave us the stars of deep space, of the Rian, of Terra, Thao, Paragon, Trithicate (the planet),Tellesco, Esperanza, Corsica, Vega, Judea...of all of Known Space, Union or not. So many stars, so many worlds, all that space condensed into a cloud of diamonds dazzling overhead.

I brought my eyes down to view the fellow congregants. Mostly *Indarrean* Tarine and Terran Human, not surprisingly, but also a dozen or so unaffiliated Terrans and three Heelies. I was really surprised at that last. Eriss had been having weekly services (usually here, but we shifted the place depending on availability) for months as part of her duties as Semi-Pelann. Anyone who wanted to attend was welcome, but we'd had more takers than I had expected. Security, of course, was very tight even if it wasn't obvious. Every single person on Eriss' 'team' was both heavily armed and more than a little paranoid. Thankfully no one had (as yet) been stupid enough to start something.

Eriss spread her wings and what little talking there had been immediately stopped. According to tradition, a Pelann read from holy documents when conducting an observance, but the most holy of scriptures had burned when Trithicate had caught fire. That was the accepted wisdom, but Eriss had told me that she believed the Pelann's inner sanctum had been rigged to ignite upon her death. Seemed more than a little believable to me. It didn't really matter, however, since Eriss had all the scriptures (and not just those of the Rian) memorized. Really.

Over the last months she had, as per the traditions of the Pelann, read passages of the *Septt,* the Rian holy book, and then spoke about it, relating the text to present day problems. She also, and this was unprecedented in the previously closed Rian Society, took important (or seemingly ordinary) historical events from many other cultures throughout history and connected them to the passage. People (chosen by lottery from those who'd registered their attendance at the service) could ask questions related to the topic. Eriss didn't always know the answers, but she'd never claimed to. We'd had some curiosity-seekers, some journos pretending to be on a pilgrimage, but for the most part the people who came wanted to hear what she had to say for its own sake.

I'd asked Marca (Hannibal's mate) once why so many came to the meetings and he'd said (since he was, as all Tarine were, a TP) that people wanted to interact with the divine, especially since all were sure such an opportunity to do so would never happen again. This thought had bothered me enough to give me nightmares for a week afterward. Eriss needed to be Eriss forever—I didn't know if I could survive her going away. Or worse.

But she was speaking at last.

"From the *Septt*, First Book, Grid five, Sections four to seven. The Book of Myrrim."

She paused, then spoke in beautifully unaccented Denethian for three minutes, then spoke the same passage again, this time in Standard.

"In a time when all Rian had the wings of angels...

Myrrim was the sister of the First Pelann, the Holiest of Holies and she was born of her father when the stars were new.

Her father, the great King Dyr, burst into being when the Home Star became hot and white. He was a wise King who piously bent to the will of God, the Holy Mother, and he obeyed Her command to establish order.

Dyr harnessed the power of the tribes that lived in shadows, afraid of the light of the stars and brought them to his own star, with its one planet, Trith, to build a great shell, a home with gleaming walls, a hive of safety. He called his great tribe Den and they became the righteous Deneth, ordained by God to conquer the Space Above and World Below.

But the air Below was heavy; there the air meant crushing death to his people, so Dyr created, born from his very side, two daughters that he hoped were to lead his people to the planet.

The First Born, Pelanna, saw God, the Holy Mother, and lived Above.

The Other, Myrrim, was Tarine and strong against the deadly air of the world Below. She flew there as the Rian flew in the cold darkness Above.

The Deneth and the Tarine always reached towards each other, unable to touch as the air Below became too light for the Tarine, too heavy for the Deneth. At first they reached, then they fought.

Upon Dyr's death Pelanna told the Queen that God had wanted order and Dyr had made order. Now God wanted peace and the Queen must make peace. The jealous Queen then struck down Pelanna, blaming Myrrim. The Deneth prepared revenge on the Tarine Below.

But God had seen this murder and stripped the Deneth of their wings, weakening them, and readied the blow of death to all in the hive Above.

Myrrim begged God for the lives of her sister's people. She promised that she would be faithful only to God, un-mated for all time, if the Deneth were saved.

God relented in her anger. Myrrim's promise was kept. There was peace.

God's Will was inexorable for, like the brave and loyal Dyr who brought order, the defiant and jealous Queen had been Her Instrument and had brought peace.

Pelanna's life and Myrrim's promise were the cost.

The wingless Deneth would live on, but they would always be scrupulously guided for God, in Her Wisdom, tied to all the Kings and Queens of the Deneth to Pelanna's daughters and sons forever, for She knew no living being could be entrusted to both rule and have God's ear.

Myrrim lived for seven hundred years on the world Below. Her last words were of her sister Pelanna, the first one of the Rian to speak directly to God.

She said, "At last I go to Pelanna and to our Holy Mother in the Space Above. At last I go Home.""

The reading concluded and Eriss began to speak about its relevance to today's issues within the Union, but it was all noise to me, words I easily tuned out. I wondered now, for the first time, whether there were any actual facts within this mythical origin story. I'd never given any thought to the creation and apparent division of the two species of Rian before. It hadn't seemed important and I wasn't sure it was now, but I needed a distraction from the cold hand of fear that seemed to have a grip on my intestines.

Tirith wanted Eriss to *be* Myrrim? Was that what this was about? To be some sort of sacrificial virginal religious figure? To be, what, celibate or chaste forever? Part of me was perfectly fine with this idea since it meant she'd have to stop fucking around. A bigger part of me was very upset that that meant she would never, ever, be able to fuck around with *me*. I was jumping to a lot of conclusions, though, wasn't I? Wasn't I?

Who the hell was this Tirith anyway that he could even make such a suggestion to a being he hadn't even met?

I tried to derail my panic with a sort of logic—there hadn't been a King or Queen of the Rian in centuries and the Pelann, despite the fairytale Eriss had just given us, had been the ruler of the Rian since the Royal Line had died out. Perhaps Tirith wanted the power for himself? Did he want to relegate Eriss to the status of religious oddity in order to be the Pelann? Shirin had left no biological heir—my guess had been that she'd expected to have more time to produce one and had waited so long to do so to prevent an ambitious child from taking her out prematurely. That seemed within the realm of possibility to me and, as Eriss and I had found as we'd researched it, there was a great deal of historical precedent. We'd read of at least half a dozen instances of Pelann meeting with 'accidents' or outright murders that had gone unsolved. Unfortunately, there was a great deal of evidence that as different as the Rian and the Humans were, violent ambition was a trait both races shared.

I needed to have a long talk with Eriss.

Obviously.

So, naturally, it didn't happen.

As soon as the service/broadcast was over Eriss engulfed herself in a whirlwind of preparations for the trip to Paragon. She needed a ship, and she needed supplies for the five-day (one way) journey. She needed to decide who went (all the *Indarrean* wanted to, of course, but there were space limitations that prevented that), who stayed and why. She gave the religious duties over to the excellent Marca, who had tried to refuse since he'd wanted to accompany Hannibal to Paragon, but one look from Eriss had made him bow his head in acquiescence. She got clearance from Corsica to refuel at the fueling ships stationed around Annaluca (the former Pace-Pallon) and messages were sent to outposts letting them know that we were coming and (importantly) not to shoot us.

She'd also had Hannibal contact a Corsican ally/friend/genius for hire, and friend of Jane's, requesting that she meet us at Annaluca 4 in four days' time.

All this she did within about twenty-four hours.

What did I do? Not fucking much.

I offered to help. I offered to take over, but Eriss was frantic to organize everything herself (not coincidentally providing a believable reason to avoid me and my pesky questions) and I eventually gave up.

I was so damned bored. I was bored enough to get irritable and antsy and soon Hannibal sent me on my way because if I didn't go he would "sever my spinal cord to get me to stop being so fucking twitchy."

That was how I found myself on-planet at a professional Macro Ball game sitting in the owner's box with Derek Pace-Taylor. I was still twitchy and anxious, but there was too much going on for anyone to really be bothered by it, except for me.

14:00 – Pace-Taylor Stadium, Washington, D.C., Terra, September 16th, 2874

Pace-Taylor Stadium was very new and seriously amazing. It was the first and only (so far) professional Macro Ball Stadium in the Union. There were Griit Ball stadia all over the Rian territories, but it really wasn't the same game anymore so they technically didn't count. As a side note, Derek was apparently a *very good* lawyer and an excellent husband since he had built this state-of-the-art edifice (with some investors) for his beloved spouse. Garrett had been more than happy to tell me about all the 'rewards' Derek had received for this gift, but I hadn't wanted to know. He'd told me anyway. I wanted the memory of that conversation 'safed' pronto. It wasn't that I was a prude, it was just that I didn't want to have to keep imagining my *friends* doing all these things, even if one of them clearly wanted me to. Just seemed wrong. Especially if it turned me on (which I will forever deny it did.)

Some information on the Professional Macro Ball Teams of the Galactic Union

At this date and time there were eight teams.
Two from Terra: The Washington Eagles and the Hong Kong Cavaliers
One from Thao: The Pessette Pirates
One from Tellesco: The Tellesco Titans (the only one not named after its town because Tellesco arguably still didn't have one)
One from Judea: The Masada Chosen
One from Novy Heliot: The Abramstown Armada (Jane had suggested the "Abramstown Assholes" but that hadn't gone past a select few of us.)
The final two were from Cyrillic: The Samara Saracens (an odd ethnic juxtaposition, but whatever) and the Becha Czars. The 'Czars' were owned by the never-down-for-long former Senator Katja Guryev and were as determined and underhanded as she was. It made for good games and a lot of bad blood.

Derek grinned at me as I settled next to him. He looked like the proverbial cat that ate the canary.

"What's got you so pleased?" I asked, smiling back.

"Tonight's roster," he said.

I noticed, then, that his husband was nowhere to be seen. Or, I amended, nowhere to be seen yet. "Got a ringer, do you?"

Derek's grin widened, if that were possible. "One of the perks of owning the team." He inclined his head towards the Macro Ball Cube. "There's always room for my baby to play." Then he looked over my shoulder. "Other people's babies, too."

Fitz took the seat next to me.

It took me a split second, but then, "Jane's playing, too?"

Fitz smiled, "It seems that, and I'm quoting, she can 'still kick Judea's ass even if she is a motherfucking Princess.'"

"Then I hope the Eagles win," I said, amused.

"They'd better. The Countess has money riding on it."

I looked at Derek. "Do they have any idea that the two inventors of Macro Ball, one of whom is the Emperor's wife, are playing tonight?"

Derek shook his head, his long braids flying about. "Trust me, though, they'll know soon enough. There is nothing subtle about how the two of those lunatics play." Then he winced. "No offense to your Emperor, Fitz."

Fitz shrugged. "The Emperor is well aware of the qualities that makes his wives great." He chuckled. "He's counting on the Countess to make their fortunes tonight."

Some extremely loud musical instrument started to play. It was clearly a tune meant to excite the crowd and it did. The time for the "drop" was nearing and people were cheering lustily.

My mind, however, was stuck on what Fitz had said. I knew he wasn't actually married to the Lady Idis, but to me (and to him, apparently) that was semantics. I just didn't know how that sort of thing actually worked.

"Sir?" I said quietly (well, as quietly as I could over the deafening organ-thing thundering through the stadium). Some moron in an Eagle Costume was walking through the aisles beating a drum. Fans started chanting "Go Eagles Go!" deliriously. Good cover.

"Yes, Ian?" Fitz said turning to me. "You know you aren't required to call me that." He grimaced. "At least not here."

"Thank you, Fitz," I said, though I was much more comfortable with Sir. "I'm sorry, but I wanted to ask you…"

"How I can make it work with two lovers?" Fitz said with a smile. Because, I realized, that Jane would have told him all about Eriss, Arrow and me. I didn't really like it since it was private, not to mention embarrassing, but he was her husband so it wasn't surprising.

"Yes." Sir.

"Honestly, I'm still figuring it out," he said thoughtfully, "but there are two things I have learned." He sighed. "One is that there can be no secrets." I nodded. "The second is that some things are private." I must have looked as frustrated by that non-advice as I felt because he chuckled. "What I mean is that we are three. Partners. A team. That said, however, there are certain things that go on between Jane and I and then between Idis and I that do not get shared. There is no deceit, Ian, but there is a certain amount of privacy."

"I see," was all I could say. I did.

"Please forgive me if I am overstepping, but if I may offer advice to you..." he looked expectantly at me and I nodded for him to continue. "Tell her everything, but there will always be those small private intimacies that will be just for you and Arrow. That way you will honor the woman you can be with and the woman you were with. You can be true to both."

"I can?" I said, hoping I didn't sound as much like a weenie as I thought I did.

"I promise you can." Fitz looked back out at the Cube. We were very close now to the game starting. "I like to think of my life as a series of glorious complications. It is a life you can have, too, if you trust yourself and your partner to have it."

Just then a voice boomed, "Welcome to Pace-Taylor Stadium, the premier venue to the Galaxy," Derek rolled his eyes but grinned, "for the finest in Macro Ball!" The crowd cheered. "Tonight the Washington Eagles," the (local) Eagles fans screamed, "battle the Masada Chosen!" More cheers (from the much fewer Judea fans) and boos from the 'screaming Eagles' fans.

"Here is the starting lineup for the Eagles: Number 14, playing Low-Mid position - Jeremiah Hill!" I saw a (relatively) small figure in head-to-toe navy with white piping 'fly' out of the corner of the stadium towards the Cube, waving. A large picture of the same helmeted man (protective eyewear off) appeared on the enormous monitor overhead with his jersey next to him. Obligatory cheers.

There were nine on a regulation (this amused me because I knew that Garrett had written all the regulations himself, with Jane's help) Macro Ball Team, plus alternates. So five more (three men, two women) were similarly introduced to similar cheers.

"Team Captain, playing Mid-Front position, number eleven - Jessica DeLouse!" A very intimidating dark-skinned woman flew out into the stadium. She did not smile or wave. She was pretty scary. I heard the crowd (even the Eagles fans, it seemed) boo her and looked askance at Derek.

"They're saying 'Loose,' from her last name," he explained. "They'll do that every time she gets the ball and scream it when she scores. It's how they show their support."

Well, that was odd, but harmless. "She looks pretty scary. She must be good to be Captain."

"She's terrific," Derek said proudly. "It's all a pose. She's a real sweetheart out of the Cube." He winked. "She's also a tiger in the sack."

God help me.

"Number nineteen, playing Up-Mid - Garrett Pace-Taylor!" There was Garrett, grin big enough to be seen even at that distance. Fitz, Derek and I stood and clapped, Derek even screaming his spouse's name.

"Aaaaaaand Number 6," this caused Fitz to both cough and blush, though I had no idea why, "playing Mid-Mid position - Jane Pace!"

There was an audible gasp as the crowd realized whom that meant and then they lost their minds as your favorite lunatic and mine raced out (god, she was fast) and paused before the Cube. Her grin was positively evil.

"Those Judeans won't know what hit 'em," Derek said happily.

"It'll be a bloodbath," I muttered. Judeans were fearless and ruthless competitors in everything they did. They were disciplined, smart and seriously driven. They were going to get creamed.

"As long as the bloodbath remains metaphorical..." Fitz muttered back.

"It'll be fine," Derek responded with some believability. Some.

The four Macro Referees then 'flew' out in their black and white striped uniforms and took up position at the four upper corners of the Cube.

"Please rise for the Anthem of the Galactic Union," the booming voice said. We did.

Why did Anthems always suck? The words were awkward, the sentiment overly patriotic (if not outright incomprehensible—you should hear the one for Gloriana-Levvon, all 'loins of our fathers' and 'birds of freedom' and shit) and the melody lugubrious. They brought a lump to your throat if you sang along anyway, though, no matter how technically bad they were. I sang and I was moved even if being moved annoyed me out of principle.

The Head Ref (different colored helmet) brought the Human-adapted Griit Ball into the center of the Cube...and "dropped" it.

The game began.

Macro Ball

The game had evolved a little since the days on Gloriana-Levvon. The goal square that lit up still had a circle to put the ball through that made two points, but the circle no longer changed size. A penalty shot was one point. There were nine positions (Lower back, lower middle, lower front, then the same for Middle and Upper) and no goalie. The person whose square the goal square lit up (in green) and whose team didn't have possession of the ball became de facto goalie. Depending on how many turnovers there were a person could be goalie one minute, then not the next, then goalie again. This was a contact sport so injuries were common, though there were rules about what sort of contact was allowed. Anything really nasty resulted in penalties. The uniforms had elbow and knee pads as well as helmets and eye protectors, but other than that the players were at the mercy of fate.

The Referees had several jobs: call violations of the rules (obviously), provide first aid and watch for cheating. Not all Macros could 'move' the ball to their advantage, but some (like Jane) could, or were at least willing to try. While Jane wouldn't cheat (she knew they'd be watching her ass like crazy) others had and the fines and penalties were severe. There had only been one previous full season and two players from the Cavaliers had been benched after only one game—for the entire season. (Garrett had been able to recruit one of them for the Furies. Elton was that rarest of birds, a full Macro/Micro hybrid, and too rare to pass up. The other player had apparently just gotten lucky with something he'd tried for the hell of it. Plus he was a known asshole so Garrett had passed.)

There were three fifteen minute periods and a two-on-two playoff if there was a tie at the end of regular play. They played until someone scored and then the game was over. No ties in Macro Ball, mostly because Jane found them annoying. Her sense of justice (or whatever) required clear winners and losers. So the rules went. The Judeans had been Union Champions last season, with the Eagles coming in second place. It must be noted that Jane had been busy being pregnant during that time and Garrett had been with the Furies for at least half the season (when he wasn't working for Dad). I wondered how much longer Garrett would be willing to be separated from his team and his spouse even half the year. Seeing the look of determination on his face, I didn't think it would be long.

Anyway, the game...

Fast and crazy for the first period. Jane and Garrett zoomed here and zoomed there, getting knocked around quite a bit, but only seemed to be interested in making sure no Masadans scored. Unfortunately, it didn't look like the Eagles were scoring anytime soon either. It was really frustrating.

"Don't worry, Ian," Derek said with a blinding grin.

"But they aren't doing *anything*," I said through my teeth. "Why the hell not?"

Derek shook his head. "Actually, they're doing quite a lot." He turned slightly to me while still looking at the game as the first period drew to a close. "The Judeans are in terrific shape, but they expend energy in bursts and will wear out quicker if they are running around like maniacs, frustrated that they can't score. The fact that *we* aren't scoring pisses them off, both because they know we're fucking with them, and because it gives them hope that they can still win."

"Plus Garrett and Jane have by now mapped out all their tics and physical weaknesses," I reasoned.

"Exactly," Derek said.

"When will they actually play?" I (almost) whined.

"Trust me, Ian," Fitz chimed in, "you'll know when they get to it."

Before I knew it the buzzer had sounded letting us know the second period had started.

A few minutes of more of the same then...

"The ball falls to number twelve Lebowitz of Judea and she's heading for the goal square in the Upper Right Section..." the announcer said calmly, but loudly. The Judean player's picture and jersey (white with a blue six pointed star on her chest) popped up on the overhead monitor. Miss Lebowitz was huge, as all the Judeans tended to be, but I wondered, as I had earlier in the game, if they had miscalculated on that. Size, in this game anyway, should matter less than speed and agility here, I reasoned. I needn't have worried. "She throws to Masada -3 Feinswog in the upper middle section at 99 miles per hour! He heads for the goal but Pace-Taylor knocks the ball out of her hand and it drops...and it's caught by none other than Number 6, Pace!"

Derek was on his feet screaming. Fitz and I stood, too.

Jane, raced to the middle of the Cube. Nowhere near the goal.

"Where is she going?" the announcer asked, "the goal is in the…" the green section of the Cube that held the goal circle went clear. "Goal shift!" Jane was in the middle still, passing the ball to DeLouse and back, just waiting. The green square popped up again...in the bottom left section. "Goal square in bottom left!"

I saw Jane look for an open Eagle. There were two people open, but both were Judean, using their bulk to block. The clock was ticking and she was close to 'holding' the ball too long. She drew her arm back and Meyer (Masada - 27) knocked the ball hard out of her hand. Really hard. I swear I heard a crack, but Jane made no sign. (Apparently Jane and Garrett weren't the only ones looking for their opposing players' weaknesses.) Meyer, trapped as they all were in their cube positions, had to throw the ball to have a chance of scoring. Jane waited. Meyer looked around wildly. The goal was going to move any second. Meyer threw the ball...and Jane grabbed it out of the air with (I noted) her left hand and…

"Pace throws it up to Pace-Taylor? What is she thinking?" the announcer screamed, reading our minds.

The goal square went dark. Garrett threw the ball to his counterpart at the top. His teammate threw it back.

The goal square reappeared...middle front.

Garrett hurled the ball at Jane who caught it, once again, with her left hand. The goal square was being blocked by Tabachnicoff (Masada - 9) who was in front of DeLouse.

"Jennifer!" Jane yelled.

With what looked like a massive effort, DeLouse ("Looooose" being shouted by the fans) shoved off Tabachnicoff and held out her hands for the ball. Tabachnicoff, however, grabbed DeLouse from behind, swinging her around. Out of time, Jane had to throw the ball somewhere or to someone.

She threw, the ball bouncing off the back of Tabachnicoff (leaving, I had no doubt, quite the bruise if not a few broken ribs) and into the goal.

The stadium erupted in cheers and screams.

"Two points for the Eagles!!" the announcer screamed.

The Cube changed to transparent white with the team's Screaming Eagle logo in it.

Music played, the crowd danced. The Judeans looked pissed.

When play resumed, there was no Jane. Seeing this Fitz started to rise but stopped himself and sat back down as he remembered the part he was playing; Jane was Fitz's friend, not his wife. A friend could go see a friend, but a lover pretending to be a friend needed to stay where he was.

"I'll go," I said quietly and Fitz nodded. I quickly left the stands and made my way to the place I was sure she was: Med station.

There she was, sitting on a table, arm being immobilized by a Med Tech and grinning her head off.

"Did you see it, Ian?" she said giddily.

"It was amazing, Jane," I said, adding 'you nutcase' to myself.

She frowned slightly and winced as her arm was moved. "Did the Ambassador see, too?"

"He did," I said kindly. "I'm to report back. He is a bit concerned about his best friend's wife, you know."

She smiled a little tiredly. "I know." She looked down at her broken arm. "I think I need to get my shoulder replaced." She sighed. "Makes this whole side weaker than it should be. I might as well have had a sign on me saying, 'sock me here.'"

"That's pretty serious surgery, Jane."

She shrugged with her good shoulder. "Tell Fitz I'll be fine and not to worry."

"You bet," I said, both of us knowing that Fitz *would* worry, of course, until he saw her himself.

"Enjoy the game, my friend."

Thus dismissed, I went back to my seat to offer reassurance to Fitz and to ponder his advice.

Garrett and his team made four more goals for the Eagles and, despite serious resistance by the Judeans, they did indeed cream the competition. Once the game was over Fitz left as quickly as he could to get home to his best friend's wife.

06:00 – Main Cabin, *W.S. Liberty*, Leaving Terran System, September 17th, 2874

Name of the ship sound familiar? Yes, Jane had leant Eriss the *Liberty* and Eriss, Hannibal and I (plus twelve *Indarrean* guards) were on our way to Paragon via Annaluca. Jane, Wilby and Dad had seen us off very early in the morning, everyone wishing Eriss good luck and then (silently) warning me to make sure nothing happened to her. Well, Jane, never one for silence, just told me not to fuck up, then hugged me and told me to take care of myself. Jane was the only one I knew who could mix a threat with affection and have it work.

Eriss' beautiful face was slightly pink (pale) but she acted strong even if she didn't really feel that way.

Before we knew it we were underway. I'd piloted us out of and away from the station, then out of the system, but handed over duty to the autopilot once we went into hyper. Much as I loved going fast (I'm a pilot, for god's sake) it's really only fun if you can *see* yourself doing it. Hyper, to me anyway, was just the amount of time you had to wait until you were out of hyper. With luck you'd arrived at your destination by then. Hyper on its own merits was boring as fuck.

So I sat on the small couch in the main room (Hannibal was already asleep in the bunk room and the *Indarrean* had taken over the cargo holds) and brushed up on my Denethian even though I didn't really need to. Eriss was sharpening her butterfly knives (and yes, I found that hot). They had been a gift from Jane, waiting for her with a note when Eriss had taken possession of the ship. I'd immediately made plans to review her knife training in the future. Eriss herself wasn't a huge fan of knives, but they were useful in the right circumstances.

"Are you worried about going back home?" she said, only looking up from her work briefly.

"Curious, not worried," I said. "Are we ever going to talk about this, Eriss?"

She put the knife she'd been sharpening down. "Some of it, yes."

"Just some?"

"Yes, Ian," she said very seriously. "Would you rather talk some now or wait for the whole picture after we leave Paragon for home?"

Was she kidding?

"Your choice," she said.

Obviously not. I sat back against the couch cushions. "Some now, all later."

She nodded, having expected my answer, and came over to join me on the couch. Her proximity was distracting as it always was and she smelled so... Jesus, Ian, get your shit together.

"When you are in command, your people come first." Eriss said this as both a statement and, somehow, a question. I nodded. "People come before your own personal concerns. Not every single minute, but generally..."

That sinking feeling returned to my stomach. "Duty must come first."

She took my hand. I really wished she wouldn't touch me, but I held on to her anyway because I really wished she *would* touch me.

"I have to save the Tarine, Ian," she said passionately. "I have to save the Deneth, too." Her wings vibrated a little, betraying her agitation. "Despite my best efforts, I've become a problem for the people I want to help, because of who I am and how Shirin dropped me on everyone. I have been wracking my brain trying to think of a plan of *any* plan that could help fix this."

That was certainly true. She had tried everything either of us (and some other very clever friends) could think of: the broadcasts, dividing up the Tarine to spread risk, reaching out to the Deneth, making friends in the Legislature. Had it helped? Yes. Had it solved the larger issues? No.

We hadn't had a brilliant breakthrough. We hadn't even had a new idea at all until...

"Myrrim," I said bleakly.

"Possibly." She now held my hand with both of hers. It was affecting me in ways that were heading in the direction of embarrassing.

"If that is the only solution, then that's it," I said, pulling away from her and standing. "You have to protect your people. Every commander knows the sacrifices, Eriss, I'm no different." I really wanted to throw up.

She rose and moved closer. "It takes me out of the running within all the power struggles."

"As a virgin queen?"

"Priestess, more like."

She stepped closer. It was getting harder to breathe.

"You're not much of a virgin," I croaked, wondering where my voice had gone.

She raised an eyebrow. "And you are?" I laughed in spite of my nerves. It wasn't as if she didn't have a point.

346

"What if Tirith is just setting you up? Making you a patsy for some kind of religious coup?"

"He might be doing just that," she said, "but I've been going over his military record. He has consistently made tough calls for the good of the Nation. Devoutly religious, he never misses a service, tithes more than he needs to and neither his spouse or his seventy-three offspring are in the military or government."

"Not one of them?"

"He'd insisted, apparently. A few years ago he was accused of only playing with the lives of other people's children because of this and he said that he'd kept his children out so that he would never be biased in their favor, but that he saw his kids in every soldier."

"Sounds like someone positioning himself for higher things," I said thoughtfully and more than a little cynically. "Spotless record, perfect on the surface..."

"Beneath the surface, too," she said. "He was one of the people I asked Huong to do background on months ago, and she looked hard at everything."

"She found he is an honorable being?" I said skeptically.

"She didn't find he wasn't." She stretched out her wings at the same time she stretched her arms. I swallowed hard. "We both know that had he really wanted me dead, I'd be dead."

I didn't have to agree with the obvious. As many precautions as we'd taken (and we'd taken a bunch) there was nothing that could stop a very determined, very clever, very rich murderer. This was true in the Rian Nation as much as anywhere else.

I looked into those big pale eyes. "We may need to stop him."

"I know."

"If that's the case the *Indarrean* will get you home somehow."

Eriss shook her head. "No."

I opened my mouth to argue, but stopped myself. I had, in my head anyway, lots of iterations of 'but you have to stay and lead your people' stuff. I knew she would have argued back but what I didn't know was... "Why, Eriss?"

She wrapped her long arms around my waist. I felt dizzy and grabbed on to her to steady myself. Is anyone buying that excuse? I thought not.

She rested her head on my chest, bending down a little to do so since she was tall. My heart felt like it was beating through my damned ears it was so loud.

"Because what Tirith proposes might keep us from ever being physical lovers," she said with definite sadness, "and that will break my heart, but I will make myself live with it because…" she took a deep breath. " I know you aren't ready and you may never be, but…but," she looked up at me, "you're in my blood."

I swayed a bit and she backed me up to the couch so I could half sit on the arm, but she stayed against me.

"Tell me about Arrow, Ian," she said gently. "What was she like?"

Was this Ok? Talking about Arrow like she was somehow a regular person that I'd had a regular relationship with? Like normal people discussed exes? Fitz's advice to trust rang in my ears. It scared me, but what else was I to do? Eriss was in my blood as well. Like my beloved Arrow always would be.

I sighed and stroked one of Eriss' wings causing her to shudder. It was so soft. "Let's sit."

So we settled on the couch, and since it was, as has been mentioned many times, small we were pressed together thighs to knees. I focused on Eriss' question, though, which was somehow easier to do now.

"She was prickly."

Eriss laughed. "Really?"

"Oh yeah," I said, smiling. "Once she liked you she was unshakably loyal, not to mention lethal, but she wasn't easy. Impossible to get to know."

"So how did *you* get to know her?" she teased.

"Unworthy specimen that I am?" I asked, amused.

"Uh huh," she said, her eyes twinkling.

I took Eriss' hand in mine. "I never gave up. I came to see her every time I was close by."

"Like gaining the trust of a wild animal."

I looked over at her, but her smile was kind and she was more than a little right. I'd never really seen a wild animal, of course, but I knew what she meant. "I suppose so."

"So when did it change?"

"One time, after a couple of months of trying to start a conversation and getting one-word answers, I came into the School yard and I saw her before she was aware I'd arrived. She was looking for me, then saw me and smiled." I stroked the back of Eriss' hand, surprised at how easy this was to talk about. I sensed Eriss wasn't as impressed by Arrow's giving me a smile as she should have been. "She never smiled," I explained and then wondered if I was making her out to be some horrible bridge troll. While she wasn't much for the social graces, Arrow wasn't a bridge troll. Eriss, however, had moved on.

"That was the first time you kissed her," Eriss said.

"That day, yes."

"You'd waited and wooed and proved you were there for her no matter what." The look she was giving me was full of significance.

Comprehension was dawning on me. "Yes." My heart started to beat faster again as I thought of the many, many months Eriss had been here, with me. How she hadn't gone anywhere. How she had wooed without wooing. How she'd been there no matter what.

"Ian?" she whispered.

She moved closer, but all I could say was, "Yes." She kissed me.

It was just a kiss (of course it wasn't just a kiss) and it was almost chaste and completely perfect. She'd kissed me as if it had needed to be done because without it we couldn't move forward. Technically it wasn't much, but it was everything.

I had the rather laughable thought, once the kiss had ended, that I'd survived. That I hadn't curled up into a ball of guilt on the bathroom floor. Not yet, at any rate. For the first time in ages I just sat with this incredible being, relaxed and talked.

We talked for hours and hours, about Arrow, Eriss' childhood (such as it was), Shirin, my Dad, about everything. And there was the private stuff between Arrow and I that was never discussed, but Fitz had been right. It was all right.

Eventually Eriss fell asleep against me and that was all right, too.

I was almost asleep myself, thinking how wonderful it was to have her by my side, when an unbidden (and completely true) thought floated to the surface.

Jane was right.

I love her.

The thought hovered in my brain for a few seconds and it was a happy, glorious, liberating thought...

…until I started to shake and sweat. My chest hurt. My brain hurt. I put my head between my knees because I couldn't breathe.

Eriss' hand was on my neck, massaging it.

"Breathe, Ian, breathe," she chanted softly over and over.

I couldn't, though. I was seeing spots.

You are a cheater, Ian.

You treat the women you love like shit.

You value loyalty but fucked Adele.

You aren't good enough for Eriss.

You are a cheater, Ian.

Cheater.

For one second I was actually angry at Arrow for keeping me from being happy. Only for a moment, though, because I really did know that this was all me.

What was Eriss saying?

"Breathe in and hold for three, then breathe out and hold for three." Again. Then again.

So that's what I did.

She never moved her hand from my sweaty neck. She never stopped speaking softly, helping me.

I could breathe again.

"When things were going wrong with Arrow, really wrong, I was a wreck," I said, knowing my voice sounded ragged. "I drank, I hid from work—not when we were in crisis, but still—and I was unravelling, almost as fast as she was." I took a long breath and counted again. And exhaled. "She told me to find comfort elsewhere and I did."

Eriss' hand stopped moving on my neck, but she didn't take it away. "Did it help?" She added, "You?"

"Yes." Admitting that was almost as bad as the cheating itself.

She took her hand away from me now and the panic returned, but only for a second because she wrapped herself around my shaking, surely smelly self and held on tightly.

"If it helped you then it helped her, Ian."

In my heart I knew it was true, but the shame…

"Do you want me to wait for you?" she asked, now unsure.

I exhaled again. Be brave, Ian, though you are scared shitless. "More than anything, Eriss."

She trembled against me, but didn't let go. "Thank God."

"Yes."

I would make this work and I would make Eriss happy. I couldn't do it for my Arrow, but I would for Eriss even if it killed me. I felt something then I hadn't felt in, well, years. I felt hope.

I turned my head and captured her sweet lips with mine.

Yes.

Just then my watch pinged. I sighed and Eriss sighed with me. It was time to train.

08:00 – Cargo Hold A, *W.S. Liberty*

We stood in the Cargo Hold (all but Eriss and Hannibal, both were now both resting) and the six Tarine and six Terran Human *Indarrean* were in a half circle in front of me. I had decided to practice with gravity this time, mostly because the next situation we'd be in would be on-planet. Paragon would be different story of course, but I thought we were in pretty good shape when it came to zero-g. Our Humans had become proficient with their jet packs, due to a great amount of pushing on my part, and the Tarine were grudgingly good with them, too. That was the problem with having only one wing—it was pretty much worse than having no wing at all. I'd worked tirelessly with the one-winged Tarine, beating into them the idea of *not* using their wings in zero-g when they wanted to move (so very counter intuitive) and it hadn't endeared me to them one bit. I hoped the plans Hannibal had put in motion would fix all that but they needed to be able to function and fight without them. Today, however, we had to deal with gravity.

"There are protective suits on the wall. Put them on, face guards down, and pair up," I ordered, and they immediately did so. Some of the helmets were blue and some were red. Not an accident. I waited until they were in their groups of two and then said, "Today we work with sharps."

The guards looked their questions but did not voice them.

"Butterfly knives and Agni Katars," I explained as I opened a drawer in the side of the hold and revealed Jane's stash of slicers. That woman, I thought, shaking my head. "Put the Agni Katar on your non-dominant arm."

They did that, too.

"This will be a fight for touch, not blood, since we need everyone whole for the next parts of our trip. Evade, block and, this is important, be aware of those fighting around you. All those with red helmets are on a team, same goes for the blue." I stared them down and said what I always said. "Protect your team."

The guards said nothing, but I knew they'd gotten the message. I'd said this same thing so often they would have had to be complete morons not to have gotten it. I had hand-picked this non-moron group of *Indarrean* myself, so I wasn't concerned.

"Prepare..." They did, assuming the fighting stance that I had drilled in them, that I'd had drilled into me so many years before on the very planet we now headed to in hyper.

"FIGHT."

They fought.

All of them ended up with cuts (as I'd expected), but only one had actually needed bandaging.

I was proud of them. I'd insisted that they be the best in the Union and they had risen to my challenge. They had to be the best so they could be there for Eriss (no longer a slouch in the fighting department herself) in case something happened to me. It was an unpleasant thought, but I didn't think it cynical. Realistic, yes, but not cynical.

I headed to the bunk room for some rack time, lost in scenarios both good and bad, but despite this I fell quickly to sleep.

Arrow visited me in my dreams, as she always did, but while she was sometimes amorous or sad and sometimes angry, this time she was shy and sweet.

This time she spoke to me and said, "Tell me about Eriss."

In my dream I told her (almost) everything and then drifted into the best sleep I'd had since she'd died. I felt at peace.

13:03 – *W.S. Liberty*, Orbit Around Annaluca 4, September 19th, 2874

I was sweating again as we pulled into orbit, but not for either very good or very bad reasons. We, Eriss and I, were playing a game. *Boltha* was a Tellescan children's game of nerves where each player placed one thin metal oddly-shaped piece at a time upon all the others. The last person to place a piece without the whole thing falling into a tinkling tinny pile won. We were both used to being steady under pressure so the structure we were making had grown quite large.

Eriss placed a precariously balanced piece on one side of the small edifice, her hands sure. She held her breath (so did I) as it slipped into place…and stayed there.

Eriss exhaled.

I picked up my next piece (shaped like a tuning fork this time) and placed it. Easy peasy.

The *boltha* sat on the table looking rather like an elegantly spiked crustacean. Eriss considered where to put her next piece as I felt a dreadful resolution take root in my chest. She placed it…and it stayed put. I picked up my next one, but I hardly knew what I was doing. I had to make some kind of declaration. Not an equivocation or a promise of future happiness. A real statement. I owed her that and, it seemed, dream Arrow had given me permission.

I placed my piece, my hand still steady.

She picked up hers (something star-shaped).

"May I tell you something, Eriss?" I said quietly.

Her hand faltered at the wrong time and the whole thing collapsed loudly, spraying pretty bits of metal all over the coffee table.

"Do you think you should?" she said, giving me an out.

"I think I must," I said, not taking it.

"May I say something first?"

Well, that was a surprise. "Of course."

She thought for a long time, long enough that the tinkling of the destroyed *boltha* had fallen into silence. "It's quite a thing, to feel responsible for a people. To feel that if you screw up, your race might disappear."

I nodded, not wanting to interrupt her. I didn't envy her this terrible burden, not that I hadn't felt it myself on a smaller scale when I'd led the Furies, but I'd never questioned her ability to shoulder it. Not once.

She smiled a very sad smile. "It's the sort of thing that becomes really terrifying if you stop and think about it." She took my hand. "Do you know why I don't just run away and hide—because I've thought of doing that more than once."

She had? "Why?" I asked.

"Because the reason I *think* I can do this is because you *know* I can."

I just stared at her, stunned.

She looked at me, deadly serious. "You are my strength."

God, I wanted to be worthy of that trust, but the fact that she had vulnerabilities even I hadn't known about was worrying. Not for my sake, but for hers. She had been trained to be perfect and she was, for the most part, but this... Did she really need me that much? Was that even possible?

Now her eyes were wide with panic. "I've tried to always be strong because that is what I needed to be and it is what is expected, by the Rian and by you."

I'd never expected her to be strong all the time, I protested in my head, and I certainly hadn't meant to put that kind of pressure on her.

Her panic was clearly growing, however, whatever I was thinking. "What happens if I fail? What if you realize your mistake in throwing in with me?" Her wings shook. "What if the being you see isn't who I actually am?" She was really shaking now. "Will you turn away from me then? When I finally and irrevocably disappoint you?"

No, that wouldn't do at all. I grabbed her hands and squeezed them hard. "Eriss."

She was doing the Tarine version of hyperventilating.

"Eriss!" I said sharply, putting enough pressure on her hands to cause pain.

She hissed and I relaxed my death grip just a bit. I looked in her eyes and I could tell she was back with me.

I spoke then, putting every bit of passion I had into my words. "I promise you that no matter what happens, even if everything in the universe goes wrong and you manage to personally fuck up all your plans, I will *never* turn away from you, Eriss. You do not have to live up to anything, whether it's what you think my expectations are or anyone else's for me to..." My throat closed, but I pushed through because I had to. "For me to love you." My heart pounded again, but not with panic. I'd freak out later, but I couldn't worry about that now.

She took a huge breath and let it out. I could see the panic receding from her eyes. I took her in my arms and held her tightly. I felt her body calm bit by bit. She snuggled closer and eventually whispered, "I love you, too."

Her eyes were bright as I kissed her. I felt dizzy but really, really happy. She needed me and I was strong.

"Miss Fenton?" Trette, *Indarrean* Captain extraordinaire, said with cool professionalism from the doorway as the Tarine resolutely stared directly ahead and not at us.

354

Eriss straightened, a little breathless but also a lot giddy. "Yes, Captain?"

I felt giddy myself, among other things. Giddy enough that I'd need a little quality alone time pretty damned soon or be really damned uncomfortable. Not that I already wasn't.

"We are being contacted both by the station and the *Chrysalis*."

I rose and offered Eriss a hand up. "The *Chrysalis* is docked at the station?"

Trette shook his head. "In orbit. The station's docking arm is not yet complete."

"First we have to pay our respects," Eriss said, voicing my own thoughts aloud.

"Please tell the *Chrysalis* that we will contact her when our obligations on the planet have been fulfilled."

Trette's eyes sparkled with excitement. Eriss smiled at him.

"Yes, Sir," he said happily.

"Have you already informed the Prince that we wait upon his pleasure?" I asked, fully aware of what an arcane expression that was.

"Clearance has already been given for the *Liberty* to land next to the Charleston Dome, Captain."

"Already?" Eriss asked in surprise.

Trette looked amused. "I gather the Prince is eager to have an audience."

"Then let's get down there," I said. Actually it made a lot of sense. One of the things that had made the selection of this system for Drs. Pace and Pallon all those years ago was its isolation. It would have to be lonely for someone not used to it, even for a Prince. Especially a Prince with things to, most likely, justifiably brag about.

15:00 – Hanger, Charleston, Annaluca 4

Eriss and I (and six *Indarrean* guards), wearing breathing masks because it would be years before the planet's air became breathable again, filed out of the *Liberty* to meet the Royal party. I had expected the pomp and circumstance (or some version of it) of the Palace and I think Eriss had expected it, too. We were both wrong.

To the South of the hanger sat the bulk of the enormous colony ships, so covered with built-up dust and dirt they looked like small mountains.

The massive doors to each of their cargo holds were all clear and there was a steady stream of people, colonists, scientists and technicians, going in and out as we watched. The ships were home, storage and laboratory for the inhabitants of the former Bane on the former Pace 4. They would be in use, I gathered, for many years to come as well, even after most everyone had moved into more permanent lodgings.

Just to the right of these landbound ships, however, I could see the forms of Prince Whitman, Princess Joyanna and another man. No guards, and certainly no pomp. I saw Eriss hesitate in her step, as if deciding to eschew her own guards but I gave her a sidelong glance and shook my head slightly. Even if *they* were safe here, Eriss was safe nowhere. She nodded back and we proceeded on.

We reached them quickly and the Prince stepped immediately forward, his smile worn, but natural. He looked thin and there was a patch of dirt on his sleeve. The Princess looked smudged as well, but equally pleased to see them. The remaining man matched them. On the whole, I thought, mussed or not, they looked good. Happy.

The Prince held out his hand to Eriss, "My dear Miss Fenton, it is an honor to welcome you to Charleston and Annaluca 4."

She bowed her head respectfully, "The honor is all mine, Your Highness." She bowed her head to Joyanna next. "Your Highness." Eriss smiled. "It was so kind of you to allow us a glimpse of what all the Union is dying to see." She shook the Prince's hand, then Joyanna's. "You remember Captain Armstrong, Sir? Ma'am?"

Whitman's expression clouded as he remembered the connection that he and I shared. Please don't say I'm very sorry for your loss, I thought. Please just skip right over it. I hadn't seen him since Arrow's death, however (I had missed the funeral, unable to face it at the time), and she had been his half-sister though they had barely even met when she'd died. Just then I felt Eriss' hand on the small of my back, giving me strength to be gracious, as if she had known what I'd be thinking. My 'door' was closed then, for the record.

She was correct; I needed to be gracious because there was always protocol.

"I'm so very sorry for your loss, Captain," Whitman said with sincerity.

"And for yours, Sir, thank you," I said, wishing the moment had already passed.

"It is good to see you here, however," Whitman smiled proudly, "back home."

Right. That.

"It is good to be back, Sir." It wasn't, but it was the proper thing to say and I just wanted to get on with the obligatory tour.

Whitman grinned and gestured the third person in their party forward, "This is Doctor Omid Shahi, our planetary ecologist." The short, rather dark, rather squat man stepped closer and shook our hands.

"You must have much to do here, Doctor Shahi," Eriss said.

"There aren't enough hours in the day, Ma'am, but," the man nodded, "one could not ask for a more challenging or rewarding assignment."

"I can believe it," Eriss said. I could, too. I mean, if reclaiming planets was what got you off, well, buddy, this was the place to be.

Whitman smiled at us, "Mr. Thal sends his apologies that he could not be here to greet you; his presence is necessary on the station." He looked amused our looks of incomprehension. "Having someone who is tireless, brilliant and impervious to space has been absolutely invaluable."

Eriss said, "Mr. Thal is a remarkable being."

"A godsend, truly."

"Will he take a surname, I wonder?"

Joyanna said, "He and the Prince have had a long discussion about it." She sounded approving. "Lady Idis thinks it would be beneficial he have one," Joyanna explained, "for the upcoming legal case, but he hasn't settled on one just yet."

We nodded, appreciating (at least in part) the courtroom nightmare that was to come for Thal and the Countess when they tried to prove his sentience and, consequently, his guaranteed freedoms as a citizen of the Union.

Whitman, apparently done with the subject, said, "Would you care for a brief tour of Charleston?" He bounced forward on his toes a bit in his excitement. "The dome was just completed last week and the city is nearly clear of debris."

Eriss' eyes went wide. "Already?"

They'd built what had to be a massive dome in under three months? Was that some kind of record? Impressive. Granted, the dome probably hadn't had to be as large as most city domes tended to be since it was covering the opening of the remains of the underground part of what had been Bane, but still...

Then it struck me how funny it was that the one thing that had survived the destruction of Pace-Pallon had been renamed. Renamed under the auspices of probably the only person (Whitman) who would have wanted the name unchanged. Then again, that at least had probably not been his decision.

Eriss and Whitman, and Dr. Shahi, started walking out of the hanger and towards the entrance to the dome, so I joined the Princess.

"I have to say, Ma'am," I said carefully, "I'm surprised the Emperor chose to name the city after himself." Joyanna grinned. Ok, so there *was* a story there. "Doesn't seem like his style." Not at all.

She laughed. "It isn't. The naming decision was made while the Emperor was indisposed," when he was off playing Ambassador, probably, "in fact it isn't official until the settlers take residence next month."

"So the decision was made without him?"

"I gather that the Princess and the Countess thought it would be amusing," she said as she rolled her eyes and laughed, "to them if no one else."

"The Emperor..?"

"Will find out at the dedication in October." She shook her head, but was clearly tickled by the whole thing.

"Jane may be a bad influence on the Countess," I said, amused.

"An influence, Captain, but hardly a bad one," Joyanna chastised gently. I started to protest that I'd been kidding, but she waved me off. "I'm just teasing. And, to be honest, I am really looking forward to the look of horror on my Uncle's face when he sees what his wives have done."

"I'm sorry I'll miss it."

"Then you must come, too, with your lady," she winked. Her amusement faded when she saw me hesitate in my step. Were we that obvious? "If you can spare the time, of course."

"If we aren't in the middle of war, Ma'am," I said penitently, "we would love to come."

She nodded, but asked, "Do you think that likely, Captain?"

We chatted about that and other things until we'd made it through the windswept outdoors and arrived at the entrance to the Charleston Dome. The Dome itself was huge (not for a dome, since I'd been right that it hadn't needed to be all that large, but still) and slightly opaque. Doctor Shahi explained that the traditional makeup of the Dome had been altered to allow the existing sunlight to be more vegetation friendly inside. So we could see almost nothing of the city even from right next to the Dome.

Corsican guards saluted the Royals and we were ushered into Charleston.

Noise assaulted us first as we removed our masks. Sounds of building, hammering, cutting, hydraulics doing something out of view. Small and obviously new buildings dotted the flat ground around the edges of the dome. Closer to the edge of the hole (no better word) that contained the actual city was a park that appeared to ring the whole thing. Paths and trees and even grass, very new grass, decorated the space up to a fenced border around the lip.

Whitman stood by this lip, his hands on his hips as he proudly surveyed the beginnings of his fiefdom. He turned around to grin at us. "There is a lift we can take, or," he raised an eyebrow, "we can take the scenic route down."

I wasn't sure I liked the sound of that, but what could you do?

"Whatever your Highness prefers," Eriss said with a warm smile.

"Scenic route it is," he said, clearly delighted.

There were two small platforms at the lip, the fence around them (and the entire border of the lower city) gapping to accommodate them. A few feet into the giant hole hung a quickly moving synthetic cable with loops every few feet. The cable moved down into the pit. I looked a couple of yards to the right and it appeared that the same mechanism was moving upwards at the same speed. People were, one by one, riding it with one hand in an upper loop and one foot (or two, depending) on a lower one. Once they reached the appropriate level they stepped easily away from the cable and back onto land. It was, I thought, actually pretty neat.

"Miss Fenton?" Prince Whitman said gallantly, gesturing to the rope.

"After you, Sir," she said with a smile.

"As you wish," he said, but he stepped back to allow his wife to go first, which she did. Joyanna took to the rope easily which made sense since she'd probably ridden it ten times just that day throughout the course of her duties. She disappeared over the side of the lip. Then Prince went, then me, then Dr. Shahi followed by our *Indarrean* guard.

The Prince started talking as soon as he began to lower.

"There was much the survey drones didn't see, it turns out, Captain. Almost all the damage to the below ground city was to the rooms surrounding this open space. Most of the inner rooms had only slight damage and the deep rooms were untouched." He grimaced. "Actually, much of our initial work was burying those that had been left behind."

"That must have been difficult work, Sir," I said because it seemed someone should say something. Picturing the Paceys that had managed to evade the *tapetia mortis* only to be wiped out by the planetary shift (not to mention the accompanying dust storm and other delights that had come with it) was not pleasant, even if the dead were certainly all Scientists. This made me feel less bad about it until I remembered that the Scientist 'masters' had all been safely in space. It had been their lackeys and outright slaves that had died here and I was ashamed of myself.

"It was, but it reinforced our desire to bring the city back. For us and for those many we have lost."

The city was coming into focus below, and soon, around us. I could see the first level teeming with workers.

"Where is Miss Fenton?" the Prince said looking alarmed. "I should alert security if she's had problems…"

Just then a shadow passed quickly over us as, for just a second, wings blocked out the pale sun. Someone shouted and the noises of the city stuttered and stopped as all of us looked over and watched Eriss fly, darting, hovering and swooping, playing really, as she delightedly viewed Charleston. I saw the look of sadness and, in some, suppressed jealousy of the Tarine *Indarrean* confined to the assistance of the rope. It made me really want to get this shit over with so we could get to the *Chrysalis*, but, as Eriss had told me many times when my impatience had gotten the better of me, diplomatic missions could not be rushed. It was the nature of the beast. Everyone else, whether of our party or city-dweller, however, was transfixed by the sight of Eriss in flight.

"Goodness," the Prince said to himself. "I'd forgotten she could do that."

I hadn't, but I kept that thought to myself as I enjoyed her freedom probably as much as she was enjoying it herself.

I heard Joyanna below me say, "Imagine being able to move in such a way."

"Regular folks like us can get close, Ma'am, in zero-g, but I don't think it is the same." Then I realized what I'd said and added hastily, "Not that I meant to imply that you and the Prince are…"

She laughed quietly. "I knew what you meant, Captain. It's all right."

That was a relief, I had to say. Her relaxation was remarkable, though, since even I knew that the Berria branch of the Corsican Royal family (by that I mean the late Prince Louis' family) was well known for being total nit-picking dicks about the observance of protocol. This was a new Whitman and Joyanna. Not that I was planning on pushing anything. That was a recipe for disaster, but it was still nice.

Eriss flew closer to us and hovered, her wings beating with great force to keep her in place. "The first level is a hot house, Sir?"

The Prince simply said, "Doctor?"

"Thank you, Sir," Dr. Shahi said. "Our meat protein is currently synthetic, though our second dome will contain a farm, but we are growing our own vegetables and trees within the city at present."

"For transplant to the outside earth, Doctor?" Eriss asked.

"Someday, yes, Miss Fenton."

We were at the second level now which appeared to be several different kinds of laboratories.

"Will you have animals?" I asked, and suddenly entranced by the idea I thoughtlessly added, "I can't even imagine animals on Pace."

"We have embryos that will be unfrozen and tubbed once the farm dome is completed," Dr. Shahi answered, but Princess Joyanna looked up in surprise.

"Surely animals weren't such a rarity on Pace, Captain Armstrong?" she asked.

Crap. How to answer that? Well, I thought, with a kinder version of the truth. I noticed as I began to speak that the Prince was very silent though he could have answered the question just as easily as I. "Animals were outlawed in the generation before mine, Ma'am." I looked at Eriss whose expression was concerned. "Too many concerns over genetic contamination."

"Contamination with what?" Joyanna asked, puzzled as well she might be.

"Human DNA, Your Highness," I said.

"You're joking," Joyanna said, horrified.

I let my silence speak for itself. Joyanna frowned as if thinking hard.

We kept moving, but I really wanted to say something else. It was burning in my brain to be said, but I couldn't say it here. At least, not to them. I opened my 'door' and spoke to Eriss, though I knew the other

Tarine would be able to hear me. It couldn't be helped. 'My grandparents died trying to protect their horses.'

'God, Ian,' she thought back, 'I'm so sorry.'

It was a little thing, that, but it made me feel better. I nodded at her gratefully and closed my 'door' back up.

Indeed, we could see rows and rows of plants, going back what looked like for miles.

We were at the third level now and I could see what had been (and probably would be again) offices and barracks. The fourth level contained residences, the fifth maintenance and the city's physical plant and what appeared to be medical quarters. At last we stepped off the rope and were on the ground floor. Eriss gracefully landed next to us.

"We're building a tunnel to connect the city with the farm dome," Whitman was saying. "The rock is so hard, however, that I think the tunnel will take as long to build as the dome itself."

"I assume the farm dome will have to be much larger than the one for Charleston, won't it, Sir?" Eriss said turning on the charm. "Such a tremendous effort. I cannot imagine taking on such a project." Her gaze of admiration covered both the Prince and the Princess. Whitman ate it up, but Joyanna still looked thoughtful as if she couldn't put aside the idea of Paceys killing all their animals because its people couldn't be trusted with them.

"I was hoping you would dine with us before you go, but I know you have other obligations," Whitman said wistfully.

By now I had moved closer to Eriss and she tucked her arm in mine as she said, "We have things to do, Your Highness, but nothing would keep us from sharing a meal before we return to the ship. Isn't that right, Ian?"

"Nothing at all," I said, taking her cue. "We would be honored, Sir, Ma'am."

I kept my sigh to myself as Whitman grinned and said, "Fantastic."

12:00 – Chamber of the Admiral-Zuerst, Paragon Station, Rian Space, September 22nd, 2874

Paragon.

Twelve *Indarrean*, six of them Tarine Black Wings, entered first, flying up to the sides and below in the ball-like room. Then I followed with my jetpack. Then, lastly, came my Eriss, in the center of the protective sphere created by her people. I hovered behind her and to the right.

We paused. Waited.

'Black Wing' Tarine, you ask? I shall explain. The *Chrysalis*, the ship belonging to Affsoon (AKA Pistil) and her husband Gabriel that had met us at Annaluca, had, over the last twelve exhausting hours, fitted our six Tarine with vests. Black vests, each with one magnificent (black) artificial wing.

The design of the vest/wing was deceptively simple: it started wide at the shoulders and covered the body to just below the waist. The back had a hole that allowed for the original functioning wing to poke through. It *looked* simple, but it wasn't. Gabriel had explained that the vest itself was, under the mesh cover, a light reinforced steel alloy that had only the minimum give for the comfort of its wearer. There couldn't be too much give, he'd said, or the artificial wing wouldn't be braced enough to function. The vest also contained auxiliary servos and sensors that fed to a processor on its back allowing the wing to 'learn' the idiosyncratic flying patterns of its wearer.

I'd originally considered objecting to everything being black (as opposed to mimicking the natural coloring of the Tarine) but had held my tongue after some thought. After all, Affie had brought out Jane's inner badass—why not the Tarine's? They looked fucking dangerous, not to mention happy, darting about like lethal butterflies.

Of course there had been a bit of a learning curve with the new wings (a lot of smashing into things like walls and cabinets), but our *Indarrean* Tarine were now in reasonable control of their new additions. I was looking forward to seeing what they could do when they really had their shit together.

All this I thought while we continued to wait/float in the darkened room.

The far end of the room slowly lit.

In the center of *his* sphere of guardians floated a being who could only be Tirith Ebata.

He was...fat.

I only mention this because I had never seen a non-lean Denethian. He was otherwise normally-sized and his dark hair was long and in many glossy braids bound together at his nape, but what had surely been wiry muscles at some point had been lost in unwieldy bulk. His long tail moved elegantly behind him, though, and his extra weight seemed to add gravitas, once I'd really looked him over, rather than rendering him foolish or infantile. So not like an idiot baby.

"Welcome, Miss Fenton," the being said in a deep, rich musical voice. "I am Tirith Ebata." There was a purr to his words, an archness, as if he knew it all and was either disgusted or amused by everything he saw. Or both. I wondered if Eriss could read him. Was he a TP himself? My 'door' was firmly shut, of course, so I had no way to test it without potentially letting him see everything in my head. (He wasn't one, we found out later.)

"Admiral," she said quietly. "I believe you wanted to see me?"

He smiled, clearly pleased. "Indeed I did, my dear." He turned to me. "Captain Armstrong, I presume, or should I call you Captain Fisher?"

"Armstrong will do, Admiral," I said, watching his soldiers. I wondered if he was going to apologize for attempting to kill me. It was a wasted thought.

"I take it," Admiral Ebata said as he turned his attention back to Eriss, "you have been considering the question of Myrrim?"

"I have," Eriss answered cagily.

"You are unsure, however, of the larger picture, are you not?" The purr in his voice had grown.

"That is correct."

"Let me enlighten you," he said, but then looked around at the, ahem, balls of guards on our side and his. "Just the two of us."

Eriss frowned and I opened my mouth to protest when she said, "Ian will stay." She gave the rather intimidating Admiral Ebata a look of pure steel that was both powerful and really sexy. Hopefully just to me.

Tirith looked even more pleased and nodded, half looking over his shoulder he said, "You may go." His guards fled the room breathlessly fast.

Eriss just looked at Captain Trette and nodded and the *Indarrean* left, too, though they didn't look very happy about it. I wasn't thrilled either, but we needed to know what the hell Tirith's plan was and this was obviously going to be the quickest way to get him to talk.

"There are two points that will allow my plan to reach fruition, should you agree to go along," he said. "One is that you are an unusual leader. Poised to be both religious and political by Shirin," he said her name through his teeth, "but not given a firm footing with which to easily be either. What I would suggest is that you abandon your Ambassadorial post."

"You want me to abandon our people?" Eriss said a little testily.

"Never," Tirith said with emphasis, "but I believe you can be more use to them in your rather nebulous religious capacity."

"I'm not the Pelann, Sir."

He practically pounced. "*That* is an opportunity for change, my dear." He took a breath. "The other point I wish to address relates directly to the fact that each family, and Denethian families are quite large, as you know," Eriss and I nodded, "chooses its *Burua,* or Capo, if you will. Very often it is the oldest living parent, but sometimes it is the most dynamic being within the family, regardless of age. This existing hierarchy is, I believe, something we can use. I will elaborate on that in a minute." He paused.

We waited.

His expression turned grave. "We haven't had a King or Queen in the Rian Nation in hundreds of years, but we *have* had a Pelann. Though they are supposed to be guided by the Voice of the Holy Mother, I believe that they have mistaken ego, or their own hubris, for that Voice."

If they weren't just bat shit crazy, I thought, though I kept that to myself.

Eriss nodded.

"Do you believe in the Holy Mother, Miss Fenton?"

"I do, yes," she said.

Belief. Interesting topic. I'd abandoned my own anti-religious upbringing easily since being cynical about god would get in the way of being with Eriss (and my feelings about the subject had never been strong), but the fact that she really did believe in a higher power still surprised me. It shouldn't have, but it did.

"Does she speak directly to you?"

"She does not."

Was it my imagination or did Tirith looked relieved?

"If you took the story of Myrrim literally, it means you are willing to give up a physical relationship with the Terran Human you love for the good of your people."

Cold filled my gut as she answered, "Yes."

He turned to me, "Will you, despite the pain it will cause you, be willing to forgo the same?" I blinked at him. "You wouldn't be here by her side otherwise."

"I want, Sir, what she wants and because it is the right thing to do."

Tirith positively beamed at us, so much so that his cynical detachment slipped for just a second. "I cannot tell you how glad I am to hear that, Captain."

"One question, Sir, if I may?"

"Of course," he said.

"Whatever you'll propose, she has the chance to say no," and here was the kicker, "and walk away?"

"She does," he said firmly.

You know, I believed him. I looked at Eriss and I could tell she did, too.

"May I proceed?" Tirith asked, the purr back in his voice.

"Please," Eriss said.

"I confess I am weary of leaders who are born to the job." We looked at him in surprise. "How many Kings, Queens, Emperors, Pelann, etc., are really worthy of their positions?" He smiled at us. "The Emperor Charles Fitzroy," he winked, letting us know that he, too, had divined Fitz's secret, "is an exception, as is Prince Pilar, but even they have brought in new blood, have they not?" Pacey blood. The next generation would be true wild cards for the first time in centuries. "I was dismayed when David Abrams created a monarchy by appointing Tania of the *Indus Felae* Queen, but even then it isn't the same. He chose her because the bloodlines were more than acceptable, but she was already equipped to lead whatever the circumstances of her birth."

"I don't understand, Sir. If you don't want a restoration of the monarchy..." Eriss said hesitantly.

"I want to give the Rian a chance to choose their leader. For the first time."

Eriss floated back a pace, shocked.

"You want a *democracy*?" she asked as if trying to confirm that she hadn't gone mad. The thought was revolutionary, but was it revolutionary in a good way? I was too shocked to be able to look at the pros and cons clearly.

"Not exactly," he said, watching her closely. "More a modified Parliamentary system. Three houses, one comprised of the *Burua* of all the families. The *Burua* will be chosen within the families as they always have—though one has to believe that the standards for choosing their Capos will have to change once the requirements of the job have expanded since the stakes will be infinitely higher. The second house will come from the Warriors, chosen by *their* peers. The third will be by popular election within the masses and the unaffiliated. Once all this is set in place we will, for the first time, have votes on laws, treaties and trade, etc., instead of decrees from a Pelann."

"Who will be at the top?" I asked. Will *you* be at the top? Was my unspoken question.

Tirith shook his braided head. "I have achieved the highest position I have aspired to attain. I am quite happy where I am." He grimaced, "I will be happier still to be commanded by an elected leader. One hopes we will finally be able to acquire one worthy of the job."

Eriss shook her head hard. "The person at the top must still be the Pelann, Sir." I looked quickly at her. "Not me. The 'office,' for lack of a better word, of Pelann has meaning and has earned respect all over the Union. Whatever his or her actual function, I am sure the Pelann must lead."

Now Tirith's smile was almost fatherly. "That is correct. An *elected* Pelann, but a Pelann nonetheless. He or she will be Head of the Holy Mother's Temple and Defender of the Faith but he or she will be *chosen* by his or her peers."

I took a second to process this. It was a fantastic proposition. Too fantastic, perhaps?

"What about Eriss, Sir?" As I said this I realized his plan, while potentially brilliant, had left out one entire segment of the Rian. "Where do the Tarine fit into your three houses?"

"She will actually lead, or a better word might be inspire, the Faithful." Tirith looked a bit apologetic. "The Tarine will help her do this or, if they choose individually, go their own way."

The real answer was that there was no place for the Tarine, but why wasn't there? Why had Tirith written them off?

"So their only options are religion or exile while Eriss is to live her life as a mythical virgin priestess?" I tried not to sound cynical but it was difficult. Especially since this status meant I could never make love to my lover. While that had been expected (what else could you glean from the fucking Book of Myrrim?) it didn't mean I liked hearing it confirmed.

"In a way," Tirith said, now very intent. He moved closer to us. "What I saw from the reintroduction of the Tarine was that they were *other*. Shirin not only wanted her place at the table with gravity-dwellers, but she wanted a warmer, fuzzier version of the Deneth so that Humans wouldn't fear them as much. They are deliberately less alien, but, I thought, as I watched the fascinating battle between the Tarine Princess," he inclined his head in Eriss' direction, "and the lethally impressive Red Angel, was that being *other* was the Tarine's strength."

"How so?" Eriss asked a little shakily as if she didn't at all like where this was going.

"They are a people apart. Another deliberate choice, like the removal of the genetic code that would have given you tails." Tirith pursed his lips, clearly preparing for something unpleasant. "You see Shirin made just enough Tarine to look like she meant business, but the Tarine are...temporary."

That cold feeling in my stomach started to take over my whole body. "What do you mean *temporary*?"

"I know what you were told," he said to Eriss. "That you could only breed by approval from Shirin. That you were infertile unless you used the tubs to have offspring." Eriss said nothing, her face pinking with fear. "There were never going to be any Tarine children, Eriss." His face became sad. "You are all siblings." His saturnine face softened. "Though technically you would be termed clones."

Oh god.

It hadn't been Tirith who'd written them off. That had been done twenty years ago by Shirin herself before they'd even been born.

Eriss' hand reached out blindly for me and I grasped it hard, trying to anchor her.

"So we were just some experiment?" she said. "Just for now. No future. Just now."

"I am truly sorry, my dear."

"How do you know all this?" I said, more than a little accusingly.

Tirith didn't seem to take offence as he answered, "I was able to retrieve certain records from the slavers who bred all of you. There was only one set of genetic material used. It is why you all look so similar, though some of you lean female and others male. It is why you all are Telepaths and it is why you cannot deed the Rian to your children."

I wanted to take Eriss in my arms, but now was not the time. She didn't cry (Tarine didn't) but her wings shook as if she was crying.

"It was her final act of control. An insurance policy in case any of you started having ideas of your own. For the most part she thought in terms of decades."

As do you, I thought bitterly as I looked him squarely in the eye. He met my stare easily, even a bit smugly, as if he'd read my thought and wouldn't deny it.

"So, even if we became a problem we would be a problem that would eventually pass," Eriss said bleakly. Tirith nodded sympathetically.

Temporary. Disposable.

I grasped Eriss' hand tighter.

"I'm so glad that bitch is dead," I muttered.

"As are we all, Captain."

I waited for Eriss to speak, but she seemed lost in her own thoughts so I spoke, "So you want to, in effect, divorce the serious religious aspect from the office of Pelann by giving it to the virgin priestess because she's just weird enough and temporary enough," I said bitterly, "to be considered divine?"

"Because she is *other*, yes."

"What happens when she and the other Tarine have died off?" I asked, though it made me sick to even consider the concept.

"They will have written their wisdom, they will have trained years' worth of Denethian priests and priestesses and their words will live on." Tirith looked a bit tired. "Longer than any of us will."

"Will that be enough?"

"Your question should be: will that be all?"

"I don't understand," I said.

"The book of Myrrim within the *Septt* was recently re-translated," Tirith said. "Very little was different even when the words were modernized. One word *was* different, however, within Myrrim's promise to the Holy Mother."

Eriss looked up.

"The older translation, the one in most common usage, says that she promised to remain 'un-mated' throughout her life, but the recent version says she was to be 'un*married*' throughout her life."

"You mean..." Eriss asked, her eyes bright.

"Provided you are discrete, I see no reason why the two of you cannot live a *full*," he leaned his head towards us for emphasis, "life together." He turned to me. "Unless you would have difficulty keeping a relationship secret?"

The irony of me, of all people, being asked that particular question was not lost on either Eriss or myself. I made no verbal answer, but suddenly feeling lighter than the air I was floating in, I took Eriss in my arms and laughed. She let out a shaky breath and laughed with me.

There may also have been kissing. A lot of kissing.

Before I end this unexpectedly long (and far too personal) journal entry, here are some headlines and journo excerpts you might find interesting.

As Jane would say, I'll see you around.

Ian Armstrong
Dep Qua, Trithicate

Guryev Free Press, October 30th, 2875
PRESS GETS FIRST LOOK AT
'SPIRITUAL' SPACE STATION

Journos invited to examine plans for a new 'spiritual station' to be built around the Trith star in the heart of Rian Space. The new station, Aise-Trithicate, will be, in effect, a large Temple devoted to the Holy Mother. Non-Hyper capable, it will stay above the holy city of Dep Qua, connected by an 'arm' and space elevator. (See article on the 'Arm' of Gloriana-Levvon.) Former Rian Ambassador Eriss Fenton, the *sagrat-Pelann,* has, according to sources, hired several firms of diverse origin from within the Union to work together to build the station. The project will be supervised by her head of security, Captain Ian Armstrong, son of High Admiral Armstrong of the Union Navy...

Masada Times, March 15th, 2876
LEADERS MAKE PLANS TO BRING X-SHIPS TO UNAV

Today Rian Admiral-Zuerst Tirith Ebata hosted Union President Hugh Leder and High Admiral Armstrong, as well as other Union dignitaries, to discuss best allocations of X-Ships within the Union Navy. Admiral Armstrong's aide-de-Camp, Colonel Alex Couvillion, said, "The Deneth Rian have speed and agility in space that Terran and Heely Humans can only dream of. Their presence in the X-ships will give all of us a tremendous advantage in the years ahead. It is an exciting time within the Union." This meeting has been one of many indications of the steady improvement of relations between the Rian Nation and the Union-at-large…

Galactic Journal, Commemorative Edition, October 5th, 2876
BLACK WINGS PAY RESPECT TO MEMORIAL

October 5th, 2876: 'Black Wing' Tarine visited Trithicate Memorial Park in Washington, D.C., Terra, on the third anniversary of the devastating crash of Trithicate Station into the planet. The Union capital came to a standstill as Terran and Heely Humans, who had stood in line for hours to see them, met the unworldly but gracious Tarine for their blessings. (See related article on the reputed healing touch of the Black Wing Tarine.)

Guryev Free Press, July 4ᵗʰ, 2877
TELLESCO RISES AGAIN! UNION REJOICES!

The much-loved *sagrat-Pelann* presided over the re-dedication of the planet now known as New Tellesco today, offering the blessing of the Black Wing Tarine for the health and prosperity of its people. Their Royal Highnesses Prince Henry and Princess Sophia of Corsica were present at the ceremony, being principal authors of the reclamation of the planet from the inundation by Heely water (see article: The Drowning of Tellesco) as well as the His Imperial Highness the Emperor Charles 6 of Corsica and Princess Jane. The Emperor and his wife, the notorious Red Angel, made the people of Tellesco a gift of twenty-five breeding pairs of *Lumina*.

New Tellesco Free State President Narazet Barsoumian made special thanks to famed entrepreneur David Abrams for his development of Heely water cleaning technology.

The 'rebirth' celebrations are expected to last all week throughout the Union.

PART 2

2881-2882

ENTRY 10-8-93

<u>11:03 – Gardens, Robin Hill, Irena, Corsican Empire, Galactic Union, December 18th, 2881</u>

Yes, it's Jane again and yes, it's been a little over seven years since my last entry. Or longer, come to think of it, since technically the last entry was Ian's. You may be wondering why I skipped seven (or eight) years in my exhaustive detailing of my little life. It isn't as if nothing had happened in those years; a great deal had, but I had found, as I'd attempted to put it down on paper, that most of the events had been, for the most part, small, personal and (who would have thought it) *happy*. In life, happy is generally what most people want. In a book, however, happy is boring as shit to read. So I thought I would catch you all up and then move on to the messes, danger and drama to come. I promise that there will be suffering, adventure and fear and, because it's me, things being destroyed or blown up.

I looked out over the lawn at Robin Hill, trimmed and perfect in the warm morning light, and had to smile. I noticed that ring of guards around the perimeter of the yard were smiling, too, though their expression blanked when they saw I was looking. Idis was laughing, her hands on her hips, as she stood in her trousers (!) with dirty knees (!!) as our now eight year old daughter, Lucy, tried to teach her how to do a cartwheel.

"Mère," Lucy said to Idis in her 'very serious' voice, "now put your hands up like this..." she raised her little arms over her head, "...take a hop, then keep your body straight as you go over like a wheel." Lucy then executed a perfect cartwheel. One of her nannies (the Terran one) had taught her how to do it and Lucy, once tears of frustration had been shed and mastery attained, had insisted on teaching everyone she knew how to do one. Charles had declined. Captain Stanley had been game and, I have to say, watching that mountain of a man attempt it had been one of the funniest things I'd seen in a long time. I'd been able to do it easily (she said immodestly) mostly because the Telespatial thing allowed me to know exactly where I was in relation to the ground. Now, however, it was Idis' turn.

Idis put her hands up, hopped…and landed on her ass laughing like a nut. Again.

"Oh, mère," Lucy said, shaking her adorable head with its mane of long curly red hair. "Try it again." Then the little tyrant helped her mother up and made her try again. And again.

Lucy. Yes, all the clichés about loving your kid beyond reason were completely true and no longer felt like clichés at all. She had a temper (like her mama) but poise (like her mère) and command (like her father). She was, in the unbiased (ha!) eyes of her doting parents, perfect even when she wasn't. Her threes had been pretty awful, even I'd had to admit, but Charles had told us to wait until it got better and it had. I still had fear for her safety, especially since she had claimed, at the advanced age of five, that she wanted to command ships in UNav like her older brother, Alex. I'd had a quiet panic attack after that one, but had recovered quickly. I'd been hoping she'd want to become a professional gardener on the estate. Or a chef. Or a shut-in.

"Good morning," said a familiar voice with a smile in it. I looked over my shoulder to see the vision of beauty that was my friend Wilby arriving after his trek across the lawn.

"Morning, love," I said but I was distracted by a number of things. One was that while he was still my friend of old, he was subtly different from the man I'd met when I was just a girl. Life had been at him one way or another, as has been documented, but this was more subtle. Something only a long-time friend would notice. A touch of bitterness in his eyes, perhaps, or maybe disillusionment would be more accurate. There were more pressing issues, however. The most pressing was the fact that he was here on Irena at all. The result of a frantic call a month before in the middle of the night.

I'd been alone at Robin Hill since Charles had been with Idis at the Palace. It had been extremely late but I'd been up working on lesson plans and teacher allocation so was wide awake. This was going to be our first year with Denethian cadets and I'd been trying to troubleshoot (and hopefully avoid) the problems we'd had with the Heely cadets. While we'd had three graduating classes with Heelies included it hadn't been easy. Actually at times it had sucked, but I'd been pretty sure we knew how to do it now and Heely applicants were pouring in. Cadet Wylan Smith was now Lieutenant Wylan Smith on the new UNav ship from Novy and doing quite well, his best friend, Lieutenant Petros Nitsa, happily serving with him. I hoped that Wylan would one day return to teach, though I had a feeling it would be a long time before he left active service. He'd certainly be more welcome at the *Schola-Terra* than on Novy, especially since he'd refused the rather dubious honor of being formally named as Queen Tania's heir. He'd wanted to serve and to fight for the Union, not lead a planet. Tania wasn't speaking to him and, since I had backed him up, she wasn't speaking to me, either.

Back to the call.

My comm had beeped. "Pace here." I'd listened with growing alarm as my usually unflappable friend had asked, no, begged to be allowed to come to Corsica right then and there.

"Of course, Wilby, but what happened?"

He promised he'd explain when he arrived and did we have a place, a safe place where we could house himself and the children.

"*All* of them?" I asked.

I'd met him in the garden, right where I was seeing him now about five days after that call. I'd risen and moved over to him, tucking my arm in his. We'd walked slowly through the gardens near the house that I had grown to love like they were my own, which in some ways they now were.

I'd felt him take a breath. "Fitz is all right with this, Jane?" he asked quietly.

"Of course, but Wilby what the fuck?"

We'd housed them all immediately when they'd arrived, twenty-five ten year old supers, their nannies and support staff, and a teenaged Shira in what had been an auxiliary barracks we'd called the Annex on the grounds of Robin Hill. Idis had managed to transform the space like so much magic in those five days. As if thinking of her had summoned the Countess, she'd appeared by my side.

"Welcome, my friend," she said graciously to Wilby as she smiled and kissed him on the cheek. He flushed slightly, but looked pleased. "Have I missed the story?"

"You're just in time," I said looking pointedly at Wilby. "All right, then, spill."

"It was two things, really," he said, looking a little embarrassed. "One was a message I'd received ten days ago from Prince Whitman."

Both Idis and I stiffened. "What was it?" Idis asked gently.

"He said, 'Your children are at the nexus. Go to the Princess and you will be safe.'"

Idis and I both frowned, but it was Idis who said, "Which Princess?"

I'd assumed he'd meant me, but now I had to think about it. "Because he referenced the children?"

She nodded. "He might have meant Lucy."

Because Lucy was a super, too. More on that in a minute.

"We need to up security around all of them if Whit saw it," Idis said thoughtfully. "I'll put it in Charles' briefing."

"I think he did mean Lucy," Wilby said heavily, still on the original point. "Since I have never known a pre-cog to be wrong, I started making arrangements to leave, quiet ones, especially since I knew Abrams wouldn't like giving us up."

"I don't get it. You've had no interactions with him, regarding the children, either yours or his," I said, tacitly confirming what I thought I knew. "What did he get from having all of you there?"

Wilby shrugged, "All our data and all the recordings of training sessions with the kids who were developing skills early, right from the beginning. It was his only requirement."

What could he possibly want with all that? "You said there were two things," I pressed.

Wilby nodded. "I knew we were leaving and I figured it wouldn't hurt to assuage my curiosity about Abrams and his children."

Oh crap, I thought. Talk about poking the dragon in the nose. *No one saw Abrams' children, not even Wilby who'd lived four floors above them for years.*

"What did you see?" I asked, frankly consumed with curiosity.

"Well, I was wandering around on their floor and I found a room off to itself outfitted with those chambers, enclosed beds, really. Five of them. One was clearly Abrams', the one we'd seen before, but the other four were... Some had pictures in them, two had stuffed animals..." he swallowed hard, looking quite disturbed.

"Four more aging chambers," Idis gasped before I could. "Like he used on you," this was to me, "after your surgery?"

"One of them was still open. A young man was just closing it, actually, when I saw him." Wilby was looking pretty freaked out by now. "He was tall, brown eyes, dark hair. About eighteen or so. He saw me, smiled and said, 'I'm Tommy. Who are you?'"

"Father in Heaven," Idis said.

What I said, however, was, *"He put his own children in the aging chamber?"* I felt the world spin around me, but took a breath and it stopped. I looked up at Wilby in horror. "That boy should be nine or ten." I was so flabbergasted I became silent.

"So Abrams found you with Tommy?" Idis said because I apparently couldn't.

"I think he would have killed me himself, but he looked pretty ill," Wilby made a fluttering gesture around his face as if marking the black lines of Abrams' disease. I nodded. David would have been in no shape to deal with Wilby in his condition, especially since he always let it go too long between treatments. "He had his Thals knock me out and when I woke I was with my kids, a ship standing by to take us away."

"What the hell is he doing to those children?" I had to ask. Why was he cheating all of them out of the childhoods they deserved? As an experiment? For a product or medical device? Were even his own kids just guinea pigs to him? The whole thing made me sick.

"We needed to be somewhere safe," Wilby said as he took one of my hands and one of Idis', "thank you so much for giving us this place to land. I'll be looking for a new home as soon as I get my bearings."

"Nonsense," Idis said firmly. "You *are* home." And if Idis said it, even though she'd probably just made the decision in that moment, it was so.

"I am?" Wilby said, his cheeks pinking again.

I nodded. "We need you and the last Paceys to grow up safe, or as safe as any of us can be, plus," and here I grinned a little wickedly, "we have a slightly unusual situation and need your particular brand of help."

"I'd hate to even think what my particular brand would be," Wilby muttered.

I whacked him on the shoulder, "A good brand, idiot," I said affectionately. I turned to Idis. "May I?"

Idis rolled her eyes and laughed. "Go ahead."

"Lucy!" I yelled across the lawn, "Come here, please." Then I added, "The fast way."

"Ok, mama," she yelled back in a clear bright voice. "Watch this."

The small distant figure on the grass immediately 'rose' from the ground, 'hovered' a second and then 'flew' at us at terrific speed.

"Holy shit," Wilby breathed.

I gently 'held' onto her as I always did the rare times we let her fly (one too many near misses) but she was fine this time and only stumbled a little bit when she landed in front of us with a flourish. I found that all of us were grinning with her triumph.

"Well done, sweetheart. Your control was very good," I said.

"Thank you, mama," she said, suddenly shy. "Was it good, mère?"

"It was perfect, precious," Idis said softly. She flashed her eyes in the direction of Wilby and Lucy immediately lit up the way virtually everyone did when they saw him. "Uncle Wilby!" she cried as she leaped up for him to catch. She hadn't seen him in two years, true, but he wasn't someone you forgot.

"Hello, dearest, how are you?" he said, laughing.

"Fan-fucking-tastic." My daughter, ladies and gentlemen.

"*Lucy!*" Idis gasped.

"Sorry, mère," Lucy said with feigned contriteness. "I am well, Sir, and how are you?"

Wilby laughed. "Quite well, Your Highness," he said, kissing the top of her head as he put her down. "I think your mothers want you to take some classes with my kids this year, would you like that?"

"Your kids that are like me?" she said, brown eyes wide.

"Yes," he said, "we're going to work hard and have a lot of fun."

"Is Shira here?" Lucy asked eagerly. "With Uncle Quinn?"

A shadow fell over Wilby's face but he hid it quickly with his trademark blinding smile. Quinn. After years of ups and downs and no permantenly happy resolution, Wilby had finally divorced his husband two years earlier, saying he wanted his freedom, yet, it was freedom by an unusual definition. Quinn still spent half the year with Wilby and the kids. When he did so they lived like they were still married. When Quinn went back to the Furies, Wilby lived single. It was how Wilby had wanted it, and I was sure Quinn had agreed only because he'd had no choice, but no one seemed actually happy. I didn't get it. I wasn't sure they did either, much as they clearly still loved each other. "Uncle Quinn," Wilby answered Lucy, "is with the Furies, but Shira will see you after lunch. Ok?"

"Cool."

Idis checked her watch. "Speaking of lunch, Lucy, it's time to get dressed."

Lucy sighed theatrically. "I know. So much time dressing," she grumbled as she trudged off to her nanny.

"You're a bad influence on her," Idis teased in my general direction.

"I certainly hope so," I teased back. "Between the two of us we'll have a real badass lady one day."

"Won't that be something?" Idis said, more to herself than to me.

"So she's a Macro?" Wilby said, still processing apparently.

"Uh huh," I said. Then I looked slyly at Idis. "Tell 'Uncle' Wilby what happened over last Frost Break."

Idis put her hands on her hips. "Jane, really."

"Tell him."

She sighed as Wilby looked back and forth between us, clearly enjoying our interplay. Yes, we'd come a long way, Idis and I. "Fine," Idis said. "I was having a meeting with the Lord Chamberlain when Lucy came in looking for her cat. Mr. Harris was about to leave when Lucy said, in a clear carrying voice, 'Mère, he isn't a horses' ass at all and why do you want to choke him with that chain-thing he wears?'"

Wilby stared and then laughed and laughed. I laughed, too, (I did every time she told that story) but waited for him to get the larger picture. I knew he'd gotten it when he abruptly stopped. "Wait a damned minute, she's a..?"

"Hybrid," I answered. "The only TK/TP hybrid I've ever heard of."

"Well fuck me running," he said.

"Indeed," Idis said, amused.

As a side note Charles had *not* been amused. In truth he'd been freaked out. Pun intended. It wasn't that he'd loved Lucy less, he doted on her, but he'd seen her with new eyes and hadn't known what to do. Eventually I'd had to tell him (not to mention train him to block his thoughts which he'd learned to do with annoying ease) to get over it or Lucy *would* feel like a freak with her own father and he'd started acting normally again. It had been a possibility, of course, that we would have a super for a child (I'd assumed we would have, as had Idis, but we'd been the only ones) but actually having one had been a shock for the normals. Personally, I kind of liked the idea of having a Super-Empress. You know, with a cape and everything.

Unfortunately, the horrid concept of dressing for an event brought me right back to the unpleasant present.

"We need to dress, too, Jane." Idis turned to Wilby. "Will you be attending?"

Wilby nodded. "He may have saved my life and the lives of my kids. I will pay my respects."

"Thank you," she said, and I could see her assuming the mantle of Countess as she straightened and started moving towards the house. She always seemed to float when she walked even without the sweeping skirts.

"I'll see you there," I said with a sad smile. "The shuttle will leave in two hours."

He nodded and I followed Idis to prepare for a sad duty.

13:00 – Imperial Cathedral, Lyonesse, Irena, Corsican Empire

I heard the murmurs of the assembled congregation as I entered our Cathedral holding Lucy's hand. I followed the Emperor and the Countess, a bastardization of protocol that gave Mr. Harris fits, not that I cared. We were all dressed very formally in black, even more formally than we had been for Prince Louis' funeral eight years before, because this was a service for a man who had fought his own nature to be good, to contribute. This time we were truly mourning.

Charles, standing grand and somber, took his place on the altar, standing to the side of the Officiant, the same man who had married us. Idis, Lucy and I joined the family in the front row. Alex, Hal and Sophia, the little Princes Simian and Henri-Charles and the chief mourner, Princess Joyanna, who looked almost catatonic.

There were about two thousand attendees, all in black, matching the crepe, the black shrouded coffin and the rain that was falling lightly on the muted colors of the stained glass.

Many people I didn't know were there and some I only knew slightly through life at the Palace and Robin Hill. Some, however, I knew intimately, I realized as I read the biosignatures of Samuel, Bertie, Ian, Eriss and what had to be half a dozen Black Tarine.

The Officiant started speaking and my mind naturally flew back to the reason we were all there. An emergency message from Thal had told us and this exclusive had told everyone else:

Guryev Free Press
December 2nd, 2881
TRAGIC ACCIDENT KILLS COLONIST
PRINCE!
Sources confirm that H.R.H. Prince Whitman Pace-Pallon-Couvillion-Bourbonnais, Prince of Corsica

and Its Environs, was killed in a shuttle accident,
along with his body guards and assistant Captain
Mirta Pace-Torva, on his way from Annaluca (Luca)
to the newly completed Luca Station. At press time
investigators have found no evidence of foul play
and believe pilot error to be the cause of the tragedy.
The colonists of Annaluca have expressed shock and
grief at the loss of their tireless leader who,
according to many, had made miracles and coaxed
life out of a previously dead planet.
Prince Whitman was a Pacey refugee who married
into the Coriscan Royal Family and many had
suspected it was merely for the prestige, but he had
pushed for the re-colonization of the former Pace-
Pallon on behalf of Corsica and was universally
regarded as a true leader of the Colony, Prince or no.
He and his beloved wife, Princess Joyanna, had
created a safe haven for commerce between all
members of the Union…

The Officiant said all the appropriate things, making us feel all the
appropriate feelings (if we weren't feeling them already). I only half
listened, reminding myself that our interference in Whit's life had extended
and improved it. Had we left him alone he would have remained a
murderer and would never have risen above his original self. I still felt
guilt and loss, of course, especially when I looked at the grieving form of
his widow. Joyanna was a Corsican Princess, trained to take it on the chin
and smile, but she was hiding nothing. She suffered and anyone could see
it. Her boys seemed dazed. They were only a little older than Lucy, but
they had barely seen their father, having grown up at the Palace here on
Irena. They had never been to 'Luca. It had been their parents' decision
and Charles, Idis and I had never questioned it. I guess none of us, not even
Whitman himself, had trusted him enough to be around his own children
every day. The thought made me even sadder, but I still couldn't say for
sure that the instinct had been wrong. Would he have tried (even
unintentionally) to push and mold them into something cruel like their
grandfather Louis would have? Or like the Scientist Prince Whitman
himself might have? We would never know.

I felt a shift in the congregation and realized that Charles had risen from his ornamental chair and was making his way to the pulpit. His expression was grave, but I knew that the guilt and loss I was feeling belonged even more to him than to me, since 'editing' Whit's personality had been his idea. Idis and I had done our best to reassure him that he'd made possible the good that Whit had done by allowing him to *be* his better nature, but I knew the guilt was still there. I could hardly fault him for this feeling; I still felt the dull ache on my back from the addition of Whitman and Mirta's names to my skin.

"We have been thinking a great deal about the man We lost ten days ago," Charles said, his magnetic presence reaching out over all of us, especially since he'd brought out the Imperial 'We,' "and how much the times he lived in shaped who he was." He caught my eye. "Unlike most of the Paceys we have come to know publicly," he smiled slightly, "and privately, he was born to privilege on Pace-Pallon and raised to rule, but even this ruling class, one known for ruthless cruelty," I felt Joyanna wince at this, "became just another group of people fleeing their system's destruction. The Paceys, born both low and high, that survived came to Terra and many thrived, but since more of the rank and file than the nobility," that was giving the Scientists too much credit, I thought bitterly, "escaped the destruction of the *tapetia mortis* the Union was able to learn the real nature of those that had controlled Pace. It is possible that the future Prince learned of this when we did as well." It was possible, I grudgingly admitted, but he hadn't cared. Not then.

Charles took a breath. "We," as in Charles the Emperor, "did not meet Prince Whitman until after he had married Our beloved niece, Princess Joyanna and, We admit, We were wary, given his people's history. We are glad to say that We had underestimated him and that he was not the man We had thought he would be. He was better, more dedicated and stronger than We had anticipated. Only he could have wrought the miracle of turning the ruined Pace-Pallon into the future Eden that is Annaluca. Only he and his Joyanna had the vision and determination to create a space station open to all members of the Union, Human and Rian alike. Only he could have created a place where business could be carried out in safety and where new friends could be made without fear of conflict. We are grateful for his sacrifice. We are grateful for his unique vision." We would miss his particular brand of vision, I thought sadly, for as much of a burden pre-cognition had been to him it had helped the Empire many times over the years, even when he'd been so far away.

Charles continued, "We are grateful for the love he gave to his wife and sons." Charles stood even straighter at the podium. "To show Our gratitude to this man who will be severely missed, We will re-dedicate the Imperial Station at Annaluca as Prince Whitman Station in hopes that this man, Our nephew, will be long remembered."

I felt the silent sob from Joyanna.

I looked up at my husband and gave him a silent nod full of pride. He did not react outwardly, but I knew he was pleased. Such a wonderful man.

Several other people, including Samuel, spoke beautifully about the work Whit had done. No one mentioned the burning of hundreds of Corsican soldiers. No one mentioned that he'd almost killed his own Emperor. Only a few even knew of it and if I had my way, no one else ever would. As much as a man could have redeemed himself, Whitman had and as much as a man could have been punished, he had been. That was all. Many spoke but eventually we finally came to the end of the service.

"Let us all bow our heads in silent prayer," the Officiant said, his soft voice carrying over the assembled.

We did as he'd commanded/asked and the great grand room fell silent. I felt Joyanna's hands clutching her sons' smaller hands. I felt her trying not to hold on to them tightly enough to hurt them. I looked slyly over at Lucy and had to hide my smile as she was looking around at everyone, taking in the scene when she was supposed to be praying. A quick squeeze on the hand of hers in Idis' custody corrected her behavior and Lucy bowed her head obediently. I had to stifle a laugh at that. Lucy flashed a quick look at me under her lashes and I winked at her.

I felt the Officiant raise his head and we all looked up just in time to see the light flicker and hear the 'whoosh' of great wings churning the air into life.

"The Benediction will be given, at their Imperial Highnesses' request by the *sagrat-Pelann*," the Officiant said as he bowed and backed away from the podium to give our visitors room to land.

Eriss, however, for it was Eriss, along with her glorious Black Tarine in flight around her, did not land at once, but hovered effortlessly at the altar for a few seconds before touching gracefully down. Her Black Tarine silently landed also, fanning out behind her.

She bowed her head in the direction of Charles first, then thanked the Officiant.

Then she turned to us. She was so beautiful, so ethereal and other-worldly it took my breath away. There was something else about her, however: surety, in herself and in her purpose. It made her have power, even more so because she didn't want or need it. I wanted to look at Ian and see if he could see what I was seeing, or had he gotten used to it, to her, but I found looking away from Eriss impossible.

"All Holy text, indeed all belief, is subject to interpretation," Eris said gently. "One person may read a Holy text, whether it be the *Septt*, the Torah, the Bariit, or any other and take from it something very different from the next person, but for me I hold certain ideas to be sacred no matter from whence the Word came. The idea, the tenet so crucial to my personal belief and the belief of so many across the galaxy, is that of the existence of the soul. Whether you feel the soul is a bit of God put inside your heart, bits of the very building blocks of the universe or the electrical currents moving within our physical bodies, the *idea* of each of us having something inside us that captures our thoughts, our spirits, our experiences, our great moments and our bad decisions, our hatred and our love is a beautiful one. It is what I believe takes us from being mere sentient animals to being the stuff of stars."

I felt my throat clog with emotion and squeezed Lucy's other hand just a little tighter.

Eriss held her hands in front of her, cupped together but empty. Her great wings beat slowly and strongly, lifting her from the ground. Her Tarines' wings beat with hers, the timing exact, and they rose, too. They moved slowly at first, then faster.

"You cannot see it, this soul," she said, her hands still in front of her, "and though it belonged to Whitman while he lived, it must now be returned, returned to the stars that created us."

She flew to the top of the cathedral with her people, bowed her head, and opened her hands.

"May you be at peace, Whitman," she said quietly, as though he were close in front of her. "Now you are free, though you are never forgotten."

Joyanna wept silently into Idis' shoulder.

Soon the Officiant had said the Mourner's Kaddish and then we were filing out of the somber Cathedral. I found myself next to my spouses (Lucy having been handed over to a nanny along with the young Princes)

and Joyanna in one of those endless receiving lines. No one was supposed
to be there to see *us*, of course, but we were there to support Joyanna.
Joyanna, however, seemed to have found some inner reserve of strength
and was coping (outwardly at least) adequately.

I ran back over the brief conversation we'd had with her as the
receiving line had been in the process of being set.

"What may I do for you, my dear?" Charles had asked gently.

Joyanna's pale face was strained with the effort of not falling apart, but
she held her head up. "Send me back home." She frowned. "To 'Luca,
Uncle. I need to finish what we've started."

Charles nodded. "Of course. Will you take the boys?"

She looked even more pained now as she shook her head. "No, Sir.
Whitman was afraid that it wasn't safe for them."

"Not safe?" I asked, perplexed. I'd thought the only danger to them
would have been their father's influence. I felt like a shit for thinking it,
but...well.

"He had a vision, about children..." Joyanna hesitated, "children who
are different." She looked right at me. "Simian is different."

"Different how," I said a bit more sharply than I'd intended.

"He's like Whit," Joyanna said, her eye filling.

"He can see the nexus...?"

Joyanna frowned, "I don't think so, but he can tell me how things will
go."

"He sent Wilby and his kids here, too," I said. "Why? Did he tell you
what the danger was?"

"I don't think he knew, specifically, all he said was that the children
needed to be here. The supernormals were in danger." All of them, or just
the kids, I wondered.

"You're sure he didn't know from whom? Or what?" Lucy, my Lucy.

"No, I'm sorry."

Idis looked at me as I tried to cover my fear and took Joyanna's hand.
"We will protect them as we would protect Lucy. You have our word."

Charles smiled. "And Our word."

"Thank you, all of you," Joyanna said gratefully as she wiped her eyes.
She turned to Charles. "Thank you for renaming the station, Uncle. He
would have loved that."

Charles smiled sadly. "I hope so, my dear."

A cleared throat from Mr. Harris called us to the line and we'd gotten to it.

A few endless hours later Samuel found me at the reception (there was always a reception), his expression serious. He looked good, despite his grave demeanor. I had to guess that Mallory and he were still going strong. They weren't married, but I had the feeling that Samuel, having two disastrous marriages under his belt, wasn't going to bother making things official again, no matter how attached he was to her. I'd heard speculation in the press that it was odd that they had been a couple for so long without tying the proverbial knot, but all I cared about was their happiness. A wedding insured nothing except that you were legally bound to each other. Besides, Samuel seemed really happy with Mallory and that was all that mattered. Oh, and the fact that it was none of my business. Funny how I always forgot that.

"What's wrong?" I asked as I stood on tiptoes to kiss his cheek in greeting.

He smiled and hugged me briefly. "You asked me to look into finding you a new TP instructor since Mr. Carmichael moved on."

Yeah, that had been a blow. Brady Carmichael (though I haven't given him too much attention in these pages) was a terrific and slightly scary TP that had been a valuable part of the ESTF Program. He'd taken a high paying private sector job a few months ago and I'd been really sorry to see him go. I'd put feelers out for a replacement when he'd left, including asking my favorite High Admiral if he knew anyone. Obviously.

"No luck?" I shrugged. "It happens, Samuel, but I appreciate the effort."

"I appreciate your appreciation, Jane," he said, rolling his eyes, "but it isn't that I didn't find any suitable candidates. It's that I had trouble finding *any* candidates at all."

I frowned. "You're saying that there's a TP shortage?"

Now he shrugged. "Some have been hired by the same outfit that took Mr. Carmichael, some haven't responded to my office's requests for contact and Alex can't seem to locate anyone else."

"That's...weird."

"It is."

"Someone should investigate that," I said thoughtfully and hopefully. "Someone should go to that mysterious employer and talk to those TPs with the cushy jobs." A mission, I thought excitedly. Yeah, I could do with a mission.

Samuel sighed. "Let Alex do a little more investigating before you go haring off into the unknown. Okay?"

I grumbled something under my breath.

"I'm sorry, what?" Samuel asked, all feigned innocence.

"You'd go, too, if you were staring down the barrel of the fifty or so parties and receptions we have to go to during the fucking Frost Festival," I said quietly.

He chuckled. "I probably would, but you aren't here for them, are you, Jane?"

Right then I saw Lucy hand in hand with Wilby and smiled in spite of the horrors of adult behavior in my future. "No," I said softly, "I'm not."

Samuel frowned again, though, as his gaze rested on Wilby. "He doesn't look right, does he?"

I stared at my friend, assessing. "He's given up his home in a hurry. I wouldn't expect him to be his normal self."

"Maybe that's it," Samuel said, though he didn't sound convinced. "I thought the divorce would cheer him up." He laughed, "Mine certainly did that for me."

"How is Mallory?" I asked.

His expression warmed, though I was sure he wasn't aware it did. "The same."

Odd answer. "And that's good, right?"

"Jane," he said with a contented sigh, "It's very, very good."

Charles and Idis joined us then and the conversation turned to other things, but I felt a little glow that lasted throughout the evening. Samuel was happy, really happy, and that was a great thing.

It was later that night and I waited in our bedroom at Robin Hill for Charles to finish undressing and be released by Mr. Beddoes. Wilby was on my mind. I had to admit that Samuel was probably right about my friend not being happy. This strange divorce-but-not-really-a-divorce from Quinn seemed to be taking its toll. I wanted to help, of course, but aside from being there when he needed me (and not the way I would have been in the good old days) I didn't think there was much I could do for him. I didn't like that at all.

Eventually Charles did appear, handsome in his pajama pants. He said nothing, merely giving me that smile that promised wicked and wonderful things. I took his hand and led him to bed.

Sometime later I lay on my lover's chest as he stroked my hair gently and he seemed to read my mind, which was something that occurred more and more often the longer we were together.

"I know you want to fix Wilby."

It's not as if I could deny it. "I don't like seeing him unhappy, Six."

"You don't like seeing anyone unhappy, my dear," he said as he kissed my forehead. "It's one of the many reasons I love you, but I'm a little concerned, too."

"Why? What's happened?"

"Nothing criminal or dangerous," he said reassuringly. "Just high bar tabs and concern that our friend may soon run out of tail to chase. In town, at any rate."

"Samuel thought the divorce would help him."

"I thought so, too, but the tie to Quinn is still torturing him," Charles said thoughtfully. I started to speak when my man unexpectedly continued. "I think you should ask Shira."

"Shira?"

"She's a very clever girl and she's been a witness to more than her parents realize." He sighed. "Kids always see more than their parents want them to anyway."

"Scary thought."

"Indeed." Charles ran his finger down my arm. "Alex told me to throw Marianna out years before she died. He was ten at the time."

I sat up, shocked. "He did?"

Charles nodded grimly. "He'd seen the other men. He'd heard how she'd talk about me. He knew it was wrong."

"You didn't do it, though."

"I didn't feel I could, in my position."

"What did you say?"

"I told him that she didn't mean it and that when you make a promise like that, you make it for life."

God, what they must have cost Charles to say. Defending that harpy. "No wonder he hasn't gotten married," I said without thinking. Oh crap. "Sorry, Charles."

"You're not wrong," he said sadly. "So talk to Shira. Perhaps she knows something that can help, even if it's something that ends it for once and all."

"I will," I promised. We said nothing and I left him to his thoughts, but snuggled closer, just letting him know that I was there and I never wanted to be anywhere else.

I think he understood.

12:30 – Swimming Pool, Imperial Palace, Irena, December 19th, 2881

I found Shira the next afternoon, thanks to Captain Stanley, swimming laps in the pool no one ever seemed to use. At almost eighteen Shira was a big, muscular girl, taking after her Judean parents, and swam both effortlessly and at great speed through the water. She reached the end of the long pool, turned in a beautiful, practiced motion under the water and rocketed under the surface in the opposite direction. And repeat. It was actually very calming to watch so I just stood there for a while, loath to disturb her.

After about twenty minutes of constant effort she finally headed for the side of the pool and easily hauled herself out. She saw me, nodded to herself as if she'd expected to see me standing there, then reached for a nearby towel.

"I know why my father is acting like a jealous asshole," Shira said.

And good morning to you, too, Shira.

"You do?"

She nodded as she dried off. "But you have to promise that, if you even want to know, what I tell you will stay between us."

Fucking great. There would have to be the promise, wouldn't there? I really did want to know what the hell was wrong with Wilby and Quinn, however. "Fine."

She looked relieved. "Ever since this nonsense started I'd been quietly surveilling Papa," Wilby, in case you were wondering, "to see if he was doing any of the shit Dad was accusing him of."

"You were a kid, Shira…" I protested. Come to think of it, you still are.

She shrugged, "This 'kid' is the child of a Judean Master Assassin and professional spy. Not that my techniques didn't improve the older I got."

"And you found?"

"Nothing, as I'm sure you'd suspected."

"Papa isn't a cheater."

"He isn't," Shira agreed, "but something was clearly wrong, so I turned my attention to Dad."

Logical. A bit creepy, but logical. "There was some sort of trauma, post traumatic something or other..?"

She shook her head, her long wet hair slapping against her shoulders. "It took some doing and a couple of favors called in by, ironically, some of Dad's cronies, but I think I know what happened." She paused for dramatic effect and I gestured for her to continue. "Papa and Dad were separated briefly, I mean, they were together," she clarified, "just not physically, when Papa took the Pacey fetuses ahead to Novy, right?"

"Right."

"The last night Dad was in Pacifica, Elysium actually, was also his wedding anniversary." I frowned. "From his first marriage. He was sad and tried to cure it by getting really fucking drunk."

Drunk and sad in Elysium was a bad combination. "Quinn wouldn't cheat on Wilby."

She sighed angrily. "He would have agreed with you, but, according to the super-secret Elysium records (and don't even ask what I had to do to get access to them), father hired an Empathic HM that night and slept with her." She blushed, looking really uncomfortable for the first time since this uncomfortable conversation had started.

"Why that kind of HM?" I asked, not sure I wanted to hear the answer.

"So he could make her look like mother. Like how he remembered her."

I wrinkled my nose in disgust. "Mother of god."

Shira wrapped the towel around herself and attempted to look blasé about the whole thing. "Apparently mimicking dead or unobtainable loved ones is more common than you'd think on Elysium. They call it ghosting…"

I couldn't stand any more. "Shira, please stop." Mercifully she did. "Wilby doesn't know?" She shook her head. "Quinn has no idea you've figured it out." She shook her head again.

"I think," she said slowly, "that Dad had always had to rely on himself, on his usually impeccable judgement. For his missions, for his personal safety, for right and wrong. Once this happened…"

"He knew he couldn't trust himself," I said, understanding.

"If he couldn't trust himself, how could he trust anyone else, even the man he loves?"

Well, crap. "So now what?"

"I'm waiting for Dad to confess to Papa."

"It's been at least a decade, Shira," I said, appalled. "He might lose Wilby permanently if he does."

"I know," she said sadly. "Losing Papa for good will break him. So I've said nothing because, even as shitty their arrangement is, at least Dad gets him sometimes, which is better than nothing."

I shook my head. "It's far from fair for Wilby," I chided, "you have to know that."

"I hate myself for it, Jane, I really do, but as much as I love my Papa, Dad is…my Dad."

On that I subject I had no argument, but the whole thing was just gross. Worse, I now had the information that might bring closure to my friend and couldn't use it. Fuck a duck. Speaking of my dear friend, Wilby…

13:00 – My Private Training Room, Imperial Palace

"Why are we here, Jane?" Wilby asked, his tone just shy of surly. We stood in the training room at Robin Hill, dressed to sweat, so to speak.

"I can't imagine," I said sarcastically as I stretched. "I mean, we're in training clothes in a training studio. My guess would be swimming."

"Corsicans don't swim," Wilby said absently, arms folded across his chest. Shira swims, I thought, Quinn's secret weighing heavily on me. I could feel Wilby's hangover from where I was and if I had to guess (which thankfully I did, even my senses weren't that good) I'd say he wore a slight odor of sex.

"So, how was she?" I asked, taking another guess.

He shrugged, hugging himself tighter.

"That good."

"She was willing and available. What more could you ask for?"

As unhappy as my friend clearly was, not much. It bothered me a lot, though. The one thing I had learned from Wilby, years ago, was how fun sex could be. This beautiful man was having sex, sure, but there was clearly no fun to be had with it.

"You know, Wilby, you could just let Quinn go," I started.

He turned on me, eyes bright with fury. It was such a fast, such an extreme change, that I took a step back. "Like you let the General go? Jesus, Jane, I thought you'd be the last person to judge me on this."

Fair point. Too fair. I sighed. "I've just never witnessed anyone suffering through it before. I'm sorry."

He blinked at me for a second, having trouble taking in my complete acceptance of his point. "It's all right." He rubbed his forehead as if trying to push out his headache. "It wasn't easy watching you do it."

I walked closer and put my hand gently on his arm. "Loving like that is awful, isn't it?"

He shuddered. "It really is." He patted my hand and I pulled away. "So why am I here?" he asked, but the annoyance was gone from his tone.

I grinned because even though I couldn't break my promise to Shira (the old Jane would have in a heartbeat, but not New Jane) I could do my best to help in other ways. "When I get low this is where Idis sends me."

"Is this your time out?" he said, his lips curling up slightly.

"Sort of," I said, amused. "She says nothing pulls me out of a funk like getting back in touch with my inner badass self."

"I'm no fighter, Jane," he protested half-heartedly, but I could see him stand a little straighter. Ah ha, I thought. Good going, Idis. "I haven't been for a long time."

I rolled my eyes, "Well, then I guess I'll have to cancel the assassins I'd ordered." Wilby snickered. "Come on, Wilby. You *were* a fighter once. You were a cocky asshole once." I meant it as a compliment.

"Those were the days," he muttered to himself. Then he laughed quietly and put his arm on my shoulders. "Back before all of you ruined me with *feelings*."

"My apologies," I said and I kind of meant it. I didn't think old Wilby would ever have let himself be so down. He would have plotted revenge, fucked someone he shouldn't but, by god, he would have *enjoyed* doing it.

"It's ok. I could never have been a good father without them, so it's all right, in the balance."

"It's a weird pull, isn't it?"

"What is?"

"The person you have to be to be a parent can be so different from the real you."

He nodded and kissed the top of my head. "It's all the 'real' you, Jane, and and you can't tell me you'd trade a hair on Lucy's head for your old life back, even if you got to keep Fitz."

My Lucy. "No," I said honestly, "I can't even think about that."

"Exactly," he said thoughtfully, "but I do see your point. At this time in my life I am a parent and a failed spouse. I'd forgotten I'd ever been anything else."

"You have twenty-six children, love. I don't see how you'd have time to remember to be anything else."

He shrugged.

"That's what made you divorce, isn't it? Not having time to be a husband and a father?" I asked carefully. I'd never come out and asked. Unlike me, I know. I guess I'd been afraid that some of it had been my fault so had avoided asking.

He stepped away from me, his green eyes snapping with anger. "There were many things, Jane. I used to be unstoppable. I wanted something, I figured out a way to get it. I taught and my students were the best. I went on impossible missions and we succeeded. Anyone I wanted to fuck, all I had to do was crook my finger and I got them. As many as I wanted whenever I wanted."

"I remember." Boy, did I and some of those memories were not appropriate to a woman very much in love with someone else, but I was human and he was *Wilby*.

His shoulders stooped slightly and I felt that power dampen. "Where is that man, Jane?"

Just the in I needed. "Let's find him." I grinned as he looked at me in surprise. "Come meet my favorite toy." I raised my voice. "ATR, power up and present!"

A full length cabinet at the far end of the room popped open and a seven-foot tall blue-skinned android fighter stepped out, walking quickly towards us and stopping about three feet from me. Like our other ATRs it was fully humanoid, both in appearance and down to the veins and arteries inside it. It stood waiting, breathing calmly. It was the most sophisticated Automated Training Remote available and had been a gift from my beloved Charles.

"Wilby meet," wince, "Bunny." Another wince. "Bunny Wabbit."

Wilby barked out a laugh. "I take it Lucy named him?"

"How did you know?"

"I have twenty-six children, Jane," he grinned, "and a feline named Mister Muffin-Pants."

I laughed. "Well, don't let the name fool you. Bunny," I inclined my head in the direction of our mechanical friend, "is no one to be trifled with."

Wilby's green eyes, however, were sparkling with the challenge. "Let's trifle with him a little, hey, Jane."

Thank goodness. "Let's."

Then, just like that, everything changed.

My comm chimed.

"Pace here," I answered and Wilby paused, watching me closely. I felt my eyes go wide. "Play the message from Officer Schulweis."

"Huong?" Wilby mouthed but I held up my finger for patience. He waited.

I listened and looked quickly at Wilby, then back straight ahead and I focused on my response. Oh it was bad. Or it would be really fucking soon. "Drexell," the on-duty comm officer to whom I was speaking, "contact all Macros within orbit or on-planet and tell them to suit up and meet Dr. Quinn-Pace and myself in Berria's orbit over Trexxa. Send coordinates with the orders. Alert the Home Navy of potential incoming fire to Berria and play Huong's message to Admiral Tracey, General Sona, the Countess of Boulton and, of course, the Emperor." I listened. "Yes, the Countess will know what to do if there are casualties. Tell Captain Stanley to get my DSS and a spare. Pace out."

"Jane, what the hell?" Wilby asked.

"Hold on, love," I said as I tapped my comm on again. "Get the the Emperor, Priority One, this is Commander-General Pace." Oh yes, I'd forgotten to mention that my marriage to Charles had brought with it one interesting duty that I'd had no problem with assuming: Commander-General of the Corsican Home Guard. Technically I was under the command of my husband (His Imperial Commander Supreme Majesterial Awesomeness or something) but he had all but handed everything over to me. The Corsican-born Generals and Admiral had been less than thrilled, but no one fucked with Charles. Or me, for that matter.

I straightened as the call was connected and I looked at my friend as I spoke. "Charles, Huong thinks there is going to be an attack on Berria. Trexxa to be specific." Wilby gasped as I nodded. "Wilby and I," I paused, finally getting around to tacitly asking whether he wanted to accompany me, thankfully Wilby nodded, "are going almost immediately." I listened again. "She didn't know." I smiled. "We'll be careful, Six," I said softly and disconnected.

The door to the room opened and the huge form of Captain Stanley loomed holding two DSS Suits. It was time to go.

11:02 – Corsican Space (In-System), Outside Irena

I went fast. Fast enough that I had taken the precaution of actually tying Wilby to my back so I wouldn't lose him. The air thinned as we left the surface of Irena, then was gone as we passed out of the atmosphere and into space itself. The moisture we'd picked up going through clouds immediately froze and cracked off our suits. Berria was the furthest out in the system's orbit around the Corsican sun and it was taking time to get there, even as fast as we were moving. We passed one planet, then another, and I could see the green world that was Berria grow in front of us. A green world but not a green and blue one, I thought. There was a tremendous supply of water on the planet but it was all underground. Underground rivers, lakes, even an ocean. I had seen these wonders in their cool crystal caves, sounds of water, both lapping and rushing, in the dim light of phosphorescent plants and animals on the cave walls. This was Idis' world; where she had grown up, where she had buried her son. I had to protect it, and not just for her sake.

Millions of Berrian Corsicans fed the Empire and beyond. They also sheltered the lost, the hurt and the disenfranchised. Trexxa was the largest refugee city in Corsica and, arguably, the Union itself. Former slaves, pacifist supernormals and even the odd dissident Tellescan called that city and that world home. They and their Corsican friends had built a new city in what had been unused (and not terribly arable) flatlands. Idis and I had approved every building, every home design ourselves. I knew Charles privately wished that the (he hoped) natural interbreeding with friendly Corsicans would improve the bloodlines but all of us had just wished these people would thrive in the shelter we were attempting to provide.

Some goddamned shelter, I thought grimly.

Then I felt it and looked up, though I saw nothing out of the ordinary.

'What is it?' Wilby asked over the comm.

'There is a massive ship coming into the system,' I said just as the system-wide comm blared into life in my ear.

'We have contact!' a heavy voice said excitedly. 'Hostile One just dropped out of hyper just outside the system limit. Weapons hot.'

Since I hadn't stopped speeding along I was already much closer than I had been and I could feel the ugly buzzing and crackling of SLPGs. God, I hated those abominations. Give me a good divertable torpedo any day. I'd divert the shit out of it.

I changed my trajectory, making straight for the enemy ship.

'Give the evacuation order for Trexxa,' I ordered, though I knew it would do very little good. SLPGs could be fired from space and cause a fucklot of damage on a planet, the distortion caused by the beams hitting the atmosphere diminishing their accuracy but not their potential devastation.

'Acknowledged, Commander-General,' the heavy voiced man said.

'Any Macros that can hear me, report in,' I said sharply. Help, I needed help.

We were passing over the continent that held Trexxa now and the frankly enormous ship was starting to come into view. With its giant SLPGs.

'Drop me here, Jane,' Wilby said. 'I can help on the ground.'

'You can help after, Wilby,' I said, distractedly. 'It's too dangerous right now.'

I felt his body stiffen on my back and I realized that I'd screwed up. 'Fuck you, Jane,' he said and then, without another word, Wilby pulled himself free of the rope and fired his jets, dropping like a stone (well, that's what it looked like) away from me and down towards the planet. I felt like an asshole but Macros were calling in by then and I needed to focus on the mission.

All in all there were only a half-dozen, four of them being part of the detail that protected the royal children, including my own. Well, better than nothing. Much better, since I had trained those four myself.

'Martinez and Nagra stay in the skies over Trexxa and watch for debris. Scout out a safe landing spot for the stuff you catch if you have time. Keep your eyes open,' I said.

'On our way, Ma'am,' the two responded and soon I felt two tiny shapes dive into the atmosphere.

'You other four, come to me,' I ordered.

'This is Admiral Tracey,' an exaggeratedly clipped voice said over the comm, 'I have two ships enroute and four more making for Berrian orbit.'

That was good, I thought, the Home Fleet had ten ships total so no planet would be unprotected. What a rookie mistake it would be to bring everything/one to Berria only to have some stupid sneak attack get the other worlds when our pants were down.

The other four Macros approached and then fanned out around me. I knew what my people could do, but it was the two unknowns I needed information from.

'Names?'

'Napia,' a female voice said. Napia? This Macro was a recovered slave?

'Blake,' a male voice answered.

'Thank you for volunteering,' I said perfunctorily. 'Now can either of you two,' I asked the strangers, "cut' metal?'

They both frowned. 'Like with our *minds*?' one of them said.

Ok. 'You two support Duarte,' who raised his hand, 'and Kosevich,' and then I turned to my people. 'Wait until Hostile One fires.' They nodded. 'If they do, carve that fucker up and gut it.'

'But if they fire..?' Stranger One said in dismay.

'Leave that to me,' was all I would say. Mother of God this was going to *suck*.

Then a familiar voice came on the general comm, 'Unidentified ship, this is the Emperor Charles.' I could hear the buried fury in my man's tone. It was a tone few people heard. Most people would only have guessed that he could sound so menacing and probably assumed he wasn't capable of being so scary. Those people were fucking morons. This was Corsican *soil*. He'd rip the heads off of anyone who seriously threatened his home.

I looked at my people. 'Go!' and they headed for the ship.

I put myself physically between it and Trexxa and waited, forming the biggest, thickest (keep your mind out of the gutter, please) shield I think I had ever made. I wished Garrett was with me. The man had a positive gift for shielding. I looked at the ship, felt the SLPGs buzzing and realized that I (yes, even I) was overmatched.

'Martinez, Nagra, Napia and Blake, to me!' I shouted into my comm. "We need to shield the planet!"

They came, the two volunteers faster than even I had hoped for.

Charles had been talking and I'd tuned him out but once my people were with me I listened again. We floated in space, shields working together like a large invisible wall between the planet and the coming beam of death.

Just breathe, Jane.

Charles spoke, 'You have intruded upon Corsican Sovereign Space. Power down and state your business. In that order.'

No response. Well, no verbal response.

'Here it comes,' I said.

Hostile One fired.

Correction: Hostile One fired *everything*.

Six SLPG beams slammed into our shield at once.

So bright. So hot. And it *burned*. My eyesight went black as I screamed in agony. I heard the screams of my people but they seemed far off somehow. I held out my hands in front of me, warding off the blasts and I felt the DSS peel back in the onslaught of impossible heat. Part of the shield failed. I knew what that meant, but had to concentrate on my part. My hands burned, but I didn't feel it; the pain was drowned out in the greater assault of light and heat. I could somehow feel the DSS heal itself over my flesh only to get burned off again, then heal again. It was too much. It just was.

We couldn't take it head on, I realized. Not and have anyone survive.

'Angle the shield!' I said too loudly, or not loudly enough. Sensory overload made it too hard to tell. 'Napia, tilt towards the planet, Nagra lift towards space.'

So I 'tipped' my shield, the other Macros tipping theirs almost seamlessly with me, aiming the blasts at what I hoped was the wasteland beyond Trexxa. The pain became slightly less since we were diverting the beams (hey, I got to divert something!) instead of trying to outright stop them, but it was still overwhelming. I felt the pull of darkness. I fought it.

The beam pointing (seemingly) directly at me stopped. I sighed in relief and started to move to help the others when the oddest thing happened…another beam diverted from its original position to take over in mine. Thank god I hadn't actually *dropped* my shield or I would have been vaporized.

Then it happened again. The beam flickered out over me, but I stayed right where I was, waiting and another beam moved to blast me and be diverted.

What specific thing was so damned important below me that an SLPG had to constantly attack it?

Another shield phased out. Then another beam stopped. Later I was told that the Navy had sheared off Hostile One's engines at that point. Then they cut it in half, spilling most of its crew into space as they did so. Most of the crew but not all because even though another SLPG went dark there were still two left.

The fifth beam cut out. There was only one left, mine. Always mine. Lucky fucking me.

I was tiring, however, my hands still burned like fire and I felt myself fading even as the others were coming to bolster my shield.

That one last beam suddenly doubled its intensity (this motherfucker had been on *half power??*) and it was all I could do to concentrate, the pain was so intense. My DSS was losing the power to regenerate to protect me and the scalding burns were traveling up my arms. Tears streamed down my face as I tried to stay strong...but it was just too much, for my DSS and for me.

I screamed my pain and frustration as I felt my shield wink out. I felt myself 'yanked' out of the way of the blast and, unable to handle the overwhelming agony any longer, I lost consciousness.

17:49 – Tent Five, Mobile Infirmary, Trexxa, Berria

I woke about five hours later to two very dear faces peering at me (hey, I could see!) anxiously. Idis and Wilby hovered over me. Their faces were covered with grime, Wilby's with blood, and they looked terrified. I realized I was on a planet, Berria, judging by the feel of it. I was alive, too, which was a relief. I moved my hands and found I couldn't. My hands and arms were covered with thick, soft bandages and were tied to the cot I occupied. I looked past the faces of my friends to see I was in a tent. I tried to bend a finger on my right hand.

"Ow." I needed information, however, more than I needed to hurt so I pushed through. "What happened?" I asked almost breathlessly. "Did we do it?" I knew we hadn't, though, not completely. I had failed at the last second. I could only hope that final beam hadn't done too much damage.

Idis hesitated, as did Wilby. That wasn't good. "Your team," Idis started, "did better than anyone could have hoped for."

Ok, but that still didn't sound like complete success. "Casualties?"

"Some," Wilby said, speaking finally, "but there would have been many, many more had not the Macros stepped in."

"Who?" I had to know and I bet that at least one of 'my' people had been injured or lost. My stomach clenched in anticipation of the tally.

"Miss Napia and Lieutenant Martinez were burned over most of their bodies," Wilby said grimly. "Alice Napia died of the burns. Martinez will make it, I think, though the first two hours were touch and go." He ran his hand through his dark hair. "Thankfully there have been breakthroughs in treatments for burned skin. He should look about normal within a year or so of treatment. If he survives." He exhaled. "Your other Macros, Mr. Blake, Captain Nagra and yourself, have only superficial burns. Lieutenants Duarte and Kosevich got a little banged up diverting debris, but should be fine." I looked down at my bandaged hands. Wilby nodded, "A couple of days in those and there should be only minimal scarring." For me, anyway, I thought guiltily.

It had all depended on the strength of the shields the Macros could produce. Ideally, I shouldn't have sent anyone in untested, but what were we to do? There just hadn't been any time. Those volunteer Macros, especially Alice Napia, deserved a pile of medals for what they'd done. I was sure Charles (or, most likely, Idis) had already thought of that, but if they hadn't, I would have to say something. I wanted to weep for Miss Napia. To escape slavery to die here..? I couldn't think about that right now, but I knew I would at length later.

"What about the civilians?" I asked, dread increasing.

Wilby looked at Idis who answered, "One of the SLPG beams got through. Four hundred thirty-six refugees died." She'd made it sound as though it had been no one's fault that lone beam had made it to the planet. If only that were true.

I felt my gorge rise. "Mother of god." I tried to sit up, but Wilby put his hands firmly on my shoulders and pushed me back down. I felt stupid tears welling up. "I tried so hard to keep going, but they strengthened the beam and I…I failed." Damn it, I couldn't even wipe the tears away. "It's my fault."

"Jane," Idis started sympathetically, but Wilby had no time for my self-pity.

"If anything is your fault, Jane, it's that thousands of people *didn't* die," Wilby said firmly. Then his voice and expression softened, "We do what we can do, Jane."

"It wasn't enough," I said softly.

He shook his head. "Sometimes, love, it just isn't, but we go on anyway, don't we?"

We did, of course. What choice did we have? Then, out of nowhere came a panicked and even more guilt-stricken thought, "Does Lucy know I'm all right?" Funny how my worries had always been for her safety. It

402

occurred to me now that I had another worry that I hadn't counted on: her peace of mind. What on Irena was I supposed to do about *that*?

Idis' voice became soothing. "She knows, though she was able to 'read' how worried and upset the adults around her were." Great, I thought. We would have to have a TP for a daughter.

"She's with Shira at the Palace," Wilby added. "She has adapted quite well, all things considered."

Quite well to having a mother who charges in no matter what the danger, I thought. I sighed internally. I took a second to think about changing, about putting my abilities and desire to rush in to help aside, but discarded it almost immediately. Not to be selfish, no. To be realistic. Oh, I thought, I'm a genius at self-justification. Blech. Plus, she had two mothers so she could afford to lose one, right? I thought sarcastically. I'm a good spare. I was glad there were no TPs around me right at that moment. Then I had the inkling of a thought, but it wasn't ready to emerge so I moved on, back to the issues at hand. "Damages to the Navy?" I asked.

"The Navy was untouched," a strong female voice said.

I looked over to see Admiral Tracey who had clearly just entered the tent. I hadn't sensed her coming, but I was just a bit out of it. I 'reached' out to sense and felt that Charles was a few steps behind her. My heart soared. *Charles.*

"Congratulations, Admiral," I said.

She snorted. "While I am glad we emerged unscathed, it wasn't due to any skill of ours. They ignored us, even when we carved up their ship and ejected their people into open space. It was as if we were invisible, irrelevant."

Charles ducked into the tent just then, looking pale and even more stooped than usual. He was tense and on the verge of adrenaline burnout. Poor Six. He hesitated once he got close to the bed, taking in my bandages with his gold eyes.

I smiled at him, trying to reassure. "I'm Ok," I said softly.

Charles swallowed hard and nodded, then seemed to come to a decision and planted himself next to me on the cot. I shifted over a bit so that we were shoulder to shoulder, pressing reassuringly against each other. I immediately felt better and I felt some of the tension leave his body.

Out the tent flap I could see corpsmen carrying stretchers with bodies. Many bodies, some corpsmen coming back over and over.

It was then the niggling thought resurfaced. Those SLPG beams always directed to the same place, no matter what, as if that spot on Berria had been the only spot that... "Where were the refugees we lost from, Idis?"

Idis produced, as if by magic, a clipboard and started scanning with a frown that deepened the more she read. "Tellesco, two from Judea," Wilby stiffened but said nothing, "Pace-Pallon, Esperanza, Cyrillic, Napia, even several from systems within Thao." Her frown deepened. "A lot from Thao, even from Levvon." She looked over at me. "Why?"

"I don't know, Idis," I said thoughtfully. "Something." I bit my lip. Just then a man entered the tent. I got the impression of smallness about him, though he was actually quite tall. I ignored him and asked, "How many were listed as supers?" The new man stiffened. I ignored that, too. One condition of refugee-hood on Berria was that you had to disclose. If you lied you were out. We didn't care what you were, we just wanted to *know* what you were. We'd never exploited the knowledge, but perhaps there were other people who had wanted to.

She shook her head, following at least part of my train of thought, "A low percentage...I would guess only about ten or so percent."

"Oh."

The stranger must have caught Idis' eye as I felt (but did not see) a tiny frown of irritation cross her lovely brow. "Sire," this was to Charles, obviously, "may I introduce His Honor, Mayor Bretschneider of Trexxa?"

Charles did not rise but the Mayor bowed deeply in front of his Emperor.

"Your Imperial Highness," the man said pompously, his accent cartoonishly clipped.

"A difficult day, Bretschneider," Charles said. "How are your people holding up?"

"As well as can be expected, Sir," the Mayor said with the attitude of the heroically suffering.

"Do you have all you need to rebuild?"

"The Countess," Bretschneider bowed officiously in Idis' direction, "has promised to provide materials and men, Sir, and we are grateful. Though," he said a little ruefully, "the area that was bombed was mostly only used by the people that lived there."

"The people that died in the attack," Wilby confirmed, "or the majority of them."

Bretschneider nodded.

Something, however, about that didn't sit well with me. "They were isolated? Was the terrain difficult?" I tried to call up a map in my head but all I could remember were miles and miles of flat plains. The land might have been bad (soil-wise) for farming, but none of it should have been hard to get to.

Now the Mayor looked frankly uncomfortable. "They were self-isolated, Ma'am."

My hackles went up and I felt everyone else in the room tense.

"For what reason, Your Honor?" I asked with an edge on my voice.

He paled slightly. "The supernormals in that area were a colony of Telepaths, Ma'am. From all different worlds." He hesitated. "They were...undisciplined about their abilities and the normals were afraid of them." He looked pleadingly at his Emperor, all pomposity gone. "We tried to make it work, Sir, but there were small acts of violence against both groups and I," and I was momentarily proud of him for taking responsibility for the choice, "had no intention of kicking them out. This was the only way I could think of to make it safe for all involved."

Much as I'd had antipathy for TPs at one time or another I had, for the most part, only known ones with discipline and a strong sense of duty and respect for personal privacy. Bad TPs could cause a hell of a lot of trouble. For the first time I had sympathy for the Mayor, but I also had the feeling that his clustering of them together had made them much easier to kill— though he certainly could not have anticipated that that would happen. None of us could have.

The Mayor wasn't done, however. "I visited their colony about every two weeks on my rounds as I felt duty-bound to do, but it was...unnerving." He looked at me, eyes wide. "They didn't speak. Not one word. They communicated, but never out loud."

Creepy. No wonder no one liked them. It didn't mean they'd deserved to die, of course, but still...

Then I started really thinking. TPs were viewed with wariness, even by other supers. Perhaps someone had a grudge against TPs and had used this attack as a cover to get rid of them. *Then* I had another thought, one that was a lot scarier.

"TPs," I said and then paused.

"You think this was all a smokescreen to take out the TPs?" Charles asked quietly.

"Were those the only ones in that colony?" I asked Bretschneider.

"Yes, Ma'am."

"Jane?" Idis asked, but I was thinking.

They waited, Charles resting his hand on my arm comfortingly but not interfering.

I turned to my spouse. "Whitman is dead, but he wasn't a Telepath." Then something came to me. "So is Mirta Pace-Torva, who definitely was." Charles' golden eyes went wide. "Maybe she was the target, Charles. Not Whit at all. He was just…"

"In the way?" Charles supplied unhappily.

I nodded. "Brady Carmichael has disappeared. Someone is hiring TPs like they are going out of style and Samuel can't find me any to instruct my TP kids at school." I really hoped Brady was still alive.

"Someone is systematically *murdering* TPs?" Wilby asked while Charles stayed silent, clearly thinking.

Admiral Tracey was nodding. "That odd firing pattern?"

"You noticed that, too?" I said.

She favored me with a look that made me feel about two inches tall. "I did." Of course she did, Jane. She's a fucking Admiral of a fucking space Fleet. She looked at Charles. "That area was targeted, no question. Had our people not stopped the other beams, however, it would never have been so easy to spot."

"So the mission to wipe out Trexxa was a cover for killing 40 or so Telepaths?" Admiral Tracey said as if not quite believing it.

I shrugged. "Had we not stepped in the whole town would have been gone and we never would have known it was the TPs they were after," I stopped, "if I am right."

I was, though. I knew I was. Then I looked at Idis and Charles and I knew we were all thinking, Lucy. Lucy was a TP. Only a very select few knew it and Corsicans never gave up secrets, but still…

"We need to talk to Sam," Charles said at last.

"I thought he'd gone back to Terra," I said.

Admiral Tracey snorted. "He'd taken an extra day to inspect our ships. For fun, he'd said." I smiled at that. Yes, that would have been fun for him. He'd designed them, after all. "Spent the whole attack over my shoulder, trying not to say anything." Must have been hard for him, I snickered internally.

Charles switched on his comm. "Ask the High Admiral to meet my team in my office in an hour." He switched off his comm and smiled at me. "That will give you just enough time to say hello to Lucy and the boys."

I nodded in relief and we got to it.

20:00 – Private Office of the Emperor, Imperial Palace

"So they fucked up," I stated with my usual subtlety.

Charles nodded seriously, as did Samuel. Idis merely contented herself with rolling her eyes. Admiral Tracey was probably horrified, being Corsican, but, being Corsican, she kept her reaction to herself.

"Indeed," Charles replied. "Whoever this was," and we had no idea who since Hostile One had been carved in tiny pieces and all its skeleton crew killed in what appeared to have been a suicide mission from the get-go, "got lucky, or unlucky as it turns out. It appears that the whole city was supposed to be destroyed so that the death of the small colony of TPs wouldn't attract attention within the larger carnage."

Admiral Tracey nodded, "Some anti-refugee nutcase causing trouble."

"Right."

"But who are 'they'?" I asked. All eyes turned to Samuel who, as High Admiral, should have been the recipient of the best intel in the Union.

Samuel grimaced. "I'm not sure." At our disappointed looks he continued, "I do, however, have a guess."

"Not the Deneth," Idis said, ticking the potentials off on her fingers, "or Tarine, thanks to Eriss, and not the Heelies. Judeans look after themselves but only defensively, Thao has been quiet forever thanks to fear of Prince Pilar, the Tellescans, Terrans, Esperanzans, and Cyrillics have no motive, at least as a people, though there is no accounting for the crazy of individuals," unfortunately that was all too true, "and the Vegans were wiped out by their own hand years ago." She looked at Samuel. "Someone new? Perhaps one of the other mercenary fleets? Limiting the number of TPs so that they are the only ones that have them?"

That wasn't a bad theory, I thought, but I didn't think it was the case. Apparently Samuel didn't think so either.

"There was a name that came to my attention when Napia and Torva were liberated. A custom slave buyer that took horrendous losses when their slaves were freed." He looked intently at me, one of the principal liberators. Yes, I remembered this name. "Cero."

"Cero," Admiral Tracey repeated. "Is that the name of a person or a people or..?"

Samuel shook his head. "Unknown."

"What kinds of slaves were they making?" Charles asked. I looked at him in surprise. It had never occurred to me to ask that. A freed slave was a freed slave to me.

"Not supers, it seems," was Samuel's answer.

"No TPs?" I confirmed. He nodded. "So what was 'custom' about his slaves? There has to be something special about them."

Samuel sighed, putting his hands on his hips. "Because being a supernormal is the only way to be special?"

"That's not what I meant." Of course that had been what I'd meant and an unfooled Samuel's response was a raised eyebrow. I racked my brain. "Improved speed, agility, vision, hearing, focus, strength, bone density, regenerative abilities…" I glared at him, "there are many options."

"Susceptibility to mind control," Charles offered thoughtfully. "Brain washing?"

I was thinking about that when Idis said, "What sort of secret is being kept that merits the murders of all the mind readers?"

"Unfortunately, we have no idea," Samuel said. "Prince Pilar is sending Huong to Terra to assist in the information gathering that might give us a clue. General Quinn-Pace will be joining us as well."

It was a good thing Wilby was going to be on Irena, I thought, but Samuel was right to ask them both since they were the best spooks in the Union.

"We need to let Stuart know he's in danger," I said quickly. "God help them if any of their brood turns out to be a TP, too." Pilar, Stuart and Ronnie were up to nine children now, via the discrete use of the 'tubs' for the most recent seven. Pilar had had enough of being pregnant after Persephone Jane. I honestly thought they kept having kids because it made Ronnie happy and it really, really did.

"Aside from a name that may or may not be useful, Sam," Charles said, "is there anything we *do* know?"

"Perhaps," Samuel said cagily as he inclined his head in Admiral Tracey's direction. "Admiral?"

The Admiral put her hands behind her back, unconsciously, I was sure, to give her small report. "We were able to scan the ship before the Commander-General's people started taking it apart, at the High Admiral's suggestion." The tension around her eyes told me there had been no 'suggesting' about it and I almost laughed. Almost. "It was a junker, barely space-worthy, so a good candidate for a kamikaze mission. Stolen from the Boneyard at Thao six months ago."

The Boneyard? Where the *Scylla*, our old Pace-Pallon refugee ship, rotted?

She continued, "It had only enough fuel for a one-way trip."

"From the Boneyard straight to Berria?" I asked dubiously.

Tracey shrugged, "From somewhere in Thao to Berria, yes."

I shivered. "Huong has some ideas?" I found myself clinging to her excellent reputation. Thao was her backyard, after all, especially since she ran all the spooks out of Gloriana-Levvon.

"A few," was all Samuel would commit to. "I'm afraid this will make for a security nightmare for you all," Samuel said, looking at Idis, Charles and myself.

"How so?" Idis asked.

"As of right now, to my knowledge, the highest concentration of Telepaths of all kinds is in two places."

"*Schola-Terra*," I said, fear in my gut. "And..."

"Irena," Charles finished, going pale. The kids. Ours (including Prince Simian) and Wilby's. Mother of God.

I looked at Samuel and I knew my face was full of fear. He was one of the few non-Corsicans who knew about Lucy. His expression softened in a way that made my lover tense. "We'll do our best to figure out what is going on and stop it before more lives are lost. I promise."

I nodded. I knew he would do everything in his power to protect the TPs that were left. I would do everything in mine to do the same.

The meeting over since we'd canvassed all the meager information we had, we started filing out of Charles' office when Samuel gestured me over to a near corner.

"Huong said something that you should know about, Jane."

I could see my lover over my ex-lover's shoulder. Charles was as close to jealous as I'd ever seen him, his body tense, his freckled face slightly flushed. I needed to make this short for his sake. "What about?" I asked hurriedly.

"She thinks something is up with Abrams."

"David?" I said with surprise and snorted inelegantly. "Something is always up with David."

"True, but she thinks you need to go see him, sooner rather than later."

"Really?" the idea was repellent at best. "Some plot? Or he's this Cero?" That seemed preposterous. While David had never valued human life all that much, I would never have believed he was an outright murderer.

"I don't know. She was being vague, I think deliberately so." That wasn't good either. Had she been told to make me come to Novy? Bribed? Coerced? Or was she just curious herself. There was, I had to allow, no one curiouser that David Abrams. "I think we can't rule out Abrams as Cero, not completely, though it doesn't seem his style."

"Except," I said grimly, "for the feeling I get that this is a plan within a plan. *That* couldn't be more David, but outright murder..?"

"I agree, but it needs to be investigated either way and, for better or worse, Jane, you are the best person to do it and, if necessary, stop him if he is behind this."

I thought for a minute and, even though I didn't want to get anywhere near David and his controlling shit-headedness, nodded. I needed just a bit of backup, though. Someone who had been able to influence David far more than even I had ever been able to. "I'll ask Thal to meet me there." I sighed. "A cooler head than either of ours."

"Yes," Samuel said, "thanks, Jane."

I wasn't sure a 'you're welcome' was appropriate (or necessary) so I just patted him on the shoulder and he left. I turned around to face Charles and found the two of us alone. He seemed upset, though I couldn't think of a logical reason why. Not that one needed logic to be upset.

I played it light, "Ready for the update?" I smiled.

I felt some of the tension ease in his broad shoulders.

"Please, Red," he said.

So I gave him the run down and he agreed with Samuel (and me) that a trip to Novy would be annoying as shit but probably necessary, though all of us were pretty sure we'd just be ruling David out as a Cero suspect.

"So you'll meet Thal there?" he asked, stepping closer...and closer to me.

"Assuming he'll agree to it, but I think he will. It is his son after all," I said as I backed up with each of his steps and tried not to grin.

"You'll take the *Liberty?*" He continued to advance, his golden eyes twinkling even as they turned black.

"I thought I would," I said, attempting to play it cool as my back pressed against the wall.

He pressed against *me*. "Just you and the ship all that way?"

Plus Captain Maass and a team of Corsican security. "Uh huh."

"Do you have room for me?" Charles leered at me as he started to move his hands over my body.

"Charles," I giggled, "You can't ask me that sort of thing when your hands are...where they are." Not and have me not laugh. Did I have room for him? I mean, honestly.

He smiled and kissed my neck. "So?" Charles wanted to come with me to Novy? Well, I thought, that could either be the best idea or the worst, though Charles seemed immune to David's what-the-fuckery, so why not? Aside from the fact that any time I got to spend with him was precious.

"Please come, Six," I said as my rather awkwardly bandaged hands moved lower on *his* body. Unlike me, though, the silly double entendre didn't make him laugh at all.

I 'reached' over and flicked on the lock to the office door just as Charles lifted me off the ground and kissed me.

13:00 – *H.M.S. Lumina*, Novy Orbit, December 30th, 1881

We had taken the *Liberty*, sort of. We had left Irena right away, sort of, too. Thal had agreed to meet us at Abramstown on Novy, but couldn't immediately get away from 'Luca and Charles had had commitments for the Frost Festival that couldn't be avoided, even when one was an Emperor. Or, to be precise, when one was an Emperor with a young child at home. Lucy was at a wonderful age, full of awe and still free of the attitude that Charles had warned me was coming in a year or three. So we'd delayed a week, put the *Liberty* within the *Lumina* and, since my bandages had been removed right before we'd left, enjoyed the hell out of our private time (the only person we'd seen was Beddoes the entire four day journey) in transit. Thank goodness we had Beddoes, however.

About five years before I'd, in a burst of...something, had, on a trip home from Terra, requested that Mr. Beddoes stay on the *Lumina* and leave Charles and myself completely alone on the *Liberty*. That experiment had lasted about two days—and about a day and a half longer than it should have. Turns out my beloved Six was a complete slob without Beddoes. Things, clothes, glasses, books, anything, just stayed where it they were dropped. Though I knew full well that Charles had an excellent mind (obviously) and was extremely conscientious and organized about his work, at 'home' he kept track of nothing and misplaced everything. Within about six hours my cabin had looked like some sort of tornado/flood had occurred. I'd been stubborn about calling for help and Charles had been game to try to clean up after himself, but it seemed stupid to force it when it was unnecessary.

We'd told Idis about it when we'd arrived on Irena and she'd been appalled by the very thought of Charles managing his household without professional assistance. Not, she'd said, because it was 'beneath him' or anything, but because ten years before Mr. Beddoes had caught a twenty-four hour Ran-Dar Virus that had sent him to the Infirmary. Mr. Beddoes had been fine after a day (though pretty damned miserable during) but there had been some kind of plumbing accident/misadventure in the Imperial bathroom (caused by Charles trying to fix something) that had rendered the room unsanitary for weeks afterward. Neither Idis nor I had tried to separate Charles from Mr. Beddoes ever again. Mr. Beddoes had been too well bred and professional to gloat, but I knew he was very smug on the inside. What can I say? He'd had every right to be.

Charles and I peered out the viewscreen of the *Lumina* at the beautiful mostly dark blue Novy Heliot. I imagined tens of thousands of free Heelies streaking through the converted oceans, cool and free the way they never could be on a station or ship. Even that spectacular tube of Heely water in the heart of the *Indus Felae* couldn't compare to an ocean. I opened my mouth to ask Charles if he wanted me to arrange Tania to give us a tour of an underwater city (there were easily a dozen within the main ocean), but then I remembered that Tania was still pissed at me. Perhaps Ambassador Synon was on-planet and I could ask him..?

"On behalf of Ambassador Fitzroy this is the *H.M.S. Lumina* requesting clearance to land at Abramstown Primary Field, Novy Control. Please respond," the *Lumina's* comm officer said through the open frequency.

"This is Novy Control, *Lumina*, you have been cleared to land on area Gamma. Mr. Abrams asks that His Imperial Highness, the Emperor, bring only a minimal security detail."

Oh, that fucker.

Thankfully our comm officer was no idiot, "Ambassador Fitzroy and Vice-Admiral Pace are our passengers, Novy Control, here to see Mr. Abrams. His Imperial Highness is not aboard."

"Acknowledged, *Lumina*. Land at will."

I rolled my eyes at Charles who sighed. David was still David, at least. Was that comforting? It was a little odd, however, that his people had evinced no surprise at our arrival. Perhaps we had been sent for after all. Or maybe he'd just been tracking us. Neither of those options would have surprised me.

"Sir?" a voice prompted from our ship-wide comm.

"Land us, Captain, if you would," was Charles' unruffled response. "Have Captain Stanley bring the minimal security complement."

"Yes, Sir."

"Not that I need them," Charles whispered to me, "I hear my wife is a real badass."

Soon we debarked (security fanning out around us) from the ship to find Thal waiting outside the main entrance to David's compound, his mobile plastic face the picture of worry.

"Thal," I said quietly by way of greeting.

"Jane," he said, trying a smile that failed, "Sir." He bowed to Charles. Thal had stopped calling me 'Miss Jane' after Idis had won him his freedom. Usually hearing him call me by just my name made me happy, but there was no room for that today.

"Mr. Thal," Charles said as quietly as I had. I felt uneasy, as, apparently, did the rest of us.

"When did you get here?" I asked gently.

"Yesterday."

I looked around me and noticed the heavy indentations in the grass below Thal's (currently) two feet. "You've been standing here the whole time?"

Thalberg shrugged. "Couldn't summon the courage to go in alone, even if he'd agreed to see me. He's still so angry with me for siding with you over the pregnancy."

"God, Thal, I'm sorry."

"It's Ok, Jane." He looked at the main door just as it slid open. "He's ready for us now."

I swallowed hard as Charles took my hand and we went in.

Hallways and hallways and levels and levels down. A bunker was David's home, apparently. I wondered if the levels that the Pacey children had occupied had been this oppressive. I'd never visited, of course, not wanting to be anywhere near David. I felt like a jerk for that right now, but it had been a relief to be away at the time.

A few minutes later the three of us (and our security) were ushered into a well-appointed bedroom that had been stuffed full of medical equipment. It was fairly dark in the room and I felt David moving around just out of actual sight. I noticed that as cluttered as the room was, there were what appeared to be well-worn paths through it. David was moving, even off in the dark corner.

I scanned him and froze. He was...wrong. His blood was sludge, his heart labored to beat and everything about the way he moved screamed of physical pain. Oh, David. The Black Blood.

"I'd appreciate it if you would leave your goons outside, Ambassador," David said. "I'm no danger to anyone, I promise."

Charles thought for a second and inclined his head towards the door. Captain Stanley and his people left efficiently.

David started moving slowly towards us, talking as he came. He sounded tired, so tired. "I'm not Cero."

He stepped into the dim light and I couldn't hide my gasp.

All his handsomeness was gone, obliterated by the thick lines of black on his skin, his muscles wasted away and his confident sexy walk was apparently long gone. The gray eyes were still very much David, but that whip-sharp intelligence was now haunted by pain and, I thought, fear.

"But you didn't actually think I was Cero, did you, Angel?"

"No," I said, still in shock, then realized I didn't know what to say next. Ask him how he was doing? Ugh. Oh, right. I did have a question. "What did you do to Huong to get us here?"

He smiled and it was a ghastly thing. "You figured that out, did you?" He turned right into one of his paths through the equipment. "It hurts to move, but it hurts more to stop," he explained. "Don't worry. I promised her what every spook can't resist to get you here."

"Information," Charles said.

"You're awfully clever for an Emperor," David said snidely as he carefully turned down another path. "I told her that I would tell Jane what I knew about Cero if she could get her here."

"What do you know?" I asked sharply. Finally, a lead.

David paused, then grimaced and started walking again. He moved like everything hurt. "I had a plan, you know," he said, looking directly at me. "All I needed was seven months."

"Seven months?" Charles said warily. "What happens in seven months?"

David laughed coldly. "Nothing now, not for me, anyway, but my kids will be eighteen in seven months."

That was too much. "Your kids will be *ten* in seven months, David," I corrected angrily.

His mind had jumped somewhere else again. "I've only had two things, two problems I couldn't solve in my life." He looked at us defensively. "How many people can say that? That only two things were unsolvable?"

"Not many," Charles allowed.

"David," Thalberg said for the first time, but David ignored him.

"What problems, David?" I asked, though I was pretty sure I knew.

"You," he said to me with as much anger as he could muster, "and this." He held out his emaciated and blackened arm. He straightened painfully. "One will beat me, but I'll get my victory with the other. After a fashion."

"What are you talking about?" Charles asked sharply.

"What 'victory'?" I said with equal sharpness. His demented plan to get me back when the 'time was right'? He was bringing that up *now?*

"I needed seven months," he said to himself, "and I'll miss it by five."

"*David,*" Thal barked, but David looked at me, still angry.

"You know what that means. You can sense it even better than I can, Angel."

I could, but I felt the breath knocked out of me anyway.

David slowly moved towards me and I backed up, but ran into some pile of something. "I'll be dead by February, love." I put up a shield to stop him from getting closer, but he'd already stopped advancing. "It's what you've always wished for, hey, Angel?"

Well, yeah, but not really.

"Not like this."

His once handsome face clouded. "No," he said in a defeated voice, "not like this."

"I'm sorry, David," I said because how could I not be?

"Tell her, David," Thalberg ordered. Tell me what?

Now finally, finally, David turned to Thalberg, furious, his body shaking with his rage. "*You* should have stayed away, Thal. Or are you here to betray me yet again?"

Thalberg stiffened but was unfazed. "You want me to tell you you're right even when we both know you're wrong?"

"Yes!" David practically shouted. "You should be on my side, *mine*, no matter what."

Thalberg's look became pitying. "I am always on your side, boy, but on the side of your better self. Keeping things from Jane then and now is wrong and you know it."

David shook his head stubbornly. "It's the only way."

What the fuck was he keeping from me this time? I shuddered to think.

Thalberg sighed. "I can't argue with your logic, son."

He couldn't?

Thalberg continued. "If getting your way is all that matters no matter how it affects the people you say you care about, then, yes, keeping secrets is the only way."

Oh.

"You don't understand," David said petulantly.

"I understand just fine, but I still think you're wrong."

"Why are you here, Thal?"

"Because I wanted to be with my son at the end."

David stared at him a second, then, suddenly overcome, he buried his face in his hands with a sob. "Dad," he whispered.

Thalberg walked over to him and put his hand on David's shoulder. David seemed to crumple against him as the construct held him up.

"Now tell the nice people what they need to know, ask Jane your question, and then send them on their way. All right?"

David nodded, all the fight gone out of him. He took a breath then wiped his face on his shirt. I could see his torso when he lifted the shirt up and it was solid black. The Black Blood must have invaded the capillaries, too, I thought. I had to pity him even though I knew he was holding something over me. Something Thalberg knew but would never tell.

"Cero came to see me about six months ago," David said, his voice still clogged by tears. He cleared his throat. "It's a non-gender humanoid alien. It wouldn't give me its planet of origin, or the name of its people," he said, cutting off my question before I could voice it. "It said that it wanted my help, my science, to help wipe out all the supernormals."

"Mother of god," I gasped. "Why?"

"For the good of the galaxy, it said."

And what in the name of fuck did *that* mean? Was this simple racism, just on a vaster scale than even the Vegans had attempted? I felt sick, even more so because Cero was such an unknown that I didn't know for sure it couldn't actually succeed in wiping us out. *Lucy.*

"Genocide?" Charles asked, his face pale with fury, probably thinking along the same lines.

"That's what it wanted, though it didn't seem happy about it."

"God forbid you should feel uneasy about murdering tens of thousands of people," I said bitterly. "What will it gain when only normals are left? Does it want to rule them? Control them?"

"It wasn't clear, but I got the impression it was a supernormal itself."

I just blinked at David as I took that in. "It wants to kill all its *own people?*"

"As I said, I don't think it *wants* to kill anyone. I got the impression that it feels it *must.*"

Charles thought for a second, frowning, then looked at me. "That sounds like the actions of a zealot or…even a pre-cog to me."

I needed to sit down. I looked around and found a chair that was almost free of junk. I cleared it and sat hard. "But a pre-cog is…"

"…never wrong," Charles finished in a near whisper. "Assuming," he added, "that he, she or it is telling what they've actually seen."

This was suddenly too damned scary. I needed a lifeline. "We don't know for sure he's a pre-cog, or even a super."

"True," Charles said with some relief. "Did you get anything else, Abrams?"

David grimaced. "In retrospect I think it might have told me more if I hadn't looked so horrified by the concept." He shrugged. "Now I wish I had played it cool, but it was, as you can imagine, a shock."

"Indeed," Charles said.

"I think it wanted to use me and thought it could play on my breakup with the Red Angel to get me to agree." David clenched his teeth. "More fool he, or it."

No, I thought, given David's obsession, that would have been the exact wrong way for Cero to proceed.

"I told it to go fuck itself," his eyes lit for a second, "and it left."

We lingered in silence for a minute, each trying to make sense of this.

"The only bit of information I *was* able to gather was from the intensive scans my people," his Thals, "ran on Cero's ship while it was pitching me."

"And?"

"His ship came from a world called Solitário."

"Solitário?" I repeated.

"It's at the far edge of the Thao Proctorate," Thalberg said. "Theoretically uninhabited."

That fits, I said to myself. Hostile One came from Thao.

"Personally, I think it wanted me to know where it could be found if I changed my mind."

Thalberg nodded sagely and, apparently feeling the interview was concluded, turned to Charles and said, "If you and I could retire, Sir, David would like a moment with Jane."

"Jane?" Charles said, catching my eyes.

"It's fine, Charles. I'll join you in a minute," I said without hesitating as I rose from the chair. Seeing me alone was clearly a dying man's last request, or close to it. It would have felt wrong to say no, even it if was David, or perhaps, especially because it was David. I'd said nothing but no to him for so many years, I guess I owed him one last yes.

Charles nodded and allowed Thalberg to escort him out.

David tried to take a step, but cried out in agony. I rushed to his side and wrapped my arm around his waist for support. "I told you not moving was worse," he said with a laugh that attempted to cover a new gasp of pain.

We walked, slowly at first, but soon his stride was stable though it was clearly costing him to move at all.

"What did you want to ask me, David?"

He laughed. "Let me work up to it."

Oh boy. "Sure."

We walked.

Finally he said, "We do have something in common, you know."

"What's that?"

"We are used to doing the impossible," he said. "I figure that if I think and work hard enough I can get around or solve any problem. You figure that if you risk everything you can do the same."

"True."

"I can't trick my way out of this, though, and I couldn't trick you into staying."

I didn't want to get into this again. "What did you want to ask me, David?"

He took a deep breath. His pulse was as close to racing as he could get in his state. "Did you really never love me?"

I should have been prepared for the question, but I still felt flushed and a little dizzy by its bluntness and by the self-pity behind it. I owed him the truth, however, though it was many, mean years too late. "I did love you, Tiger."

His body shuddered against mine. "You did?"

"Just...not enough," I said guiltily. "Not enough to love the man you actually are, not just the fantasy I had in my mind. Loving someone on the condition that they change is deeply unfair. I'm so sorry, David."

I felt the tears falling from his eyes again. "The man I actually am is tragically flawed, Angel."

"We are all flawed, love, tragically or no." I took his hand as we walked. "The things you have made, however, the lives improved and saved by your genius, will live on. There has been and will never be another like you."

"You'll say nice things about me to the journos when I'm gone, won't you?"

My throat clogged and I had to swallow hard to speak. "I will."

"We'll part as friends, right?"

"Yes."

"We've never been that. Friends, I mean." He stopped walking. "That's something."

"It's a big step for us," I agreed.

The door opened and Thalberg reappeared. He waited patiently, but it was clearly time for me to go.

I stepped closer and saw David's big gray eyes staring at me. I leaned in and kissed him gently on the lips. "May you be at peace, David Abrams," I said quietly, quoting Eriss's standard funereal benediction. *"Nawr eich bot an rhat ac am ttim, er nat atach an cael eu hanghorio."* Now you are free, though you are never forgotten.

And David responded, *"Nit war an ei ben ei hun ar eich carer bob amser an ra nghalon."* I am not alone for you are always in my heart. Bastard had learned Pacey.

I felt a sob of my own building and I needed to get out of there. I kissed his blackened hands and hi-tailed it out of the room, leaving David to Thalberg.

As I ran for it I heard David say, in almost a child's voice, "Dad?"

"I've got you, Davey," Thalberg said soothingly, "I've got you."

David George Thalberg Abrams, Jr., died in his sleep on February 10th, 2882, his children and Thalberg Abrams (the Union's first non-organic legal citizen) by his side. Many, many journo articles and T.I. specials ran about his unparralleled achievements in medicine and technology. I said nice things about the tragically flawed man I had once loved in every single one.

Had I known the full extent of his 'plan' for me, however, a plan I only fully understood five months after his death, I would have told all of them to go to hell.

David, too, but I was pretty sure he was already there.

Entry 11-8-94

Author's Note:

Yes, I know I teased about the last of David's horrible secrets, but it will have to remain a tease for a little while longer. Crappy of me, true, but there it is. Besides, I don't get the lowdown myself until July 2882 and there are some serious things that happen before then that cannot be skipped. So, please, have patience. I'll share it all in good time. I promise.

<u>11:00 - My Office, ESTF, *Schola-Terra*, Terra 1, Terra, January 5th, 2882</u>

I was feeling antsy. Nervous, actually. Today was the first day of the new semester and the first day Deneth Rian cadets were being admitted. Somehow they had ended up under the jurisdiction of the ESTF, though as far as I knew (and I knew, trust me) none of them was a supernormal. Or super Rian, I should say. The overall Director of the Academy had broached the idea with Marston and me and we'd thought about it a great deal. Technically the Rian didn't belong with us at all, *but* we were, of all the departments within the *Schola-Terra*, the best equipped to deal with the unusual. That was the word the Director had used. The word Marston and I used (in private) was freaks.

In the end we had agreed to take them, as least for the first few years of their inclusion, partly because we wanted to protect the new Cadets and partly because we were excited/curious to see what they could do. Some of the ESTF staff had been wary, some afraid, but most were as curious as we were, so we'd worked together to hammer out a curriculum, find Zero-G classroom and bunk space, appropriate teachers, etc. The first class was small, a dozen students, but I thought that was a good thing. We needed to be able to really pay attention and adapt to each kid as they learned (or didn't) and evolved (or didn't).

I wasn't just antsy about the new program, however. I was crawling out of my skin because even though I needed to be right where I was, where I wanted to be was in Thao, Solitário to be precise, with Alex and the battleship and small fleet Samuel had sent to try to meet Cero and stop wherever the hell it was doing. Samuel had cursed long and hard about the fact that he couldn't send any TPs with Alex from the Academy to get information out of Cero, but it had been (correctly, I thought) too dangerous to include them, at least at this stage of the game. I'd desperately wanted to go, of course, but hadn't argued with them when they'd told me I couldn't. Strange for me, I know, but the program and my kids (space-dwelling and otherwise) needed me. The fact that I thought this *and* followed through on doing the right thing (and not the emotional thing) made me feel mature and really fucking old.

The ship, the *T.S.S. Actium*, was still three days away from reaching Thao so there was nothing for me to do on that front. I told myself this about once an hour.

I looked at the clock. Time to head to Zero-G D Classroom One. Orientation.

11:30 – D Classroom One (formerly Cargo Hold S-45), Terra 1

Marston, Clydan (now one of our Heely instructors), Acting Instructor Victor Ha (a graduating Senior in the TP Program drafted to fill the TP shortage), Vice-Admiral Aaron Pazman (transferred from the non-super part of the Academy) and myself floated in front of the twelve newly minted Cadets. I had been around the Deneth enough now that I could tell them apart (though the genders I'd had to look up and memorize) but they really did look close to alike. I suppose that was alienist of me to say, but I am only human. Marston, who found telling them apart hopeless, had insisted that *all* Cadets of all stripes wear name tags this year so that he wouldn't completely embarrass himself. Well, it did make getting everyone's name right a lot easier in general, so that was something.

I hadn't wanted Vice-Admiral Aaron Pazman, or Paz, as he was called, involved in our show, but we'd needed him. Only about half of the instruction we gave our ESTF Cadets was from the standard Academy "book." The rest was our own stuff. Necessary stuff, of course, but not for these Cadets. We needed to be able to make these beings 'regular' soldiers, too. Right. Paz was the best at that on the 'regular' side. So there he was, floating along with us.

A bell rang, indicating the start of class. The Deneth stilled and quieted.

"I am Vice-Admiral Pace," I said, "and this is Admiral Manthorpe, Acting Instructor Ha, Instructor Clydan and Vice-Admiral Pazman." Some of the Cadets nodded, most stared straight ahead at attention. Either was fine. "This day, the entry of beings of the Deneth Rian into the 2886 graduating Class of the *Schola-Terra*, has been a long time coming." I smiled. "You are the best and brightest of our applicants. We know you will do the Academy and the Union proud."

One of the Denethians smiled, clearly excited. Cadet Dnnh. (She'd chosen the Standard name 'Donahue' for fear of being given the name 'Duh.' It had been a wise choice.) I smiled back at her.

I switched to Deneth, "Most of your classes will be conducted in Standard, since that is the official language of both U-Nav and the Union itself, but, as part of your duties, you will also be assisting in teaching Denethian to non-Denethians, as Cadets from Heliot," I nodded at Clydan who nodded back, being already fluent in Denethian, "do for Heely."

Some of the Cadets looked visibly relieved. I nodded. "Denethian is an unusual and beautiful language and we believe it should be shared with everyone." The same could not be said for Pacey which was used as battle language within the Furies. Still an abomination, it was, however, a useful abomination.

"I am sure you are aware that this Program will go through growing pains," I continued now in Standard. "Human-Denethian relations are still comparatively new, just as the Heely-Terran Human one was less than a decade ago. There will be problems. There will be prejudice, on both sides, but hazing and intimidation will not be allowed. *By anyone.* A gross infraction will lead to dismissal and, if it is really heinous, prosecution." I moved closer. "I know that you are all faster in space than any Human, Terran or Heely alike. I know that you are also stronger and much more lethal without weapons, but remember that you aren't going to be sharing class time, training time or quarters with your run-of-the-mill Humans. These are supernormals, kids. They may look soft and squishy, but underestimating them would be a serious mistake."

Some of the Cadets just blinked at the seriousness of my warning. One of them, Cadet Zeus (Zsse) raised his hand.

"Yes, Cadet?"

"You said, quarters, Ma'am?" He looked a little horrified. He wasn't alone.

"You will be living in Bunkrooms D-46 and D-47, just down the hall. Six Deneth and six non-Deneth will room together, lotteries at the beginning of each semester will determine who among the Humans will live with you, unless requests are made in advance. We will honor those unless there is a good reason not to."

"What about the Humans that do not want to live with us?"

"They will immediately become your roommates."

Cadet Zeus didn't look too thrilled with that idea and I didn't blame him, but keeping everyone separate was not going to make anything better in the long run, though intergration might make everything tense as fuck in the short-term.

I looked at Clydan who floated forward. "As the Head Heely, so to speak, at the ESTF, I may be able to offer some perspective on the challenges you will face here. My door will always be open to anyone who needs it," she frowned, "though my office would be death trap for you." Oh, Clyde, I thought, stifling a laugh. "Then reach me on your comms and I will come to you. I will be supervising your fight training between Heely ATRs and Deneth." She looked at me. "Vice-Admiral Pace will be responsible for your Denethian ATR training. Instructor Mallory will train you to fight Terran Humans."

Cadet Lincoln (Lnl) raised her hand, looking at me. I nodded. "We will learn to fight supers, too, Ma'am?"

"Most definitely. And carefully. That will come later, though, once we have an idea of your control." I grimaced. "We have no ATRs that can do what Macros, Micros and TPs can do, so you'll be facing the real thing. Instructors such as myself," a few of the Cadets gulped nervously at facing down the Red Angel, "and later with upperclassman." At the same time the Humans would be learning (as they had all along) how to take out Denethians and Heelies. This was going to be a very exciting year.

Then Marston spoke for the first time, "Then there is a part many of us here at the ESTF are looking forward to: Human, whether with jet packs or self-powered, speed training with our new Denethian Cadets." He grinned. "Personally, I can't wait."

Neither could I and neither could the now grinning Cadets. *No one* touched Denethians in open space. I could get close, but even I was pretty sure they could lap me. Of course the new Cadets didn't know how I planned to use their speed and agility to increase the effectiveness of *everyone* who flew with them. That would come later. Now it was Paz's turn.

I looked at my colleague and he jetted forward. "Vice-Admiral Pace told me something once that I think will be useful in this instance, though with an addition." My eyebrows raised but I didn't butt in. "She said that, as the refugees of Pace-Pallon neared Terra, then General Armstrong," I saw some recognition in the faces of our new Cadets, "told his people that the key to success here was to offer the Union talents and abilities that it didn't have access to and could only get from the supernormal Paceys. He told them to make themselves invaluable and if they did so, they would find their place." I'd given the same story when the Heelies had started at the Academy and every semester since. Samuel had been correct as usual. I'd told the staff this just the previous week; I just hadn't been aware that Paz had been listening.

"I will say the same thing to you twelve, but with an added caution." He paused, but we (myself included) were hanging on his every word. "You all have skills that we not only do not have but need and can make great use of, but do not neglect your academic studies. Your history classes, your tactical training, rules and regulations for U-Nav, especially if you want to eventually attend Command School."

Several of the Cadets gasped. Command School? I was surprised myself. My, Paz was ambitious for these kids.

Paz nodded, acknowledging his possibly unrealistic dreams for these Denethians. "It isn't open to you right now, but last year it became open to Heelies, and only the best, whatever their species, are allowed in. To succeed you must be better, smarter and more knowledgeable than anyone else. To fit it you must make yourselves indispensable. To lead you must be extraordinary."

Cadet Pinky (Pnn) raised a hand. Yes, I'd tried to talk him out of the name, but it was, as he put it, his first adult act and he wanted to be called Pinky, goddamnitt. Still seemed like a terrible idea to me, but at least it had been *his* terrible idea. "You really think, Sir, that Humans will follow Denethians? Into battle?"

Paz's expression became serious, or, more serious. "I think some Humans will, at first, then more to come, but it all depends on a truly special Rian. One must be worthy of being followed, Cadet. You won't have to tell anyone how worthy you are; it will be clear to everyone without your having to do a thing." Then he shocked the shit out of me. "Vice-Admiral Pace?"

"Yes, Vice-Admiral Pazman?" Lord, what was he doing now and why was he involving me in it?

"Back on Pace, when you are where these Cadets are now, would you have thought you would have been a leader?"

Samuel had thought I would be, I thought. "No, Paz."

"So how did it happen?"

It just happened. "It just...happened."

"Did you work hard to become one?"

Not even a little bit, but I didn't want to come right out and say that with impressionable minds listening. "I worked hard to be the best super and the best team member I could be. The strongest, the fastest and," I thought for a second, "the one most likely to bring my people home in one piece, even at my own expense."

Pazman looked satisfied, as if he'd known this was what I would say. Perhaps he had. "There, Cadets, is your mandate. Absorb everything, learn everything, work harder, take care of your Teams, no matter their makeup, and you're futures will be bright indeed."

I looked at Paz with suppressed astonishment. I could see him hiding a smile. He'd energized the Cadets masterfully. Interesting. Now, however, the speechifying was clearly back to me.

"This is, effectively, a pilot program. How you conduct yourselves here, in your classes and in your downtime, will affect how future Denethian Cadets are dealt with or whether there will be any more period." I straightened. "We have X-Ships to fill and, at some point, will have battles to fight. I am sure all of you will prove worthy of this Academy and the faith we have placed in you." I smiled warmly. "Welcome to the *Schola-Terra.*"

"Thank you, Ma'am," they said quietly, some happy, some worried.

Ah, but I'd forgotten something and I turned back as I'd been about to leave. "One more thing: fraternization with non-Denethians."

The look of horror on Cadet Lincoln's made me stifle a giggle. Cadet Pinky looked intrigued.

"There will be a mandatory sexual safety course tomorrow morning at 09:00." Someone snickered. Another looked like he was going to throw up, Denethian style. "Some of you will never take advantage of what you learn there, but some of you may. I don't care who you have sex with within

your own people, since that isn't physically dangerous," though the
Denethian bonding (creation of *Shann*) that came with sex could make
things tricky, but one thing at a time, "but there are life-threatening issues
involved when Denethians and Humans get together. The staff and I will
take the endangering of *any* life extremely seriously." I floated much closer
to my new kids. "Anyone who fools around with a Human in an unsafe
manner leading to that Human getting hurt will be put in the Brig and
dismissed. You get me?"

Oh, the conversation we'd had about Denethian/Human sex in the staff
room. Then there had been the hours spent with the med techs in the
Infirmary putting together the presentation. I'd wanted to call it, "How to
fuck your Human without killing him." I'd been overruled on the name,
unfortunately. Putting together my intimate knowledge of Heely anatomy
with what I (also intimately) knew about Denethian bodies had been
interesting, too. I hoped the couplings (assuming there were any) would be
fun for somebody. Finally a positive from my years as Jane The Galactic
Slut. I mean, how many people could say their sex life could directly affect
the life or death of others? I'd been so proud. Kind of.

Marston had argued that Denethians needed to take a chastity oath
upon acceptance to the ESTF to take the danger and the mating bonds out
of the equation, but I'd been against it, as had Clydan. The Academy (all
parts of it) was considered a good place to meet a mate no matter what you
were. We'd decided to take a 'wait and see' attitude with Denethian
fornication. I really hoped we hadn't just let ourselves in for a nightmare.

Threats issued, I dismissed the kids and the staff and I floated out of
the room and into the newly created Zero-G 'hallways' connecting D level
rooms to each other. Leaving this I let the door slide shut behind us. My
feet touched down and we filed into the corridor before I turned to Victor
and asked, "So?"

"I got a lot of worry from them," Mr. Ha said, though he didn't look
worried himself, "but nothing out of the ordinary. Some of them were
scared to sleep with Humans." He snorted. "In either sense."

"Scared of what they would do?" Clyde asked, "or of what the Humans
would do to them?"

Good question.

"Afraid of the Humans causing trouble for them, mostly," Victor said.
"No one in the ESTF, wherever their place of origin, is an out and out
bigot, obviously," we screened the shit out of them for that, Victor having

done a good portion of the screening himself, "but there are culturally created fears on both sides." He looked in Clyde's direction. "Just like after the Heely War."

She nodded as did I.

Marston looked unfazed as per his usual. "There will be a couple of bad eggs. There always are no matter what." It was true. We'd had to dismiss two to three Cadets each year (the regular *Schola-Terra* dismissed ten times that) for one reason or another—not always for anything racist or alienist. Sometimes you got people who simply couldn't work with a team, especially if it was a team he or she didn't like. Some people cheated, cut corners or lived for excuses. Some had thought they were ready to risk their lives for the Union but when faced with the reality of actually serving found they weren't up for it. Some people just flat out changed their minds, no reason given. We'd tried to find jobs for the 'good' eggs who just hadn't been temperamentally suited for U-Nav. The 'bad' eggs we monitored discretely, feeling a little responsible for teaching them skills and then unleashing them on the universe.

"That was quite the pep talk, Paz," I said.

He shrugged. "Most won't make it to even apply to Command School, even if Deneth are allowed in, but I always encourage Cadets to reach for it. Beings can surprise you."

"True," I said half-heartedly.

He smiled. "Not all surprises are bad, Jane."

Uh, sure? I sighed. "That hasn't been my experience of late."

"I've given some version of that speech twice a year for over a decade." He started off down the corridor. "Gives me hope, too, every time I give it." With that he left.

Clyde watched him go, her expression sly. "He's cute for a Terran."

"I suppose so," I answered absently. I hadn't noticed. Paz was short but powerfully built. Good dark hair and had all of his limbs, so I guessed he qualified as cute. I guessed. I had Charles-induced tunnel vision, I happily admitted to myself. Yes, I still thought he was the greatest thing in the universe (Lucy excepted) even after all these years. Ah, Charles.

"Your eyes get all dreamy when you think of him, you know," Clydan said, pleased.

I was sure they did.

She looked like she was going to say more, but shook her head. "Let's say hello to Sy and Missy at Aronoff's before we have to do this all again for the Human Cadets."

"Sounds like a great idea."

We got to it.

For the record, the Human Cadets (Heelies and Terrans) were no longer separated in any way, either at orientation or anywhere else, with the small exception of some classes that were tailored to Heelies only. The Humans reacted with much more curiosity than fear to the promise of the sexual safety lecture than the Denethians had, which I thought was a good sign in terms of everyone getting along. I wondered when I'd be getting letters from concerned parents, though, saying things like "I didn't think *sex* would be part of my little Waldo's education. Can't you keep your perverted immorality out of the classroom?" Which I would counter with, "When little Waldo ends up in the Infirmary with burns on his dick you'll scream that no one was looking out for your child. What do you think these kids *do* when they're not in class or studying?"

Yeah, this was going to be fun.

05:03 – Corsican Ambassadorial Apartments, Terra 1, Terra, January 10th, 2882

I heard the distant chime of a received letter on my computer and was instantly wide awake. It had to be from Alex at Solitário. I managed to stop myself from leaping out of bed and scaring the crap out of Charles and slowly turned over to kiss his cheek as I carefully disentangled myself from his warm grasp.

"S'Ok, Jane," he mumbled. "I know you've been waiting for it."

"Thanks, Six," I whispered as I got quickly out of bed and ran over to the computer.

Personal Message to High Admiral Samuel Armstrong, Vice-Admiral Jane Pace, Information Officer Huong Schulweis, Information Officer Quinn-Pace and Corsican Ambassador Charles Fitzroy from Captain Alex Couvillion, T.S.S Actium, _Solitário, Thao Protectorate, January 9th, 2882_

Sirs and Ma'am,

While we found a massive training facility and make-shift shipyard, Solitário _was deserted when we arrived at the planet. Recently deserted but not quickly vacated, it appears; it was as if they had known we were coming. It is unclear how the Cero could have been warned of our impending arrival since this mission was dark, but the facility was not only cleaned out but sterilized for any biological residue. No fingerprints or even stray hairs were left._

Awaiting orders on how to proceed.

Alexander Couvillion, Colonel

I read the letter aloud to Charles as he got out of bed. He frowned, worried as I was, though perhaps not as disappointed.

"If whoever was there is gone, where did they go?" he asked, voicing my own thought.

The station shook, rocking violently in some kind of explosion.

All the lights in the room (not that many had been on) turned red.

The rarely-used station-wide comm blared on. "Terra 1 Station is under attack! All inhabitants report to your designated escape pods!"

"Mother of god," I said even as I ran for the closet to skin into my DSS.

Mr. Beddoes and Stanley burst into the room as Charles threw on pants. I'd never seen him get dressed so quickly.

"Charles!" I cried as I fixed my seals on the suit.

"We've got him, Miss Jane," Stanley barked and Charles gave me one last fleeting look as he was bundled out of the room and, I assumed, safely off the station.

I clicked on my comm as I headed into the corridor, homing in on the nearest airlock. "Marston, what's happened?" My kids. Someone was targeting my kids. I felt it in my bones.

"Someone set off a bomb in the ESTF offices."

"The offices?"

"Blew a hole in the station hull but the force fields caught it before the section decompressed. We're evacuating the kids to the surface."

"Tell everyone to suit up before they get in the escape pods."

"Already did, Jane."

"I'll supervise from outside. Pace out."

What the hell? Why do that? Why not just take everyone out at once? If they could have assembled a bomb and set it off there they could have set it off anywhere in the ESTF, even the dorms. How they were able to get into our offices was something we'd have to deal with later.

Even without answers I had to go, so I went out the first airlock I found immediately adapting to the floating of Zero-G.

I soon saw hundreds of small personal pods shooting out of the station and I moved closer to them. Most of the pods kept up chatter over the comm, giving status to Marston, the *Schola-Terra* Director, or Docking Control (depending on who was in the pods, civilian or otherwise) and checking in with the Emergency Co-ordinator at the designation landing field assigned for this part of Terra, somewhere over the Asian continent. I found the chatter comforting, normal. I moved closer to the herd.

The evacuation path, as I well knew since that sort of thing was drilled into the heads of anyone who lived in the unfriendly habitat of space, took the pods (depending on where the station was in relation to the planet below) around the station and through the corridor of empty space between the station itself and the massive docking arm Beta. Docking arm Alpha held the U-Nav ships in port. Beta held the civilian ones.

Right then the first of the pods passed the middle of Beta that four of the ships attached to it opened fire.

'I think that ship is shooting at...' and the voice on the pod's comm went silent.

I saw five pods burst into flame and blow apart.

Oh god.

Dozens of small torpedoes shot out of each of the four ships, targeting with deadly precision *some* of the pods. Most of pods, however, went right through, apparently safe.

'This is Pace,' I said, speeding up. 'Get any suited Marines and Macros to pick up and pod any survivors of attacked escape pods. I'm going to take out the Hostile Ships.' Then I felt small quick figures in space behind me, coming out of the airlocks near the Zero-G Bunkrooms. Thank god.

'Denethian Cadets, this is Vice-Admiral Pace. Zero in on my coordinates. Hostile ships are firing on the escape pods. We need to take these fuckers out.'

I heard twelve surprised voices acknowledge and within seconds they had caught up and matched my (slower) speed.

More small torpedoes flew out of the hostile docked ships, hitting clusters and still (seemingly) deliberately missing others.

'Do any of you have pods?' I asked, meaning expandable personnel pods not to be confused with the escape pods. We needed a different name for one of them.

'We each have ten pods, Ma'am,' a voice I recognized as Lincoln's said. I had a dozen myself.

'Well done,' I said. 'Rip apart any ship that fires on our escapees and capture as many live hostiles as you can find. *We need them alive*, Cadets. That is a direct order.'

'Yes, Ma'am,' they said.

'Now go and don't wait for me.'

They went.

Pinky and Lincoln were the first to reach the closest ship as it was still firing perfectly aimed shots at my kids as well as the other escapees. The torpedoes never missed. Pinky extended those terrible claws and ripped through the hull like butter through a hot knife, expelling at least some of the people inside into space. Lincoln attached himself to the far side of the hull and shredded the torpedo launch bay just as a device was launched. For a horrible second the armed torpedo faced him and he froze, but I 'grabbed' it (still at the very outside of my range) and 'threw' it aside, 'crushing' it once it was clear of the Cadet. Lincoln (good boy) went right back to destroying the ship.

By then the other Cadets were eviscerating the other three ships and the firing stopped. The few pods, both civilian and those from the ESTF that were left, made it through unmolested. I ordered the Denethian Cadets back to the station since they, obviously, could not come down with me to the planet.

I 'pushed' myself into the first Hostile ship and found it empty of life. The dead floated, their bodies distorted with violent decompression and the living, if there were any, were gone. Podded, I had to assume, by my Cadets. It was the same on all the ships but the fourth. There I found two people, barely alive, in engineering and podded them. What I found on the bridge, however, was purely horrifying.

Blood floated in giant frozen blobs. Dead Terran Human bodies bobbed around, their chests and backs showing the unmistakable marks of angry Denethian claws. I knew the feeling behind the carnage, but that could not stand. Later, though.

It was clear by now that there was no one left to either capture or save. Stanley had sent me a signal that let me know Charles was safely on-planet, so it was time to go to Earth and see how bad this all was. First, however, there was something that I had to gather.

I was just 'pushing' myself out of Hostile 4 when all four ships exploded.

Acting on pure instinct I curled myself into a ball and wrapped myself in the thickest shield I could make.

I woke up a minute or two later spinning out of control and trying not to throw up in my DSS. So gross. I was fine, though. Nauseous as fuck, but unharmed.

'JANE!' Marston was screaming into my comm.

I saw the station receding from view. Shit, I'd gone far.

'Gimme a second to get right, Marston,' I said.

'Thank God,' he said. 'Was anyone else on the ships?'

'Not to my knowledge,' I said just as I stopped spinning. Oh, that was good. 'I got thrown in the blast, but I'm heading back now.' Only a few minutes had passed between what should have been the end of the murderous mission and the destruction of the ships they'd used. A suicide mission all along. I wondered if the perpetrators had known before they'd left Solitário that they'd been marked to die. I had to assume that it was only the terrific speed of the Denethian Cadets that had allowed us to capture any of the murderers. "Are you still on the station?"

'Yes, Jane,' Marston replied, now sounding more like himself.

'How many of the Cero's people did we get alive?'

Marston hesitated. I wondered why. 'Two.'

'That's all?' I asked surprised. I know they'd used many more pods than that.

'Seventeen were dead by the time they made it through the airlock, though we're still going through the pods. We have the two known survivors in the grav Brig heavily sedated. Very heavily.'

'Good.'

'About the Denethian Cadets, Jane...' His voice was grim.

I remembered all the blood and bodies on Hostile 4. Didn't help with the nausea. 'I take it you know which of the Cadets acted outside of their orders?'

'Donahue and Franklin," or Dnnh and Fkk (that one had just been begging for a bad nickname), "came in with Terran blood all over their claws.' Marston sounded defeated and very tired. 'They are in the Zero-G Brig.'

'Good,' I said, more than a little worn out myself. 'Do you want me to deal with them after I assess our losses?'

'I think you'd be the right person to do that. Paz is beside himself.'

I bet he is, I thought. To have so much go wrong so damned quickly was a real shock. For all of us. 'Tell him all is not lost, even with those two, though I'll know for sure when I talk to them.'

'I don't know that he'll believe you, but I'll tell him.'

Four days, I thought. These kids had had *four days* of training before they'd been thrown in the deep end. I sighed as I passed into Earth's atmosphere and felt its gravity start to pull at me. 'We just ran right into a cultural difference I didn't think we'd hit nearly this soon. There is still hope. They saved a lot of people today, all of them.'

'I know, Jane, but how many?'

'I'll let you know when I do, Marston. Pace out.'

11:49 – Inner Mongolian Plateau, Old China, Terra

Ten thousand or so escape pods (individual and twelve-person, depending) littered the dry grasslands as I landed on the Inner Mongolian Plateau. The area set aside for the emergency evac of the Station was barren of villages or, seemingly, local peoples. Hastily erected temporary shelters dotted the land but it was, for all intents and purposes, pastoral and empty. I pulled my helmet back and took a deep breath of unfiltered air. Off in the distance several transport ships had landed, preparing to move the wounded and, once Terra 1 had been declared safe, take everyone else back to the station. I 'flew' towards what looked like a command structure. I saw all the Cadets sitting together quietly and many, many unhappy Station civilians (most still in the sleeping clothes) loitering about, some demanding answers of anyone in uniform.

A medium-sized woman in U-Army fatigues stood at ease next to Samuel and, thank god, Charles (surrounded by a phalanx of Corsican Guards) in front of the tent.

Both Charles and Samuel looked relieved when they saw me approach. The woman just nodded, clearly unsurprised.

"Jane," Samuel said at the same time Charles said, "Are you all right?"

"I'm fine, Fitz," I said to Charles, then I turned to Samuel. "How bad is it?"

Samuel merely said, "Vice-Admiral Pace, this is Colonel Meng, Evacuation Co-Ordinator."

"Good to meet you, Colonel," I said politely.

"You, too, Vice-Admiral."

"Thank you for taking us in," I said, doing my best to pretend I gave a shit.

"We've had a plan for this for over fifty years and have never had to use it." Meng looked a little worn out. I was right there with her. "It has been an interesting day."

"That it has." I looked pointedly at Samuel, who cast a quick look at Charles, who stifled a sigh.

"If you will excuse us, Colonel?" Samuel said.

"Of course, Sir," she said, "Ma'am." She saluted Marston and myself. "Ambassador." She bowed to Fitz and left.

Samuel's expression immediately became very grim.

"So, Samuel?" I asked quietly.

"We lost forty-seven TP Cadets," he said. "One hundred and twelve others, but it looks like they were," he gritted his teeth, "collateral damage."

I felt the world spin and my eyes filled. In sadness, yes, but mostly frustration. We'd *known* TPs were in danger and that knowledge had availed us nothing. I could not speak; I just shook my head in denial.

Finally I swallowed past the lump in my throat. "We only had fifty-nine TPs in the whole school." I couldn't look at Charles. His sympathy or empathy would make me lose it.

"I know," Samuel said softly.

I wiped my damp eyes and straightened. "So no one else? No civilians? Regular Cadets? Merchants? No one?"

"Just our Cadets. The supers were all travelling together."

"I guess we should be grateful," Charles said reflectively, "that Cero has stopped trying to hide what it's doing."

I supposed so. I took a breath. Actually, he had a valid point. Tens of thousands of people in pods flying virtually unprotected through the atmosphere? It could have wiped out every one of them. Or at least given it a good shot.

I had one question, however. Well, I had several, but one was foremost in my mind. "How did they know who to target? How could they be so precise?"

If it had been possible for a man to look even more grim, that was Samuel. "Come inside."

Samuel led Charles and myself into the tent. There, wrapped in a blanket and probably in shock, sat Victor Ha. He looked up when the three of us entered and tried to rise, but all three of us waved him down.

I pulled up a camp chair and sat across from him. "Victor, are you all right?"

He looked at me dumbly as if fighting to process his thoughts and words. "Fine, Ma'am."

Well, he wasn't fine, but it was the best he could do. "Do you know how the TPs were targeted?"

His eyes were unfocused. "We were passing by those ships in the Beta Arm and I saw horrible things."

"I don't understand, Victor."

Victor continued as if I'd said nothing. "A family being beaten and raped and then murdered. Children." Big tears rolled down his face. "Then burned alive." He started to sob. "They screamed."

I took his hands and squeezed them hard, trying to get his attention back for just a few seconds. "This was put in your mind?"

He looked at me, fear and pain in his eyes. "It was…fast, was done in less than a second. Like it was compressed. I couldn't block it and then it was over." He rubbed his head with both hands as if trying to push the memory out. "I'd had my 'wall' up and it cut right through it."

I looked up at Samuel in horror, but Samuel stepped forward.

"Who would do this, Sir?" Victor asked him desperately, his voice full of grief. "Who would shoot down people escaping?" His breathing got faster and hysterics were on the horizon. "My friends…"

We knew, of course, but there weren't many of us who knew. Problem was that the escape pods were meant for escape only, not protection. The planners had imagined a technical problem with the station or even evac before an attack. Everyone in those pods had been defenseless. I'd have to speak to David about shielding for the pods...when I remembered I couldn't speak to David. I realized then how much we'd all taken his genius for granted and what a loss (at least in the technical aspects of our work) his death would be.

"We're working on it, Victor," Samuel said.

I, however, answered a different way. "They will pay."

Victor looked into my eyes and apparently saw my murderous determination and relaxed a bit. The Red Angel had said it, therefore it would happen. I hoped he was correct.

"You've done well, son," Samuel said. "Now you can rest."

"Ok, Sir." Victor was starting to shake. "Thank you."

Samuel led us out of the tent and ordered a Med Tech in who, I was sure, was going to sedate the hell out of poor Victor.

"None of the non-TPs my staff and I interviewed have mentioned anything like that. Only the surviving TPs."

"The images are all the same?" Charles asked.

"Yes."

"So," I said, "Cero has at least one very powerful TP working for it."

"So it would seem."

Charles folded his arms over his chest the way he did when he was upset. "Someone sets off a bomb in the ESTF, in a part of it they know will be empty at that time in morning, causing a mass evacuation then waits to target only TP supers, having put, probably over the previous weeks, four civilian ships in place to do just that over the planet." He looked at Charles. "Aided by a tremendously powerful TP."

"Right."

"How many evacuation plans are there for Terra 1, Sam? For the escape pods?"

"Half a dozen." Samuel was frowning.

"How many of them guarantee everyone passes by the Beta Arm?"

"One."

Yeah, nothing about this was random.

"But who set off that bomb?"

Yes, that was the big question. Well, it was one of them.

Just then Samuel straightened and turned his head to click on his comm. "Armstrong." He listened. He looked sharply at me. "On our way." He clicked off his comm. "Marston needs us on the station."

Charles nodded and looked at me, lowering his voice. "I'll see you at home."

I nodded and gave him a reassuring smile.

He (discretely protected by his guards) walked into the thick of the makeshift and camp and immediately started talking to people, asking them questions and helping. I watched him, full of pride and outright adoration.

"Put your helmet on, Jane, before you give the game away," Samuel said, chuckling.

I stuck my tongue out at him, while privately acknowledging he was right, and put my helmet on while he did the same.

'Need a boost, old man?' I asked through my comm.

'I'll manage,' he said smugly as he launched into the sky like a rocket.

Well, I thought, as I scrambled to catch up. Someone has the new jet pack.

13:58 – ESTF, *Schola-Terra*, Terra 1

Samuel and I walked quickly into the undamaged part of the ESTF to find Paz and Marston waiting for us. I was immediately set upon by Paz.

"What the hell, Jane? Marston says you know what is going on? Why don't *I* know what the hell is going on?"

I looked at Samuel for permission and he nodded. I said, "There is a being called Cero who is targeting and killing Telepaths. Though I haven't confirmed it, I believe that it is responsible for today's attack."

Paz froze and just stared at Samuel, Marston and myself. "Someone is out to *murder* the Cadets we are responsible for and you kept this knowledge to yourselves?"

He was right to be angry, of course. "We thought the Academy Cadets would be well protected here, of all places," I said because it had been true.

Paz just stood there and fumed.

"How many TPs survived, Sam?" Marston asked, clearly dreading the answer.

"Just under a dozen."

"God in Heaven," Marston murmured.

I felt the odd stirring I got when Samuel turned on his projecting and he turned to Paz. "We were dealing with the situation, Vice-Admiral," he said in a voice that reminded everyone that he was very much in charge, "and it was only just before the explosion that we had exhausted our best lead."

Paz, chastened, said, "Of course, Sir." Nothing like the beauties of a command structure to shut someone the fuck up, even if he'd been perfectly justified in being angry.

"There a couple of things you need to see, Sir," Marston said as if informality was now out of bounds.

Samuel nodded and we all followed Marston.

We ended up in the morgue. Not a good sign, I thought. It wasn't.

Seventeen bodies in bags were lined up on tables in the cold storage room.

"We have two still alive, you said?" I asked Marston.

"Yes. They are currently sedated, their suicide capsules removed, in the locked Infirmary under guard. Though we only have them at all because Cadet Pinky realized that they were offing themselves either while or right after they were getting podded." Marston grimaced but still managed to look pleased. "He hit them in the head until they passed out."

Well, I thought, one adapts to the situation. "Good thinking on Pinky's part. Let's just hope they wake up."

"Let's hope," he concurred.

Samuel looked at the rows of black bags. "Anything unusual about the Cero Agents? Anything that can tie them either to each other or to their boss?"

Marston shook his head. "We're doing DNA identification but we don't have anything so far. Terran Humans. All adults, but not all young. All fitted with standard poison capsules in a fake tooth."

"What kind of poison?"

"Cyanide."

Nothing unusual about that, unfortunately. It was a classic and very common. Attempting to trace it would be a waste of time.

"Anything on the registration of the civilian Hostile ships?"

"The MPs are investigating, but we don't expect to get anything from that either."

"Yes," Samuel said thoughtfully, "that would be too easy."

Asshole Cero. Couldn't you give us *something*?

"You wanted to us to see something?"

"Yes, Sir." Marston walked over to the farthest body but one and unsealed the heavy plastic bag. Inside was a Terran Human, unremarkable except for the projectile-made hole in his temple, complete with powder burns.

"Cadet Phillip Dresden," Paz said sadly.

"One of yours?" I asked. So not a super? Was my implied question.

Paz nodded. So Dresden was not. "I knew him from my years on the 'normal' side of the Academy. Very bright, very duty-conscious." He shook his head. "Just accepted a post on the *Romanov*. It would have been waiting for him after graduation."

"I'm sorry, Paz," I said quietly. Paz didn't respond, but I felt some of his tension ease.

"We tested the body for explosive residue and it was all over him," Marston said.

"So he played his part by setting off the bomb and then killing himself?" I confirmed.

"Evidently."

How could anyone have gotten to him, though? Even the 'normal' Cadets had been screened by TPs for the past five years. "But he'd been scanned by Brady before he'd even been accepted to the Academy, not to mention getting re-screened every Fall since," I protested, though I wasn't sure to whom.

"Not again since this Fall, however," Samuel said thoughtfully. Yes, a lot could happen in a little more than four months. "We need to know where he's been and who he's seen since that screening."

"I can handle that, Sir," Paz said. "I probably knew him best of all of us."

Samuel nodded, "Work with Agents Schulweis and Quinn-Pace. They've set up shop within my office. You'll coordinate with Colonel Couvillion once he returns."

"Yes, Sir."

Samuel then said to Marston, "And the last body?"

Now Marston seemed even more distressed and Paz flatly looked away. I felt dread in the pit of my stomach.

Marston unzipped the, I now realized, unusually-shaped bag.

There, pale white with large blue bruises all over its delicate skin, was a dead Tarine. It's artificial black wing was missing, it's remaining real one maimed, almost shredded. The expression on the being's lovely face was of pure terror, its mouth wide. The poor creature still screamed for release, even in death.

"Mother of god," I whispered.

"We wanted you to see him or her before informing the *sagrat-Pelann*," Marston said reverently.

My heart hurt for Eriss. I didn't think any of her flock had died (since the Trithicate attack) before the being in front of us had. Just awful.

A few minutes later Marston, Samuel, Paz and I stood outside the Infirmary's lockdown ward, staring at the unconscious figures of one woman and one man. They wore civilian clothes and looked disappointingly ordinary.

"We had the MPs process the DNA of these two first, for obvious reasons," Marston said. "Dr. Mary Blackthorne, Ph.D. in Theoretical Physics, Ph.D., in Philosophy, Master's Degree in Romantic Literature."

"What the hell?" I asked. No one answered me.

"This is Berkshire Bentley," he continued. "Calls himself a 'Herd Activist.' College dropout but full time agitator."

"What kind of 'herd' is he protecting, exactly?" Samuel asked but no one heard him over my exclamation...

"He's a *Bentley*?"

"Yes," Marston confirmed distastefully. "One of those Bentleys."

The Bentleys were a family of immense wealth and infamous reputation. They'd been war profiteers in, well, every war we'd had in the last hundred years, including the Heely one. They'd been very disappointed that the potential Intra-Union War between the Deneth and the Humans had been derailed by peace. What in the hell, though, was this idiot doing here?

"According to the dossier, this Bentley was the black sheep, publicly appalled by his family's lack of respect for human life, etc., etc.," Marston said. "He was finally disowned a few months ago, but was smart enough to move his fortune out of family hands before it actually happened."

"He broke with his amoral family in order to kill Telepaths?" I said, trying to wrap my head around it all.

No one responded to that statement either.

I peered closer at the faces of the two living murderers, trying to divine something, but I didn't see much.

"What we have here," Samuel said, "are true believers."

"Brainwashed?" Marston asked, "or the real deal?"

"I don't know."

"Either way, Sam," Marston said, "they won't talk. Not easily anyway."

"We need an experienced TP," Samuel said. "Something we have in very short supply these days."

I was still looking at the people. "The Tarine are the best in the Union, but right now..." Samuel nodded. "Victor isn't up to a serious interrogation and the rest of our TPs are kids."

"We can contact the Furies..."

Then I had it. "Stuart."

Samuel thought about the idea for a second. "Stuart."

"Who is Stuart?" Paz asked.

18:05 – Docking Bay 02-12, Terra 1, Terra, January 13th, 2882

Two days later Marston, Samuel, Paz and I waited outside the airlock as the *G.L.S.S. Prince Hector* completed its docking procedure. Our old friend had actually been in the neighborhood when he'd received our urgent messages so our expected 4-5 day wait had been drastically reduced. While I had assumed he would come (his sense of duty would have taken care of that), I hadn't expected him to do it so quickly, but he had, and soon enough his now almost portly figure was stepping quickly down the umbilical arm from the ship and into the airlock.

The airlock signal turned green and the inner door popped open.

"Stuart!" I cried as I threw myself into his arms. The extra padding made him a fantastic hugger, though I kept that little thought to myself.

"Jane, love," Stuart said, chuckling as he hugged me back. "It's good to see you."

"Thank you for coming," I said as I let him go.

Stuart straightened as we walked and stopped before Samuel and Paz.

"General," Stuart said with a bow.

Samuel held out his hand, which Stuart shook with only the slightest of hesitations. "One day I'll get you to call me Sam, Stuart."

Stuart grinned, "Not a chance, Sir."

Samuel smiled back.

"Good to see you, Marston," Stuart said to Marston.

"I'm relieved you're here, Stuart." Weren't we all?

I stood next to my friend and said, "Lord Miller, may I present Vice-Admiral Aaron Pazman of the ESTF." I looked at Paz. "Paz, this is Lord Robert Miller of Gloriana-Levvon." I'd kept to the ultra-short version of Stuart's title. It got longer each year.

Paz's eyes had gone wide with the revelation of Stuart's identity. Apparently the short title had been enough. I shouldn't have been too surprised. Pilar's alliance with Stuart (and Prince Ronnie) had changed everything about Gloriana-Levvon, not to mention Thao itself. Everyone knew who Stuart was no matter what name he used.

"Nice intro, Jane," Stuart said.

"The Countess made me take lessons," I grumbled.

Stuart shook Paz's hand. No one explained why we called Bobby Stuart. It made me happy. That was still 'ours.'

"It is good to meet you, My Lord," Paz said, sounding a little shocked.

"Bobby, please," Stuart said, but then rolled his eyes, "at least when it's appropriate."

"Thank you, Bobby."

"Shall we get to it?" Stuart asked, turning on that focus I so well remembered.

"Yes," Samuel said and we started walking quickly towards the Infirmary.

"How long can you stay?" I asked.

"Until the threat is over, Jane," Stuart said quietly. "I can't be anywhere near my family."

His family? His children. The biological children of a powerful Telepath… My expression must have given me away because Stuart grabbed my arm and pulled me off to the side of the corridor we were in. He leaned in close.

"*None* of my children are Telepaths, Jane." His brown eyes bored into mine. "Do you understand? *None.*"

I saw so much fear. Too much. Oh, god.

"I understand, love," I whispered.

We turned to the rest of our party, who had stopped ahead of us, and rushed to catch up. Samuel caught my eye and I knew he knew Stuart's fears. They were the same ones I had for Lucy.

Within a few minutes we were all standing outside the Tenorium, looking in on the still unconscious forms of the Cero conspirators.

Stuart was eyeing them as though they were the fly and he the spider. "I'll need witnesses."

"I'll go," I said automatically, dying of curiosity. Samuel and Marston also wanted in. Stuart 'sharing' what he got from these people would allow more people both to remember and interpret. Paz stayed mute and that was just as well. I didn't think Marston had been through anything like this, but he was tough and experienced in many other ways. Paz? This might have been too much for him since for him all things super were still rather new.

Stuart turned to the Med Tech on the other side of the Tenorium. "Wake them up."

If you're wondering what happened to my Denethian Cadets, the ones who'd screwed up during the 'Evac Attack' as the journos were calling it, here you go…

I had waited a full day to speak to them, letting them cool their heels in the Zero-G Brig, not because I was consumed with anger and getting myself together, but because they deserved it. Paz had been furious that Donahue and Franklin had killed those Cero operatives and he was right to be. I *should* have been equally angry, but I really wasn't. What I was bothered by was that they hadn't followed orders. *That* was a serious offense. Yes, they had taken lives, but it mattered whose lives they'd taken. They'd killed murderers (which was, of course, why they'd killed them) who had targeted their classmates. The Denethians had punished killers the best way they knew how, with razor-sharp claws. Within the Rian this act would have been praised. While I didn't praise it myself, what they did showed, to me at any rate, their loyalty and a sense of right and wrong, even if it wasn't in the way U-Nav would find acceptable. This was all aside from the fact that the bodies had been on Hostile 4, meaning that by the time the Cadets had gotten to it, it had been clear that all of the operatives were killing themselves to avoid capture. I assumed that the Cadets had wanted the last minutes of these criminals' lives to be painful. It wasn't as if they hadn't earned the pain.

The interesting twist to all of this was that it really was in my hands— but only because no physical evidence remained. If Hostile 4 had survived, the whole situation would have been different, but it hadn't. This had given me options.

I'd floated in the corridor outside of the Zero-G Brig for just a second before the kids had realized I was there. They'd immediately risen from their sleep hammocks and had floated to the Tenorium at attention. Though I hadn't planned on spacing them, I *had* still been displeased and I was letting them know it.

The security cameras and recording devices had been switched off.

Time to let them have it, in my own way.

"You know why you're here," I said.

"Yes, Ma'am," they answered.

"Tell me."

Franklin looked at Donahue who answered, "We disobeyed orders and took revenge on those murderers."

Concise. "Why did you do that?"

Franklin raised his chin defiantly. "Justice, Ma'am."

I sighed. "*Rian* justice."

"Yes, Ma'am," Franklin said proudly, not realizing I was setting him up.

"I see. Were you acting as an officer within the Rian, or as an officer of the Union?"

"The Union, Ma'am," Franklin said, "but..."

"That is the material point, Cadet." I floated towards the glass, they took a 'step' back. "Every being that comes to the *Schola-Terra* has cultural traditions, ingrained prejudices, quirks or sometimes laws that conflict with Union regulations. You can ask Vice-Admiral Pazman. He's dealt with it for years. The worst of it now gets ruled out with the TP scans," would we even be able to continue doing that now? I wondered, "but there are still issues. We cannot be the Union Navy, however, if we aren't all using the *same* rules. The same code."

"But they were murderers and they were going to kill themselves anyway!" Franklin said. Donahue looked like she was willing him to shut the hell up, but I was personally glad he was being honest. It was much harder to make a dent in implacable silence.

"Did you or did you not disobey a direct order, Cadet?"

Franklin paused, desperately wanting to disagree. Eventually, though, there was nowhere to go but to the truth. "Yes, Ma'am."

"Did you or did you not take an oath to obey the officers above you in the chain of command?"

"Yes, Ma'am."

"So you felt that your four days of training as a Cadet gave you the right to break your oath and overrule my order?"

Franklin said nothing.

"Cadet?"

"Yes, Ma'am."

"You know what we are trying to do here, yes? Trying to make the Rian Cadets as good and then better than the other Cadets, super or normal. This behavior of yours and Cadet Donahue's, aside from being criminal, will set you apart as unreliable, untrustworthy and dangerous to our side."

"But back home…" Franklin said, still holding on.

"There are other 'back homes' in the Union, Cadet. 'Back homes' whose inhabitants would turn on the gravity in your bunkroom because you are 'filthy aliens.' Others who would puncture your skin to keep you out of space and trapped inside. Similar to the people who contaminate Heely water or hunt down supers to get them out of the gene pool."

Both Donahue and Franklin stared at me, horrified. Yes, all these things had happened, though they were mostly anecdotal, but we at the ESTF kept an eye on all of it. We'd come a long way, but perfection would always be out of reach.

"Think of the rules of U-Nav as stifling if you like, but they aren't just stifling *you* and orders are orders. If you can't be trusted to follow them, you can't be trusted at all and you need to resign and go 'back home.' Is that what you want?"

"No, Ma'am," Donahue answered immediately.

Franklin took about a second longer, but his answer seemed sincere, "No, Ma'am."

I gave them a long look (for effect) and then said, "You are both on one year's probation. One inch out of line and you're gone."

"But we killed those pe…" Donahue protested. Interesting. She'd wanted justice for the murderers and then justice for *their* murderers.

I nodded. "Only Admirals Manthorpe, Pazman and I know what really happened, but I have made a sworn deposition with my personal attorney telling what I witnessed on that ship. If either one of you ever makes a serious mistake like that again I will release it to the MPs." I would probably go to prison for obstruction of justice, but I didn't really care.

"Forever?" Donahue gulped.

"There is no statute of limitations on murder, kids," I said, "and whether culturally sanctioned or not, that is exactly what that was."

The next day I'd let them go. They'd quietly gone back to their bunks, their classes and their lives. Though they, especially Franklin, would probably have never admitted it, I'm pretty sure both of them worked ten times harder in the years following than they would have before.

Perhaps, Jane, I'd thought, we'll get two good officers out of this horror. Perhaps.

Back in the present, however, all of us, save Paz, were standing over the two conspirators as they opened their eyes.

Stuart kept his eyes fixed on Mr. Bentley as the man's eyes fluttered open before growing wide with terror. "Wait to open up," Stuart commanded us.

Bentley looked around him, not knowing, of course, that all it meant was that Stuart was making sure it was safe before we opened our 'mental' doors.

"Where am I?" Bentley asked. "What are you doing?"

Stuart ignored him and nodded at us. It wasn't a trap, at least not as far as he could tell.

We opened our 'doors.'

I had been prepared for the usual disorganized mess a person's mind was. Scattered thoughts, repetitive worries, bits of music or well-won bits of old conversations or arguments. What I found, through Stuart's projection, was quiet. Order. As if all of Bentley's memories, feelings or plans had been sorted and neatly shelved. Fear was front and center, of course, and dismay. Even that, however, was somehow contained.

I felt Bentley chewing hard, evidently still trying to find that poison tooth, but the tooth was gone.

"Why are you so desperate to die, Bentley?" Stuart asked.

I felt another 'box' open up in Bentley's mind as he answered, "The Great Cause."

"What is the Great Cause?"

Another 'box' opened. "The Master will meet you at Levvon 47-22A on January 28th."

"Cero."

"Yes."

"Where did you meet it?"

All the 'boxes' closed up tight, retreating to their shelves, so to speak.

"Did Cero reorganize your mind?"

Nothing.

"Why is it killing off Telepaths?"

Bentley's light brown eyes looked up at Stuart, this time defiantly. "All life is precious."

"Except the lives of Telepaths," Stuart said.

Then a 'box' opened and we saw what had to have been a memory. It was a person, a being, large and amorphous. If this was Cero, I thought, David's description of it as humanoid had really been stretching it. Just as I thought this, however, the amorphous shape appeared to grow arms and legs and head. It didn't get smaller, it just rearranged itself.

The creature spoke but we heard nothing right away, then I could see a disc hanging in front of its mouth. After a second, words in Standard came out of the disc. A translator.

"We have a story, back where I come from, of a tribe. An ordinary tribe with a chief," the translator had had trouble with that word, "spouses, offspring and the like. They were ordinary by anyone's standards. Unremarkable. Except there was one child in the tribe, Arva, who saw things happen in its mind before they happened in real life. Arva told the chief and chief believed the child and told him to pay attention to the visions. Many years passed and the child grew and the visions kept coming. The tribe avoided many dangers, found food more easily, even won a war without bloodshed all because of the visions of Arva. Then one day Arva came to the chief shaking. He had seen a river of fire blanket the planet, then spread to all the other planets. The chief asked who caused the fire. It was the chief's oldest child. Arva knew that the child had to die. To stop the fire. But the chief would not act, it could not take this life, even to save all the lives of the universe. Arva stayed quiet after that. Things became worse for the tribe. Wars were lost, food stores were spoiled, preventable diseases spread. The visions still came but Arva kept them within himself. And one day when the then long-dead chief's child, now old himself, started the fire that consumed all, Arva stood by his side and wept as they were all carried away by the flames."

I could feel the horror of Bentley, whose memory this was. "The fire...the fire is coming here, Master?" he asked.

The translator again took a second to catch up, "There are all kinds of fire, child, but it is coming."

"I can help you stop it?" Bentley's voice was full of hope and an overwhelming desire to please.

"Yes, but know that if you do, you will not live to see our success."

448

"But I will have done the right thing? The good thing? You will be proud of me?" Desperate need was pouring out of him.

Cero pushed the translator aside and said, in heavily accented Standard, "*Yes.*"

I felt relief wash over all of us. Then joy.

The 'box' closed and we were still inside Bentley's head, but the silence and oppressive order was back in place.

"That is all he said to you?" Stuart asked.

Now Bentley smiled. I wanted to punch him in the mouth.

Stuart ground his teeth and started poking around in Bentley's closed off mind. He got nothing. The boxes wouldn't open for him. At least not yet.

I clenched my teeth in frustration. Tens of thousands of people were going to die, including *children* and this sterile mind had to have something in it that could help us stop it.

'I *know*, Jane,' Stuart thought at me as I belatedly remembered I was linked up to all of them. Then he spoke aloud, "You all may want to get out of his mind. I'm going to dig until I find something."

"Stuart..." Marston started to protest.

Stuart just glared at him and I felt Marston disengage. Then Stuart looked at Samuel, determined. "General?"

Samuel straightened and I saw an image from his mind; Lucy. He'd seen her once four years before and he saw her like she had been then, a little red-haired child who looked, now that I saw her through his eyes, like her mother. I felt tears building behind my eyes. Oh, Samuel. "Proceed, son," he said gruffly. He did not disengage and neither did I. Not because I wanted to be there for the violation of this fool's mind, but because Stuart needed to know that I, as his friend, supported him and also because if Samuel was going to suffer through this to protect my daughter, and through her protect me, I couldn't leave.

Stuart nodded and I steeled myself for the worst as he began.

It was brutal. Stuart, no longer holding any of his power back, ripped through the mental 'boxes' like so much tissue paper. Samuel and I were flooded with childhood memories (of neglect and derision, beatings by people who had to be his parents), abusive love affairs, loss of the one good one he'd had, drugs, violence under the influence, spending sprees, getting thrown out of several schools, nightmares, loss and then, finally,

Stuart stopped speeding through and paused and we were really inside one memory instead of just skimming the surface of hundreds.

Bentley/I was lying in a pool of something, vomit I/Jane realized, and his/my head hurt like a son of a bitch. He/I was lying on his/my belly in what looked like a space station corridor that, from the smell, had been used as an impromptu toilet.

He/I heard a voice, but only I/Jane knew it was the translator speaking. "You are lost, boy," the voice said gently. He/I looked up but it was too dark to see much. The voice continued, "Would you like to be found?"

He/I felt so awful and was so lonely and it had been so long since he/I had heard a kind word from anyone that he/I just burst into tears and nodded.

Out of nowhere, seemingly, what looked like an arm of flesh appeared. The end quickly changed into an articulated humanoid hand. He/I stared at for a second, then he/I reached out and took it, the owner of the hand lifting him/me to his/my feet with incredible strength.

"You may call me Master, Berkshire."

"Master," he/I repeated. We felt his joy.

Stuart kept looking after that and he found some other things including the conversations that had allowed the ordering of Bentley's confused mind—which had been outright fascinating. Cero had picked Bentley up on Levvon, had trained him, helped him and, at least as far as Bentley believed, loved him. Bentley had loved him back, not in the sexual sense, but as one would love a god.

Then suddenly we were in another memory infused with a very different kind of joy.

Bentley/I was sitting in a gun chair in a space ship, firing. Hostile One, I/Jane realized from its position in the Beta arm. Bentley/I stared out at tiny pods flying by the ship we were in and turned back over his/my shoulder and yelled, "Keep marking, little bat!" He/I saw the Tarine, beaten and bloody, with a man I/Jane didn't recognize holding some kind of wand next to the being's chest. The Tarine stood in a tub of water, remaining wing mangled, wrists tied to the ceiling. "Are you sending out the signal?"

The Tarine just wept and the man with the wand touched it to the being's skin. He screamed. "I'm sending it," he whimpered as the rod was pulled away. I/Jane saw a monitor in front of the alien. Each blip on it had a number, from their pod transmitters I/Jane surmised. Who could have known those signals would allow them to be picked off so easily? "Pods

48, 51, 22, 90, 643, 13." As he spoke the marked pods glowed red on the monitor and the ones further away from Hostile One disappeared as they were picked off by the other Hostile ships. The clear spaces on the screen soon filled with new numbers. More prey.

"You're a good little bat, aren't you?" Bentley/I cackled as he fired at each of the closer ones, laughing as each exploded and the TPs inside died.

"Let me go," the Tarine begged and I/Jane realized with a chill that his voice reminded me of Eriss, as if it were Eriss begging. It wasn't Eriss, of course, but they were clones… Oh, god, it was so fucking hard to hear 'her' plead for mercy.

"Keep marking them, little bat, and you'll be free once they're all dead," Bentley said.

"You have to leave my people alone," he said. "You promised."

"Numbers!" Bentley growled and he cast his eyes to the man. The electrified rod was touched to the Tarine's genitals and I/Jane felt that scream in my bones.

"127," the Tarine said breathlessly, sobbing, "289, 421, 1056, 827, 1,609."

Bentley/I shot each of the closest of those down cackling with glee. I/Jane was weeping. So many gone. My kids. Ah, my kids.

Then the Tarine fell silent, its bloody eyes staring into nothingness. Then he turned to Bentley/me.

"More. Numbers," Bentley/I demanded.

The Tarine then smiled a ghastly smile, full of blood and missing teeth.

The rod was applied to the marked skin and the poor alien shrieked and cried.

"Give me a number!" Bentley/I screamed.

The Tarine's smile almost split his face.

"One."

A sound above caused them/us all to look up to see a claw tear through the ceiling revealing both the stars outside and the big black eyes of the being I/Jane knew as Cadet Pinky. For a fraction of a second everyone froze.

Then were sucked out into space.

I was gasping for air I didn't actually lack as I came back to myself in the Infirmary. I took staggering steps to the nearest wall and leaned against it, desperate for its support. I wanted to cry, to rage, to beat the ever loving crap out of the piece of shit Bentley who had had such fun murdering innocents. *My kids.* Samuel and Marston looked sick.

Stuart, however, Stuart looked murderous.

My 'door' was still open though I wasn't in as deeply as I had been and I, along with Marston and Samuel, saw Stuart go to work, slashing and smashing everything he could find in Bentley's mind. *Stuart's* justice was swift and violent. Justice for the gleeful murders of those innocent TPs. For the torture and death of that still-nameless Tarine. For the fear for our children we'd probably never shake.

Though Cero was ultimately to blame for all, Cero wasn't in front of us and when Stuart was finished there was nothing really left of Berkshire Bentley.

Now, finally, we were out and I gratefully closed my 'door.'

Stuart looked at Samuel, Marston and me, as if daring us to challenge him on the havoc he had just wreaked on the defenseless man's mind and, I thought, hiding his shame.

I said nothing, though I felt gutted by all I had witnessed. Samuel didn't say anything either. Marston just stared at his shoes.

Bentley looked around, dazed and vacant. He didn't speak; I wasn't sure he still could. His gaze slid over Dr. Mary Blackthorne with no sign of recognition.

Dr. Blackthorne was on the verge of having a good old-fashioned nervous breakdown.

Without a word Stuart started walking towards her.

She backed up on the bed, but there was nowhere for her to go.

"Please, please! I'll let you see everything! Just don't do that to me, too! Just kill me before you do that!" she screamed.

"Co-operate and you'll keep your mind, Dr. Blackthorne," Marston said in a message more for Stuart than for her. I wasn't worried about Stuart losing his shit again, though. He just looked wrecked though he was trying to hide it.

"I'll do anything, anything!"

"Then open your mind," Stuart said calmly.

Mercifully she did.

She gave us everything she had. She kept her mind, but not her freedom, but as the MPs hauled her away to hand over to the court system, it seemed she got better than she deserved.

452

Throughout all this I could feel Paz standing outside the room, tense and sick. He kept opening his mouth as if to speak, but no words came out. He didn't fall apart, too controlled for that, but he could tell that Bentley had been damaged, seriously damaged by Stuart and I was pretty sure that the fear Blackthorne had felt was something Paz now shared.

I fully understood that, but he hadn't seen what we'd seen.

17:13 – High Admiral Samuel Armstrong's Office, U-Nav Headquarters, Terra 1

Classes were over for the day, finally, and I felt it was time to stop by Samuel's office to see how the intel gathering was going. Alex (along with Garrett) was still on his way home from Solitário which was a shame, in my view, because…well, because I had made up my mind to meddle and wasn't sure of the reception I would get for my trouble. I was still very shaken by what we'd seen in Bentley's mind, but I needed to put it behind me. What better way to do that than to interfere in something that was clearly none of my business?

It was large, Samuel's outer office, and when I walked in I saw it teaming with its usual activity. Aside from Alex not being there, the only things unusual were the presences of Huong and Quinn, who both looked up when I entered. I belatedly made sure my 'door' was closed. I thought that letting Huong (whom I had forgotten was an Empath more than once) into my mind would be cruel after the day I'd had.

Unaware of my musings, Huong, beautiful, tiny, delicate Huong, rose from her chair and embraced me. At least that was nice.

"Good to see you, Huong," I said truthfully. "It's been ages."

"That is has," she said with a smile.

Quinn had risen, too, but he stayed where he was. "Jane."

"Hey, Quinn," I responded.

Huong, who, one way or another, knew everything about everyone, did not miss a beat even though Quinn and I were the awkward twins. "We've been going over the information from Bentley and Blackthorne."

"Anything new?"

She raised her perfect eyebrows and looked at Quinn, who said, "Not as yet, but we did come to a conclusion, based on Admiral Pazman's work tracing Cadet Dresden." Yes, the bomb detonating suicide.

"And?"

Quinn answered. "All roads lead to Levvon."

"The Blackthorne woman met it in Levvon, too."

"She did."

Now Huong spoke, "Lord Miller found absolutely no evidence of coercion or brainwashing, right?"

I shook my head. "None."

Huong shrugged. "Lost souls." She turned back to her monitor.

"Lost souls?"

She turned back to me and nodded. "You'd be surprised how many people who do bad things are just people who desperately need...something. Some people in that position find a purpose by throwing themselves into contributing, some only want to punish the universe for their own suffering. Some are so desperate to be seen that they don't care who wants them as long as they are wanted."

"Which do you think Bentley was?"

"From what Lord Miller said," she sighed, "he was all three."

Depressing thought.

"The High Admiral's people are now checking every person who has been unaccounted for, so to speak, on Levvon over the last six months," Quinn said, leaning back in his chair to stretch.

"Take eight hours, Quinn," Huong said. "You've been working non-stop since you got here."

"I don't need a break," Quinn said a little defensively.

"I know," she said placatingly, "but I do and I won't leave if you don't. The Admiral's people will have data for us when we come back."

When it was put like that, even Quinn had to give in. So, seeing my opportunity, I pounced. "Care for a drink?"

Huong smiled, "Another time, Jane. I'm beat."

"Quinn?" I asked.

Quinn eyed me warily, as well he should. "Sure."

A few minutes later we were seated at the bar at Aronoff's. It was busy and having all the people around us made it seem somehow more private than if we'd had the place to ourselves. Quinn pounded down several shots immediately, apparently girding himself for whatever mischief I was planning. I nursed my one glass of spirits.

"So, Jane, what's on the agenda for this evening?" he asked, shooting back another one. His tolerance was impressive.

"Why do you ask?" I said innocently.

"Because we've said more to each other in the last twenty minutes than we have in the last eight years."

It was true, of course. I'd stopped telling him to fuck off all the time years ago and, the rare times we'd seen each other, I'd treated him as a distant acquaintance. My grudge against him, on my behalf and on Wilby's, had lost strength over the years but had never really gone away.

"Wilby is settling in well. With the kids and Shira."

"So he's said in his letters." Quinn tapped the bar, indicating he needed more shots.

"Seems pretty unhappy otherwise."

Quinn looked at me sharply. "Did he tell you that?"

I laughed without any humor. "Like he needs to."

The shots came and Quinn downed them all efficiently. His eyes were turning a little red. His body language was softening, relaxing a bit with the consumption of alcohol. "He's been getting his dick wet."

Gross. "He's allowed."

"Yeah." More shots were ordered.

"What will you do if he meets someone?"

Quinn sat bolt upright, still drunk, but as tense as he could manage under the influence. "Has he?"

"Not to my knowledge."

Quinn stared at the bar and drank the spirits as they were placed in front of him. He was moving slower, but the need for alcohol was still there.

"It will happen, you know."

"I know." Quinn rested his head on the bar.

I had to be careful now; I didn't want to break my word to Shira, but I needed him to man the fuck up. "You need to fix it or let him go, Quinn." I leaned forward. "It's cruel to keep him like this."

"I have no choice, Jane."

"Bullshit."

"You don't understand."

"You're right, I don't," I said, disgusted. "Did you do something? Something you need to tell him, but are too chicken shit to open your mouth and say?"

Quinn raised his head and stared at me, his green eyes wide with fear and then anger. "What do you know?"

"So there *is* something?"

"*No!*" he almost shouted. The bar was loud, though, and no one noticed.

"You know," I said as I got up from my stool, "I thought you were jealous, but now I know that you're just a coward."

Quinn rose so quickly I almost didn't have time to react. Before I knew it I was on the floor, his huge hand around my neck. I was, for the record, in no danger from him, but the booze had made him forget that and he snarled at me as he held me down.

All conversation at the bar had ceased.

A pleasant calm voice, Missy's, I identified easily, spoke, "Everything all right here, friends?"

"Fine, Missy," I said though my voice was understandably choked. "Just a sec."

Then I 'pushed' the giant man off of me and threw him on *his* back. He just stared at me in surprise. "What did you do?" I hissed. "You've been acting like a jealous maniac for years now and this isn't you. What. Did. You. Do?"

"The MPs are on their way," Missy said calmly.

"Thank you, Missy," I said.

"Let me go," Quinn said.

"Tell me."

He shook his head.

"You have about one minute before they get here," Missy said, clearly getting that this was not just an argument between former friends, but an interrogation.

"You're trying to scare me with *jail*?" Quinn scoffed.

Then I played the eternal parental trump card. "I'll have Shira bail you out."

His face went ashen and he stopped resisting.

"She knows, doesn't she?" he asked, his voice that now of a little boy.

"Why would you say that?"

He snorted. "She was spying on a *spy*, Jane." He closed his eyes. "She's just better at it than the old man." Or he'd let her find out even if he hadn't made it easy for her to do so. I'd had my suspicions.

I heard the commotion that could only be the Military Police arriving. "It's now or never, Quinn."

He exhaled hugely and nodded. "Fine. I'll talk."

I shook my head. "Don't talk to me. Talk to him."

The look of fear returned. "I'll lose him."

"Khaver," I said gently, "he's halfway gone already."

His face fell and I thought he would cry. Eventually he nodded again.

I 'released' him and he stood. The MPs reached us and I painted on a big drunken smile. "Sorry, officers, my friend and I got carried away. Fucker can't take a joke about the game."

Quinn smiled, too, though his smile was far drunker and much less convincing. "Her Eagles beat my Chosen in November." He stepped forward sloppily and put his hand on the MPs shoulder, almost knocking him over. "I lost two hundred credits on that game." He pointed at me. "Her fault. Red Angel don't," he corrected himself, "doesn't play fair."

The listing MP went to attention at the mention of my nickname, recognizing me. "Vice-Admiral Pace."

"It's Ok, Sergeant," I said, glad for once of my rank. "Just a misunderstanding."

The Sergeant looked at the (comparatively) diminutive Vice-Admiral next to the mountain that was Quinn. Only next to Quinn could I look small.

"It's true," Missy volunteered. "Macro-Ball is good for business, but you've seen the trouble it can cause."

Apparently this wasn't the first time the Police had been called to Aronoffs. I'd picked a very believable lie. Good one, Jane.

"If you and the Vice-Admiral say so," the Sergeant said.

"We do," I said.

The Sergeant and his partner saluted me and I saluted back and then they departed. Fun over, the noise of the bar started up again, heading quickly for its usual volume.

Missy came around the bar. "Are you Ok, Jane?"

"I'm fine, thanks, Missy."

I looked at Quinn as Missy's name was called from behind the bar. She went back to work and Quinn stood straighter, his incredible Judean metabolism already fighting off the effects of the shots. He already looked better, however, but in different way. It was as if, now that he'd given his word, something had settled in him.

We started out of the bar. "I can't tell him in a letter, Jane," he said quietly. "I'll go see him after this is all over."

"Really?"

"It's not a dodge," he said. "I will do it." He sighed. "If, after that, he wants to be free, then I will let him go."

I put my arm on his massive shoulder comfortingly.

"I am sorry, Jane," he said softly. "For keeping you from your friend. It was a mistake."

That was something at least. I didn't know what to say because agreeing with him (which I did, of course) seemed cruel under the circumstances so I kept quiet.

"I've fucked up so many times, Jane." He wiped his eyes as we walked. "I don't know how to get back."

"Give all of us your best from now on, Quinn." I rubbed his shoulder. "You've fucked up but you aren't a fuckup. Be the man I called friend, be the man Wilby fell in love with and you can make your way back."

"You think so?"

Well, I certainly *hoped* so. "Absolutely."

Then I was struck by the memory of Shira telling me that losing Wilby would break him and Huong's speech about lost people needing to be found by the right people and added, "If you do lose him, Quinn, and need a friend, you come to me, Ok?"

"Why to…" he stopped, confused. "After all I've done…how could you offer..?"

"No one deserves to be lost, love."

He ran his hand over his face. "I'm not so sure about that, khaver."

"I am."

08:00 – High Admiral's Office, U-Nav Headquarters, Terra 1, January 14th, 2882

I entered quickly the next morning since I was actually on my way to class, and saw the usual activity in Samuel's outer office. Quinn and Huong were bent over Huong's monitor, studying it intently. Samuel himself stepped out of his inner office at the same time I arrived.

"I was just about to call you," he said and since he was projecting calm stoicism I knew something was up. Something serious.

"What's the word, Samuel?" I asked lightly.

"Levvon," he responded succinctly. "Among other things." He didn't elaborate. In fact, he looked like he was waiting for something.

I had places to be so stepped over to Quinn and Huong. "Have you tracked any lost souls who went through there?"

Quinn looked up at me. "We have been able to track some, though not all." That wasn't a surprise since Levvon handled ninety percent of all shipping (passenger or freight) through Thao. That could be upwards of ten million people over a four month period. Sorting the lost from the found had to be quite the undertaking. I didn't envy them.

"Where have the ones you've tracked gone?"

"Nowhere interesting, really," Huong answered, frustrated. "Some here, and," she added, "we are bringing those in for questioning with Lord Miller," I kind of shuddered at the thought, "and others back to their home worlds."

Marston then appeared at the doorway of the office and Samuel waved him in. "In my office, if you would."

The four of us followed him into the inner sanctum and he shut the door behind us.

"I have briefed President Soto," Mary Soto, the Esperanzan who'd succeeded Union President Leder's after his retirement, "and she has given her orders."

He paused, clearly very unhappy.

"Sam?" Marston prompted.

"Mindful of the various attacks Terra has sustained and taking into account the recent violence around Terra 1 the President has ordered the temporary closing of *Schola-Terra* until this matter is resolved."

We all just stared at him. "She's shutting down the Academy?" I summarized numbly. Had that ever even happened before?

"The normal students will be sent home to await orders for a resumption of classes."

"And the supers?"

"Will be sent to Paragon."

For a minute the words 'sent to Paragon' refused to make sense. Slowly, however, things computed. Paragon was the Rian capital, hell and gone from anything in the Union that *wasn't* Rian. If they had to go somewhere it wasn't a terrible place to send them under the circumstances. Still…

Huong was frowning. "How will they get there?"

"Initially the plan was to send them in a transport ship with a small escort fleet supplemented by one of the merc fleets but no merc fleets were available."

Huong's frown deepened.

"It was also decided," or Samuel had put his foot down, "that concentrating them within one ship was asking for trouble, so the Cadets will be distributed within the new Union Fleet Paragon-Gamma."

"Strength?" Huong asked.

"Twelve ships."

"Commander?"

"Admiral Tree."

Huong shrugged as if displeased she couldn't argue with the choice.

Samuel folded his arms over his chest. "I know what you're feeling, Huong, but the President does have a point and while I can't think of a good place for the super Cadets to go, Paragon is at least out of the way."

"It's not that, Sir," Quinn said unexpectedly. "It's the unseen hand that is pushing all this along."

Samuel sighed. "I know. You're not the only ones who think we only *feel* like we're making our own choices."

Huong was on another worrisome topic, however. "We have, to date, five mercenary fleets, including the Furies and *none* of them was available?" I was now afraid her pretty face was forever going to be marred by her frown.

"Not one," Samuel answered.

She started making notes on her screen. "Worrisome."

Everything was worrisome.

A Note on the Five Major Mercenary Fleets within the Union

There were more than five, of course, but the five biggest and best were the ones with supers, not surprisingly. Some supers came from the Furies, seeking greener pastures. Some were former Academy dropouts, but some were graduates who preferred the freedom and monetary rewards of a private enterprise. The leaders of each of these Fleets were paying top dollar for qualified supers and everyone knew it. The one that paid the least, however, was the Furies, though most vied for a spot there. The Furies were known for good treatment, fair (if not extravagant) pay and strictly enforced tolerance. They were the only Fleet with Heely supers and

Pacey Marines. Though they were not the largest Fleet, they had the best reputation and the lowest mission casualty rate (percentage-wise) of any Fleet including U-Nav. It's not that the other Fleets were awful, but the Furies was the only one founded and run by Paceys and Paceys always took freaks to their hearts.

So, the mercs:

1. *The Three Furies Fleet, Five ships, 1,000 personnel strength, Commanded by Captain Atalanta Pace (Captain Paul Friedman had been KIA on a mission two years before.)*
2. *The One Eyed Jacks Mercenary Group (OEJ), Eight ships, 3,500 personnel strength, Commanded by 'Admiral' Sylvester Roykirk.*
3. *The Ryuu, Ten ships, 900 personnel strength, Commanded by Commodore Seiko Hashimoto.*
4. *Forløpere til Undergang (Harbingers of Doom), Four Ships, 5,000 personnel strength, Commanded by Captain Hansen.*
5. *Les Renards, Seven Ships, 2,700 personnel strength, Commanded by General Bertrande Fox.*

The Ryuu's Fleet was, forgive me, the fleetest, with the smallest, newest and fastest ships and their commander was ruthless and clever. The Forløpere had the oldest, most labor intensive Fleet, but their firepower was unmatched. I'd seen simulations of some of their battles (Felix had shown me) and their inventiveness in using what they had was impressive. Their maneuverability was limited but they planned around it and when they got you in their sights you were toast. Les Reynards was the sneakiest, always just this side of breaking the law (though there were rumors that they had crossed over the line many a time) and the OEJ was run by a man with more money than sense.

These five groups, made up of cast-offs and misfits, did the work U-Nav either wouldn't or couldn't do and, at present, they were all too busy to be hired. Odd, that.

"Jane, contact our people with the Furies and see if you can get more information," Samuel said. I nodded. I knew, from my correspondence with Atalanta, that things had lately been slow with the Furies Fleet. Like, not going to make payroll slow. I didn't blame them for jumping at a job, but the timing was unfortunate. I only hoped that was all it was.

"I need to talk to my kids," I said, "before we go to Paragon."

Samuel shook his head. "Talk to them before they go, Jane, but you're not going to Paragon. At least not right away."

"I'm not going with them?" I asked, fear clenching my gut.

"You, Quinn, Stuart and I are going to Levvon. Huong will keep monitoring everything here." Huong nodded. Then he checked his watch. "We'll leave as soon as Alex gets back to keep an eye on things. Which should be in about six hours."

"Our instructors will be with Paragon-Gamma?"

"Yes," Samuel said. "With Marston." Marston looked relieved.

"I…" I sighed, "I can't say I like this, Samuel. I feel like I am abandoning them." Again. Letting them down again.

"If we have a chance to catch Cero and stop whatever is coming before it comes on Levvon, we need to take the risk."

I looked in his handsome (to me) face and saw two things: that he believed it and that he was afraid. That was all I needed, though I still wasn't happy about any of it.

"Right."

"The Home Fleet has already been placed on high alert as have all the Fleets within U-Nav."

Quinn looked at Samuel. "What will they be told?"

Now Samuel looked really unhappy. "The President will send out a message to the Union warning that supernormals, both military and civilian alike, are being targeted for extermination by an outside force and that in solidarity with the many supernormals who live among us as friends and fellow citizens and in remembrance of those supers who have given their lives for the Union in service, we must prepare to stand up for them as they have stood up for us."

"That…" Marston said, "…is not how I would have chosen to go."

"Nor I, to be honest," Samuel said, "but it is what she will say."

"It will be open season on supers," I muttered. Every asshole with a grudge about the 'unfair' and 'preferential' treatment of supers will get out their axes in the name of avoiding a war. Why would they want to die for freaks? "Has the President been living under a rock all this time?"

"No," Samuel said, "but she sees only the progress we've made with supers, not the bad. She got elected on hope. Fortunately, or unfortunately, it wasn't a pose, it is how she views everything."

"So a few villagers with torches and pitchforks will be ignored, too." God forbid you were a super *and* an escaped former sex slave. What were your chances of survival then? I took comfort, though, in the fact that a lot of the former slaves had taken advantage of one of the last acts of President Ledger's administration: a 'Clean Slate' bill that allowed any refugee without a criminal record to erase his or her history and take a new name (obviously not Napia or Torva) and start afresh. Hopefully many of them now functioned in quiet anonymity, though with this announcement they'd be looking over their shoulders for sure, new name/life notwithstanding.

I started at the attention signal and we all turned to see Samuel's desk monitor switch on. The pretty oval face and dark eyes of Union President Mary Soto appeared on the screen.

"My fellow citizens," she said solemnly. "A threat to the heart of our Union is upon us…"

She spoke for quite a while, but I didn't listen. I nodded goodbye to everyone and went to see my Cadets and tell them it was going to be all right. And hope I wasn't lying.

ENTRY 12-8-95

<u>12:46 – Ambassadorial Suite, Corsican Embassy, Terra 1, Terra, January 14th, 2882</u>

"How did it go with your Cadets?" Charles asked, still trying to catch his breath as I lay, half-clothed, over him on the couch in his office.

I sighed and snuggled closer, not caring that I was wrinkling his already wrinkled crisp white shirt. I hated to think of the state of his trousers…which were currently around his ankles. "They got it, though many of them wanted to stay and fight whatever it is we're fighting."

Charles chuckled and I could feel the sound rumble through his broad chest. Lovely. "They want a chance to be badasses like their hero, the Red Angel."

I made an irritated sound. "Sounds like a good way to get yourself killed." I sat up reluctantly. Unfortunately, there were things I had to do before we left in about two hours. "Not everyone can have my luck."

Charles frowned. "What worries me is that even you may not always have your luck, Jane."

It worried me, too, really. Not so much for myself, but for the life and people I'd be leaving behind. "It doesn't do any good to dwell on it, love."

"I know." He rose, pulling up his pants as he did so.

I stood up, too, quickly putting myself back together with a speed my beloved spouse would never be able to match. The thought made me smile. I straightened his tie. "You're all mussed, Six."

He smiled down at me as he pulled me close. "I've earned it."

"That you have."

He looked thoughtful as I pulled my long hair back into its ponytail. "I think I'll go back home while all this is going on."

I looked at him, surprised. "You will?"

"Lucy will pick up on our worry and I think…I think I should be with her." *In case you don't come back* was left unsaid.

"That is a good idea, Charles." While the implications were disturbing to me, I really wanted him away from Terra. Bad things always seemed to happen to Terra. "Give Lucy and Idis my love."

He held me tightly and said, "What do *I* get?"

I kissed him and said quietly, "Everything I am and everything I have."

He nodded. "Back at ya, Red," he whispered against my lips as he kissed me back.

15:23 – Main Cabin, *T.S.S. Liberty*, Hyperspace (bound for Levvon)

I'd seen my kids off. Admiral Jennifer Tree had been anxious to go and I hadn't blamed her. I'd hugged Marston, seen Samuel tenderly kiss Mallory (who was going with the Cadets as well) goodbye, and had seen the Denethian Cadets safely settled in the X-ship attached (in record time) to the *U.S.S. Jefferson*, Admiral Tree's flagship. I'd wondered about their reception at Paragon; some Rian weren't as thrilled as I'd have liked about training their youngsters to be Union officers. The majority seemed all right with it, though, and the newly elected *profà-Pelann* (the secular leader as opposed to Eriss, the *sagrat-Pelann*, who was the spiritual one), backed by our ally Tirith, had been completely onboard with the idea. I was pretty sure that had been one of the main reasons that particular Rian, Tresso, now *profà-Pelann* Tresso, had been Tirith's protégé in the first place.

Either way, that was their problem (at least for now) and we were going to face down Cero, assuming Cero was there, since we were much earlier than Cero (through Bentley) had told us to come. I wasn't worried, however. One of the side effects of dealing with a suspected pre-cognitive was that it probably was well aware that we were coming and it'd either be there or it wouldn't. Or perhaps it had no choice either. This all sucked. I just preferred it sucked more for Cero than for us.

So now I sat on the small couch in the main cabin of my ship next to former flame, Samuel, and across from former sexual partner, Stuart. Quinn was already dead to the world in my cabin. The two teams of U-Nav Marines were safely ensconced in the Cargo Holds and our military pilot in the cockpit.

Samuel leaned back and closed his eyes, an expression of fatigue I knew he would have allowed few to see.

"How are you holding up, Samuel?" I asked, thinking there were few who could even ask him that. My mind flashed back to a time so long ago it was back on Pace 4 when he'd told me how hard it was to be treated as a regular person when one was addressed as 'sir' or 'ma'am.'

"Any luck fixing Wilby and Quinn yet?" Samuel asked, dodging answering my question. Silly man. Just putting off the inevitable.

"I've shaken things up a bit," I said, "now it's up to them to see if they can put things back together."

"Because it wasn't always?" Stuart said archly.

"Sometimes people need a little push, Stu." I threw a pillow at him.

"I wonder, Jane, what you would do if all the people you loved suddenly did everything right?" Stuart said, his eyes twinkling with amusement. "Communicated? Were always the best person they could be? Completely unselfish and generous? Perfect people with no problems to sort?"

"I don't know, Stuart," I said, glaring at him, though I knew he was teasing. "Find new friends?"

Stuart dissolved into laughter. Even Samuel cracked a smile at that one. "I think I'll get some rack time," Stuart said as he rose out of his chair, then grabbed my hand and kissed it, by way of an apology for the teasing, and toddled off.

I turned back to Samuel and I felt his sigh. "So, Samuel, how are you holding up?"

He sighed again and actually answered. "Pretty well, Jane." He tipped his head back and closed his eyes again. "But for so long the supers were *our* supers and then when it turned out there were more than just Pacey supers, they became our supers, too. That's a lot of people to feel responsible for." No shit, I thought. He sat up and looked at me. "You know, we left Pace twelve and a half years ago."

"That long ago?"

"That long," he confirmed. "So many of our people have grown into their lives here. They've gotten jobs and careers and spouses and lovers…"

"And children."

"Yes." He rubbed his hands over his face. "So many are supers." He cocked his head to one side. "You must be even more afraid for them than I am." Lucy. Always fears for Lucy.

I thought we'd only be picking at Samuel's feelings in this conversation. Bastard. "I am afraid, Samuel, but as long as I'm alive to fight to protect them I will fight."

"I never doubted that, Jane."

"I never doubted it for you, either, my friend."

Samuel was silent for a while.

"Do you think it's weird that we can sit here and be friends like this?" I blurted out. Why the need to say this had come over me was inexplicable, but there it was. I wished I could take it back, but, well...

Then Samuel smiled, "It's a first for me, I will admit, but, I think we can do it because we liked and respected each other before we were together. Somehow, that never disappeared even after we had to fall apart."

I nodded because, though I hadn't thought about it before, he was right. I wanted to know if he was happy, though, I wanted to know if he loved Mallory and not with his usual cute deflections, but for real. Because he was right, I did like and respect him. I always had and always would. I loved him, even if it wasn't the overwhelming passion it had once been.

Samuel rose. "I'm going to look for food."

"Good luck," I said distastefully because the fare had only been interesting when Thal had been around to look after it. When it was left to me there tended to be two hundred-fifty packets of reconstituted chicken bites and that was it. Then I had a thought. "Hey, Samuel?"

He'd made it to the door but turned back. "Yes, Jane?"

"What does Mallory call you?"

He frowned at me. "What does she call me?"

"Sam or Samuel?"

"Oh," he said and he looked off into space as if picturing her. His cheeks pinked just a little. "Samuel." He didn't meet my eyes, but his private smile was adorable.

He left but I couldn't stop smiling myself. Samuel. She called him *Samuel*. Something in my heart kind of settled. He was happy. He was in love and that delightful thought cheered me up quite a bit. It couldn't do that forever, of course, since we were still facing some scary shit, but it was such a wonderful thing to know.

I went to go sharpen my knives. Like most people did when they want to relax and distract from impending doom.

A Reminder Note about Levvon

Levvon still reigned as the premier shipping hub of Thao and had done so for over two hundred years. One of the reasons for this dominance was its four enormous orbital barges. They were called barges and they looked like barges but there was more to them than that. Floating in space around Deen (the secondary planet and the shipping center) these barges looked like a vast set of boxes, stacked almost unevenly giving the illusion of a giant's block set. These 'block sets' were roughly the size of small cities and could hold a tremendous amount of cargo. The cargo would be picked up either by another Levvonese ship (which would simply detach the containers needed) or (once fees were paid) by the end consumer. Some of the barges even contained massive, though not luxurious, living quarters, shopping and restaurants.

Each of these orbital concerns served a particular section of the galaxy, though that could change at the drop of a hat. Everything was modular, everything interchangeable. Whether shipper or consumer you could hold anything and anyone (though not slaves anymore) in your containers and move them anywhere.

You could even, if it came down to it, hide a mass murderer from a race unknown.

21:09 – Tubular Hallway Outside 47-22A, Orbit around Deen, Levvon, Kingdom of Gloriana-Levvon, Thao Protectorate, January 18th, 2882

Samuel, Stuart, Quinn, twelve armed to the teeth Marines and I walked/climbed/slid down the outer connecting tubes that allowed access to the containers, specifically to Container 47-22A.

We emerged at the proper airlock and, after a glance from Samuel, Quinn pounded on the door. He waited a second, then started turning the wheel that unlocked it. Eventually he pulled the heavy door open and we went into the airlock itself, the outer door closing behind us with an imposing metallic thud. He banged on the inner door and we just stood there. It was hard not to feel trapped in the space especially since the twelve giant Marines (not to mention Quinn) didn't make it seem any larger. Eventually the inner door clanked as its wheel was turned and it finally swung open.

We entered a vast space. Metal walls and a false floor oddly comprised of strips of metal with gaps between them large enough to catch a human-sized foot if one wasn't careful. There were lights overhead, way up, too high to really make out and it was dim even with them shining. It was a cargo cube, but there wasn't, as I scanned, anything in it but us and something in the far corner. A dark corner. The set up was something, I thought, out of one of those T.I. horror shows. I strengthened the shield around us that I'd automatically put up when we'd entered.

We heard a scratching noise, then, through the translator, "Let me tell you how this will go, Humans." A pause then more scratching sounds. "You will talk to me for six minutes, you will get very angry, you will try to kill me and I will escape. I'd skip the whole process if I could, but this is how it has been foretold."

"You are Cero," Samuel stated.

Scratching. "I am."

"Why are you trying to kill the supernormals?" Samuel must have figured that he only had six minutes, so why waste time with preamble.

"Some must die so that all may live," it said.

"But why?"

"Fire that burns all the worlds," it said. "You heard my parable, if you took any of my people alive." So he'd planted that in *all* of them? Geez.

"You'll have to be more specific."

The creature/being moved closer and I stepped in front of Samuel. Quinn moved in front of Stuart, who didn't try to hide his annoyance at being protected this way. Cero came into the light and we could at last see whatever form it had taken. What it had taken was green and a hexaped with the head of a Tellescan Balla (like a Terran lion but with fins instead of a mane). "Not really. You are going to attempt to stop me no matter what I tell you."

"True, but we'd like to know anyway."

"Tell your Attack Dog," me, I guessed, "and your Professional Killer," Quinn, "to back off and I will." It blinked at us, though I was pretty sure the creature, in its natural form didn't even have eyes.

"Jane," Samuel said and I moved to his side. Quinn, however, stayed right where he was.

"I saw a Terran Human, a male, a superhuman with the power to amplify energy," it said. "He was a living weapon of tremendous power, but he could not *make* energy himself." The creature sat up on two of its hind legs. "He wanted to have his own power and set about absorbing as much energy as he could. He tried small explosions and found he could hold their energy and then use the power later."

"Like a battery," Stuart said. I felt the 'knock knock' of a TP wanting in and I opened my 'door.'

"Yes," it confirmed, "but he was greedy and kept looking for a bigger and bigger bang. All this I pieced together myself from many visions, but the first vision I had was the last one in his time line: he tried to harness the nuclear reaction of Proxima Centauri."

A red dwarf star close (in galactic terms) to Terra. "Oh god," I whispered.

"It worked for a fraction of a second. He held all that power just long enough to be the most powerful being in the universe and then he lost control and the star went nova."

Suddenly I saw the vision, taken from Cero's mind and placed in mine (and, I assumed, Samuel's and Quinn's) by Stuart. A man in a very unusual DSS floated at a good distance from a red star. The star shook, then went dark and the man glowed, waves of energy emanating from him in incredible color. The man took a breath as though to laugh in triumph and...everything went blinding white as the star went nova.

"However, he hadn't merely caused a star to explode, you see," Cero continued, "for his abilities allowed him, as I've told you, to multiply energy. He took that nova and multiplied it 10,000 times, spreading it throughout the galaxy."

The vision then backed up from Proxima at an incredible rate as we watched the blinding light of the destruction of the star expand through its own system and to the next, the next, the next and so on.

"Even the worlds that were untouched by the amplified nova were affected...some by being shifted in their orbits either a few feet or mere inches. Some died from debris."

The vision zeroed in on one quadrant of the galaxy that, once hit by the nova, was followed by nova after nova after nova.

"Beta quadrant, where Thao and other centers of trade exist, was wiped out by a nova chain reaction. Of course there was no one left to be amazed by it once it was done."

The vision changed and became a little boy sitting in the dark in a shed with a candle. He looked to be about six. He looked at the flame, held out his hand, and the flame went out. He smiled and held his hand out again.

The floor caught on fire and he ran out screaming as the shed burnt like tinder.

"This boy, who will become the man that, effectively, ends the galaxy, is a descendant of the supers now living."

"Whose descendent?" I had to ask.

"I do not know, Attack Dog," Cero sneered through the translator. "Perhaps yours?"

"There is no way to that figure out?" Stuart asked.

"No, Telepath Prince," Cero said. "There are no future birth records."

"Can't we stamp out any, what did you call it, 'energy amplifiers' as they are born?" Quinn asked. Gruesome thought, but still a bit better than wiping out tens of thousands of supers.

"He is unique," Cero said. "A genetic anomaly." He looked disdainfully at Quinn. "Killer."

"So," Samuel said, back to the main point, "you aren't just limiting yourself to killing Telepaths, are you? You really plan on murdering *all* the supers to prevent the birth of *one* super?"

"I did not and do not wish to kill anyone, Boss Man, but my vision tells me that *now* is the time I can act if I wish to save all life."

"Even your own?" Stuart said, but Samuel said, "You are a *nexus* pre-cog. Like Whitman was."

Oh, now that could be interesting. "So there are other points, other times you can stop this, right?" I asked, childishly hopeful. "How far off is this event?"

Cero hesitated, then the scratching resumed. "Hard to say. Feels like five hundred years or so."

Stuart laughed in relief. "We have plenty of time to prevent this, then."

"*NO*, Telepath Prince!" Cero practically screamed. "It is *now* and only *now*."

Silence for a second and then Samuel's rich voice echoed in the large room. "Do you succeed?"

"It is a nexus, Boss Man," Cero said quietly. "I do not know."

"Why did you say you would meet us on the 28th?" I asked.

"It was one of the options. I should have known you would be too impatient. You moved your supers away from Terra 1 faster than I had anticipated."

Fear grabbed a cold hand on my innards. It knew about the kids. Oh fuck, it knew.

"I had, of course, anticipated this possibility and here we are."

I looked at Samuel who appeared calm, but I could read adrenaline crackling through his system. Stuart read the same as did Quinn.

"Don't worry, Attack Dog," Cero said. "Enough of the freaks will be together soon enough to make a difference."

What the fuck did that mean?

"What have you done?" Samuel growled. Four of the scariest words in Standard—or any language, come to think of it.

"You, Attack Dog, have you ever had a blind mission?"

The implications of that question were terrifying in this context and I felt sick. "No. The Furies won't take them."

Blind missions were rare and ethical mercenary fleets wouldn't do them at all. An employer would hire mercs and install a program in their tactical computers that would prevent any access to navigational systems during the mission—except by the program itself. The stated reason for this would be so the fleets could claim deniability afterwards. The fleets would then drop out of hyper wherever and into whatever, perform their mission (it was usually way too dangerous to back out by then) and try to get out before they were arrested or killed. Or arrested and then killed. The employer would also have their own people within the fleet making sure that no one changed their minds when they saw what kind of water (so to speak) they were in. It was gambling at the most dangerous level. I had heard of the OEJ (the One Eyed Jacks merc Fleet) taking on a job or two like that, but I'd thought it was only rumors started by their 'Admiral' to make him look like a badass.

Why did anyone take them, if they were so dangerous? Because they paid. One thousand times more than the same job (assuming there could even be an equivalent) under normal circumstances. These blind missions, however, were the stuff of legend and so rare they weren't even technically illegal. It would be like passing legislation against ghosts or the Loch Ness Monster. They just never happened.

However, there had been no merc fleets to hire when we'd needed them and the Furies was hurting for money so badly that Atalanta had talked in her last letter about putting one of the ships in dry dock and laying off all its crew.

"You didn't…" I started. Mother of god.

Samuel spoke, his voice hard. "You hired all the merc fleets with supers on a blind mission to..?"

Stuart looked pale enough in the dim light that I thought he might faint. Fainting sounded appealing to me, too, but we hadn't time for such luxuries. "Where did you send them?"

Cero laughed (or something like it) and said, "Don't worry, Telepath Prince, we'll be coming for your little ones soon enough." It turned its 'head' to Samuel. "Were I you, Boss Man, I'd take your Attack Dog home. Right away."

"Not to Pace," Samuel said. Funny that that had been his first thought. "Her real home."

Home. Corsica. Lucy. Charles.

I couldn't breathe. I fought off a panic attack with my blinding rage.

I 'reached' out and 'grabbed' Cero, intending to rip the motherfucker into bits, but the creature simply smiled...and slipped down through the bars in the floor.

Gone.

Sure, I 'pulled' up the bars and dropped into the sub floor, chasing after it, but none of us, Marines included, Quinn included, could find it.

Gone.

Corsica.

We raced to the *Liberty* and disengaged from the box we'd been attached to. The pilot immediately put in the coordinates Samuel had given for Irena and we went into hyper almost instantly, whether or not it was safe to do so.

There was only one message waiting for us on the ship, once we'd been able to focus on such things. It was from Huong from the day before.

URGENT Personal Message to High Admiral Samuel Armstrong, T.S.S. Liberty, January 17th, 2882

Sir,

Irena has sent out a planetary distress call, having received intelligence of an imminent invasion. All Fleets except Home Fleets have been called to defend the Corsican system. Paragon-Gamma has been rerouted as well. I had to get this message out through unauthorized channels because all the communications grids have been failing, one by one. The T.I. satellites failed a few minutes ago.

I think the information about the invasion is false, but no one else thinks so.

My spook network will not last the day if whoever is silencing us is as good as I think they are.

I hope you had good luck at Levvon, Sir, because there is none to be found here. I will keep working on getting communication back to normal unless I receive further orders.

Huong Schulweis, Information Agent

Samuel's response to Huong was bounced back. We couldn't reach anyone else, not because our equipment was bad, but because no one else's appeared to be functioning.

So we ran. We ran for Home.

05:02 – Orbit around Irena, Capital Planet of Corsican Empire, January 21st, 2882

Two and a half days. It had taken us two and a half days of running like hell to get to Irena. If I'd slept it had only been by accident. Samuel and Stuart hadn't done any better, though Quinn had slept like the dead. Judean training, apparently. I'd been tempted to take a sleep aid, but I'd been too afraid I'd be drugged when something bad occurred so I'd just stayed awake. Terrified. I'd sharpened my knives to the point where I'd come close to ruining them. My projectile guns had never been so spotlessly clean. Had there been a rug on the hallway that lead from the main cabin to the cargo holds I would have worn it to the weft with pacing. I'd only forced myself to eat because I didn't want to be any more depleted than I already was, but food was supremely unappealing. The four of us had done endless hours of fight training, trying to stay sharp and also, though it didn't work, trying to wear ourselves out enough to be able to rest.

Nothing worked. Fear prevailed.

One conversation had added to the fear.

We'd been sitting, the four of us, in the main cabin, trying to play cards to pass the time. I say trying because no one seemed to have the focus to carry the game except Samuel, who won every hand of poker, and Quinn, who was a surprisingly bad player. I kept folding unless I had something brilliant, but even when I did I bet stupidly.

"What do you suppose Pace 4 is like now, Jane?" Stuart had asked out of nowhere.

I'd answered him with an eyebrow raise.

He'd shrugged. "I wondered if it looks anything like it did when we lived there."

"No idea," I answered honestly. I could have gone to see it any time I'd wanted, but I just didn't want to. I raised the bet too high and everyone folded leaving me with a pot that was worth dick. Or half a dick. "Underneath it will 'pull' the same as it used to. That much won't change."

"You can feel that?" Quinn asked, intrigued.

"Every planet has a different bulk, different speed, its own unique pull. I'm sure I would know it was Pace no matter what it looked like."

"Is that comforting, in this case?" Stuart asked as he shuffled the cards.

"I have no idea, Stu." I really didn't. "I refuse, however, to feel nostalgic for a planet that made me a slave."

"I know I *should* feel that way, too, Jane, but I'd still like to see it," Stuart said quietly.

"Then you should. Once this is all over."

Stuart nodded and dealt the cards. "This is baseball. At night." He dealt us each a stack of nine cards all face down.

My focus on the game, however, which had been pretty terrible to begin with, was now completely gone. Slave. Slaves. Cero's slaves. I must have frozen as this hit me because Samuel asked, "Jane? What is it?"

"Cero's slaves," I said. My hands felt cold. "Where are Cero's slaves?"

Thanks to the 'Clean Slate' Act they could conceivably all have new names, new backgrounds with sealed records to protect them. They could be anywhere.

We all looked at Quinn who looked very unhappy as he put his cards down. "Huong and I started searching for them and had even managed to hack into the super-secret DNA database that can prove who is who, but the database had been wiped."

I stared, unseeing, at my cards. Napians, Torvans. A former Napian slave had died protecting the city on Berria so not all were Cero's pawns, but...there were almost six thousand Cero slaves I *didn't* have a location on. I put my cold hands on my thighs to try to warm them up. I took a deep breath. I knew where they were.

"The blind mission."

Samuel just waited. "The blind mission..."

"The Union Fleet..." I tried to catch my breath but it wasn't easy "...the employer always has its people onboard. They know the mission and they keep everyone in line..."

"You think the Cero slaves, the loyal ones, have infiltrated the *Union Navy?*" Stuart said, "That's insane." His face paled, however, when he realized that neither Samuel nor Quinn was saying a damned thing. "They get scanned every year, don't they? How could they hide it?"

"We've had a TP shortage," Samuel said, "as you well know, and even then the focus has been on new recruits and we only started scanning *them* five years ago. Even if the Ceros had been scanned, they could have had the Great Cause 'safed' in advance, and, if they've had TPs working with them all along, that would be easy enough to do. Only a well-trained TP with experience would even have known what to look for."

Another piece of the puzzle fell into place. "Which they have because Cero's been hiring them. Brady and all the others. With that database gone, we'll never be able to figure out who we're even looking for."

"So," Quinn said carefully, "Cero is using his people in U-Nav to control the Fleet and it hired the merc fleets to come in, guns blazing, and get wiped out by this same Fleet in, effectively, self-defense."

"So it would seem." Samuel's eyes were moving as though he was running over scenarios in his mind.

"What about the supers on the ground?" I'd asked, making my voice flat so it wouldn't tremble.

"You can bet he has a plan for them, too, Jane," Quinn had said heavily. "For my kids and yours."

"God help us," Stuart had breathed.

If there was a God, I'd hoped she would do just that.

So now we were dropping out of hyper into lord knew what, DSS suits on, weapons ready. Quinn and I had flipped for whom we were going to protect and Quinn had gotten Samuel. I had Stuart. I knew Samuel and Stuart were slightly offended that we'd thought they would need our protection, but that was irrelevant. They were people with many lives depending on them. They needed their backs watched.

We returned to normal space.

Irena's orbit was bristling with Union ships, perhaps a hundred of them, SLPGs hot. I heaved a small sigh of relief. The ships looked menacing but thus far untouched.

The pilot tried to hail the Fleet, but couldn't get through.

Then I felt… "They're…*firing!*"

The lead ship's SLPG roared to life and I could feel the hot beam slicing through space, heading right for my little (and by comparison) defenseless ship. There was no time to fight back and not enough firepower to do it successfully even if we'd had time.

Samuel switched on his personal comm. 'Abandon ship! Repeat, abandon ship!'

I pulled on my helmet and sealed it…just as I felt the beam cut my beloved ship right in half, right through Cargo Hold A.

I heard screams as I was violently decompressed and flung out into the space over Irena. I spun for a minute, out of control, but then righted myself before I could throw up in my suit. I scanned for Samuel and found he'd been bear-hugged by Quinn. Both seemed unharmed. I found Stuart flying end over end away from the planet. I created a vortex and 'pushed' myself to him, catching him to stop the spinning. Two halves of (I thought) different Marines floated by. Other Marines were masterfully using their jets to converge on the High Admiral. I counted thirteen of us. Thirteen that had survived.

I spared one small look at the two halves of the *Liberty* as they floated like so much debris in the cold of space. I felt a lump in my throat that I had no time for.

'Samuel,' I said into my comm, 'we need people on the ground and people to try to stop the mercenaries.'

Samuel didn't even hesitate. 'I'll take the full Team of Marines to the *Jefferson*,' Admiral Tree's ship, 'and get to the Admiral. Once I've gotten through,' assuming he was able to, 'I'll take reinforcements to the planet.' He looked at me, his helmet light made him look cold and blue, 'Jane, you get to Atalanta and the other mercs when they arrive.' Then his eyes went wide as he looked at Stuart. 'I'll need your help.'

Within five minutes Samuel, Quinn and their six Marines were jetting off to the *Jefferson* at full (but non-Denethian) speed. I had considered trying to get to my Cadets, to get their assistance, for they were somewhere in this mega-Fleet (and some were with Admiral Tree) but so many of them were so green… For now I wanted them right where they were, semi-safe. At least for now.

I felt Quinn use his considerable brute force to open an outer airlock door on the *Jefferson*. I could not hear it, but I knew Stuart was sending a targeted TP message to Jennifer Tree, telling her what was going on. Telling her to let Samuel and company in.

I waited with Stuart and my three Marines.

I felt Samuel's crew go all the way inside the ship.

'Her Executive Officer is a Cero slave,' Samuel reported over the comm. 'Our Marines have overpowered him and two minor members of the command crew. They will sedate them.'

'Good,' was all I said because I was waiting for the next step.

'Ready, General,' Stuart said.

'This is Admiral Tree,' Stuart then broadcast (in her voice) through all our heads so loudly I put my gloved hands against my helmet in a useless attempt to block out the sound. Stuart paid no attention to my foolishness. 'A being named Cero has used agents to infiltrate the officer corps within the Union Navy Fleet. These may be officers you have known for years, but anyone who tries to fire at will on the so-called invasion Fleet we are expecting will be disobeying a direct order from High Admiral Samuel Armstrong. Repeat: do not fire offensively on the incoming fleet. Defensive fire only.' Because, I thought, we can't just leave the UNav Fleet as sitting ducks if we can't get to the mercs and stop them. 'We believe they have been infiltrated as well. That is all and Godspeed.'

I wondered how many fights had broken out on all those ships now that the cat was out of the bag. I also wondered how many of those fights were won by our people.

A few minutes later I felt a mass exodus of, from their size and equipment, UNav Marines (plus Samuel, Quinn and *our* Marines) flooding out of the *Jefferson* towards the planet.

Still we waited. Waited for the mercs.

Then, something I hadn't expected (or wanted) happened. More people flew out of the *Jefferson's* airlock. Twenty or so, I guessed. They moved quickly. They were Humans but weren't wearing jet packs.

Mother of god, it was my Cadet Macros. I opened my mouth to tell Stuart to send them back when the side of the X ship opened and twelve Denethians streamed out, moving so quickly they put everyone else to shame.

Damn it damn it damn it.

Thirty-four mercenary ships dropped out of hyper right on top of us.

All but five opened fire on the Fleet. Our five. *My* five.

'Holy shit,' Stuart murmured. 'Brady Carmichael says to tell you…"

Brady? Brady was with the Furies? I didn't have time to wonder how the hell that happened, however, because dozens of Fleet ships started firing on the merc fleets.

'We have to get out of the way,' I yelled into my comm, 'or we're going to get fried.' I suppressed a scream as a bolt of energy got a bit nearer than I would have liked. 'Get on the other side of the merc fleet, away from the planet.'

'Roger that,' my Marine Captain said and we started moving quickly around the ships, putting them between us and the Union Fleet's fire. I knew some Union ships were back under our control only because they weren't firing, but I also knew it was just a matter of time before the 'bad' Union ships started firing on the 'good' ones.

'Mercenary fleets! This is Vice-Admiral Pace,' I yelled (through Stuart), 'you are being set up for destruction by your employer—get the fuck out of here before you are destroyed!'

It took about four seconds before the Ryuu Fleet disappeared back into hyper.

We don't have enough people to stop both the merc fleets *and* the Union Fleet, I thought despairingly.

Then I 'heard' Atalanta's voice in my head (also through Stuart) as the Furies started to fire on her fellow mercs, 'All is not lost, Jane,' she said, 'we've brought friends.'

Two things happened at once: A group of twelve ships dropped out of hyper right over us and three hundred or so pale figures (in specially modified space suits) sprinted out of all the Furies ships.

The new ships...I recognized one of them...it was the *Actium*. It was Alex's Fleet!

The pale soldiers were led by a bio-signature I knew very well indeed, a jet-packed human by her side. Eriss and Ian.

They waited, though, and for a minute all of us just floated in space, no one moving, not even the Union ships.

Then I felt something: tiny (by comparison) ships, open ships, coming at us from all directions. They weren't more than missiles with handles on the sides...

Mother of god, I thought, as I felt goosebumps all over my skin.

It's the Denethian Navy.

Then a powerful voice appeared in my head, in all our heads, even more powerful than Stuart's. 'This is the *sagrat-Pelann* and you are involved in an illegal operation. The Terran, Heely and Rian Navies are here to take you down if you do not immediately surrender! Stand down now or you will be destroyed!'

I imagined a collective 'oh shit' running through both fleets.

Another merc fleet disappeared (the Forløpere) into the safety of hyper.

I felt Furies Marines pouring out of their ships, heading for the remaining merc ships. Mercifully the mercs, apparently realizing they were in over their heads, stopped firing and started retreating, all but one now going into hyperspace. Atalanta's people would deal with them, the Union Fleet was the larger problem now.

Now half of the mega-fleet was quiescent, but the other half started firing at us, at the Furies, at Alex's Fleet and the Rian.

I heard a command in my head (through Eriss this time) from the Denethian commander in Denethian, 'Open them to space.'

The Denethians let go of their transports and moved faster than I had ever seen them as they streaked towards the Union ships that were still laying down a scary layer of fire on us.

Someone screamed as they were cut by one of the beams, then more screams. We needed to do something. The one remaining merc Fleet (OEJ) was still putting up resistance.

'Cadets,' I ordered, 'disable that Fleet and then report to the Furies. Captain Pace will look after you.'

'Yes, Ma'am,' someone said and they all, Human, Heely and Denethian, took off.

The Rian Navy, however, had reached the Union Fleet and was decimating the ships that were still trying to fire on the Furies and OEJs, their claws ripping the hulls to pieces easily and tossing their crews into space.

'Stuart,' I said as I realized how badly that could go unchecked, 'we won't have anything left...'

Stuart said nothing for a second and then almost shouted, 'Close your 'door', Jane.'

'What?'

'Close your 'door.'

I did, and even with it closed I could hear the following, though it didn't affect me. You'll see what I mean in a second.

'CEASE!' a voice, Eriss's voice said.

Everyone who couldn't (or hadn't) closed their mental 'doors' simply froze. Really froze. Atalanta told me later that it had been the oddest sensation. She'd told her body to move but she'd stayed still.

Jesus, how powerful *was* Eriss?

I watched the Tarine (in groups that averaged about four each) use their jet packs to go to each of the ships. They went inside. Those ships didn't fire anymore.

Then I felt something wrong, really wrong.

Half a dozen ships were moving, on autopilot, I guessed, and heading straight for the surface of Irena.

I felt Eriss' power fade, weaken, then flicker out. I couldn't even imagine how much energy it had taken to do what she'd done, but it no longer mattered for the main Fleet.

The six ships, however, had sped up and, despite not being made to land anywhere, let alone on a planet, were pushing for the surface.

'Felix, Garrett!' I said into my comm, hoping someone would relay my cry for help. 'Stuart, grab onto me,' and he did.

We flew. Not quite Denethian fast, but really fucking fast.

I soon felt the bodies and bio-signatures of over a dozen Furies Macros (Felix included) behind me.

'Garrett is on his way from the *Actium*, Jane,' Stuart relayed.

A tremendous shudder in the planet at the first ship landed/collided in the field outside the Palace.

'First ship impact,' I said into my comm wishing the whole comm grid was back up and running because this was stupid.

'Atalanta's comm people are working on it, as are Admiral Tree's,' Stuart answered me, though I technically hadn't asked the question.

We neared the planet, edging towards the atmosphere. I could see the large outline of the Palace now and knew that my people, from Charles, to Idis and Lucy, to the Princes and Wilby and the Pacey kids were already barricaded in the bunker down way below the surface. I didn't know what Cero had seen in his vision, however, so that knowledge held only some comfort.

A second ship crashed (and really crashed) into the ground taking out a good chunk of the forest that surrounded the South border of the Palace Grounds.

Another ship crashed into *it* a minute later.

Suddenly my comm was alive with chatter. Thank god.

'...intercepting Hostile forces on the North-West corner of the Palace. We're holding position but the Corsican Guard is outnumbered...' Samuel was saying.

'Admiral, this is Pace, we're on our way,' I said.

'How many are you bringing, Jane?' he said, sounding relieved.

'Twenty Macros,' I responded.

'We can't use Union soldiers from the mega-Fleet,' he said, and he was right since we hadn't checked them for traitors yet.

I shivered in cold (though there was no way I would have felt it in my DSS) as we passed through the clouds over the Palace.

'Call in the Paceys, Jane.'

I knew what he meant. Send in the Furies. Send in the freaks.

I switched my comm frequency. ''Lanta, we need you.'

'Get me the *Actium*,' it was Samuel again, but he was speaking to his comm officer. 'Alex?'

'Sir?'

'Send in the troops and take out those ships in space or on the ground.'

'Yes, Sir.'

The fourth enemy ship didn't land, however, but hovered over the Palace, though I imagined that I could hear the engines groaning as they fought the gravity they were unaccustomed to. Denethians would have made short work of this ship, but Irena's pull kept them in space.

The fifth and six ships crash landed to the East of the Palace, one of them immediately exploding upon impact. Though I was really very sorry for the innocent lives lost there, I was relieved the ship had saved us the trouble of having to disable it.

'Furies personnel are five minutes out, Admiral,' Atalanta reported calmly. 'Handing over command to Captain Daniel Pace.'

So she was coming was she? Excellent.

We were right over the floating fourth ship now and my fellow Macros and I stared at it. I wanted to crush it and roll it up for disposal, but I was pretty sure most of the people on it were being held against their will.

'Nullify the other ships so no one can escape,' I ordered. The other Macros, including Felix, went off to do just that, but Stuart stayed with me.

'What will you do?' Stuart asked, clearly curious.

'Go long,' I said as I 'grabbed' the ship and spun it on its axis, faster and faster. Then I 'threw' the whole thing, a small cruiser, thankfully, away. Away from the Palace, from Irena, possibly from Corsica.

One gone, one exploded, four left.

I felt something strange overhead. It was Humans, Terran and Heely, coming from what was probably the Furies ships but they were moving fast. Too fast for either the Macros or the jet packs. Only Denethians moved that quickly.

I repeated that thought in my head. Only Denethians moved that quickly.

'We're coming, Jane!' Atalanta's exultant voice said in my comm. 'Some friends are giving us a lift.'

The super-swift (ha!) Denethians were carrying them.

'Holy crap!' I said.

'Disengaging now,' a voice said in Denethian and I felt the Humans essentially being thrown from the backs of the Deneth into the atmosphere.

'Thank you,' I said in Denethian over my comm as I landed, dropping Stuart down next to me.

'Make the murderers pay,' the voice responded.

'I will,' I promised.

Over six hundred Furies personnel, Terran and Heely, non-Macro supers, Marines, everything we had that didn't leave our ships empty, rained down on the field next to the Palace...at the same time scores and scores of Cero agents broke out of their four ships and headed for the Palace.

It was time to go to work.

I drew my knives, Agni Katar in my left hand, one butterfly in my right and the other one floating on my left. Stuart unholstered two projectile guns.

'Protect the Palace! No one gets in!' I shouted as the Furies people lined up behind me. 'Godspeed!' I started to run, Stuart close behind.

A male Cero pointed an LPG at my heart and I 'knocked' it away and broke his neck without pausing in my stride. I could hear the sizzle of other LPGs and the crack of projectile bullets being fired. People screamed, in fury, in pain. Knives clanked together. Bodies fell to the ground.

It was chaos.

I stabbed a Cero woman who was running at me, murder in her eyes, pulled my knife out of her and kept running.

"They know, Jane," Stuart said as he tried to catch his breath from all the running. "They...know...where the bunker is."

My stomach knotted.

He nodded. "It was in that woman's mind." A deep breath. "They all know."

Atalanta appeared by my side, an arsenal of weapons hanging off her petite body and an absolutely huge gun in her hand.

"Get to the Palace gate, Jane," she said. "I'll cover you." She looked over at Felix, who was already bloody but still fighting and jerked her head in my direction.

'Half the Macros go to the North Wall and back up the High Admiral,' I ordered as I kept going, Stuart and Atalanta keeping up deadly fire as we moved. 'Garrett, take them.'

'You,' Garrett's voice said, though I wasn't looking at him and was too intent on my goal to try sensing him, 'follow me.' I looked over my right shoulder and saw Garrett and his crew lift into the air and 'fly' for the North Gate.

I looked back towards my goal only to see the backs of the Ceros running ahead of me. I 'swept' their feet out from under them as Atalanta and Stuart fired behind us to buy us time. I made a giant 'fist' and 'smashed' it down on the prone Ceros. Some of them struggled to move. Some didn't.

I could see the giant ornamental gate quite clearly now. I heard the unmistakable hiss of a jetpack and saw a Cero fly into the air, making it halfway over the gate easily. I 'reached' out, 'grabbed' him and threw him away, but more were flying.

Atalanta, with machine-like precision, was shooting them out of the air, Stuart following her lead, but even their excellent aim wasn't enough. One got over. Another. And another.

"Jane, go!" Atalanta shouted.

I 'picked' them up and 'lifted' all of us over the gate. Bodies of dead Corsican guards littered the yellow moss of the lawn that separated the main wall from the Palace itself.

I was popping heads off bodies before I'd even touched down. Atalanta shot the ones I missed. I could tell Stuart, by his breathing and silence, was scanning them for intel before they died, but had nothing new to report so far. Damn.

'Samuel?' I said into my comm.

'We're holding the wall right now, Jane, but more are coming,' he said, sounding breathless. 'Where are the Macros?'

My stomach clenched. They should already have been there.

Another wave of Ceros, and, apparently, their Marines, flew over the stone wall. I made another fist and 'punched' some of them out of the air. More kept coming, then more still.

'How can there be so many?' I asked, almost despairingly.

'The ships that made it through were almost completely Cero,' Stuart answered, standing over his last scanning victim.

'How many people?' Atalanta asked.

'Several thousand at least,' Stuart said.

I heard Felix grunt as he fought, 'All with goddamned jet packs. Hold on a sec.'

Fucking awesome.

At least a hundred Ceros were over the gate now and more arriving all the time. I saw Felix 'fly' over the gate with some more Furies Macros. He landed to my left, next to Stuart and Atalanta was on my right. The other Macros quickly assembled to each side of us, the only things keeping the Cero from the Palace doors.

There was a brief pause as we eyed each other.

They ran at us, screaming defiance.

I 'grabbed' bunches of them and 'threw' them carelessly over the wall. Another group was tossed over the wall. Felix was doing the same. Atalanta threw down her now empty big gun and grabbed two more from her holster.

Then I felt crushing despair. Suicidal despair. It washed over me and I felt tears welling up in my eyes.

'Jane!' Felix yelled, 'Your 'door.''

I did and the hopelessness quit, like turning off a switch. Atalanta had stopped firing and was standing tautly next to me, sending everything she had at them. They were slowing. Not stopping their advance, but slowing.

I pulled heads from bodies I could as fast as I could. People were dropping but more were still coming over the wall.

I felt a burning pain in my good shoulder. I looked at it. Damn it, I'd been shot. Ow. Thankfully, the DSS resealed over the wound and I felt the cool of the anesthetic take the edge off the pain.

I started 'pounding' out the Ceros, smashing some of them flat, but Atalanta's spell had been broken, at least a little, and the Ceros pushed through their artificial despair and started advancing again.

I felt the ground shudder. Impact tremor.

'We pulled the wall down when they were trying to scale it!' Garrett crowed. 'We've held the North Gate!'

Thank god for that, but we, however, at the Main Gate, were no better off than we had been.

Suddenly the Ceros outside the gate stopped.

Atalanta paused, unsure. She raised her weapon and I gathered my strength and felt an odd form rolling across the yellow lawn. It rolled across it up to the wall, then up and over, changing shape only as it touched the ground on our side.

The blue blob then stretched into a humanoid shape with the head of an eagle.

Cero.

"Even you cannot win here, Attack Dog,' it said through its translator. "You doom the future by trying."

"Fuck you," I said eloquently.

It laughed. "The longer you resist, the slower your kids will die."

"You're never getting anywhere near my kids, you asshole."

I grounded on the planet below me.

I launched myself in the air, knives in front of me just as I heard screams of dismay from the Ceros outside the wall.

Everyone but me looked up but I could feel the shadows of massive wings block out the sun. The great 'whooshing' sounds those wings made filled our ears. I flew over the Cero rabble, feeling many pieces of burning hot lead hit my chest and legs. Pain was intense, but I did not waver.

I 'reached' down into the dirt, making 'fingers' of large hands. I 'ripped' the earth apart, stealing the ground itself from under the feet of the murderous Ceros. They fell screaming into the chasm I'd made. The Tarine descended picking up any still standing on the side and dropped them over the wall.

But Cero was mine.

I neared him, closer and closer.

He rolled quickly up the wall but I 'held' him in place and rammed all three knives right through him.

I let go of my blades and floated for second as he stayed there on the wall, thoroughly impaled. He had no real face to show his pain or even his surprise. Perhaps there wasn't any. Perhaps he had seen this coming, too.

I was starting to shake. I was starting to fall. My vision was blacking out.

I felt strong arms around me. Felix's. And, as I always did at the end of a battle, I passed out.

I awoke, gasping for air, a few minutes later. "The doctors have you, Jane," a once beloved voice said.

An even more beloved voice said, "You did well, my love. And you're going to be all right."

I retreated back into the darkness, relieved.

The next few hours were a delirium of pain as I drifted in and out of consciousness. I heard more than I saw, but even that was not much.

"Cut the DSS off her, I need to get in there," a woman hissed. "Felix, get out of here."

I felt my body pushed and pulled. It hurt so much.

The pressure of the DSS on me was gone and I felt my blood draining out of me. I felt floaty as it left me, but they touched my right leg and I screamed.

"Father in Heaven," someone said. Charles. Why was Charles seeing this?

"She's losing too much blood," Wilby's voice said.

"Jane," Charles said, his voice strained with fear.

"Make it stop," I begged. I knew I was scaring Charles, and I didn't want to, but, Holy Mother, I needed it to stop.

I felt Charles shudder against the wall. His arm was grabbed.

"Fitz." Samuel's rich voice. "Fitz, you have to let them work. Come with me."

"We need her in surgery," the woman said.

"Is Quinn stabilized?" Wilby asked sharply.

"He can wait, Wilby, she can't. We have to go now*," the woman said.*

"We're going."

Then the pain receded and I went away.

15:34 – Infirmary, Imperial Palace, Irena, Corsican Empire, January 20th 2882

About two days later I opened my eyes to see a worried Charles sitting next to my bed.

"Jane," he said.

"Six," I whispered, so glad to see him.

He shook his head. "Six *bullets*, Jane," he said, as he stared at my hands.

"My lucky number," I joked weakly though my voice was clogged from disuse. He looked pale, too pale, so I said, "I'm Ok, love."

He took a big breath, clearly pulling himself together. "How do you feel?"

"Drugged, but fine."

Charles took my hand, still not meeting my eyes, and kissed it then, unexpectedly, rose. "I'll tell Lucy and Idis you are awake."

"Ok..?" I said, confused, but before I could question him on his odd behavior Samuel came in with Felix, Garrett and Atalanta. Charles was already down the hall and on his way.

"Are you cleared for visitors?" Samuel asked with a smile.

"Fucked if I know, Samuel, but come on in."

Samuel took Charles inexplicably vacated seat and the others clustered around him.

"So, what did I miss?" I asked.

"We're still clearing the Fleet of the Cero slaves, ship by ship, scanning the hell out of everyone with the help of Stuart and the Tarine. The slaves we've already identified have been rounded up and are on their way to Terra for trial," Samuel said promptly. "Union Med Ships arrive tomorrow to deal with the low-priority wounded and take them back to Ter-Med."

"How many did we lose?" This was always the scary question. Samuel's grim expression didn't make it any less so.

Atalanta answered, "Almost two hundred Furies, two thirds of them Marines. Twenty-seven Cadets including one of the Denethians, Pinky, I think her name was."

"Pinky is, was, a he," I corrected automatically. "But how...I left the Cadets with the OEJ? What happened to Pinky?" Not my baby supers. Please.

"The 'Admiral' Roykirk," she said the rank with distaste which seemed appropriate since the owner of the OEJ had bestowed the title on himself, "attempted an escape. Pinky tried to stop him but Roykirk got caught in some cables outside the ship and, far as we can tell, accidently stabbed Pinky when he was trying to free himself. Pinky died of cold and decompression before anyone had realized he was punctured."

Poor Pinky. "And Roykirk?"

"Is on his way to prison."

"Well, that's something." Not enough. Pinky had just gotten started. He would have been brilliant had he had the time to learn. I wanted to weep, but kept myself together. It was not easy.

"But why didn't my kids stay put?" What the fuck was the point of giving orders if no one followed them?

Atalanta sighed as she sat on the corner of the bed. "They knew we were in trouble and they came to help." Her dark eyes narrowed, "Just as you would have done once upon a time."

"Not to mention any time since," Felix muttered.

I ignored his commentary. "How did Brady end up with the Furies?" I had to ask because what the hell? "I'd assumed all the TPs Cero had hired were dead."

Atalanta frowned. "I'm sure they are now, but Cero held them for a long time. He'd needed them, you see, before they had to be stamped out. Brady told me he'd realized he'd made a mistake by the time he'd reached Solitário. It took him all those months to escape."

"I'm glad he did," I said, but back to grimmer matters. "How many ships were lost?"

"Five of the six mostly-Cero Union ships, plus minor damage to about twenty in the Fleet. Just two were permanently disabled during the battle, but we only lost sixteen non-Cero Union personnel," Samuel said. "It could have been much worse."

That was certainly true, but even some deaths were too many.

"Cero?"

"Dead, though not from the knife wounds," Felix said.

"I don't understand."

"The surgeons here had, not surprisingly, never treated a...whatever it was and it turned out it was severely allergic to the anesthetic they used trying to save it."

I barked out a laugh. "As long as it is dead, how it happened is irrelevant."

"Agreed," they all said.

"The children are all right?" Then I had a terrible thought. "Quinn? Wilby? Eriss? Ian? Marston? Stuart?"

"They're all fine," Samuel said. "Wilby stayed with the children, ready to fight for them, but, thanks to all of us, the Cero never made it into the bunker. Marston got his arm broken disabling a Cero Agent on the

Jefferson, but is recovering well. Stuart earned a bullet wound in his arm, but it turned out to be just a bad scratch and he'll be fine. Eriss and Ian were unharmed and Quinn was seriously injured, but will recover." He winced. "In time."

Oh god. I had a fuzzy memory of Quinn being 'stable' when I was being taken in surgery. "What happened to him?"

Samuel looked a little distressed, "Apparently a Cero LPG blast at *very* close range. Vaporized everything below his right knee."

"No."

"But the DSS applied a tourniquet and Quinn finished the battle, saving my life half a dozen times before we got that wall down."

"He is one tough motherfucker," I said, awed by his prowess and thinking how good it was not to be so mad at him anymore. However, Samuel's remark about the Wall reminded me of something. I turned to Garrett. "Why was your Macro Team delayed getting to Samuel?" Then I realized how shitty that sounded, like they'd stopped to eat on the way, and I backpedaled. "I mean, he was asking where you were…"

"Relax, Jane," Garrett said easily. "Apparently a large team of Cero fighters had been trapped in the fourth ship when it crashed, that was the ship closest to the North Wall. They freed themselves right as we were passing by. Bad luck for them," he grinned, "good luck for us."

"You and your team were real badasses, Garrett." I smiled proudly at Garrett who looked very pleased with himself. He'd certainly earned the feeling.

"Takes one to know one, Jane," he teased, dimples emerging with his smile.

He really was too cute. Adorable, really. My expression clearly gave me away as he laughed and said firmly, "For once and all I. Am. Not. Cute."

"Whatever you say, love," I said.

"Impossible woman," he groused, amused.

"How much longer am I here?"

"A week, they said," Atalanta responded. "Wilby has been overseeing your care, of course."

"Of course."

"Quinn's care, too?"

Her lovely face clouded. "Yes, but he hasn't woken up yet."

Oh no. "But they expect him to?"

She nodded. "They just can't say when."

"The man is strong as an ox," Garrett said confidently. "Once he's awake, I can induct him into the club." I raised my eyebrows and he blushed. "Not *that* kind of club, Jane. Geez, keep your mind out of the gutter."

"Never gonna happen, my friend."

"I mean the fake limb club." He rapped his knuckles on his prosthetic. "One way or another we always have a leg to stand on."

"Oh, Garrett," Atalanta groaned.

The joke was so stupid that I had to laugh. I was still laughing when I fell back to sleep.

Days two and three in the Infirmary were uneventful. Mostly I slept, but both days Charles and Idis brought Lucy to me and I got to hold her for a long, long time. While I knew the fear I had for her safety and happiness would never disappear (nor should it) that made me feel better than any medicine. The medicine helped a lot, however. Getting shot six times sucks balls.

Day four found Samuel darkening my door.

"Hey," I said with a smile.

He smiled back and walked in. "We've finished culling the Ceros from the Union herd and I'm heading back to Terra with Alex's Fleet."

I patted the bed and he sat down next to me. "Did Charles get to see him?"

"He did," he said, but then he frowned. "Why do I know that and you don't?"

Good question. "Charles isn't…himself right now." I shrugged. "I don't know."

Samuel patted my arm. "Just remember, Jane, that as hard as it is for us to go out and risk everything, it is sometimes harder to stay at home and wait. Give him a minute to catch up." I read that as: think of him and not yourself for a minute, Jane. Excellent advice, I knew, but I still missed him. I missed my Six. I nodded dutifully, however.

"You know, I've been thinking about what Cero said," Samuel said in an abrupt change of subject.

"About the allegory? The worlds bathed in fire?" I asked, guessing that's where his mind had gone.

Apparently I had been right on the money because Samuel sighed. "The chief didn't kill his son and we didn't let the children, and all the supers, die." He looked at me, his brown eyes sad. "We may have doomed everyone in the future because we couldn't make that choice."

"But you didn't hesitate and neither did I."

"No."

I turned that around in my mind for a minute. "I suppose a lot of parents would say that they would do anything, sacrifice anything to keep their children safe."

"All parents *should* say that, certainly."

"That is what we had to do, Samuel." I took his hand. "We protected our own and damned the future."

He patted my hand with his other one as he rose. "Was that kind-hearted or colossally irresponsible?"

"Both, probably," I said, "but the future isn't written, Samuel, no matter what the damned pre-cogs say."

"Even though they've never been wrong?"

An unfortunate truth, but too awful to stand. "We have to have faith."

He paused at the doorway. "I guess it is all we've got." He shook off his gloom and grinned. "I've gotta git. I've a lady waiting for me at home."

That brought me to a point I felt I needed to bring up. I didn't want to do it, but I really felt I should.

"Samuel?"

"Yes, Jane?"

I hesitated, feeling emotion welling up inside me. "Do you want me to stop calling you that?"

"Stop calling me by my name?" he looked surprised.

I nodded. "Do you want me to call you Sam, like everyone else?" Because I'd thought, after he'd told me that Mallory was the only other person alive that called him Samuel, that maybe that was a distinction meant only for the woman he loved. Perhaps he wanted to take back his name from me but didn't want to hurt me by asking. It would hurt, of course, but if it made him happy then I would do it.

"Don't, please, Jane," he said. "Whatever we are now, we were real then." He shook his head. "I don't want to forget that even though we've both moved on." Then he grinned as he walked out the door. "Besides, Baby, you are *nothing* like everyone else."

Then he was gone, but he was still Samuel even if he wasn't mine. Thank goodness.

Day six Idis came to see me by herself. She brought food and a bouquet of the little yellow wildflowers I loved so much. They made me miss Charles something fierce, of course, but I was glad to have them all the same.

We chatted easily about Lucy, the Princes and Wilby's kids, but soon Idis turned the conversation to more serious matters.

"I sent Charles to a counselor."

"You did?" I asked, shocked.

"A discrete one, of course," she said. I realized, then, that an Emperor couldn't just go asking for mental health advice. An Emperor had to be perfect, his armor (whether physical or mental) impenetrable. When I stayed silent she said, "You have to have noticed that he's not himself."

"Of course I noticed. He won't even look at me," I said irritated. "I just thought he needed time."

"He needs to process what's happened."

"He was there, Idis," I said quietly. "When they brought me in." I felt angry tears falling. "Why would they let him in?"

She looked at me like I was an idiot. "You try telling your Emperor to back the hell off when his wife is dying."

Well, when she put it like that. "I just…I would have spared him that."

Her expression softened. "I know. Me, too."

"So…what is he...?" I stopped talking because I didn't know how to ask what I wanted to know.

She bit her lip. "He really isn't like himself at all. When he gets scared he gets angry." Yes, he did, I thought, recalling how he'd blown up at me after Stoney had put my own knife through my chest. "*That* I can deal with, but this…"

"He'll be our Charles again, though, won't he, Idis?" I asked. "Eventually?"

Idis smiled at my use of 'our' in reference to the man we shared. "He is strong, my dear. It will be all right."

I took her hand and kissed the back of it.

Charles didn't see me that day at all.

Quinn stayed in his coma.

18:02 – Imperial Bedroom, Imperial Palace, Irena, January 27th, 2882

On day eight I was wheeled (since I had taken three bullets in the legs and they weren't up to walking just yet though they would be soon) by Mr. Beddoes into Charles' room in the Palace.

Mr. Beddoes had fussed over me and set me up in a comfortable chair with food and drink within easy reach and had disappeared, but not before reminding me that he was only a comm call away when I needed to be moved or to (ugh) relieve myself.

I was alone.

No Charles.

No Charles for two hours.

I just sat. Sat and waited.

I was worried and, I am ashamed to say, a bit angry. I *had* been shot trying to protect his Palace and our child. Couldn't he have turned up for my arrival?

Eventually I heard the doorknob turn and Charles entered the room. His walk was unsteady and his motor skills in general were fuzzy.

He was drunk.

I was annoyed. I opened my mouth to make a snarky comment about being on time when I saw that his face was wet. That stopped me cold.

Charles *never* cried. Not ever. In the eight years we'd been married and the over ten years we'd known each other I had never seen him this…lost.

Just like that my irritation evaporated. He must have been so afraid. Oh, Charles.

"Charles, love," I whispered as I held my arms out to hold him.

He took a shaky breath and stumbled over me, ending up on his knees, his face buried in my lap. It hurt, but I couldn't have cared less.

"I'm sorry, my beloved, so sorry."

I stroked his hair as he let go.

I never called him 'Six' again, the number too much of a reminder for Charles of the six bullets that had almost taken me from him, but as scared as he had been and as much as he clearly wanted to wrap me in cotton and tuck me safely away, Charles never asked me to quit living as I had always lived. I was (and am) in awe of his bravery and unselfishness. I knew I didn't deserve such a man, but I also knew that there was no force in the universe that would make me let him go.

494

10:09 – Hallway Outside Quinn's Room, Infirmary, Imperial Palace, January 28th, 2882

The next morning I'd woken to the news that Quinn had regained consciousness an hour before and I, after Mr. Beddoes had assisted me in getting showered and dressed, had 'wheeled' myself quickly over to see him. Charles, very deeply asleep, hadn't even moved when I'd left. I'd just been glad he was sleeping peacefully so I'd let him be.

I'd turned the corner in the Infirmary that led to the hallway outside Quinn's room and found, to my surprise, a whole bunch of people there, Shira included. No one was going in and everyone was eerily quiet.

"What's going on?" I asked and was shushed by pretty much everyone.

Shira looked at me. "Dad told me he was going to confess everything to Papa," she whispered.

"You did *what?*" Wilby's voice said loudly from inside Quinn's room. "Jesus, Nathan, that was a decade ago."

"Here we go," she said softly and, creepy as it was, we all listened in.

"I was ashamed, *shatzi…*" Quinn said.

"Don't call me that, Nathan," Wilby said angrily. "Not right now."

"I won't," Quinn said, "but I did something I couldn't believe I'd done and it made me doubt everything."

"Even me. The one person you shouldn't have doubted." A pause. "You should have come to me. *I* knew who were you were. *I* could have reminded you. Wasn't that my job?"

I scanned inside the room. Wilby's body was taught with fury but Quinn, still lying in his bed, was shaking. "It was and I can see it now, but then… I never really believed you cheated on me, Wilby. I was so angry with myself that I…fucked up."

Wilby was pacing back and forth.

"I am so sorry. I will never be able to express how much."

Wilby huffed at that, still pacing. Then he stopped. I wished I could see his expression. "You've broken us, Nathan. Even if we stayed together it would never be the same as it was."

"I don't care. It can be however you want it to be," Quinn said his tone desperate. "Other men, other women, anything you want. I don't know how I would survive without you."

"Strong words," Wilby said, though his pacing did not resume.

"The strongest I have."

I felt Wilby walked a few paces and sit down across from Quinn. "You'd be all right with my continuing to fuck around?"

"Yes."

"Or taking on a permanent lover, say, here on Irena?"

"Yes," but Quinn's voice wavered.

"Or marrying someone else and keeping you on the side."

I could feel a sob building in Quinn's chest. "Anything."

Silence. "I never wanted any of those things."

"I know."

"All I wanted was you."

Now Quinn shuddered and I imagined tears running down his face. "I know."

I felt Wilby get up and kneel by Quinn's bed. "I need time to think about this, Nathan, and I need you to think, too."

"I *have* thought about it…"

Wilby shook his head. "You haven't, not about this." Wilby sighed. "I let you lead us because I thought you knew the way. If we were together again I would have to be myself, the man you knew before all this."

"The man I fell in love with?" Quinn's voice became lighter. "I liked that man."

"I did, too, but you aren't used to him anymore."

"I won't stop wanting you, even if you leave me for good."

Now Wilby's face stretched into a sad smile. "Give me until summer, then come back here and…we'll see."

"Thank you."

I felt Wilby then lean in and kiss him. A quick kiss, a chaste one, but it was something.

Wilby stood up again.

"I love you, Wilby," Quinn said.

"I love you, too, *shatzi*," Wilby responded and then headed for the door.

We scattered like rats as he came into the hallway. Well, everyone but me since the crowd had made it difficult for me to move my chair. Wilby stood in front of me, hands on his hips and said loudly, "Everybody get all that?"

There were a few giggles in response. He looked down at me, rolling his eyes.

"Are you Ok?" I asked.

496

"Not really, but at least I know the truth. That's a start."

"Can you forgive him?"

He shrugged his broad shoulders. "I have to, Jane. For better or worse, he's mine."

12:00 – Defender's Field, Imperial Palace, Irena, January 31st, 2882

Another funeral. The once pristine lawn in front of the Palace's main gate had become 'Defender's Field' and was littered with lines and lines of open graves, their pale blue headstones standing guard. The dead Furies, Union soldiers, Corsican Guards and even the dead Cero slaves would forever line the walk up to the Palace once they'd been laid to rest. There were so many. Pinky had been taken back to Paragon with the Rian Navy, as per their custom, but everyone else who had died lay waiting in stacks of coffins.

The chasm I had made during the battle had been filled in, the yellow mossy grass replanted but now with sprinkles of yellow flowers, making the lawn between the Wall and the Palace the same yet not.

The lawn outside the Palace, however, was different forever. Now it waited to receive the dead.

Charles had decided to have the service there, instead of at the Cathedral, and the morning had dawned cold and fine for the ceremony.

Eriss officiated with all the Tarine living, the sounds of their pale wings a constant beat behind her words of comfort and strength. We, the mourners, stood throughout the stones, I on crutches, and paid our respects. Felix and I 'lifted' each of the coffins as their names were read and 'placed' them gently in their graves. Gidi, the poor Tarine who'd been tortured and murdered by the Cero, had been brought to Irena as well and was laid to rest with them.

I looked at the grave markers with satisfaction, noting that the only difference between the gravestones of the heroes and those of the Cero was that the Cero's stones were blank. Eventually they would be forgotten. I hoped they would, at any rate. The lines and lines of the named dead would not be.

Once the service was over the Tarine made straight for their ships, bent on returning home to Dep Qua. I kissed Ian on the cheek noticing his two startling blue eyes (he'd *finally* agreed to get a replacement for the one the Pelann had taken from him) were full and sent him on his way with his beloved Eriss. They never looked back, clearly content to be together wherever they were.

Stuart left the next day for his own home with the thanks of the Empire.

Quinn had gone back a few days before with the Med Ships to Ter-Med to be fitted with his new prosthetic leg. Garrett had gone with him, determined to keep his spirits up. Wilby had seen Quinn off with a deep kiss and a smile. Shira, who was staying on Irena, had looked both grossed out and pleased all at once when she'd seen it happen.

The Furies were last to leave, but that was all right, too. Daniel, Atalanta and Felix still seemed delighted with each other and dinner at the Palace the night before they left had been both loud and fun.

I was sorry to see my friends go, of course, but I was fine.

I had Charles. I had Lucy. I had Idis.

I had Home.

18:34 – Gardens, Imperial Palace, Irena, Corsican Empire, July 4th, 2882

It was five months later.

You all know that David Abrams passed away on February 10th, 2882. I'd mourned him, of course, partially out of guilt and partially out of genuine loss. The Emperor had gone with me to the funeral on Novy and dozens of other Heads of State had flocked from all parts of the Union to pay their respects. In David's will he hadn't wanted Tarine Officiants, so Eriss had not come (she'd probably been glad to miss at least one funeral). He'd wanted Heely ones. The service had been almost entirely in Heely and I'd found it moving and beautiful. Fifty of David's newest fighters had flown overhead at the end shooting off fireworks.

Charles had then gone back to Corsica and I'd returned to Terra 1 and the reopened *Schola-Terra*.

So I'd waited, waited for July 4th of 2882, for the 18th (or 10th) birthday of David's kids and for the other shoe to drop. It had never occurred to me to doubt David's word on it. Not even for a second.

It was early evening on July 4th and I was walking the gardens around the Palace as I so often did when I was in town, so to speak. I'd planned on refamiliarizing myself with them, having just returned to Irena the day before at end of term, but even so I barely saw them, too wrapped up in my own thoughts to notice much of anything.

It had been exactly thirteen years since my friends and I had fled Pace-Pallon. We'd looked out the view screens of the *P.S. Scylla* and watched the last lights of our home flicker out and die. David had known this date, of course, and I wondered why he'd picked it for the birth of his children (or the opening of the 'tubs' would be a more accurate description of the act). With anyone else I would have put it down to coincidence, but there were no such things with David. Was he sending me some kind of message from beyond the grave?

I'd been antsy and nervous all day. I'd had no attention for much except Lucy but eventually she'd had to go for dinner and I'd found myself at loose ends again. I'd just decided to go inflict myself on Wilby at the Annex when my comm clicked on.

I turned my head to respond, "Pace here." I listened. "Of course, Charles, I'll be right there." I frowned and 'lifted' myself into the air to be able to get to him faster. He hadn't sounded scared or hurt (and Stanley would have reached me if there had been any danger) but something was clearly very wrong. It had to be the bomb David had promised to drop on me today. Once again I was correct, though I could never have anticipated the form it would take.

I landed at the doors and ran down the hallway to Charles' private office. Stanley was not there but a dozen other Palace Guards were. What the hell was going on?

I burst through the door to find Charles and Idis, both looking shell-shocked, Stanley, six more Guards, four young people and Thalberg Abrams whom I still thought of as *my* Thal, though he belonged only to himself.

Thal looked both guilty and relieved, but flicked his eyes to the teenagers, David's kids, forestalling my questions. I'd seen them for the first time at the funeral but no one had been allowed to talk to them. The Thals, apparently led by my Thal, had prevented any contact.

I stopped in front of everyone and looked at Charles for an explanation.

"Jane," Charles said calmly, though his body told me he was not even close to calm, "these are Abrams' children." He looked at the tallest boy who seemed to be their spokesperson. "Would you introduce yourselves again as you just did for the Countess and myself?"

The tall, serious boy with dark wavy hair, David's olive skin and the unexpectedly brown eyes stepped forward. "Of course, Sir."

He cocked his head to one side and said, "It all starts with our names, Vice-Admiral."

My heart started to race as a sense of déjà vu overwhelmed me. "Your names?"

He raised his chin and said, "We found out our full names five days ago, as per our father's will, and immediately set course for Irena."

"Why here?"

He ignored my query and said, "My name is Tomas Atticus Pace-Abrams."

I just stared at him as my brain struggled to process his words.

One of the girls stepped forward. "I am Magdalene Annabelle Pace-Abrams." David had called her Maude my confused brain reminded me.

The second boy who had reddish blonde hair and David's gray eyes. "I am David George Thalberg Pace-Abrams III," then he grinned, "but you can call me George."

I felt like I was going mad so I stayed silent so no one else would know, but *Pace-fucking-Abrams?*

The last girl who had dyed black hair and stared at the floor, clearly annoyed, said, "Cherie Tania Pace-Abrams." Then she added, "This is stupid."

"What…I don't understand," I said almost breathlessly. What I meant, of course, was that of course I understood; I just really didn't want to.

Tomas, Tommy, then stepped forward and held out his hand. In it was a black stone.

He stared at it and it 'lifted' off his palm and floated in the air.

He looked me in the eye.

I felt, for the first time in a long time, the crazy truly calling me. The farm wanted me back, but I fought it and stayed right where I was.

"I am your son, Jane." He looked over his shoulder at his brother and sisters. "*We* are your children."

Thal stepped forward then, reaching into his chest cavity and removing what looked like a hand written letter, which he handed to me. "This is the last of my son's secrets and the hardest one to keep from you."

Everything seemed so surreal. I felt Charles and Idis move to either side of me supportively. I tried to think outside myself for I knew they had to be freaking out, too.

"Jane," Idis said quietly, "is this really true?"

500

"Do I have four apparently grown children, at least one of whom is a super…"

"We all are, Jane," George interjected brightly. "Wanna see?"

"Perhaps in a bit, George," I said. "I'm still taking all this in."

"Oh, Ok."

"As I was saying, who are all supers, apparently, that I had with David without my knowledge?" Or consent. I sighed as I started to open the letter. "Seems so, my friend." I turned to Charles who looked pale beneath his freckles. "Shall I read it?"

I felt him clench his fists. "You might as well," he said quietly. "We need to know the worst."

"All right, love."

Here is David's last letter, apparently written the day before he died. In retrospect I shouldn't have read it aloud, but my curiosity had clouded my judgement.

February 10th, 2882

Dear Jane,

By now you have met our children and are angry at me yet again. As you probably have guessed, I'd saved your DNA samples from our time together on the Foudroyant. *I wanted you. You know that I wanted to marry you and create children with your abilities and my brains. Children that could change the universe. You refused, paralyzed by the fears for the safety of any children of yours. Enemies could get to you through them. You had nightmares of them crying, hurt or even abandoned if something happened to either of us. You told me you couldn't bear it.*

I knew then that the only way for it to happen was to make the choice for you.

[Idis gasped in horror. I felt a bit sick, but, honestly, none of this shocked me at all. Charles put his arm around my waist but no one said anything. They just waited for me to continue.]

The first plan, as I'm sure you have figured out, was to nullify your birth control shot, which I did easily, but you failed to get pregnant by me and instead, which was worse, got pregnant by Fitz. I knew that the call of marriage and your baby would make it more difficult to get you back, but by then our four children were already born. I was sure you would get yourself sterilized as soon as you could, so I would have the advantage of numbers at the very least.

["Advantage of numbers," I muttered. "Four to one. Fucking David." I read on].

I was very well aware that the vulnerability of young children scared you, so I'd reasoned that you would be happy, happy with our family and with me, if that was taken care of. Since I had the means to fix it, fix it I did.

[That stopped me cold. I looked up to see four human and one plastic face staring at me. Then I did what I should have done at the beginning. "Thalberg, dear, would you please take them into the other room for a few minutes?"

"Of course, Jane."

"You mean we're not going to hear the rest?" Cherie said, dripping sarcasm. "Oh no."

"Yes," Thal said with equal sarcasm, "you're such a terribly clever girl. Let's go."

They left and the Guards went with them except Stanley and one other, both of whom pretended they weren't there.]

The plan, of course, was to 'age them up' for you, eliminating your fears and allowing all of us to be a family once they'd turned eighteen and were able to fend for themselves. You and I would be together as we always should have been. I wasn't even going to ask for your divorce...

["And that's bullshit," I added.]

...because divorcing Heads of State is notoriously difficult. I just wanted you and I didn't care how I had to have you.

["Truer words were never spoken, apparently," Idis said under her breath.]

Even before they were a year old it became clear that the children were supers, though not all the same kind. I needed to know how to train the

Thals to nurture their abilities, so when Wilby adopted that truckload of Pacey super babies, I jumped at the chance to take them in and learn from them and their instructors.

["Well," Idis observed, "*that* mystery is solved." She put her hands on her hips. "It also explains why Abrams flipped out when Wilby discovered Tommy and the aging chambers."

"Yeah," was all I could say, because...yeah.]

I've known many women and a few, when I was younger, had even been real girlfriends. They said they loved me, they said they didn't care about the money, they didn't care about the black lines on my skin. They did care, of course, but dealt with it because they loved the wealth and prestige more than they were disgusted by my body. I've thought many times that you and I could have been happy for years, had you only been a whore like all the rest. I could not buy you, though. Perhaps that was part of the fascination.

[Charles' grip on my waist tightened and I was grateful. The pressure was comforting.]

The children go to you, of course, since they are legally underage. Justine will be discharged upon my death with a hefty payout completion of services. Thal destroyed all the aging chambers yesterday. Things for the kids will be normal now.

[I'd forgotten about his wife/prostitute entirely. I wondered how much of a mother she'd actually been to these kids. David's firing of her upon his death seemed par for the course for David; the feelings of either the children or Justine were irrelevant once business was completed.

His sociopathic coldness to Justine (though I hadn't liked her personally), however, was so typical it made be abruptly angry on her behalf but mostly on mine. Thanks, David, I thought scathingly, for dumping four children on me who look like adults, who had (I had to assume) the hormones and strength of adults but the minds of ten-year-old children. Yeah, that was going to be a cakewalk, wasn't it, fuckwad? Oh, and don't forget that they're supers and, very likely, miles smarter than I am.

"Jane?" Idis asked, concerned that I had paused in my reading for that long.

The prospect of attempting to parent these four strangers was daunting to say the least, but…but I wasn't alone, was I? Please let me not be alone, I begged silently. "I'm feeling a bit overwhelmed."

"That seems appropriate, Jane," Idis said. "I'm feeling it a bit myself."

"Charles?" I said, trying not to sound pathetic.

"Finish the letter, love, and then we'll talk to the kids, and Thal, and make a plan." He kissed my forehead. "We can do right by these children." He looked over at Idis who nodded. "Give them a real family since I think it's pretty safe to say they haven't had one before."

"Besides, Jane," Idis said softly, "The son of a bitch did give us Lucy. Now she'll have four more half-siblings her age." She frowned. "After a fashion."

I turned to stare at them in awe. "Are you two really this perfect or has being with me just worn you down?" I was trying to tease, but mostly covering up the fact that I was trying keep myself together. It was proving difficult; I was so damned grateful to them. I looked away and tried to discretely wipe my eyes with the back of my scarred hand.

Idis hugged me and said, "Let's finish the letter, my dear."

"Ok," I snuffled.]

I have never understood people. They are the only things in the universe that have truly baffled me, but I tried with you and am trying with our children. I make the effort because, though you won't believe it, I can love. I can be better. I was never good enough for you, Jane, but, I hope I was good enough for them.

[My eyes filled again, but I kept reading, though my voice was clogged.]

I had planned on leaving you the P.A.U. but I figured that since I thought that was a good idea that you would think it was the worst idea ever, so I left it to Thalberg, Dad, to look after for the next eight years until the kids are of age.

What I want you to have from me, aside from our own flesh and blood, is the only thing I thought you'd actually accept: my little ship Annabelle. *It is the fastest small ship in the galaxy, faster even than your precious* Liberty. *Maybe you can teach George to fly on it one day. He wants to be a pilot this week. Last week he wanted to be a janitor. The week before that a trampoline.*

I'm going to go now, Jane. Please tell the children that I love them, that they were my greatest creation, my greatest joy. I never wanted to leave them and no matter what happens to them as they grow up let them know that their father thought they were perfect even to his dying breath.

And for you, Jane, my only love, I will tell you that I will be all right. Nit war an ei ben ei hun ar eich carer bob amser an ra nghalon.

Goodbye,

David

"That was Pacey," Idis identified. "What did he say?"

Oh, David. "I am not alone for you are always in my heart."

Charles held me as I broke down and cried and Idis patted my back until I was done.

A few minutes later I'd pulled myself together and the kids, and Thalberg, were called back in. We had tea. We chatted about their lives, about their father, and about being supers. Or rather Charles and Idis chatted and I listened, racking my brain to try to find a way to connect to these people. I had seen time and time again that it was committment that made a parent, not biology, but biology was all I had at the moment. So I sat and smiled and hoped I would think of something.

It came to me towards the end of tea.

After about an hour I'd noticed that Tommy was shaking. It was subtle, but I knew what I felt. I started to speak, to ask him what was the matter, when I realized what he was doing. There was a large and very ornate multi-level server-thing full of cookies and pastries on the side of the tea table. He was staring hard at it, concentrating so intently he was trembling and starting to sweat. Were he a true Micro, this would have been at the very outside of his range, if he moved it at all. It rose just a swaying centimeter off the table. Nice.

I came over to sit next to him and said, "That was good, Tommy."

He dropped the server with a small crash and everyone looked up. "Sorry." He turned bright red.

I leaned closer and said, "May I offer a suggestion?"

He sat back with a huff, clearly frustrated. "I can't do it, J-" He paused, now even more annoyed. "Do I call you Jane?"

"Sure," I said easily. "Don't quit now, Tommy. You *can* do it." If he'd gotten it off the table at all, yes, he could. "It's *how* you do it that makes the difference."

He shrugged. "I can either 'lift' it or not."

No, kid, I thought. It wasn't that nearly simple. "Will you try something for me?"

"I guess." Good enough.

"The key to 'lifting,' whether it is for Micros or Macros, is to remember that it is your mind that 'lifts,' not your body."

"I know that," he said, offended.

I let that go for the moment. "You've had anatomy study, correct?"

"Yes," he eyed me warily.

"Scan me and find my heart."

He closed his eyes and concentrated.

"Eyes open, my friend," I said gently. "Don't give up the advantage of sight when you don't need to." I had said this to hundreds of students over the years and I thought of Wilby (back in *my* student days) saying it to me every time.

He opened his eyes. Yes, he had it.

"Now widen the scan to my whole body, keeping an eye on muscle tension."

"Ok."

I 'reached' out and carefully 'grabbed' the tall server, 'lifting' it off the table and around the room. Conversation stopped as all eyes followed it. No, that wasn't true. Idis watched me, a smile on her face.

"The 'lifting' I'm doing isn't being assisted by my physical strength at all."

"But..." Tommy said.

"Because even though my brain used to think that it knew what moving something meant, effort in the muscles, balance corrections, strain, even pain in some cases, it was wrong." I 'put' the server back on the table. I didn't dislodge a single cookie doing it. "I had to train my mind to divorce anything physical from Telekinetic lifting. Once I did that I could 'lift' virtually anything within my range without hurting myself." Felix's remembered voice was in my head. *Mass means nothing.*

"How could you hurt yourself moving shit with your mind?" Cherie asked, masking her curiosity with disdain.

"The heavier the object, the more stress you put on your body."

Cherie shrugged but Tommy was unabashedly enthusiastic. "You've always done it like this, without effort?"

I wish. "No, it took me years and a very good teacher for me to get it. Before that, however, I got hurt a lot." A *lot.*

"What's the biggest thing you've ever lifted?" Tommy asked at the same time Cherie said, scornfully, "You got *injured* 'lifting' things with your *mind?*"

I was getting a bit annoyed with her tone, but, it turned out, Charles was getting even more so.

He spoke and everyone stopped in their tracks as people usually did when he said something. "The day after I first met your mother she broke her back destroying the Aquaformer missle that was going to annihilate Terra. Right after *that*, though she was broken and in unspeakable pain, she saved my life." His anger in my defence was quiet and a little scary. I can't say I didn't love it. "If she says you can get hurt by moving things with improper technique *you should believe her.*" And, by the way, don't use that tone with my wife, child. I added that bit in my head. Oh, Charles was so getting laid later.

Cherie looked at the floor, chastened.

"That's true?" George asked, aghast. "I thought the book made that up." Great, the fucking book. Why would David let them read that piece of shit? Fucking David. A phrase I would use often and for many years to come.

Charles said nothing, waiting for Cherie. I was pretty sure she'd never been put in her place by a true Alpha male, not one with an Imperial presence, certainly. David, for all his genius, had certainly never had that.

"I apologize for my disrespect, Sir."

Charles nodded, but it was Idis who said, much to my embarrasement, "Jane is an extraordinary woman, Cherie. All of you have the potential to be extraordinary yourselves, but that takes effort, training and, above all, listening to the people who have come before you."

"Yes, Ma'am," Cherie said, "Sorry again, Sir." Cherie looked like she'd rather disappear into the couch cushions.

He smiled. "Call her Idis," he corrected her playfully. "You may call me Fitz."

Then Maude piped up, "That's what they call the Corsican Ambassaor." I tried not to laugh at that very apt comparison. She continued more slowly, "You know you really look...a lot like... him..." She stopped speaking and really stared at his, face, analyzing it, as Charles' smile broadened. Her gray eyes went as wide as they could go. "Oh my."

Diplomatic manipulation at its finest, I thought, as I shook my head slightly at my spouse. He winked at me. I sighed, but still had to appreciate his method of gaining trust though, from her expression, Idis would have preferred he'd discussed the revealing of that state secret with her before he'd told anyone new. Charles looked at her and shrugged. She sighed, too.

"May I try again, Jane?" Tommy said, still intent on the serving tiers.

"Do you think you've got it?" I asked.

He nodded distractedly. "I think so."

"Then show me."

Nothing happened for a second as we all held our breath. I felt him trying to force himself to relax, which was good, and then the server swayed and lifted off the table, spilling its contents all over it. The server hovered in the air for a few seconds...and then touched back down a little loudly.

I grinned at him. A very good start. "Wonderful, Tommy."

He flushed as we all applauded. "I spilled everything."

"Yes, but you spilled everything the right way," I said. "If you like, I can come see you tomorrow morning and we can try lifting all kinds of things." Though perhaps I'd wait to teach him how to inflict pain and immobilize nerves. Giving a ten-year-old boy in an eighteen-year-old's body too many tools for mischief seemed like a bad idea all around, at least for a few years. When he was mature enough, though? It was going to be a fuckload of fun.

"Really?" he asked, eyes bright.

"I would love it," I said.

"Cool. Thanks, Jane."

The next morning Wilby (who had been gratifyingly shocked by the sudden appearance of my four "new" children) and I started training Tommy and George (who was a Macro) on the finer points of Telekinesis. Within a week Brady had joined us to look after Cherie whose TP abilities rivalled Eriss.' Quiet Picture-Maker Maude had had to wait a while for a visit from Alma Gonzales (with Srihas), but once they had worked with her awhile she'd been able to show us visions of improbable beauty. Charles, Idis and I were amazed at these kids. Amazed and proud.

That first morning we'd begun working together was the start we'd desperately needed. It was the same morning they'd met our darling Lucy who'd immediately took over 'big sister' (so to speak) duties in terms of acclimating them to Irena and the Palace. True to her nature she'd treated them as equals, as siblings, not overgrown freaks. She more than anyone else, I think, helped them to know that *they* were now *us* by accepting them just exactly as they were.

That morning, because of Lucy and because the adults all wanted it so badly, we were able to begin the long (and occasionally very bumpy) road towards becoming a family.

I knew David wouldn't have understood what we had, but I'd like to think he would have been pleased anyway.

EPILOGUE

I stood in the middle of a large, deep circle of friends and colleagues on a dirt plain, mountains off in the distance, one of them missing its top. All of us wore breath masks, though I'd been told that eventually there would free air and grass where we were standing. Another twenty-five years or so might do it.

I looked around me, seeing Samuel and Mallory, Stuart and Prince Ronnie, still dressed in mourning black, with their son, King Hector 2, Queen Tania and Marston, Atalanta, Daniel and Felix, Garrett and Derek, Wilby and Quinn with Shira and all twenty-five of the last Pacey super babies long since grown up, Prince Alex and his wife, Felaysa, Prince Hal and Sophia, Princess Joyanna and her adult sons, Missy and her husband Ambassador Synon Aronoff, Captains Wylan Smith and Petros Nitsa, Hannah Three and her husband Jonah, Alma and Srihas Gonzales, Affie and Gabriel, Samson and his wife Ro, Huong Schulweis, Tommy, Maude, George and Cherie, Bertie Nylander and his Tarine wife Ulla, any and all living Paceys, most of the Furies, many of my ESTF Cadets, Eriss and Ian, Lucy, Idis and the Emperor Charles 6 (who had quietly retired from being Ambassador Fitz a decade before).

The sun was directly overhead and it was time.

"Today," I said, "is July 4th, 2889, and the twenty-fifth anniversary of the fall of Pace-Pallon. Here, on this site, was the School where many of us met. It was our home." I looked at Maude and tapped my temple. I knew the proper people had seen this signal and had 'opened' their minds as well.

Suddenly we were in the Quad on a typical sunny morning. The courtyard filled as the bell rang and students streamed out of the dorms above us, laughing, shouting and moving quickly to get to class on time. More students came from the Refectory and some more from the old Choir Room. Up above in the Guard Tower a much younger Samuel paced, watching over his kids. The day was bright and cheerful. A stunningly beautiful teenaged girl smiled as she passed by on her way to class and we felt, since this was a day from Felix's mind, joy.

The scene shifted and we looked out over the fields of Pace 1 from the window of a shuttle. I heard several people gasp at the feeling of disorientation, but the flying continued uninterrupted. I had never seen Pace 1 at all, let alone like this. This was Garrett's memory, one of stripes and stripes of green, red, blue and yellow color lining the ground in endless flat fields. Thin sparkling rivers snaked through the colors. The extreme flatness of the land made the sky seem to go on forever.

The next view that surrounded us was of black rock and red fire, magma and ash. Walking together on a wide expanse of rock the huge Pacey 3s in their heavy protective suits were dwarfed by broken mountains surrounded by frighteningly beautiful rivers of glowing molten rock. You could smell the ash in Wilby's memory and feel the blistering heat. I thought that as beautiful as Pace 1 had been, 3 was almost more so, deadly as it was.

Then the scene shifted to view out the glass wall of an elevator at the top of a building. The center of the structure was open to the air. It was the main Government building in Bane, Pace 4's capital. This memory was from one of the workers within that building, a man whose name I couldn't remember, though I had helped sort through the offerings when the request for Pacey memories had gone out. The view from the elevator into the massive busy building was stationary for only about a minute before it started to descend into the lower levels. It went down, down, down, passing offices, storage, the Infirmary, the PX, food services, more offices, security, all soon swallowed with us as we passed into the darkness below the planet's surface. Flags of the noble Scientist families stuck out from the balconies and waved in the wind the car made as we passed them. Down, down and down we went until the car finally stopped at the bottom in front of guards with automatic projectile weapons. Their badges read 'Office of the Director.'

Mallory's images were of training her students.

Stuart's were of Irrfan, smells included.

Samuel's, however, took us to a dark corridor, empty save for cold blue lights overhead and Tenorium windows next to locked doors. Inside the enormous warehouse-sized rooms were rows and rows of hundreds of machines. 'Tubs.' There was a small window on the front of each and the windows showed the gestating fetuses floating. Over each row was a number. A woman with dark hair streaked with silver walked with two men who carried portable monitors. "238-77690 is developing as expected," she said. One of the men typed something on his pad. "Check them again next week." She passed to another row. These fetuses were larger, almost full term and kicking in their 'tubs.' She frowned. "Has there been any evidence in 238-77885 that the mutation desired has manifested?"

"No, Doctor," the other man answered. "We could wait another week."

She shook her head. "Dump them now. We can use the 'tubs' for stage two of the next project."

He made a note. "Of course, Doctor."

She walked to the last row. That one had only one 'tub' and one fetus. "The Founders Project fetus is viable?"

The copper-skinned baby inside swam around energetically. "Yes, Doctor."

"Good," she said. "Inform the Director."

I wasn't sure anyone but Samuel, Mallory, Ian and myself knew that the Founder's Project baby we had just seen had been Arrow, but I heard outraged muttering among the non-Pacey within the assembled.

One after the other more scenes from the people of Pace-Pallon's past, taken (voluntarily) from the minds of those Paceys present, were lived again. So much of both the good and bad were brought to light after so many years tucked away in memory. The Breeding Program. The powerlessness of the supers. The cold cruel indifference of the Scientists.

However uncomfortable some of these memories made everyone, however, we shared them. These were *our* stories. *We* were the survivors, introducing friends and family who hadn't been there to these past lives. There was no press to see any of it. There were no tickets to the event. No strangers. Just our very personal history of a world and a culture long gone. Twenty-five years gone, to be precise.

We'd spent an hour in the past, but there was one memory left, one that I had insisted be included. I didn't want to relive it but it seemed dishonest to leave it out of our collective story.

I took a deep breath and welcomed Maude into my mind.

The Quad again, but now all was chaos, people running and screaming because of what was coming.

The ground outside the School shuddered with movement.

"They're coming!"

Through a small gap between the open double doors that led into the School thousands and thousands of creatures, carpeting the fields surrounding us, heading towards the School, towards sustenance. The sound of all the crab-like creatures moving inexorably towards was a low rasp of claws on earth. The sound grew in volume.

[Someone in the present screamed.]

Atalanta and Felix ran up the gangway of our rescue shuttle.

"Where's Arthur?!?"

"I'm sure he's on board, Jane. Come on!" Felix yelled. They disappeared into the crush of evacuees flooding the shuttle.

A new sound added to the rasp of claws. Chewing. Scraping.

[I felt my body start to shake and my skin crawl just as it had years ago, but I suppressed it.]

They were eating through the doors, their progress slowed by only a few seconds. And then they were through. The few remaining humans that weren't on the shuttle screamed and ran for it.

["Oh, God," someone said, "I can't bear it again."]

Ian bellowed from the ship, "Get up the goddamned ramp! I have to retract!"

A small cluster of people was running for the ship, Arthur among them.

"Wait!" Arthur shrieked, "We can make it!" just as the creatures swarmed his group, running over them like they were nothing. It all happened in a few seconds and, when the wave of creatures receded, Arthur and the others were gone, gone so thoroughly it was as if they'd never existed at all.

Then the shuttle walls were around us and Ian slammed his fist into a button on the wall. The doors closed and the gangway retracted at rocket speed.

"Get us in the air, Janowski!"

"Aye, Sir."

The ship rumbled and everything went black.

I opened my eyes to the quiet of the present day earthen plain. Some people were crying, some were shaking, but most of those of us who had lived through it were simply remembering and, probably, feeling guilty for surviving at all. At moments like this I was certainly one of them.

"We will," I said, "come here and share our memories, see our pasts again, every quarter century until there are none of us left to come. This world has been given a second chance, thanks to the sacrifice and dedication of many, but we remember how it was then because it would be wrong to forget."

I stepped to the side, revealing a plaque in the ground that read:

Carlamter-Pallon bu rarw a tiwrnot hwn, 2869 4att Gorrennar. Gatewch cenetlaethau'r tarotol gorio bot bawat an werthrawr. Battet ittant ei trin gata pharch ac an caniatáu itto rhattit i rot ar han a mae'n tamuno ei rot.

Pace-Pallon died this day, July 4th 2869. Let future generations remember that life is precious. May they treat it with respect and allow it the freedom to be whatever it wishes to be.

I bowed to everyone in thanks and farewell then walked to over to my family. Idis wiped her eyes and smiled proudly. I thanked Maude for her images and hugged her and the rest of the kids, my hands lingering a bit on Lucy's cheeks as I wiped away her tears. I saved my husband for last, of course.

Charles, his golden eyes black with emotion, simply wrapped me in his strong arms and held me tightly. I felt I could breathe again. A river of friends, familiar beloved faces, enveloped us briefly as they said goodbye and then passed on.

Idis, after taking a long look around at what had been Pace so long ago, said, "Let's go home, my dears."

I nodded, but, as I watched Idis lead the kids to our ship, I was thinking about how lucky I was. How I had come of age in destruction and death, but was somehow still standing. Overcome, I leaned in to Charles, the center of all my joy, to say something, anything that would express what I was feeling, but my throat was clogged and no words would come.

Charles smiled, somehow understanding, and he pulled off his breath mask to kiss my temple whispering, (almost) as he had on our wedding day, *"Ein un ni. Corrr ac enait." Ours. Body and soul.*

Yes, I thought. *Ours.*

Within minutes the *Annabelle* had lifted itself from the ground and we were gone, bound for Corsica, but already home.

END OF BOOK EIGHT
August 19th, 2895

JANE'S TATTOO AS OF 2895

Pilar Julia-Callas
David Abrams
Pinky
Alice Napia
Whitman
Mirta
Paul Friedman
Lita Utat
Arrow
Adele
Stoney
Soames
Peter
Winifred
Duncan
Thal
Gladys
Criss Utat
Ian
Samuel
Wilby
Andrew
Anan
Julianne
Sig
Paulette
Arthur
Irrfan

A NOTE FROM E.V. COMFORT

Jane Pace was a character that first appeared to me over five years ago at night when I was trying to get to sleep. I usually prefer to make up a new story every evening, but there she was again and again, night after night. She was a mere seventeen when disaster struck her placid school world and she fell in love with a generous and kind older man who eventually was called Samuel Armstrong. Eventually I embraced the character and wrote the first chapter of what would be an eight book series. That first day I sat down to write she felt the impact of the *tapetia mortis* Objects in the Quad and we were off.

Jane has had a hell of time in the thirteen years that have been covered in these novels and I truly hope that you have enjoyed adventuring, suffering and loving along with her. She was an interesting person to write and I have loved the work and the challenge of bringing her story to the page.

I wanted to thank every reader who has made it to the end of her recorded journey. If you have had half as much fun imagining her story as I did in writing it, then my efforts have not been in vain.

Though I will miss Jane, Samuel, Wilby, Ian, Arrow, Eriss, the Trio, David, Thal, Synon, Soames, Quinn, Garrett and Derek, Criss, Idis, Lucy and, of course, Charles, it is time for new challenges. Thankfully, you and I can always visit our old friends anytime we wish just by opening a book.

Godspeed to you.

E.V. Comfort

Ladera Ranch, California
November 19th, 2016

www.ingramcontent.com/pod-product-compliance
Lightning Source LLC
Chambersburg PA
CBHW050018030726
47506CB00001B/9